# The Big Tide

# The Big Tide

Marc Heberden

*Camerado Press*

ISBN: 978-0-692-39080-1 (Camerado Books)
www.cameradopress.com

*For* Christine Suzanne

Maurine Elvina

Joyce Eileen

& Clifford Georges Lloyd

# THE BIG TIDE

*There is a tide in the affairs of men,*
*Which, taken at the flood, leads on to fortune;*
*Omitted, all the voyage of their life*
*Is bound in shallows and in miseries.*

Julius Caesar – Act IV, Scene III

# Chapter 1

THE GRAVEL in the parking lot crunched cheerfully under his feet as he made his way across to the boatyard. Although late in the summer, the early morning air was cool and moist and in the long shadows of buildings, cold. With a bright sun coming up into a pale blue sky the freshness of the air that morning and the sharp crackling of the gravel beneath his shoes simply added punctuation to his deeply happy mood.

Eric Sumners was a very rich man who was also handsome, intelligent and well-mannered and he was married to a strikingly beautiful woman who loved him.

Of all those things that morning it was his money that was making him so happy. Because he was going to be able to do something in an offhand fashion that even moderately wealthy people would have spent a lot of time thinking about.

Although he had, indeed, thought quite a bit about this. It was just that he hadn't found it necessary to squander his time worrying about finances. Simply, he was going to buy his wife a boat.

Really, it was an inspiration. More than just a rich man's gift. It was a gift of love. Eric liked how it contained so many perfections. Considering his wife, her love of beautiful things and her appreciation of naturalness, a boat—specifically a sailboat—was sure to delight her.

If he hadn't been paying so much attention to the specifics of his happiness that morning he would have laughed outright. He realized he was being practically a boy.

But he caught himself, casting a wary eye around the yard filled with the gleaming white hulls of sailboats, on the lookout for anyone there. It was no time to start smiling like a fool when you are getting set to invest hundreds of thousands of dollars.

Eric strolled among the boats, appraising the advantages and disadvantages of one against the other. But this was more for the exercise of it than anything else since he already knew exactly what he wanted.

Clyde Moore was at the far end of the yard washing down a couple of thin, racing sloops. With his longish, combed-back hair, thick sideburns and shiny, striped shirt and white pants, he looked vastly out of place in that job. He looked more like he belonged in some Vegas lounge. Clyde and his wife Annie owned the boatyard. As it was, Eric couldn't have chosen a better morning to stride onto their property. They'd been having a terrible summer. So terrible in fact they'd started discounting some of the boats a month earlier than usual.

Neither could say why it had been so bad and so could only guess. And as is usual when a couple is only guessing why they're having a hard time they put the blame on each other. There had been a lot of bitter fighting at Moore's Boats. About everything.

Clyde recalled the last fight and made a face, rolling his eyes and sighing. As he passed the soapy mop over a smooth fiberglass craft, he told himself for the hundredth time how, what with all the washing and polishing, and little else he'd done that summer, he may as well have owned a car wash.

He'd just turned to grumpily dunk the end of the mop back into the sudsy bucket, when around the end of one of the sloops came the crisp, light summer suit of Sumners.

Clyde's heart jumped.

Few business suits walked into the yard, fewer first thing bright in the morning, and none at all that summer.

Clyde pulled back behind the racing sloop again, staring thoughtfully down into the bucket full of soap suds. Truly, he thought, this was more than just curiosity. This was a sale. From the look of that tailor-made summer suit, a big sale perhaps.

Maybe even the ....

He stopped himself, not wanting to jinx it.

Clyde's face jerked with a grin. God, he thought, would that ever cool Annie's jets.

Clyde peeked around the bow of the sloop again, watching Sumners walking slowly past the boats.

Clyde nodded. It looked good. No reason to rush it. Act casual. The man out there looked like serious money, and serious money liked things done professionally. He smiled. Even Annie would be proud of the way he had control of things that morning.

*

Annie Moore had been doodling on a scratch pad in the kitchen, drinking a cup of instant coffee and staring out the window into the bright morning sunshine in the boatyard, when Eric Sumners came out of the parking lot.

Like Clyde, she'd seen that Eric was all business. And like Clyde, she'd sensed a tightening in her chest, and felt her throat thicken in the same way a hunter feels his throat go hard at the first sight of game.

She took a slow breath and then looked away, taking a sip of her coffee.

They needed the money that year. It was getting to be a crapshoot whether they'd come out with anything at all. Of course, they weren't sinking or anything. They'd get by somehow.

But it would just be nice, she thought, to have a year without worries. A year they could take a holiday or something. Otherwise, it was just the usual old grind ... only this year a bit worse than the usual.

Scraping. Little different from what it had been like when she'd first met Clyde, when she'd been working as a barmaid up at Celeste's in Fairhaven.

Annie frowned. Clyde had been a good talker. Good looker, good talker. Ten years later, for all his looks and all that talk, she'd found herself surrounded by a million dollar inventory and two hundred dollars in their checking account. As bad off as if they'd owned a Mom and Pop.

She glanced back out the window at the boatyard. It was as if, she said to herself, the only things Clyde could sell anymore were boathooks and seat cushions.

Well, she sighed in sudden excitement, here at last is a chance. Maybe a big chance.

As she thought that, she noticed Clyde glance around the sloop he was washing, taking a peek at the handsome man in the beautiful suit. The look on Annie's face changed from hope, to disbelief.

What the hell was he doing?

There he was, with a prime customer in the lot who was really looking at the goddamn boats, and all he was doing was just going on with washing down some shit boat back in the corner.

Like he didn't give a damn.

But when she saw Clyde take his second peek and hide again, her

3

disbelief turned to bitter fury.

"Fucking idiot ...," she breathed out, sharply rapping the half-full cup down on the counter.

What was he doing out there? He had to have seen what the guy looked like. He must realize what he's got in the yard that morning.

Annie thought quickly about Clyde. The Clyde she knew. She thought about all the possible reasons he would be playing some small cat-and-mouse game out there. It was probably some half-assed psychological reason. With Clyde, there was never really any way of knowing.

She only hesitated a moment before she got up, smoothing her dress and patting her hair.

She skipped lightly down the office stairs and strode firmly out across the clean, carefully raked gravel of the lot.

Damned if she was going to let this guy get past them. Clyde's theories about sales notwithstanding.

*

Eric was looking at a large and beautifully made ketch floating at the sales pier.

"That's a world-cruiser, sure enough," he heard behind him.

Eric nodded.

"It's perfect," he said in turning, and found himself looking into the blue eyes of an attractive auburn-haired woman. She had an attractive smile as well although somewhat worn.

He understood. At any level, business was business. He smiled back at her.

Annie felt him taking her in and she returned the appraisal. In Eric she saw an athletic man of about her own age, closing on forty, who was matinee-idol handsome in a masculine, Danish sort of way, with thick, longish sandy hair and dark blue eyes.

She was also very much aware of how he was dressed in a suit Clyde could only have bought once every two years, and would have never had an appropriate occasion to wear.

A rich man's light summer suit.

Annie had never seen so much money go into something so ... seasonal. She felt awed and yet at the same time reassured. This one, she thought, wouldn't fluster at the price of things.

"Really," she said, "it's not merely the best we have, but it's one of the best boats anywhere."

Eric smiled and looked at it.

"I know," he said.

"You know about boats, then."

"No. But I've been studying a little."

Annie tried to appear calm. "You've heard of the Nickerson ketch?"

Eric knew the effect he was making, and managed to keep a straight face. "I've read about it, yes."

He turned back to look at Annie. "Is it true that a minimum crew can handle it?"

Annie nodded quickly. "Yes, it's really quite simple. They've really made some very interesting arrangements with the rigging. Amazing really. In fact, if it gets right down to it, this boat could really be sailed single-handed. That is, alone," she added, careful to not get too nautical with him.

Eric tried not to grin at how everything was really this and really that and glanced back at the boat.

"That's what I read," he said, then looked back at her with a smile. "But sailing it alone wouldn't be all that much fun, would it?"

He knew he shouldn't tease the saleswoman. That his every statement would be interpreted in light of a possible sale. But he was enjoying himself.

Annie knew the rich man was thinking of his girlfriend or wife but when he turned his sharp eyes on her with a hint of mischief she felt it was possible he could contemplate going for a sail with her.

What with her excitement at his handsome build, his beautifully casual suit, his obvious money, and a sale, she actually felt her face begin to flush. In her embarrassment, all she could do was smile and nod. Luckily though, Eric was again looking at the boat.

As fiberglass sailboats went, it was beautifully big. Ninety feet with teak decks and mahogany cabins.

Eric knew it was spacious, with a separate main cabin and two smaller double-cabins. In total, it could sleep up to ten people very comfortably.

As well, it had an exceptionally large parlor and a separate and large galley. Two people could live as comfortably on board it as they could at home.

And even better ... almost the most important thing ... it was also finished beautifully with inlaid woods and special touches that Deborah, his wife, would appreciate.

Artistic things, fine and natural things that along with the beauty and naturalness of the sailboat, would appeal to her fine and artistic sensibilities.

Eric, now standing close to the boat, could reach down and touch the robust curve of its hull swelling up from the water, could picture clearly how it fit his idea so perfectly.

This time, even with that woman standing right there, he allowed himself a big grin. A grin of money, and the sheer joy with what he could do with it.

"Boy," he said aloud, throwing restraint to the winds, "what a beauty!"

He marveled at the boat, and at the same time marveling at his life.

Enraptured, he didn't hear the sigh of relief and happiness that had suddenly escaped, uncontrollably, from Annie's lips as well.

She knew the boat was as good as sold. That was the main reason she sighed.

But another reason, which she wasn't fully conscious of but would have been if it hadn't been so mixed up with the moment of actually selling the ketch, was that she'd just fallen in love with Eric Sumners and everything he stood for.

"Would you like to see inside?" she forced herself to say. "I could unlock the cabin for you."

"Yes," Eric said, bringing himself back to earth.

Annie felt herself flush again, but could no longer hold herself back.

"Are you very interested?"

Eric turned with the somewhat startled look people get when their minds are being read. But then, realizing that it wasn't going to matter in the end, he smiled.

"As a matter of fact, I'm very interested in buying a boat. Especially this particular boat. So, if you don't mind, while I'm looking around inside, would you please bring me all the information you have on it? You don't have to bring information about the accommodations. I know all that quite well. What I mean are the financial specifications and insurance figures and so on, if you know anything about what they might be. That is to say, I have a close idea, but I want yours. Okay?"

At all that, Annie kept nodding her head and smiling and she brought a key purse out of her pocket, found the right one and handed it to him.

As soon as Eric had stepped across from the dock onto the ketch, she turned on her heel and headed for the office, this time almost on the point of breaking into a run as she went.

When she got there she found Clyde had come back to the office and was sitting behind the desk.

She half expected he might be angry, but from his guarded expression it was impossible to know. That is to say, whether he was angry or not. Because she knew what that guarded expression of his meant.

He was suspicious.

Immediately, she was on edge, and was ready to be angry again, whether he was or not.

## Chapter 2

CLYDE HAD felt more disappointment than shock when he saw Annie walk out from the office across the yard over to the man. Sales, as he'd repeated to her often enough, was his side of the operation. Hers was the books.

But what could he have done? He couldn't have just run out and cut her off. That wouldn't have been professional at all.

Clyde had warily eyed Annie as she approached Sumners. And then had crept back around to the office to wait.

"Jesus, Annie," he said, watching her as she went to the file cabinet and began rifling through manila folders.

"Jesus what, Clyde?" she said at last.

"What are you looking for?" Clyde's voice gaining a belligerent edge.

"For your information, I'm looking for the finances on the Nickerson ketch," she announced with some belligerence of her own.

She pulled out a folder, turned and looked at her husband ruthlessly.

"While you've been fiddling with yourself, I went and introduced our baby to the most expensively cut summer suit I've ever seen."

The color which had risen in Clyde's face slowly paled. Somewhat deflated, he raised his hands in a pitiful way.

"You didn't give me a chance, honey," he said. "And I thought I'd already told you anyway. That's my job."

"It's your job if you do it," Annie cut in, having no time for her husband's delicate feelings. "But I didn't see you doing anything. As a matter of fact," she lied, suddenly realizing how she could get around Clyde and get back down to the boat, "I didn't see you out there at all."

Clyde, without being able to trust her completely, did feel soothed. But he was also aware that he now had small or no chance to take over, as he'd planned to do before. She had made it so he had either to accept her version, or bury his pride at a heavier price. So he chose to accept.

"I was washing the Sharktails," he offered, reinforcing things, trying to find a way to work it around to his advantage.

"See?" Annie said, going through the papers on the ketch, weeding out all but the most pertinent.

"Ok. So let's think about this a second, honey. What now?"

She knew Clyde was trying to find some way to take over. He always asked her for her opinion when he wanted it the least. But that time Annie wasn't having it.

She looked over at him and, for that moment, appraised him in the way wives appraise their husbands when the family security is at hand.

What she saw wasn't too flattering.

While selling seat cushions and boathooks or even Sharktail racing sloops was well within his range, this perhaps wasn't. She was going to keep Clyde from getting anywhere near Eric Sumners. That would be up to her, strange as it might have seemed to anyone who'd known who she was.

Former beautician, secretary, barmaid, her solitary claim to fame having been voted Miss Date in high school. Something she hadn't been all that proud of, but it had somehow compensated for how difficult it had been to get any attention at all. But even so she still felt, suddenly and completely, that she was better able to handle this serious business than Clyde with his glad-hand and sucked-in beer-paunch.

Clyde had never been voted anything, anywhere, by anyone.

"What now?" Her voice was hard. "What do you think, what now? I started this, so I'm going to finish. With all your psychology of sales you should know that this isn't the time to switch gears on the customer."

Annie never gave a thought to mentioning how there had been next to no sales work involved.

Despite Clyde's powerful sense of a lie somewhere, he went along with her. There was no reason, logically, or without damaging his newly recovered sense of pride, that he could argue against any of it.

"Well," he said slowly, "it seems now that you're into it, that the best thing for you to do is continue. If it's all going well right now I see no reason to step in. That is," he added somewhat sternly, "if it's going well."

Annie sighed only slightly.

"Yes, yes. It's going fine, Clyde."

"Okay," Clyde went on, now fully into the role he was developing for himself, "but at the first trouble, now, if you get into the slightest problem, you get me quick. All right?"

Annie nodded rapidly.

"I will, Clyde."

She flapped the folder shut and shot out the door before Clyde could think of anything else to say.

He watched her cross back over the lot, listening to her fading footsteps on the gravel, and let his mind go as blank as possible. Except to think of how friendly and warm he and Annie had just been towards each other, and how, if the sale was made, that warmth would be a good sign of things to come. Also, how a big sale with that particular yacht could set him and Annie up for a real smooth year ahead, with even a good vacation thrown in.

Annie would love a vacation, he thought as he let himself recline back lazily in his swivel chair. His gaze wandered around the room until it landed on a big poster advertising one of his lines of sailboats. There, one of the boats floated in the peaceful solitude of a small Tahitian cove, the sky and water brilliantly blue and the satiny coral beach shaded here and there with lush stands of overhanging palms. In the mysterious distance, dark high mountains looming.

He imagined himself with Annie there on that beach, in the evenings, maybe naked beneath the palms, tanned and happy, making love.

"Annie would love Tahiti," Clyde said aloud.

He never went to church, never gave a thought to anything like that. But with vestiges of a Sunday school superstition somewhere, Clyde often formulated his wishes in a semi-religious manner. That is to say, out loud, in the way children pray. As if that could somehow make them not only realizable but perhaps already real. Putting his hands behind his head, he started to hum some unknown song.

Of course, he thought, looking again at the poster, they would fly there. No sense going there in a stupid fucking boat.

# Chapter 3

IN ITSELF, as far as the sale went, there wasn't much to do. By the time Annie got back, Eric had been sitting in the main cabin of the boat long enough to feel like its owner.

It didn't matter to go through any bargaining. He already knew the base price of the boat and what he knew to be a regular markup for the boatyard.

As long as what the woman was going to show him was close to what he expected, he wouldn't quibble about the odd few thousand. So, having all that settled in his mind he'd sat there thinking of his wife, Deborah.

It was like a dream. For she was like a dream. Thirteen years younger than him, she'd married him the same year she'd finished college.

He'd been thirty-four. That might have caused problems, taking what was little more than a girl and pulling her straight into an adult world. Except their love was so special, and had grown so much more solid in the seven years since, that now there was no longer any need to wonder about how easily it had come to be.

Sweet Deborah.

A dreamlike, floating angel.

Eric smiled to himself.

It was a silly way to think of her, a silly way to put it. But he had never met anyone like her.

He would never have guessed, if he had fully known what she was like before they were married, that they could have made it last. For he felt anything but anywhere near the angels.

She'd always been special. A little other-worldly ....

When they got married, Eric had figured it was her age that made her that way and that with the passage of time she would grow into what passes for normal womanhood, full of real-world passions and pragmatic sentimentalisms. But she hadn't changed and instead had simply elaborated and perfected as a woman what she so mystically had been as a girl.

Eric smiled. It was rare he so freely allowed himself to think

11

about his wife. But today was special. Because today, for once, was a day where everything he did and said, was about and for her.

Deeply, honestly, Eric could only describe her as a dream. He had no other way of looking at her, especially from his position in life. Where he was constantly in touch with what made the world run, with its business dealings, contracts and the shifting sands of the money supply, she was unconcerned with all that. Occasionally her lack of interest or, it had to be admitted, her outright ignorance of the financial truths of the world pained him. After all, it hurt to have the largest portion of your make-up left out of a relationship. But he would always forgive her that. Because whatever those dreams of hers were, he knew he was somehow part of them.

Eric sat back into the richly tufted cushions of the sofa in the main cabin. Given her artistic and charitable impulses, anyone would think she would have looked for someone more in line with her own tastes. Instead, she had turned her instincts towards her husband and sought out those same qualities in him.

She had, by unveiling to Eric his own sensibilities, made him into a whole man. Because of her, he could appreciate talents in other people he would never have considered useful before. When he contemplated himself, through the eyes she bequeathed him, he was happy with what he saw.

There he was, a successful businessman—successful to an incredible level of return. At the same time he was keenly appreciative of beauty. That last, so-called human, quality which made him feel so whole was because of his wife's influence.

He reminded himself that, of course, that was not to say that money wasn't the product of deeply human qualities. His well-known abilities to manage it were a sign of his superior abilities in general. But to mix that with the fine appreciation of the other things in life, the world of the senses and of thought, only helped make him so much better.

If he was superior in the development of his worldly abilities, Deborah was superior in her artistic development. Between the two of them, they became greater than their sum.

As individuals, of course, he was the one that profited by getting the best of both worlds. She probably never would arrive at appreciating his understandings of the real world.

What matter, he thought? One, in a couple, would always be more fortunate than the other. Could he help it if only the worldly knew how to add up worldly blessings?

In the meantime, they had a love few people could boast of. They loved each other, were contented with each other, much more than many people who were not so dissimilar.

He looked around the richly appointed cabin and signed. He read the papers. He knew the statistics on divorce. He knew how love quickly became tragedy though no change ever occurred—inbuilt failure that had simply been ignored in the beginning.

But what he and Deborah had, what he had been so amazingly blessed with, was that thing the poets only allow as an ideal and never a possibility.

Real love, which is supposed to occur to one in a hundred, or a thousand, chances.

One in a million, perhaps.

Eric liked that number. It was a number he knew something about. Like someone else might know what a hundred or a thousand means.

And half of that million was about the same as the number of dollars he was about to put down in purchasing one of the world's most luxurious pleasure boats.

But it was worth it because for each dollar there had been a corresponding possibility of unhappiness. Five hundred thousand chances of bad love.

Knowing the size and weight of that number gave him reason to wonder, and even secretly feel smug. A magic number perhaps.

He smiled.

Deborah's influence, and this purchase, had led him off down these lanes of thought like some cabalistic occupation, half sorcery, half accounting. But he would not allow it long. He believed as little in numerology or astrology as he did in the alchemic creation of gold. Nevertheless, he liked how the present circumstances presented a tidy, summed up feel to them, and he liked the fitness this surreal sense of snug security gave to the actions of this morning ... if not his entire life.

The morning's extraordinary offering of happiness hit him again and he luxuriated in his exceptional good fortune. No one could say that life was fair, and some thought it somehow evil for so few to have so much. But he believed that it was exactly because the world was so unfair, that it was somehow a great and wonderful thing that at least a few could actually touch the substance of their dreams.

Someone had to, or none ever could. There was the undeniable logic of how he could enjoy all this. Eric, suddenly, was deeply at peace with not only himself, which was rarely not the case anyway, but also with all that was around him.

At that moment Annie arrived with the papers.

*

Eric and Annie were stepping back off the boat to the dock when Clyde made his appearance, sauntering across the boatyard.

Annie cast her eyes over her husband. He had changed into a charcoal suit and tie and replaced his floppy boat shoes with cap toe oxfords. While Clyde had his failings of common sense from time to time, she had to give him credit for his ability to spruce up his appearances. She saw he was even carefully arranging his face to resemble intelligent concern, and she was glad. Unlike what was usual, here he looked quite the serious man. Annie felt sure everything would work out as long as he maintained it. Or as long as she could make sure he did so.

"Good morning," Clyde said to Eric. "I see my wife's been showing you around."

Eric nodded and stuck out his hand. "Eric Sumners."

Clyde took his hand.

"Clyde Moore. My wife, Annie," he tilted his head in her direction.

"Of course," Eric said. With the arrival of the owner, it was obvious that things were now developing in more consequential directions. Not that Annie hadn't impressed him with her businesslike manner, but Clyde Moore, he could see straight away, was the man to deal with.

On reflection, the way Annie had jumped him the moment he'd got near the ketch showed signs of being overeager. Not that he was chauvinistic about how women did business, but it was often the truth that women overreacted at any indication of interest. Whereas this Clyde Moore was evidently a man of self-containment, content to let a customer arrive at his own conclusions in due time.

Probably, Eric reflected, Clyde Moore had shown up not simply to join Annie in helping things along, but also to make sure things didn't stray off track into unnecessary considerations or conversations. Which was quite proper.

Eric approved of how the air was now drained of the previous emotional charge. Expectations were back in the realm of the possible, rather than the hoped for.

Eric had to smile. Only he knew how close and how certain the Moore's hopes were to coming true, and he suddenly enjoyed the prospect of the effect he was about to make. But he wasn't about to play with them, either, just for the sake of drawing out the admittedly pleasant feeling of power it gave him.

He gave them both a significant look.

"I think I may as well tell you now, so as to get it out of the way, that I've decided to buy this ketch. All I want, past preparing the papers, is to go out for a run with her one of these days this week."

Clyde, to Annie's satisfaction, neither danced for joy nor greeted the statement as though he'd known it all along. He simply smiled benignly as though there was the slightest chance his leg was being pulled.

She glanced back at the expression on Sumners' face, comforted by the look there of relaxed sincerity.

Clyde, though, did indeed have a momentary and frightening impulse to make a wise-crack. Who wouldn't have in the same position?

But there was something about Sumners, something dry and lifeless to Clyde's way of thinking, that held him back. Unlike his buddies up at the Fairhaven Bar, there wasn't that glint of fun in the depths of the rich man's eye, the welcome flag for good spirits.

Clyde could never imagine really liking Sumners. Sure, he might be a regular enough guy and all that, but there was something stuffy about him. Maybe his money made him that way.

He glanced at Annie, and saw her looking all too obviously in awe at the man. Well, okay, he could play it cool too, and she would finally see how things were really done. He smiled back at Eric just as easily, and nodded amiably.

"Oh, good."

Eric liked that. These were intelligent people, he thought. Neither was going to be a believer until the check cleared the bank.

Yet, there was something ... he couldn't put his finger on it, but he could somehow feel something in the air, as though something quite important was happening.

Other people, he supposed, might have missed it. But he had a sixth sense for these sorts of things. And in this case, he knew exactly what it was all about. These people were like himself. They lived in the real world. They knew the cost of things. They knew damn well by looking at him that his one word was worth a hell of a lot more than entire speeches by most other people.

He liked them. They were of his tribe. So he had no regrets for having just washed out all the business apprehensions. With anyone else, he might have considered some prolonged haggling. But they were his sort.

Once again it was confirmed, he thought: wherever you went the best thing in life was to come across people who understand.

The fabric of commerce was the way of the world, little as most people wanted to accept that fact. To find people for whom that reality was part of the air they breathed, of the ground they stood on, had a comforting side to it, as though finding brethren in a foreign country.

"Well," Eric nodded at what had obviously been Clyde's gentle jibe of non-belief, giving him another small, conspiratorially understanding smile, "I guess under most circumstances it does seem a little jumpy, but that's all there is to it."

Clyde pursed his lips like a banker, but also seemed to drop all pretensions. "Okay," he said cheerfully, "then I guess we won't try to talk you out of it."

For a split second Annie's breath caught, but Eric's laugh wiped away her momentary fright. She could even feel confusion in Clyde seeming capable of doing everything right. She let her attention wander away, in order to gather her drifting thoughts.

The rocky substrata upon which she had carefully constructed, over the years, her impressions about her husband and their life together, was suddenly becoming a little intangible. Perhaps because of the general circumstances of their lives she had never noticed some facet of character. Success had always seemed an impossibility for him because he had seemed incapable of bringing it on. But now it looked as though that might have been only bad luck, and that Clyde in fact could easily handle success. It made her suddenly feel guilty, and even ashamed, remembering a few of the things she had said or thought.

She didn't look directly at Clyde, feeling suddenly shy of his presence, but she felt a glow of support rising in her. She would have to do her best, as well, to maintain a solid front.

"Do you need to see anything else?" she asked Sumners as they all, in an automatic sort of way, began to walk towards the office.

"I don't think so," he said. "I think the figure you quoted was right."

"Mr. Sumners will be paying in full," Annie told her husband quickly, almost apologetically, knowing he would be startled at the knowledge they'd agreed on some sort of figure. She was suddenly concerned he would be angry and upbraid her on the spot.

"Please," Sumners said, "call me Eric."

"All right, Eric," Clyde said smoothly.

He did, in fact give his wife a momentarily searching look. She had no idea he was just hiding a momentary confusion and mistook it for a reproach. It nearly withered her. She could only give an imperceptible, pleading shrug.

"Well," Clyde said, looking back to Sumners, "how you want to handle it is entirely up to you."

For Eric, things were said and done. He decided there was now no harm in expanding his explanations. In fact, all things considered, he had a desire to share his enjoyment of the significance of the purchase with these like-minded people.

Nearly a feeling of camaraderie.

"You know," he said, with an oddly satisfying feeling of diffidence, "this is one transaction I'd like to make differently from the normal way. You see, it's a gift in fact, and the way it's arranged is part of the whole thing, the feeling of the whole thing, altogether it's ...."

Eric was dissatisfied suddenly with the explanation, and cut it off. As much as he'd wanted to explain it, he could see it was impossible. It was just too deeply connected to too many things.

Both Clyde and Annie registered that he'd wanted to say more. But it was Annie who found a way to smooth it over.

"Of course," she said. "Something like this is always going to be meaningful."

Eric flushed slightly. As much as he'd wanted to, he now could see he'd been too intimate. He cleared his throat.

"So ... I'll have a certified check sent up from Seattle later this week, after the trial cruise. And we'll arrange for delivery somewhere after that. I suspect the moorage will eventually be over in Squalicum Harbor."

"Fine," Clyde said, relieved to hear the businesslike tone return to things. "That's just fine."

Clyde and Annie now made purposefully towards the office, Sumners in tow. And just as purposefully, they said nothing.

But where Annie would give quick, encouraging glances at Sumners, Clyde was striding straight ahead, nodding his head as he went, as though they were still talking and as though he was agreeing with everything being said.

As though, somehow, that ensured it would happen.

But if he felt a sense of urgency, he was surprised by how there was no feeling of panic. And suddenly, with each sure step they took going along across the yard, there now rose up a blissful feeling. As though he were falling warmly into a large feather bed of happiness.

The dream of the blue water and creamy sand came into his mind again and Clyde automatically glanced over at Annie walking along on the other side of Sumners. He allowed himself the pleasure of noting how her breasts pleasantly filled out against her dress, rounding out the light summer fabric there ahead of her arms. Near forty, she was definitely at her prime, and the thought of her fine figure beneath the thin cotton dress brought on an automatic, hot tickle of interest.

Clyde suppressed a smile at that, and shoved his hands strategically into his pockets so he could continue to enjoy whatever the morning had to offer.

Happy, he even allowed his concentration to drift, letting himself indulge in actually thinking about how nice it would be to finally get Sumners on his way. Considering the way things were moving right along, Annie wouldn't resist anything. Clyde damn near whooped out loud.

Walking towards the office Eric, too, was sinking into a reverie of his own. They were most of the way across the boatyard, passing in step amongst the smooth and gleaming white hulls of the other boats in the yard, when he caught sight of the little rowing shell.

"What's that over there?" he asked casually.

Clyde turned to Eric with a smile, and then looked in the same direction. "Oh, those are just our regular line of small, cruising sailboats."

"No, no. I mean that little boat behind there."

Clyde followed Sumners' line of sight and spotted the little wooden boat that had been built over in the work yard next door. "Oh, you mean the rowing pod."

"The what?"

Clyde shrugged with professional ease, and enjoying the way life was unrolling, let himself expand.

"It's a rowing pod being built next door." He laughed, as though it was a joke. "Built!"

Neither he, nor Sumners, saw Annie's horrified face.

# Chapter 4

"WOODEN, isn't it?"

"Of course," Clyde said, and seeing how Eric seemed interested, went on, "come and see." He led Eric over towards it, barely noticing how Annie had tried desperately to pluck at his sleeve, just giving her an irritated glance.

They walked past Clyde's boats to a gate in a chain link fence, passed through, and went over to the big, covered boatbuilding shed next door.

It was a tall, weather beaten shed, with an open first story and, for some reason, an enclosed and windowed second floor high up above them. Below, the disorderly shop, smelling suspiciously fishy, was cluttered with piles of dirty iron and dull lumber scraps, everything covered with thick, oily looking dust and sawdust. In a corner of the shed, braced on two sawhorses where Eric had first noticed it, stood the little wooden boat.

It was undoubtedly some form of classic rowing boat. But of a type Eric hadn't thought existed anymore, except in a Currier and Ives print, with its graceful lines, its delicate ribs curving gently against its overlapped planking.

Across the trim stern, in neat, dark-green letters with gold edging was painted the name *Isabelle*. As old-fashioned as she was, she seemed an unabashed flirt, as though daring anyone to deny she wasn't a beauty. Eric smiled.

"It's what's called lapstrake planking," said Clyde, taking the opportunity to show off his boat knowledge which, though not extensive, had strangely eclectic little pockets. "This particular technique, that is."

Eric looked thoughtful.

"It's quite old, and yet brand new."

"Oh, yes," Clyde said, ignoring the ever more frantic looks coming from Annie. "The builder just gets himself some old plans and duplicates the boat exactly. You can see how perfect it is, right down to the cast-iron armrests for the back seat. You know, where your beloved would sit as you rowed her across the lake."

Clyde chuckled deprecatorily for his choice of that elegant word, and for the exclusive intelligence it had rendered to his speech. Clyde was overflowing. This was the sort of day he was born for.

"It's an absolutely lovely thing," Eric said as he looked over the little boat with its insides glowing beneath rich varnish, the wood there a deep reddish brown, its flawlessly painted hull beautifully cream white. Eric had an inspiration. "It's a work of art, isn't it?"

"Yes, it is," Clyde responded, looking at the boat.

Of course, he thought, it was also a hell of a lot of trouble, these little specialty things. The more precious they seemed, the more headaches you got with them. Bad as a woman, they could bleed you dry for the little pleasure you could get back.

But then he thought suddenly, what the hell, maybe Sumners would like an unusual dingy for the Nickerson ketch. He certainly had enough money to deal with the selfish whims of the little bitch's maintenance needs. And no doubt, a little twelve-footer like that would look great, mounted like a trophy, on the deck of some fathead, rich-guy's boat.

"Jack Colby made it," he said, feeling swell enough to mention his neighbor.

In fact, it was more than swell. It was pretty goddamned magnanimous, considering how he didn't have any great liking for the owner of the boatworks.

Colby was a blowhard, always talking about his big plans for the place even though he'd only been in there a few years. Nobody liked the guy, nor the way he acted like he knew everything there was to know about boats. How he could build any boat you wanted.

The truth was, Colby spent most of his time scraping off fishing trawlers ... down under their hulls, his head and shoulders covered with the stinking, smashed guts of barnacles. Which was part of the reason Clyde could dismiss him as a loser.

In any case, he reasoned, giving Sumners another glance, psychologically it did no harm to put in a word for his neighbor. It was a hell of a lot more relaxing to be chatting away like this, than if it seemed as though Clyde's sole concern was in steering Sumners continually towards his office and the dotted line.

"This is all he does?" Eric was looking around the boatshed.

"This is all he's done," Clyde corrected. "If you mean things like this. Mostly workboats, you know. Repairs. Cleaning." Clyde gave Eric a light grin. "Barnacles and so forth."

"Never anything bigger?"

Clyde didn't change the expression on his face, but a heavy warning bell had finally reverberated ominously. He had no need to ask Sumners what he was referring to. The rich man was being thoughtful, somewhat vague, and evidently reflecting about the method Clyde had mentioned for recreating old boats.

"Oh, no," he said quickly. "Of course not." And he instinctively turned and stepped away from the boat.

As he turned, Clyde flashingly saw Annie's now deeply worried face, and realized why she had been so skittish about wandering over in this direction.

She had known somehow, from something Sumners had said before, that the guy would feel a more than ordinary tug at the sight of the little matchstick boat.

"Just workboats," Clyde said, taking a step, turning back towards their yard.

Sumners moved, with almost a reluctant air, to join him. Clyde, his mind racing, was now consciously and carefully intending to avoid anything resembling full answers now. But he couldn't help wanting to bury deeply any interest.

"You know," he said easily, as though just being conversational, "times have changed. The upkeep, both in time and expense, is astronomical for such things. Fun as they are."

Clyde knew immediately and crushingly that his off-the-cuff argument, thrown in so briskly, wouldn't have the slightest effect on Sumners. Deep fear pounded in his stomach. Cost, he thought bleakly, was going to be the smallest part of what this bastard was going to worry about.

Clyde looked at Annie. Her face was pale. He gave out a slow breath, and let his voice go light, and even gave a light-hearted laugh despite the leaden feeling in his body.

"In any case," he said, "they're sort of like history anymore, you know."

He now took three firm steps to get out of there, causing Eric to automatically join in. There small solace for Clyde in the successful use of body language.

"Yes," Eric said, coming up alongside. But even so, taking a last glance at the rowing boat. "I guess you're right, at that."

"Yes," Clyde repeated, nodding his head forcefully. This time, instead of strolling casually as before, he firmly guided Eric back through the fence and the line of his own boats, past their gleaming, easy to clean white hulls, and then across the crisp gravel of the lot.

The morning had become hot, the gravel sending off heat like the coals of a barbecue. They went up the steps into the office and got out the papers, and got Eric's concentration back to the ketch.

Only when Eric had driven off, having been escorted directly to his car by Clyde and Annie, did either of them feel as though they were breathing again.

When they got back to the office Clyde shook off his jacket and threw it into an armchair. He yanked loose his tie with a hand still half-clenched in a repetition of the firm handshake he'd forced upon Eric out in the parking lot.

He sat down at his desk. But instead of any of the other things he'd thought he'd be doing at a moment like this, he just sighed.

But Clyde, ever the optimist, wasn't one to worry about things perhaps sliding off the edge. Or, at least, before they'd actually slid.

He felt himself get irritated. Why should he be so worried? Just because Annie was? Just because the guy had looked at a little whiff of a rowboat whose appeal was little more than skin-deep?

That was all nothing, he told himself. Then he looked over at Annie, sitting silently across the room at one end of the big sofa they'd reserved for customers. He could see she was ready to go any which way. That also irritated him. Because of the many ways it could go, it could go against him. He'd get blamed. So to throw her off balance he smiled at her.

She couldn't return it. "Christ, Clyde. That scared the hell out of me."

Clyde stopped smiling, nodded, and then took to frowning. He knew he was going to have to beat her to the punch to keep her from getting some sort of domination over the way things were going to continue that morning.

Of course, in the best of all worlds, they could both end up sharing the same feelings about it. But theirs was far from being the best of all worlds. So either he was going to have the right to be angry, or she was. He planted his flag first.

"I don't know why it should have, honey. I mean, I agree it sure felt funny there over at Colby's. But it couldn't be helped. He wanted to go, and the pressure over everything just made it seem necessary. Or else we'd have seemed too pushy."

Annie looked up at him, and then back at the floor. She stared at the pattern of the rug there between her feet, and suddenly began working her hands and fingers nervously.

"You should have heard him on the ketch, Clyde."

Clyde waited a moment. This was exactly what he'd needed to hear. "Why?" he said, feigning innocence, giving her a chance to develop what he could already imagine. He'd seen her face before going over to the Colby's and now understood how far into some sort of fantasy Sumners had been. But then, suddenly, changed tactics. He could see Annie was already well into whatever regrets or even guilt she might feel. She was too far gone to notice subtleties. He prodded, rough.

"It wasn't good for me not to know what he was thinking about, Annie. It would have been better to have known his reasons for buying that boat, if you'd known them. I just assumed he was a real sailor." Clyde had her on the spot, and he drove the point home. "Wasn't that it?"

Annie had nothing to defend herself with, even if she had been thinking of doing so.

"That's exactly the problem," she said. "He isn't buying the boat for himself. Well, you heard that a little bit. It's a gift. I mean," her voice became miserable, "it's a goddamn present for his goddamn wife."

Clyde rubbed his face, but said nothing as she went on.

"The way he talked in the boat. When I was there with him. Talking about her. His wife, I mean. The artistic side of it, how she would love all that wood. How what she was about, more than anything else, was how she was artistic. I don't remember. I mean, I didn't pay that much attention to it. But most of all," she looked at Clyde in a pleading fashion, "I do remember how he kept looking at all the woodwork down inside the cabin, and how he kept repeating that thing about his wife, saying how buying a sailboat for her was right because it was a romantic object. How sailboats were romantic and artistic. And how she would love all that wood because it was so natural. That was the thing, most of all, that she would probably appreciate."

Near tears, Annie's eyes were very bright. She'd been so angry with Clyde. So sure of herself. And sunk in her despair, she didn't recognize, as she normally would have, how Clyde was playing her into a corner.

Annie, in that morning's despair, had completely forgotten how it worked, the true tragedy in her marriage to Clyde. How she had never been able to be dishonest with herself in the presence of her husband, who was unable at any instance to be honest with her.

It rarely had consequence, but when it did, it left her as naked as any one human being can ever be in front of another. As she was right there.

Because all she could do, at that moment, was to condemn herself. Whether that was fair or not.

Clyde looked at his wife thoughtfully for a moment, and then looked out into the yard and down to where the Nickerson ketch sat off the pier—big, fat-bellied and expensive. Then he took a breath, his next line coming as though from a play where everybody knows the ending.

"Wood," he said, with husky, perfect delivery.

The reproach was complete, unassailable. If he'd known, it could have all been different.

Clyde eyed his wife. Of course he was unhappy about how this dangerous element had been introduced into what had very nearly been a sure success. But Clyde had an unsinkable quality to his nature which came about simply by his inability to project himself into the future. Carpe Diem could have been his life's motto. Not that it was anything he could have been proud of, because it was a result of an unimaginative, irresponsible nature, not as a result of some process of having learned something from life.

But regardless of how shallow it was, it meant he would never refuse whatever spoils were available, even in defeat. And in spite of the very real gloom present in the air, he enjoyed having Annie absolutely convinced she was entirely in the wrong. An occasion of such rare occurrence, he was unable to resist capitalizing upon it. Who knew when it would happen again?

What was so good about it was that, as long as he didn't say anything more about it, he could keep it that way. She was completely unsure of herself and he was going to get his own back for all the months of nagging and bitching she'd put him through. Goddamn if he wasn't.

He looked at her over there where she was sighing attractively with distraught emotions, and had the return of an earlier thought.

True enough, the other had been in mind of a celebration of success. But this was, he said to himself, a success of another sort. Maybe not the same, but still with a sweet spice of victory.

He felt himself stir again, and this time very seriously.

"Well," he said, somewhat thickly, eyeing Annie carefully. "He's gone now and all we can do is wait and see. That's all the fuck we can do."

He got up from his chair and came over to her, the embodiment of sympathy. He sat down next to her.

Annie nodded, looking dejectedly at her hands. It was true, there was no way Clyde could have known. She felt so awful. Of course, she thought with a brief feeling of defiance, Clyde could have stayed put and let her reel Sumners in. But then the feeling evaporated in misery, falling flat against her larger despair at what had been her failure to cover all the possibilities, at how egotistically she'd handled it.

She felt utterly lost in her self-loathing, and leaned into Clyde as he sat down beside her and put his arm around her. Then at last she let it all go and turned her face into his shoulder and cried, feeling how good it felt to have Clyde comforting her, obviously comforting himself.

While Clyde had a lot of rough edges, she thought, at least, on occasion, he could be an understanding son-of-a-bitch.

Clyde, with a slight smile of anticipation on his face, could only have agreed with that assessment.

Pulling Annie ever closer, he reached up to grasp the pull chord for the drapes hanging behind the sofa.

# Chapter 5

Sᴄᴏᴛᴛ McKᴀʏ, several days beforehand, had been leaning back against the heavy, tarred timber, basking there in the sunlight alongside the boatshed. He'd reached down and found his pint bottle of whiskey. It was a little after one, but he'd drunk most of it already.

He examined what was left, and then took a long swallow. It wasn't as if anyone was working that day, he thought, putting the bottle in its ever more reduced state back alongside the heavy timber. Then shifting himself for comfort, he resumed his long inspection of Bellingham Bay.

A warm September day without any wind, there was little activity out on the water except the working boats of fishermen going out, or an occasional tanker appearing between the islands. It was just a dead, dog day. Which was all right with Scott. There was nothing happening at Colby's boatworks. Scott and Jack Colby had finished the little rowing pod the week before. With no orders for anything else, Jack had gone down to Seattle for a few days to do some carpentry jobs, leaving Scott and Jack's wife, Ellen, to watch the boatyard. So he was in charge, for whatever it was worth.

Scott looked around himself at the empty shed full of old, moldy sawdust. Graying lumber covered with dark-stained canvas tarpaulins was stacked haphazardly along one side, and strewn along the other were greasy bits and pieces of boat motors and winches and other mechanical paraphernalia. Everything was covered with gray dust and dark grime gone brown and black.

Down at the far end, the *Isabelle's* clean white strakes and gleaming woodwork made for a little clearing of light in the jungle of all that disuse and filth. There on the ground around it, like a golden halo, were the clean orange and yellow wood shavings and pale sawdust, the by-product of all their labors, looking like what it was—wasted efforts—and strangely out of place and forlorn in the reality of the rest of the shop's more worldly seeming unconcern for artistry.

If the rest of the shop was ignored, you could have convinced yourself things were taking place. But Scott knew that between the time the *Isabelle* went away with her new owner and the time the next job like that ever again came along, all that freshness there would have turned to gray as well. Because in reality, scraping barnacles off the weed-soured bottoms of fishing boats was the true business of the boatshed and its so-called artisans, and scraping barnacles didn't make the place look like a boatbuilder's yard at all.

To be square about it, they were just a garage for boats, a pseudo-artisanal environment. And a filthy one at that. It was the *Isabelle* there, and her virginal little fantasy of fresh beauty, which was out of place at Colby Boatworks.

Scott eyed the little boat. It had been good to build her. The owner had seen something like her in an old drawing and had come down and asked on the off-chance whether Jack knew how to build something like that.

While anyone familiar with what went on at the boatshed would have had a hard time not smiling at that hopeless, belly-laugh of a request, Jack had decided they would indeed build it. Or Scott and he had decided they could.

Jack, in fact, had been very much against it. Not out of lack of ability, of course. But out of a stubborn, defeated temperament.

Both of them had constructed wooden boats. Jack just wanted to be realistic and despite his knowledge and skills, wanted to turn his back on the wooden boats thing. As far as he was concerned, it was a dying trade best left alone. And, as well, it was as much of a commercial decision as an emotional one. Fact was that time and effort, measured against profit, ruled out those sorts of projects. And that was Jack's position about how to run a boatyard.

Scott, who had argued in favor of the project, who would have argued in favor of anything that was as far from barnacle scraping as possible, knew another reason. If he'd learned anything about his employer in the two years since he'd started working there, it was that Jack didn't have an ambitious tendency anywhere in his makeup.

Time after time Scott had seen Jack turn down one project after another which might have called for the slightest business risk. If the project didn't have a guaranteed foreseeable deadline, or profit return, he rejected it out of hand.

Of course, Jack had never been overt about his decisions, keeping them to himself. Scott had been there in the shop, had overheard him turning things down or simply had known of certain projects which never materialized, and had come to understand the process.

But despite how he disagreed with it, Scott had always gone along with it, never said a word, and certainly never to Ellen, who, Scott knew, was even more in the dark about her husband's business manner than Scott was. As far as she was concerned, there was nothing more to the business than what she had seen being hauled up the shop's ways.

With the *Isabelle*, though, Scott had pushed a little, Ellen having been near enough to hear the offer that day. Scott had taken the opportunity to put his employer on the spot.

Ellen had pushed for it as well, innocently thinking it was the thing Jack had genuinely been looking for all those years. And he had found it too difficult to say no, there with Ellen listening.

So Jack had given in, gone out and researched for plans, and found some that fairly matched the boat in the customer's picture ... only consoling himself through irritability on the days that followed. And from then on it had been easy enough.

Scott knew it was a fluke or a joke, and a heartless one at that. Because he knew as well as Jack, although in a philosophic rather than constitutional way, that building a wooden boat had little to do anymore with wooden boat work. Most of what work they did get was in winter when those fishermen who hadn't yet converted to new boats, and too lazy to do their own dirty work, came in with their old plywood and plank gill-netters and trawlers for minor repair work. Or else some mechanical work. Or else the usual scrape and paint job for the season. So the little rowing skiff had benefited, as well, from the slack of summer.

Now it was finished. The varnish was curing. Jack had gone down to Seattle to make up the difference pounding nails. Scott was in charge.

Scott grunted as though to laugh. He knew what that meant. That while Jack was gone he should find a way to show that he'd been busy around the place and not just screwing off the whole time.

Although nothing had been said, Scott had always felt vibrations of censure concerning his drinking, even though he knew no one, absolutely no one, could reproach him when it came to the job at hand. He looked around himself again, suddenly feeling inspired by a small flash of self-righteousness.

Goddamn right no one could say anything about his drinking.

He'd shown everyone time and again what he could do, and it was nobody's business but his own. What burned him up were the unspoken expectations, most particularly the one that figured any time there was nothing to do, he would just drink the time away.

Blinking now in the sunshine he looked into the darkness of the shop.

He could clean the damn place up. How about that for a little tactical shock? He would sweep out all the old sawdust, for starters. Really brush it out until everything was clean. Then he'd degrease and soap down the board planking on the floor of the shop, getting the slippery grime up. And he'd clean and grease the iron ways upon which they hauled up the fishing boats out of the bay.

Hell, he'd do it right. Maybe go up and sweep out the loft. Even though the idea of actually lofting plans up there was another heartless joke. Why not? He'd even wash the goddamn windows. The place, as he envisioned it, would at least look good.

That's what he'd do, he thought.

With that resolution firmly in mind he leaned back against the sun-bathed timbers and closed his eyes.

*

Scott had been up in the loft, quietly cleaning out and reshelving yellowed old boat plans, when Eric Sumners and the Moores had stopped below to look at the skiff.

Three days later, when Sumners wandered back in again, Scott had actually accomplished the entire cleaning of the boatworks. And he was now sitting on a restacked and clean timber pile by the waterside, having what he considered a well-earned, celebratory drink.

When Sumners came this time, he was alone.

At first Eric thought he'd come into the wrong place. Clean, swept floorboards of a dull white-gray ran the length of the shop. Down the center, going right out and down an incline into the water, were two glistening rails upon which sat a cradling dolly. Old, but immaculately clean lumber was carefully stacked along one side of the big shed and a canvas awning was rigged out above it as a protection from the weather. Along the other side were some shiny and expensive looking boat motors, also rigged over with canvas awning.

While there were no projects in the place, Eric could see it was in a state of readiness, very professional, and that the owner of Colby Boatworks was a well-organized man. He liked that.

He would never have guessed that what he was being impressed with was the by-product of a man too bored to stay drunk, and even less did he understand that nothing is as devastatingly revealing of troubles in a boatbuilder's business, than spotless inactivity.

Eric walked over to the rowing skiff. This time, with no one to interrupt his thoughts, he examined the work very closely.

The fitting of the woodwork was flawless, like finely built furniture. The smallest detail, from the brass oarlocks to the seats, was perfect in design and execution. The boat was obviously the work of a master builder. Eric hummed appreciatively.

He looked around himself at the boatshed, judging the length of it. A good two hundred and twenty feet long. He felt sure his hunch was right.

With an approving eye, he walked along the glistening rails down towards the waterside end of the boatshed, every detail convincing him of the appropriateness of the business. It was only when he approached the far end that he noticed, there lying on a pile of big, square timbers, the supine figure of Scott McKay.

Scott had just, for a short while, abandoned his recreational drinking when Eric came up to him. Actually, he'd dozed off. The sound of footsteps woke him enough so that he turned and squinted at the figure approaching him.

He didn't like what he saw.

Tennis whites. That was, what tennis whites looked like in 1930: white, full-trousered pants, and a white shirt with a white, v-neck, sleeveless sweater.

It was a fashionable, upper-class, yachting club sort of get up which made it difficult for Scott, with a knee-jerk dislike for purchasable class distinctions, to suppress a reaction of distaste.

Eric could see he wasn't making much of an impression on the stubbly-bearded man lying on the woodpile. Not wanting to start off wrong, he thought he'd try the friendly tack instead of going straight to business. After all, this wasn't exactly his terrain, in more ways than one.

"Looks like a hell of a good way to spend the morning," he smiled.

Scott wanted to say, sure it was, if your favorite way to spend a morning was that of going slowly bankrupt. But he just said, instead, "It does?"

Scott's first impression about the guy seemed confirmed. That opening line itself proved he was not only a rich snob, but a phony. Maybe worse, an idiot.

Eric grinned, Scott having given no clue about his frame of mind.

"Damn right."

That was the second time he'd sworn. Something he rarely did, and hardly ever at first meetings with strangers. But he somehow felt that the beat looking guy in front of him found cursing and swearing second nature and so would be more inclined to feel at ease.

Eric didn't know why though, exactly, that he cared to put the man in front of him at ease. It surprised him. Generally he didn't think twice about what people thought of him. He knew who he was and what he wanted, and that was usually enough. This was different, though.

The casual and impertinent manner of the man lounging there on that pile of lumber, combined with the extreme professionalism of both the work of that little boat and the neatness of the shop, made him feel out of his depth.

He rarely wanted things so badly that it put him off balance. Which he would have been, he knew, if he hadn't had the solid self-confidence of his immense wealth to provide its massive steadying power.

Money, in the end, would bring order to things. So despite a twinge of shyness brought on by his appreciation of the professional skills obviously at display here, he persisted.

"Sure," he threw back, showing he wasn't concerned in the slightest whether the guy wanted to be friendly or not. "It's a beautiful day, so why not?"

Scott continued to look at Eric, and then, giving a short cough which was more the announcement of movement than anything to do with irritation in his throat, swung his legs around so that he was sitting up straight on the woodpile.

"Do you need something?"

Eric nodded his head, agreeing not only to the question, but to the obvious implication in the voice that he was perhaps not in the right place. He couldn't deny it wasn't entirely true. Yet.

"Well, yes," he said, feeling himself shift briskly from his somewhat apologetic course. A change he was relieved to feel.

"I noticed that little boat, that wooden one over there, the other day and ...."

"It's not for sale."

Eric looked hard at Scott. He didn't like being interrupted. Ever. Even by someone of possibly exceptional skills.

"I'm not here to buy that boat. Actually, I was curious about what you do here. You do build boats, don't you?"

"We built that one," agreed Scott, unable to keep it from coming out as dry as it sounded.

For what it was worth, even if Mr. Tennis wasn't to his tastes, one never knew. He certainly looked as though he could afford a few things.

It would be a hell of a deal to tell Jack that they had another little boat job lined up. Two in a row. Jack couldn't refuse what had already been done, and maybe, if Jack didn't want to do it, Scott would be given the entire project. Which would bump up his earnings.

Scott had always been paid by piece-work. Most months were all right, but those months where Jack looked elsewhere were tough and Scott was a little tired of living from hand to mouth during the dry spells.

"You like the rowing skiff, huh?" Scott went on, deciding it was probably wise to change his tack on the off chance there really was something to the guy. Much as he doubted it. "Not much like that around anymore."

Eric looked back up towards the little boat, now far up at the other end of the shed.

"You're sure right. It's very good work."

Scott nodded, for a moment losing himself in a small flash of pride, but then quickly brought himself back.

"What's surprising," he said with a sudden, much more personable warmth, "what people don't know ... is that it doesn't take as much time to do, considering what you get in the end." Scott gave the guy a straight look. "Or cost as much, either."

At the mention of cost, Eric was suddenly all of himself again. He looked straight back around at Scott.

"I came down here to find out if you can build me a boat."

Scott's eyes narrowed. For all the earlier effort at being the soft touch, there was evidently some sort of hard kernel, a money sort of kernel he supposed, just come up in the guy. It was a strong force as well and Scott went flat against it, as though bucking a headwind.

He could see that the guy was used to getting his way as soon as business began. But if Scott could respect that, his earlier dislike hadn't entirely disappeared and he was damned if he was going to start letting himself get led all over the place at the smell of money.

"You want a boat built ...."

"Yes. If it's possible."

"You can see that for yourself."

Eric felt now a real prick of annoyance at the shopman's manner. A sudden impulse almost caused him to turn on his heel and let the whole thing go. But it was too important considering what he had building in his mind.

Then he realized that it was precisely that, the importance of the project, that he had to get across now. He'd see then, perhaps, a different attitude.

"Oh, yes, of course that sort of thing is possible," Eric said smoothly. "But I was thinking of a sailboat."

He stared at Scott, waiting calmly for the interest he was sure he'd be seeing when that statement sank in.

Scott wasn't one to show too many signs of inner emotions, outside of an occasionally unsociable frown, but he couldn't help his eyebrows from going up a little.

"You want a regular sailing boat built? Like one of those over there?"

He nodded in the direction of Clyde Moore's boatyard.

"Yes, exactly. Can you do it?"

Scott looked around the shop. His estimation of this rich guy had changed, this time from distaste to a sort of weird sympathy. Maybe even pity.

Obviously, this was some sort of eccentric. Who knew? Perhaps he was the serious sort of eccentric who was capable of more than just thinking up stupid questions.

So he wanted a whole goddamn wooden sailboat built? Scott's head suddenly gave a little spin, and he couldn't be sure if it was because of the idea, or because a few too many shots of whiskey had just decided to take a punch at him.

He was thinking simultaneously about the job and what that would imply, and then the money involved, which wouldn't be a negligible amount, and finally what Jack would say to all this.

Scott knew that last thing already. Jack would be back-peddling the whole way. He always did. So the best thing was not to worry about it, take things one step at a time. If the project was a good one, there was always a chance he could get things too far down the line to have it all turned down.

Why not?

They could certainly do a sailboat, although it had been years since either one of them had done anything larger than a rowboat. It could all work out. That was, if this guy wasn't a complete nut.

"So what are you thinking of?" he said.

Eric could feel the effect he was about to make, and enjoyed the moment.

He could easily guess by looking at the contrast between one little rowing boat in a big working shed, and the crowded hulls of the fiberglass boats in the yard next door, that wooden boats were the rarity even at the most insignificant levels of the example.

So, as it had been at the Moore's, it was with a certain pleasure of the anticipated surprise that he raised his arm and pointed towards the Moore's boatyard.

"I'd like something more or less like that."

Scott looked at where Eric was pointing, and was immediately disappointed and even a little angry.

Eric's finger went in a straight line directly to where Clyde Moore had parked the little, shining, eighteen-foot racing sloops.

This guy wanted a wooden Sharktail built.

Scott gave Eric a look of barely concealed disgust. Why in the hell would anyone want something which was made strictly for speed, and by all rights would be much more sensibly constructed in fiberglass in order to attain those speeds, to be made of wood? As boats, they weren't even all that esthetic. Mr. Tennis, thus, was in fact nuts.

"Well," he said slowly, "sure, we could do one of those. But I don't understand why."

Eric was startled. "Why not?"

"Why bother?" Scott said, no longer giving a damn about potential customer or not.

Money wasn't enough, sometimes. He could easily live without putting tons of time and effort into something so ridiculous. Maybe that was the difference between rich and poor, but Scott didn't care. He barely offered an explanation, just wanting the man to leave.

"I don't understand what would be the use," he said.

Eric felt himself heat up. What business was it of this workman why he wanted a boat built? Also, what sort of idiot would argue about a project proposal?

And who the hell was paying, anyway? That, above all else.

"It's a gift," he said stiffly.

Scott heard the edge, but ignored it. He'd had enough, and was going to now send it all on its way.

"Gift or not, I don't think it's worth the trouble. Those things are built for speed, for class racing, and that's all. They're not comfortable, there's no real interior to sit in to admire the woodwork. For that matter, once it's painted, you'd have a tough time even knowing it was made of wood. Except for the fact that it would have all the speed, in comparison with those, of a tugboat. In the end, you've got a boat no one else, ever, would want to buy if you decided to sell."

It was enough of an explanation. Scott didn't feel like lecturing the guy any more than that, and wished he'd now just leave and go play tennis or something.

But, suddenly, he also felt himself get angry, and decided to continue on to the end of the whole thing. Just to have said it once and for all.

"Anyway, as far as those boats go, as far as I and most other people are concerned, if there's any beauty in them at all, it's strictly functional, you know." He put a stress on the *you know*, making the translation of *you damn well don't* plain as day.

Eric had gone from an anger of his own, to a renewed feeling of pleasure listening to Scott's rebuke. His own estimation of the workman had been renewed, for he found he entirely agreed with his attitude and feelings about boats, even though he knew very little about them himself.

As he listened he recognized a hard-headed logic mixed with an esthetic appraisal which seemed correct enough. Time now to see what the real reaction was to be.

"Oh," he said, showing a mild smile of appreciation and concurrence, "I see. No, I wasn't talking about one of those," he looked at the Sharktails, "I meant, I want something like that."

He made his arm go like he was pointing over the Sharktails to the other side.

The sole thing lying in that direction, other than some boat-trailers, was Clyde Moore's Folly, the sixty-five foot Nickerson ketch.

Everyone in Fairhaven Harbor had been secretly laughing behind Clyde's back for over a year now since it was delivered and had lain, unclaimed, at Clyde's dock.

Clyde's shot at the big time.

Even though anybody with an IQ above moron knew that anyone interested in a big boat would go looking around Seattle where there were boats aplenty, of all sizes to appraise. And certainly not some jumbo-sized luxury number sitting out at some godforsaken lot in Fairhaven … where the markup was bound to be top dollar.

Scott, to Eric's obvious satisfaction, was indeed surprised. He was also worried, which didn't show.

This guy might not be a total eccentric, Scott was thinking, but simply and utterly ignorant. Which was possibly worse as far as wasting time. He and Jack could build eccentric, stupid boats, but they would never build a boat dreamed up out of some very basic misunderstandings.

"That, Mister, is one hell of a boat."

"I know it is."

Scott eyed the tennis whites again, but wasn't prepared in the slightest to believe the extent of what the guy intended to show by wearing them.

Hell, Scott thought, he himself could put on a similar costume and go strolling around town as though he was a millionaire. He squinted at Sumners.

"Have you got any idea how much something like that costs? Do you know how much even that one over there costs?"

"As a matter of fact, I know the cost of that one to the penny."

"Maybe so. So it could very well cost you half again as much to see a wooden one built, maybe even double." Scott shrugged to keep things as inexact as possible. "Depends."

"Is that right?"

"I'm guessing. I don't think anyone around here could tell you right off how much one would cost. I mean, nobody builds things like that anymore. Or, not much. And certainly not out here."

"Could you do it, though?"

Scott nodded, but was wary.

Eric nodded back. "And even bigger?"

"What do you mean, bigger?"

"How big could you go?"

Scott tilted his head a bit, considering. If this guy wanted to play Fantasy Island, he could as well:

"If it came to that, we could put a hundred and fifty footer in here, and still have room for more."

"We'd be talking a lot more, I suppose. I mean, in terms of cost," Eric said softly.

"You'd better believe it. Over a certain size, the price begins to go up not arithmetically but exponentially. You'd be quickly up into four, five, six million or more, depending on the luxury."

"And you could do it?"

It was like falling off a roof, but Scott saw no reason to say anything otherwise. Meaningless as it was.

"Sure. Comes down to it. Yeah. That's beside the point."

Eric looked over at the ketch, then back up towards the little wooden boat. And then smiled.

He disagreed completely.

It could be done, and that was exactly the point.

# Chapter 6

IT HAD simply been an idea. One that had come to mind that first morning when he'd seen the little boat. It was … a piece of art. Then all the way back home he'd been thinking of Deborah and how if he'd shown her the two boats side by side, the ketch and the rowing boat, her heart would have gone out to the pretty little wood boat. Gone out to it the way some people's hearts go out to homeless animals. Captured by love. No questions.

The more he'd thought about it as he drove out around the tree-lined shore drive of Lake Whatcom, the more he'd known he'd have to go back down to that boatworks. Just to see.

He'd guessed right. Yes, of course, it would end up costing much more, take so much more time to realize. But he knew he would have to do it or forever live with the knowledge that he'd only done half as much, in the pursuit of perfection, for his wife's sake. And he went down again, and was now standing next to Scott.

Eric found himself staring out across the smooth blue water of Bellingham Bay and he blinked and looked back at Scott.

"I know," he smiled, "I know the design wouldn't be exactly the same. But I do, generally, like something along those lines."

"She's a beauty, for sure," Scott said, a little mechanically, not yet used to the idea the conversation might have been situated dead-center in reality that whole time. But he wasn't too stunned to have an inspiration.

"Follow me, won't you? I think I can show you something else you might find interesting."

Scott led him across the boat shed to the stairs and took him up to the big loft, high above the shop. There, big bright windows lit up the smooth, gray-painted lofting floor spreading beneath even higher rafters.

Scott went over to the shelves where their library of plans lay, and pulled out a number of books on boat designs. After flipping through them quickly, he found the section on classic cruising yachts.

"We can get plans for any of these," Scott turned the pages

showing big ketch-rig boats. "Or we can have a marine architect make a variation or modifications."

Eric looked at a few of the boats for a moment, skipping back and forth between several that caught his eye. One especially, at a hundred and thirty-five feet.

"You can do modifications, eh?" he said, somewhat lost in his thoughts and thinking them out loud, nearly forgetting the presence of the workman beside him.

"Yes, sir."

Eric nodded, pleasantly noting the "sir". Finally, things were beginning to be understood. He continued for another minute or two before shutting the book. "May I take this with me?"

"Sure."

At that there was nothing else to say. Eric pulled himself up, put the book under his arm, and stuck out his hand for the first time to Scott. But not to shake. He held it level, as a request.

"I'll check back with you. Have you got a card?"

With all this business precision, it was suddenly Scott's turn to feel off base. He pulled out a leather wallet, well-worn and shining, and cracked it open to extract, a little apologetically, a somewhat less than flat business card with Colby Boats on it, and a telephone number for the office downstairs.

Eric took the card without looking at it. Then he stuck his hand back out to Scott again, this time as an offer to shake.

"By the way," he smiled, "My name is Eric Sumners. My office is in the Bellingham Tower if you need to contact me."

Scott shook his hand, but didn't say anything, his mind suddenly caught on processing that information.

Eric didn't mind Scott's lack of introducing himself. A slight slip, he thought, but quite excusable. He gave Scott a sudden and large grin.

"Thank you for your time. It shouldn't take me too long to go over this," he waggled the shoulder under which he held the book. "So, goodbye for now."

"Goodbye," Scott said as Eric turned and disappeared down the stairs. Scott looked out the loft's window, watching Eric cross the lot, get into a shiny little yellow pickup, and drive away.

For a moment, Scott stood there, silently. Then, finally, he reached up and rubbed his hand across five day's growth of beard, scratching his calloused palms with it as though trying to get in contact with some sort of sensation somewhere.

"Well, I'll be goddamned," he let out in a breath. Then he felt his beard again, suddenly wishing he'd shaved.

*

Eric was very fast and very clever. The next morning he began making calls to a variety of places. At first general, finally narrowing himself to the eastern seaboard. In the end he connected with a man named James Aston who owned a boatworks in the Providence area.

"How is Jack?" was Aston's first question.

Aston was sitting in his office, a small shed built into the corner of a much larger building which stretched, much like Jack Colby's boatworks on the other coast, down a long incline to the edge of Providence Bay. The office was cluttered with plans and loose-leaf files. Filing cabinets stretched around the lower walls. Above them, prints and photos of sail and working boats hung thickly, some of them built by Aston himself.

As he sat there, listening to the slight crackle of an imperfect long-distance connection, he found himself looking at one photo of a completed restoration of a Chesapeake oyster boat.

A crew stood alongside the hull, some with tools in their hands, half turned from their work to pose for the photo. Among them was a young man with a dark, serious face half hid by a large mustache and many day's growth of beard. There was little in the photo to show how close the young man had come to being an actual member of the family.

A certain bitterness, mingled with sadness, went through Aston. That, of course, had been a long time ago, he thought. What was done was done, and nobody, and certainly not his daughter, gave much mind to that time anymore. Funny though, how the ghosts of the past could reappear.

"He's got a good setup," Eric was saying to him.

"So he stuck with boats after all."

There was a moment's pause on the other end of the line, the slight whispering of three thousand miles ran on for a space.

"Is there any reason he shouldn't have?"

Aston shook his head to himself meditatively, looking back out through the door into the work building where his workmen were setting up forms for a double-ender.

"No," he said finally, "Jack was a good craftsman. Very good."

"I've seen some of his work. A small boat he's finished here recently. Quite remarkable."

Aston nodded to himself, unsurprised.

Eric went on, "I wanted to check. You see, I'm hoping he can build me a boat. A substantial one, that is. I hope you don't mind me asking you these things by way of reference. I mean over the phone. But I am about to invest quite a bit of money, you understand."

Aston made a humming noise. "What sort of boat is it?"

"A ketch. About a hundred and forty feet."

Eric heard what sounded like a low whistle, and then Aston's voice came on, cool and professional.

"Nice. And out there on the west coast at that. He'll have to have much of his wood shipped over."

"I've come to understand that will be the case."

"Good." Aston said, and for a moment hesitated, but then firmly and decisively shook away the memories. "Jack Colby will know what's required."

"That's exactly what I wanted to hear. Then you have confidence in his work."

"He can certainly build you your boat, Mr. Sumners. It'll be a fine one, too. I'm sure. Jack Colby had the abilities to do remarkable work."

"That's fine," said Eric. "Fine."

"Good luck to you, Mr. Sumners. I suppose you won't be mentioning this conversation to Jack."

"It wasn't my intention, but I suppose I could. After all, this is a business call."

"No, no," Aston said. "That's all right. No reason to, I suppose." Aston looked down at his desk at a few small framed photos, and at one with the laughing faces of his grandson and granddaughter to which, after a moment, he smiled back. "No reason at all."

"Goodbye, Mr. Aston."

"Goodbye, Mr. Sumners."

Two days later, following several other phone calls, Eric called the Colby's and got Scott out on the shop telephone. The boat was to be built, and he wanted to start right away.

Scott, saying nothing else, set up a meeting for later in the week. By when, he hoped to himself, Jack would be back.

Eric then called the Moore's and told them he'd decided not to buy the Nickerson ketch after all. He didn't give many details but did mention he'd gotten another idea. Although they would have never dreamed how the idea had landed right next door, the Moores knew they'd lost out to wooden boatbuilding.

That night, putting to use all the practiced vindictiveness they'd stored up all summer, Clyde and Annie Moore had one of the biggest fights of their ten years of marriage. No dirt left unturned. Clyde then went off to get whacking drunk, anywhere, with visions of Tahiti long since blown all to hell and gone.

*

During the first two days of arrangements on the biggest project Colby Boatbuilding had yet contracted, neither Jack nor Ellen Colby had been aware of what was going on. For that matter, Eric Sumners didn't realize he wasn't dealing with the owner of the place, thinking Scott was the boatbuilder.

Despite feeling a slightly precipitous sense of danger, Scott found ways to get around telling Sumners. Scott was half surprised at himself and how all this went in direct contradiction with his systematic avoidance of putting himself on the line. But for the moment, he became an efficient and businesslike arbiter of the project and tried to get as much of that side of things tied up before either of the Colbys returned.

He wanted to build this boat, and he knew this could be, perhaps, his last chance to build something which with each passing year became rarer. That was the good side.

The darker side was a half-hidden desire to place himself in a certain light, a contrast with his employer, for a certain reason. But he would not allow himself to dwell on that other reason.

Ellen got back first.

For a week she'd been up in B.C. in New Westminster visiting friends and family. A late Thursday night she drove her car into the parking lot in front of the boatworks, and noticed a light on high up in the windows of the loft. Possibly, Jack had returned. Why though would he be up in the old loft? Most likely Scott had been up there for some reason, drinking perhaps, and had forgotten to turn off the light.

A bit of irritation swept through Ellen. She didn't need late night lights to be on. She was tired from the drive and her sole desire was to take a bath and go to bed. But instead, she had to deal with carelessness.

She went past the small house and office Jack and Scott had built alongside the boatshed, and went over to the shed. She switched on the lights to the shop below, pushing up all the switches on the light panel next to the door, carefully looking for a moment at the shop space, then went up the stairs to the loft.

She found Scott sitting at the drafting bench at the far end, working over a file of papers, the deep shadows of the loft dispersed there in a small pool of light thrown by a draftsman's lamp.

It wasn't at all a customary sight and for a moment she was a little taken aback. In fact, it was shocking. As though she'd surprised a thief.

At the sound of the step of her foot at the head of the stairs, Scott looked up and felt his breath catch. It was the moment he'd been waiting for.

"What's up?" Ellen said, going across the loft floor and moving into the warm pool of the light.

Scott gave her a smile, and quickly moved his tongue across his lips. Then he looked down at the figures he'd been working on, a little shyly suddenly, as though a schoolboy rechecking his work at the approach of the teacher.

"Going over some things," was all he could say.

Ellen registered his unease, and was even more mystified. She could see Scott wasn't drunk, which was one thing, and so she was less worried than she might have been.

"Trying to turn a profit, or something?"

Scott looked back up at her, suddenly defensive.

"Shouldn't I?" he said. "Don't you think it possible?"

Ellen looked at him for a moment.

"I don't know what to think. Here I come, back after a week and, first, I see the shop space downstairs is spotless. Then I come up here and find you burning the midnight oil. Next thing, you'll be telling me you've got us contracted right up until the winter jobs cruise in."

Scott took a breath.

"More than that, I should think."

Ellen inspected Scott's face. She had seen Scott McKay in many ways, happy, sad, hung over—often that—but rarely had she seen him looking determined, and calmly so.

As the scrap of driftwood that had washed up in front of them two years before, Scott rarely seemed more content than when the work day was finished and he could resume his ever constant appreciation of getting drunk.

She knew from Jack that Scott was a man who had acquired, somehow, a great deal of skill and knowledge about boatbuilding in spite of his carefully cultivated appearance of not having worked anywhere steadily in the past ten years.

She knew, or rather felt, two certain things about Scott she didn't like. The first was that he thought he knew more about boatbuilding, or life in general, than Jack did. The second, that he didn't think she knew any more than Jack. But she had to give him credit for one thing. She had never known Scott to lie. A particular quality she was particularly sensitive about.

"That so?" she said. "Jack will be happy to hear about it."

"Maybe you, too." Scott said quietly, not looking at her.

For a moment, a slight drift of conflicting intentions floated up in him. That bad drift ... again. Then, quickly, he suppressed it, moving back to safer waters. Ellen moved towards the drafting table and examined the papers under Scott's hands.

He watched her. Even though she was tired from having driven down from B.C., even so late at night, she was a fine looking woman. Maybe not beautiful, her face a little too square, too plain. And her figure, although neither fat nor thin, was nothing for a bathing suit competition, either. But there was something handsome in her eyes, something strong in her carriage. Her hands were the capable hands of a woman with few pretensions; hands which sought work rather than avoid it. Scott considered her one of the most attractive women he had ever known.

She was leaning next to Scott looking at the file, her hands flat on the table. Scott sat back in his chair to give her room, feeling slightly disturbed by her nearness.

As always.

Even so late, she gave off a delicate whiff of perfume, mingled now with a faintly mustier odor and he could feel the warmth coming from the heat of her body.

She had long, heavy brown hair, almost black, and it was smooth and full when down but which she always kept twisted softly up behind her head, softly enough so that it was still full, and the weight of it fell upon the back of her neck like an invitation for a hand to let it fall loose.

Scott quickly moved his gaze to the table before him but his senses were swirling around him, and he could feel more than see the way her breasts hung forward as she leaned beside him.

"What a boat," she said after a moment. "Whose is it?"

It was remarkable, Scott reflected, how one body could be so aware of another without the other having the slightest knowledge. Into his sentient perceptions, the sound of her question fell brutally like the heavy, dull strike of a hammer.

"A guy named Eric Sumners," he responded dryly. "He lives out on Lake Whatcom and he's rich."

"Rich, I'd guessed." Ellen surveyed the papers again, and noted that Scott was indeed setting up some work.

It was a little surprising to get a job along these lines when there were boatworks elsewhere around Puget Sound which were known to have done large yacht work.

"Why'd he choose us?"

"He saw the *Isabelle*. Passing one day." Scott said.

Ellen was silent for a moment.

"Sure," she said, "I told you guys we should have found a way to use her for advertising. Put her out front or something. A full-color ad somewhere. And see?"

"We could still do it. In one of those sailing magazines. I'm betting this job here," he waved his hand over the plans, "is going to open every door you could ever dream of having opened."

Before Ellen had met Jack she'd known next to nothing about boats, her limited exposure to them having been those few times when she'd gone out fishing in row boats with her father, or on a rich kid's family boat for a party. After her marriage she'd learned most of what the business was about, if not the technical side, and she knew that the largest part of that business was generated by word of mouth.

Of course, up until then, the only mouths with words that had been keeping them afloat were those of the local fishermen. The yacht trade had never come about.

Back in the early days of the business, when she and Jack had found the boatshed and secured a lease on the property, they had both expected at least some of that business. Although realistic, and knowing there were few wooden yachts around, they might have expected one to come along once in a while up there in Bellingham.

But after a while it had become clear that it was a vain hope for a young boatbuilder in a dying trade to expect the few wooden boats still in use to be entrusted to an untried yard when there were some very old boatworks still in operation down around Seattle or Tacoma.

Early on, Jack had begun to shrug his shoulders at the idea. He now disparaged the wooden yacht trade at its mere mention.

That, of course, was just inevitable bitterness, she thought. All it would take was one good job and the sun would shine upon what she knew were his hidden dreams. He couldn't have worked all those years back east in those boatyards for nothing. She knew that, deep down, he loved the wooden yachts and time after time Ellen had dreamed of the day someone with enough of a sense of inquisitiveness might come around and investigate Colby Boatbuilding.

Jack didn't talk about it much, but that gave her all the more reason to think it was what he wanted. His seeming to be insensitive or unconcerned was just his way of making things easier for the both of them.

A little bit secretive, maybe, and Ellen might have wished him to be more open about it, more open about a lot of things instead of being so silent all the time, hidden behind his thoughts and thinking she didn't know what they were. Although she did. She understood him to the core. But that was the man she had married, and she got along. But now, perhaps, they finally had something.

"You say it's a big job?" she asked.

"Are you kidding?"

Ellen bristled at the slight tone of professional scorn in Scott's voice. As a man, he might have been a mess, but she was aware all the same that he was a knowledgeable workman. And so it was important, as one of his employers, to not seem ignorant. Her musings, she could see, had taken her too far away from the business at hand, and she brought herself around to make an attempt to be focused.

If she had learned anything about workmen, it was that when it came to their work, few words and gestures were wasted. To be respected, and show one's respect, one must try to show the same seriousness. Even with a workman like Scott.

"She must be in bad shape," she said, making estimates about the truest things she could say. "What are those plans? She must be a seventy-year-old tub by now."

Scott saw that she was beginning to see, but suddenly wanted to sustain this moment with her.

Ellen was an intelligent woman, and it had often galled him at how little she knew of what went on around the shop. All the time, it seemed, she gave the entire credit for what happened to Jack.

As little as it was to ask for, Scott could have wished to be considered more than merely a workman around the place. And now, there was suddenly an opportunity to reinforce her understanding of what was going on.

He let the moment continue, as though imprinting as much of the moment on her mind as he could. Make it stick.

"No," he said slowly, "those plans are that old. But they're not the plans, either. A naval architect has already started doing modifications to her lines. Above the water line she'll look like a classic ketch. Below, she won't have the deep keel, but a flat run, with a fin keel and fin rudder. That'll make it possible to have accommodations practically the full run of her hull and make her easier to handle. We'll be changing the rig design, as well, because she won't have to support heavy canvas the way they used to."

He now looked up at her, wondering at what moment she would begin to understand. And he didn't take his eyes off her, wanting to see, exactly, the moment that happened.

# Chapter 7

ELLEN NOW saw clearly, in the way Scott was describing the boat, something very unexpected was happening.

Whenever big old wooden boats needed substantial repairs, outside of replacing planking or ribs there could never be major changes except perhaps to the interior layout. She knew that much. But never to the shape of the hull itself. That would mean rebuilding the boat from the keel up. Or, in this case, from the waterline down.

Which was ridiculous.

Yet even with that knowledge she was unable to make the final leap to what was going on. It was impossible. So if the next question wasn't as firmly grounded in expertise as she could have hoped, she felt unable to change it to anything else.

"When's she coming in?" she said, and pitied herself for how small her voice sounded asking it. "We'll have to clear out a lot of space. I mean, God, will it even fit?"

Scott smiled. It was a petty thing, he knew, but he couldn't help enjoying how, for the first time since he had ever been there, that he had Ellen's complete attention. She was deferring to him. And he enjoyed that as well.

"Better to ask when she'll be going out."

Ellen wasn't as shook up as she seemed. Despite everything, in the end she was a strong, independent woman, and lack of knowledge or not she didn't care to be toyed with as she sensed Scott was doing.

"Don't riddle me, Scott. Why don't you just tell me what the job is."

Scott could see he'd angered Ellen, and he knew he deserved it. He'd been going too far with it. He also knew that aside from curiosity there was another reason for his slowness in filling her in, and he frowned a little. The other reason wasn't just game playing, and in fact was a pretty serious reason. It was time to get honest.

"Sorry, Ellen. It's true, I'm not making things very clear." He took a breath and looked at the plans. "It's just that it's so amazing.

I guess I'm afraid that nobody will be able to believe it. That it might get screwed up somehow."

"How, screwed up?"

Scott leaned back in his chair again and looked at her for a moment, gazing at her handsome, stern face, and was reminded again of many a bitter moment when he had often felt like getting the hell away from Colby's before he was driven right out of his mind.

Her clear, straight gaze came back at him, waiting for him to speak and, as usual, totally unconscious of him as a man. He looked away down into the darkened gloom of the other end of the loft.

"Oh, I don't know," he said finally, his own voice suddenly as small as Ellen's had been earlier, "I suppose by getting some sort of negative feeling about it right at the start. Getting things off on the wrong foot right at the moment when everything needs to be running the smoothest."

It was as close as he'd ever come to telling her his feelings about Jack. About how the largest negative aspect to everything around the shop was, in fact, her husband.

Scott had been working on how to line things up. He'd been consulting with Sumners' naval architect, talking to wood suppliers, fitting suppliers, checking prices. As though there would be no problems. But now he could see what a waste it all was, how all his work was little more than steam and smoke … until Jack and Ellen were into it.

If it had been himself, of course, that would have been another thing. But Scott knew he had long ago cashed in his right to have these sorts of responsibilities and decisions, his right to this sort of business. In fact, he'd never tried to have them.

And here he was, playing Cock-o'-the-Hill, when there was no hill, and no one, anywhere, to compete with him for it. Such a huge mistake he'd been making. All too easily they might not want to do it, let alone envision how the damn thing could even be built there.

Ellen's eyes had narrowed. "Why would I be negative about it?"

Scott winced, but looked straight at her and let it out. "You might not think it possible."

Ellen went expressionless again, placid as a statue as she glanced at the plans again. Then she knew all about it.

She checked herself though and looked at where Scott had been doodling figures. Prices for African mahogany, white oak, teak, prices for bronze and monel fittings. All very big numbers.

She suddenly winced, herself, as though in pain.

"My God, Scott. It's a joke?"

"I don't think so."

She looked up from the plans and stared at him. "This is crazy."

Scott nodded, but was now trying to be as unobtrusive as possible. "Could be."

"This rich guy. I mean, the guy could buy one couldn't he?"

"No doubt. Wait until you meet him, then you'll see. He wants … this is the way I understand it … he wants us to build it for his wife. As a gift, you see? But he wants as part of the gift for her to see it being built. I don't know much about that. I haven't met her. I get the impression the guy feels that that is going to be a large part of what the boat is about." Scott smiled uneasily. "An experience."

Ellen nodded, getting slowly used to the idea. But with none of the negative feelings Scott had so feared. Regardless of how long they'd been together, she and Jack were entirely different people.

"An experience," she repeated. "I'll say. This is, indeed, crazy. What will Jack think?"

Scott sighed inwardly, careful to make no outward signs of his worries about her husband.

"I thought about that. I don't know. But I do know one thing for sure. If we want to, we can do this."

"You sure?"

"Yes. Absolutely. I've done it. Jack's done it. It's just a matter of time and work. It's not like you have to carry her on your back or anything. No matter how big she seems on paper. Anything this big is always done one way. One piece at a time. And all you have to do is make sure all the pieces are done right. Like the *Isabelle*. Except that there's just a hell of a lot more to her."

Ellen could see it, and believe it, and she had gone from a sort of fright and awe, to a comforted sense of faith in what Scott was saying. She had never placed so much confidence in Scott's estimation of things before. But she did so now, without knowing it, and beckoned further proof of what she so deeply needed to hear about something which came so close to what she had so long dreamed for.

"It doesn't scare you?" She smiled.

"No."

"It scares me."

"It won't." Scott had never felt so much of his presence with her before. Never so strong, never so helpful. It was not so much for himself, but with a sort of chivalric sense of responsibility, that he now said his next words. For her.

"Believe me."

Ellen suddenly noticed that Scott was perfectly sober. He was shaved, combed and clean, and looking, beneath his curly brown hair, every inch solid and steady. In a rough way, he was even handsome with his clear, wide-set blue eyes and his square, freckled features. An honest face, and she knew suddenly that they couldn't, mustn't, turn the project down. At least not out of hand.

"Well," she said, "if you don't mind, I'll continue being scared for a while."

She bit her lip, her mind suddenly awhirl with plans of her own.

"So, now what? What to do? What did you tell this guy? I mean, Jack won't be back for another week, maybe longer."

"You need to meet this guy and see, then you'll know what to do. I think we need to keep things moving along somehow though. Not commit anything to paper, or orders, of course, but keep things going."

"Yeah?"

Although it was a question, Scott could see she was sold. Now he could see he was going to have to start laying the terrain for the hardest thing to come.

He didn't care anymore about impressing her, or making her feel his presence, or anything else like that. Because now it was exclusively the building of the boat that mattered, and he would do anything to make sure Ellen would fight for it as hard as he would—even if she didn't know all the reasons she would be fighting.

And fight for it, he was now convinced, was exactly what they would have to do.

"I figure it this way. No matter what, Jack should do this even if he doesn't want to. It's the big thing of all time. I suppose I could have gone down to Seattle to talk to him …," Scott could hear the lie coming on, but he knew he had to go with it, had to create a sense of urgency to prod Ellen into feeling the same thing, "but it couldn't wait. I had to make Sumners feel things were moving right along."

"So, it's sort of begun?"

"I'll say."

For a second, Ellen reeled with what was happening. Then suddenly she was utterly taken.

51

"Oh, Jesus!" she cried out at last. "Jesus, Jesus, Jesus!"

Without warning she threw her arms around Scott, hugging him as though he was the oldest friend she'd ever had.

"Oh, what's Jack going to say? My God!"

Scott was smiling, and when she finally stood up he looked at her, feeling that peculiar, frustrated pressure which comes in living a day-to-day life where nothing has been happening, being released within him. Just as another sort of pressure was obviously being released within Ellen in some other way.

Scott noted all that in secret pleasure. Almost as if a small, private, victory of sorts. But at the same time, fully realistic, he could also only note dryly that, regardless of whatever were the things in her own life bringing on pressures and pains, it would never occur to her that he had relieved her of them—even if only temporarily here.

Or that Jack never could have done so.

## Chapter 8

THE NORTH-WESTERN border of Washington above Bellingham was as good a symbol as anything of the sometimes bizarre inconsistencies of the region.

Of course, borders are borders. Things must start somewhere.

The northern border of the western United States was no great Evil as some borders are, but just an arbitrary line drawn straight from Lake of the Woods in Minnesota to the Pacific. The only real iniquity was in how, a good century and a half earlier, that line had been ruled along that latitude by men, thousands of miles distant, who had the barest notion of what the bisected terrain was like.

In itself, of course, that should surprise no one. The usual system of international hoodwinking and elbow-twisting, and not the suggestions from the actual inhabitants—whether soldiers, surveyors, trappers, settlers or Indians, especially not the Indians—had settled the placement of the mark. For most of its length the long border made no difference up across the high northern plains of Dakota and Montana. It cut nothing as it swathed towards endless horizons of grass. It divided nothing in particular among the northern Rockies of Idaho as it ripped through the heavily jagged wilderness homes of mountain sheep, cougar, elk and bear.

But the last twenty miles or so at the far western end disconcertingly made up for the previous thousands of miles. For that was where the border suddenly tumbles off the Cascade Mountains down onto a broad valley and runs out to the sea, there to cross with blind abandon miles of water to snip off, in a geographic joke, the southern jutting point of a small Canadian peninsula. And those last few dozen miles back on the mainland between mountain and sea, with absolute disregard, separated two small but identical swatches of natural country.

Enclosed by foothills, that broad lowlands through which runs the Nooksack and Fraser rivers should have rightly remained as a piece, either Canadian or Washingtonian. Instead, the entire country was simply lopped in two with all the graceful appropriateness of a meat cleaver halving a birthday cake.

The people living in the region were used to the unnaturalness of that separation. But to come upon it from the outside, from Vancouver in the north, or from the Puget Sound region to the south, one felt how one was crossing into a different country.

Not the false feeling one has at a customs post straddling a road. But the real physiological sense of atmosphere and style.

A thing different.

On the Washington side, Bellingham's domain could not be easily dumped into that general urban basket engulfed by the bustling expansion of the south Puget Sound. Physically, the region was separated from all that by a thin but vigorous barrier of seacoast foothills covered with Douglas fir, spruce and hemlock, the dark forest punctuated along the rocky shorelines with red madrona.

With its southern back against the last gentle efforts of that coastward mountain spur, Bellingham patted itself in between a compact bay and a five mile long, glacier fed lake, Whatcom, to the east. The town itself crept westward around its south facing bay, out to the far end where a long, thin peninsula of coast curled down, making the home of the Lummi Indian Nation. Off the end of the peninsula, standing like a sidelong cork to the bay, was the high humping dark bulk of big Lummi Island.

North of Bellingham, in Whatcom County, the land lay open as it spread flatly towards Canada. A land of dairy farms and hayfields.

There were few people who even knew, or agreed on, what to call the valley. For some, it was an extension of the Canadian Fraser Valley. Few on the Washington side would call it that even though everyone knew the origins of the famous, sub-arctic wind blowing down in winter through the valley, bringing a reminder of the ice-age cold locked into the Fraser Glacier lurking far up to the north.

Some called it the Nooksack River Valley, after the Washington river sweeping through it from its source near Mt. Baker. Some called it the Sumas Prairie. But most, with an imprecision inherent in its origins, simply thought of it as the County.

A number of small towns, homesteaded once the forest was cleared off, were scattered across the valley with names reflecting the mixed origins of its people. Indian names like Nooksack and Sumas intermingled with pioneer names like Lynden, Everson, Lauriel and Lawrence. All were fiercely independent towns and very conservative, unlike their liberal counterparts to the south, and especially unlike that decadent, neo-liberal monstrosity, Seattle.

Some of those towns carried their own view of the world to the point of belligerent reactionarism—the town council in Lynden at one time had actually thought fit to ban dancing ... not the go-go variety, but that of couples ... in its public bars with the aim of preventing the erosion of morality such close body contact would obviously lead to. Oddly, this action was not taken during some obscure year of an earlier, more prudish epoch, but eighty or so years into the supposedly liberated 20th century.

Of course, in those days, a new-old president had recently been elected, as conservative and as religiously righteous as the Lynden town council, and they were flushed with victory and had gotten carried away with the triumph of the return to traditional values.

But despite the fashionableness of the time, the decision was an indication of very real sentiments. Supposedly, one of the highest ratios of churches per population in the United States was to be found dotted throughout the dairy country with its lush grazing meadows.

They didn't lack for congregations.

A good, God-fearing population, therefore, dedicated to the proposition that if man had descended from anything it was not the obscene monkey, but the placid, modest cow.

It was no accident that Bellingham, perhaps of a more worldly if not exactly liberal outlook on life—cradling up high on its hills a small, supposedly progressive but eagerly elitist state university—should have seemed to have backed itself in protectively upon those tree-shrouded foothills coming to water's edge. Yet everything of the valley mixed there.

And it was there, in all that—the isolation, the screwed up regional frontiers, the strange hodge-podge of fundamental Christianity mixed with rough, horse playing logging and fishing, liberal academics and struggling Indian nationalism—that Jack Colby had made his home.

For a man to convince himself he owns rock-solid and mature qualities, whether he does or not, little is better than to live in one of the world's semi-designated demographic stewpots of nothing and everything. What is good, is that in comparison, one can dispense with the need to examine the reality of oneself.

Jack Colby was from nowhere, his parents the migrant mercenaries of army bureaucracy. Born in Fort Lauderdale, weaned in Tulsa and Santa Fe, schoolboyed in San Diego, blooded in two tours at overseas hellholes, and apprenticed to his trade in New

England, he ended by getting married—and to his particular mindset, finished off—in New York City.

Having made one lateral crossing from the southeastern part of the United States to the southwest, and then to the northeastern, Jack, in a subconscious desperation for the last throw of the dice—sickened by his travels as all unintentional travelers often are despite their just as common inability to find some other modus operandi to replace it with—had not chosen Bellingham as a home out of any particular knowledge or attraction. But because it seemed he'd already been everywhere else.

Ellen had thought it was a careful career plan to evade competition. Jack, a man more appreciative of the trappings of marital consensus than with the piercing passions of human, spiritual understanding, hadn't seen the necessity to tell her any differently.

# Chapter 9

IT MUST have been a woman, Jack was thinking, who decreed that you can't have your cake and eat it too. Women, being rock-bottom philosophers—that is to say sexual philosophers—were the only ones who could profit from such an either/or categorical imperative. A man might avoid the issue, smooth sailing might be a positive result, but for women the idea of monogamy was more than just a lazy ethic.

What guy, Jack thought, wasn't aware of that?

He believed in the conspiracy theory of history. There were the rulers, and the ruled. If in times gone by it had been more obvious, with poor peasants being herded around by the lords and their ladies, the fact that there was now such a thing as so-called democracy hadn't changed anything. The ruling power had simply become more subtle. People were led to believe they wanted what the rulers decided. You could put that on the world stage, and you could put that in the bedroom. He liked to tell anyone who might listen that women were the natural rulers of the bedroom. Or tried to be. If it wasn't implicit control, migraine headaches and so forth, it was by sayings and proverbs that every schoolboy was expected to learn by heart.

Not that Jack had anything against controls. God knew how most people had to be shoved into their place in the scheme of things, most being little better than dumb cows or mindless hyenas.

Of course, men had their little reverse controls, the implied threat of flight being the most workable. All that sort of thing seemed pretty disgustingly basic though, and Jack felt more insulted than threatened by the rules of the game.

It wasn't a question of love. Love was love whether a man's form of it or a woman's, and he had always figured that Ellen was satisfied with what she saw of it. But guilt was also guilt, and Jack could feel secretly annoyed. The truth was, he had reasoned out, guilt was what you handed yourself based on what you figured others would hand you. Second hand punishment.

Jack resented that anyone would dare to judge a man, an

essentially good man, based on covert rules of conduct made up in the darker recesses of human politics. Guilt was a Machiavellian mercenary in the war between the sexes and, as it always goes, mercenaries are only brought in when you can't trust, spare or find your own forces.

Ellen had nothing to fear. Jack had long ago decided there was no reason to play games fighting some made-up battle about something that didn't exist. Jack wasn't ever going to leave her, not for anything in the world. She was no student of philosophy though and wouldn't be much in for objectivity if she ever found out Jack had tripped across some casual sex in Seattle.

Very simply, she would hit the roof.

So, obviously, Jack would never tell her.

It wasn't as though he was systematically unfaithful to her. As a matter of fact, he had never been deliberately unfaithful to her.

It wasn't as though he had sought out the company of another woman. It had just happened the way it always did.

He'd been sitting there in the bar, thinking about how far his paycheck would take himself and Ellen—that in itself proof of his innocence, his faith and consistency—and the woman had materialized out of nowhere.

The way things had been for that woman, and for him, it would have been like a cruelty, and an idiocy, not to have come together. Nobody needed to know, nobody needed to get hurt. It wasn't as if he'd been expected at home and the dinner was going to waste.

If he'd gone back to his motel alone, the world for Ellen would have been no better or worse, since it wouldn't have changed his marital vows.

He examined himself and saw that he wasn't changed by the encounter in the slightest. On the other hand, if he'd done nothing, there would have been a lonely woman out there who had only needed a little human comfort, willing to give something similar in return.

At the memory of it, he slid his hands momentarily around the steering wheel as though again caressing the woman's hips and thighs, remembering that smooth flesh, more well-padded than Ellen's muscular body, and remembering the thankful abandon the woman had shown in exciting him.

Foreplay.

Who got around to much of that anymore?

Foreplay, for men, is what you used to do when women's bodies were still a foreign country, and also what you used to think you had to do to make sure. The unlocking of the treasures. There wasn't much thrill in it anymore.

That youthful thrill of not knowing, the tentative advancement of fingers and lips, and later the sort of gourmet-like consumption of a woman's body. To spend hours doing the pre-diddling was in fact sort of stupid, Jack thought, like making soppy exclamations of love that nobody would exchange for the real thing.

With that woman though it was all new again, and it was fun to be able to touch and probe everywhere in a conversation of thankful lust, where they had shown what they had learned.

In fact, he had learned something new. At one feverish moment in her living room, she had stopped them.

"Wait," she had said, her voice sounding like bells to Jack's ears. "Not yet, I want to do something for a while."

Being in a perfect state of excitement, Jack was all for prolonging the moment as though, in a realization of impossible fantasies, it was possible to imagine doing nothing but this for the rest of his life.

She held him, then moved him slightly away, having them in a way both different and unknown. It was a little kinky, like being in one of those sweaty, overseas servicemen's bars again. But mesmerized, he did as she asked and time faded into nonexistence.

He had understood. She had wanted to make it seem they were one being, and not two. A momentary metaphor for what the true and final state of what a man and a woman should be. She'd even had a name for it. Sex Knot.

Jack blinked hard and brought his attention back, just as hard, to the highway.

He let out his breath, feeling his pulse racing. He was driving in broad daylight in a heavy stream of traffic heading north on I-5.

Reality was back.

He took a few more, deliberate breaths, cool air coming in his window. Too bad, in a way, it was all now fading into what was little more than a daydream, he thought. She had certainly been something. But then, he laughed suddenly into the silence of the car, there was always Ellen.

Jack thought of Ellen, and occupied himself with transferring his excitement from the Seattle woman's body to hers. He clutched his steering wheel firmly again, looking forward to getting home.

Reunions were always good, he was musing. Obviously, there

was no reason why Ellen couldn't benefit from a few new things, somehow, herself. He sighed, turning to other things.

Although Jack hadn't been thinking of them right then, he suddenly realized how there were plenty of other things that might have preoccupied his thoughts on his drive back up to Bellingham. Not the least was that Ellen now wanted to have a baby.

That new desire of hers had taken some serious getting used to.

Of course marriage had pretty much always meant someday heading towards a family. The thing is, you get used to one way of life and when changes finally arrive, it's like you are dealing with them for the first time. If for Ellen it had always been a forgone conclusion, Jack had often put it right out of his mind.

Time, though, when applied to expectations soon makes for imperatives. What might have been better earlier, done with deliberation, now seemed like a duty. What man, especially a man who has known what duty is all about, doesn't resent it?

Jack had had plenty of duty in the military. First the duty, never spoken but there because of his parents, that made him volunteer. Then the duty of the rank and file.

He'd gone where they told him, shot at what they told him to shoot at, and he hadn't got too involved with thinking about it very much although he had seen right from the start how things were a complete mess over there.

A few of the guys tried hard to pretend they were doing something big, something for their country or for democracy, but for Jack, if he'd gotten blown away, it would have been only for duty. Luckily, he had survived getting killed for duty.

Well, now he had other duties, although not so demanding.

If Ellen said the time had come, the time had come. He had been thinking about it, and had come to see that things were going to have to change. Duty aside though, there was something else he had gotten fed up with.

Where he'd got the idea of becoming a boatbuilder, he would have liked to know. That he'd spent a lot of time hanging around with vet buddies back on the east coast, getting high and pretending the world was shit, had probably been the main cause of it.

Maybe it was guilt. Guilt again.

A lot of his buddies tried to find ways to live down the war, pretend like they weren't the sort of people who would go marching off somewhere and blow up huts and holes in the ground just because they were told to. That in fact they had some deeper sense of integrity.

If they didn't, and most were too dumb to even come up with a good lie, they were able to mystify about it a little, make themselves into seeming humanists. Talk a good game.

Some became artists, because that was the easiest way to mystify everyone. No way could an artist have been overseas mowing down donkeys with LMG ammunition and not have some secret Other deep in the soul.

Well, those had been his buddies. Maybe he'd just fallen in with the wrong sort of losers.

There had been plenty of other jerks who'd found different ways to deal with it, either by a threatening sort of bitterness that shut everybody up, or a bellicose sort of patriotism that no one had felt over there but which put people back in stateside off balance. Those suckers were even worse off than the ones Jack had hung out with because they'd had to continue fighting the war even after they'd come home.

Jack had taken up boatbuilding, a human level occupation, an old-timey sort of thing to do harking back to simpler days of more innocent values. He and his friends had been pretending to be like new age hippies, who had pretended to be like something else again.

Jack had gotten sick of that, just like all the old time hippies had gotten sick of working so hard at being confused. Now all he wanted was the real world.

The Bellingham he'd come to had been, in fact, a sort of hippy sanctuary, like many backwaters in the United States. And still sort of was that. The hippy movement died out in cities first, the retreating tide of the movement crept further and further back into the small towns, and then the hills, and lastly to the mountains. It was easier to be an earth person the closer you lived to the dirt.

But in Bellingham, even with the sheltering forest and lost-cabin mountains so near, even there Jack's latent fear of reality's duties had begun to die out—as had Jack's supposed love of building wooden boats. And so much the better.

Besides getting you nowhere, he thought, it also got you nothing.

What few artisans there were, Jack now looked upon as being pretty strange people. People who were nerds, repairing and using things that anymore had little use outside of a museum. Nerds as much out of it as the nerds who'd grown up to be computer whizzes—those nerds who'd now inherited the earth—except that the artisans didn't have the computer nerds' redeeming quality of

61

making money.

So Jack wanted out, and wanted back into the real world where work was just work, and money was just money, and things didn't have to mean anything else than what they were.

He'd made a lot of money in Seattle pounding nails and pouring concrete. Hard work, but just work, and not work that stood for anything else than the building of a big house some other realist would buy to install a family.

He was ready for the family thing, but no way was he going to keep playing around with the blind alleys of the past out in a rotting, fish-oil soaked boatshed. His kids would grow up knowing what was real and what wasn't.

Good money in Seattle. God bless Boeing's. It looked like things were going to be good there for quite a while now, too. Finally.

Real good money, and even if he had to put his back into the work, he had good health, and there were good unions and pensions and they wouldn't have to spend the rest of their lives depending on whether some rank-smelling bottom fish boat had run over a log.

The highway, after the dreary stretch between Everett and the Skagit Valley, finally went up out of the Puget Sound basin, climbing into the foothill barrier north of Mount Vernon that cut off Bellingham from the southland, and Jack sighed, rubbing at his month's growth of beard.

Only in his beard did the years show on him, gray hairs thickly sprouting amongst the black.

Time indeed, he thought. And not just for a shave.

# Chapter 10

Ellen had already put in a long day, the morning spent first with Eric Sumners working out a contract, and then seeing about their business insurance. She'd returned to the house and was making a late lunch for herself when Jack drove into the lot.

She waved at him out the kitchen window and then went over and held open the screen door for him.

"Hi," she said.

"Hi," he smiled, setting his tool belt down in a chair and then catching her around the waist.

She grabbed his beard and tugged.

"Looking pretty burly."

"Imagine so."

"At least you're clean."

"I remembered the last time."

Ellen was embarrassed by the reminder. She'd been so tired that day and not expecting him. He had, in fact, been filthy. What woman wouldn't have drawn away? She didn't want to talk about that, of course, but couldn't help defending herself.

"You know I don't mind a day's worth of sawdust and sweat. I'll just never understand how you could have stood yourself after a week like that."

They'd already had the discussion, but Jack picked it up again. Married couples often save and treasure arguments having neat resolutions. So much better than the messy and uncertain business of coming up with a fresh argument which might go anywhere.

"That was a special job," he said. And it had been. A remote job, high up in the mountains.

"You could have jumped in a river."

"Have you ever jumped in a river that high up? Do you know where the water comes from around here?"

"Snow, baby."

"My eye, baby. Glaciers."

Same discussion, same words, but they were just being together again. Ellen gave him a hug then, and he gave her a long, good kiss, and then she went back to finish making lunch, now making more. Jack began some coffee.

"So," Ellen said, "how'd you do?"

"Over four thousand."

Jack peered down into the bottom of the coffee can to decide whether he still had to measure it out or just dump what was left into the filter.

Ellen nodded, and felt her pulse increase. Not so much about how Jack had done, or even his being back, as at the thought of her news.

Not that she rarely had any. Things often came along while Jack was away. Not big things. Normally just small troubles or small jobs. Scott maybe having gotten into a scrap somewhere, or a customer making an early appearance in the season. But that was all.

This time though. Good grief. There was not only the news, but what she would have to do to get Jack to go along with it. She cleared her throat.

"How about you?" Jack said, punching the coffee maker's on switch with his thumb.

She almost choked, stumbling across what she was trying to find a way to relate. But a funny, jerky sequence of thoughts stopped her and all that came out was a long, deep-throated sigh.

Jack turned to look at her. "What's the matter?"

Ellen sighed again, but this time breathily.

"Oh, Jack. You're not going to believe it, but we've got a boatbuilding contract."

She'd practiced it for days, having come to feel, herself, daunted by the size of the project. As the days went by she knew he would deeply love the idea. But he was the sort of man who didn't like to show things like that. He would pretend he didn't. She knew him so well. And if his back got up ... ? She felt increasingly unsure.

There was little more awful, when hopes were based on mutual decision, than the insecurity of badly wanting something which could be easily crushed by a simple use of common sense or, worse, pride. Things this big, she had realized, needed a leap of faith beyond any powers of logic or persuasion. And especially beyond the need for saving face.

Jack smiled, but then felt annoyed. Not so much with the boatbuilding, though, as at the mention of an actual contract.

His annoyance had both a public and a private side to it. Publicly, of course, Jack and she made decisions about work together, often taking on work without discussing it with the other.

Big or special work though needed that discussion and here she hadn't done so. Jack was on solid enough ground to complain without having to disclose any other reasons he might be against it.

Privately, there was the instantaneous annoyance of feeling as though he'd been pushed into another corner.

Naturally enough, Ellen didn't know about his distaste for boatbuilding. He'd kept that to himself not solely for reasons of privacy, but because up to then it had been more or less a business sort of thing, irrelevant.

For him, work was just work, and whatever work he did was, or should have been, little concern to Ellen. Their marriage needed funds, and how he brought the funds through the door didn't matter. Now it did matter, because Ellen had gone right past him and bound him into work that, by all rights, he shouldn't have to do. Or at least had the right to discuss beforehand.

He didn't let any of his irritation show, though. After all, he thought, contracts could be broken, and certainly those contracts made when he wasn't there.

"Is that so?"

Ellen, indeed, was unaware of his reaction, and was beginning to warm to her pride in the contract.

"It's a real good contract," she said. "As a matter of fact, unbelievably good."

Jack forced himself to keep his voice mild.

"Yes?"

Ellen saw the hesitation in his manner, and knew she had to get it out.

"I just hope you don't get angry for me signing a tentative contract without you here. I just felt, like Scott, that it had to be done fast. The client is awfully rich and I don't think waiting would have been a good idea."

"Scott thinks it's a good idea, huh?"

Jack's irritation now swept into something close to anger. He was being pushed not only by his wife, but by his employee.

He looked at her flushed face, and decided to be unfair and petty, just for the hell of it. Show her that he wasn't going to allow her obvious enthusiasm to have any effect on him.

"Anyway, why are you so excited? You've done this before." He paused a moment, and then opted for a snide irony he hoped she'd recognize as being his right: "It's as much your business as mine."

He knew he had her there. The unspoken rule of discussing big projects was now alluded to simply by pretending that what she'd done didn't matter that much.

Ellen went from flush to a hot blush.

"Maybe so," she said. But instead of getting sidetracked into secondary issues, and unlike her husband who was unwilling to go straight to the hearts of the matter, she just laid it out. "But I don't build them, and this is a building contract, not a repair contract. It's not a building contract like the *Isabelle*, though, either. This time it's a real sailboat. So I was worried, but I went ahead anyway, figuring, at this stage anyway, there was no reason to say no."

"Of course not. You're right," Jack said, a little put off by how she had countered all the public arguments. Being as logical as she could about it. "And you signed the contract?"

"This morning," she said, beginning to read his thoughts. "It can be broken, you know."

Jack waved his hand curtly, now feeling irritated she should be moving in advance of his own arguments.

"So you must have the plans then."

"Not yet, they're being worked on right now down in Seattle. They're modifications of an old design. I've got some general plans."

Ellen pointed over at the kitchen table where there was an already thickening folder full of the boat's paperwork. Suddenly exhausted with the effort to explain, she decided to let what was there speak for itself.

Jack went over, pushed the expanding straps off the corners of the folder and flipped it open. The first thing he saw was a cover letter from Eric Sumners. Beneath that a cover letter from Sumners' attorney.

Jack's eyebrows twitched at the sight of the legal letter.

Beneath that was an insurance letter showing rates, to be readjusted weekly or daily, depending on the stage of work accomplished. No total figure, but it was still quite a proposal. The sort Jack had only seen or heard of a very few times. It had to be a very special boat.

"This is some contract you've got here," he mumbled, for the moment lost in a professional appreciation of what lay before him.

"You haven't got to the money part yet."

"Or to the boat," he added tightly, not bothering now to conceal his feelings.

He turned over the insurance letter and found, beneath that, the list of boat costs, all roughed out concerning labor and material and insurance, and was left open for possible, mutually agreed upon charges.

"Good labor cost," he admitted, a bit stunned by the material costs.

"I thought I should push it up a bit."

It was actually quite a bit. Jack only grunted and picked up a brown envelope beneath the letters and cost forms. Inside were study plans and he took them out and unfolded them onto the table.

On the top plan was the simple, drafting-line profile and sail plan of the boat. The more detailed draftsman's plans were underneath. But he didn't need to see them. He saw and understood in one second flat what was there.

Ellen stood off to one side, watching him, holding herself by the shoulders. He was silent, and there was a sudden look of far-away concentration in the shifting of Jack's back and hunched shoulders as he bent over and examined the other plans.

She looked away, in the need of finding something to do. She forced herself to go finish making the lunch. It seemed like she was doing that forever, hearing papers being turned, occasional sighs and mumbles, until finally Jack cleared his throat, preparing himself to say something.

She turned to find him looking up at her from the plans.

"We can't do this," he said.

Ellen didn't say anything. She certainly didn't smile. But from the tone of his voice, defeated and defiant, she knew she had him once again.

Of all the things she knew, she knew her man.

# Chapter 11

THE BARS in Fairhaven had been quiet for the most part. Except that each had been quickly visited by Scott since noon. And during the time it took him to have a couple of drinks, he'd managed to make it easy to see he was intent on getting himself a long way past soberness before evening. In fact, by only three o'clock he had become the sort of customer who immediately put any bartender on full alert.

He was obviously an incidental drunk. A drunk by default, by the snapping of some event. He was the sort of drunk looking for catharsis, a violent release. If he wasn't necessarily going to start a fight, or break something up, he was no less capable of being a menace to peace.

There he was, the street outside plain with daylight, but there inside the bar his mind a downed midnight. He was something a bartender didn't ever like to see pull into a bar, but especially not during what could have been its quietest hours when the regulars sat and slowly tanked with the television going.

But that was all. Scott wasn't on a mission of mayhem. And not being aware of the small distress he'd been causing higher on the hill, he finally trundled homeward, back down close to the shore road near the boatyard, stopping for a final drink at the bar on the end of the street from his house. His home away from home. It was there that Micky, the bartender, became the last, unwilling and sole audience to the handiwork of Scott's afternoon destruction.

Micky, well-suited to his occupation, was a constitutionally easy going man. An ex-athlete battling fat, he had a big gypsy mustache hanging over the corners of his mouth.

At that moment his mouth was slightly pursed in concentration and there was a definite squint of pain in the deep-set eyes.

From a bartender's point of view, no matter who you dealt with, any man really drunk was never the same as the way he'd been the last time he'd been really drunk.

Totally unpredictable, although there were little threads of expectation. Some got mean, some got pathetic, some got loud and stupid and clumsy, some got quiet—which was all right—and some, like Scott, the worst as far as Micky was concerned, got playfully cryptic.

Demandingly and confidently cryptic.

Having a confident, unpredictable drunk like Scott at the bar was like being out on the water watching a storm coming from a long way off ... and maybe it was bad, or not, and coming fast or not, but always it would have been better to have a bigger boat and especially better not to have been there at all.

Wiping beer glasses with a rag, Micky nodded at his sole customer. The hair-trigger monologue coming across the bar did not give Micky much desire to do anything else. Except perhaps to calculate at what point he was going to just throw Scott out.

For Scott, regardless of what it looked like to anyone else, the drinking had just been a thing that had happened. It had started early at home and got far enough along so there was no reason to stop and do something else. So he had left his house and walked down quiet backstreets, ambling up into Fairhaven and to the bars where a certain logic pulled him from one to the next without his needing to think.

Nothing was going on, nothing was happening at the boatworks despite all the staging work he and Ellen had worked out. Nobody needed him around.

Whether they were going to have at it or not was all up in the air. He'd done as much as he could for the moment, pushed Ellen as far as he could, pushing her even though she was already pushing herself. Nothing else could be done until Jack said something.

A sort of jumping off point. But rather than feeling the tension of the unknown, the tension of decision, Scott felt free. Things now would take their own course.

The feeling of freedom, though, is never the same, or for the same reasons, on the different occasions it comes along.

There is the freedom of escape, the freedom of going towards a sure thing, and the freedom of not giving a damn anymore about things that you shouldn't have given a damn about in the first place.

For Scott, that morning, it was somewhat a mixture of all that. Which was fine, except that one of the ways freedom also works, when you've spent a lot of time ignoring some of your thoughts, is that suddenly you've got plenty of time to dwell on them.

Lately, Scott had felt a certain discontentment getting up into him again. The same one as usual, the general one that he

69

customarily suppressed by the habitual method everyone employs: thinking of themselves not as what they are, but as what they are going to be.

Something would happen, maybe, tomorrow. Who knew what tomorrow might bring?

Scott, right then, was in a flat, not very energetic state. It took energy, of a minor sort, to live into the future, a sort of self-willed blindness to the discontent surrounding the present.

It took another sort of energy to live in the present. A big energy. Because it was hard work accepting that what you got on any given day was all there was.

Just the general thing, but enough so on that day that it had got to him, and helpless to it, he'd finally allowed it to get dragged out into the open. All morning long, and now all the afternoon.

At first, the general thing could be plenty of things. But then, to make it more concrete and focused, he'd narrowed it down to women, or lack thereof. Since he had none, a woman could only be a part of the future, and since he didn't have the energy for living in the future, he was depressed and thought he'd better have a drink.

He'd worked himself around the bleaker parts of it already. The day was too sunny and bright, in between the bars, to be depressed enough not to notice the girls down from the college on the sidewalks.

Laughing and distracting him from the mood he was working on. But also helping augment it the moment he ducked into the darkness of another place.

God knew he was too drunk to say anything to any one of them: he was an experienced and prudent drunk, conscientiously well-mannered for what it was worth. But if he was too drunk not to get an overpoweringly bad rush of sex, he was also too sober not to find it all a pathetic joke.

He knew how it was. He could not approach any of the girls without, at best, scaring them half to death or, at worst, disgusting them. Certainly not approach them with a plea for mercy, which was about all he could find to feel right then.

But for all that, he also knew that even if there was a God in heaven and dreams could come true, alcohol would have had the last, humiliating, word on the subject anyway.

Scott looked up from his shot glass and saw how Micky's gaze was quickly averted from eye contact.

Good Old Micky. A true blue son-of-a-bitch.

Scott felt a warmth of camaraderie go out to the bartender. He felt he owed Micky something. Micky'd always been a gentleman. Never too much shit. He owed him an explanation, at least.

"Well," he said, getting Micky to look at him again, "some days are bad, and others are worse."

Micky squinted suspiciously, and then had an inspiration. If cryptic it was, cryptic it was going to be.

"More than you think."

He watched Scott for a moment, but saw no response. For whatever it was worth, Micky thought to himself, it had worked.

Scott was nodding to himself, feeling the planes within slipping and overlapping in other directions, edges appearing and melting away, floating up and then sinking.

It wasn't easy, he thought, to have been working for a guy who had what you'd like to have, even when what he had wasn't that much.

But suddenly, God knew, when that same guy was about to have quite a lot more ....

It was hard enough even if you liked the guy. But again, God knew, when you didn't like him at all ....

Scott struggled not to go down the list with it. Even if you didn't like the guy. Even if you did. Even if he wasn't your friend. Even if he was.

He didn't want to go down the list. Even if you didn't love his wife. Even if you did. Especially if you did.

The goddamn sweet business of Jack's now potentially golden business and of having that one thing outside yourself with all its good parts to make a man concentrate on the outside, and then the goddamn sweet business of Jack's good woman, Ellen, who could make a man relax about the inside.

"I'd better get a girlfriend," Scott said to the wet rings made by his glass on the wood counter. Micky didn't answer and made like he had something to do at the other end of the bar. Of all the subjects he didn't like to deal with, that was at the top.

Scott, into the silence, sat like that, maybe five minutes, maybe twenty, and then he looked up and accidentally caught his reflection in the mirror behind the bar. And it all ended there.

He went home to make cold, rolled burritos. His special meal for special days, spooning refried beans onto tortillas with grated cheddar and a thick blot of hot sauce to remind him he was eating something. He finished the day drinking thin, mortally bitter lemonade, watching the news and fingering his old electric guitar, tweaking tinny little unamplified blues licks into the silence of the evening until finally, with relief and without a prayer he might have recalled, made it into bed.

# Chapter 12

Aſter dinner Jack walked out into the boathouse. With the deep violet evening going dark, an orange sky still glowed down low over Lummi Island. He stepped down in the direction of the waterside, noticing the state of the shop. Even that irked him. Too neat to work in.

He walked over to the *Isabelle* and stood beside her for a moment, running his hand along the smooth rub rail protecting her gunwale. He'd never meant her to lead to something else. She'd been his swan song. Now she'd become a siren.

He looked out to the last rim of light over Lummi, saw the reds and purples deepen over the blackening island. Inside the boatshed it was darker. Looking the other way he could now see the lights up on the hill. Fairhaven was beginning to take on its distant glow of nighttime garishness caused by the newer restaurants and bars. Merchants up there were trying to develop it into a touristy village or something and it wasn't as familiar seeming as it once was. Although nothing, anywhere, was quite so easily familiar suddenly.

Ellen had been adamant in a way he'd never seen before. So sure of herself.

He'd made a certain number of retreating actions, but now with deep misgivings. Let alone all the rest, she also had no understanding of what she wanted them to get into. Or any desire to understand, either. A form of insanity. Jack had seen how it wasn't just a surface thing either, and how the project had got itself entangled into all sorts of other things Ellen had inside. It was a sign of something, because people don't let something get such a hold on them, get so wound down in their guts so quickly.

God knew what it was. Jack had no room to move, so little he could logically counter with. Even his warnings about the dangers an operation like theirs faced going so damn big so fast, had no weight with her. Even to himself it had sounded lame, although it was also a truth. It was goddamn irritating that she couldn't even allow some concession to the truth.

She just didn't realize how big that boat was.

Just to find a breathing space he'd called Eric Sumners. Sumners said he'd be down Saturday with his architect and accountant and they'd be able to get everything set then. Jack had said nothing, later realizing his mistake in having called with nothing of his own to say. Not even when Sumners had talked about doing all the contract paperwork on his side.

Jack had, right there, also allowed the guy the opportunity of getting involved. Another mistake.

Although no boatbuilder welcomed it, if the owners got involved in the process there was little you could do to discourage it later. You ended up having to let them see the whole thing as though they were doing it themselves. Hanging around.

Although it had the one benefit of them not being able to complain about anything afterwards.

Jack sighed. He imagined it. The horror of it, the huge mess of it and how it might be done.

They would need help, for one thing. Although not with the boat itself. He and Scott could do it, even if it would take much longer without help. Much, much longer. But that was how it would have to go, at least at first. He already didn't want to do it, and hiring another dozen workers didn't appeal to him at all, telling himself that it would be just too hard to find experienced boatbuilders. That fast. There just weren't that many around, and especially not out on the west coast. The operational term for wood workers anymore was carpenters, who were just cutters and framers. Curves were not a modern condition. He and Scott would just have to do as much of it as possible. Given the time.

At the thought of Scott, his mind wandered angrily for a moment, but then he passed on. No, the building they could do, but they'd need help with the orders side, of which there would be a lot and which, in fact, had some seriously managerial aspects to it.

Which made him want someone else other than Ellen. He already felt himself backed into a corner by her. And if they actually did it, well … he'd be damned before he'd let her get more of a hand into it. Somewhere, somehow, he had to give himself a little breathing space. Someone would have to make all the orders, keep lumber and material coming in ahead of the work, not too much and not too little, and getting a secretary would be a fitting sort of revenge.

Jack shivered although it wasn't cold out. He found he'd been staring out over the bay, now ink black, and he turned his back on the last feeble scrap of defiant red sinking behind Lummi's inevitable bulk, and made his way slowly up the ways to the house, where Ellen was waiting.

In spite of everything else, she'd been waiting for whatever it was they had to offer each other.

He sighed again. Maybe it wouldn't be the best of ever, but he decided to take things a day at a time ... and it would be enough for right then. They at least wouldn't have to pretend, like they had to when things were going badly.

Giving in and ... sort of like giving up, Jack thought with a touch of bitterness. Doing the Marriage Knot.

# Chapter 13

FIVE SECONDS after Steven began talking to her about marriage, a subject she'd been trying to lead him around to for months, Catherine Wilkins knew she'd had enough of him. It was a strange sensation to know that ... suddenly cast off and away from it all immediately. Like floating.

All that time. To have been tied to this man, thinking of him, lusting for him, occasionally admiring him, and designing all her being so that reminders of him drifted constantly around her life like dust motes in the air, shaping or simply adding substance in one way or another to everything she did .... Then, like reaching over at night after the last of the ecstasy has died away, flicking off a switch.

Love, or whatever, was dead.

Sitting next to him on the couch, suddenly indifferent to his presence, Catherine shook the cubes of ice in her glass as Steven went on talking in that confident, overblown way of his. She finally stirred, got up and went over to the bar to pour herself another scotch. A lovely single malt from Islay. Steven Elgin had taught her about scotch. He knew all the refinements. For a few seconds she looked at the flows and eddies of the rich, golden whiskey drifting around the ice, and smiled sardonically at how it would probably be one of the best things he'd given her. Outside of literature.

Steven could never have guessed on such short notice how he'd suddenly become, in Catherine's inner diary, a slash in the section she reserved for Almosts, Close-calls, or Also-rans. He was just getting warmed up to his subject.

He was a great conversationalist, very nearly a great orator. He knew it. But, true, he knew he always needed to develop his background before he got to the meat of the subject. Some might consider that a minor failing but in the end, he felt, it was worth waiting for him to collect all his thoughts, his qualifications and foundations, because the end result was so rewarding. His students had, on several occasions, told him so, and he had come to believe they were right.

Subliminally, her sudden change of mood had registered as only a token, formal resistance to the sudden sea-change of his intentions. Pride and all that. He was willing to admit he'd been a bit of a bastard. She had a right to think it. As any divorced woman has a right to ruthless pragmatism. Tough thinking.

That made two of them, though. Two self-centered and self-contained people attempting, for reasons altogether different but nonetheless well-developed, to maintain separate identities.

He could recall with pride how he hadn't really thought of getting on with another step in their relationship until that very moment. Not once! He was sure of it.

As pathetic as male pride in liberty might be, it was a real enough emotion which Steven wasn't going to downgrade. He had simply made up his mind, as every other man must do, and had made the leap of faith, albeit nonchalantly.

Besides, his nonchalance had a certain, justifiable trace of indifference in it. At the start of everything, it had been less him than her. He could quite clearly and truthfully recall that there had been only two things about her that had caused any reaction at all in him, besides the primal imperatives of lust. The first was that she seemed to have an undeveloped yet possibly deep intelligence, which stirred every Svengalian nerve in his professorial body. And, more importantly, that she seemed to be an utter, compulsive liar.

The secret thrill of those challenging discoveries, in themselves, were enough to swerve his interests toward her.

For ego-fulfillment, Steven had struck a Mother Lode. To ensnare a blatant liar possessed with a fledgling, as yet undirected intelligence—and then to dominate her hard sensuality—had an irresistible pull. This was a woman worthy of epic existential potentialities. His Zelda. His June. Steven taught night classes on contemporary literature at a local community college, and he was well aware of what he'd stumbled across.

Catherine had wandered into his class the semester before, obviously in a semi-desperate effort to alter fate. An alternative to the endless singles bars grind. He hadn't felt insulted. Attractive women rarely wandered into his classes. Bored or desperate, often. But attractive ... no. From the moment she took a seat demurely in the back of the classroom, he'd wanted to sleep with her. The way she held her body, ripe but prim in a stiff attitude of attention, sent out signals of experience, cynicism and well-feigned modesty that few men not yet dead could ignore.

While some men might have held a more evolved, call it kindly, appreciation of her, Steven nonetheless felt he gave her exactly what she needed in body and soul. He wasted no time and the result was brutalizing, as it always must be when one of a couple holds the cards of objectivity. In the end, and what now counted of course … was that he had finally come to admit that he actually liked her.

At first a game, he had molded her ideas about life, via literature, along his own lines. He had manipulated her capacity for shameless lies, going along with her pretensions of self-assuredness to the point she could refuse little he demanded, in bed as well as out, without seeming to have faltered. He had grown to see her as more than just a collection of idiosyncrasies molded within vibrantly responsive female flesh.

As she stood over by the bar now, seeming to be thinking about something, he remarked to himself once more how she was one of those pretty women who was managing to brush along the boundary line of true beauty. There was nothing wrong, he reflected, with the idea of maintaining critical appreciation within the realm, even, of love.

Usually, only deep wells of experience can etch enough character into a pretty woman's conventional features to make her beautiful, he was thinking as he looked at her. But a well-honed intelligence can do it as well. In Catherine's case, it was both.

For all the world she might seem only a curly blond with a good figure and a little bounce in the walk. She did have a wonderful voice which could be at times light as air, and at other times husky and vibrant. But the immediate impression was not one of much depth. That was wrong. He had discovered that she was one of those women who had something, somehow, which could make a man ache for them. And it wasn't just the usual reason, consisting of resistance or rejection.

All this, of course, was a dilemma. Steven's heretofore indifference, up to then a secure method of steering past excesses of commitment, had become suddenly the obstacle stumbling him up in the face of decision. His experience with women had made him quite proficient with the first circumstance, but he had very little knowledge of how to handle the second.

He was sure of his situation though, sure of her need and vulnerability, so he decided the thing to do was to let her see a slight signal of intention. A confidence builder, as it were. Let hope appear, and then relief.

It had taken most of the evening, and it had been working.

Everything was drifting without a ripple in the usual directions, that was to say, cozy sofa to be followed by a torrid bed. Then, with a convincing ease surprising even himself, he had smoothly and casually, almost unconsciously, turned the discussion to marriage. As a thing, of course.

Which, on Catherine's side, didn't fool her for one second.

From the top to the bottom, from the beginning to the end, she saw the structure of their relationship finally come to sharp focus. Steven, at that precise moment, belonged to the ages.

Catherine swirled her double scotch and then turned to look towards where Steven sat negligently upon the sofa with his arm negligently along the back, holding there comfortably the space she'd vacated, holding it there for her return.

There was an indentation in the cushions where she'd been sitting and Steven fully expected its refilling. As he always would. He was still talking in an offhand, supposedly mindless and innocent way, about The Subject.

He was being generous about the general idiocy of the institution, and shrugged his acceptance of realities, nonetheless. Finally though, he awakened to the odd hardness of her smile from across the room.

"What?" he said.

Catherine gave him one last careful glance. He was a good dresser. His tousled hair, only graying as yet at the temples, was still as plaintively attractive as she'd thought that first night in the classroom. His eyes still as charming with their crinkles and sly lights. Just lovely. She took a sip of her scotch.

"Well, honey," she gave her voice the accent of a southern vamp, which fit her humor as to how she was to sound in the general circumstances, "I guess it's time you left."

Steven didn't get all of it at first.

"What?" he repeated. The genial light in his eyes gave way to blank questioning.

"I mean to say, that it suddenly occurred to me that you and I, regardless of all the effort we've both been putting into it, or not, add up to zero."

Steven frowned.

"Zero," she said again, liking the nasty sound of it.

Then she realized that, in the heat of the moment, she had just invited him to get out of his own place. And without warning an immense, throaty laugh bubbled up out of her, filling the room with a hilarity she rarely felt.

It was obviously going to be more trying than she had expected; that it would cause a great deal more confusion than her feelings of self-worth would have asked for.

The sudden question was now whether she should stay and maturely talk things out to the soured-off note of finality, or clear out and settle the dust later.

Surprisingly, she blushed. Something she hadn't done for years. She always blushed when her innermost motives became utterly obvious, there, hanging out in the air of the room, the tattered and not so noble scraps of her fraughted soul.

She knew what she was doing though. With less time than it would have been thought possible, and in fewer words, she'd collected her things in a sweeping fury and blew out of his apartment into the night. Steven had been too stunned to be able to work up a visible show of indignation, or whatever it was that he was capable of feeling in such a moment.

She was never to see her night school professor again, in the flesh or otherwise. And there were even fewer telephone calls than she had expected.

Life, then, was pretty much as it had always been.

She worked as a bank secretary in one of the larger, downtown Seattle institutions, her social life almost exclusively—before, during and after Steven—that of joining a few of the "girls" and making the singles bars circuit. With them she prowled up and down the bright metropolitan stretch, and even out into the dusky outlying suburban sprawl. In search of the magic evening, or its equivalent.

It wasn't altogether bad. She was attractive, and when she decided it wasn't too, too bad … that is to say not too fucking awful … or else that she was sufficiently numb from drinking and dancing not to think too much about it, she got what she felt she was looking for. If not, there had always been the hopes that Steven would eventually come around.

Of course, there was nothing particularly striking about any of the men she met. That was the irony of having to go to the one place you hated the most, because it was also the one place you could systematically find the one thing that seemed the closest to what you were looking for. But only close because you didn't want to meet anyone like yourself. You wanted to meet someone whose life was in one piece.

It was a fact that the people you met in those places were people who were in the same boat you were in. Or, to be honest, the same sinking ship. Nobody loves anyone who's drowning in the same water.

Catherine's weekends seemed a depressing succession of deadening descents to morning sobrieties and emptiness. Except for one strange encounter, just before she left Steven.

It had been impossible. He was a carpenter or something from up around Bellingham. He was married. They'd made love to each other one warm night in her place up on Queen Anne Hill, with the lights of the city coming faintly into her room over the dark rooftops below.

In the morning he left, making no connections but leaving her feeling so good and clean. Natural, for once.

She decided that whatever it was about him that he had, that was the thing she would be looking for. A guide. Unlike with Steven, with whom she'd had to pretend so many things, she finally felt free to acknowledge the truths of her desires as a single woman—those of need and hope for the future, rather than the pretense that the present was the limit to her existence.

Steven, smugly, had always assumed she represented only that, and for that she despised him. Steven saw no potential forces in her, only the cardboard figures of her actions.

As for the carpenter, except for the occasionally useful fantasy, she never gave him a second thought. That was during her Utter Realist period, when she was combating reality with all her might.

And since realism always demands a casualty, Steven became the unwitting victim of this sudden, impulsive resolve.

Shortly enough, shaky loans to shakier institutions in the Midwest and in South America almost brought about the downfall of the bank she worked for. Few people outside of those at the very top realized how close it had been.

Outwardly, the bank was just as impressive, its building, one of the original big skyscrapers in Seattle, darkly imposing and solid, gave no clue to the jellified accounts within. Frantic restructuring, hidden behind a stiff public projection of assurance, resulted in the tossing of more than thirty percent of the staff.

In Seattle, getting laid off was no earthshaking revelation. Years of industrial domination by Boeing's had accustomed everyone to that unblinking corporate instrument of financial adjustment.

This time though, cutbacks coming in the middle of miraculous economic recovery a few had once ventured forward to assert was only Voodoo Economics, took everyone by surprise.

Catherine was relatively lucky. She was reoffered her job as long as she didn't mind relocating up to the Bellingham branch. She was given two weeks to decide.

She took one day, and signed.

It didn't matter, she thought. There was nothing keeping her in Seattle anymore. Bellingham wasn't far north, and she would be equidistant to Vancouver. She liked the idea of living near the international border, the vaguely international flavor of the area, even though the people were roughly the same.

Perhaps things would be interesting in Bellingham. A working city, it was also a college town. Catherine had never lived in a community where only one or two elements defined the town. She envisioned something nice and simple. Perhaps, she was thinking, smaller places offered more, were more open or friendly. More clean. Straightforward. More of a chance for ... opportunity.

She recalled that one evening as a talisman of expectations. She thought of that tender carpenter. She refused herself the luxury of expanding upon the possibilities but the memory instilled itself into the framework of her dreams. She recalled specifics, but only as one remembers the vague outline of a lesson, to be used years later as a way of measuring something entirely disconnected with the original subject. She'd seen his doubts. He'd just got off his job, and had gone into that bar to get a beer and cool off before going somewhere to get his dinner.

He was feeling out of place. Dislocated, somewhere, to her eyes. So he hadn't really been thinking of much outside of the movements of his immediate actions when he nodded at her there next to him.

Things, as though simply unleashed, had gone forward with an irresistible logic. Neither of them would have ever continued with it if there had been any deeper currents of deliberation. She knew that. They'd been too soberly surprised by events to have had any expectations.

She remembered how, in the morning, sharing the shower, laughing and soaping each other, he'd then kissed her and told her he'd never be back. She remembered how that seemed to make it all seem wonderful.

She'd nodded and said, yes, it was that way for her too, how it was better than all right and how she was so happy, really, at how nice it was not to give a damn, for once.

When he left she knew he'd keep his promise. Which, strangely, was exactly the way she felt she wanted it to be.

To be free to accept possibly complicating situations, without then complicating them after all. It seemed a new road, and a new direction, and she took it with the lightness of a heart that had discovered a new meaning of freedom.

As she was packing her things, putting her apartment in Seattle behind her, she remembered. But as a haze of pleasant memory and not as some tangible goal.

She certainly wasn't going on any safari. She wasn't going to chase that particular poor guy down. It was simply comforting to think of the possibility that he was something, in spirit, of what Bellingham would be all about.

Not even the nervous bustle involved in the moving van's arrival could interrupt the calm, happy flow of a new life's sensations.

# Chapter 14

MORNING came misty, gray wisps of fog moving in with occasional gusts of cold, fishy breeze from the still bay. From the blanketed, opaque sky fell a drizzle not heavy enough to make the early hours seem wet, yet steady all the same.

Into the fog, Jack and Scott breathed out steam on the sighs of first effort, having begun boarding up the sides of the open boathouse. The job, once contemplated and then forgotten, had now returned as a prerequisite to serious woodworking. It was one thing to scrape and grind and slam things around in the blustering open air with only a shed roof high above for protection, and another when the work involved careful measurement and execution.

They didn't plan to board up the entire length of the building, only the hundred and fifty feet or so at the head, leaving the other seventy feet toward the water as it was. If the weather got bad by winter they could rig up plastic, as they always had.

Using old shiplap that had been lying around the shop so long as to seem more of the building than of building material, the work went fast. They'd planked-in the end where Jack and Ellen's house was attached to the boatshed, when Eric turned up.

Scott was inside the shed getting another sack of galvanized nails when the Mercedes turned into the parking lot and three men got out. Jack, perched up high on the ladder, could easily guess which of the men approaching was Sumners.

Eric was dressed for the weather in a snug windbreaker, corduroy pants and a pair of brand-new calfskin boat shoes. The other two wore suits and overcoats.

Jack backed down the high ladder. He wore a yellow rubber raincoat with the hood pulled up. When he got to the ground he pushed it back and stuck his hand out to Eric.

"Morning," he said.

Eric took his hand.

"Eric Sumners."

"Pleased to meet you. I'm Jack Colby."

84

Each man looked into the other's eyes for a moment with a more than casual curiosity, seeing enough in each other for the moment to convince themselves things were serious.

"This is my accountant, Newell Briggs, and the architect of the *Muse*, William Fletcher."

Jack shook hands with each man in turn.

Briggs was a thin, angular man with an ascetic, sallow face beneath thin black hair. His general expression was severe, but there was also a look of hard humor in the deep-set eyes, a hawk-like humor which was a little piercing. A man of calculation, there seemed more behind his dark eyes than he was willing to show. He would certainly be the sort of man Sumners would want around when it came to his money.

As for Fletcher, Jack could see nothing but a man of drafting boards and waterlines. It could have been the moment, the architect meeting the man who was to realize his design, or it could have been the occasion, with his own position somewhat excluded from a meeting reeking of finances, but the short brown man, clothes, eyes, mustache, hair and skin all of a brownish tint, carried himself with a withdrawn air behind brown, tortoise-shell glasses.

The introductions finished, the four stood there an awkward moment, the possibilities for conversation slowly dissolving within each man. The situation was simply unique. Even Fletcher, a marine architect, was not used to it. The building of large wooden yachts was that uncommon.

The screen door of the house banged behind them and they turned to see Ellen holding a pot of coffee in one hand and some mugs ringed on the fingers of her other.

"That's okay," Jack called to her. "We'll come inside." He turned to the other men.

"Coffee, gentlemen?"

"Sounds good," Briggs said, and then with a crooked, wolf's smile on his thin face, turned to Sumners.

"You know," he said, "this is infectious. I'm beginning to feel salty, myself."

Jack had never heard anyone describe, to his memory, the atmosphere around his place as being salty.

"It feels good, doesn't it?" Eric said, taking then a deep breath of the morning air drizzling around them.

Jack swung a flat, upturned hand backwards.

"Come inside."

Ellen had cups and saucers now set out on the kitchen table.

"Morning, Ellen," Eric said, enjoying the familiarity of his greeting to her. He and the others were hanging their coats and overcoats on a coat rack behind the kitchen door. "I guess now, with all of us finally together, we can say everything's off and running."

Ellen smiled at Eric, bringing up the coffee while the men took their seats around the table, but didn't reply. She had the diffidence right then of when a married couple is talking with strangers. The situation where there were two conversations happening, one for the strangers, and the silent one passing between the man and his wife. Sometimes the silent conversation is humorous and represents two minds in agreement, sometimes it is not. And sometimes it is neither and something else entirely different and makes them both feel like they're not married at all—but will have to face the consequences later, when they're married again.

Jack felt a small surge of panic when Ellen smiled. Regardless of what he felt about the project, he wanted no one else to see or guess at discord between himself and his wife. His diversion tactic was simple, lifting his cup.

"Here's to the *Muse*."

Sumners automatically lifted his own cup, but then made a toast of his own.

"To the *Muse*'s inspiration ...."

There Jack noticed, for what would become common, a faraway gleam in Sumners' eyes. A strange light in the depths of sea blue.

Then he noticed how Briggs and Fletcher had raised their cups quickly but held their faces woodenly neutral.

It wasn't as though anyone was embarrassed by Sumners' sentiments, but the two men gave the impression there was something odd about it, although one wouldn't have thought so.

A movement on Ellen's part caused him to look at her and he saw her give him a quick squint. She made him realize he'd been on the point of staring at Sumners. He nodded.

"Your wife," Jack said.

"Yes."

There seemed more emotion in the air than a rain-dreared morning was capable of, but Jack fell in with it for Sumners' sake. And, he thought, for Ellen's sake.

"Well," he said, still holding his cup in the air, "here's to both of them, then. Without the second, we wouldn't have the first."

A small frown crossed Sumners' face.

Jack immediately regretted making the toast which, although not very witty, had been innocent enough. He could see he had touched a nerve. But there was no way in telling anything from Sumners' face except that there had been some form of misplaced logic in what Jack had said.

Briggs though seemed to find the logic complete enough in its own way, perhaps more than it really was. He laughed outright, with a surprisingly good-natured sound.

"Yes," Sumners said, taking a sip of coffee. He then put his cup down and with an authoritarian sound, cleared his throat, and things began ....

It wasn't a long meeting. Over coffee, Fletcher made a presentation of his modifications to the study plans. Jack could see how much more efficient the yacht would be in the water.

He liked how Fletcher had designed the hull below waterline along more modern lines. She would have a semi-long fin keel, longer than deep, permitting her to manoeuver more easily than a traditional full keel, and let her enter shallower waters, with a separate, fin rudder. But he had kept the long bowsprit which would permit the main mast to remain forward and better balance between the jib and the mizzen. Even interior arrangements found his approval. The main salon and private cabins forward, with the cruising salon, galley, crew cabins, and navigation stations aft. He especially appreciated the eight crew cabins, finding a way to give crewmen separate berths, with half the bunk from one cabin fitting over half the bunk of the one next door. He smiled. Fletcher had either rode in, or was familiar with, the old sleeping compartment arrangements in the days of the Northern Pacific intercontinental trains.

"I had the freedom to go with what I like," Fletcher explained slowly in a quiet voice. "Eric's not so concerned with speed as all that. So I widened and deepened the hull for half and even double deck accommodations, and designed the rig with enough sail so that there would be more flexibility than with the old plan, and so that she'll present a more balanced appearance considering her size."

Jack found himself studying the man as much as the plans. It had been a passing thought, but Jack adopted it as probable that William Fletcher was actually some sort of poet. Much later Jack would see how that fit in so well within Sumners' project, but that morning it simply helped to explain the architect's alterations.

The most fully romantic yachts ever built had been the racing cutters of the last century, those extremely narrow and incredibly over-canvassed boats then thought to be the fastest combination of hull and sail in the world. While that had turned out to be false, the image of those boats with their huge main booms forty feet long, and with what looked like acres upon acres of sail filling above a knife-thin hull, was something out of an artist's dream. The dream of artists such as small, brown William Fletcher, who gave no clue to his inner thoughts except an occasional, solemn blink to punctuate an explanation.

If Fletcher knew he was being scrutinized, he gave no sign of that either. But if he did it wouldn't have mattered to him anyway. All that mattered to him was what was before him.

This boat.

"It's a beautiful set of lines," Jack said. For what it was worth, he could appreciate quality work in that business.

"Thank you."

"Where did you study, if you don't mind?"

"New York."

The school was too good to comment on, except that Jack might have said it was one more reason to be pleased in building the boat.

Jack's mind wasn't working in those directions, though, realizing that knowing Fletcher's training made it all the more difficult to get around the project. Not that he was planning to, of course. He'd already committed himself and wasn't going to try to cheat his way out of it. Whatever else, he'd always openly maintained, loud and strong, his feelings about people remaining true to their words.

After their discussion Jack took the men out for a tour of the boatworks. Passing outside they went by where Scott was working on the siding and stopped long enough to run through introductions again.

Scott wasn't into the formal mood they were in, having been amusing himself with a variety of lurid thoughts about a previous evening downtown. So he remained discrete, nodding quickly at the architect and accountant and giving Sumners just a nod.

No matter what efforts were being made to be relaxed and social that morning, Scott could see that what was walking around Colby Boatworks was more like a tour of inspection than anything else.

Jack took the men up the stairs into the loft, showing Fletcher how there was plenty of room for laying down the full-sized lines of the boat.

As though having passed all requirements for the project to proceed, Jack was then presented with two large cardboard tubes carrying the detailed set of work plans. His diploma.

It was awkwardly done, formal once again, and once again it was only the accountant, Briggs, who permitted himself to comment on it in some way. With another of his sudden, mocking grins, he brought a checkbook out from his breast pocket.

The checks were held in a heavy binding of rich, dark leather, embossed on a lower corner with what Jack would learn was Sumners' logo, a stylized fir tree encircled with a line. It was a nice checkbook, the padded leather softly glowing, and in it Briggs wrote, using a gold-tipped ebony fountain pen, a check for eight hundred and twenty thousand dollars.

"This should get you started," he said, fanning the check slightly in the air to dry. "At least, that's what I believe I've understood to be necessary for the preliminaries."

He gave Jack another, but this time wan, smile.

Jack took the check from Briggs and looked at it for a moment, suddenly aware that none of them had mentioned money that morning. So what he'd been handed was based on conversations Ellen had had with Sumners.

Another small thing to be bothered about.

He would have liked a moment to think, to be able to make some fast calculations about what he would need to start with, prices for the primary backbone timbers, tools and delivery costs, but he couldn't without giving the impression that he and Ellen were not in complete coordination. But the number staring back up at him from that check stopped him dead.

So he said nothing and, without folding it, slipped the end down into his shirt pocket.

One thing though, he thought. More than ever he was determined to hire a secretary. Get someone else in to act as a buffer between himself and the Sumners side. Someone who would be just a secretary, an employee, who would have to consult with him.

Someone who was anyone other than Ellen.

Nevertheless, that slip of paper in his pocket, suddenly felt real good.

More than good.

In fact, almost dizzyingly good. Like what he imagined it must be like to win the lottery.

But where Jack was beginning to swim around in that unaccustomed sense of something like happiness, Briggs managed to, again, find a way to throw cold water on things.

"It's quite an old building, isn't it?" he said, glancing up at the boathouse. "Goes right back to the 20s, I'd say."

"More. 1898," Jack said. "It's the last of a dozen places like it."

Briggs smiled. "Maybe you should have it declared a historic building. I hear there are plans to really start rebuilding Old Fairhaven again, I mean right down to here. With their old-timey looking buildings and all. Like they've started."

Jack twisted up what looked like a smile. "People are always talking about doing this and that, down here."

"Well," the accountant said, "you can't stop progress, even if it's backwards." He looked up at the boathouse again, and then looked at Sumners.

"We need to set up insurance not only for the construction, but for the site."

Sumners nodded. "Make it incremental, as per accruing cost."

Jack frowned.

"What do you mean, also for the site? I've got insurance."

Briggs took a look at Sumners, almost with a humored gleam in his eye, and then looked at Jack.

"No. Whatever you've got, wouldn't cover this. Because the truth is ...," his smile was still there, but his eyes were flat and anything but humored, "anything involving your old boathouse would take our boat with it. Until we get our boat out of here, the two are like one building together."

It was the way he said it. *Your* old boathouse would take out *our* boat. Jack felt a simmering heat come up, but kept his temper.

"My ... *old* boathouse is completely up to code. You just have your insurance agent come down and check."

Briggs nodded, and looked off towards the bay.

"We did," he said.

At that, Sumners smiled at the two men. All was settled.

With Jack's acceptance of the check the morning ceremonies were complete. If there had been liquor or cigars up in the loft it probably wouldn't have seemed out of keeping with anything else to have brought them out.

As it was, four men stood looking at each other there in the gray mid-morning light of a drizzled day, the only sounds being the increasing frequency of raindrops falling on the shingles of the open-trussed roof above them, and the steady, muffled plop-plops of Scott's hammer down outside.

For quite a while Sumners had been quiet, lost in his thoughts. Now, with all the preliminaries made, he seemed to come to life, a friendly smile now spreading on his face.

"So," he said, "when do you think you'll be starting?"

Up to that point, he had shown noticeably little emotion about the project except during his earlier mention of his wife. But there was now, within that mildly, but obviously impatient request, the enthusiasm of a sudden boyishness.

Jack had already explained the procedures involved in going from plans to construction. Sumners knew that actual building was still a few weeks off. So it was clear the billionaire wanted to know when they would begin laying down the plans.

Or else, Jack suddenly thought, as he took another glance at Sumners, it meant he was going to be an irritating client who asked insistent, driving little questions at any slack seeming moment.

In fact, Jack was convinced enough of the latter that he had a perverse desire to answer, *never*. But he nodded.

"As soon as I can get a roll up here."

He paused to consider the delivery of the sort of thing he wanted. Might as well show as many good intentions as possible, he thought, and patiently explain everything. At least for the moment. Later, he could make it clear he didn't care to have someone looking over his shoulder all the time.

"I can probably get going by Tuesday or Wednesday."

Sumners nodded. "Great," he said, putting his hands together. "That's great. You know, I'd like to watch some of this taking place. You won't mind my dropping by once in a while?"

Jack's worst fears, confirmed.

"No problem," he said smoothly. "None at all. As a matter of fact, I'd recommend it. It's good for a man to know his boat from the paper up."

He figured he might as well go all the way with it, seeing as how there was nothing he could do about it anyway. Sumners obviously had his mind made up.

"That's what I was thinking, myself," Sumners said. "Especially, for my wife. She's the one this is all for anyway." He now shifted his eyes from Jack and gave a steady look at Briggs. "I know she'll love to watch it."

Briggs smiled back at Sumners.

Jack didn't say anything, although the situation called for his extending a warm welcome to both of them to come down anytime they wanted.

But because of the momentary intensity with which Sumners and his accountant were looking at each other, he didn't think the invitation would have been particularly noticed. And besides, he was getting tired of all the social particulars weighing heavily in the morning air, and of the continued necessity to humor the byplay, and of Sumners' heavy, boss-like presence, and especially of Brigg's wolf's grin. But the worst was how it was turning into something that didn't seem to be going anywhere, as though it could now go on that way for hours.

What he wanted more than anything else was to get rid of the three of them and get a breath of air.

"I'll call you when I'm sure we'll be starting."

Sumners caught his breath, as though having been jolted out of his thoughts, but then nodded and stuck out his hand.

"Okay," he said, shaking on it as though they'd struck the deal then and there.

It was true that, in a semi-guarded way Sumners was enormously happy. He was enjoying all the details of those minutes talking in the loft … breathing in the fresh tidewater air, smelling there the odor of old sawdust and tar in the building, heavy but somehow also invigorating, listening to the mewling cries of the gulls planing outside in the drizzle. He could have stayed for hours in this new atmosphere he had thrust himself into, surrounded by the famous sensations of the waterfront. And he would have willed it except for seeing that this man Colby had a tugging adherence to an inner code of time and place; there was a resolute quality about him, perhaps a quality of self-denial, which bespoke of a man concerned with his work more than with the sharing of the consequences of it.

All morning he had been trying to watch Jack, making a private estimate, and had confirmed in his mind the impression he'd received over the phone: that Jack was the competent sort of workman who could be counted on to not waste time or energy. That he had the sort of sureness that would create a sure boat.

Eric reminded himself about how he had a theory about men and their work.

A man with confident abilities would always create work which, while subject to whims of material and conditions of fate, would at the very least carry within itself a sense of completeness and surety.

Those were the sorts of working men Eric sought out.

It was why he had Briggs on retainer. Briggs was a smooth-faced smartass, a cynical shark to be exact, but he knew how to balance the books and keep a steady hand on the cash flow, and Eric could forgive the rest—although this morning's performance was something he was going to have to deal with somehow.

And there was Fletcher, who was uncomfortably, pathologically shy, but who was so obviously at home with boats that Eric easily trusted him despite personal discomforts.

If there had been any doubts about Jack, they were gone now.

As Eric had moved the morning's conversations, subtly, towards the professional side of boatbuilding, he had observed Jack's personal deployment within that realm of experience, his relation to it.

It was reassuring to see with how much ease the boatbuilder anticipated those aspects which seemed the most difficult; unconcerned and graceful. It followed that the *Muse* would be graceful as well.

Eric took a sudden keen pleasure from not only having these sorts of men to work on the project, but also from how it confirmed his skill of being able to attract or select the most competent people to work on his projects, to enter into his circle of endeavor. It was a skill and a talent every bit as impressive as those skills and talents these men had mastered.

As a matter of fact his skill for identifying competent people was the cornerstone of his most cherished ambition: to enter politics someday.

The years of mastering the intricacies of high stakes land development had taught him that understanding how a system operates wasn't enough to make it work. The real secret was to find and motivate the right people to carry things through.

There were as many ways to get people to work for you, as there were people. The trick wasn't to know why someone wanted something, but to simply learn what it was they wanted. That ruled out psychology completely.

Any businessman who ever explained that he got things done through psychology, Eric knew was either a liar or extremely lucky.

# Chapter 15

ERIC DIDN'T believe the rags-to-riches measure of success was any more admirable than the way he had done it: taking his father's moderate wealth and building a true corporate fortune which made an impact on the economy, albeit regional.

His company was relatively small, but then, because he was not a manufacturer and so not needing production lines or a distribution system or any of the rest of the company hierarchy necessary for getting a product out onto the market, he did not need large numbers of people working for him.

Eric believed his main talent was for taking his staff and remodeling the lines of power in such a way that there were almost endless ways to give his people a sense of power and self-respect, if they earned it. And they did.

All told, Eric's teams had managed to build a third of the major housing developments of the Pacific Northwest within the previous ten years. If some people wondered why the Puget Sound region sometimes looked like a strange, dislocated collection of shopping malls and roadways sitting out in the middle of forested nowheres, it was exactly because of the long range speculation process taking place in the offices of a dozen or so companies such as Eric's.

That speculation was still somewhat the frontier tradition, a fallback corporate tactic of Northwest companies. You could look at the history of the region, following it from one decade to the next over a hundred years, and regardless of occasional wanderings from the main course you would always be able to rediscover the thread winding down through the years. From men like James J. Hill to Eric Sumners.

Jim Hill had thrown his railways across the undeveloped expanse of half a continent, with the sure knowledge that one day there would eventually be more there than just prairie gophers and Indians.

Eric Sumners, in the same tradition, knew that no matter how hard they tried to protect themselves from too much growth, the communities of the Puget Sound Basin would continue to expand.

And that expansion would cover every scrap of waterfront that wasn't declared natural shoreline, every tulip farm, dairy, private forest or market garden. All of it, one day, would be covered with housing or commerce.

Agriculture would be banned to the eastern side of the Cascades, where it belonged, and the Puget Sound would be a megalopolis equaling anything the East Coast had to offer.

The setting was too stunning to keep out the people. The economic connections with the Pacific too important to keep out the commerce. After a certain point of internal fusion, commerce and population would begin to grow upon each other. That was all there was to it.

But the people of the Northwest didn't want to look at things like that. Quality of life was still good. There was still plenty of undeveloped area up and down Puget Sound, so it was easy to ignore the scattered, half empty malls, the curbed and sewered roadways winding around empty house sites cut out of the forest, the sudden upgrading of small country roads into double-lane highways.

One day, though, very simply they would wake up and discover they were living in a compact, complex urban environment which had melded itself together out of hundreds of growth points.

That was the sort of thing that happened when people were sure it could never happen. Which was why any referendum or proposed legislation to curb the growth always got resoundingly defeated. They only voted down things they believe can happen.

If all the developers in the Puget Sound had been working together, and growth took place as a solid, well-planned, ecologically and demographically sound entity spreading out from Tacoma or Seattle, people would have been up in arms as the surrounding land was slowly overtaken as though by a lava flow.

But they didn't see anything.

On their way to their beach homes on Fox or Whidbey Island, or up to the ski slopes at Snoqualmie or Stevens Pass, or up old logging roads to do a little huckleberry picking, or out to Ruby Beach to dig for geoducks and razor clams, or up into the Olympic Peninsula to do some trout fishing, or out to the nearest lake for some water-skiing, they barely noticed each year's further dispersion of unchecked suburban development.

They barely noticed how there were more and more houses along lake and waterfronts, how there was less and less forest and field separating commerce and housing development up and down the I-5 Corridor. And by the time they might notice it, they wouldn't know it was gone.

He could see it.

It was a wave that was already building, as though a tidal wave far out in the ocean that no one yet suspected. But Eric knew it was there, that it was coming. And he knew he had to be on that wave when it came.

He was on a familiar footing with top people from all the major players in the region. All of them. Whether old money, within companies like Boeing's, Weyerhaeuser, the Seattle Times, or old money families like the Denny, Nordstrom or Bell clans ... or all the new money with faddish companies like Starbucks or, especially, with those having Microsoft as the center to the universe, including even the quirky internet spinoffs grown monster such as Amazon. And they all were more than happy to listen to him, if he had something to say. And secretly, he knew that even some of the tech company superstars admired or were even a bit jealous of him for being nearly the only northwest billionaire who hadn't got his fortune out of information technology gadgets and code.

But for all that was worth, Eric's ability to get things done was always accomplished from the position of outside looking in. Commerce was done within a region from a position of opportunism. But opportunism was the ploy of the outsider—you could only apply your will and vision of the future upon those small parts and parcels that came under your control.

Only as an insider, in politics, was it possible to coordinate all the separate pieces into one, sustained move forward. Not only then just to ride the wave, but to help channel its force. This was his new goal: to get in.

The problem, for Eric, was that of any political outsider in the Northwest. Unlike back East, there was not yet a true ruling clique which looked first to its own to find suitable candidates to promote. People such as those who had grown up in families managing power in the eastern Senates or Governors' Mansions for decades, if not centuries. People you could trust that, if they weren't particularly brilliant, energetic or imaginative, at least wouldn't seriously screw it all up.

But in the Northwest, those families were, in a sense, just getting started. And the voting population didn't instantly recognize those people, and did not equate a vote for them as being a vote for stability.

Northwesterners still had a tendency to vote for someone based on the vague idea that a suitable political figure was someone you also wouldn't mind sharing a park bench with. A mom in tennis shoes. A gumshoe reporter.

Some of the most powerful and popular politicians ever to come out of Washington had also been men who had possessed in their natures that elusive quality all Northwest politicians desperately sought or tried to create, of seeming like someone who lived just down the street. Homespun heroes. Which made it tough for the local parties.

Of all the things Northwesterners weren't used to thinking, it was that your next door neighbor was someone who had gone to Harvard and had a company worth roughly eight hundred million dollars, and was personally worth more. In other words, the political parties had to deal with a sort of regional reverse snobbism.

Eric knew the local party organizers. Bill Groenwald, Fred Shaw, Tom Hoaglund. Most of them were attached in some way to the college people. Activist intellectuals, or the social elite of Bellingham, that was to say, those people whose grandfathers or great-grandfathers had staked out their claims in the county and eventually built those big houses on Sehome Hill.

He'd attended their fundraisers, and had never made the mistake of trying to host one of his own. When he went, he gave generously, but not brazenly. His wife, although easily the most beautiful woman at any of the functions, was quiet, charming and unassuming. And at home, she was the perfect host, making everyone and anyone, feel relaxed and happy to be there. Nobody could outdo her or outshine her, not even Melinda. Bill had admitted as much. In fact, to date, Deborah had been Eric's biggest social asset.

Although there were perhaps occasions when he would have preferred she was more astute at understanding the social ramifications, and not needing him to always be explaining all these things to her during the drives into town, she had never given him cause to worry about what she might say. The men naturally took to her, attracted by the beauty and flattered by her attentions, so flattered in fact that none of them ever realized that the reason she seemed to like each one individually and specially, was because that was her way to treat just about everyone.

But the result of all that, and bolstered by his efforts to publicize his efforts through the help of the press ... not only the local paper but also the Seattle papers ... was that he was still out in the political desert.

Not once, delicately stalking along the fringes of the political hunting grounds in a conversation with one of the decision-makers, had Eric ever been able to flush out even the slightest sign of interest. And he knew damn well those people were constantly looking, comparing, taking notes.

When political party officers went to fundraisers or balls, you knew what they were up to. Every conversation a chance to discover new talent. But, even after ten years, not once even a jovial slap on the back or nudge in the ribs to encourage Eric's hope that they at least felt friendly towards him.

If the world had been one of true justice, men like himself would be acclaimed automatically and lifted into the seats of government. But, unfortunately—and oddly enough, partly as a fault of the democratic process itself which forced superior men to battle it out with the mediocre—even men of superior ability such as himself had to wait to be summoned. Could not just walk up to the door and knock.

Perhaps that was the most galling thing of all. Because Eric knew in his heart he was superior both in intellect and in energy to the party officials, and yet they held him down. If only he could get past those middle men, past the great mediocre muddle which always separates the worthy from their proper place, then people would truly appreciate what he had to offer.

But, evidently, that time wasn't for the immediate future, and he would just have to show as much a superior ability for patience, as he had for everything else.

Eric almost sighed at that thought, looking around himself suddenly at the loft.

Once again, the realities of life were such that even the wonderful experience of having this boat built could become slightly soured when he thought about what he truly wanted in life. And how he was being stymied by men he would have never personally hired for anything.

He looked back at Jack for a moment, and then nearly shook his head.

Here he was, getting himself upset at a moment which was actually quite marvelous.

With a firm set of his jaw, Eric gave Jack a friendly nod,

contenting himself on that point alone for, once again, having engaged another capable employee in a project.

"We'll be waiting for your call," he said, and he turned and made for the stairs.

Fletcher and Briggs followed suit, shaking Jack's hand in turn, Fletcher vaguely and Briggs with a sly pressure.

Jack followed them to the parking lot, thinking that he needed to do that in case anyone thought of another question to ask. But they never did. He just watched them all get back into that huge Mercedes and drive away.

He couldn't say he wasn't glad to see them go. He turned back towards the boathouse.

## Chapter 16

PULLING UP the hood of his raincoat, he retrieved his framing hammer and stepped back to the ladder.

If he was thinking anything, he didn't let it show to Scott, who came up to him carrying a long plank of shiplap and handed Jack one end. Scott went over to his own ladder and they walked the plank up into position on the side of the boatshed.

"Had any trouble?" Jack said as he tapped the plank in place.

"No, had to balance them up is all," Scott said, banging in a nail as soon as the plank was fit, and then he looked over at Jack.

There was no doubt Jack was holding back discussing the morning's meeting. Not that there was any necessity for Scott to hear how things had gone along, if you got right down to it. But there was little reason not to, either. Scott felt himself getting impatient, and even a little stubborn.

Although nothing had been said by anyone, Scott was absolutely sure that Jack had been angered by the contract. Probably feeling steamrolled, he thought. Or worse, usurped.

God knew.

But if that was so, that was just too damn bad. It was for the good of everybody, whether Jack was willing to see or admit it.

Scott wasn't going to permit Jack any slack. He had a right to know what was happening. It was a monster contract, and they were going to be up to their ears in it, all of them.

There would have to be a sense of teamwork.

"So?" he said.

Jack eyed him for a moment, and then looked back at the plank. He was indeed feeling sour right then, but it was mixed with a number of other sentiments he would have liked to contemplate in silence. He fixed another galvanized nail, and made the first, setting, tap.

"You say you saw a roll of template paper over at G.P. last week?" he said.

"Yeah. Two hundred pound Alexandrite."

"How wide?"

"Six feet."

Jack pounded the nail home and set another. "It's awful heavy. And expensive."

Scott pounded a patient nail of his own home.

"I suppose," Jack said, "once we have it we'll have as much of it as we'll ever need."

Scott stretched out to put a nail in the next stud over.

"You want me to go get it Monday morning?"

Jack didn't look at him, feeling down into his nail pouch for another nail.

"Yeah," he said. "I'll see if I can get Moore to run his forklift over here."

At the mention of Clyde Moore they both looked at each other.

"You seen Clyde yet?" Scott said.

"No."

"He's not too happy, I suppose."

"Since when was Clyde ever happy?"

"He was for at least a day or so last week."

For the first time that morning Jack smiled, but as quickly as it had come, it disappeared.

He glanced back over his shoulder at Clyde's lot, the boats there huddled sadly in the drizzling rain ... colored plastic flags Clyde had strung up in their rigging and across the yard drooping wetly. Then he looked over at the big Nickerson ketch, looking more than ever like an old maid in among the fleet of daysailers and island cruisers.

"I knew he was asking for trouble when he got that thing in."

"What'd he say? That it made him seem more legitimate?"

"Legitimate. And broke."

"Sumners damn near unbroke him."

Jack looked away from the Moore's and contemplated the boatshed wall, reaching for his nail pouch again. There was nothing he could, or wanted to say about it, whether pertaining to luck, competition or life in general.

If Sumners hadn't bought the boat, it wasn't Jack's fault. Clyde hadn't lost his customer to him. If Sumners had decided against it, then it could be explained that he'd never really been a buyer. In spite of any misgivings Jack had about the project, he was damned if he was going to feel guilty about it. Winners and losers.

Scott waited through the entire sequence of avoidance. He could see that if he didn't say it right out, Jack would go on like this forever.

"So," he said, making it sound as if he was amused by the obvious reluctance on Jack's part, "how did we do this morning?"

Jack nodded. Scott, he could see, was irritated with what seemed like evasiveness. But he hadn't been evading anything. He'd simply not wanted to discuss anything, period.

He shrugged. It didn't matter, he supposed. What the hell did anything matter? He patted his raincoat on the spot where his shirt pocket held the check.

"If this thing clears, you're getting a raise and a thousand dollar bonus."

The amount didn't really interest Scott. All he wanted was to hear Jack say something positive for once. While he still hadn't heard anything quite like that, nevertheless, Jack's mentioning of the size of the check in relation to the business had a ring to it Scott liked.

"You realize," he said to Jack, "that this guy is a crackpot."

"I realize."

"He could have it built in Turkey, or India, New Zealand or wherever, for less. For half."

"Yep."

"But he wants to watch it happening."

"Wants *someone* to watch it, yeah."

"Ah … so you caught the stuff about his wife?"

Jack hadn't seen it that much, but Ellen had gone on about how Sumners was so obsessed with the project for his wife's sake. And that he had to keep that in mind.

"Something."

Scott nodded.

"I don't think I've ever seen a guy so wrapped up in an idea."

"I don't know," Jack said, trying to be abstract about something he hadn't seen, outside of a few small signs that morning. "If that's what it takes to keep it together for him, who's to say? Anymore, I don't see that you have to be any one particular way to keep a woman happy. To tell you the truth, I'm getting to think that the most important thing is to be predictable."

Scott half-smiled the way men always half-smile when exchanging their most recently invented truisms about life. Then he shrugged.

"The thing is, it's hard to figure out how to take him when he gets like that. I don't know if it's a private thing he's letting get away from him or if it's a public thing we're going to have to join in on.

If it's private, you ignore it. If it's public, it's crank and it's fucked, and he's fucked."

If there was one thing Jack admired about Scott, it was the easy way Scott exposed people to the logical obliteration of his hypothetical code of behavior. Jack laughed.

"We'll see. Have you met her?"

"Nobody has."

"I can hardly wait."

"She's going to have to be a disappointment."

"You never know. He's as rich as they get."

"No. She's got to be a bimbo. I've been imagining it."

"You've got too much imagination. That's what you get for living alone."

"You mean ...."

"I didn't say it ...."

"Well, you're right, I suppose."

The myriad times they'd had this conversation, it always went the same way, and Jack stated what he'd always state.

"So why the hell don't you get married? Just do it and get it done with."

"You're right. OK."

Jack laughed.

"You're just a lazy bastard. You don't even bother to look around to see if you can't find someone nice, instead of what you usually get. To be honest, I think you drag those things of yours home to prove to yourself there's nothing out there."

Scott knew it wasn't just a joke, and felt it an unfair judgment: that of a married man making assumptions. Especially when the guy had been married for quite a long time.

"Where am I supposed to find this someone? The bars? The college? You imagine me up there strolling around campus? They'd have me arrested."

Scott began backing down the ladder to get another plank, but continued the conversation as he went.

"Yeah, yeah, not all of them are taken up, but there is no approach. Unless they fall on me, I'm no good." Scott paused for a second, then almost to himself: "I need to be able to talk quietly somewhere. Every time I try to do it different it doesn't work."

"No," Jack agreed. "You can't try to do it any way but your own way. They can sense it."

Scott stared for a second, an amused look crossing his face. Jack always augmented the twists of a conversation as though he had come up with all the points of view himself.

"Yeah, well anyway, just try to get a girl to go off somewhere quiet, out of the blue. What they want is a lot of noise. They resist the quiet thing so hard that it makes you feel like an animal. You've got to give them noise, and then you've got to make yourself louder than the noise."

Jack was backing down his ladder to help carry up the next plank.

"OK," he said. "So don't get married."

Of all the different sides of their association with one another, this one where women were discussed, as it is with all men, was the most natural. They enjoyed each other at this time. Better, as one married man to one bachelor, they had full, non-overlapping situations which permitted the positions of the one freely giving advice and the other not taking it.

Finished with any interest for further conversation, Scott drifted off into the work again, happily, because it was work he had helped bring about.

But Jack quickly found himself feeling bitter again. Nothing worse, he was thinking, than to get cornered into jobs by people who didn't know what they were asking, no matter how much money they might be willing to pay you. It was bad policy.

You start that way, and you end up slowly giving away all your freedom of maneuver. Just like it had been in the military.

How many times had he sat in some sweaty village watching a field officer taking orders over the telephone from someone sitting in an air-conditioned command post? Watching the jerk twisting there on the line, trying to convince someone who had never set foot outside an office that the orders wouldn't work, and knowing that if he argued too much he would probably spend the rest of his hitch wading through dust.

End result? They all got screwed.

Jack shook his head. He knew how messes felt, how they come creeping up on you. And he had that same creepy feeling right then.

But nobody was going to listen to him. No sir. They were all so goddamn ecstatic about the fucking job they couldn't see straight.

Jack backed down the ladder to get another plank, looking over at Scott who was also coming down.

For a second, Jack thought of just getting his anger off his chest for once and for all. Let Scott know how he felt about things, just so there was no mistake. Sometimes that was a good thing to do when there wasn't much else to do. At least, he was thinking, you've got yourself covered.

He hesitated though, and then just gave up on the idea with a tired mental flip of fatality.

Just get on with it, he told himself, and hope it all didn't blow up in their faces.

They grabbed another long plank and began walking it up the ladders, balancing themselves with its steadying weight.

Scott had just started tacking his end in place when Annie Moore's voice came up to them from below.

"Hey, Jack," she called up. They both turned and looked down.

Annie was standing on the other side of the chain-link fence at the edge of their property, dangling from one hand an empty plastic bucket, and from the other a mop. Under a wide rainhat she wore a tight smile on her face.

"What'cha doing? Building a dog house?"

Annie grinned with her own joke. It wasn't too bad, she thought, for having just occurred to her. She felt it a good sign that she could come up with any joke at all, all things considered. She had rarely in her life felt so depressed as when they lost the Nickerson Ketch sale. But at least she, if not Clyde, had decided it was best to pretend nothing had happened.

She told herself that the best thing was to pretend as though they would never sell that big tub, and that it didn't matter. It was a way of thinking that was like self-therapy for her. And she felt it had worked. Enough so, in fact, that she could easily prove it to herself just in the act of joking with Jack Colby and showing him there were no hard feelings.

She stood there, as Jack shifted himself around on the ladder to look at her better, preparing herself for whatever series of quick comebacks she would have to laugh up to match her good-hearted, but rough, little joke.

Jack stared at her for a second, and then clenched his teeth into a smile.

"That's right, Annie, I'm building a doghouse." He nodded his head as well. "But it's for boy dogs only."

Annie, momentarily still lulling herself with a feeling of conviviality, almost laughed. But then the smile on her face, which had been somewhat forced to begin with, suddenly felt set in concrete. She stood there for a moment, unable to say a thing, and watched Jack turn his back on her. Even Scott, who was still looking at her, seemed somewhat frightening to her.

She had never meant to insult anyone, but she could see that her depression must have rendered her practically incapable of making proper judgments about things.

She was embarrassed, suddenly. But also she was horrified by Jack's nastiness. True, they had never become very friendly with each other, but she never realized to what extent he disliked her, at least not to the point of practically telling her off. Even as she stood there, Jack seemed to have forgotten her, setting a nail with a quick plop of his hammer. Annie walked away.

Jack could hear her walking away across the gravel, and knew she had been looking at him. He also knew that Scott had been looking at him, and he glanced over at him.

But Scott was now back at his own work, and you might have thought, by the looks of him, that he hadn't heard a word even though he was only twelve feet away.

That's right, Jack thought, pretend nothing happened. You and Ellen got your way and you don't want to do or say a single thing to jeopardize what you got started. Which also meant avoiding difficult decisions on how to best humor your grumpy boss.

Fine, we'll get on with it. But now, you bastard, at least you know Jack Colby isn't going to take any shit about it from anyone.

Jack looked back at the nail he'd set, and drove it home with one heavy smash of his hammer. Then he reached for another nail, and as he did so he remembered Annie's face.

God knew she'd asked for it, he thought. But for all the world, she'd looked as though he'd shot her. Which was pretty goddamn funny and sensitive for someone throwing shit at other people.

Well, fine. Everybody's sensitive.

But now they knew that he had a right to be sensitive too. He set another nail, that time with a regular workman's tap.

# Chapter 17

DARK GREEN and silver grey, Lake Whatcom lay flat and shimmering beneath the rain. No one seemed to be anywhere out on the lake, not even the most intrepid fishermen, although at the town end of the lake it was rare to see anyone fishing. Along its shoreline at the private docks of lakefront homes were rowboats wetly tugging on mooring ropes, or powerboats, covered with canvas awning, or small sailboats, stripped dead and naked, slack running lines slapping slick to dripping masts and booms, all laying beneath the hissing spray of rain spreading across the water and up into the heavily wooded shore.

Eric drove along the north road, winding out past the older clusters of lake houses built earlier in the century. Out to the newer and larger houses, increasingly newer and increasingly larger, where newer and larger wealth pushed slowly out around the lake.

He was enjoying the idea of his impending announcement to his wife.

He was hardly happy. That, an inadequate description for the sort of muted ecstasy he felt.

Everything, even the powerful swipes of the Mercedes' windshield wipers in the downpour, as though a heavily joyful counterpoint to the rhythm of his heart, seemed to add to it.

He was as materially prepared as he would have been going into a business conference with his board of directors. He had a complete set of study plans and a theoretical work schedule. He had a beautiful book on wooden boats he'd found in Fairhaven. Inside, besides photos of boats sailing about, and of their construction— construction evidently as large a part of their mystic as the actual boats—was a text that, to Eric, was more like poetry than prose. Precisely what Deborah would be needing.

Last of all, his special treat, was a folio of large watercolors done by William Fletcher representing the boat in a variety of different settings and from different viewpoints.

Fletcher had turned out to be somewhat of an artist in the usual sense of brushes and easels. In his office there'd been hanging a number of his watercolors, the subject always boats set against typical or famous regional sights. Fletcher, showing neither modesty nor pride, said he had actually sold an occasional painting at art fairs. Once, he'd even had a show.

Eric, seeing they were well done, if a little romantically, with the mountains of the Puget Sound always looming cozily up in the background and at least one seagull balancing in the sky, realized nothing would be better to help Deborah imagine the boat than to see it represented pictorially. So he had commissioned Fletcher to do a series and the architect, quite rapidly, had brought out four scenes.

One was of the boat under full sail on smoothly rolling water, Bellingham Bay and the bulk of Mt. Baker receding in its wake. Another portrayed the ketch at rest in a quiet cove, a clear, deep blue twilight descending and the forested cliffs of the cove going dark and green, and on the boat the cabin lights were already glowing warmly out over the still, black water. In another the big boat was at dock alongside the more numerous fiberglass craft, and it was obvious a rain burst had passed for there was water standing on wet dock planking and the decks of boats were wet and there was a gray, rather foggy appearance to the other boats as though, still, a gentle fine mist was moving amongst them.

It was perhaps the best of the series because it showed how beautifully, even on that soaked and dreary looking day, the boat stood out against the others. While some of the smaller boats did have teak decks and other wooden details, they were nonetheless cold, plastic boats, their whiteness looking vaguely uncomfortable, the whiteness of refrigerators and washing machines, compared with the gleaming woodwork of the *Muse*.

The painting showed how, as well, while the basic plan of the boat was classic, there was none of that slightly awkward, horn-piped-sailor appearance classic deckhouses often had. Fletcher had designed elegantly shaped, aerodynamic deck profiles to the cabins, with clean, unobtrusive lines. Next to it, the other boats would look like bathtub toys.

The last picture of the series had been the most imaginative of Fletcher's ideas, showing the boat pulled up in dry-dock for scraping and painting. The sheer grace of her underwater lines as she stood naked by waterside, shored up by heavy timbers as workmen went over her hull, cleaning and smoothing the proud, secret bottom, was clear.

All four paintings, taken together, were as good a representation for Deborah as Eric could have ever tried to explain in words.

At least, Eric sighed slightly, he hoped so.

Five or six million dollars was a long way to go, all for the sake of love.

For himself, it wasn't so much. For others, Newell Briggs for example, it certainly was.

Eric felt a small, heated anger go through him at the memory of Briggs' unrestrained performance down at the boathouse that morning. Eric would have loved to have killed the son-of-a-bitch right on the spot. Anyone else, and they would have at least been fired right then and there.

Unfortunately, Briggs was also very simply the best accountant around, and Eric, when it came to the money, wanted only the best to handle it. So he'd let it pass. Although there was no doubt he was going to get that bastard into his office and chew his ass come Monday morning.

For something.

God damn if he was going to allow that sort of thing in public again, expert accountant or not.

But Eric wasn't going to dwell on it. He had so many, and better, things to think about.

Coming up around a small hill along the lake, he slowed, pressed a button on an electronic gate opener, and entered his property with the big gates already swung back, ready to close behind him at the signal from electric eyes.

He went slowly up the drive, swinging the car through a heavy stand of Douglas fir. Nearing the top of the hill where the house overlooked the lake, he drove out of the trees and up along manicured lawns to the turnaround in front of the house. Through the pouring rain he could see the lights in the living room's great, all-glass front. The lights, hanging from long chains, made for a yellow glow near the bottom of the cavernous room.

He parked the car by the door, grabbed the plans and paintings off the seat, covering them with his raincoat, and made a quick sprint to the door.

As he got there the door opened automatically, like the gate down at the road, but this was not a feat of technology. He expected it to be Mrs. Mesquita, but instead it was his wife.

"Whew!" he said as he swept past her into the hallway. "It really started coming down a few minutes ago, huh?"

Outside, the rain beat in with a vengeance, making a muscular hissing in the gravel of the driveway and out over the short grass in the surrounding landscaped lawns. Deborah closed the door and turned to him, giving him a smile.

"You're home early," she said.

Eric looked at his wife for a moment. It was true, he was very early that day. So early, her glowing hair, laid up full on her head with a strand falling loose here or there and the heavy weight of it pulled down in a gently rolled mass behind, gave proof Deborah hadn't had time to prepare herself for dinner, as she did every evening they were to be staying home.

She was wearing a bulky, sea-green sweater over jeans, the sweater a pale version of the dark blue-green of her eyes.

Her eyes were darker than those of most blue-eyed women and were topped by dark eyebrows, making them distinct from her remarkable, flame-red hair and golden skin, giving her face the character and accent often missing from the smooth pinks and sky blues of the conventional beauty of blonds and brunettes.

Deborah's beauty was world-class. Her features were perfect, fine, long and distinctive. Her nose was straight and narrow above wide, firmly held but otherwise full lips and a somewhat obstinate chin.

At any time, Eric would always be struck by her beauty and loved her. As much as he loved her, and her beauty, he also loved the ease with which she carried her beauty; her poise and dignity.

She could have been on the cover of any magazine, but she'd never sold this beauty professionally or otherwise. Of course, as far as modeling went she was too full bodied for fashion work, which then only left the pin-up trade. That, though, wouldn't have entered any realm of thought, at any level.

Naturally.

As though in a private gallery, Eric could look at her whenever he wanted and find himself lost in that flow of perfection, in the impeccable rightness of each part relative to the next. And he did so with pride.

It was he, and not someone else, who possessed her. It was he, and not someone else, that she had come to live with.

"You look lovely," he said. He gazed at her there by the door, admiring the rare instance of casual attire.

Deborah smiled. "Right," her light voice laughed. "Well, this is what you can expect if you catch me during the day."

"Maybe I'll start making a habit of it."

Deborah smiled again, but then gave him her version of a stern look of warning. But not too much. Exaggerated expression either angry or joyful was something she'd never learned to compose for her features. Or desired to.

Then, seeing he was saying something he meant, she set her head with a serious look flickering almost cross.

"Eric," she said, "you know that whims are nothing to base fashion upon. Yours or mine."

She pulled herself up stiffly in front of him in her jeans and sweater, now denying them the comfort they offered. It was a point she would not let him shrug off. These were work clothes, not house clothes, and she wasn't about to start living in overalls in her own home, husband or no.

Deborah Sumners' parents had both been hardworking and successful professionals, her father a lawyer and her mother a doctor in Salt Lake City, offering their only child access to the best life possible. Although they were faithful adherents to the Mormon church, eschewing direct comparison or competition to the manners and aspirations of the old-moneyed eastern elite, they were followers of the ideals of those families.

Her marriage to Eric had been painful for her parents at first. His utter wealth ... even as a young, self-made businessman he was enormously successful ... had been more upsetting to the Johnsons than the fact he wasn't Mormon.

Here was this handsome, rich and gracious young man in love with their daughter, and as a member of the ruling, Anglo-Saxon protestant class he represented all that they would forever be denied, regardless of how high they climbed in Salt Lake City.

They had gotten used to it. For her, though, she was still very much their offspring.

They had struggled to give her the opportunities. In all her years in school, there would have been nothing about her to make one guess she was not a part of a lifestyle of clambake summers in Cape Cod or chalet winters spent skiing in the Alps. Even Eric had never had a clue when he'd first met her, thinking her only the most beautiful and accomplished amongst any number of beautiful and accomplished young women drawing breath within that society.

Deborah finished her degree in Art and Literature to satisfy her parent's dream, and then went out to the coast with Eric, out to the part of the world where he was building his empire. It was there that her decision had been made. For all the liberal accommodations Eric made within his adopted class, she would never betray the lessons she had learned which had made all this possible.

Eric watched his wife's chin rising in stubbornness, and smiled.

"Yes," he said, finally, "of course."

Deborah was able to give him a true smile. Regardless of his occasionally irreverent attitudes, she always relied on his sense of deeper principles.

She noticed his slightly bedraggled appearance then, like a lost dog, and how he was scrunching papers and things up under his overcoat like some itinerant salesman.

"Good God, come get a towel for your hair. What brings you home so early, anyway?"

Although he was hardly wet at all, he followed her to a small alcove beneath the main stairwell and allowed her to pat his hair with a towel.

"News," he told her.

If there was one thing she'd learned from Eric, it was how to tease in his manner, and it was a natural thing for her to do now, a natural part of how their relationship had developed.

"You've retired early?" she said.

"I could, I suppose," he said with a flat, serious voice. Eric always enjoyed when his wife tried to tease him, giving the opportunity to tease back and show her how much better he was at it.

It worked. As usual, he was able to startle her.

"You must be joking."

Eric gave her a complacent smile. He was suddenly impatient. "Come into the study," he said.

She followed him into a room off from the main entryway, a fairly long room with large English landscapes overhanging low bookshelves. There were a number of overstuffed leather armchairs and floral patterned sofas, and at either end of the room were bureau desks, both belonging to Eric.

He took her over to one of them and cleared off the pen set and a number of file folders piled there.

"Stand here," he said, pulling her up to the big desktop, "and shut your eyes."

"You're not going to have me do that, are you?"

"Yes, shut your eyes," he said sternly.

Of all the most difficult things to do, getting her to play along was one of the hardest. He persisted, knowing the end result was worth it.

"Isn't this a bit much, Eric?" she complained. But she closed her eyes, taking on a small, disgruntled line in the set of her mouth.

Eric took out the portfolio and quickly spread the study plans and work contract on the desk. Above them he placed the four Fletcher watercolors with the photo book, and then stood back.

He looked at the arrangement for a moment, and suddenly worried whether she truly would find anything in it for herself; if he had not made a terrible mistake. You could never completely tell with Deborah. There was always doubt how she would react, even to the best of intentions.

"Eric," she broke into his reflection, "am I going to stand here all day?"

"Okay," he said. "You can open them now."

The first thing Deborah looked at was her husband, giving him a glance of semi-disbelief, and then she looked down at the top of the bureau.

First she saw the watercolors. Her immediate reaction was of disappointment. Eric and she were art collectors, had access to the best galleries and auction houses and had spent a great deal of time buying works that had pleased them both. Fine works. Some of them masterpieces.

Here, before her, although well-executed in their own way, were some unremarkable watercolors of sailboats. Very regional and charming, but not exactly along the lines of the great, museum quality works they had hanging throughout the house. She began to suspect that Eric had allowed himself another whim.

She then noticed all the paintings were of the same, long, somehow older looking black sailboat. She could appreciate, despite the mediocre value of watercolors which just managed to avoid kitsch, that the boat had swift, classic lines.

Then her eyes noticed the plans. She reached out and brushed aside one of the watercolors, and read quickly down over the front page of the contract with Colby Boatbuilding.

She didn't say anything. Eric was standing silently to the side and behind her, watching her. She let her gaze go back over the watercolors and the plans. She opened the photo book and began turning through the pages. Then she flipped back to the front and began reading the opening essay, a short thing poetically describing the beauty and increasing rarity of fine wooden boats.

She could feel Eric's seriousness, in a sense, coaxing her, and she felt it necessary to take in what he was showing her. It was her duty as his wife. She knew little about boats but she read the essay with concentration.

In a short paragraph or two she began to get the idea and emotion of it, registering the author's deep sentiment that whatever the real truth and beauty of boats was about, the best of it was to be found in the wooden boat.

Well, she saw the contract, and the boat, but that there was going to be a boat built was hardly the point. Her husband was a man of many depths and facets. A careful, clever man, and while he often had light whims, he never had whims about things meant for her.

So she looked at the whole array there glowing beneath a bright table light, and tried to be careful. Eric was obviously implying it should say something to her, or that it said something about her.

Simply, the boat was to be made of wood. Eric evidently believed that detail would please her almost more than the boat itself. Strangely enough, it did please her.

It was enough, she decided. She had plenty of time to understand all the rest of it.

"How did you ever come to think of this?"

Eric could hear the approval in her voice, and felt his breast, heavy in suspense, lighten. With a barely reigned-in enthusiasm he explained the broad outlines of the story, how it had occurred to him and how the contract had developed from the beginning, through the accidental discovery of the little *Isabelle*, and then from that point onward to the final development of an even better idea.

"So," he finished, "believe it or not, work will begin Tuesday."

"This Tuesday?"

Eric could hardly hold himself back at the look of amazement on Deborah's face, but he managed. "Yes."

She then stared at him for a second, and then it broke over her like a crashing wave, and she laughed.

"You're sure of this."

Eric knew, then, he'd been right. He'd been absolutely right, and he was as happy as the day he'd gotten the idea. Funny how instincts can be so absolute, he thought.

"Almost the whole way," he said. "It was a revelation."

"Well, it's amazing, darling. I love it already."

She turned her eyes back to the drawings and went thoughtful for a moment, and then she made a small sound.

"You know," she said finally, "I think I'd like to see her."

"You will. But it takes some time."

She continued to look at the display of papers for a moment, and then smiled.

"Sorry," she said. "I meant, I would like to see, I think, the *Isabelle* sometime. Before she goes away. I would like to see everything about this, the way you have."

Eric nodded, he was elated. Things were turning out altogether the way he'd hoped for.

# Chapter 18

THAT EVENING Deborah sat and read the book about wooden boats by a crackling, alder stoked fire, the flames jumping and flaring in the large open fireplace, making the beautiful boat pictures seem to dance and shimmer as though cradled in the light.

She also had a number of regular yachting magazines she'd scooped up from a newsstand. She hadn't been able to wait, running into town, and even stopping by the boatworks to see the little rowing skiff. Nobody had been down at Colby's, it seemed everyone had gone off to early dinner, but she'd managed to peek inside and take a look.

Back home, by late in the evening, she'd begun to appreciate the extent of the boat her husband had commissioned.

"This is going to be quite a boat, isn't it?"

She looked up from the book to where Eric was reading one of the yachting magazines in a chair on the other side of the fireplace.

"I guess so," he laid the magazine aside. "She'll be unique."

"She'll be big, right? One hundred and thirty-seven feet."

Eric nodded.

Deborah looked back into the boat book.

"They really are works of art."

"Aren't they?" he said, looking at his wife and how she'd become engrossed in the world of wooden boats.

As he watched, he saw her eyes slowly glassing over as she went out of herself into art. He didn't always understood it, but he was happy when he could encourage it, and somehow become part of it.

"Well," she went on as though a school exercise in appreciation, "I suppose it could be considered a work of art. They are created and one of the results of them is more than a pleasant functionality, but of actual beauty. Some are built almost more to be beautiful things."

She stopped her thoughts, catching herself and interpreting his look as amusement.

"You're right," she smiled. "If we say it's beautiful, and it looks that way, then it is."

"It's art as far as I'm concerned."

"Like the *Isabelle*."

"Yes."

Deborah's hair, down now for the evening, hung forward with her reading and she shook it back across her shoulders, the light of the fire momentarily creating a halo of brilliance around her face. Eric gazed at her in admiration as she went on:

"What an exquisite thing. Beautifully made. More than just the work. You could see the attitude which went into the creation of it. You could feel the presence of the builder's soul."

On that note, Eric suddenly felt uneasy. This was the thing he didn't like, the way she'd go so far out with this stuff. But he quickly smothered the sensation as well as his irritation.

"Jack Colby is quite a capable man, I agree."

"He must be."

Deborah was impressed by the man who'd been able to create such a strangely lovely object. She felt, for a moment's flush, something deep and warm stirring, a thing she could not put a name to, nor would have wanted to, at the thought of such a craftsman.

Almost instantly she was embarrassed. And with the guilt that often comes when the subconscious catches out the conscious, she got immediately up and went over to sit on the arm of Eric's chair.

She put her arms around her husband, somewhat stiffly.

"But then," she said, as though reciting a potent against evil, "that makes you something special, too."

Eric knew she did love him. He just wished she would outgrow this inept, slightly cloying manner. She was as clumsy as a novice actress learning her lines, paying more attention to the words than the emotion.

But, looking up at her, he brushed away his habitual discontentment. He felt she was truly happy and that he'd made her that way. Regardless of her difficulty in feeling spontaneous emotion, she had managed in only a few hours' time to fall in love with the idea of the boat.

Although it was he, not Jack Colby, who had planted the idea and pleasure in her, he refused to feel jealous of her seeming inability to make a clear distinction.

"Actually," he said, "the boat will mean quite a lot to Jack Colby, too."

She moved her shoulders in thought. "How so?"

"Well, it's plain they could be better off down there."

A small frown crossed Deborah's face.

"Are they poor?" she said.

"Not exactly. But not as comfortable as you might expect."

"You mean as comfortable as *you* might expect."

Eric smiled. "I'm not making comparisons."

"What else can you do?"

If Eric rarely noticed the inflections of her feelings about their wealth, he always noted her implied criticism of his attitude towards the less well off.

"Oh, come on," he groaned, once again impatient that he had to deny such a thing.

Deborah shook her head.

"It's true," she said. "The simple fact is, from your position you will always be better off."

"That bothers you. I know."

Eric felt himself getting upset. But not because of the subject. But because the idea of the boat was to have given them, among other things, something else to talk and think about in the evening other than his life, his work, and his money.

"You know it doesn't bother me. How many times must I tell you that what you are, and how you are, is what I'll always want. I don't look at you through your money, and I never have except that first time. It's you who does that."

She felt she never used it as a judgment point. She was sure he did, because it was natural for him to do so. If there was a single hope she had about changing anything for him, it was to free him of the iron bonds of his wealth-bound perspective.

Eric looked away at the fire. It was not a satisfying conversation. And the damnedest thing about it was that it was exactly the conversation that only a poor couple could have produced.

He didn't know. Maybe it was her Mormon background. Mormons, like a number of other groups that had been forced to pull themselves up by their own bootstraps, had an obsession with money. They seemed to adore it when it was their own, but look down on it in the possession of others.

Of course, he was sure she didn't look down on his, their, money. She simply didn't fully appreciate the extent of good it could accomplish in the world and what a privilege it was to make use of it for that good. How that good could be extended to others. Like Jack Colby, for instance.

As for what she had said about not looking at him through his money ... true, that sounded nice in a modern way. One shouldn't do that if one were intelligent and generous. But it also smacked of an irritating naiveté he could not seem to help her out of, no matter how he tried.

Wasn't it simply a fact that his life, and what he did, was constantly revolving around what he was to do with all that wealth? So why then shouldn't he be looked at through the excellence of his own craftsmanship the way a baker is judged by the excellence of his bread, or a tailor his suits, or a boatbuilder his boats?

Eric knew it was an impossibility though. The world was yet a long way from considering the use of money as an art form, and that world included his wife.

She respected art, and loved him. She did not find any respect for his money. Respect he gained from his business associates.

Jack Colby would inspire that same respect in Deborah only because she had no idea, and had no desire, to see how money could be anything else but the result of the power of exploitation.

Eric's chin dropped slightly, and then he yawned. He looked up at his wife's face glowing with a reddish cast in the gentle firelight. Perhaps, he thought, with Deborah actually seeing him in charge of a project, seeing him directing the building, she would not only be artistically delighted but also come to understand at last how he was, with his money. Out in the world. Creating.

She would see how beautifully he handled his wealth and position in ways she never had.

What she would need was to see it being constructed, both the boat and how he made his life, dealing with money and people. Then she would see how it did not separate people into those superior and those inferior, but how it was a catalyst, and agent of change and freedom.

Just possibly, he thought, the boat's inspiration was maybe one of the greatest ideas he would ever have. Even the name, now, seemed a perfect inspiration. The *Muse*. It was exactly that, and in more ways than one. She had liked, as well, and agreed with the name's implication. Although for her own reasons, whatever they were.

He could see that there was the chance that what had started as a simple gift was becoming a moving agent in finally joining them together as one. A privileged merger ... impossible unless he'd been able to achieve its purchase. He felt sated.

One of his deep beliefs was that to will something as though already a fact, was as good as making it a fact. If you were strong enough. And here, he was doing just that. Creating the future.

He shifted his shoulders more comfortably in the chair, feeling the warmth of the fire and of his wife's body.

He felt the glow of his love for Deborah as well, and the comfort of their future spread over him like an old-fashioned quilt blanket as he listened to the heavy sound of rain coming down high above on the vaulted ceiling.

He then reflected on how there was nothing like the sound of rain outside, for making you feel safe inside.

*

Jack felt a little differently about the rain, listening to it in a sleeping bag up in the loft at the boatworks. The wild storm passing in from the Straights over Bellingham had caused no one at Colby's to feel happy at all.

In the late evening, when they'd all come back from a Mexican restaurant in Fairhaven, Scott had gone up into the loft to check on ways to set up new working lights and had found a near catastrophe. The gusting wind, easily over seventy miles an hour at times, had torn three gaping holes in the roof's old cedar shingling. With that foothold a sudden hard blast of the wind could have easily torn the whole old roof away, if not the whole building.

The entire loft was soaked. There was no way, if it wasn't dried out, that they would be able to start the lofting of Sumners' boat on Tuesday. No way could they put the drawing paper down on that floor.

That was neither here nor there though, considering how it looked improbable they would have any loft to work in, at all.

Scott got Jack and they began with trying to get the loft protected. The driving rainstorm was only growing in ferocity, and they could not leave it for morning.

They had dragged out some big canvas tarpaulins to temporarily cover the holes, manhandling the heavy cloth up onto the roof and spreading them out.

It was like trying to set the topsail of a square-rigger in a hurricane, the rain whipping and blasting around them from all points of the compass, blowing up inside their raincoats, wetting them throughout and threatening to turn the coats inside-out like blown-out umbrellas.

The canvas billowed up from underneath, or the ends were blown away into the dark rain by the wind. Tearing itself out of cold, numbed hands, the heavy cloth resisted their every effort, once nearly being ripped away and blown off the roof into the bay before they got it down at last and nailed the edges securely.

It had taken more than an hour and a half of constant, slipping exertion to fight the canvasses into place, working on the wet shingles in the absolute darkness of the storm, smashing fingers clutching nails, landing heavily on unpadded knees and elbows, until they were able, finally, to climb down.

They had gone then up into the loft to see what could be done.

All the wood was soaked. With the cold, humid air of fall now having arrived, it would take a week to even get the surface dry. But surface dryness was not enough. If there was wet wood underneath when they laid down the alexandrite paper, the moisture would be drawn up, and despite the paper's heaviness, there would be nothing to expect but a sad, crumpled mess.

They went down in the boatshed and wrestled up a couple of old, jet engine style, kerosene space heaters—five feet long and a foot and a half in diameter—used in the winter when they were working with fiberglass materials. In time enough, with those big heaters roaring away, there was a noticeable increase in warmth in the loft, but that was all and there was also a massive rise in humidity attesting to the amount of rain soaked into the heavy old flooring.

The fact that the flooring was heavy was one of the few fortunate things, not having then to worry about warping. The only problem was that there was no way they could leave the space heaters unattended up there.

Too old, the heaters could very easily break down, get too hot or throw a spark. And between the kerosene and the old timber of the boatshed, no matter how wet it seemed, a fire would be a foregone conclusion.

And a fire would mean the end.

No matter how fast they caught it, or how soon an engine from the closest station arrived, there could be no way to stop the total consumption of the boathouse. It would simply burn to the ground in the time it took to make the phone call.

They hadn't arranged for any complete insurance yet. Only the basic. They had always planned on larger business coverage but had never done it because of the cost.

One look at the building, and insurance agents became very unsympathetic.

Even the electricity in the place was well below code. Something Jack had hedged on in front of Sumners, but which he did mean to fix.

So it meant that as long as the old kerosene heaters were blasting away up in the loft, one of them would have to stay up there and watch. With a fire extinguisher at hand.

Jack said he'd take the first shift, Scott could get some sleep. But he'd have to return early in the morning because of an appointment Jack had.

So Scott left and Jack had gone up into the loft with a sleeping bag to lay on, and an alarm clock set every half hour in case he went too deeply to sleep.

The space heaters made a shrill roar up in that enclosed space, the temperature climbing up to where, with the steaming floorboards, there was the suffocating feeling of being in the mid-summer depths of an equatorial rainforest.

The rain and wind beat drums across the roof, howling and whistling through the eaves and sucking and slapping at the canvasses.

There was nothing comfortable up there. The sleeping bag offered little padding against the hard floor, the noise was deafening; and laying on the bag in his shorts because of the heat Jack went off to sleep easily.

Sheer fatigue beating all the rest.

He slept, every half hour on the half hour. A watchman at the gates of disaster ... it had very little to do with what Deborah's idea of the craftsman's life entailed.

Although, to Jack, it represented very much what it entailed.

# Chapter 19

THE FOLLOWING Monday, even as the first lights of morning spread through low clumps of fog shifting across the surface of the water, the sound of hammering could be heard echoing down at the Fairhaven waterfront. Jack and Scott, with the storm now but passing gusts of drizzle, had begun patching the holes in.

The shingle work wasn't difficult. There was a certain problem in manhandling the cedar bundles up the forty or so feet to the roof's eaves and then hauling them onto the steep-pitched roof. It was also uncomfortable working on the roof with only makeshift roof ladders made of two by fours. Soon enough though they had the roof patched shut, the fresh cedar patches standing out bright against the rest of the roof's old and blackened roof shingles.

When they'd got everything down and were standing back to survey the job, Ellen had said it was too bad the entire roof couldn't be redone.

"Why bother?" Jack said.

"Imagine it with the shakes painted or stained, and the siding repainted." Ellen liked the idea more and more as she talked about it. "It'd be good for business."

"Maybe so."

Scott looked the building over and had to admit that, all in all, the building looked even more tattered than before. Just another dying waterfront establishment from the looks of things.

Thinking of Jack's windfall, which Scott had certainly contributed to, he felt he had a say in what seemed not a bad idea. Why not clean themselves up on the outside, as he'd done to the inside?

"Appearances work," he added.

Jack raised his eyebrows and gave a little sigh.

They all stood there for a moment thinking about different things. Then Jack headed for the stairs and went up to look at the loft.

The floor no longer showed any signs of dampness, nor was there any feeling of humidity in the heated room. Even the paper towels they had put here and there, weighted down with boards, were bone dry in contact with the floorboards.

They shut down the space heaters and went down to the house for lunch where Ellen had set out salads, a platter of toasted cheese sandwiches and a bowl of creamy potato soup.

Jack and Scott got off their work jackets and stood turns at the sink cleaning forearms and faces, scrubbing nails and wringing hand cloths.

"Eric called," Ellen said when they took their seats. "Just to check up, I guess."

"That so?" Jack looked at her. "What'd you say?"

Ellen smiled. "I told him you were getting busy remodeling the boathouse."

Scott laughed. But Jack jammed a fork into his salad.

"So you told him what happened."

Ellen's face went blank. "I was just joking."

Jack nodded. "You could have," he said.

"He just wanted to know when you would start because he said he'd finally told his wife and she was excited about it and wanted to see it being built right from the start. He said she would appreciate it, was all."

"Sure, sure," Jack said. "I just hope this thing isn't going to get too crowded."

"I don't think it'll wind up like that. Eric said that if it was in any way inconvenient, they would stay completely away during working hours. He was very specific about that."

As though there was anything he could have done about it anyway, Jack made it appear he didn't care.

"I don't mind if Scott doesn't. I just don't want it all to turn into a zoo."

Scott pushed away his salad plate and reached for the soup ladle.

"Well, it's not like the Sumners are slumming or anything." It was the least of his own worries right then, but he wanted to bring out into the open what Jack seemed to be insinuating.

"Aren't they?" Jack said.

Ellen made a noise of disagreement. "I don't think so. I think this boat means a lot to them."

"It's certainly going to cost them," Scott said.

"No, more than just the cost. I get the feeling that it's becoming a very special thing between them and they naturally want to be close to everything as much as they can."

"I think it's good," Scott said. "It's good that they care more than just whether the cupboards look nice or whether the cabin mattress is lumpy. Although that's important too."

"Yeah," Ellen said. "Everybody likes to fuck on boats. It's the sound of the water."

There was a little pause, then Jack said flatly, "Maybe we should have someone find a way to work that into our prospectus."

It was obvious Ellen and Scott were feeling good about everything. The high spirits were too much though and he wasn't especially happy about Ellen's light-hearted crudeness. Scott, he thought with irritation, had an erratic attitude about women, too much like a stray animal looking for any scrap it can find. And he didn't like Ellen coming anywhere near it.

Scott cocked his jaw sideways, and said dryly. "So the day has finally come when sex is a factor in boatbuilding."

Ellen waved her hand. "That's progress."

"Not bad. Soon enough, everything will be that way. Everything you do a form of sex. Might even replace love."

It was common knowledge how Scott's last romantic effort had gone, and Jack and Ellen, being of one mind where Scott was concerned, had figured a lot of his drinking had been based on self-pity.

He had never alluded to what had happened. But now, perhaps had. They both felt a bit embarrassed. Yet where Ellen might have been more discrete, Jack had no problem being blunt.

"Seems there's already a replacement for it," he said.

Scott wasn't going to say anything about how he lived his life.

"It's just a thing to go through," he said. "No bigger or worse than any other thing. That is all."

Jack was not to be put off. That the conversation had turned directly towards what he'd been thinking—and thankfully away from Ellen's lurid comment—made it impossible not to want to moralize a bit. And with Ellen there, it was made easy. It was always easier to make moral points with a woman present.

"It's too bad," he said. "You should try to be more selective."

Scott now regretted the maudlin, if not feeble-minded idea he might have been able to confide in either Jack or Ellen.

"Okay," he said. "Next time I'll be more selective."

Ellen felt Jack had been a little too preachy. But she couldn't resist commenting. Scott just didn't take things seriously enough.

"You know what we mean," she said.

Scott looked at her. But instead of thinking about her comment found himself once again making a comparison between her and the women he'd known. Wondering, despite his momentary irritation with her, where in the world such women were to be found. It was impossible to tell if Ellen had any inkling of his attraction to her. If Jack did, it was a banished thought. But he was nearly convinced that Ellen, in that place where she was a woman to a man, could not just put it away. He was sure she had to register it and, he felt, it probably accounted for this motherish tone she occasionally took on towards him.

As for Ellen, she was in fact consciously aware of the presence of Scott, which wasn't all that displeasing—on a philosophically strict, man-woman basis, of course.

"Maybe," she said, now in a somewhat softer tone, "you're already too selective."

For just a moment, totally deniable and ignored by either of them, a small ember passed between them. That thing from which within any relationship, whether it will go on to last five minutes or another fifty years, everything builds. Or is allowed to fade away.

Being the most fragile part of the human experience, it was the easiest thing to either simply fall upon, or ignore.

Scott, trying to ignore those thoughts, deliberately took her words at face value, as a form of news about himself. But Ellen's opinion gave little solace or real insight for understanding his motivations and actions. He therefore had to lump it amongst the many others that didn't really matter either.

Helpful opinions, he had found, aggravate rather than relieve the feeling of human aloneness. He had never heard one opinion that could replace the one solution to loneliness. If that had been so, the most terrible aspect of the human condition would have long since been jettisoned from the human experience. Just by the act of having others chew it over.

"I don't know," Scott said. "That seems a contradiction in itself."

"Then," Jack said, "maybe you just like to complicate things."

"I don't get any satisfaction from it, if I do."

"Maybe you don't want to be satisfied."

Scott smiled. "That explains just about everything then, I guess. I wonder why I try at all."

"Your luck might change."

"Luck."

Ellen could see Scott was annoyed. And she was now embarrassed at how obvious it was that she and Jack had developed a mutual viewpoint about Scott's private life.

She smiled amiably.

"Best not to think about it, perhaps."

Scott looked over at her for that suddenly dismissive remark. The first thing that came to his mind was a sarcastic retort about how someone *else* had certainly seemed to have been thinking it over, as well.

"I'm afraid I'm not that philosophical."

"Or too philosophical," Jack said.

Scott grimaced. As far as he was concerned the subject was finished.

Jack saw that Scott was not amused and tried to end on as diplomatic a note as he could find.

"Never mind," he said. "Life always works out in the end."

Scott, who had been at the point of lazily letting the conversation die of its own accord, felt a hot flash of deep anger. At the banal triteness. Let alone the solicitude.

"I hope so," he said. "Plying liquor on horny middle-aged barflies to get a half-drunk dogflop leaves a little to be desired."

Sympathy aside, that was it for Ellen. "You crude bastard."

She actually felt shocked somewhere, and deeply, because she could feel how it had been more than an offhand cynicism. An actual confession, if hot with anger. And the way he'd said it, looking directly at her, made her feel it hadn't been a response to Jack, but a message meant for her to receive. Alone.

On the surface, she permitted herself to be infuriated with his deliberate show of crass indiscretion, throwing his sordid bedroom details right out there for her to see. But in fact, she was suddenly feeling something Scott had suspected. His choosing to be ugly about things made her angry, but what made her even angrier was the sudden realization that—despite herself—he had caused her to feel, indeed, a sudden surge of her mothering instinct. The one that didn't have anything to do with mothers and sons.

Bastard indeed.

# Chapter 20

Early afternoon, past the downtown sidewalks full of late lunch-goers, Jack and Scott drove to the Georgia Pacific plant to buy the alexandrite paper.

There, a forklift loaded the six foot roll into their pickup, putting its rear end right down on its springs. They had to explain a number of times what was happening out their way. It made people happy to hear of a boat being built down in old Fairhaven, a place where, once, many had been built. People like it when parts of the past were preserved, or cropped up again. It was reassuring.

Back at the shop they borrowed Clyde Moore's forklift in exchange for having to listen to only a few hollow wisecracks, and got the roll hoisted up and through the access door to the loft. With that done they called Sumners, telling him they'd be starting the lofting that afternoon.

Neither Jack nor Scott made any outward sign of it to each other, but the moment they both got up to the loft floor they could feel the change: Where before they had been a boat repairing yard, suddenly they were boatbuilders.

No matter how many times Sumners had come down, or even when he'd dropped off the check, it hadn't been a reality. But looking at the big, empty loft, the bulky roll of Alexandrite resting heavily down at the far end, the truth finally sank in.

Scott, in silence, bent to unlace his boots and set them by the head of the stairs. Jack followed suit.

For as long as the plans were laid out on the lofting floor, the top of the stairs was as far as shoes would ever get.

They went down the smooth floor of the loft to the roll of paper, shoved it around and began unrolling it.

The heavy paper was stiff, wanting to hold the shape of the roll. To keep it from following them across the floor, they weighted it down with lumps of lead. All told, they unrolled four strips, making a surface twenty-four feet wide and about a hundred and forty feet long.

Pushing what was left of the roll into a corner, they set to getting the edges of the paper strips well butted together and then went along and tacked all the edges to the floor.

They studied the work plans to check the height of the boat from the keel to the sheer line at the deck, and then measured off enough room from the edge of the paper and began the transferring of the horizontal lines, called waterlines by boatbuilders, from the work plans to the full size plan on the floor. The lines were drawn in pencil by Scott, checked for accuracy, and then made permanent by Jack with a medium-tipped indelible blue ink pen, using a four-foot steel ruler.

From those they began to mark off the position of all the perpendicular station lines, rechecking and then fixing those in blue ink and numbering them in sequence, starting at the bow at zero. A few hours later, when they had traced the last station line and had stepped back to look at the finished grid upon which all the curving lines of the yacht would be plotted, Deborah Sumners had appeared at the top of the stairs.

They'd been at the far end of the loft, too far to say anything without having to yell, but they hadn't needed to. She noticed the footwear there at the top of the stairs, and the work in progress, and before she stepped out onto the floor she placed her expensive pair of high heels alongside Jack and Scott's heavy work boots. She stood there in her nyloned feet as Jack plodded down to her and shook her hand.

Ellen, behind Deborah on the stairs, didn't stay to make introductions, just waving at them and leaving her behind. Scott could have sworn he'd seen a glint in her eyes. Something that almost looked like humor. Almost.

Informing them of who their visitor was hadn't been needed. It was there that Jack and Scott could see the logical connection between what they were doing and Eric Sumners' enthusiasm.

Scott, coming up from behind, wanted to say hello, but waited for Jack to do the initial greeting. Not surprisingly, Jack managed to begin awkwardly.

"We just got the basic grid down," he said, as though they'd known each other forever.

Deborah, for the moment, could say nothing to that. So she didn't.

A few long seconds passed, then Scott coughed. "Pleased to meet you," he said to her, sticking out his hand. "I'm Scott."

She took his hand, giving him a warm smile. "Deborah Sumners.

My husband told me of you and your help."

She gave Jack a brief, neutral look, then glanced at the planning grid stretched away down the floor. A flicker of a smile crossed her face. Eric had also told her what she might expect from Jack, and he was right. Introductions would evidently form themselves.

"It looks like an awful lot of paper," she said, looking back at him with a smile only the slightest bit ironic, "Jack."

Suddenly aware of the faux pas, he did what he normally did. He ignored it, wrapping himself in excuses of democratic informality. But in truth, the awkwardness wasn't lack of upbringing. He was simply doing the best he could in that first encounter with her shocking beauty. He'd guessed at its existence. You expected it of a rich guy's wife. But no one could have been completely prepared. It was a beauty to be categorically feared.

An odd thought crossed his mind at that moment. He could say he was almost glad he had never had the occasion to meet, or had wanted to meet, a woman like her.

He looked away from her to gather his thoughts.

"It's big," he said, "because the boat is big and we have to make the plans full size." Then, with another small moment of lucid awareness, he added: "Mrs. Sumners."

A puerile attempt at swapping the acknowledgement of social blunders? Jack suddenly sensed, glumly, that even if they got past all this, he was never going to feel completely comfortable around her.

"I see," she said, with just the slightest stress on *see*, looking politely at the plans. "Oh, and how rude of me, Mr. Colby. I hope you'll call me just Deborah. The thing is, I've heard so much about you, I felt like we already knew each other."

She looked at Scott, who gave her an easy, encouraging smile. She then looked back at the plans, shaking her head in admiration. Jack, still a bit tongue-tied, looked at her as she gazed about her at the loft. He knew he was coming close to staring. But she didn't seem to mind. As though she was used to it.

Work evaporated. All he could think of, right then, was her.

Of all the incredible harmony of her parts, he could see that the greatest attraction of Deborah Sumners at close range was the hypnotic effect of her eyes.

Deep ocean green between the dark lashes, they were now looking at the loft with a dreamy sort of diffidence, soft with some sort of feminine humor. But deeper still there seemed something else Jack couldn't quite name. Something at a misted distance, far back from intelligence, humor, or even the beauty itself.

He could feel the pull, and he knew then how a man, even one with all the wealth the world could offer, might get lost in those eyes.

With a mental jerk of violent embarrassment, he looked back at the loft, hoping his thoughts hadn't been showing and damning himself because he knew they had. But she was probably used to that, as well.

"Yes, right," he said, filling in until he could figure out what he was going to do with her up there, "I suppose it does look big. But wait until you see it growing down below, in all three dimensions."

She smiled then at them. Brilliantly. Radiantly. Easily and warm-heartedly. And everything else disappeared. For both Jack and Scott. Whether it was worries about lack of manners, of being tongue-tied, of her being the paying client. All gone.

Jack and Scott were immediately in love. But badly. Like boys. Unconsciously jealous of each other's presence, and not so unconsciously hoping any of that was noticeable. To anyone.

"That's amazing," she said. "That was exactly what I was thinking just now."

Deborah, herself, had a sudden and momentary feeling of shyness. But love had nothing to do with it.

She had registered Jack's reaction to her physical appearance. That was something, though, she had long before learned to deal with where men were concerned. What had suddenly struck her was how it was *her* that was the central figure to the project. It momentarily swept away her mechanisms against self-consciousness.

It didn't last long. Shyness, with her, was fleeting, and she was quickly drawn out of that towards her commitment to place things within an artistic framework. Or, lacking that, business. As Eric would have done.

"I was just looking at all that white space, and then I filled it in and put it upright like this."

She turned her head a little as if to look at the plans sideways, Jack and Scott watching her every movement. But she seemed disappointed with that and she brought her head back up to level.

"No, I guess I can't do it, at that. It's just a big space that seems too big to actually be the size of a boat."

"Uh," Jack said, "Right." His tone was guarded.

Scott, for himself, was fascinated. Seeing how incredibly easily it was for this outrageously beautiful woman, even in front of virtual strangers, to follow the whims of her mind. She actually seemed to have forgotten about herself, and especially of herself as a woman. It was unsettling, and in a masculine context, even a little insulting.

It was though, in her world, extreme beauty, in the same way extreme wealth did, dissolved all social cares or concerns about what people thought. She seemed capable of paying no more notice to them, than she would have paid to a couple of curious steers.

In fact, though, she did notice how Scott was looking at her. And how it was a different way of looking than Jack's looking. But she wasn't intrigued. She just laughed. At both of them.

"I see," she said. "That's not the way to do it."

"Not really," was all Jack could say.

"*Ah!*" She laughed again, and then raised her eyebrows. "Then I'll just have to *learn* how to see all this." She looked back at him, obviously just short of teasing.

Jack looked at her carefully. What man would ever have admitted to her that her manners were as unsettling as her physique? He wanted to shrug with irritation, but just took a breath.

"I suppose so," he said and looked back at the plans.

It was sure, he was thinking, they were all going to have to learn. But if he had wanted to just get on with things, he was too late. She had now taken her mind away from the boat, and was watching him. She could feel his uneasiness.

Like many unordinary people—which she believed absolutely of herself—she also felt keenly those things she thought made her distinct. And one of those things was how she also was inordinately kind.

"I hope," she said from her well of compassion, "I won't be in the way, in *any* way, if I come down here to watch."

She knew, the moment she said it, it didn't sound quite right, although she couldn't exactly say why. But she didn't care because, of course, she was being sincere. That was all that mattered.

If Jack had noticed that devastating use of utter kindness, muttered as though she hadn't noticed his embarrassment and distress—although she all too obviously had—he didn't show it.

Scott though, did, and suddenly had to dig something out of his eye. Beauty, evidently, could flub things up as well as anyone else. He then looked over at Jack, but saw no reply coming, so he decided to move things along.

"Not at all," he said. "Look around all you want. If you want, you can walk around the plans and watch us. We're getting ready to draw the actual curves of the hull." He pointed at the floor. "These are just grid lines."

"Hmmm," she said, as though that meant anything to her.

Jack didn't mind Scott's taking the conversational burden off him, and it gave him a second to reflect. He could see that, among other things, a large part of the building of the boat was now to be exactly this: constantly explaining to her what they were doing, taking him, or him and Scott, out of their work.

Of course, it was his own fault. He was now going to be responsible not only for the success or failure of a project he was in no way sure he could accomplish, but also for what Deborah Sumners understood about it.

While he couldn't actually bring himself to feel ill will towards Deborah Sumners for having been the ultimate reason for his position, he felt galled. He was the only one who had bothered to cling to reality. Yet he was the only one who had lost out.

"Listen," he said suddenly, with a faint spark of hope in his heart, "maybe you won't find it very interesting. This stage, like a few others, often isn't very spectacular. I mean, even for us it isn't all that interesting, just marking off points and lines. But at least we're doing it, you see. That makes all the difference in the world. I'd hate you to feel bored."

It occurred to Deborah that Jack might think there was some sort of tacit agreement between himself and Eric about her coming down there, but that she might not be really interested. She could see there was a need to have things out in the open.

"Believe me, Mr. Colby," she said. "This is the most interesting thing I've ever seen. You can't imagine what it means to me. Ever since Eric showed me the plans, I've thought a lot about it. In a way, this is a bit like an event for me, an event of my life. It isn't often that a person has the opportunity to recognize important events at the outset, and then participate in them."

Jack forced a smile. "I don't know if we're capable of being that much of an event. All we're going to do is try to build this boat for you. The rest, I'm afraid, is up to you."

Deborah laughed a light, sparkling laugh that finished on a dry note. She felt they were hitting it off very well, coming to some very important preliminary understandings.

"You," she emphasized, "don't have to do anything for me, I assure you. Please concentrate on the boat and I'll provide myself with the rest." Seeing they had agreed on arrangements, she felt she could now apply a more philosophic tone to show how she would be handling things for herself.

"You only have to do this," she went on, "in the way you would do it if I weren't here. It will be for me, then, to get anything else out of it. Your job is to create, mine to spectate. I don't feel I can make all this clear just now, but I would prefer if you could try to forget I am even here. All right?"

"*That* may be difficult," Jack said honestly. But he suddenly, mixed with a bit of shock at how that had come out, had enough presence of mind to elaborate over the top of a comment which flirted with the naked truth.

"We're not used to people watching. This isn't performance art, is what I'm trying to say."

"Of course not, Mr. Colby," Deborah said.

But that, on her part, was a flat-out lie. Her intentions, whether they liked it or not, were exactly to consider the project a long presentation of performance art.

Otherwise, there wouldn't have been much of a point.

But the last thing she was about to do was confuse them all down there with things she doubted they'd understand, anyway.

Jack nodded, as if he was agreeing to something, and then finally breathed out: "I ... uh ... I'm j-just ... Jack will do."

# Chapter 21

Work in the loft was resumed. For Jack and Scott—and especially a red-faced Jack whenever he thought of that Jack Will Do and the flicker of merriment it had caused—it was at first difficult to let the work slide into that solitude of thought it normally had. But as time wore on the initial discomfort subsided.

They made no sign to each other, but they separately began to enjoy having a silent witness to their work. When one's work is rarely seen except in final form, it's a pleasurable, almost flattering, opportunity to be demonstrating talents and abilities few except other professionals are aware of.

To show those talents off, as well, to an incredibly beautiful woman who was sincerely fascinated, was very nearly the Mother Lode of flattery. It was suddenly a craftsman's paradise down there.

By the end of what seemed a very short afternoon they got the main lines down. When they finally stood up and cleared away the long batten strips they'd been using for straight-edges, there, on the sky blue lines of the grid, the full-size profile of the ketch lay in indelible black ink. There was no question how big it was, filling three quarters of the length of the loft. They couldn't take it all in from one spot and had to move to make its size appear.

"Damn," Scott finally said.

Jack nodded, suddenly reminded of something Ellen had once told him about Native American language. How the white man had never understood the Indian, and vice versa, because in certain Indian dialects, in the way they organized their world, man rarely did anything. Instead, everything did things to man. A man did not die, as though dying was an action he could control the same way a man might walk, or ride a horse, or eat a meal. Instead, death happened to a man. Just as life happened to a man or the world happened to a man. Anyone who thought it was the other way around was crazy. Like white men, who thought they did everything that happened.

A swell theory, all that, Jack thought. But everyone knew, in the end, that the white man hadn't not only just happened to the Indian. But had sure as hell done them, as well. The real lesson was

135

that there were people who had things happen to them, and others who made them happen. Jack wasn't all that happy with his sudden suspicion that things were beginning to happen to him.

After a moment Jack and Scott turned to see how Deborah was taking in it. Noticing them looking at her, she gave them a smile.

"Are you sure it's not too big?"

Scott wasn't bothered by whether things were happening to them or not. He'd simply been happy all day, seeing how each minute took them farther and farther towards a point where nothing could stop the momentum of the project.

"Well," he said, "the lucky thing about it, the thing people don't realize and so they get scared off, is that it all goes together only one little piece at a time. So you take it one thing at a time."

He knew that little lecture was more for Jack's sake, than hers. But it wasn't hypocritical. He truly felt it.

"If you get too far ahead of things," he went on, "think too much about the whole thing, to the end, you end up too small for it. And you end up excusing yourself out of something that you could have handled."

The words, strictly speaking, were still aimed directly at Jack. But seeing with what intensity she listened, Scott became suddenly and extremely aware of how voluptuously she was hanging on his words. He felt a tightening in the stomach. And it made him feel wary for some reason.

"I don't know about you two," Jack said with a tone that sounded flat, "But I've had enough for today and I'm hungry, so I suggest we get down out of here."

"All for that," Scott said, and headed for his shoes, suddenly tired of the day's work, and the day's thoughts.

"What say?" Jack said to Deborah. "Would you like to have dinner with us this evening? By the smell," he nodded in the direction of the end window of the loft which gave over the kitchen of the house below, "I'd say it's spaghetti. When Ellen makes spaghetti, we always have plenty."

"Survival fodder ...," Scott said from the stairway. His voice had risen in amusement, preparing to tell a funny story, but he dropped it, seeing a hard look on Jack's face.

"I don't know," Deborah said. "Although Eric has a business dinner tonight."

"Then it's settled," Jack said.

"All right," she smiled at his insistence. "I'd love to join you."

It had been a light enough offer, lightly taken. But there was a weight behind it now that none of them could ignore.

The three of them, for three separate reasons, regretted both the invitation and the acceptance.

In an almost formal manner they all descended to the first meal shared between the contractor's side and the workmen's side, down in Ellen's kitchen.

It was a forced affair, but luckily—at least as far as Scott was concerned—there was also plenty of wine.

# Chapter 22

ELLEN WAS going through her morning routine. As with most people, to go through it unconsciously and for a string of days on end, gave her a feeling of security. She would have denied the idea that she needed the security of routine in her life. But there in the morning, with Jack and Scott out in the boatshed, and taking a seat at the kitchen table again, a quiet cup of coffee gave her a point of departure to reflect on the entire day. Lately she hadn't been able to do so, what with morning visits by Eric Sumners or his proxies and the setting in of the new patterns of work around the boatyard. But things were calming down. Even with Jack things had settled down. His evening routine: dinner, television and early sleep.

Ellen was content and thought about developments. She decided she liked Deborah. The dinner the night before had been comfortable and friendly. At least, for her. For the boys, it had been more difficult, although Scott—she had to admit—had made a better job of maintaining a light sociability. But in the beginning, she'd withheld judgment.

Deborah was the most beautiful woman Ellen had ever met. She would have expected that the responsibilities of Deborah's appearances would have weighed more heavily on her. It had turned out there was a strange lack of consciousness about appearances which, in truth, was the largest part of Ellen's decision she could like such a woman. There was no threat.

Deborah didn't seem the sort of woman who would consciously do anything out of simple, vain curiosity. She seemed, to Ellen, quite married to Eric Sumners even when he wasn't there, and also genuinely interested in the building of the boat. She certainly wasn't at all the spoiled rich woman come down to relieve her boredom at the expense of the working class.

If anything, it was exactly that strange interest in the boat which helped Ellen feel that Deborah's womanliness, at her deepest point, was checked. When Deborah talked about the boat something distant came into her eyes.

Whatever it was, a fabricated romance of it, or some individual philosophy, it was not something concrete. For Ellen, the domain of the concrete was where you had to worry about things. And that was her definition of womanliness.

Ellen knew exactly what she had, and how much it cost. It was that knowledge which allowed her to believe in Jack. She knew his realities. She didn't want to be smug about it, of course, but she knew how deeply she could push herself into him, how she knew him absolutely and completely. And he couldn't help but feel, if he didn't know, the truth of that.

With other women she had been put to the test and convictions and confidence notwithstanding she couldn't say she enjoyed the battles. Not that any actual war for her husband had ever taken place. But many women would do challenging things—tough, hard things—almost for the hell of it. Women's form of curiosity.

But sometimes not just for the hell of it, and those had been the times it got rough. A challenge of some kind was made, and usually without the woman having any idea of doing it. Almost a reflex action. And because it was unconscious they would go much farther with it. Innocent. A lovable, friendly somebody just clicking along on the mechanical imperatives of pure biological instincts, with all her claws and fangs at the ready.

If men, or her man, said they didn't see it, Ellen couldn't entirely believe it. Men often submerged the reality, either ignoring things or pretending to women that they didn't notice so as to be supposedly free to react or not react.

Ellen took a sip of her coffee and then smiled grimly. It was always amazing what men would tell themselves.

As far as feelings of freedom of reaction, men were extremely vulnerable at that point. Because—exactly—rather than making it possible for them to proclaim exclusionary rights to the control of things, it made them profoundly easy to trap. Nothing traps men so easily as their own pretensions.

Jack got himself into these corners all the time. If it wasn't serious Ellen let him get out, although giving him a few kicks just to let him know she was no fool. But occasionally, she took outright advantage of him.

That was the paradox of couples, how they by necessity had to work in fusion and yet maintain a certain separateness for functional reasons. It was what made it possible for men to live with themselves. And it was what made it possible for women to live with men. Without eventually killing them out of frustration.

Ellen had been raised to deeply understand all this. Her mother explaining how it was only women who had the insight, the instinct, which allowed them to understand men better than the men understood women, or even themselves. Her mother was very systematic with the viewpoint, even going so far as to bring it into the modern age by explaining how it was a by-product of male or female hormones on the nervous system. According to her mother, testosterone gave a man a decreased capacity for internal sensation in an equivalency to the external increase in physique and resistance to pain.

Her mother read a lot of articles on the subject. Ellen wasn't that sure, yet couldn't find a way to altogether disagree.

But whatever it was that permitted Jack to fulfil her life as she fulfilled his, whether it came from glands or kindergarten conditioning, it didn't matter. All Ellen wanted was to be able to get into him deep enough to make her own convictions stick. That had been the effort, and of all that, as Ellen had looked into Deborah's eyes the night before, she had known there was nothing there to shake anything.

Deborah's appreciation of what Jack was doing was quite disconnected from any hint of sex. So, for Jack, there would be neither instinctual pretensions of honesty nor outright lies to deal with because there was nothing there for him to get his teeth into. Or anything else.

She stretched, luxuriating at having for a few minutes the men of her life, out of her life.

When she finally got up to rinse out her cup in the sink she smiled at the thought of the two men up crawling around on the loft floor beneath the steady gaze of that ripe-bodied but somewhat vague young woman.

Her boys. Crawling on their knees.

They would show off for that beauty. She expected that would help get an awful lot of work done.

But that was all.

Because of one simple, obvious fact: this Deborah, this feminine-worship inspiration for the building of the *Muse*—in spite of her money ... in spite of her face, or hair, or the long legs and shapely ass, or those big tits and that body that would turn any man into a dog—was also one of the most neutered females she had ever met.

An unsexed statue in the form of female perfection. A sexless

140

Barbie doll.

A good woman had a right to be smug, Ellen told herself, beginning to hum as she dried her coffee cup.

Because no good woman has yet lost a man to a perfect statue. Or Barbie.

*

While she'd only been in Bellingham a month or so, Catherine was already sick of her new job.

Perhaps smaller cities were better places to live, she'd been thinking. But working in the branch office of a big city bank there, wasn't the way to prove it. The office society was even duller than it had been at  headquarters to the south. If not dead. The women were reduced to carefully constructed innuendo about each other. And the men, few of whom were even attractive anyway, were well-trained to avoid anything smacking of sexual harassment. She would have traded half a month's salary for one sincere, if misplaced, leer.

So it couldn't have come at a better moment, reading the local paper at lunch in a small coffee shop on Railroad Avenue, when she noticed a three-line ad in the jobs classified. A secretarial position with a local boatbuilding company.

Anything. Whatever. Just to get out of that bank.

She called from the coffee shop, talked to a woman, and found she could go straight down if she wanted.

Which she did.

By the time she got back to the bank at one-thirty she owned two jobs.

She gave the bank two weeks' notice.

Her boss tried to get four weeks from her, training time and all that, but she held firm to her rights.

That evening, driving out of the staff parking lot, she felt truly, truly free for the first time since she had left Seattle.

# Chapter 23

UNDER NORMAL circumstances, regardless of what Jack or Ellen might think, or even himself, it made in reality only an negligible strain upon Scott not having any steady female companionship. Out of an occasional feeling of emptiness he would daydream about Ellen. Or he would go to the bars and torture himself watching college girls. But mostly, he wended his way along without getting too twisted up about it.

But with Deborah's stunning physical presence around at the boatworks all the time, his shaky equilibrium collapsed. He could not remember a time when he had felt so energized with all-consuming flashes of lust. Which was strange, because excepting the impetus of Scott's physical loneliness, she seemed as sexless as a ninety-year-old nun.

Partly, his desire was fed by fantasies which, at the age of thirty, were more independent of absolute realities than ever before. As well—as is the case generally for the more innocent forms of guiltless lust—her allure was heightened by the simple fact that he wasn't connected in a personal way with her husband.

Not that Scott felt free to test married women. He had made his peace with the subject years ago by the way, as it is with most men, of matured ethics based on bitter or embarrassing experience.

But if he had a general rule about such activities, he fully allowed speculation free reign. Perhaps, he conceded, he would someday have to make a rule about that as well. But it didn't seem a pressing matter.

Each morning, when he saw Deborah show up, he felt his pulse quicken and an amorphous desire began to form. Sometimes that was all. But sometimes the desire continued to feed upon itself, flirting with that terrible abyss of lonely despair where innocence and strange purity were ready-made victims to the spirit of rape.

The over-all effect, though, was that Scott was simply more clean shaven than usual. Which Ellen noticed, and correctly interpreted. She told him flatly it was an insult, but that all things considered she preferred it to the alternative.

Scott had laughed, not embarrassed at all by being caught out.

Fact was, he was feeling more responsive to the possibilities of life than he had in a long time. Just because of the ethereal presence of a woman who seemed more image than real.

*

Luckily for both Jack and Catherine, Ellen had gone shopping early. Before leaving she had only told him to be on the lookout for the new secretary.

He and Scott had lofted all the lines of the boat by then. The myriad markings, in black for profile and water lines, green for the buttock lines, dark red for the deck line and diagonals, and purple for the body lines, made long graceful tracers of color across the loft floor.

The little brown architect, William Fletcher, came up from Seattle to inspect the precision, and had dryly given the go ahead. In his taciturn way, even he seemed enthralled by the intricate web of full-sized lines from which the boat would arise.

Given that green light, they set to making the hull molds, each representing a slice through the boat, a working template to shape the hull. And on that first morning of actual woodwork, Jack looked out the window at the sound of a car below, expecting to welcome the new secretary. And saw Catherine emerge.

At first he thought it pure coincidence. Hoped. And then fleetingly entertained the sordid possibility she'd come looking for him, even though she had said she wouldn't. But then he realized it was just the sorry and incredible fact that she was the woman who had answered their ad, spoken to Ellen, and taken the job.

Panic.

The first concrete thought he could muster was that she had to be, quickly and definitely, talked out of it. Yet, a second later he realized how difficult that would be. He had heard she'd given up her old job, excited by the prospect of the new one. She was excited, he'd been told. It was like a new lease on life for her.

Well, it would be a new lease on something, he thought.

He watched until she went out of sight towards the kitchen door, and then called to Scott.

"It looks as though someone has shown up for the secretary job."

Scott, thankfully, wasn't an overly inquisitive man. Or, at least not when he was concentrating on work. That spared Jack any audience. The fact that Deborah was there also helped stabilize idle curiosity.

He went over to the stairs and headed down to the office. Difficult or not, he knew what he was going to have to say. Things were complicated enough.

Catherine was standing on the porch, knocking lightly, when Jack came up behind her. Hearing crunching steps in the gravel of the parking lot, she turned with an excited, hesitantly hopeful look. It was quickly replaced by a look of shock that would have easily rivalled the one Jack had worn.

"Oh, my God."

Jack held up his hand.

"Go in there," he pointed into the kitchen as he went up next to her and, opening the door, partially led and partially pushed her inside.

Catherine was open-mouthed, confirming that it was a complete accident. Which was unfortunate, for if it had been any other way he could have simply told her to get the hell out.

"I don't believe it," she said to him as he stared at her. "Oh, my God. I had no idea."

Beyond exclamations, they could only look at each other, embarrassed and curious. It was embarrassing to be meeting in broad daylight. It was almost more naked than the time they'd spent together. Yet there was also a form of satisfaction to place a frame of reference around who this other person truly was.

"Well," Jack finally said. "Hello again."

Apologetically, Catherine nodded. "Hello again."

There was something poised and graceful about how she said it. Jack, despite the overall mortification, could affirm to himself that his original attraction to her had been no fluke. That was one more good reason for letting her down, and quickly. So he got right to it.

"Okay," he sighed. "So, here you are, and here I am, like a dog chasing a tail."

Jack winced inwardly. He had a personally uncomfortable bad habit of making ambiguous, off-the-cuff analogies when stressed. It arose out of his difficulty with explaining things. And as usual, he found himself hoping they'd be taken neutrally, or even ignored.

They weren't. For Catherine at that moment, any declaration about what was going on had significance. And although she felt an immense chagrin herself, she was damned if she was going to allow

144

it to look like she had planned something.

It might not work out. She was willing to admit that. The next few minutes would be crucial in knowing what would happen. But she felt a sudden surge of pride. She wasn't going to hand any free outs to him on a silver plate. Somewhere, an old and stubborn anger set itself.

She gave Jack a level look and said flatly, "I'm not chasing anything except a job."

"No," he said. "I'm not saying it's you chasing your tail. It's that night coming back around. You know, what goes around comes around." Jack swung his hands in the air as though that was the entire explanation.

Catherine was soothed by that. She could see he was more confused than angry. Or determined. And so she decided to take a soothing tack, as well.

"I guess so. It's just an amazing coincidence, is all. It's amazing I'm even in Bellingham, for that matter. If you'd told me two months ago I wouldn't be in Seattle, I wouldn't have believed you."

There was nothing much either one of them could say. It was one of those hopeless situations where if there was anything to be done about it, it was too late. What was worse was how the general feeling of forward movement in life and work, for both of them, had come to a standstill.

Moments before, Catherine had been heading towards a new job, and Jack had been moving along as best he could with the project. They were now both faced with a future that was, for Catherine, no longer simple, and for Jack, even more complicated.

The fact was, there was no way to not think about their passionate encounter in Seattle ... pretend to ignore it in some way they could call being adult. One of the lessons to be learned on becoming an adult is how often it's impossible to act like one. So Jack said the obvious and left the rest unsaid. Which was the only adult thing to do.

"You realize this isn't the best thing that could happen. For me or for you."

"I know, Jack," she said, her voice softly agreeing.

She, too, knew that pretending there hadn't been a connection between them would be a futile act. She didn't welcome the complications, herself, either. Suddenly, though, she saw what the end product of too much agreement here would be. Another way out for him. Too easy. They would just find themselves mouthing platitudes about how it was an idea that hadn't happened at the right time or place. And then it would just be *sayonara sailor*, she'd go away, and Jack would be relieved, and that would solve his problems in one shot. Another one shot. For him.

At another time Catherine would have ignored it. But she was fed up lately with the way she'd been moved around.

Of course, she'd agreed to take the banking job in Bellingham. The pressure had been either that or nothing. Which, when everything has worked out, is nothing to get bent out of shape about, either. But if not, can be a very irritating thing to remember.

Now this.

Just be a good girl, Catherine, and walk away and everything is all right in the world at Colby Boatworks.

It was unfair, and she suddenly wanted things to be a little more even. She was tired of losing. She didn't need to win anything. All she wanted was the feeling that, for once, she was able to break even.

"Listen, Jack. I know what the best thing for you would be. That this isn't good. As a matter of fact, it may be worse than bad. But this has got me in a spot that may be even worse than all that put together."

She watched Jack's face, and saw it was hardening as he realized that the easy way out wasn't going to happen. She knew, now, she was in for a fight. And it was right there she made up her mind. She was going to have the job whether he liked it or not. Whatever it took. And she knew how she could make that happen, if she really wanted to. But she wasn't at that point, yet. She moved her head slowly from side to side.

"I really have to have this job. I'm not looking for pity. But I didn't save a dime, between the move, the new house, and only a month on the job, to let me get by without work." She shrugged and then, despite the seriousness of the situation, she suddenly remembered the puffy, angry face of the bank manager when she had forced through her leaving, and—startling Jack a bit—laughed freely.

"I can't go back to the bank," she went on. "Believe me. So, okay, I agree this isn't good. But I'm in too much of a spot to just walk. You understand? So maybe we can work something out. Just let me work here long enough to find something else. Who knows, I might find something tomorrow for all you know."

It seemed reasonable enough to her.

146

Jack felt a little ashamed of himself. It was true that it was unfair to wish she'd just leave. But although it wasn't as though she was a sinister vamp who was out to wreck his life, a man had a right to hope things could be just a little simpler.

"Are you sure?" he said. "I mean, you've stepped right into the middle of the one thing you weren't meant to ever come near. Isn't that bad enough?"

Jack watched her eyes closely, hoping to see agreement there. As he did so, he couldn't help noticing how pretty they were. Intelligent and soft at the same time. A woman who had been a pretty girl, and had managed to become an attractive woman and not just a pretty girl grown older. And he was suddenly aware of her in the way he had first found her attractive, and could not pretend that her presence wasn't having an effect on him again.

It made him all the more adamant about his fears. He hadn't just forgotten about her, of course. And in the past few weeks, feeling stressed and irritated by Ellen, the memories of Catherine had occasionally come back to him. He had felt the strong pull of her. Which was normal, he had figured, considering how their needs had been so strong that night.

He had been able to avoid any other thoughts about the subject, though.

There had been no right or wrong to worry about since there was no reality to deal with afterwards. Where, for some people, memories and thoughts can be as much a part of their physical reality as their actions, for Jack it was only the exterior circumstance which counts. It is an attitude only capable of being sustained in a closed off world where people and things are carefully arranged. It is an attitude which suffers the most when those people and things refuse to be closed off. Or disappear.

It had never been considered a betrayal because it had no effect on the arrangement of things. Her presence meant that he would now have to be continually responsible for making sure Ellen never knew anything about it. Active concealment.

If that wasn't as good a definition for betrayal, he didn't know a better one.

"I don't know," he went on. "Ellen's not stupid. I can't imagine her not figuring something out, sooner or later."

Catherine—despite knowing it was a bit absurd—couldn't help beginning to feel betrayed, herself.

Where before, the incident hadn't meant that much to her, she now felt rejected. Scorned … to put it in its most ridiculous form.

But ridiculous or not, the feeling was there and so was the return of the earlier, slow burning infuriation.

"It's a possibility," she agreed.

She didn't mean to sound flippant about it. God knew his worries were on solid enough ground. But she also had some physical and emotional dilemmas to suddenly face, herself.

Despite the reception she was receiving, the mere sight of Jack sent an upheaval through her. He now had a name, a place and a life that was truly outside her own. She no longer fully owned her dreams of the one man she had been able to have fully as her own. That man was now gone, through the simple process of appearing again.

The images flashed through her mind. She had never denied herself the luxury of thinking about him. The memories filled her yearning bed, her hollow fantasies. Him holding her, kissing her, of his legs, the memory of the soft hairs of his thighs moving upon her smooth skin, his gentle hands and fingertips touching her, and holding her quiet. How he had thanked her forever and told her she was wonderful and beautiful, and how he'd always be grateful. Later, she had sometimes used those memories to move herself in her loneliness. She had never expected to see him again, so there had seemed no danger in it. The dream of sharing that again with him had seemed safe.

And now here he was. And now that she had found him again, she had to lose it all and banish the shadow of his generous sharing of something like love from her mind, training her body to forget as well. What before had seemed a gift, now seemed a punishment.

Her loneliness, like a secret bank account of bitterness, came over her in a blood red wave. A thick, choking force. She did not cry. She knew she mustn't. That was the last thing she should do. Right then.

"Listen," she said slowly, "perhaps your wife might be able to figure something out. But that's not for sure, and it wouldn't be by any fault of my own. It's totally up to you. If you make such a big thing out of it in your mind that you can't shake it or reign it in, it'll go over to her. I know I have no reason to make her wonder. I won't because of how I feel about you, and that I don't want to have this go wrong for either one of us. Just to get it out, for once and for all, all I remember of that night is that it was good. I want it to stay that way. The only way I can think of doing that is to make sure nothing bad comes of it. You see? I can do it, because it means a lot to me to keep things like that. If you can trust me, then we can get by. If you can't ...," she lifted her shoulders.

It was an ultimatum, in a way, devoid of blackmail, and she immediately regretted how it gave him a sudden out. He could admit he couldn't handle it and it was all over. She knew she mustn't now make it a real possibility by simply saying it aloud.

She had no idea, though, that she had said exactly the right thing. Because for Jack, an admission he couldn't handle something was an impossibility. And all other considerations were momentarily forgotten. He could no longer ask her to leave on her own accord, admitting she could handle herself better than he could handle himself.

"You think this is possible then," he said flatly. As he did so, he saw a slow smile creep onto her face.

Stuck, he thought bitterly, once again.

It was getting to be a pattern. First Ellen and Scott with the boat, then Sumners with his wife, and now Catherine. Once again, there was nothing to be done about it.

"Okay," he said quickly and somewhat brutally, wanting somehow to bully the smile off her face. But then, feeling his sudden anger was unjustified, and ashamed of himself, he lowered his voice and sighed out slowly, "okay."

Catherine now smiled openly. She had won. What she had won was debatable, but for the moment, the feeling of victory was enough. He was going to have to trust her.

"All right, then," she said, giving a sympathetic sigh of her own. "Oh my God. What a deal. But I think this will work out all right."

If the crisis had passed for Jack, there wasn't much to feel good about.

"It'll have to." He gave her a long look. "It'll simply have to."

Where that should have been the easy end of it, Catherine couldn't resist one last matter. After all, she was now there and had a right to know a few things. It seemed no mistake.

"One thing," she said, her confidence restored to her. "I mean, this is just because I need to know it. I mean, although it's now impossible for us. I'd like to know how it is with your wife. I don't know ... do you have some sort of arrangement with her?"

Jack looked at her with a sudden intensity, and Catherine read his thoughts.

"You're wrong," she went on, "I'm not on a fishing expedition.

It's a form of protection, if you want. I'd just feel safer knowing where things stand."

Jack recovered enough from the shock of almost having had his worst expectations confirmed, and nodded vaguely. Honesty, at this point, wouldn't hurt.

"We've never discussed it," he said.

"So what does that mean?"

"It means that, no, we do not have an open marriage."

An irrational feeling swept over her. He was being honest and open. And she truly expected nothing from him. But, then, why did she have an odd and sudden feeling of being excluded? As twisted as it might feel, as tortured and unjustified a position as it might be, it was maybe a necessity for her to put herself into it as though she was, indeed, a part of it. Create an artificial jealousy where none was possible. Invite rejection even where there was none.

Of course, she would deal with this all later. But for the moment she was unable not to scratch the itch of their former intimacy.

"You know," she said. "Even though I shouldn't, I feel a little ridiculous."

"I don't mean to make you feel that way."

"No. It's not you doing it."

"Then don't feel that way."

Catherine gave a plaintive smile. "It's just a part of the package. I had a boyfriend who told me that the modern package is to always be stuck having to feel old ways about new things. We never catch up."

"There must be a better way, somewhere."

Catherine looked at Jack, and then around the kitchen. That particular conversation, now over and dead, would never rise again and she must now begin a new way of life, and a new way of guarding her dreams.

"Yes," she finally said. "There must be another way."

Jack, too, had trouble imagining it. But maybe everything would work out just the way it had to. The way everything should always work out, everywhere.

But on the other hand, he suddenly thought, probably not.

\*

Catherine declined taking a tour of the place. She would start work in a week.

Jack returned to the loft. Scott, concentrated on the work and silently warmed by the aura of Deborah, did not notice the worry lines now creased deeply into Jack's unhappy forehead.

But where concentration can create ignorant bliss, it can also cure anything.

Jack turning his concentration to the work, put his worries back into the boat.

If, for Jack, there was one absolutely redeeming quality to the work he found himself doing, it was to be found in how he could lose himself within it. As though no one, himself or anybody else, could find him. It was how he, and many people, hide in plain sight.

# Chapter 24

Scott and Catherine were never to know whether they might have hit it off. As is often the case after a certain age, life's patterns of busyness interpose. And so two mature, reasonably intelligent, reasonably attractive, and reasonably interesting and good-humored single people, both wondering why they were alone, never had a chance to see or talk to each other when it might have counted.

Not that something might have happened. People put a lot of weight into the idea of missed chances or bad timing. As though that was a preponderate ingredient to success or failure in life—when in fact it's mainly a hindsight consideration. But in any case, by the time the two really did have the opportunity to get to know one another, it was too late. They'd both been too distracted. And other things came along.

By that time, as well, the work on the boat was deeply in swing.

Compared with the stressful concentration necessary for putting down the lines correctly, making the molds for the boat was no difficult thing. Using the highly exact body plan laid out on the floor of the loft, they set closely spaced, two-sided tacks along a line and then pressed planking upon the tacks. When they lifted the planks, there were a set of tacks, curving to follow the lines, which they could cut the wood down to.

Some of the molds at amidships were large and heavy, and it was an effort to jockey them down into the shop using blocks and tackles. It was hard work but they went at it in a haze of effort, and over the next few weeks most of the molds would be built, numbered and carefully stacked along the edge of the shop near where they would be set up in their stations.

In the evenings Jack and Scott, together or singly, would go out and look at the fantastic forms, the glowing, fresh-cut wood in the dusk there taking on the shapes of giant punch bowls and fancy dessert dishes. Some would be overtowering, twenty feet wide at deck level and twelve feet deep to the bottom where the bottom of the mold would rest upon the spine of the keel.

In themselves, although a temporary part of the building process to be used for forming and then to be removed, the molds still held their own functional beauty. They were well made, as carefully made as possible, as though they were a trial run for what was to follow. There were tight joinings and fittings, and it was satisfying to run a hand over the sharp, smooth edges.

The days of summer were nearly ended. Soon, the Colby's would be getting their first requests from the local fishing fleet to have repairs done. Jack and Scott had discussed it, and decided they didn't want to turn their backs, entirely, on their traditional autumn work on fishing boats.

Many of the fishermen preferred to leave scraping and painting for deep winter, to try to keep a fresh paint job from going into the water until as close to the next season as possible. But some of their boats would have suffered damage, and would have to come in even in the early fall. Colby Boats had always taken that work, and would continue.

Three boats would come within the first two weeks of September. At first they tried to handle the work themselves. But soon enough they decided they needed help. And for once, could afford it. Neither of them would have admitted that the need to maintain Deborah's interest, mattered in that decision in any way.

Thinking it over, Jack decided against advertising for experienced boatmen, ship's carpenters or yardmen. For the trawlers and bottomfishers coming in, there wasn't much need for extensive boatbuilding skills. Jack would say, and Scott agreed, it would be a shame to hire professionals to work on minor jobs where, alongside, true boat construction was going on. Of course, there was no need to mention how experienced boatmen wouldn't come cheap, no matter how difficult it was for them to find wooden boat work anymore.

Jack hired a couple of locals. One, a high school graduate named Tom, and a Lummi Indian named William. Tom was a somber young man, black eyes looking out suspiciously beneath a heavy bowl of black hair. He'd been around boats all his life, his father running a local marina. The young Indian, William, was newly out of the army. He was also quiet and, like Tom, seemed to know his way around woodworking tools. And that was all that Jack cared about. The regular business would go well down at the waterside end of the boatworks.

But the work wouldn't be steady down there yet, still a few months before the regular, more heavy rhythm of incoming fishing boats settled in, so Jack couldn't just forget about them. With them around, he sulkily agreed, at Ellen's insistence, to put his extra help to another use.

During the times when the work was slack, paint drying, or waiting for material to come in, he would set the two apprentices to refinishing the boatworks. Ellen chose the colors.

The roof, old and new shingles alike, was to be stained a dark red, the trimming, sashes and gutters painted a creamy, light gray, while the siding would be a fresh blue-gray. Small details, doors, window woodwork and railings would be done in a blood-red enamel to match the roof. Surprisingly, it wouldn't cost much and the effect would be spectacular, she said.

No one who had lived in that area for any time would have guessed at how a little paint could have transformed the sprawling old boatshed. Jack nearly laughed the day a young reporter, over from the Herald, wandered in asking if this were some new business going up. Jack just said it was a paint job. Standing there, the reporter noticed the big molds and learned about the boat. He also noticed Deborah, and before too long knew all about what was happening down there and who it was being built for. He told them all, and especially Deborah, that it was a good story, that people would love to know all about it. Maybe do a running series showing the different building stages.

Jack and Scott saw how most of this was directed at Deborah, who smiled intriguingly and said little … although she did mention that maybe the reporter should talk about it with her husband. The young reporter seemed pleased with that idea, as well, asking for Sumners' phone number. He then turned to look at Jack and Scott.

"This'll be great," the reporter said. "You watch. You'll be famous, and this'll be great for your business." He looked back at Deborah, and arched his eyebrows. "Famous."

She smiled uncommittedly. Jack and Scott gave each other a blank look, and then Jack made a slight movement with his head. Scott took a step towards the reporter and, with a smile, led him out of the boat shed.

As the reporter headed for his car, he kept yelling back how he'd be getting back to them whenever there was something to take a picture of. Saying he was the sort of reporter who hated writing stories where there were no pictures.

"Whatever that means," said Scott when he came back in and walked up to Jack and Deborah.

"Well, one thing it does mean," Jack said, "is that it's a warning to us all to make sure we look appropriately picturesque."

"If it's us he wants in the picture," Scott said, with a slight smirk at Deborah. They had gotten familiar enough with each other for small jokes. She gave him a droll look.

And for a second, she almost made a small joke of her own. Maybe something about not being down there to model bathing suits. Or something. But she didn't. Familiarity had its limits. But she did manage:

"At the very least, we'll all be famous."

She was pleased to see they were, indeed, amused.

And they genuinely were, although the code of manly behavior for this sort of thing—the question of fame being something no one would treat but as silly—meant they could only smile enigmatically.

And for the first time, they actually felt a bond of friendship between them. Proving, once again, there is nothing better than the presence, actual or eventual, of a newspaper reporter—and especially a young one still flattering himself with illusions of self-importance—to make people feel co-conspiratorially superior.

# Chapter 25

I<small>F</small> D<small>EBORAH</small> had shown, though, the slightest degree of understanding of what she could do to them, Scott, at least, could have been easily miserable.

An irritated, agonizing awareness of the sex of the other. Or, as she would have put it: awareness manifested within the ponderous mass of social limits preventing the ultimate disaster of explicit recognition of that awareness ... for someone who would have never have shared, for a second, the same thing.

Or something like that.

Thank God, Scott thought, for the privacy of the mind.

Of course, there was evidently to be no lurking disaster with Deborah. No sudden awareness. He was in no way certain he could have survived even one knowing and ironic smile from her. Acknowledging yet another infatuated fool. Blasting his manhood back even farther than the stone age.

He now realized that that one danger wasn't there. He even began to relax a bit when she was around. Putting things, mostly, out of his mind.

But if he was coming to terms with her spectatorial presence, she began revealing what she thought about all of that. Which, in a way, became even more bothersome.

Philosophy had strolled through the door. And at first, as he always did when that happened, he'd ignored it.

He was enjoying the work like he had rarely enjoyed anything before. As one of the first steps before building the spine, he and Jack began making the keel blocks which would hold and steady the big keel timbers and, eventually, the boat itself.

Taking railroad-tie sized lengths of fir, they were drilling holes and bolting on the heavy side blocking that would prevent the keel from shifting. While these were of a very pedestrian construction, there was a functional beauty in them as well.

Deborah, who was constantly there, had even begun to bring them their tools, and then began talking to them. About things. And mostly about the things they knew intimately, like keel blocks, and their functional beauty, and picking at their thoughts. Thoughts which they didn't need to have edited by someone else. Especially by someone who didn't know a keel block from a chunk of brick.

And who seemed intent on turning it all into something else. Philosophically, that is.

Scott hadn't listened to her much in the beginning. What attention he usually gave her was mostly wrapped up in unwrapping her. Scott had become adept at doing so, no matter what she wore, and what he finally was able to imagine was practically an end in itself. He realized he'd never seen anything like her except in magazines.

He'd gotten used to her being around, but he would never get used to her haunting physique. Or, at least, hadn't done so yet.

The airbrushed perfection of adolescent lust is a hard thing to pretend to have forgotten, let alone actually forget. And in her case, impossible. In the same way she was impossible.

He'd seen things almost like it, a face here, a figure there, a pair of legs somewhere else. But never all together at the same time. It was something you only found pictures of. Never on the street.

Yet here it was. Every way she turned, bent, twisted, sat, or leaned, with her shape moving within an ever more precise vision of her in his imagination, gave reality to the glossy dreams.

Which had nothing at all philosophical about it.

It was amazing to Scott how she could live so easily with it. She had to be aware. How could any woman not be aware of how the vast majority of men would kneel at her feet? How they desired her, and would practically destroy themselves to possess, even momentarily, a beauty which was almost immortal. She seemed unimpressed with it. Merely so much flesh to get up in the morning and bring down to the boatworks to watch Scott and Jack saw wood all day.

Frankly, so much the better.

But now she had begun talking, and the contrast between that carnal reality of her physical body, and what went on in her mind ... was unsettling. He listened, at first amazed. Then something else. She gazed at things, it seemed, as they could be. Not at what they were. She saw potential. Reality was the temporary state.

"Don't you see," she'd said. "These too are a form of the boat. It's all integral."

"Of course it is," Scott had agreed as he cranked a long lag bolt into place. Then he looked around at her.

157

"All I said was that these were just blocks for the keel. When they're done with, they might be saved. Maybe we'll be building something else on them. Another great yacht. Or maybe we'll use them to hold a garbage scow in place, or maybe we'll just burn them next year as firewood."

Scott turned back and made a last twist on the bolt and looked up at Deborah patiently. It wasn't often someone wanted to argue the metaphysical nuances of a piece of wood. She seemed so sincere, though, he gave her as pragmatic a viewpoint as he could muster.

"Look, if anything, because these are going to help build the boat, I figure they're more a part of the category of things like this building, or my tools. I certainly don't consider my tools to be an integral part of this boat ...." He grinned at last.

Deborah smiled back at him and his blunt, let's-get-realism, but she wasn't to be put off.

"I think you're deliberately confusing the issue. I think you're doing it partly so you don't have to think about it, and partly because you think I'm nuts. They are beautiful, and you can't deny that."

Scott looked with her down at the blocks, and had to agree with her. They were set in a line down the middle of the shop, waiting for the keel. Each block was of fresh wood, cut, smoothed and beveled against splintering, with gleaming bolt heads and their washers recessed neatly, binding parts strongly together.

"When you work, I've seen how you approach it," she said. "I know better than what you're saying. It does mean more to you."

Well, fine, he thought. So everything means more than what it appears. After you got to that point, there wasn't much left to say. From there, you could go on and on forever. Or ... until you ended up forgetting whatever the hell it was you were talking about in the first place.

Scott had a sudden realization about her and her husband. Something he hadn't understood before. About how she, who disdained so much the material world could be with someone who was one of those responsible for it. It was now obvious. Simply, her habit of constructing levels of meaning got her around having to deal with the realities of Sir Moneybags.

He could end up being anything she wanted to believe.

Lucky him, Scott thought. Sumners wouldn't have to work so hard for her. Which was a little cheap, if you thought about it.

But Scott didn't have anything against Eric Sumners. In spite of his seemingly infallible luck, he did evidently make an effort to put things back into his marriage. Even though that effort consisted mainly of throwing money at it.

Understandable. And yet ....

These people were a strange breed. Sumners was out of no neighborhood Scott had known. A guy who didn't quite fit the description for someone you could take for granted: a regular guy.

A regular guy could be your best friend or the biggest asshole to come down the road. But at least you knew where it was all coming from. And a regular guy had the other regular guy quality: he thought of you in the same way.

That wasn't Sumners.

At all.

Sumners ... he came at you like he had a radar on, examining you and trying to form opinions.

He gave the impression, early on, that he thought the whole world down there at the boatyard was a simple thing. Part of a simpler world ... that he had set in motion.

Making them all a part of a simplified working class that was simpler than it was. While his wife, not much of a regular guy either, had some sort of radar assuring her that it was all undoubtedly much more complicated ... than even the inhabitants could know.

On top of all that, the inhabitants were all supposedly so happy being either way.

Happy simpletons for the husband, who evidently saw such a thing in a wistful eye. Wishing—non-judgmentally, of course—he could only have that simplicity, too.

Or happy schizophrenics for the wife. Who not only wistfully hoped they were like that, but was actively trying to convince them of it.

He gave Deborah a careful look, making sure he didn't sound irritated.

"You're saying, maybe, I don't appreciate what I'm doing? Is that it?"

"No," she said. "Of course not that. I mean you're just not fully aware of it."

Now, he was careful in how he spoke.

"You know, I don't just do this as though I'm stamping out parts in a factory. There wouldn't be any point, if I wasn't aware of the beauty in it. Both in the product, and in the work itself."

"Ah!" she said, almost triumphantly, as though she'd just taught him something, despite himself. "Then you are aware!"

Scott had a rueful moment, but let it pass.

"Believe me," he said finally, "Sooner or later, I'm plenty aware."

# Chapter 26

THE WEEKEND following Catherine's appearance at the boathouse, a Saturday evening, and after a quick bite at a nearby eatery, Scott drove to his place, picked up his guitar and drove around the bay to downtown Bellingham. A piano player Scott had once unloaded fish with over at the icehouse docks had got a gig at one of the big college hangouts and had asked Scott to sit in.

Scott was no virtuoso on guitar. But unlike the untold millions of other American youth who learned to play at least three chords in order to impress girls, he'd managed to develop his playing beyond the Machiavellian stage into the hobby stage. That netherworld of any art form—the stage from which one might accidentally, and fatally, become serious about the thing.

Just out of high school, strumming like a Neanderthal and thus fitting right in, he'd played with enough bar bands to learn at what low levels of skill music can be performed in public. And still be got away with, let alone paid.

The experience had almost had an effect. He'd even given the guitar serious thought for a while, practicing quite a bit, getting at least competent with a fair number of the more standard American clichés of blues and blues-rock. One day though he arrived at the breakthrough point: his technique improving enough to allow him to understand how truly bad he was. And how many years it would take to really be able to play the thing. Whereupon, with no regrets, he immediately quit. Or, at least, the so-called serious side of it. To play was now another thing, and enough in itself.

He was glad for the chance to join in.

For one thing, it was fun. For another, it was always good to be able to go into bars and be able to actually have something to do besides drink and stare at women.

He could even feel happy, and felt free, for the first time in weeks, to think about nothing and also Deborah Sumners—whatever it was that Deborah Sumners represented—without getting bent out of shape about it.

They had developed a mutual use for each other's needs.

161

He fixed her as an object of abject lust, she fixed him as a sort of happy complicated dumbshit to be instructed. He smiled to himself as he drove, wondering what she would make of him now, in his role as Working Class Hero, a lower form of life striving to evolve, now heading over to town to play caveman guitar for other members of a loose social grouping of hominids known as a bar band, for another group, called a bar crowd.

All in all, whatever she might think of it, it was a pleasant enough prospect.

When he got to the bar he found the band had already set up. His friend was idly warming up on an old upright piano as the evening crowd began to slowly trickle in. An amp was set up for him by the drum kit, and he only had to tune to God only knew what key the piano was in, to be ready. At a table near the dance floor the band had got some pitchers of beer set out. While there weren't many people in there yet, it was obvious they were in a mood to party. Scott liked that.

Two hours later, with the music, the beer, and sweaty bodies stumbling all over each other, it would have been easy to believe he'd been there all his life, far from complications of any kind.

Then life, as it's said to happen, happened to him.

# Chapter 27

Her name was Sydney, of all things. She was out from West Virginia, studying Nutrition and Health Sciences, and would graduate in three years instead of four.

That was not to say she was a genius. But she was interested in things she did and very intense.

She loved skiing, sailing, and liked to do fun things like clam digging. She'd never done that before and had found it really great. Couldn't believe how great it was and had he ever done it? Wasn't it really great with a big clambake out on the beach, dipping the clams in melted butter around the fire? God, they were so delicious!

She was enthusiastic, to put it nicely. And also young, which made it all fit together, as youthfulness seems to be able to do so gracefully.

Every once in a while she got quiet, and her beautiful eyes which had a tendency to flit all over the place, also showed that she could really look at things.

But one thing was for sure. She was all party, when it was time to party.

She had a great mound of dark blond curls that shook down over her face and shoulders all the time, and especially when she danced. Sort of the wild woman thing where she could let go and get down hard with the music.

She liked drinking beer.

She thought Scott looked "tough".

Scott hadn't heard that one since he was eleven years old and wasn't sure what it meant anymore. In those days, it sort of meant "cool", or "bad" in the good way. Maybe, anymore, it meant what it was always supposed to mean. It seemed like a compliment, in any case. He'd tested it.

A couple of times he had moved away from her, once deliberately and once not, and both times he had turned to find her there in some way.

When he was up chunking out his old-fashioned rhythm guitar style, the noise of the band ripping out through the dark swirling mass on the dance floor, he saw her dancing out there and most of the time alone. For the one number the band didn't really need a guitar, when he had gone down to dance with her on a song they could somewhat hold on to each other to, she had grown passionate to him in a detached way. Or at least comfortable. Somewhat unsure.

It could have been the beer. Or it could have been that she did like him more than what partying at a bar required. He had no idea when they stumbled out of his car and into his house.

But she seemed to still like him the next morning. More than a morning requires, as well, with her up and wandering around his place in one of his old shirts.

He didn't mind her being around, either.

He had no idea, of course, if anything was meaning anything. That they might stretch things beyond that one night. But with breakfast looking to be shared, he could see the faint stirrings of something they might agree on if they wanted to acknowledge the fact.

Since she hadn't packed out of there at first light, and was up making coffee and toast, she had already done just that, for the most part. She was saying nothing outright though. Waiting politely for Scott's first reaction.

He sprawled in bed, alone with his thoughts and considering it, pretending to be asleep. With a sober mind back in a sober body, one needs to readjust slowly. Decisions which might have taken days, weeks or months have been acted upon in a very recent and hazy past. He thought he actually liked her, and quite a bit.

But to him, she was still something of a little beast he had tripped across in the dark. Except for what she had been like at the bar, he had no real idea of her.

And certainly not after the sex, what he could remember of it. Perfect strangers can have sex. Real intimacy is the acknowledgments of the nitty gritty.

It had been said that nothing is more revealing about people than the way they make love—yelling, whispering, strangling, crying, praying, biting, laughing, clawing. But drunken lovemaking was never the best condition under which to test out that theory. Alcohol can make the most generous act selfish, or the reverse, and no matter how good it was Scott figured the real truth of those nights only found exposure in the stunned early moments of the heartless day that followed.

He rolled around with a moan, pulling a wad of blanket with him and trying to forget about the aspirin he had forgotten to take.

He slid a glance out from under the blanket to the living room where Sydney was now sitting in an armchair, waiting for the water to boil. He could see she still had it, even then. The sensual cunning he had thought was drunken impetus. But, alongside that, he saw a girlish timidity. Which made him see a lot of other things as well. Things which could make that morning more than another morning. An acknowledged loneliness of want, perhaps even of need, in the way she sat. The same way he would have sat. Quietly. Wondering what the hell was about to happen next.

If anything.

The question wasn't so much getting past a night, and a morning after. But simply waking up into a new day.

He looked at her some more, and he could tell she knew he was looking at her. But she didn't seem to mind, and that made his mind up. He really did like her.

Really liked her.

And enough to want to do something about it, like saying the hell with it and just go find out. Like that.

He got himself up, forgetting his nakedness, and went out to the living room.

She turned at the sound of him coming in. "Oh, shit."

Not that he was into strolling around in the buff in front of women. But it seemed a right enough way to reintroduce two people to each other. The naked truth, he thought.

Giving way to impulse and flinging aside consequences, he pulled her out of the chair and gave her the friendliest hug and most prudent kiss on the cheek he could manage.

"Hiya," he said.

She nodded and brought her arms up around him after a moment and then smiled up at him from under her curls. In the light of day she had beautiful, clear blue eyes under all that hair, disturbingly clear considering how he had barely been able to see them the night before. He was trying to get used to how she looked. With those curls and everything.

"So," she said finally, a type of intelligence and purpose in her voice and eyes that he hadn't noticed before in her, "what do you think we might do today?"

It was the showdown. He could see she was scared, but she was no coward.

He didn't answer her. He could only give her a momentary tightening of his arms. The truth was, he didn't have the slightest idea what they were going to do at all. Maybe nothing.

But suddenly, that was exactly what he wanted to do ... and with her ... and all day.

Chapter 28

At the same moment Scott was beginning to track blindly along some new arrangement in his life, Catherine had already been up for three hours. She had done her shopping and was back, now having a cup of coffee and reading a nicely bound version of a universally well-appreciated novel, underlining sentences as she went along.

That bad habit she'd learned from her former boyfriend.

But if it was bad for that edition of the book, at the very least it helped slow down her greed to inhale the contents of Steven's legacy—her reading list.

Self-improvement 101 would continue, where he wouldn't.

She read through the vast ocean of his list of great books, some classic and some obscure, like some voracious sea monster moving ponderously though its domain, swallowing everything it crossed paths with.

Somehow, all this obsessive reading frightened her. She had never read as a girl, and only occasionally as a teenager. Who had? The only "serious" book she had tackled outside of what had been required for classes had been America's supposed War and Peace, Gone With The Wind. At the time, she had thought it was a great book. Now she realized it was anything but. In fact, really, it was pretty bad. But it had made a hell of a movie.

Maybe.

When she'd been young, reading and books and even art for that matter, hadn't mattered. There didn't seem much use for it and, worse, it caused you to spend an awful lot of time alone. Alone is not a place where pretty young girls want to be. Even school was better than that. Although school was basically where you and all your friends went to not study. College was where you went afterwards, except that your parents paid for it and so you were supposed to come out of there with something.

Though they never said it, meeting the right guy was as good an accomplishment as getting a useful diploma. Failure, on either count, wasn't a disaster but in a way not getting married was worse because everyone knew that a girl would then have to take her chances at the office or wherever it was that graduated, unmarried coeds ended up.

It seemed to Catherine now that while not meeting the right guy had seemed the worst thing, the really bad thing was how she had missed an education.

She had gone on after college, in fact, to join clubs and so forth, and it was no absolute irony that her first, post-college softball team was named the Desperados. Her friends there had called her Guppy for the way she drank her Margaritas, White Russians and beer. Or else—it had recently occurred to her—because of how easily guys could reel her in.

All that as a joke.

Which she had laughed at.

The years upturned themselves, and onto that heap went her first marriage, then the second. Each time with a happy-go-lucky guy who had bubbled up out of seemingly golden days of softball matches and picnics at the park. Luckily, those two jagged episodes of futility had produced no children.

Well, she liked to think it was her fortunate sense of survival, but she was honest enough to suspect it was also because both those great guys had shown all the paternal instincts of back-alley tomcats.

Maybe she had taken it all to seriously, what friends her age had liked to espouse: that marriage was a trap. And she and all her friends had fashionably and meticulously avoided those quick slides into the suburban nightmare everyone thought was so awful. Mainly by getting a divorce at the least sign of what was deemed masculine indifference. Her generation pulled up stakes or upped the ante at the first signs of trouble. Diplomatic domesticity the all-time dirty concept.

Now she felt she'd been cheated. By her friends and the fashions of the time. And by herself. Let others have what they though they wanted, but she now could wish for a house and home, and some man of her own who would be there every night. A man she could join with in figuring out how to make things work.

Regardless, she knew she was getting aloof. Each divorce had demanded its own form of mourning where she had buried, each time, another piece of her life.

Then came the rest, and Steven, too. If there was one thing for certain, it was that you always got older. For every day you didn't find something to give of and to yourself, someone or something, you just got more stupid. Being alone made you stupid, and remaining ignorant made you stupid.

She had come to believe that she'd had the wrong perspective, which had caused her to be with men who, on some deeper level, corresponded exactly to the sort of man who would prove her theories. Now, she needed a man to prove that all wrong.1

Catherine sighed, passing her hand across the open novel in her lap, and looked out her living room window towards Bellingham Bay.

Well, she didn't have much in the way of company, perhaps, but at least she still had a brain. If she couldn't have someone around right then, she could at least fill her mind with something more than self-pity, or the self-centering dribble of the more sensational women's magazines which amounted to the same thing.

So she was reading. At least, as long as she was going to be alone, she might as well profit from it. It wasn't an act of entertainment so much, as a search. She saw it as a form of exploration. And it was working. She felt she was discovering things, new ways of thinking and seeing. She had come to feel a resurgence of hope, seeing that with a new world opening up in front of her, new options could open up as well. If she had stayed within the old patterns of her life, and her thoughts, time would have slowly diminished her options.

A sudden contentment came back over her, and for two simple reasons.

She had a great new job, with an interesting—almost literary—twist to it with its dirty laundry subplot. And she was unshackled to any particular society and could develop whatever she now wanted, based on new ways of feeling, in any way she wanted to go and find comfort where she could.

And, right then, it was her books that comforted her. It was liberating, no longer feeling as though she was no longer a complacent part of a continual tragedy of ignorance.

A tragedy perhaps as great as the one she was reading about. She looked down at the book in her hand, where the youth was ignoring his father's prophetic advice not to go to Tchermashnya.

She went back to it, amazed at how clearly it was shown how a person could be making an awful mistake, at the exact instant they believed they were doing the right thing.

# Chapter 29

WITH MOLDS and keel blocks finished, Jack and Scott began making the casting box for the lead part of the keel. The steel keel would be fin shaped with a torpedo shaped ballast at the bottom and would be attached near the exact center of the boat into the timbers along that part of the spine. It was really the last thing they would do, attach that fin, but they didn't want to be doing any foundry work towards the end, with a big wooden boat in the shop. They built the molding box using templates from the drawings and allowing for shrinkage as the lead cooled.

The form was completed in two days and placed inside were the tie rods and plates which would permit it to be attached to the steel fin. Inside, a thin layer of plaster was smoothed over the naked wood to prevent burning. When it had dried they brought Tom and Will up to help, their job to keep the fire roaring and maintain the level of molten lead in the cauldron.

It was a hot, beautiful, smelly job to melt the lead. The fire, contained within a mortared firebrick enclosure at one side of the shop, was steadily fed from a pile of old, dry cherry wood Jack had bought. The wood had belonged to a friend of his who lived out on the Mt. Baker highway. Originally it had been meant for firewood use but for some reason hadn't, and over a period of years had dried out too much. In a fireplace where a slow burning fire giving off moderate heat was the ideal, the cherry wood burned so fast and hot that its fire became too powerful and destructive for the home. But for them, it was a true working tool,.

Each time a log was thrown under the pot there was an immediate flash of combustion. The smell of the cherry wood mingled with the thick, greasy smell of the molten lead and of the sweat of the workmen as they began ladling the heat-shimmering, red and silvery flows into the bottom of the keel mold.

Jack and Scott took turns ladling the lead in, or puddling and skimming the lead in the mold with iron rods, working up and out any bubbles. In a continuous pour, the mold was filled in less than an hour. Left-over lead was poured into pig molds.

It was a fast morning and when they were done, Ellen told them that Eric had called down and had offered to take them all to lunch over at Micky's.

Jack glanced at the others, then looked back at Ellen and nodded. She went back inside. A half hour later Eric drove into the parking lot.

As they all ambled up the street towards Micky's, the warm September air filled with the cries of seagulls, Jack was thinking that regardless of whether Eric was a nice guy or not he would always be the man with the money.

Even this lunch spoke of that.

In spite of the fact that Ellen had planned a special lunch to take advantage of the fact there wasn't much to do until the lead cooled, they had all quickly changed their plans.

The simple way Eric was able to impose a new order on even the little things spoke volumes about the way he had been able to impose a new order on Jack's life, as well. No matter how Jack might have learned to dominate the physical action of his life, Sumners had the abstract control on life that money brings.

Jack suddenly didn't have much appetite for the lunch. All he hoped was it wouldn't be obvious.

Not surprisingly, Eric had been thinking similar thoughts, and had decided that forthrightness was the best policy. Get things out in the open. Upon reaching Micky's tavern, he said, looking at Jack, "I hope nobody minds eating with the money bag."

So closely mirroring Jack's apprehensions, the words shattered his thoughts as though a stone had dropped through them. Jack was speechless. Scott was therefore, and as usual, the first to say something to it, grinning as he went through the door ahead of everyone else.

"Not when it's open."

Looks, amused or otherwise, were exchanged.

Eric could see he'd made a blunder. Even among blunt people there were times when the obvious had no place in the conversation. In fact, it rarely did, and to have joked about it only showed he was nervous, or worse, unsociable.

They took a table by the window, and Eric found himself sitting across from Scott. He looked around at the bar for a moment, and then looked back at the workman. It reminded him of the first day they had met, but he noted the difference between then and the present.

Before, there had been casual suspicion and frank dislike. Now there was a casual, if slightly humored appraisal and expectancy, or perhaps curiosity for its own sake.

Evidently, Scott was waiting to see how many other ways Eric could manage to make a fool of himself.

But if there was something cold-blooded about that, the workman also seemed quite bland about it, with a pure indifference barely over the line from actually wishing to see it happen.

From the look on the faces of the other workmen he could see that Scott's was perhaps the most tolerant disposition towards him.

He had his work cut out for him.

But Eric was also surprised to realize how badly he wanted to win these men over. Generally, he had no burning need to be liked by men he worked with, let alone those who worked for him. Scott, especially, he wanted to focus on. Why him in particular, it wasn't clear. Jack, who anyone including Eric would have thought the logical choice of being the first needed to be won over, lacked something. The thing Eric wanted to conquer. A cynicism perhaps, or maybe an obvious indifference, in Scott.

Eric had a sudden, uncontrolled urge to take the earlier blunder and probe at it, unable to simply leave it alone.

"Never mind the crack about the money bag," he said to Scott. "You know, I don't mean to always bring things down to money."

Scott gave a look around at no one in particular. It was obvious he was being picked out as a lightning rod, of sorts. The shop floor spokesman. Scott wasn't particularly flattered.

He shrugged.

"Why shouldn't you?"

It was an honest enough thing to say, and something Eric couldn't have agreed with more, but strangely enough his first reaction was to bridle.

"Of course," he said smiling, but not in the friendliest way, and he picked up a menu and began examining it.

Scott smiled back.

The guy was basically all right, he thought. He was rich and a little strange, and his wife was beautiful and a little strange, and there was a strangeness in the combination of the two of them he couldn't quite figure out.

But regardless of all that, there was nothing to be gained, for himself or anyone else, by being antagonistic towards him. He obviously needed to talk about the money, so why not put things on the table? Diplomatically, of course.

"Don't get me wrong," he said good naturedly to Eric. "I've got nothing against money. But there's no way for me to look at a dollar bill the way you do."

Eric grunted, not in any negative way, but continued to look at his menu ... intent on dropping a subject he'd been fool enough to introduce.

Micky came over and set a pitcher of beer on the table and Jack poured out the glasses.

Eric held his up.

"Here's to it." He looked straight at Scott.

Somewhat awkwardly, the others followed suit, raising their glasses. Scott nodded, and then took a long drink.

Jack wasn't feeling very comfortable with what was passing between Eric and Scott. Mainly, he felt that he, in his position as owner of the boatworks, should have been the one to have discussed the subject of money, or whatever, with Eric.

He didn't mind the idea of the others talking with Eric, but if they were going to get into philosophy, or personal things, it should have been left to him. What galled him worse was the realization he couldn't have managed to be as blasé about it as Scott.

There was also something about how Scott carried himself that made Jack uneasy. Without saying much at all, he'd managed to say a hell of a lot and was now in the process of creating a personal relationship with Eric, while Jack only had a professional one.

What was worse, Scott now seemed deeper than Jack was. What the hell were you going to do? Easy, superficial people with easy, superficial conversation always got their toes in the door faster than people who had to take a longer run at explaining things.

Jack glanced over at his working partner and felt a small glow of angered frustration. Scott was too much of a hedonist, boozed up and horny, to see the complexity of things. And yet managed to get away with it, at all times.

But as screwed up as things seemed, he could see there was nothing he could do about the situation. Certainly not make his feelings known. It was bad enough without letting it be known he felt threatened by it. Or have it mistaken for jealousy or something.

If Scott didn't give a damn about the social complexities of Eric's money, and Eric admired that somehow, then Jack could easily pretend to the same attitude.

He made himself relax.

It wasn't easy, and especially not with Eric's next question and to whom it was put as he folded up his menu.

"So," he said to Scott. "What's the next step?"

Scott, himself, was surprised. Easily guessing how Jack was feeling, and regardless of how little he sympathized, he nevertheless also considered that that was a question for the boss to answer. He responded quickly, glancing at Jack as though seeking telepathic counsel:

"Well," he said, "it'll take a couple of days for the lead to cool. So in that time we'll try to get the keel timbers tapered down to size." He looked over, significantly, at Jack. "Right, Jack?"

The idea was to get Eric to turn to Jack.

But Eric didn't take the bait, and just nodded back at Scott. "You literally think one piece at a time, don't you?"

Scott looked over at Jack, but Jack didn't react and respond to the prompt, either. So he just gave up, and looked back at Sumners and shrugged. Again.

"Once you get going, you have to. We can't afford to make mistakes, considering how big these timbers are and how long it takes to get them here."

Eric liked the way Scott put it. It was the opposite of how Deborah thought about the process of building the boat.

When it was only Deborah talking about it, he could feel a little worried things were getting out of hand. She spoke as though the boat already existed.

Always one step beyond. Reality catching up when it could, like some sort of backwards looking wish-fulfillment. Which was all right for her. She was protected enough to afford the luxury of that attitude.

But for the boat, or for anything else in the real world ... Eric's world ... there could not be a more dangerous attitude to have. Eric almost sighed.

God knew, even after eight years of marriage he still couldn't figure out what it was about her that had him so enthralled. Like a beast staring at a whirling kaleidoscope. Either she had something no other woman he'd ever known possessed, or it was the opposite, that she was so absolutely lacking something that the resulting affect, the perfect void of that quality, made her seem utterly pure. Maybe it was her imperative defect.

On the genuinely beautiful woman, or in the beautiful soul of a woman, it was perhaps an unswerving necessity to have an irregularity, an imperfect feature, a microscopic disaster, to render the rest perfect. The asymmetrical mark of the beast which denied impossibly statue-like and characterless completeness.

Untainted, unmarred, a perfect creature would be doomed in an imperfect world.

Well, they weren't going to discuss his wife at the table, but Eric wanted to keep things relevant. So while Micky showed up with lunch platters of deep-fried oysters, jo-jo's and barbecued ham sandwiches, he launched himself into a discussion of people the workmen would have little contact with but who were also important to the project. He even brought himself to joke about Newell Briggs. An accountant, he said, who could make Simon Legree seem a philanthropist.

"He keeps his suits that tight," he said, "to keep himself from breathing too fast. Fast breathing, you know, spends too much money."

"Just the man you need," Scott said, with a plainly hooded irony.

Eric laughed out loud.

"I think he loves money in a way neither you nor I would understand."

"Neither rich nor poor", Scott said, with genuine thoughtfulness, "nor anything in between. What would that make him? Free?"

"I once almost thought that too."

Jack knew he had to insert himself into things at some point, or else spend the rest of lunch munching away on fried oysters in silence.

"So what does he think of you spending all his money."

Eric looked over at Jack. "What would you guess?"

"I think he's an ironic guy," was all he could say.

Luckily for Jack, Eric didn't pursue it or he would have discovered it was Jack's standard description for anyone he didn't understand.

Eric, now nodding absently, dipped one of the last of the batter-fried oysters into a tub of tartar sauce. He had never had oysters this way before although it was a common enough fare in the Puget Sound, if not all over the country. He rather liked it. Something rough-hewn and down-to-earth about eating oysters like French fries.

"As far as that goes," he said, "Briggs thinks you're one of the luckiest bastards in town."

"Because you wanted a boat built?"

"No." Eric bit the oyster cleanly in half. "In relation to the unluckiest people in town."

Jack frowned, and then realized who Eric was talking about.

In spite of his own ability to forget the Moore's, he felt shocked by Eric's glacial ability to not only dismiss them entirely, but joke about them openly. And of how it was obvious he could do that with practically anyone. Jack pursed his lips and nodded.

"You mean my neighbors."

"Yeah." Eric dipped what was left of the oyster in a tub of ketchup.

Jack simply couldn't help what came next. Whether it was true or not, and it definitely wasn't true, it just slipped out. And he regretted the words even as he said them.

"That does bother me."

Eric finished off his oysters in an easy enough fashion.

Jack could see he'd said something stupid, but could no way to back out of his statement without making up a few, very careful lies.

"Well, sort of," Jack went on, thinking of a fairly usable one. "I might as well admit, if this thing gets successful, Moore might have to leave to find greener pastures."

It was actually a giant lie. There could never be enough competition between the Moore's and the Colby's to make a difference. Jack was banking on the idea that Sumners would not be knowledgeable enough of the details.

"So ...?" was all Sumners said, seeing that Jack was dissembling for some reason. Also, he was knowledgeable enough to spot the untruth, but there was no way he would ever say so. In any case, he wasn't interested in the Moores in the slightest.

But he was now extremely interested in how Jack was going to explain his way out of what his college chums at Harvard would have called an extremely "wet" remark, even if unintended. Exactly the maudlin sort of sentiment one might expect from the lower classes. It had been a disappointing remark, to say the least.

"So," Jack went on, unaware of all that, "it would be a goddamn shame. Because nothing I could think of could make my wooden boats look better than Clyde's plastic boats sitting over there next door like ...," Jack struggled for an image, "... like a bunch of styrofoam cups littering up a parking lot."

It wasn't bad, and Eric smiled at him for the first time during the entire lunch. Jack felt good, and everything was all right with the world. Everybody could be pleased with themselves again.

And they almost were, except for Scott, who had picked up on the one little disaster in Jack's statement—let alone what a goddamn lie it was. Something much worse than pretending to worry about the Moores.

There was Jack, taking a position which, a few weeks before, had to be forced down his throat. It was that little slip about his wooden boats. His wooden boats. Where it had been Scott's idea to build them in the first place. First the goddamn rowing pod, and now this goddamn yacht.

If Scott had felt earlier the necessity to smooth a diplomatic course through dangerous waters with Jack, it was now gone.

Jack noticed the glittering eyes staring at him from across the table and realized that all was not well with the world. But he had no way to stave off what he knew was coming. If he'd gotten one over on Eric, he suddenly knew he'd dug himself in very deep with Scott.

"Yeah," Scott said blandly, staring straight at Jack as he spoke to Eric. "Although our production already has him on the run as it is, you know. And it probably wouldn't matter, in the end, how many projects we bring on board."

A noticeable strain in Scott's voice caused Eric to glance up at Scott, and then look over at Jack with a certain curiosity. But what he saw, and what he thought, he hid well. Although he had to admit: he was enjoying it. He was now a foil, rather than a fool.

Jack had a bad moment. But suddenly he rebounded into a sense of hot indignation.

He didn't care anymore. Not about any of this goddamn situation.

What the fuck, he thought angrily, was all this shit? What did he fucking care if Eric and Scott got on together? So much the better.

He was still the goddamn boss and he was still going to make the most profit.

When it came right down to it, Eric knew that as well as he did. So it didn't matter, and neither did Scott's pitiful attempts to make sure he got recognition.

Well, so be it, Jack thought. He'd give Scott some recognition someday. He'd recognize him for sure. And maybe a little more than he'd wished for. But for now, he thought, the first thing was to just get finished with what had become, for him, the Last Supper.

He'd be damned if he would ever do this again. At least, not if he could help it.

# Chapter 30

BEFORE THEY could begin shaping the keel, lumber sorting needed to be done, looking for grain patterns or defects. Of the latter, there were few.

All the frames and backbone members—the keel, stem and deadwood—were to be made from only the best quality New England white oak. Catherine had specified to lumber dealers the timber had to have been cut in winter. This was not so much because Jack or Scott believed in the old superstition that oak was more durable if cut when its sap was down, but because they could rely on there being less chance of fungus or insect attack on the fresh-cut lumber during the cold New England winter.

Catherine proved herself up to the task, quickly learning a general theory on cut wood, and then searching New England by internet and telephone for the right lumber at the right price. Those two factors, she was to learn during several days of searching and patient calling, were often miles apart. She finally found a lumberyard in lower Maine that had big lengths of white oak, air-dried down to fourteen percent moisture content. For the framing lumber she found the same mill had plenty of riff-sawn stock, and ordered a complete shipment with a surplus. She secured guarantees against defects, arranged the cross-country shipping, and confirmed by letter and scanned email orders.

Jack was pleased. She was obviously a quick study. She read a number of technical manuals on wood and could speak easily about the subject within a few days, her understanding completed in conversation with Jack and Scott.

That was more than Ellen had ever bothered with. She'd always left the technical side to Jack. Of course, Ellen had never had to deal with an actual boatbuilding project. Her experience went little farther than small or medium-sized orders, never having to bargain for the best. Fishermen weren't so picky. Even so, she had never felt it necessary to be able to recall technical information off the top of her head.

Jack joked with Catherine about how deeply she had plunged

into the work. She reminded him, he told her, of the old men who used to hang around the yard where he worked as an apprentice, and of how they commented on everything.

The boatbuilders would say those old guys knew everything about how to build a boat, except how to build a boat. Catherine had laughed. But secretly she was beginning to think she might just manage that too. She felt very happy with her new job.

Of course, that job was no ordinary one, and she was sensitive to the undercurrents of her being there, which could never entirely go away. One morning, as she sat waiting for a lumberyard back east to return a call, she finally allowed herself thoughts of how things were.

There were plenty of possibilities.

Perhaps things were not really hidden from Ellen. She might indeed know what Jack was capable of when he was on the road.

To Catherine, it now seemed a contradiction how he had shown no guilt or uneasiness that night with her. There had been no hint of a leer, revealing a sentiment of wrongdoing, nor clumsiness, exposing the tiny indecisions of the heart. It was strange, considering how careful he was being, now.

That night in Seattle, he had been tender in a way expressive of gratitude for what she had offered. It was just so unbelievable to think Ellen wasn't aware, on some level, that Catherine and her husband had shared so much tenderness.

Occasionally, she would imagine herself and him together again. Why not? Besides, there wasn't much she could do to stop it anyway. Sometimes she permitted a daydream at work, but mostly she saved thoughts of him for later, at home, where recalled images relieved the sharp pains of the physical solitude.

There, not so much a yearning as it was during the day. More like an exorcism at the approach of the night and those much darker dreams.

But that was the extent of things. Even if a deeper chord was being struck somewhere, nothing in the general atmosphere around the boatyard could give it explicitly away. Catherine was sure of it.

Feeling safe though, she told herself, was not enough. Don't let yourself get too relaxed about it. Perhaps there was no suspicion. Or better, there was a self-willed blindness. Or, at the worst, there were twitchings of suspicion which were currently being ruled out as the usual, irrational little jealousies.

The truth of the matter was that if Ellen ever became fully aware of all the tiny signs and signals that were inevitably in the air between Catherine and Jack, after what they had so fully shared, she would see it all at once.

Instant Armageddon.

Catherine got up from the desk and went to refill her coffee cup. Standing there at the kitchen window, she looked pensively out over the parking lot. Whatever else might happen, that last must not.

No disasters, she thought, of the self-made sort here.

She had gone through a lot of things which she hadn't been able to control. But if there was one thing she had learned, it was to avoid bringing it upon herself by her own hand.

Catherine nodded to herself. She wasn't going to worry. But she would keep control, remain vigilant.

What had happened, had, of course, happened. But she was going to let it flow out of her, let her life empty itself of all that, and let the future have its own.

She was absolutely lucid on this whole thing.

But even so, when she thought of Jack and Ellen, or more precisely, Jack, a smile of pleasure formed on her lips. After all, she had a right to her memories. And she felt no guilt, either, about the fact that regardless of what she'd told Jack, she had no intention to look for work elsewhere.

She knew when she tripped across a good thing, and if life had taught her anything at all, it was that when a good thing comes along the worst mistake was to think you had a choice between it and something better down the line.

Catherine had spent too much time farther on down the line, and she knew she was there at Colby's for good.

# Chapter 31

Puget Sound floats more pleasure boats for its surrounding population than any other place on the face of the earth. Each weekend fleets of half-drunk sailboats, sport-fishing runabouts and luxury cruisers set out to jostle and skip amongst themselves and the Sound islands, and mingle out in the sea lanes with plodding tugs, barges, fishing trawlers and purse seiners, the dead-pan naval boats, coast guard cutters and nuclear attack submarines, and the ocean freighters and tankers, obese and aloof, gingerly edging their ways down from the Strait of Juan de Fuca to the ports at Seattle or Tacoma.

But in spite of that vast flotilla and the regional mania which could produce it, neither Jack nor Scott were all that big on being out on the water.

Jack contented himself with doing a little salmon or cod fishing ... once in a while clamping an outboard on an old twelve foot pram and going off by himself for a few hours. Sailing, never.

Scott, if anything, spent more time on the water. But that wasn't much to speak of either. If someone called needing a crew member during one of the season's regattas, and if he had absolutely nothing else to do and the crew was well fed, he might agree to do it.

Maybe once or twice during the summer he would rent a little Flying Dutchman and scoot it back and forth out on the bay, and maybe out around Lummi Island if the day was nice enough. Which it usually wasn't. He refused cold or rainy weather and let those who said they liked it have it all. To stay warm and dry in the Northwest is practically a synonym for staying home.

But one weekend he took his new girlfriend for a sail. She had never been sailing in her life, was mortified at the idea there was no motor and was uneasy about being out on waters that Jacques Cousteau reruns had told her were alive with sharks, killer whales and giant octopi, all prowling around with evil intent down below in the deep. Even mewling seagulls looked vicious to Sydney Pryce.

Terrified, she had felt a tremendous pressure to accept. She had come to understand that nobody could live out there very long without eventually going out in boats. She was sure that none of her friends up at the college would have given it a second thought. She had listened to them discussing nonchalantly an afternoon's sail in the same way as any other college sport like racquetball, volleyball, tennis, drinking, dancing, car rides, and dormitory boys.

Sydney decided then it was inevitable, and carefully hid her apprehensions. At least at first. She had, after all, gone clam digging. Which was also an idea she had been initially bothered by.

One thing about clams, though. You didn't have to swim around to catch them. They just sat in the sand and you dug them up like rocks, being that they couldn't swim at all. If you put them in water they also sank like rocks. Which was something Sydney had in common with them.

Why she had never learned to swim was easy enough to explain. Water in her ears deafened her, in her eyes blinded her, and the trick of keeping water out of her nose totally defeated her.

To be in the water meant drowning.

But she had been unable to ever confess it to anyone. At the beach, with people splashing around, she avoided going in even if it meant risking that a few of her friends would think she was just trying to protect her fluffy head of curls.

Nevertheless, she couldn't avoid the boating excursion with Scott, and was secretly glad he forced her to put on a big, ugly lifejacket. She wore it even as he puttered back and forth on the dock.

Bellingham Bay was fresh that morning with a skin-tightening breeze moving up from the southwest. Despite that, it was warmer than usual for the time of year.

Scott had already loaded some cooking utensils, and some briquettes in the case no driftwood was handy. Sydney brought the lunch: a cut-up chicken, potatoes and carrots, a half-gallon of something called "California" Chablis, potato chips and onion dip, tomatoes, avocados, a head of lettuce, a bottle of salad dressing, a lemon cake she'd made herself, and a big thermos of coffee. Scott ran up to Micky's and bought a half-case of beer and bought as well a loaf of the sour dough bread Micky used for his sandwiches.

With the breeze coming straight across the dock to push them off, they were able to let go lines and the boat was able to sail out smooth and quick directly away from the landing at the boathouse. As the shore receded Sydney felt only misgivings. But with Scott's calm handling of the sails and rudder, she discovered her fears were diminishing beneath her enjoyment of the motion of the boat out upon the water.

Looking continually back towards Bellingham, she watched how the town went flat beneath Sehome Hill, the college clinging up there among its trees.

Funny how that teeming campus life now seemed so insignificant, if not inexistent. She could see her dorm room window and thought of how her friends, if they had known, could have seen her and Scott setting out.

Straight back of town from the bay was the sharp rise hiding Lake Whatcom with its cold glacial depths, and then hills farther beyond, and poking up at first like the top of an ice cream cone, and then rising higher and higher until they rode serenely over the ranks of foothills, were the gleaming, snow-filled flanks and pearly glaciers of Mt. Baker. Sydney had rarely seen so clearly the mountain, usually shrouded in mists or low cloud cover. Looking to the north, she could also see Mt. Garibaldi in B.C., jutting up like a huge, cracked molar.

Overhead were high flying streamers of clouds like jet trails, and a few big towers of clouds escaping over the mountains far to the east. As the day progressed the last few filigrees directly above dissipated in the warming sunshine. A beautiful day, and Sydney was suddenly so happy.

She looked at Scott then, at his wind-burned face. The fair, lightly freckled skin was rough and reddened, and his eyebrows were bleached all but white. With his light brown hair, curly and tousled in the breeze he could have seemed a boy except for the lines and well-etched crows-feet around his pale blue eyes. He looked back at her from time to time, but didn't talk much, only to point out this thing or that on the water or back on the land. He didn't fit at all any of the categories of guys she had been used to up at the college.

That was a problem for Sydney. Because of all the things those guys could be, they could not be out making their livings from one day to another. No matter how serious they might be about studying, which was a form of work, they certainly weren't yet in the world the quiet way Scott was.

Compared with what she had known, he was a man.

It felt funny to be with a man and she felt it was necessary for her to be responsible about it in some way. Quite suddenly, she felt fear return. But of a different sort: replacing the fear of being sucked down to her death in the waters of the bay, was that of being alone with a serious man for whom silence was an eloquent partner to conversation.

The fear of silence.

She was used to and loved noise. It was like a bubble of safety having a crowd of friends laughing, talking, clowning around. So easy to get excited and join in, pitching into it with a laugh and without a care what you or anyone else said as long as the music of it went round and around. But if this nerve-wracking, many-voiced silence she shared with Scott was difficult, she wanted to be a full partner in the quiet exchange of time spent together. It seemed infinitely better, for some reason, although she could see it meant you had to both concentrate and completely let go.

Later, it was even more difficult as they sat amongst storm thrown logs and driftwood at the summer, high tide line, recovering from lunch, gazing lazily across the waters of the Sound.

The slow movements of boats and seagulls in the far distance from that uninhabited island beach gave the impression that theirs was another world. Bellingham was now a smudged line of barely distinguishable buildings, the plume of steam from the paper mill rising imperceptibly into the light air. Only the whisper of small waves rinsing across the pebbles at water's edge accompanied the conversation.

Sydney suddenly understood what it meant, when people talked about how life wasn't just a situation, but a series of possibilities. And the question then wasn't so much how you dealt with them, but how you choose from among them.

But then a comforting thought struck her. Being there with Scott … within that world of few and quiet words where a wink or a nod of the head made more for conversation than anything else … had been a choice. And in the same way, Scott too had chosen to be there. A shared choice.

Which meant that within that silence which she wasn't used to, was something that made silence something that didn't matter.

She suddenly realized it was something only real couples ever shared.

## Chapter 32

IT WASN'T all silence, of course. Occasionally, even in the first few hours, Sydney and Scott found themselves falling into fairly lengthy discussions about something. In the very beginning, sailing away from Fairhaven, there hadn't been much for Scott to do but handle the boat, or for her but to watch him or the scenery. And talk had sputtered along.

At first, when some subject had worn itself out, Sydney would continue on for a while, just to keep the talk going. But whenever Scott had finished, he would just stop. Later in the day, she realized she could do the same thing, and not even feel uncomfortable about it. Just waiting, companionably, for something else.

Life seemed to take on a new dimension, more profound in its consequences, with details standing out where, before, everything had carried an equal weight. When she first realized that, at the very beginning of their trip out across the water, she felt stifled to the point she could barely think what to say.

Sydney, at the age of twenty-one—of an age and maturity she felt she had fought hard to attain—suddenly had felt as though she was five years old and having to learn it all over again. With the only difference being that it was easier when she was five.

Scott hadn't shown he was aware of her nervous soul states. Which was just as well and probably saved the day. The truth was, he hadn't entirely forgotten what it was like to be twenty-one. He was just disinclined to care. So the more distracted she became by her own commentary, the less he listened. Sometimes, not listening is a form of being polite. The fact that she was there was enough, and he let his thoughts drift away across the bay. Of course, that meant that when something did occur to him to say, there was a risk he would be interrupting her.

As he suddenly did. "It's funny …," he said.

Sydney stopped speaking, mid-stream, completely losing track of what she was talking about. A small twinge of irritation came over her, realizing he hadn't been paying attention to her. But on the other hand it hadn't been much of a thing to talk about anyway: a bit of griping about library costs up at the school. Or school costs in general. Or lack of money in general.

"What is?" she said.

"This whole thing with Sumners."

"What's funny about building a boat?"

"It's not the building of it. It's who we're building it for."

"Lots of rich people have boats," she laughed, happy to suddenly have him in another conversation again.

"Yes, and lots of not so rich people have boats."

Scott stretched his arms up, and then brought them down, putting one around Sydney's back and pulling her towards him as they sat against a big drift log. She hugged him back, suddenly cozy there with his relaxed unconcern. He sighed.

"It's just all funny. I didn't see it before because I wasn't looking at the Sumners like they were just people."

"It's a pretty different world."

Scott liked the pragmatic and unjealous tone in her voice.

"Not like you think", he said. "I've talked to Sumners. He's like anyone else except that he's got one hell of a pile of money, and that's how he identifies himself."

"Why shouldn't he? That doesn't make him strange."

Now Scott laughed. "No. It's not strange at all to have so much more than anyone else. What's strange is how they are to their boat. I know how rich and poor people usually are and it's close to being the same thing, normally."

"Rich people and poor people are the same? You've got to be kidding."

'No, I mean about their boats. I mean, what the boats mean to them. Tell me: what does a boat mean to you?"

"Me?" Sydney said quietly. She threw in a joke. "You mean as a poor people …?"

She suddenly felt on the spot.

But not because she had nothing to say. But because she had to find something, anything, which wouldn't give away the fact that she was horrified by them. Normally, all she carried were horrendous images—ships struck by icebergs, wave-tossed lifeboats, sharks attacking small boats. Gigantic, storm whipped waves swallowing all, to infinity.

She clicked her tongue in frustration, but managed to bring herself down from all that to something positive: whatever it was she had enjoyed about the trip across the bay with Scott.

"Well," she said, "I guess the main thing is that they're fun."

"Fun?" Scott was clearly disappointed.

Sydney quickly caught his attitude. There was a long moment of silence. Then she decided not to let him get away with it.

"What else did you want me to say?"

Scott knew what he'd done. But instead of apologizing directly to the implied insult, tried to talk his way around it. Philosophically. He hunched his shoulders amiably, as though they were talking about nothing in particular.

"There are so many things people do with boats, the same word can't apply. It isn't the same. Not even if you just stick with recreational uses. You take a guy fishing out in his boat, or people who sail in races, or people who are living on their boats, or others who go sailing off to Tahiti."

"Or who build them," Sydney said, seeing what he was doing, and even more angry. "So what? Those all sound like fun. Or enjoyment, if you want to use another, less simple, word."

"… or those who build them," Scott nodded. Still sidestepping, and at the same time wondering why he was doing it. "But that's getting into something else. Because I build things anyway. If it wasn't boats, it would be something else with wood. The boat isn't the main thing."

"So … building with wood is fun for you. Like boats are fun for other people."

Well, yes, Scott thought, realizing he was just making things worse.

And … why? Because she was a college girl, and that was the way she and her friends talked?

He felt ashamed of himself. Obviously, he had tried to stifle her simpler reactions, force her to come up with a more complex view of the Sumners. What now seemed more important, was to figure out what he expected out of his girlfriend.

Which included not lording his age and experience over Sydney. The fact was, although he hadn't known her long, he had an instinct she was a more decent person than most of the people he'd come across.

Being good and decent was a lucky attribute, like being born beautiful or talented were lucky attributes, and which didn't need anybody's applause. But it was also something not to be taken for granted and then to expect more. Always expecting more from people is worse than a bad habit, he thought. It was selfish.

But if Scott was getting himself around to making himself a more tolerant, attentive boyfriend—let alone a man—he was wrong about that as well. Sydney, in fact, had the capacity for being just as insightful and complicated as he was.

"You like getting drunk don't you?"

"You mean like last night?" he gave her a look. She didn't know him enough to know that he had lately also been turning himself around on that as well ... turning that form of escape into a minor occupation. But maybe what seemed minor to him, to her might seem pretty substantial.

"You seem to have quite a capacity."

He knew it was true, in any case. He had got drunk, and often. And did have a capacity. But he had always felt he hadn't gone into his drinking like a pure drunk: he had indeed also thought about it, and his motivations, often. Too often. Removing from it the drunk's desire for it to be just a pastime intended to blot himself and everything else out.

It didn't seem, therefore, like it was a black hole he was being sucked into. So he could laugh at himself.

"I'm the primal man. I also like ...." He was almost to say the really crass joke, but stopped himself. Suddenly, his instinct for being obscene and cynical about things when they came back and landed on him, no longer seemed quite right. The sort of self-abnegation ... joking himself down into the ground ... was absurd. Because he knew he was, in the end, better than all that.

She was doing this to him.

He'd started the joke, though, and Sydney knew what he'd been about to say. She squinted her eyes. "That doesn't make you special."

"Think not? Some people might consider that an extreme example of lack of imagination and degeneracy."

Sydney evidently didn't find the subject worth exploring, or joking about—if that strange remark of Scott was joking—but she had a sudden inspiration.

"Do you think Eric Sumners is being extreme? The way you talk about them getting off on their boat and all. It's like they're getting drunk on it, treating it like the big art thing. "

Scott nodded, and then damned himself for being so patronizing. There, he'd been trying to put his finger on it, and she had come up with the answer.

Just like that.

"That's it ... that's all there is to it." He smiled.

"Anyway," Sydney went on, "it's nice the way he's giving it to his wife."

"This is going to sound awful, but giving something like this to her, and calling it a gift, is shocking. I mean, it's embarrassing."

"What does that mean?" For Sydney, there were limits. Open cynicism was one of them. She gave people the benefit of the doubt, and expected them to do so with her. When she gave something, it was out of love, or a show of love. She felt that was an important thing to do. And that was all there was to it. "That's really," she went on, "and I mean it .. really terrible. If I understand you. Which I might not. Because I really don't know what you're talking about."

"Yeah, I suppose so," he grinned. "And I guess you probably figure now I'll never give you anything, and it'll be impossible for you to give me anything."

"You're awful."

"Don't worry. If you ever give me something, believe me, I'll love it."

Sydney didn't know why she suddenly felt embarrassed, and somewhat angry with him again. "Don't be so superior about him."

"Why not? Look, it's true. Although, maybe it's just jealousy."

"Probably," Sydney said. "But that still doesn't explain what you meant."

"All right, " he said, "this is what I meant: If I give you something, or you give me something, nobody else would know about it except you and me. The best gifts are private. But think about Sumners, or just rich people, when they give their money away in gifts. First thing, they end up getting a plaque put on a wall saying what swell people they are. Have you ever noticed they still can't let go of it but make sure it's spent exactly on the right things? Try to get some of that money sometime for something you think really needs to be done, and you'll see. Who says you can't buy love? The rich do it all the time, and get adored, admired and respected for it." He spread his hands. "Well, anyway, here we are working on this public monument to his love for his wife, and we're supposed to admire and respect him for it. And feel delighted for her."

Although she felt sure he was making fun of her somewhere, she played along. "And he's drunk with it."

"Extremely. What's worse is that besides getting drunk on all the big-time gift-giving and love of art or whatever else is going on, the weird thing is how the most obvious thing is missing."

Scott paused, and waited for Sydney to ask him what that thing was. He was liking the role of wise, older guy to her young, naïve soul. What guy could resist? But there was something else as well. Despite her age, her enthusiasms, and how she'd dropped into his bed like a shot duck, he was aware there was something solid about her. The fact that she was solid somewhere, reassured him about himself. Because, in truth, it was like finding approval.

And there, as though she was perfectly in tune with him, which she might actually have been, she said, "which thing is that?"

"The fact that, of all the things they've said about it, not once has either one of them mentioned what they plan to do with it when it's done."

It caught Sydney by surprise. Because despite Scott's belittling her for the word fun, it was, exactly, the same thing he expected from the Sumners. She smiled. She might be younger than him, and not the most artistic or creative, the most cultivated and intelligent person he might know ... but at least he, and they, both knew she would have found a way to have fun with it. He was just finding a way to get back around to agreeing with her. Their first lover's spat resolved.

"Huh," she said finally. "That doesn't sound like rich people to me. Just sort of weird."

"Yeah," Scott sighed out. "Maybe though it's the same thing."

It wasn't bad, he thought, talking to Sydney. An independent soul, who could sometimes be quick as lightning. Of course, it wasn't a strongly independent soul tempered with experience, which was a disappointment in the sense of fantasy. He was well aware of that long-standing desire of someday being loved and appreciated by an attractive, strongly independent woman. What man wouldn't?

It was with no small bitterness that he had come to realize such women were rare, to meet them rarer, and the fact that they were often with men who could not fully appreciate what they had, was the case more often than not. Jack with Ellen, for instance.

Yet here, reality had come fluttering on its feeble, fledgling wings, young and enthusiastic. Not exactly the soaring he'd often imagined it could be like with someone like Ellen.

But maybe, soaring wasn't really the better place to be.

As for Sydney, she now just gazed out across Bellingham Bay. Wondering how she could have ever been frightened of such a day.

# Chapter 33

JACK AND Ellen, in a way they rarely did, were celebrating.

They'd driven up to Vancouver and spent the day, first by wandering around the downtown with its crisp office towers. Ellen did a little shopping and studied the city women. Jack studied the city women. Then they drove out to the aquarium at Stanley Park.

They wandered around the outdoor tanks for a while, looking at the whales and porpoises and watched the sea otters playing around, and then went to look at the marine life tanks. The aquarium was dark and quiet, people huddling in front of each tank pointing out this or that small Georgia Straight creature they could find, some in brilliant display, others shyly reclusive. While neither Jack nor Ellen were particularly interested by marine biology, it was hard not to become fascinated by the carefully reconstituted marine environments in the tanks. Ellen especially was touched in a strangely comforting way.

At one time, it had scared her.

But unlike Scott's new little plaything Sydney—what else could you call her?—who had gone around confessing to everyone that her fears had been based on the simple, concrete fear of drowning, Ellen had been uneasy about the ocean for other reasons. Mostly about the invisibility of what was there. How the surface was the boats, and the wind and islands and shore birds. All so familiar. Yet below the surface, and then into the depths, was a hidden secret of movement. Secret and very deep.

The local waters were unquestionably in the realm of the darkest, wildest places, where you couldn't know if something bad was going to happen to you until it did. You might get a last second warning, but even if you knew something was out there, menacing your life, and it was very serious about doing so, you also could do nothing about it before it hit you.

Or maybe not, and with a mysterious flick or a ponderous sliding, it would move away into the murky dark. Worse, was the terror of not knowing what it had been, which was even worse than drowning, that already horrifying suffocation of the deep. Ellen hadn't let those sorts of things bother her on days at the beach. She was a strong, smooth swimmer and exalted in the feeling of moving quickly through the water. She would often swim far out from shore for the pleasure of swimming a long way back. What it was, that sudden terror she would have formerly felt at contemplating hermit crabs, sea anemones and sea perch, let alone the wolf eels and sharks, had been strictly limited to this idea of the unknown.

She had hated with a special vengeance the unseen threat. In her person, she was a graceful woman who could show tenderness easily enough. Beneath that existed a fierce hardness that few, and certainly not Jack, could have guessed the extent of.

She had always known that hidden away in her own silent and mysterious depths was something very old and untamed. And for no reason she could put her finger on, before each glass exhibit, before each creature, harmless or not, that distant chord was being struck. But the fear was no longer there. She had vanquished it. Because, simply, she now could see it all, right to the bottom of it. She knew it, and so now owned it.

If her hard-eyed, oddly triumphant gaze now became ever more intense as they moved with the eddies of the crowd there before the glass-enclosed sea life, Jack never noticed it. For him the sight of giant chinook and coho salmon swimming imperviously around in their nice, safe tank, was about all he could really get interested in.

There they were: big, fat, lazy salmon which could never realize what fortune they had. Jack would have loved the chance to throw a hook down in the tank sometime. Show those complacent bastards—each one a barbecue in itself—a thing or two. He would have even paid for the chance. Why the hell not? But despite Jack's general indifference, his only real problem with the aquarium was that they seemed to have toned down ... for political reasons probably ... the shark exhibit. Don't scare the kiddies.

That evening they had dinner in the B.C. Tower. Like Seattle's Space Needle, the restaurant on top revolved around a central bar. Vancouver's was the newer, and nicer, with an old fashioned feeling. Comfortable and cozy with brass, chintz curtains, lace, and blown glass lighting. Undoubtedly kitschy, but it was better than the revolving cafeteria to the south.

The food was more expensive than it would have been down at sea level, but it was also of a guaranteed quality and neither of them regretted the price. Ellen had a tender sirloin served with a white wine and Roquefort sauce. Jack avenged himself on his aquarium buddies by having a thick salmon steak with au gratin potatoes. They had a bottle of local wine.

Then another.

They got quite warm as they ate their dinners, looking at the sparkling city spreading out beneath them from the port and the Fraser River mouth, and then across the Lion's Gate Bridge to the northern part of the city, going away in a million lights into the dark foothills of the looming coast mountains. It was a romantic dinner and a romantic city below.

Earlier in their marriage, not having known any better, they might have somehow wasted such a magic occasion by assuming such moments were commonplace. But there are all manner of wisdoms which come with age and they didn't bother to drive all the way back to Bellingham that night. South of town they found a cheap motel where they allowed the expensive view, the expensive food, and the expensive wine have its way, and they expanded on the theme of their usual, minimalist, three-act lovemaking of pre, during, and post. The morning brought them just before noon, blinking, partly exhausted and not a little hungover, out to their car.

It was a nice morning as they drove back down to Bellingham, the sky a high, thin blue streaked with the wispy trails of some long-dead ocean storm. Both of them, each for their own reason, felt quietly happy, and quietly content. Jack had even managed to forget for the moment about how Ellen had so recently been burning him up in anger about the goddamn boat, and enjoyed her companionable silence as they swept down towards the border crossing at Blaine. Ellen, for her part, felt herself as though floating on her back, uncaring and in a way contemptuous of the unknown, in waters where the ebb and flow had a rhythm familiar and predictable. And controllable. Where sea creatures were just something that got, mostly, eaten.

Very simply, one little night of completely forgetting about everything but herself and Jack, was enough to restore their marriage to her with a fullness of security that day to day life tends to drain away in a drip here, a tiny rivulet there.

OK, she conceded, glancing over at Jack with a secret smile, it was a little conceited. But when she came to a point in her life that she *knew* there were no more sea monsters, a woman had the right.

# Chapter 34

As was now her custom, after Deborah instructed the maid about the morning's duties, she went down to see the progress on the boat. She enjoyed the process, but mostly enjoyed the fact that she alone was capable of appreciating it.

The workmen, so energetic and briskly confident, could of course get a tactile pleasure from their work. But it was she who was able to see the entirety of it.

Finally ... finally ... she was in *her* element.

Her training in art had gone on for years. It had been difficult at first, a thing to be hidden from her parents, an artistic temperament not necessarily being an asset in the pragmatic, Mormon view of life.

She had been unsure, when growing up, where to look for the answers to the mysteries which seemed to involve her and no one else. At home, even with the strictures of that wrathful faith bound tightly around her, she had always felt as though cast adrift.

At school the feeling became worse. She had felt deeply lonely, baffled by the emptiness of life and the all too eager readiness of her friends to accept that emptiness with full hearts. Why was such a price put on things she couldn't find value for?

Her quickly developing beauty didn't help things. The reaction on the part of parents and peers was something along the lines of astonishment. Girlfriends became obsequious or estranged. Boys became bumptious or morose.

The boys, especially, had been horrid. Their unrestrained instincts spilling forth as though uncontrollable. Worse, they seemed to blame her for their tight-jeaned discomforts.

If it was with pride that she could look back on those dark days, it was to recall how she had held strong to her purposes. How calmly she had continued her search for an ideal beyond society, beyond corporal existence.

College fulfilled her dreams. Truthfully, it made her.

At Brown she discovered intellectual freedom. While she had yet to discover the philosophy of art, she was on her own, free of parents, childhood friends, and Salt Lake City. Two events were to change her ways of thinking about school and, eventually, life. One was Dr. Marion Banks, a wonderful and lively professor of art.

Marion Banks was a poet, teaching the plastic arts and their history. As she gave her lectures she would seem, at least to Deborah, to lose the physical world. Her fine, light voice tinged nasally, even nostalgically, with the accent of the Midwest, would drift off into verbal reveries about the transcendences of art.

The second, which seemed a trifling thing by itself, came when she had learned by accident of the geniuses, slackers and lazy cynics inhabiting the back rows of the classrooms. As wonderful as Marion Banks was, perhaps more important were the heretics in the back of the class.

She had been late to class one day and had been forced to take a seat far in the rear. She had suddenly found herself in a different world. Of ideas and critical thought. She had never imagined sitting anywhere in a classroom except at the front where all her concentration could be given to her teacher. And she discovered the stratification. The front row scowled and took heavy notes, the middle rows dozed and doodled, and the back rows carved up the desks and the lectures with a furtively confident egoism.

Deborah listened with astonishment to what was being said on either side of her in that back row, and learned things sometimes more interesting than what was promised in the curriculum.

Between the two, the honest attempts at teaching by Dr. Banks, and the well-honed and jealously guarded skepticism in the back of the class, she came to understand the true responsibility of having an independent, superior mind.

Of course, she maintained her social distance, fending off the expected invitations from the motley, bumptious iconoclasts—mostly male—in the back. As interesting as they were, none of them showed any sign they had any concept of, let alone interest in, being serious about the concrete things Deborah thought were still important. The back row, interesting as it was, seemed to her as well the ultimate train wreck disaster of unrealistic ambition and wasted intellectual talent. They all seemed interested in being writers.

*

Perhaps with any other professor, the circumstances would have meant little. Dr. Banks was no fool, and twenty years in university had taught her to loathe most college students as so much flotsam thrown into the academic system through the wave action of their parents' money. She had little to say directly to any except the few she could trust were listening; most of whom, she had found in the same way Deborah had, lurked in the back of her classrooms surreptitiously passing jokes and critical innuendo amongst themselves.

Not all of them, of course. There were the hooligans there as well, and idiot savants. God knew where they came from. But that was her true audience and out of self-esteem she worked for their benefit. Occasionally, a rare spark of life sprang forth.

Sometimes it was a smile, sometimes a shadowed acknowledgment of gratitude, and sometimes it was as forthright as a defiant, shocking or hesitantly imaginative essay. Which, upon reading, would make Dr. Banks pound her small fist on her desk in her office, shaking with either anger or happiness.

It wasn't long before she noticed the tall, dreamy-eyed girl with the auburn head of hair, who, it might have seemed, would have been more interested running for Miss Something-or-Other.

Marion Banks soon transformed Deborah, in her mind, from student into personal project. On occasion, her lectures were delivered in a package tailored exactly to the mesmerized excitement the girl seemed to have.

Somewhere, there was something unethical about that. But she couldn't help it.

To have one student like that, absolutely hanging on each word, every explanation, was just too good to ignore.

*

Deborah, of course, didn't see any of this as having her obsession preyed upon by a lonely teacher, and transposed those lectures into what was to eventually become a personal manifesto.

It was the observer, the spectator or the reader, she was told and came fervently to believe, who truly received the message of art.

Artists created. Which was fine for all that was worth. But from their vantage point there was never the possibility of also receiving it: a pure message arriving a priori from another. Artists, thus, were blind, creating visions of glory for the sighted to appreciate.

It made so much sense to Deborah, framed by the incredulous wisecracks whispered near to her, that she accepted it in full.

Perhaps, if she had sat in front, listening to the lecture in unimpeded purity, Marion Banks message would have had less power. But given cynical approbation in the back of the class, the words rang with truth and vision.

To fulfill life was to place it in constant reference to art. To watch was greater than to be watched, to listen greater than to be heard. That was the soft-spoken credo of Dr. Banks.

It became a well-spring for a cosmos. Where, before, she had felt the constraints of having to deal with the idea that she herself was a creation of beauty for others to contemplate, she was now freed to another plane where the material world could be shed like an old skin. Art, that was the contemplation and appreciation of it from the objective-subjective viewpoint of the spectator, was that plane.

She became anchored to it, free then to swing upon the tides of the universe, safe from destruction. Art was a signpost in the soul, a direction for the will to take. It was the image, and the determination to recreate that image, of heaven.

In gaining her faith in art, she lost for all time her faith in the Mormon God.

This was in her second year in school.

In her third year she met Eric.

*

If Eric had ever guessed at how much of her personal philosophy she put into her interpretation of him and everything else, he might have balked at the idea of marriage. Not that he was one to doubt himself. But few men could say they enjoyed the prospect of being suspected to be perfect. Or being married to someone who carried that ruler permanently around with them.

And he never was to know. Or, at least, not for a long time. To Eric she seemed just a great beauty who happened to be a bit of an intellectual. It simply tickled his pride such a woman could love and respect him.

Following the marriage, each year brought new resolve and insights to Deborah's faith in truth and beauty, the two pillars of the temple of art. She applied her insights everywhere, observing the art within man and its mirror of the artificial beauty in nature—nature taking a sad second place to the only real realm of beauty: in the spirit of art's godhead.

Of course, it pained her that she could not share all this with

Eric. But she didn't mind. He was a good man. And even among the good, few were the elected.

It became her silent, sweet dream of a God more potent than any religion's God could be. Whatever it was in, that early uncertainty of her childhood was at last defeated. The calm she received glowed within, taking form in the womb of her spirit, in the now truly beautiful image of herself. She became a saint within her faith. Art was her habit, her sacrament the blind strivings of artists, their blessed self-deception and martyrdom the object of her great pity and devotion.

It was her deepest self, and the wellspring of that enigmatic smile she wore. A smile of knowledge which few could understand. Perhaps notice, of course, as Leonardo da Vinci seemed to have managed. But not fully understand, he being only an artist.

Thus, each morning now, as she went to the boat, it was to make a sacred blessing, to favor Jack and Scott with beneficence upon their toiling efforts. Jack and Scott, simple workmen at their labor, unwittingly thought the *Muse* was named after Deborah.

Even Eric thought that. Dear Eric.

Deborah could smile her little Mona Lisa smile at all of that.

Her secret joke.

# Chapter 35

"SHIT," he said to no one, thinking of something Deborah had said. Then tried to dismiss it.

In the early hours, the morning still and dark, Scott sat out in the boathouse with a cup of coffee waiting for daylight to come. Feeling restless and uneasy, Sydney still asleep, he'd made coffee and had brought a full thermos bottle down.

He surveyed the work in progress, and then looked down the boathouse. Re-accustomed to the darkness after the glare of his early morning kitchen, he could make out the shapes, down at the far end of the shop, of two trawlers hauled up the rails. One needed a new shaft and propeller and its steel rudder straightened, having touched ground somewhere out by Decatur Island. The other was receiving sheer planking along the port side to replace the splintered and smashed results of a rough docking. Both jobs were easy enough for Tom and Will, and easily supervised. Scott knew Jack wouldn't spend much time thinking about them. Except to perhaps realize that his regular business was as good, if even better, with two new customers brought his way by their own bad luck. Once again, someone's bad luck was good luck for Jack.

Scott took a sip of coffee, glanced at the inky smoothness of the waters of the bay beyond the fishing boats, and then turned to look at the ketch. Or, at least, what was becoming a ketch.

It occurred to him that watching a boat go up was approximately the opposite of watching a whale rot on a beach. Where the whale starts as a whale and is slowly reduced to a bleached skeleton, the boat starts as its spine, and slowly accumulates ribs and a hull.

They had managed to finish the *Muse*'s backbone. The massive lead keel had been hoisted from its mold and moved outside, making way for the laying down of the boat. At the aft end, set in the waterside direction of the boatshed, the spine of the boat angled gently up from the keel blocks through a series of timbers, shaped and fluted to receive other structures, the whole finishing in the wide transom plate. At the opposite end the curving stem, going up and outwards, described the elegant shape the bow would make.

Though it was dark, Scott could see the entire structure, amazed at the sheer size of her all the same. All the timbers they had put into her were big. It was doubtful that a classic, plank-on-rib wooden boat of that size had been built in the last five years. A real wooden boat.

Scott had nothing against plastic boats. Relatively easy to maintain, relatively cheap, they gave a relatively enjoyable sailing experience. But the aesthetic equation of the sea and wooden boats, was absolute.

Of course, that made him as much an anachronism as the boats were. You make a choice like that, he thought, and you're immediately divorced from your own world.

What a boat though, he thought, staring at the keel running a hundred-plus feet and ending fifteen feet in the air at either end. It was hard not to be awed.

Sumners, his wife, even Jack seemed awed. Scott fought the feeling.

He thought about Deborah again, sourly.

What he had told Deborah was the truth. Her mystic boat was not building itself based on its final *perfection*. She really irritated him for that, because that was exactly the worst thing anyone working on a project this big could start thinking. You have to reduce things to the one thing you can do at any given moment. Each piece fashioned with nothing else in mind but to make that piece perfect for where you were going to put it in.

Anyone could sit around daydreaming of the entire boat finished in all its complexity. But to get it there depended on a way of thinking that had nothing at all to do with immaculate perfection. Or whatever.

Lately, it had seemed a constant battle to keep Deborah's billowing transcendentalisms out of the atmosphere of the shop. Difficult, even for Scott, who had long been immunized against flighty idealism.

But he worried about Jack, who was vulnerable to easy discouragement and had not been completely happy with the project in the first place. The sole way for the work to go on, was for it to be done as work.

It was all well and good for Deborah Sumners to get big and airy about this thing. But nothing leads the working man more quickly towards chaos than to lose his grip upon the immediate details.

It was like having non-stop brain fever, Scott thought suddenly, the effort to fight off her intrusions. Once, she'd gotten so worked up with explaining one of her ideas, she'd distracted him to the point of having nearly cut off several of his fingers. A whirring band saw was no place to get distracted by metaphysical arguments.

In an impatient gesture, he threw cold remnants of coffee into the gravel of the parking lot, and then poured himself a fresh cup. Then winced in pain at the first sip, having taken in too much.

He was upset now, he realized.

And mostly about being upset.

If everyone were like her, there would never be a single goddamn boat built, mystic or otherwise. Or anything else, for that matter. You wouldn't have the courage to begin.

The way she looked at things all at once, without learning what each step of the work might entail, automatically meant it had to be done by someone else. But the way she talked about it, she was somehow taking credit for it. He couldn't figure how. But she was.

As if he and Jack had nothing to do with it.

Perhaps what was bothering him was … that. Every time she began going on and on about it, how it was this and that, and something else, when in fact she couldn't have managed the first thing about it, it all had a tendency to destroy what boatbuilding held for him.

Worse, he knew that, now, all that was part of the package.

Somewhere, because she had studied the bigger thing and believed he couldn't have—that people like him only barely learned how to pound nails and cut wood—she had come to the conclusion she knew more about what he was doing than he did himself.

That was the crux of it. Ugly and somehow childish. But she wouldn't give them credit for having any aesthetics of their own. How could they, being so stuck to the daily grind?

Only someone like her, who was above it all, omniscient, could appreciate the beauty of it. Not once realizing that—in fact—if they didn't have a sense of aesthetics, the boat they created could look as much like a garbage scow as a sailing yacht.

A fine little piece here, a well-shaped piece there, but without an inbuilt sense of balance and harmony you ended up with a Frankenstein's monster.

Scott grinned at the inanity of it. Of her conviction she was what was making the difference.

When the truth was, that he and Jack were putting a fair amount of themselves into it. And not just technique, but—what?—a love for their work? That's what it came down to for Scott. Either you had something very real and true to put in or you didn't, and the result was based on that.

Sure, it was nice when someone came along who knew something, saw what was good about it. It was always nice to be appreciated by people who knew something about the work. Knew what went into it. The planning, the general idea, of course. But also the intense necessity to make each detail harmonious. And have the skill to carry out that detail.

That was what made Deborah Sumners' presence all so damning. Because she had no idea what they were bringing to it. As though she was watching a movie or whipping through the pages of a book, unconnected with the mass of knowledge, experience, planning and thought that had created it.

Which was all right. Those things were made to be enjoyed. But it wasn't fun having someone like her around watching you create the goddamn thing, thinking all the time this was coming from somewhere else. A divine mystery.

Scott took another sip of coffee, and then thought of how someone else had been doing something like that lately. Catherine.

But where Deborah Sumners was on Pluto, Catherine at least was somewhere nearer to home. If Left Field counted. Or maybe not even that, but something else. Trying to start up conversations that only made sense if you were hitting on someone. Which he knew wasn't the case, since he knew Catherine didn't have much interest in him. Which he didn't mind. It made one thing down there simple to deal with. She was, without a doubt, an attractive woman. But there was something about her that said she was angling in other directions which, absolutely, excluded someone like himself. A man, despite himself, could be jealous despite himself about that sort of rejection—but he wasn't. Because regardless of Deborah's or Catherine's nonsense, he now at least had someone to talk to about all this. Or gripe or complain about to.

Who did sort of understand. And sort of in the right way. Someone who wasn't battling anybody's gods.

He filled up his coffee again, and let his thoughts wander on to thinking how one of worst temptations people had, was to judge or impose their points of view on others. And how the great thing about being with someone honest, was how that temptation basically had nowhere to go. Or if it did, not very far.

## Chapter 36

IF SOME people were battling the gods—or someone else's gods—those days, Catherine felt no need to either complicate or simplify things. With things going well, the desire in fact was something else: to just make it all fit together. To create meshings and networks and build up a mighty edifice of new, crawling, teeming life. Then plunge in.

She had the impression, at last, something very good was just around the corner. Everything she did was in expectation, making herself ready, uncaring and full of life. She wasn't going to push. She allowed the tangles to grow, not only with the Colbys and her work, but even with the boat. Deborah Sumners had started it but Catherine had come up with a few observations of her own.

It was a strange truth to boatbuilding that the boat, the shape of its mass that is, got built twice—that the real boat itself, with its ribs and planking, was only a filling in of a shape that has already been realized.

Of course, there was a first building that preceded all that. The building of the ideal shape as conceived by the marine architect, which could be considered the first construction. But when talking of the first physical manifestation of that shape, it was the molds and molding ribbands which gave that shape existence, even if the boat itself didn't exist. The first building.

Everybody had been excited as the workmen, piece by labored piece, erected the great molds in the shop. Slowly, as in the unfolding of a vision, the boat's shape began to take form.

Regardless of other chores Catherine would run out to the shop every so often to watch the process, reinforcing her idea of how the shape, not the boat itself, was being built. Shapes of things to come.

She would have loved, even, to have pointed all this out to her ex-beloved Steven. So vain about being an Aristotelian that he would have missed, she was sure, the wonderful chance this afforded to appreciate the form of what yet had no form.

Catherine got an occasional pang at the memory of Steven. Even in his egotism he had been able to talk about these things with her.

Of course, he would have disagreed with her, argued her down and attempted to supplant his own theories. But his cheating vanity would have been large enough to concede that she had made a great deal of progress. Ego is a direct function between self-consciousness and intelligence. And in his case, his ego would have allowed him to feel proud of the ... obvious ... result of his influence.

Irritating as that might have been, she would have been able to at least share her thoughts with him.

At the Colby's, of course, she had little of that. Evident to her eyes everybody, including Deborah Sumners, saw the shape as the shape. With nothing ironic. The fact that Deborah even brought down champagne to celebrate the last mold being put in place, did nothing but confirm to Catherine that emotion didn't necessarily have to be based on reality to be very real to people.

Catherine, though, did not expose her thoughts to anyone. Nobody down here, she thought—and she knew it was vanity, but the truth was the truth—would understand.

None of these people, as far as she could see ... well ... *read* anything.

Of course, it was disappointing to not be able to share her insights and feelings with these people. Especially since what she could share could, in fact, reveal to them some things which would make them feel more deeply about what they were doing.

Live their lives more deeply.

But she was no teacher. No Steven Elgin. And certainly not needing the ego-feeding his form of teaching consisted of.

She wasn't going to start doing that. Going all sort of mystic sounding about it—because that's obviously how it would sound to them. And certainly not the way Deborah Sumners was doing, turning everything into an opportunity to *transform* things.

Although she'd very nearly slipped in her determination not to be like that.

One day, she'd noticed Deborah pestering Scott about it. And she'd seen his obvious irritation at her metaphysical groundlessness.

Not that she gave a whit for Scott. Except that she'd come to appreciate his simple, fairly good nature, which he spent a lot of effort in covering up with cynicism, sarcasm and vulgarity. And she'd flattered herself with the idea that he would appreciate hearing how she could do better—in terms of understanding how he felt about the boat—than Deborah Sumners did.

Sidling up to him a little later, while he was relaxing, she'd tried it out on him as a conversation, pointing out the form of the boat and all that. But the look in his eye immediately told her that of all the things he might feel or think about what she was saying, it wasn't appreciation.

Well, the hell with him, then. Pearls before swine. And leave him happy in his ignorance.

If anything, hers was a tolerance. Let people take what they thought best, regardless if there could be something better.

She'd just leave Scott alone, then.

And leave him as he was. Happily whatever. With whatever it was he had ... like his fluffy-headed girlfriend.

Proof, if any, the man didn't seek out depth in his life.

# Chapter 37

INDIAN SUMMER swept back into the Pacific Northwest that year with a true intent to dazzle. It didn't often happen. Usually, the weather began turning daily grayer, if it had been blue at all, drizzling towards the steady, wet sloppiness that is the Northwest winter. But that year, a miracle, and the days were hot and bright and the nights were warm and still, and there couldn't have been a more opportune time for the first real get-together around the boat.

Out in the shop, in the warm semi-darkness of the October evening, with dim yellow lights high up in the rafters casting shadows through the ghostly shapes of the huge boat molds, Jack and Ellen built a barbecue grill over the firebrick forge and set steaks and pork chops to sizzle. There was a wonderful smell in the shop of fresh cut wood shavings and wood resins and the fire and the cooking meat and barbecue sauces mingling with the warm sea air off the bay. Even Eric showed up, and they all sat in deck chairs sipping champagne or beer, eating happily off plates balanced across their knees and laughing about anything.

Eric was able to forget, for once, his anxieties about his relation to these people. He decided he really liked them, and was more than just pleased at how they seemed to like him too. He liked how even Deborah seemed to get in the spirit of things, relaxed and easily laughing, even getting a bit tipsy. Almost too good to be true.

After dinner, the party's general grouping broke into more intimate patterns, individual conversations developing and then fading, to take up elsewhere. Everyone had little moments with one another, punctuated by large, general acknowledgments of togetherness. It was during that time that Catherine and Eric found themselves together.

Jack, Scott and Sydney had gone down to the other end of the boathouse to look at one of the fishing boats drawn up on the skids. Ellen and Deborah had gone off to the house. Eric and Catherine were left sitting in the dim, warm shed by the forge, watching the glowing embers of the fire, the looming shape of the boat filling in the boatshed behind them.

Eric had been talking about Bellingham, about where he thought it was going and, in a general sense and carefully, what his plans were for taking part.

Although he, too, noticed how he was getting a little drunk, he managed to remain vague at first about what he said. But it was obvious he considered himself a part of the history of the area despite acknowledging the fact that he was sure that people saw him differently, as an exploiter.

Catherine listened, nodding and occasionally making an observation of her own, but maintained a certain discretion.

In the beginning he was very diffident about his money and business, conditioned by being married to Deborah. But eventually he found himself speaking to Catherine as an equal of sorts.

She proved to be more knowledgeable than he would have guessed, finally discovering that she had worked in a bank. Soon they were talking about his world in a way Eric usually only practiced around investment counselors or lawyers.

Not only did Catherine have a knowledge of money, but he found that she also had an unthreatened sense of humor about it. A rare possession, indeed.

"So, what do you think?" she said at one point, making a small wave back towards the shape behind them. "Are you getting your money's worth?"

Eric laughed, glancing towards the construction, and then looked back at her, eyeing her appreciatively. She was wearing a cool summer dress, white and light greens with strings up on bare, dark shoulders, her skin glowing dusky in the reflection from the coals of the fire. She was attractive, he noted, sensual and feminine.

He quickly looked at her face again. When he did he saw the playful look of a woman who knew she'd been measured, and saw her clever eyes watching him knowingly and steadily in spite of whatever the champagne was doing.

Just a small moment of mutual understanding on yet another level. Nothing but that.

But why not, he thought? No harm in it.

"So far, so good," he said, squinting his eyes at her and permitting a tiny flirtation of innuendo to then creep in: "But you know how these things go. Each investment often brings unexpected returns. Some good, some bad."

She smiled, noting the flirtation, slight as it was and easily ignored. But she suddenly didn't want to ignore it. She had enjoyed it, and now didn't want the small thrill she had felt in the realization he had appraised her, and had liked what he'd seen, disappear completely.

"In other words, you're not taking the risk yet of getting excited about it." She hesitated, wanting to find something flirty of her own, but not wanting to be too obvious about it. Just in case. He was, after all, the money. And married. And …. But she couldn't help it. It was just something she needed. She was enjoying the flirtation. It was a break from the basically sexless atmosphere around the boathouse. She gave him a smile meant to be ambiguous. But her gaze, bold, was anything but that.

"Despite what you see right before your eyes," she said.

Eric eyes, whatever they were seeing, flicked instinctively towards the door to the house. He hadn't expected her to respond so strongly, in terms of the flirtation. He looked back at her and tried to make his voice sound normal. Because, regardless of how innocent and fun it all was, he could feel his heart beating.

"I guess I'm careful, when it comes to my investments."

"Especially when the payoff can be so big."

Eric looked at the way she was holding that smile. It was fun, but he wasn't sure he could keep up with her. She, evidently, had boundless resources when it came to this sort of thing.

"Not just when the payoff's big. I'm afraid I get very prudent about even the very smallest investments. You can never be sure of anything."

They exchanged a laugh.

"I see," Catherine said. "So if I can't get you to make," she paused for effect, "an outright declaration … about whether you feel you will get something out of your investment, what would you say if I were to ask you then about an appreciation of … oh … craft and art, then?"

Eric felt a bit at sea, the way she had so quickly shifted things as though to a different subject. Although the flirtation was still definitely there. "Depends on what crafts and arts you're talking about," he said, thinking immediately it sounded clumsy and heavy.

But Catherine was feeling light-hearted. Bubbling. Enjoying herself confidently in a way she hadn't known in a long time. She could see Eric was, too, having fun. Of course, there was nothing serious in it. So why not enjoy it, while it lasted? She laughed.

"How about the ones concerning making something out of nothing, rather than the ones which use what already exists."

It came out like that. What already exists. She, of course, was playing with her metaphysical idea of form and reality. But if it was pulled straight into what they were flirting around with, there was only one meaning. And she knew she had perhaps ruined things. A small fear went through her as she watched for his reply.

But, in fact, Eric hadn't noticed the allusion Catherine was making between herself and his wife. Caught up in the flirtation and the knowledge he wasn't really good at such things, he was suddenly feeling glum. And worse, he only focused on what had sounded a bit like philosophy. He knew all about the passionate intellectual life from Deborah, and he was just a bit disappointed to find it here, again. Right when he was beginning to have fun about something he really wanted to have fun about, for once. And trying very hard not to think about the reason why he wanted it so bad.

"Yeah. Well, actually," he said aimlessly, "I am getting a kick out of this. It's quite an impressive job the guys are doing."

He looked at her, and saw how he was dampening things for her. He had no idea how to fix it, and found himself wanting to go into full retreat. From what he was thinking about, from looking at the boat, from the flirtation with Catherine. With everything. And his next words came out, brutally, almost a non sequitur to everything else.

"I mean, look at that thing. Suddenly sprung up from fucking nothing, nowhere."

Catherine, like Eric, was more aware of her thoughts and feelings than the words being exchanged. She only noticed his sudden, uncharacteristic and blunt-edged use of that word. As though, to everything else, it was a tiny coda. There was no way to know, of course. But still, she had a quick stab of excitement go through her. You could ... *interpret* ... his words to mean something entirely else than just the boat. If you felt like it.

Obviously, she thought, it could be interpreted that Eric had felt it necessary to sum up all the flirtation between them in a brutal, heavily sensual way so that it would not be lost on either one of them. Now, it was Catherine who could feel her heart beating. She knew there was no way to go farther than that, though, and so just went conversational. Warm and comfortable.

"Answer me something. I'm interested in your reaction. Look back there and tell me, when you look at what's there, what do you see?"

Eric, a bit distracted by an unpleasant thought he was trying to suppress, didn't look. And not only because it was exactly the sort of thing that Deborah did.

"A boat," he said.

She heard the flatness, but didn't care. She now felt confident about what she could say, or not say, with him. And she just wanted to continue to enjoy the moment.

"No. Look."

Eric turned, looked, and then turned back and smiled at her.

"A boat."

"Okay. Now I want you to look again. No, not yet. When you do, I want you to be very exact in what you describe. Be specific, as if there were a punishment for not exactly describing what was there. As if something, somewhere, would be destroyed if you didn't get it right."

She smiled at him and sat back to wait for him to answer. Eric, in spite of all the rest, turned to look again. As he did so, Catherine took the opportunity to examine him as well. He wasn't exactly what she had been used to seeing among the young rich.

Most of those people ... well, you could spot them. Not the ones with the family money. Those were fairly insufferable, and didn't come around the banks much anyway. But the self-made guys.

But even with those guys, Eric was different. There was a split of some sorts. There were the fast-food millionaires, and there was Eric.

There were the glitzy sorts who were basically extremely successful used-car salesmen in fifteen hundred dollar suits. And there were those on the serious side of it, where the real sharks swam ... where some of them ended up deeper in politics, for instance, than politicians. Ended up owning it. Despite the charm they often seemed to have, you could smell the blood on them.

Eric was definitely on that side of things, but at the same time seemed different.

He was as confident as they were, of course. He would have to be. Even as he sat there, now turned to look at the boat, she could see the ease of his athletic body, an obviously, beautifully trained body.

That ease was also a sign of the ease of his mind, a relaxed physical confidence relaying a relaxed mental confidence.

She could admit he wasn't the most handsome man she had ever seen, although attractive enough with his straight blond hair slung back casually from his blunt, squared-off features.

But there was something about his eyes. The intelligence there, in spite of how it was wrapped up in his money and power, was somehow tender, with an honest glint of steady good humor.

Right then, before he turned back to her, Catherine realized that in only two months' time she had found herself in the presence of yet another remarkable man. Two remarkable men, in two months, both of whom obviously found her attractive.

And maybe even signs of love.

Jack, of course, represented a symbol of the simplified forms of love, the reduction of form and flesh to its most intimate and tender acknowledgments of basic truths. Eric, in some way, was more the shape of the spirit.

Both were unpretentious. Both clear about who and what they were.

She found that Eric was talking, and as she regained her senses to listen to him she was shocked by his words.

"…well," he was saying, "What is there, precisely, is the keel and the molds set up along the top like so many slices of bread. A very prettily shaped one, that is. But not a boat at all."

It was precisely her theory! He understood!

Catherine removed herself entirely from her reverie, feeling now a total excitement, sexual and intellectual, course through her body.

"So, tell me this. Why did you first say it was a boat, if there was no boat there at all?"

"Because that's what is suggested back there, and that is what will be there in the end, I suppose. It seemed the efficient way of wrapping things up."

She wasn't sure if the flirtation was back, but let herself go towards the jagged edge of it, anyway.

"Getting a little ahead of yourself, though, aren't you?"

His eyes, clear and focused, looked at her calmly.

"Sometimes, you can't help yourself."

It was difficult, but she was proud of how she kept her voice as calm and flat as the surface of a windless lake. It was a beautiful voice, when she wanted it to be so. She had once been informed, to her surprise, of it having *shimmering* reflections. She now let it out with just a hint of heavy, breathy sensuality.

"That's the difference between what we see, what we want to see, and what is there."

Eric was not entirely deaf to the music of her voice, and plainly saw that they were back to double meanings. Given what he'd just been thinking about—a bit angrily—he didn't mind it a bit.

"What if what we want to see, is what is there?"

Catherine saw they were both on the same page, right then, flirtatiously and otherwise, and just gave him as straight a look as she could.

"Then," she said, "I suppose, that is just one of those extremely fortunate moments when you just know. When, most of the time, you can take nothing for granted."

"An appreciation of reality."

He admired the fact she could talk this way. And ... once again on what was not a completely tangential line from this train of thoughts ... he was well aware that his wife could not have done this. Deborah would never have approached an intellectual subject from the direction of casual conversation, let alone finding a way to flirt with it.

"You know," he said, and not without an inner bitterness. "This reminds me of a course on aesthetics I took at Harvard."

Catherine was surprised. But after a moment's reflection, realized it wasn't as remarkable as that. "So ... you do know."

"About image versus reality? Yes. But I've got to admit, I didn't take that particular class by choice. I'm afraid I was pretty stubborn about what I felt was going to be useful, and what wasn't."

As he spoke he now looked at her indirectly, which is the way men look at women when they want to really look. Her smooth legs were crossed and her dress had slipped upwards, exposing her thighs a bit more than she knew. He could easily follow the shapes and promises of her thighs upwards under the light dress, seeing her there almost as though nude. The image of the form of what was there, without really seeing it, brought a sudden, warm reaction of its own. He struggled for words. A bit bitterly. There are times, he reflected, when there is nothing you can say which doesn't sound like what you shouldn't be talking about.

"Yes," he said finally, "I did imagine, and then act upon the final possibility as though it were the reality. But that's normal, don't you think? Otherwise, how could anyone ever take any initiative, unless we could more than just imagine the results?"

Catherine had noted his appraisal and her eyes narrowed slightly with that old and familiar sensation she admittedly enjoyed. But she was also slightly embarrassed, and found herself getting flushed.

She felt suddenly exposed, her legs too naked with a fluttering quiver in the thigh muscles as though they desired to shift all of their own accord. The small thrill of feeling surreptitiously, but deeply, looked at, and yet a small fear that that was all Eric's mind was suddenly getting focused on.

"But perhaps it's not the truth," she forced herself to say, calming herself again with her own words. "Perhaps the efficient way of looking at things is perhaps an efficient way of avoiding the truth."

"Or an efficient way to get at it."

Catherine swallowed, but before she could say anything, a voice suddenly boomed behind her.

"Hey, you two! Do you have any idea where Deborah is?"

# Chapter 38

Scott's voice shocked them both out of wherever they were. Which didn't bother Catherine at all. The conversation had become a little too much for her, too, or for that matter Eric's eyes, which seemed now too bright and sharp, unmistakably predatory.

"She's in the house, with Ellen," she said. Scott nodded and he and Sydney walked in that direction. Catherine didn't bother to ask herself why Scott, who normally did just about everything he could to avoid Deborah would suddenly be looking for her. She had other things to deal with here. She felt her hands twitch nervously, but she kept them quiet in her lap, forcing them not to move, smooth her dress or fly around in expressive gestures.

She said lightly, responding to his previous question. "I want to know why that is. Tell me."

Eric looked at her for a long moment, acknowledging now to himself the definite wisps of desire. And suddenly as well, of the fact he didn't care if he was feeling them.

"Okay," he said to her. "I'll have to look again, because whatever it is, no, wait, I can see it again. The shape is there. The form is there again, and there is nothing I can do about it. No matter how you think about it, even if you know better, it keeps coming back. Insistently." He smiled at her. "Your turn. Why were you asking?"

"No big reason," Catherine smiled. "I'd been thinking about that today, and wondered if anyone else would notice it. It's just that even the most obvious visual, physical truths can be misused, you see. It just seemed a little strange and a little hard to get used to."

Eric wanted to both nod and frown at the same time, feeling how she was—quite rightly—withdrawing herself from the conversation. A bit.

"So don't tell me you go around trying to drape things onto philosophic frameworks all the time. Because, I think I can tell you, it doesn't work very well."

"Oh, no," she laughed. "Not all the time, no. But you should be used to that."

Eric looked back at her with a steady intensity for a moment, almost to the point where she thought she'd made a very serious gaffe.

"Yes," he said, finally. So that was it, he thought. Just Deborah's name had been enough to throw cold water over everything. Which was nothing to be surprised about.

"But Deborah's concern with aesthetics seems to be quite different from yours," he said easily. "I mean, you're both quite different. So there is obviously a different motivation. I'm used to my wife's form of it. Excuse me, but I'm not used to yours, and it may well be that I am automatic in responding in a certain way and it's hard to break the pattern. Maybe."

There was a hint of criticism, but Catherine went nowhere near it.

"That's all right. Anyway, I'm not used to talking with people at all about these things. I hope I haven't gotten carried away."

Eric said nothing to that. They were evidently at a point where they were either going to start saying too much, or nothing at all. The choice was all too obvious. "So I take it you read a lot. Probably too much, as they say. I've always thought reading is one of those things which could be considered a gift and a curse at the same time. You learn to appreciate things but you become separated from them as well. The only thing you can hope for then is that it might take you out of yourself."

He laughed. He'd always wanted to say something like that to someone. Especially to an intelligent and attractive woman. He had to admit he had enjoyed finding someone who responded to the seductions of art as though it was possible they were also the seductions of the hormones.

He looked again at Catherine, suddenly realizing to what extent he was attracted to her and couldn't help wondering to what extent she was—really—attracted to him.

Not that it mattered, of course. But it was there.

But how much?

"So, tell me. What do you get from all these books, besides your famous calm. Or," he gave her a sincere look, "what do you believe you get?"

Catherine had to digest that statement. Her famous calm? Her teammates on the Desperados had considered her practically a hysteric. But those had been other women and women often look at each other as though looking in a mirror. It made her wonder.

"I don't know," she said. "Books, I suppose, if anything, give me the feeling that the future is predictable."

A happy glow spread on Eric's face. He picked up a bottle of champagne and filled their glasses.

"Swell," he said. "That's wonderful. I can't believe it. Where do people like you come from, I'd like to know? Here I am in a boatyard in good old Bellyburg, talking with the secretary about the future as made possible within art and literature. Can you predict the future then?"

For a moment there was a hint of earlier feelings, a chumminess of flirtation, but she was no longer uneasy about it.

"No. I just get the feeling there are no real surprises out there."

Eric held his glass out to toast. Finally he leaned forward towards her, looking intently into her eyes. She stared back.

"Catherine, I feel I do, now, know you quite a bit. I mean, I know a great deal about you, because I know about these things too. I can appreciate the idea of having ideas. Even my wife doesn't see this in me, at least not all the time. I can see other things about you as well. I don't want to be impolite, but I feel I can tell you something about these things. That is, I feel you haven't learned yet how things can be useful, or not. I think you're still trying different ideas out. The important thing is that it's very important to be selective, in the end, about where you apply all the things you come to know. Because it often works, once you learn how some things fit together. But ...," a strange, choked emphasis came into his voice with his conclusion, "that doesn't always make it worth the effort, either. I used to think it was always worth the effort to figure everything out. To try to make it all fit. Sometimes," he set his glass down and then took a breath, "the best thing is to leave well enough alone. Can you understand that? I just want to say it's so pleasurable to meet someone who feels the same way about things."

She had sat through the whole thing. Dumfounded. It had come spilling out of him as though ....

Maybe he was a little drunk.

Even so, it didn't matter.

What mattered was that she truly wanted to understand, and she wanted him to think she understood. So she nodded at him.

Sharing with him a bit of an acknowledgement of a dream. Any old dream. Although this one had to do with the dream of understanding. As though whatever he felt, she too was feeling. It was a very old dream, as well. Being the one thing women were able to give men, that men tended to believe unconditionally. Men aren't very good at intangibles, and the wisest of women know it. And once in a while—when they're not too sore at their men for being so obtuse—they let them feel as though they really are understood.

And on that, she gave him a smile of encouragement. Quite happy in being able to give him that, if only perhaps wishing she might have known exactly what it was they both felt the same way about.

As though it might matter.

# Chapter 39

LATER THAT night she would find him so good and sweet.

And Jack then, too.

Doing the Knot.

Oh god, she thought.

Doing anything.

Her breathing became soft and still. The quiet caress of sleep coming over her.

And that night, as she hadn't for a very long time, longer than she had ever been able to remember, she dreamed of herself in her childhood.

Of just herself.

*

"You liked it tonight," he tried again.

It didn't bother him too much anymore that she wouldn't respond. In some ways, he had found ways to pretend she responded in how she didn't respond.

"I love it, you know, when it's good for you," he went on. "You really liked it."

She surprised him.

"Yes," she whispered.

It was like finding gold, and Eric couldn't stop, saying with almost as much urgency as what had just passed, "What were you thinking?"

"You mean when we were ...."

He wanted her to say it. He wished it. She never had.

Deborah lay silent for a moment, and for a moment he thought she was going to go away from him again. As she always did.

Then she sighed.

She did want to be there with him still, and she wanted to make an effort. She knew what he wanted her to say, but she couldn't do it.

She did, however, feel she should give her husband something.

"Oh, you know," she tried, "I always love when it goes like that. You're like, I don't know ... like my Apollo then."

She hadn't ever been able to tell him that before, and it felt exciting to admit it. She even felt nervous.

He was very silent. Finally he kissed her, and resettled himself.

He had nothing else he could say to her the way he wanted to. Not after that.

It wasn't possible to talk about fucking, and talk about Apollo, at the same time.

Apollo rides again.

What a small thing to get hung up on, he thought.

Now it seemed like such a small, ridiculous idea.

As though he had been wishing her to be someone else.

## Chapter 40

HE HAD been quiet in the kitchen for a long time. But that didn't mean everything had calmed down. It was hard to find what to say to him. There seemed either everything to say, or nothing at all.

It had been nothing. An incident which meant nothing, if nothing meant anything, but which suddenly seemed much more serious than anything she'd ever known. To the point where it now seemed a fatal mistake. Sydney could feel how everything was so much closer suddenly. How it had clarified what had not seemed serious before. And she could even now imagine the other words.

Marriage. Kids.

Too soon. Too fast. But how could you know what the right amount of time was? How could you anticipate going from never thinking of such things, to suddenly having them very real on your doorstep? Normally, one might think, you don't start even hinting around about those things, or you shouldn't really even be thinking them, until some serious time has gone by.

She found herself thinking about how her grandfather had met her grandmother, and then courted her, mainly by letter, and finally proposed marriage. All of that across more than a year.

Nowadays, you woke up in the morning alongside each other and then pretended to go through a long process of getting to know each other before making up your minds.

Sydney could see how their own relationship had seemed less substantial than even that. But now she and Scott were at a point of making it more substantial, or letting it all fall apart. Which didn't fit into any of the regular patterns she had known. And all because of something that didn't seem like a mistake, but now did. A mindless, social fling.

Which had brought on this. A sort of instant put up or shut up. Which had caught both of them by surprise. Unsure if they had really meant things to go this far. And worse, now, because of the earlier murkiness of it, it was hard to know if it was meant to continue, in itself. If they, as a couple, were … what could she call it? … valid? Whatever validity, in a couple, meant.

That whatever they had, together, was good?

She had seen the stupid expressions people liked to blather around. Slogans. That a couple was greater than its sum. Things like that. Love is, they'd say ... and then follow it with some damn whatever somebody else had said. Greeting card style.

When in truth, there was no truth to love. Except, perhaps, in accepting moments as they came, knowing other moments would be different but they would be accepted as they came along. One at a time. And, maybe, the validity came from knowing it would always work that way.

Or ... whatever. She had no idea. All she could do was wait. Look for signs. It was just awful, all this not knowing.

Because the first real moment had come.

She heard him make a sound in the kitchen, making his presence known although still not wanting to say anything. Sydney wondered if he was feeling the same way she was. Groping.

She looked out his window for another moment, looking out across his roughly hacked down lawn, looked at his car, looked at the other dumpy house across on the other side of the potholed side street in the gray, troubled light of morning.

Not exactly the sort of view you admired in quiet contemplation for hours. Which meant, of course, the next step was bored irritation. Sydney decided she was going to have none of that.

"So," she said flat out into the silence, her voice not loud but easily heard in the even more silent kitchen. "What now?"

More silence. Then a scrape in there.

Then she heard him say quietly, almost as if he wasn't talking to her at all, "What now?"

She tossed her hair back, her chin rising slightly.

"Yeah," she said, her own voice now stronger. "What happens now?"

Another scrape, and silence.

She knew it had sounded defiant. But she was also scared. Then the voice came back out to her again, also defiant, but also with a note of brutal uncertainty.

"I don't want to feel like I'm in bed with Western Washington University."

Sydney looked down at her hands. Her courage wavered.

"You won't," she got out, not loud enough for him to hear. She had made a decision. But she couldn't make herself heard.

Scott suddenly laughed from the kitchen.

"Don't laugh," she cried out. "It sounds terrible."

"You don't think it's funny?"

"Stop it."

There was silence again, and then: "Yes, stop it. It's not funny. Even though it's pretty fucking funny."

He wasn't giving in an inch on it. Blocking completely.

Sydney felt herself get angry.

Now, especially that she'd made her decision. Now that she had to start knowing things. She turned towards the kitchen.

"What the hell can I say? You want me to solemnly swear I will not go to bed with anyone but you?"

A risk. It wouldn't take much now to undo all of it.

Scott came to the kitchen door and looked at her. She didn't look back at him and continued looking out the front window.

At first she thought it was the one thing. But as the silence continued she realized it was something else, and her heart began beating hard.

Her courage returning, she looked back at him and although she wanted to seem calm, and mature, her eyes suddenly watered and she felt her voice shake:

"Really?"

Scott looked at her, and thought: she's not much past a girl, all right. But he felt a bit of a sting in his own eyes as well.

Moments of truth worked that way for everybody.

*

Work went slower in October. Putting ribbands onto the molds was time consuming. Even on a smaller boat the pace would have crept.

To keep on schedule, they worked long hours and began eating breakfasts and dinners, as well as lunch, together. It was then that Catherine and Ellen finally became friends, which seemed a wonderful thing for both of them.

Ellen, herself, had been longing for a woman friend to talk to. She was occasionally depressed about how few opportunities she had to meet other women. But then, she also knew she wasn't an easy friend to have, quickly shunning those she didn't like. She wasn't very inclusive. Especially, she didn't like the ones who preferred mutual misery, the stronger of the moment helping the weaker.

Ellen had a theory, admittedly somewhat bitter, that if men had one thing in their lives which could make up in some way for not being able to experience motherhood, it was they could have friendships based on strengths and viewpoints. Rather than weaknesses and opinions. An agreement to let the smaller things ride. Even Jack and Scott, far from the best of friends, were an example of that.

As solitary as men could be, there was definitely a herd instinct. Some people psychoanalyzed it, but mostly it was some sort of dopey group hunting instinct, like a bunch of clods trudging around with spears and knives looking for something to bring down.

Sadly for them, in the modern world the only thing the poor bastards had to bag anymore was either a salary, or women. The latter either in the flesh, or the spirit. But that made their friendships no less legitimate, and Ellen could envy them.

She often complained to Jack about the fact that she had no women as friends. His response had been predictable: that she had no friends because women, when not competing with each other, allowed their friendships to invade each other's private lives ... which was something she made it obvious she didn't like.

Of course, Jack's opinion was slanted. To Jack, women were an interference in his home life ... he especially didn't like the idea that he, himself, might become fodder for dissection. Nevertheless, his words had a slight ring of truth to it somewhere.

But now, in any case, there was Catherine Wilkins. And it was a stroke of luck because they shared the same problems, and had had time to sort each other out. Ellen enjoyed Catherine's company more each day. Part of that enjoyment stemmed from the fact that she felt no stabs of savage suspicion when Jack was around. Something ... knowing him ... she would have sworn should have been there as a matter of course. But down there at the boathouse, nothing.

Ellen had never known such a non-sexual atmosphere could exist around Jack with an attractive woman around. But she was prepared to believe it—despite a surprising confession from Catherine one morning, that should have sent warning bells swinging violently. But, strangely enough, didn't.

They were sharing a coffee after having cleared away the breakfast plates. And something made them feel confidential.

"There are simply no men in my life right now," she had told Ellen one morning.

"I can't believe that," Ellen said.

"It's true. When I got here, I didn't get much of a chance to settle in. Ever since, it's been so hectic that I haven't got out and around. But then," she smiled, "that might just be the luckiest thing. There's a big difference between wondering how bad the possibilities are, and cruising around and confirming it."

Ellen laughed.

"That's not very optimistic. But you wouldn't really go out alone, would you?"

"I don't care about that anymore. It's less depressing than to pretend you don't want it and that you actually like drinking with the girls. Another girl makes it easier to say no, is all. Actually, anymore, the last thing I need is a bunch of spectators to whether I want to say no, or not. And I'm old enough to take care of myself."

Ellen laughed again.

Catherine waved her hand.

"Let's face it. There isn't all that much out there, anyway. After a certain age, cruising around is a matter of diminishing options. It's always so depressing, you know, to have to make yourself feel resolved to your fate. It's not always a wonder the guys kick you the hell out in the morning. Sometimes I've got to admit it's surprising they can even get it up."

"They can always get it up."

It was Catherine's turn to laugh. "If only they knew that's just an extra option, like getting a stereo and a sunroof."

"I like sunroofs."

"Who doesn't?"

Ellen groaned sympathetically. "I wish I could help. But Jack and I have so few friends that we could have over. Guys, I mean. Jack doesn't know many single guys, anymore. And guess where most of the guys he does know go."

"To the bars."

Ellen shrugged.

Catherine shook her head.

"Believe me," she said, "it doesn't matter all that much, anyway. You see, this is all so new. I spent so many years in Seattle doing the same thing. You know, all my friends down there were like me. You get to the point where there seems one way to live." She gave a little sigh. "I can't tell you how good it feels to be free of all that. Sort of exciting. I think that when you get out of a rut, you don't want to start thinking about guys, or options, or things the old ways again.

224

Uh … yeah, you know … and even my house. And anyway, you'll have to come up and see the place. I got a hand woven rug from Peru."

Ellen could admire how cheerful Catherine was about herself, and relaxed. So free and easy, except for having changed the subject—understandably—when Jack had come striding into the kitchen for a cup of coffee.

But that was as it should be, as was the slight cough that ended her speech.

Ellen, in a chatty mood, went on with the subject of Catherine's new rug while Jack was in the kitchen.

Well, okay, she was thinking, even if Catherine wasn't being absolutely truthful about her private life—how could she not care?—she was certainly being courageous about it. Ellen liked that and how she wasn't looking for someone to listen to her woes. Nor make any noises about how Ellen was so lucky to have her home.

When Jack finally cleared out … giving them both the grimace of a busy man … Ellen gave Catherine a smile. But momentarily didn't know whether to go on with the new tack, or return to the earlier subject.

She came close to saying something about Scott, to make a joke about the only single man in the proximity. She would have liked to see if Catherine had the same impressions of the man. The main being how he was easily one of the most unsuitable prospects imaginable. But although he was on the periphery of the subject of single men, she checked herself. She had seen how Catherine had never shown anything but a willingness to joke around with Scott. Whenever he was in a good enough mood for it, that was.

So the conversation turned towards their material surroundings. But that was just as pleasant and intimate, women often choosing to reveal themselves to each other through a discussion of the world they drew, like a blanket, around themselves. That was also what a friendship with another woman could be, Ellen was thinking. A certain transparency at all levels.

But where Ellen was preoccupied with the present, Catherine was suddenly preoccupied with the past. What had been building up in Catherine all month, all her loneliness, all her needs, compounded by the daily exposure to the man … had come pouring up into her consciousness, unchecked, because of the subject of the conversation.

And then … the sight of Jack's face turning to her from the sink, out of Ellen's vision, giving her a quick, furtive glance, a look of questioning strangely vulnerable and forlorn, made her heart jump a beat. And the forbidden thought came swooping in.

If he'd said anything to them, inviting a response, she might have even stuttered. Luckily though, before she'd seen the look from him, she had already given a short cough and Ellen had picked up the ball.

But now, as Ellen talked, the thought struck Catherine with a blinding clarity. Regardless of what they'd said, and regardless of what they would do, she knew she wanted Jack again.

The thought was simple, honest ... and utterly horrifying.

But her reaction to the thought stunned her even more than the idea itself.

Peace.

It was incredible.

Ellen was talking happily away, and Catherine was smiling back with a profound calm gone through her, quieting a storm long and secretly raging.

It didn't mean anything though, of course, she thought. So she didn't feel bad about anything. Nor pity for Ellen.

If anything, she could feel closer. As though the simple admission to herself had suddenly made them sisters, or at least sisters-in-law. Naturally, she liked Ellen very much, and wanted her friendship. But there was that natural curiosity of thinking about what would happen if fantasies came true. And of course, because there were a million variables against the idea, there was no harm in letting those fantasies roam wild. Jack wasn't the only man she could consider, either, although his was the most exciting and dangerous situation to think about.

She indulged herself, and could almost smile. Looking at it clinically, just objectively, Catherine knew that Ellen would not see it because, if it happened, it would happen without guilt.

It was making her feel good, all these thoughts. And not to forget: there was also Eric Sumners, and his obvious show of attraction. In a way, her ability to admit honestly these desires for Jack, had sprung from a confidence Eric had helped her to regain.

She was feeling sexy again. There was no longer any need to flee from hidden desires in order to avoid the pitfalls of doubts about herself. She could feel glowing, and expansive, and happy to be talking away about nothing at all with Ellen. If she wanted to think about Eric Sumners, she would. Or about Jack, if she wanted. And it didn't matter at all.

She could even think about Scott, although she barely knew anything tangible about the man. Catherine smiled at the idea of it, because as the third man around there, he was the oddball, and in fact brought in a vulgar sort of element. Sort of titillating.

Scott could be a very funny guy. He was also a good craftsman. But no way was he as desirable as either of the other two men who knew what they wanted and how to get it. Scott wasn't as deep— more a reflex, like a twitching muscle. Which was all right for some women. Like his current little girlfriend, for instance.

But for some women, like herself and Ellen, muscular reflex was a little barren for the imagination. What *that* meant, she told herself, was that if you wanted something good out of a man, you had to give a great deal of stock to not only what you could see, but to what you should be able to imagine.

And with that thought she knew she was free again to imagine whatever the hell she had a right to imagine.

With Scott, not much … but as for Jack and Eric …

She looked at Ellen, who was sharing something about the furniture she and Jack had owned when they'd first got married. And she smiled.

As any friend would have.

# Chapter 41

WITH A miscalculation in the stock needed for ribbands, work stopped at a point about three quarters of the way up the sides of the hull molds. Regardless of its incompleteness, though, it was now a wonderful sight, the great construction crouching in the woodshed like some beast. The initial framework was almost in place to the point where the real construction would begin, the point where whatever it was they were making together would finally begin becoming reality.

But it had been difficult work, straining long ribbands upon the forming molds carefully, making sure no distortions took place. Making sure that everything in place would correctly inform the final structure. Every important detail taken care of. And care had been taken not to overbuild the form, making it too weighty, considering what was to follow. Already, they had been forced to strengthen several key rafters and stress points in the boathouse itself. To take the load. One hell of a lot of work. So it was with relief that Jack and Scott were able to take the forced break.

Very nearly half way. Or, at least in terms of the mental effort. The boat would take more time, in sheer days, but from this point forward there would be much less calculation needed. The stage, as Deborah had come to call this work on the frame, was set.

Ellen, on the day of the stoppage, had decided to go up to Burnaby to visit what Jack called her "cheese head" friends. She had never liked that Washington nickname for British Columbians, the result of an unfortunate television advertisement thought up many years before by the B.C. Dairy Council. But transfrontier nicknames were inevitable.

In that country there were Yanks and there were Canucks. And God knew if they didn't love each other, at least they didn't hate each other.

She had invited Catherine along, but Catherine said while she would love to go some other time, she was going to take advantage of the break in mid-week to take care of a few domestic things.

She had really meant to.

As it turned out, Jack didn't go up with Ellen, Deborah went home, and Scott and the apprentices took off, declaring a general strike if everyone else was going to declare a general holiday. It was a sunny day, and seemed unfair to make them work. Everybody laughed about it. Within a half an hour, Colby's was deserted.

With everybody gone, and Catherine putting things away and preparing to go herself, she realized Jack was out in the shop, also alone.

She could smile at the thought, let a little fantasy run through her. As she'd been permitting herself to do, lately. But then, also, she finally put it firmly aside. As she did on each occasion.

Freedom, she had come to see, also meant the freedom to be in absolute control.

She finished her filing, backed up all the documents, and then went out of the house.

Before she left she went over and poked her head in the shop door to say she was leaving. She didn't see Jack, so she went in farther.

She had been alone with Jack before. At those times there had been a slight extension of intimacy. But that was all. That was to say, that had been all it could be with the agreement in force. A tacit, mutual avoidance of even thinking about what had been.

Now, though, things were different. She had broken free of it, declared her independence of what, she could now see, was a silly enough thing anyway.

She had been allowing free play to her memories, gratifying her needs to feel desirable by assuaging herself with what had passed that night. She had even become a little militant about how unjustly she should have been denied access to her own mind.

She had every right to feel good about herself. If he had been a part of her life, and had represented something good, then he had no right to deny her what he had been for her.

An intellectual victory, then, for her. But if it was intellectual, she could not avoid admitting that it changed the physical atmosphere. At least for her. Which didn't bother her either, of course. Because it didn't matter.

As she stepped gingerly around the dark shop looking for him beneath the looming hull molds, sunlight filtering down in rays through the fine dust hovering in the air, she could suddenly feel an electric tension surrounding her. Why that was, she couldn't say. Although it was perhaps connected with her new feelings of freedom, and the fact she'd be having them, for the first time, with Jack around. Alone together. So she was unnerved when, looking one way, he surprised her coming up silently from behind.

But where, only seconds before, she wouldn't have given it a thought, she suddenly realized something.

She wanted something. And from him.

It was like a dam breaking. All that time, she had hidden from it. But no longer! Freedom meant just that, and included her right to be exactly as she felt she was, or needed, to be.

She was sure of herself.

She had the right to her thoughts, she had the right to her fantasies. What was more, she had every right, very simply, to ask it of him.

And it wasn't wrong, because it wasn't as if she had calculated it … had been lying in wait for him to make a mistake, or a sign, or a movement. It was pure emotion, and true feeling, which couldn't be cheapened by the jealous ethics of those who couldn't feel such things in the first place.

If it had been premeditated, she would have talked herself out of it. But it was upon her, like a violent storm come up at sea. And all there was for her to do, was but to run before it. Just trying not to get swamped.

Despite a racing pulse, and a tight throat she made up her mind.

"Hiya," Jack said to her. "I thought everyone had left. It was so quiet around here I've been sort of standing in a daze wondering why I wasn't working."

She said nothing.

Waiting.

He laughed, crinkling his eyes at her, and then looking around at the molding frames and ribbands.

"It's looking pretty good, isn't it," he said. "The way things are going we'll be able to set up a steam box in a few weeks and start setting ribs. This is sort of a Never-Never-Land time right now, where you've got just moldings and ribbands. The point of no return, where you really haven't started actually putting the boat inside it. If Sumners wanted to say stop right now, there would be no huge loss. There's no boat. We all would have just been very well paid to build a boat mold …."

Jack was running on but all the while, Catherine was thinking of what she wanted to say, and how to say it.

She finally blurted out his name to interrupt his flow.

Lost in a reverie about the boat, dazed as usual with this giant thing squatting in his boatshed, he looked around at her blankly for a second.

Completely unaware.

"What?" he said.

Catherine felt herself flush, and then said haltingly, "I need to talk to you about something important. I mean, it's important to me."

For half a second he actually played with the possibility this was about a raise. But only that long. Because even though Jack was better at denial than most other men, he was honest enough to not always go there. He could see easily enough this was going to be much more complicated than just money.

Understanding things, though, doesn't necessarily make you feel better prepared or provide intellectual tranquility. Far from it. In fact, Jack was immediately and thoroughly alarmed.

Trapped. And worse, he was alone there with her.

Nobody to show up and stop what was about to occur, or be occurring.

Anything could be said without fear of discovery.

Anything.

And, anymore, Jack didn't trust himself with words. Actually, he never really had. Gift of the gab, and all that. Which had taught him to remain silent, mostly. But lately, with both of the Sumners around, he'd become more sensitive than usual to his lack of verbal abilities.

He'd gotten worked around. By Scott, by the Sumners, even by Catherine about this job.

And now ....

For just a second, a passing regret. As though mourning something. Which, in fact, he was: his recent and fragile sense of safety around her. It, of course, had been based on the fact they were unable to stumble into these sorts of situations. And so had never really been tested. He could see it had been a mirage.

He looked at her as quietly as he could, trying to make it clear to her that he would discourage any attempt at an intimate conversation. Which encouraged her. His tight face and defensively rigid posture just made her feel more belligerent.

"I wish I didn't have to put so much of a preface on this," she said. "But it will make for less misunderstanding. I want you to know right off exactly how I feel. Okay?"

For a moment, Jack had another fantasy. That she wanted to quit.

A faint hope, and instinctively he tried to encourage her with an even more neutral stance, folding his arms complacently in front of himself. As if.

"Okay," he said.

And, of course, it wasn't to be.

Catherine gauged his resistance, and went ahead, now remembering to relax her voice in order for its naturally musical qualities to exert themselves.

"First off, you know how I feel about you and Ellen. It's the same way I felt the day I came here. I told you then, and it hasn't changed ... that I'm not out to take anyone away from anyone."

Jack's arms began to droop.

"For what it's worth," Catherine went on, "I can see that Ellen and I are quite similar in some ways. For you, there would be no reason to leave her. Thank God for that. I certainly would never want a thing like that. But ...."

She now hesitated. She had been keying herself up to discussing the situation briskly. Pragmatically. Make it all a logical outcome of the situation. But suddenly her feelings swelled up and came pouring out. Unwilled, and undesired, she felt her eyes begin to smart.

"Oh, Jack, I'm so lonely. I come down here and it's always here. You and Ellen and everybody have so much. There are days when I can't stand it. I just watch and ... I don't know ... all I want is to feel like a woman. That's all. But it's so hard. You don't know what it's like. I can't find it anywhere. I can't even pretend to make it happen a little bit, either. I can't do that anymore. I don't want to go down to a bar and get crawled on by drunks. I need, I don't know, a friend. Someone who understands. Me. And this."

Her voice had started shakily, but by the end it had risen, tight and harsh and bitter. She looked at him. Jack was now leaning back against the ribbands as though pushed there by a strong gale, shaking his head dumbly.

"Jack, if you're worried that I might ...."

"Wait, wait," he finally found his voice. "Hold on."

But she wouldn't hold on, wouldn't stop. No matter what he tried to say or do now, her sense of urgency, and his obvious desire to push it all away, forced her to the ultimate demand.

"Just be with me sometimes."

Five words.

Said simply and calmly.

But they hung there in the heavy, exhausted air, echoing over and over like the tolling of the biggest and deepest toned bell ever cast.

At first, Jack felt nothing. Then, when something did come it wasn't complicated at all although its simplicity was pretty complicated, and he felt a profound depression.

He was reduced to examining his work boots. Each and every crack and crevice in the scuffed, once-black leather.

His mind seemed just about as old and faded as they were.

Then, slowly and carefully and completely, he damned himself.

Heavily and honestly, with a deep, heartfelt anger and hatred.

"Jack ...."

He didn't look up at her, but was thinking again. Coldly.

It was his own damn fault, he thought. He knew this would happen. How could he have ever believed it wouldn't?

Go climbing into bed with a woman, showing her what a wonderful, honest guy you were.

Be Mr. Wonderful, because you'll never see her again and you won't have to deal with it anymore.

Then, there she is. And there you are. Unable to find any way to show her how it was a lot easier to be a wonderful, honest and caring adult a hundred miles farther to the south.

What. An. Idiot.

"Jack ... don't look like that. I mean, it's not as though this is weird or anything. I'm not being weird about it, you know. You've got to admit, it's fairly normal, in fact."

Jack looked at her ruefully. "Yeah, it's normal."

"Are you angry with me?"

"I haven't said that."

"I can see it."

"No, you don't. You don't see anything."

"Listen," she said, "I didn't plan this."

Jack couldn't seem to think anymore.

"I don't know."

Catherine knew he wanted to brush all this aside. But it was too late. There now had to be a resolution. One way or another. "I'm sorry I've surprised you. I really am. It's just the way things are."

Jack looked at her tiredly. "Just the way things are."

"That's right."

It came out just a bit too bossy, a bit too affirmative, and she thought she saw an angry light come into his eyes. And what he said, confirmed it.

"So, what do you want?" he said quietly, shaking his head. "It's ... I mean, can't you see? How big a mistake it would ...?" He stopped, a bitter exhalation like a laugh replacing whatever he was going to say. He squinted at her. "What do you want?" he went on. "*What?* Once a week? Twice a week? I mean, I think it's obvious what wasn't a mistake, now is. Now *is*. And we'd just be making it worse. Much, much worse."

"I don't see how. What would be changed?"

Jack waved his hands furiously.

"Everything," he said. "Everything. Everything is changed. Even right now. And it was already bad enough as it was." He looked away from her, down the boatshed to the water, and said, half to himself, with a quiet sigh of sarcastic self-mockery: "Although I was *hoping* ...."

Where a short time before, Jack could have considered himself a contented man, with his wife, his boatyard, his work, life ... now the world was a bleak place, all prospects bad, and no exits.

He'd lost control.

Of everything. The whole world was shit.

First one thing, then another. It was like a trap had been set for him.

God knew, he had plenty of things which could have caught up with him.

OK, women, that was one thing. All his life he'd been nonchalant about women. It had never seemed wrong before. If not exactly happy, nobody had been left weeping. No strings ... hearts not broken ... perhaps a few bumps and dings, but nothing really noticeable.

Now this. Right back at him and all over him. First her. Well, not really her at first. Down there. It had seemed all right at the time. But then her showing up again. And now it seemed like just another part of what was the beginning of one giant unholy mess. With him just treading with his head barely above the muck.

First, really, a doubtful, secret act. But like the butterfly wings in somewhere creating a hurricane elsewhere, it had come back to haunt him.

Scott and Ellen with the fucking boat. With Sumners pounding on him like a nail to be just whacked into place, and his goofy wife to watch. And now, here, Catherine and ... *that* ... back to life again. Sex as vampire, resurrecting itself on its home turf. Making it seem as though everything was always guaranteed to blow up in his face from the very start.

He sighed.

"Oh, come on," she said. "It hasn't been that bad for you."

He couldn't tell her any of it of course. No, it hadn't been all that bad. But he'd felt, off and on, bad about it for reasons that no man who had any pride at all in himself, would admit. Jealousy, ego ... of who had done what, who controlled what, who decided what, who said what, who was liked by whom, who ....

Just thinking of trying to explain all that seemed pathetic in itself. There was no way out.

It would have been easy. He could have just spilled his guts and crawled out of there like a cockroach and that would have been the end of it. He could have lowered himself so much in her eyes that she would have gone from attraction to repugnance. But he just couldn't do it. He was just too battered. He could not permit her to think of him as small.

"No," he said. "But do you think it's been easy for me? You being around? You're not the only one dealing with it. But we both knew it would be like this."

She saw he was trying to find a way to change the challenge. Ignore the question. She pushed closer, making her voice go serious. She would play along, for the moment.

"It's been difficult for you?"

"Sure it has."

With Catherine so close to him, the way they were talking ... he couldn't help how it did, indeed, bring back whispering memories. He did, after all, like her.

But that, he caught himself, was of course beside the point.

Catherine's eyes narrowed.

"You know," she said carefully, "I'm not meaning it to be like how you're thinking maybe. I couldn't ... I don't want ... to expect anything else. I really don't want it to become .... I don't know ... like making little plans. Little meetings. Sneaking around."

She was trying to stay calm. But as she spoke, her need—the one she felt she had every right to have—once again swelled within her and her eyes grew large with an emotion that stabbed with seeming honesty. "For me," she said, her voice nearly choking, "I think most of it is to know you might be willing. Just to know.

That's all. Just get me through this until, I don't know. Until someone else can really come along."

It let him off the hook. A bit. But in other ways, she knew it caught him as surely as though he'd swallowed it straight to the bung. Just a quiver, a hesitation, and it was done.

Or else a flat out No.

And, no, she had no intention of blackmail. No, not that.

She was nervous, but she knew she had to seem as calm as she possibly could. She had to be calm and sure for both of them.

Jack, in the meantime, was doing his best, trying to think through the tangles. Trying to be nice about it, if that didn't seem too stupid a thing to do. But at the same time keep to the line of how it was just too complicated.

He wanted to be fair. Or at least have her feel that. No, she wasn't being psychotic. In truth, she was being pretty straight. He could feel sympathy for her. God knew it couldn't be easy for her to be alone. He knew how even a few days of it felt. She, though, had it for weeks at a time. He wondered if he could just get through it with a sympathetic conversation.

It was worth a try.

"Have you," he said quietly, "really been miserable?"

She felt his sympathy and wondered where it was suddenly coming from. And why. But what happened next just happened. She could never have planned it.

In answer to his question, of course she had never really been miserable. But with some people, talking about the possibility of having a certain condition is enough to make them momentarily believe they have it.

And that was it and she now did.

The tension inside her burst into what sure seemed like pure misery, and she cried openly. Not in her voice though. Nor did her features contort. But the tears streamed down her calm face.

And that was what killed him dead.

"Badly lonely," she said, and then smiled, her eyes still streaming. "And sometimes a little old."

She wiped her face.

"Oh, shit. This is all I need, to start blubbering like an idiot."

For a moment it was as though she was all alone there in front of him. Jack: a wooden statue. But then Jack just put his arms out and gathered her in. Holding her then for a long time until it seemed they'd been holding each other forever.

At last they started murmuring to each other, and then she spoke into his shoulder.

"This is awful. You can't know how sorry I am."

He stroked her hair, stroked her back, his mouth moving.

"It's okay," he said. "It's okay."

She buried her face into his chest, now embarrassed.

"Not very impressive, was I?"

Jack continued to stroke her hair unconsciously, staring off into the church-like gloom of the boatshed, looking at the half-finished project.

And only for a second did he find himself wishing he'd never let it see the light of day.

"It's all right," he said. "It's going to be okay."

# Chapter 42

Deborah went down to the boathouse again that afternoon but found it deserted. She went across the parking lot and stepped into the cavernous shed. The small windows high up beneath the rafters allowed in the late afternoon's golden light—dark shadows and beams of light in the finely dusted air alternating down through the giant wooden molds and long ribbands. But it was still fairly obscure.

She switched on the small bulb lighting, not bothering with the big floodlights Jack and Scott used while working. She then made her way gingerly in her light summer shoes across the sawdust strewn boards.

Her first impulse was to touch the shape of it. But she drew herself up suddenly with an impatient breath.

A small frown. Disciplining herself.

Yes, it is, she thought. This is a wonderful thing.

She glanced down the length of the clean, sharp-edged ribbands where they curved around the series of molds, defining the shape of the hull. With a faithful geometry the ribbands combed across the three-dimensional planes like plough furrows across a rolling field, converging at some far distance.

At some inward curves they disappeared with perfect regularity, first one and then another, some then to be rediscovered emerging from the other side of the curve seen between the ribbands. The internal curve no one would see when the hull became a solid plane.

This was what she had always wanted, to see this for herself at a quiet moment, to enjoy in peace her understanding of the perfection of the boat. With the sweeping lines open from both sides the hidden mathematical structure was for the moment caught in the open. She could feel as though she had discovered the underlying symmetry of reality there.

A passing fancy. But a pleasant one, and it had overtones of the discovery she dreamed of, the possibility of seeing the underlying structure to everything.

It was a metaphor, the naked three-dimensional curves and lines, perhaps of God, or of Truth. Here, a form made by simple men who she felt it important to think were also conscientious and kind, and dedicated to what they were building even if they did not understand the extent of how the form transcended their humble simplicity, their dedication and kindness.

Drawn suddenly, her hand went out instinctively to touch, stroking her hand lightly upon the grain of the wood. She stood near the thick stem where the heavy timbers of the keel curved up from below to her.

Her hand ran along the rabbeting grooves where the planks would be screwed in along its length, her fingers dancing there with a small tremor. The groove was perfect, sharply cut and clean, and her breath deepened. She leaned against the stem with her eyes closed, gripping it with both hands. Too beautiful to be real, let alone to touch. This gift which had sprung from the depths of her husband's heart, a projection of his soul mingling now with reality.

She had spent so much time trying to make it all clear in her mind. Yet the illusive truth of it still managed to escape her. She had tried to explain to Eric what it was to see living art being performed by men unconscious of what they were doing. Real art. And for once, her husband seemed to understand.

After the boathouse party he had mentioned something to her about the shape versus the reality. God only knew how it had ever occurred to him. But there it had been and she had been gratified, if not astonished, and secretly proud.

Of course, Eric was different from the others. Good as they might be, the others—Jack and Ellen, Catherine, Scott and that girl—could barely have a clue.

Deborah frowned. Especially that girl. So confident and pleasing, so ready to enjoy everything. Enthusiastic and, most probably, popular. And so utterly shallow.

Deborah suddenly flung her hand away from the stem of the boat with an impatient wave of despair and began walking slowly alongside the forms. That girlfriend of Scott's, the one with the strange name, was a perfect example of ignorance.

*How* she had gone on and on at the party about what she would have done with a boat like this one.

Sail it here, sail it there. Parties, endless parties. Live on it.

Every time Deborah had tried to even hint that there might be more to it, the girl had brushed it away, not able to even begin to understand, and would then continue, talking about all the other things she could do.

Not once could you detect the slightest presence of aesthetics, barring one little discussion concerning what the color scheme for the cabins would be.

Interior decorating. As though it were a house.

Well, to be honest … as transparent and simple as she had been, the girl had puzzled Deborah in one way: she could not see what in the world Scott saw in her. She was exactly the sort of girl Deborah had tried to stay far away from in school. Not loud, but opinionated and active. Never worrying about what she was going to say next, or who it was to, as though nothing she said would ever be taken amiss.

It rather pained Deborah, this evident—if dismissible—element of vulgarity brought in by one of the craftsmen. One would have said it was practically deliberate, an element of self-destruction.

In general, she thought, Scott was a likable, simple man, with polite eyes and a modest humor. A quality of artistic sympathy. Perhaps more than the sometimes unsubtle Jack, in a way, but ultimately in a lesser sense. Because the fact was, Scott didn't seem to be aware of … *it* … or else took it all so lightly. Where Jack had a smoldering awareness of things, readily seen in his brooding, troubled glances whenever he looked at the boat.

She thought about the two of them, and their relation to the boat. The differences were enlightening.

Scott loved his craft, and loved the materials as well as his tools. He had a way of bending to his concentration as he grooved a rabbet channel, planed a scarf or carefully bored a hole. His hands never left the surface of his materials, always carrying something, a drill or hammer, a finished piece of timber, or simply a waste scrap of wood he'd idly picked up. When he touched what he had created, she had seen the bonding there. He caressed his work.

Jack, though, tended to give his work a guiding, somewhat fretful squeeze as though it was a sort of companion with whom he was trying to coax toward better behavior, the necessity to follow certain ethics. Deborah agreed with that necessity. It was, as well, a sign of a higher plane of thought.

Of course, as professionals they were both perfectionists and produced exacting work, but from personalities sprang work habits.

Jack seemed to believe in things faster. He checked his measurements and adjustments less, going more on the faith of his calibrations, his artistic instincts, but then carrying out the actual work quite deliberately. Scientifically.

Scott, though, looked things over more carefully beforehand as though a hunter stalking his prey. But once he had made up his mind he executed things with a nonchalant degree of rapidity. Athletically. His comfort more in the action, where Jack was best at the calculation.

That, for Deborah, said it all. It was gratifying to her sense of the rightness that it was through Jack, in fact, that the project was taking shape.

There was a certain shape to men's destinies. Once you came to understand it, you could see why some men, like Jack, were in charge of their lives, where others simply responded.

As interesting as all that was on a minor scale, neither of those men, in the end, could really conceive of what they were doing. It was all too obviously true, Deborah thought once again, that the closer one is to the creative act, the less chance one has of fully understanding all the values of its creation. It was distance which truly supplied the beauty, as in a magnificent range of mountains. Up close, you just had stones and plants. Too close, all an artist could see was a vague shape within the swirling details.

A sudden insightful thought struck her, and she smiled. Oddly enough, an artist was obviously someone who basically didn't have a clue what it was they were doing or what was happening to them.

It was a sad thought, but a sad truth, and Deborah gave her head a shake. But as she did so, also discovered how she had been staring away at nothing there in the shop, almost like she'd been in a trance.

She gave a small laugh at herself, and glanced around the shop as though worried someone might have seen her like that. But the place was empty; and it had been that emptiness which had got her started on all these thoughts in the first place. Emptiness was at fault.

And then it struck her. Where, indeed, was everybody?

She looked down at her watch and sighed. Perhaps it was getting late. She still had dinner to plan and Eric wanted a small reception, drinks before dinner, and she would have to get prepared for that. Back, she smiled to herself, to the real world.

She went over and turned off the lights, taking one last appreciative look around, and then walked out of the shop. Funny how there wasn't a soul around, she thought as she closed the door. It seemed eerie. As if everyone had abandoned the place. She felt as though she had just visited a deserted fort or town where all the inhabitants have fled because of some cataclysmic event. A final attack, or pestilence.

"Oh, brother, Deb. Don't be so dramatic." she said aloud. Calling herself the name college friends had not been able to refrain from using, and which she now used against herself whenever she felt she had betrayed principles of good taste.

More than anything, she thought, this place needed to be above all the kitschy, mundane reflections one could apply anywhere, to anything.

No, leaving the quiet shop behind like that, empty and waiting, was more like the feeling of having just left a cathedral at the hour of closing.

That was better, she thought, and headed towards her car.

You have to watch yourself, she decided. It's one thing to try to slowly and painstakingly develop a personal philosophy. But to maintain it at all times in all places and around all people, was another. Even in the face of people you liked and respected for their own sense of integrity … a Jack or an Ellen, or a Scott or a Catherine. People who meant the best, in their own way.

But the deep truth was that sometimes you had to be a little selfish about your needs, even when you knew people were being generous. You had to tell a few lies, even around honest, simple souls. A small betrayal, in the short term, to keep yourself from a much larger treason in the long run.

As much as she enjoyed knowing them all, she knew she must never allow her thoughts to drift downwards, become crass. Not that these people were that, but when you placed them in comparison to her own ideals … well.

A lonely idea, she thought, and one that could almost make you feel guilty.

Except for the knowledge that it was the only way to keep some things pure.

In the end.

# Chapter 43

Ellen came back late that night and found the house dark. Jack had already turned in. But he wasn't asleep. When she went into their bedroom he called out.

"Hello," she said back.

"Have a good time?"

"So-so. You know Helen and Roy ...." She didn't want to talk about it.

"No big scenes, though."

She sighed, shrugging off her jacket.

For a while all Jack heard was the sound of running water, and then it stopped. She came out, clicking off the bathroom light, stepping blindly over to the bed and crawling in. He put his arms around her.

"Warm," she said.

"And you're cold."

"How was your day?"

Jack was ready for that sort of question, having already gone over several possible responses. He had built a few complicated ones, let them go, built them up again, and then let a few of them stay as though they had actually happened. Then definitely had let them go, in the end.

"Nothing much," he said.

"What'd you do?" she yawned, moving her cold feet between his.

A yawn wasn't a bad idea, so he made a long one for Ellen's sake.

"Oh, a little catch-up work. Did a few errands."

He rolled onto his back as though too tired to even hold her. She snuggled close to him, moving a leg across his, and placed her hand on his belly. Jack didn't move. She laughed.

"I suppose a few of those errands ended up over at Micky's."

Jack almost agreed, but caught himself. *That* would have been verifiable. "Yeah," he said sheepishly, "but not at Micky's."

"Figured something like that."

Jack chuckled at her.

Ellen stopped rubbing his stomach and moved her hand up upon his chest. It was late, after all.

"I suppose," she said, "there's plenty to do tomorrow."

"First load will be here at eight."

Jack heard her yawn again. He was relieved.

"Goodnight, honey."

Gradually, Ellen drifted off to sleep. Jack listened to her breathing go shallow and soft while he was thinking.

His immediate instincts about Catherine told him everything would be all right. There was a separateness about everything, a partitioning.

They had driven off from the boathouse separately, and had gone all the way around beyond Squalicum Harbor for lunch. He and Ellen almost never ate over there.

The fact was, it had all been incredibly exciting. Even in remembering it hours later, Jack felt himself move heavily again.

They had ordered so much, had felt such an overpowering appetite for everything, eating halibut and mussels, prawns and crab, and later, cherry and lemon pie with coffee. Sated, but still excited with each other, touching knees and exchanging breathless glances like a couple of kids, their bodies tugging at each other.

Then they got out of there, driving straight to her apartment on Sehome Hill.

He had left his pickup parked around on a back street, and walked around the block.

Being told he was the first visitor to her place, he had done his best to look at it carefully while both of them tried to compose themselves. Later, on reflection, he could still agree with his appraisal of her good taste. Her apartment had an abundance of comfort. A large, overflowing couch stood in the center of the living room, covered with a light-colored fabric of a flower and grass design. To sit on it was like dropping into a cloud. There were matching chairs by the bay window and on the polished oak floor between them and the couch lay an oriental rug of pale brick-reds and yellows. Opposite the big window was a fireplace, large and old fashioned with a mirror above. There were some prints and framed art posters hanging on the wall, a few large plants.

But it wasn't a simple room. On both sides of the room were two long, low, white-enameled bookshelves absolutely crammed with books. Hardbacks, paperbacks, stacks of magazines. Not at all a show library, the jumbled reading material gave the impression of tremendous activity. Books made any room complicated, and called for comment.

But at the time, the need for impressions, remarks, social pretensions of polite conversation, soon fled swiftly from his thoughts. As hers did as well, and there upon that couch in her living room they had at last taken hold of the excitement of each other, the pull of each other's body finally irresistible.

At first frantic, they were like two utter strangers, hurriedly taking as much as they could before it disappeared. But then, with the growing realization it was all safely there for them, that it would not go away, they slowed, and became deliberate, restoring the same tenderness they had shown each other before. Except this time, with a full knowledge of each other.

With appreciation as well as desire.

If that wasn't the definition of what love was supposed to be, he didn't know what was.

But if that was the definition, then it couldn't have been closer to the definition of what a mistake was all about, either.

Jack, laying now next to his wife, staring fixedly up into the darkness of their bedroom—had the excited cries of his mistress still ringing in his ears. Remembering it all. Sexual appetite for Catherine had drawn him in a blind rush across town, chasing her car as though a wild madness had possessed him. It had been electrifyingly obvious how she loved the act as much as the situation, herself. The amazing way she threw herself into a state of frenzied sexual stimulus and reception, the carnal desire for expanding the possibilities of arousal, all of which was deliberately kept in check beneath a quivering control of tenderness .... tenderness itself becoming a silent scream of pleasure.

Then she stopped them, and once again she had them there as she had had them before. A knot of something, he recalled. But where before it had been a knot of pure sex, it was suddenly something else—and they had remained like that until he could no longer help himself.

When they were finished, exhausted and breathless, they both knew they had crossed over to a place far beyond their original agreement.

Which, Jack thought, that was a hell of an understatement.

All he had to do was think of Catherine and it was immediately with longing and a poignant need.

What else could it be?

He loved her.

*God* ....

People talked about how impossible it was to know another person. How even the most consistent efforts might take years. It had been that way with Ellen. A forever of getting used to things.

With Catherine everything was an explosion of understanding.

It proved once and for all, Jack thought, that if people misunderstood each other, it was mostly deliberate. Human understanding was a lot closer to the surface. The total connections he had experienced that afternoon could easily be made. People evidently spent a great deal of their time avoiding making those connections. For control, for politics. For a million reasons.

Jack was amazed with the discovery, and delighted. But also very afraid.

Because of all the things he could see about it, the most obvious one was that something so complete between himself and Catherine, would be impossible to hide.

He floundered in that feeling for a while, but it was all too much and even that simply became a dull state of sensation. As though his body was laying there receiving encoded messages from the static silence of his bedroom, as if expecting something. But knowing, all along, there was nothing to expect.

Except the morning.

With that thought, he rolled upon his side, away from Ellen's deeply sleeping warmth, and went to sleep.

## Chapter 44

A FRIDAY in late November, Scott and Sydney went to one of the downtown bars popular with the college crowd. They stayed later than they'd planned. As the night wore on the music seemed to get louder and the air thicker. The ground itself seemed to be shifting beneath them the more time passed. Everything up in the air. The only things to remain constant was the consumption of beer and the argument that had loomed up over them like a bad dream.

Especially since it wasn't really the argument they were arguing about.

"I didn't say I wanted to live there," she said. "But with all the time we spend together ... I don't know. I should just have a key because coming and going is sometimes difficult now."

Scott sat back in his chair and gazed blurrily around at the crowd. The bar was long and narrow with a high ceiling and walls of naked brick hung with mirrors and glowing, neon beer signs. The band, a raw blues-rock and country band from the north of the county, was blasting away over the small dance floor. Already at high volumes, they were made piercingly louder by the narrowness of the bar and the hard acoustics of the brick walls.

He took a breath.

Nothing could make a guy feel older, he was thinking, than to go drinking in the perpetual riot of a college town bar.

It had been her idea. Which he'd gone along with without thinking about it. And which was now about the only thing he was thinking about. Having watched her, for the past hour or so, rejoining all her friends and letting herself rejoin, as well, the atmosphere of fun, as she had defined it for herself before they'd met. And as time went by, a voice, at first just a whisper, had become ever more insistent in his inner ear, asking him just what in the world he was getting himself into. Her life seemed to have nothing to do with his.

"What?" he said. He had heard her, but wasn't trying in the slightest to carry through.

He wasn't being fair and he knew it. But he also knew his sour mood wasn't because of any residues of resentment. He had gotten over the "fling". She had openly admitted it, and admitted it was a huge mistake. Getting swept up among her old friends and all and forgetting things had recently and rapidly changed.

Didn't he still, she'd asked, occasionally, forget himself too? Not being used to this, and all? And, anyway, they had gotten past that, hadn't they?

He had agreed and they'd gotten past all that.

But coming down to that bar, with the college crowd in there, and watching how easily she went back into it, was triggering something else now. What that was, he wasn't sure. Or, at least, it wasn't something he wanted to admit openly to himself: that he wasn't sure he could compete with her age group, and especially the college men, who had something to offer, other than youth, which he wasn't sure he could offer anymore: a future of large possibilities, of hope and opportunity. The worry that his future was all, now, in his past.

Everything about that bar just fed into the inner logic of his insecurities. Each wave of her chirping girlfriends coming to their table made him increasingly morose. Cynical and morose. Feeling older by the second. And it didn't help watching how easily and eagerly Sydney went into all that. As though he wasn't there.

"Hey, Sydney, how you doing," someone yelled through the music. A good looking boy approached, all confidence and swagger. He was suddenly in front of Scott and Sydney, hunching his shoulders decorously with his hands thrust into his trouser pockets.

If Sydney wasn't delighted, no one could have told by her face. She gave him a bright smile.

"Hi," she said.

He closed on the table and leaned across to talk in a more normal voice, although it was still loud enough.

"What's up with you?"

She knew him well enough, from parties and all, and had at one time found him amusing. Matt something. But he was no longer amusing, and in fact he now seemed incredibly rude ... not even looking at Scott, as though Scott wasn't even there.

Normally, Sydney, who considered social inclusivity a virtue, would have repaired the situation, introducing them. But, suddenly, and for perhaps the first time in her life, she realized there were some situations where instincts of friendliness and social cohesion were a waste of time in the face of a complete lack of manners.

"Not much, same as usual." she said.

Sydney, usually, never had to make an effort at developing social conversation. She was an attractive girl and the boys customarily supplied the rest. But here, it was now on purpose. Not surprisingly, though, Matt didn't notice the difference.

"Not dancing?"

Sydney didn't look directly at Scott, but from the edge of her vision he seemed relaxed enough.

"I'm resting."

A flashing smile.

"For what?"

Sydney could have killed the guy. Was Matt stupid, or what? There, sitting right next to her was, all too obviously, if not her boyfriend then her date for the evening.

And yet, Sydney couldn't help thinking how maybe there was something about Scott that made it so this guy wasn't worried about what might happen. It wasn't very flattering.

Matt laughed for some reason. "C'mon and dance, Sydney. I know you like it."

"No, thanks," Sydney said. She didn't know whether to look at him or Scott, but somehow knew it was less wise to look at Scott. "Maybe some other time."

Involuntarily, she now did glance at Scott.

There, she thought. She had just said no, and that should take care of it. And, as well, she suddenly felt better about the evening because she had figured out what had been bothering Scott. Just this sort of thing. Her college life, or some parts of it, that was.

She could see it now. As he had seen, and had been feeling. Their lives were now going somewhere else. Together.

All evening, Scott had been trying to tell her that. And she agreed now! She agreed. She wasn't all *that* much interested in hanging out in college bars, and letting her old life spring back to life. And she was sorry. It had been a miscalculation to think she could mix both worlds.

So now she just nodded, planning to get through the next half minute as diplomatically as possible.

Unfortunately for her Scott didn't give a damn about the next half minute, or her social ramifications, or his own for that matter. And certainly not for those of the guy in front of him who seemed to be pocketing Sydney's casual remark as though some sort of victory.

"Maybe some other time?" he said, just loudly enough to be heard.

Matt made a wry face. As though surprised to discover that Sydney's date for the evening, this lump of hamburger, not only had nothing interesting to say, but had no class. He gave Sydney a look saying, obviously, where did you dredge up this muscle-headed Friday paycheck?

"Okay, okay," he said to her. "Sometime later then, huh?"

Sydney wasn't thinking about Matt at all, now. Warned by Scott's remark, she was highly aware of how still his body had become. She realized there were things about Scott she hadn't learned yet. One of which was whether he was the sort of man who took the slightest excuse to make all hell break loose. She found herself nearly holding her breath, mentally urging Matt to leave.

And it seemed to work. Matt looked at Sydney and Scott thoughtfully for a moment, and then shrugged.

"Well, OK. I guess I'd better go see how they're doing at my table. I'll probably have to cart half of them home."

There was a moment of silence.

Then Scott said, "Good-bye."

Scott wasn't particularly bothered by Sydney's friend's presence, at least not as much as Sydney dreaded. But he wasn't amused, and even less so when he saw the boy, looking casually out into the bar, make a sudden sneer at the sound of Scott's voice. For what it was worth, Scott's insecurities about himself as far as Sydney was concerned was one thing, based as they were on his own perceptions about himself. But he wasn't going to accept any sort of judgement coming through the supercilious eyes of some college kid who didn't know him from Adam.

Matt, evidently not willing to be dismissed, gave a contemptuous shrug.

"I'm bored," he said.

Sydney saw a flicker of a smile on Scott's face and, for a blissful moment, thought that would be the end of it.

Then Scott suggested, with a quiet rasp, "Try suicide."

It wasn't loud, but there was no mistaking the tone, nor the open invitation.

Sydney couldn't believe her ears, and even felt an unaccustomed thrill, if you could call it that, of real fear. Expecting the worst.

But nothing happened. Matt didn't look at them, and didn't seem to have heard Scott. Although, for a moment, he didn't move, either. Then, suddenly, he smiled as though seeing someone, and even raised his hand in a wave. Sydney, on a reflex, looked in that direction but couldn't see anyone in the crowd looking back. Matt walked away.

Sydney looked out at the crowd as though nothing had happened. When she finally looked back at Scott, she found him looking back at her. They gazed at each other for a moment and, suddenly, broke out in grins, finding themselves smiling at each other for the first time that evening. Scott winked.

Sydney chuckled in relief. "I can see you're thinking again."

It was true. Scott was indeed suddenly thinking a number of things.

One being about the lessons of life ... and how more often than not we learn what to do from what we shouldn't have done. And certainly not from the stupidity of good advice, which nobody wants anyway.

"And which is impolite, even ..., " he mumbled, as though she'd been reading his thoughts. Which of course she hadn't.

"What?" she said.

"Nothing. Just a thing about how we figure out how things work by doing the things that don't."

"Yeah, right?" she agreed.

"We're not coming back down here anymore."

"Not for a long time," she agreed again. "No."

There was a moment of silence, then Scott said, "I guess I'd better find the spare key."

"That too."

## Chapter 45

At nine in the morning, Eric sat in his office, waiting and looking out over Bellingham. The December sky was one big gray cloud, cold and ominous, but Eric's thoughts were nowhere near the weather conditions.

Bill Hartman of Hartman and Associates of Los Angeles was back in town and Eric hadn't seen or heard from that little bulldog of a man since the summer before. Not that there had been any reason why he should have. He and Hartman were competitors. Their previous discussion, about Fairhaven, had simply contained a small kernel of mutual possibilities.

Eric had no idea what Hartman and Associates were going to propose for the Fairhaven shoreline. He knew, however, they had been doing their homework; and what Hartman would say would now be based on what he had learned about Eric's position. Mostly, that morning, Eric had been thinking about whatever it might be that Hartman might have found out.

At nine-thirty sharp, Eric's secretary ushered Hartman into the office.

Anyone meeting Hartman for the first time didn't really notice the receding hairline or his heavy jowls. All they would see was the thin, grimly-compressed mouth and hard, direct eyes. Especially the eyes.

Eric knew top-level corporate types by heart, the CEOs, presidents, vice-presidents, general managers, and all of them approximated the thing he saw before him. But Hartman's eyes made a difference. Corporate presidents never looked as though they were trying to find anything out. Smoothly cagey. They seemed as though they already knew everything and it was up to everyone else to prove them wrong. Hartman didn't seem to care. His eyes were questioning and sharp, and as he began outlining his proposal, Eric had to stifle a smile at his personal predicament.

There were two other men in Bellingham with about the same stature of Eric, and long ago whatever there was to be cut up, had been. In the world of local business, if it were diagrammed like a food chain in nature, Eric and the two others would have been at the top with no natural enemies. The threat, therefore, could only come from the outside. It was a very serious morning for Eric. He pointed to the sofas, and they sat down facing each other.

Hartman wasted no time, and hid very little ... launching directly into his introductory remarks.

He knew a great deal about Sumners' company and so in describing his own, only explained those areas which had any relevance.

Hartman's was a high turnover network specializing in the redevelopment of commercial property. Their main emphasis was to pinpoint sectors of outdated or unused property which had fallen through the cracks, as he put it. Peripheral property he liked to call dormant, which if left as it was, would eventually be assimilated into other uses—at best a real estate shelter, at worst residential.

They located these dormant properties as time changed the face of towns and cities, land use shifting from one sector to another as the town's configuration logically followed new needs for efficiency. Which was what happened often enough in western towns where original settlements were found to be, with time, not the best organization of use.

Like for Bellingham ... where, when the original settlement at Fairhaven towards the southern end of the bay slowly became obsolete, industry had moved north around the bay. Sliding out around towards the Lummi Reservation which, unfortunately, would have been the best place for residences. That, of course, not to be regretted. Just a detail of history to be worked around.

Hartman wrangled cheap, and resold upon three scenarios: reconditioned for redevelopment, which meant bulldozing everything flat; rezoned into entirely different use, which meant parceling off lots to the highest bidders; or packaged. Hartman liked packaging the best. That scenario gave him two options.

The first one was that after reconditioning with his bulldozers, he drafted a redevelopment plan which met all local and state regulations. Thus armed with a potential redevelopment, he could sell it to those who liked the idea and liked how time was saved buying the entire package—the naked land, the plans, the environmental impact statement and other regulatory details—all in one neat bundle.

Or, in the second, Hartman could sell the property to those who hated the package and wanted to forestall the development.

253

Often as not, it was the second case which generated the most money. By going somewhat public with the plans, horrified townspeople would often force local legislatures into committing matching local funds to surpass outside bidders.

There was one last scenario though which Hartman held in private reserve. He could go ahead and develop the project himself. That, of course, meant a lot of good credit standing.

Eric knew that not only did Hartman have a lot of credit momentum, but in fact could pull off any but the largest project by himself. At one time, Hartman and Associates had self-financed two skyscrapers from the ground up. A frightening, white-knuckle thing to do. Rumor had it that Bill Hartman had done it as a stunt. Whether to prove something to himself, or to everyone else, didn't matter. Because he had pulled it off. That had been fifteen years back. A young Turk testing his power. The end result was that if Hartman was talking business, there was no danger of bluffing.

His company now, as always, preferred short-term projects. Two to five years maximum, mostly in the Southwest—Arizona, New Mexico and Southern California. But they had several long term developments in Tampa, New Orleans and Brownsville and, most recently, in Portland, Oregon.

The Northwest, despite its recession-vulnerable dependence on lumber, was the new mother lode for developers who were scrambling for toeholds. Hartman had been fortunate and had got in early, making a few, oddly far-seeing investments back in the bad old days in the years after Boeing's had crashed and taken the entire region with it. It was boom time now, though. Seattle, quite naturally, was the prime targeting area. A great deal of short-term development was muscling its way around, jamming up permits processing and raising a political ruckus, looking, for all the world, like a supermarket sweepstakes.

But though Hartman considered the mad rush for land amusing, he had very quietly taken a look at the area. He saw how compact it was, how natural rail and water linkages meant there was no place which could be considered on the periphery. Which caused him to look beyond Seattle at the smaller ports.

He had looked at Tacoma, and Everett. The first had a great harbor and bay, but a terribly located city center. The second was basically an overdeveloped beach. Then he had discovered the Bellingham-Fairhaven situation. Everything he could have hoped for was there: a bay with a well-protected port, the closest access to the sea lanes out in the Strait of Juan de Fuca, and best of all an inconspicuous city government.

Less meddling and infighting. Less scandal. Rather unimaginative and unambitious.

In a short time his company had spent a lot of effort studying the town. And in the end, the situation at Fairhaven was the natural choice.

It was an old town, out of the way at the south end of the bay. In those days, there was little left except for a few half-empty brick remnants a half a mile up from the waterside that the locals were having declared historic, constantly working to get developers interested in rebuilding.

Hartman always found humorous the concept of "historic districts". Although he could almost see where he could make that work for him, this time around.

"We have a duo-fold proposal, showing both public and commercial aspects," Hartman said. "I've left a set of plans with your secretary for you to look at later. But I think it's simple enough to describe it right now as a multi-use convention center with a yacht basin and a docking facility for passenger and container cargo ship handling."

He paused, letting all that sink in.

Eric said nothing. Anyone else telling him something like that, he would have laughed out loud. It was that preposterous. But this was Bill Hartman.

Hartman nodded, and continued.

"The container handling is the real commercial aspect, and so the bigger problem. This is a strange area of the country. The voters crush any legislation which might limit individualized development—you can build two hundred used-car lots and fast food restaurants side by side right through the best agricultural land in the Puget Sound. But the moment a developer comes in with a single, solid package for any one particular spot, and if there is the slightest whiff of heavy-weight business about it, the same voters scream rape. But we think we've got this one solved. The problem with container handling is the storage."

He pointed out of Eric's window there overlooking downtown Bellingham, towards the distant Fairhaven.

"You wouldn't be able to park a thousand containers anywhere down near the Fairhaven waterside, even though there is quite a bit of room where the old docks and the old streets of the town down there used to be. For one thing, there's a bit of a slope. And for another it would be too visible from that historic part up higher, especially if they get it all rebuilt it with specialty shops, apartments and offices, like they've begun doing about. The local housewives won't want to be sitting up there drinking their high-priced espressos looking out over a container handling yard. Even if it did mean jobs. And anyway, it would eventually get too cramped, throwing blue collar industry and white collar office building development in each other's' faces like a dog's dinner. Like what happened down in Tacoma."

He looked back at Eric.

"But what is great is the old rail spur running around the bay, up from Seattle, straight along Fairhaven's waterfront and up around to Bellingham's waterfront and beyond. Completely out of the way. We were astonished it hadn't been torn out."

Eric nodded. He had to admire how well Hartman had come to understand the lay of the land. But surprised as he was, he was even more so as Hartman continued.

"Of course, there is no other shorter way the railroad could have come up here. If they had to, they could send trains the long way around, another thirty miles or so from down at Marysville, around to Sedro-Woolley and up through that valley back there and then around back to Bellingham. But they didn't. And are we ever lucky. Because it means we can put a dock and some cranes down there, but everything gets loaded on flatcars and hauled around to the other side of the bay where there's room. And what do we have?"

He paused, but not for effect. Hartman never did anything for effect. He wanted to gauge whether Eric was beginning to see how good it was. Satisfied, he went on:

"It's an existing, port authority right-of-way from here. It was never rescinded. That's what's so great, and it was the reason I thought this was so interesting last summer. Can you imagine what mountains would have to be moved, what butts we'd have to kick, to get a right-of-way recreated, or just created? And here we are, sitting on an unused gold mine. We put a spur up to the track, and we can shift the containers around the bay, and the whole thing dressed up for the voters as a pretty little yacht basin, convention center. Put in even more specialty shops. Just have to raze all that punky, existing property flat."

Hartman spread his hands. "There's even a little wedge of waste land running along the shore, cut off by the railroad and impossible to develop. So," he smiled, "we'll make a park out of it to make the local tree-huggers happy." He smiled. "Funny, when I was a kid, parks were always in the middle of the best of everything. Nowadays, a new park means land nobody can do anything with."

Eric could only stare at him.

It was incredible, he thought. The man knew it all as though he'd spent his entire life in the area. Geography, even down to the name of backwater towns. Economics. Commerce. As well as the arcane rights-of-way conditions.

The only thing he hadn't mentioned was politics, but Eric could imagine he was well-versed in that as well.

He pursed his lips, knowing he was expected to now say something. Show some interest or, at the very least, that he was impressed.

With a thin smile he said, "would you like a coffee?"

# Chapter 46

WHILE THE coffee was coming, Hartman made as though he had a call to make and wandered over to a far window to talk to someone. It was to Eric a chance to gather his thoughts.

With the coffee finally laid before them, Hartman sat back down on the sofa. Eric hunched over the table, poured two coffees, and offered the sugar bowl which Hartman didn't take.

"I think you've got the right idea there," Eric said. "The county commission has a very localized outlook, and the situation is stable politically. True, the commission seems like musical chairs. Voters up here are small-town provincial, as you might imagine. Emotional. They make every election seem like a bar-room brawl. They like to lose their tempers and feel they're voting the bastards out, all the time, although you couldn't tell one commission in the past thirty years, from the next."

Hartman was nodding, and Eric expanded on the theme.

"All that makes for a pretty careful bunch over there at the county building, resisting efforts by local, radical parties. The city is another thing, there could be some holdouts in the mayor's office. He's visible with the university people and has a few people around him who are up to their necks with that crowd—they have to be. One of the trustees runs the newspaper."

"I thought it was part of a group," Hartman said.

Eric shrugged. Hartman's hadn't been a question, and went on with his outline of the area.

"It's a quirky town, all right, but it's a one-newspaper town, and you'll find it no surprise that the paper won't start any public push until everything has been politically sewn-up. We show how public opinion will go for it, and they'll steamroll it for us."

Hartman, who never chuckled at things he didn't agree with, chuckled.

Eric felt comfortable. He liked all this, and could see that as big as all this was, it was possible. They were now both sitting back deep into their respective sofas, looking at each other across the coffee table, and Eric momentarily luxuriated with the prospect of

258

what had to be easily one of the biggest opportunities, biggest chances, he had ever had come his way. Maybe the biggest, period. Golden. But even as he was enjoying the moment, there was one nagging little problem suddenly in the back of Eric's mind.

Despite all the talk and how obvious it was things could start moving, for the first time in his life Eric was in the strange position of being aware of a flitting guilt. A sort of wayward scruple, based on actually knowing people who were in the direct path of a proposed development site. Meaning: bulldozers. People whose worlds would be buried beneath the projected commercial marina, convention center and container handling facility.

To put it simply: people who, unless they were land owners, would never profit in any way from that development. Or to put it brutally: people who were going to get screwed.

There was only one stretch of Bellingham which could possibly support the project, and smack in the middle of it all sat Colby Boatbuilding.

It wasn't good knowing people who could be affected when property development and a positive political climate came together on a project. It could be, perhaps, very expensive trouble.

Eric looked at Hartman, who was now checking some emails on his phone—another polite gift of silence—and felt a sudden worry.

He would have to check, knowing the size of what Hartman was now proposing. There would have to be a necessary and covert research on the Fairhaven land titles.

He wondered if Hartman perhaps already knew something about his connection to people down there.

Eric was suddenly suspicious. Hartman was too thorough not to know, and hadn't said anything. Which was strange, because no developer worth his salt permitted connections which could result in speculation accusations. Insider information, however it came.

That was the old-school way of doing business, of course, anointed since time immemorial up there in that land of land-grabbing lumber barons. But times had changed and even politicians got skittish. County councils and commissions got worried, and let off the lease like a pack of dogs those bureaucratic mechanisms which could bring everything to a screeching halt.

Did Hartman know of his connection? Was it something he might use somehow to reduce Eric's position? It didn't seem possible, but one never knew. It was easy to sideline partners on the very hint that there could be a conflict of interest. People knowing people who could eventually know. Eric had done it himself. It was time to find out.

"So," he stated flatly as soon as Hartman was finished with his cellphone, "what are the lessors like?"

For a second, Hartman's eyes narrowed. Then, with a nod of his head, he accepted the invitation to get down to specifics.

"In fact," he said, "we've got all but two pinned down. We've got two local, and another down in Seattle. And we've got two more out-of-state. Houston and New York. This one …," he pointed at a large property cut into sections, one of which included Clyde Moore's marina, "the Houston one, we think we can close the negotiations next week with a ninety-day positive notification clause if the project falls through. Otherwise, we think it will all go like dominoes once we get the big one."

It was rough play, even as far as Eric was concerned. But not unusual. It meant that the project proposal could be all but on committee tables at the county seat before anyone down at the shore got their first notice.

Or the newspaper caught wind of it.

Everything, if it got set up right, could trip exactly like Hartman's dominoes. So fast that no one could try to outbid or even out-think it.

Very rough. Very professional.

But it still didn't answer Eric's other worry.

"And the others?"

"Just a stretch of beach running along the trunk line to the south of the bay."

Eric was surprised. "Really? That *isn't* railroad right-of-way?"

Hartman, up to then all business, suddenly grinned.

"Believe it or not, this is one of those old lady stories. A Bellingham woman has still got the family deed, and that deed has a history running back to a British naval survey two hundred years old. Nice, huh? Anyway, she's plenty willing it seems, and the lease has a provision for discretion."

Eric's eyes widened in open amazement. Hartman smiled, almost apologetically for how outlandishly lucky that was.

"It seems one of our representatives managed to sweep her off her feet."

Eric, to make himself seem unconcerned, poured them some more coffee. No more beating about the bush. He addressed the crux of his worries.

"What about the land at the bottom of the bay road?"

"That's the New York lease." Hartman took his cup and nodded again, easily, now directly addressing the issue about the land parcels crowded under and around the Colby's.

"That's been in the bag for three months ... except for a leasing clause for the present business property improvements buyout. I guess there have been a few, which is too bad. Just time on their part, but the cost won't be much. One thing though, this place, a boatbuilder's, has a negotiable clause for releasing, which—it has to be admitted—could be a problem. Because I guess the guy has the option to go for a long-term lease any time he wants. Or even buy it. Tomorrow, for example."

Hartman shrugged while Eric eyed him with unconcealed intensity. And then went on:

"That would obviously be a problem for us down the line. As it stands though, the way I understand it, the boatyard owner has been very reluctant about long-term leases, and has repeatedly rejected the idea of buying it. The New York owners, up to now, didn't mind. It's a drop in the bucket for them. Or, I should say, it was."

"They won't warn the guy?"

"Why should they? We've taken every precaution and they are unaware of any other movements. We've made them, for now, only suddenly interested in unloading the whole package: as things stand, and as they understand things. We've made a very attractive offer for the entire property, and not bit by bit. Which means taking over all leases and clauses. Becoming our problem, only. So it's in their interest to keep the status quo long enough for us to take over, and then let us deal with the business owner's contract."

He looked up at Eric, but there was still no sign of hidden knowledge.

"It's a little chancy," he went on, "but we've also got a very short notice clause to work with. Basically, once we retain the property, it would be like pulling the rug out from under the owner of that boathouse. He would have to decide to re-lease or buy, and come up with the financing so fast that I doubt he would, based on his previous refusals. Or whether he even *could* do it. From what I understand, he's not in debt, like his neighbors, but he has no bank rating at all. Not at all acute for business, let alone ambitious. Last notice, he's got nothing going on worth a dime down there. So, in effect, I think we can safely say we've got all these pieces tied up. As

I said, all we'll have to do is scrape whatever is on it, off."

Simple as that. And what was more, it was now obvious Hartman had absolutely no idea of any connection between Eric and Jack Colby.

And, amazingly, nobody from Hartman had been down there lately to see how things had changed.

But, suddenly, Eric realized there had never been anything really to worry about in the first place. Jack Colby, indeed, could present a huge problem for Hartman, and Eric eventually. Colby, getting wind of the project, could buy the land and then hold out for some astronomical price permitting all the lands to be conglomerated. Hartman, if he'd had even the slightest idea that Eric had the power to hold, either by himself or through a surrogate, that sort of knife across his throat, would never have walked into his office to outlay the project, openly, in the first place.

Eric would have been identified and relegated by Hartman's team to those local interests needing to be worked around. Meaning: kept in the dark. Right from the start.

Eric gazed out the window across town towards the Fairhaven waterfront to the south. As he did so, he realized suddenly how everything down there would soon enough be gone, one way or the other, whether Hartman's project was picked up or not. The land was too valuable not to be reworked eventually. There was a law of nature about these things.

Eric's mind was made up. If he could manage it, he was in.

"Who else knows about this, here in town?"

Hartman took a sip of coffee. And took his time doing it.

"Well, the port commissioner had a conference with us. No details. Off the cuff. He's very safe, and sees how this could help him in the next reshuffle. Then, as I said, there are the local property owners. But all that is individually handled. There is no idea of the size of the buyout so for the moment I think we've cut speculation off at the root."

"Anyone else ready to jump in with their own proposal?"

"No way. I only have five people on my staff, two on the ground, who know anything at all about this. And I have total faith in them."

Eric stared at Hartman's complacent smile, lingering with curious reflections on how such a man would guarantee himself loyalty. But at the same time, he felt another surge of the earlier happiness sweep over him. It was an incredible opportunity and he fitted perfectly as a very necessary part of it. Hartman was powerful, but not enough to pull the whole thing together alone. Eric was the only developer in the area who could gather the strings quickly enough to fit Hartman's hit-and-run tactics. In the end, it was like a gift.

There would be the one-time profit for Hartman off the project sale, but all the long-term benefits would be left, like table scraps, to Eric. But what table scraps! A tie-in with the oil people, a share in commercial waterfront property, a future stake in an industrial port, and most of all: political benefits he could pick up like fallen apples.

If Eric had any naïve wistfulness or personal concerns about his own connection with those people down there, they were gone completely.

Of course, thinking the unthinkable, if he was only interested in turning a quick and dirty, if extremely sizeable, profit, he could betray Hartman, becoming his main obstacle, by convincing Jack to let him, Eric, take over his lease. At the same time, his payoff would be huge, and he'd save Jack from getting thrown out on the street. More than that, he'd put Jack in the position to even improve his current business situation, because even a small timer would know how to leverage a comfortable windfall from such a situation.

But that would be a penny ante victory in comparison with all the other benefits.

As far as the personal side with those people down there, it was all very well and good to befriend or want to help people, but there was also a point where that was simply puerile.

"Very good, Bill. Very good. I'll look the plans over tonight and get back to you. It doesn't need to be said—but I will anyway—that I can assure you that no one else will see them."

They went straight up to the restaurant afterwards for a quick brunch. From time to time as they chatted Eric would glance off across town to where he could see, even at that distance, the bright red roof of Jack Colby's place. As well, he could see the white blurs of Clyde Moore's boatyard ... almost in a direct line over the top of Colby's to where he was sitting in the Bellingham Tower.

Dominoes, he thought at one point, indeed. Almost like fate. Like a wave of fate, coming in relentlessly.

And as well, like fate, the simple truth: when you had things over people, try as you might, you usually kept getting even more over them.

# Chapter 47

THE LAST thing Jack would have been thinking about at that exact moment would have been of Eric and the world of big development and finance. He was in one of the worst depressions he had known.

He was sitting beside Scott in the kitchen at the boatworks making an early lunch of sandwiches. No one else was around. Ellen and Catherine were having lunch with each other somewhere in town. Lately, they had been doing a lot of that, a suddenly blossoming friendship.

Jack wasn't worried. He was also worried to death. A strange mixture he couldn't straighten out.

He didn't worry about Catherine and what she might say. She had too much at stake as well. But God knew, it made him feel queasy.

There was also the mortification of realizing for the first time what every man with a mistress eventually realizes: that he shares more secret knowledge with his mistress than with his wife.

The thing was, Catherine wasn't really even a mistress.

He wasn't keeping her, wasn't necessarily in love with her to the point he wanted her for always. Although there was, somewhere in there, some sort of shared emotional equality—a sameness—with the feelings he had for his wife.

He saw Catherine was very happy. As Ellen was happy.

He glanced over at Scott for a second. Even Scott seemed happier.

Everybody was happy, he thought. Just so goddamn happy, and that was exactly what was making him feel so miserable.

Scott noticed the glance, but didn't look back. Given that Jack wasn't exactly a stoic, Scott had noticed the undertow of gloom, and had been wondering about the cause.

Some people ... he thought. They've got it all, or at least a lot of what they should normally be happy about. And yet it wasn't enough.

Who knew what the hell it could be, this time ...?

Scott thought back over the past week or so, trying to remember if anything had gone particularly wrong. Or even a bit sideways. But he couldn't see it. The work was advancing, and what they were building, in all ways, was perfect. Elegant and precise. Deborah Sumners hadn't launched any particular inanities which were any more beyond the pale than normal. Material for the project came in exactly on time and when needed, thanks to Catherine. Ellen said the cash flow had never been better. Even the work on fishing boats down at the far end of the shed was ticking right along. And as for himself, he hadn't remembered a time when he'd found himself getting along so well with Jack. Not one snide comment, no grating exchanges. They'd been downright chummy.

There seemed no reason at all for whatever was causing such a deadened look on Jack's face.

Of course, he thought, the guy was a natural pessimist. If things weren't bad, they were bound to be.

But even with that, he didn't always go around like this, looking like Walking Death.

Scott grabbed a sandwich off the plate and gave Jack a long look. Despite himself, looking at the sourpuss there, he had to finally grin. But he decided he should ask Jack if he was all right. It seemed the correct thing to do.

"So tell me, what the fuck is the matter with you?"

Jack, caught off guard, looked quickly over at Scott. He hadn't realized it was visible.

"There's nothing the matter with me."

Scott nodded as though he'd learned something important.

"Oh … okay. Sure."

Jack eyed him for a second. "Come on …," he said.

"Come on yourself."

Jack didn't answer, but his face showed he was thinking a lot of things. And suddenly, where before Scott had felt it could be helpful to offer his ear, now he didn't want to know. This much resistance, it was bound to be screwy.

"Hey, whatever," he said equably. "Whatever you want. You don't want to talk about it, don't. You want to walk around looking like the end of the world, that's your business. As long as it *is* only your business. Didn't have anything to do with me, for instance."

"I'd tell you if it ever did."

"Would you?"

"Of course."

Scott looked at him for another moment, calmly, but then went back to his sandwich.

"OK. But you do look a little down in the dumps, anyway."

"I'm not down."

Scott couldn't laugh with his mouth full, so he could only snort.

"If you're not," he said between chews, "you sure do a good imitation of how to fool people into thinking you're not happy. So, what are you? So happy it embarrasses you? With how bad you look, then, you must be the happiest fucker on earth."

Scott was able to finally swallow, and then laughed.

Jack glared at Scott, who had his elbows planted on the edge of the table, one hand dangling a half-eaten tuna and egg sandwich, a huge grin on his face. Jack suddenly had the uncomfortable realization that, if anything, Scott was as close a thing to a best friend that he had.

For whatever that was worth.

Which wasn't very much.

Because one would think that, normally, a friend was someone you could hash over the difficult things with. But this thing … it could be hashed over with nobody.

Scott's not knowing was as important as Ellen's. So he was just stuck with it.

But, at the same time, he could also see he was going to have to watch the way he looked. Evidently, if even Scott could pick up on it, anybody could.

He was being much too obvious. An enormously dangerous thing. And, yet again, another thing to worry about.

He turned back to his own sandwich.

"There's nothing. Drop it."

"Really?"

"Really."

But Jack could see that wouldn't do. His bad mood had to be explained somehow, or else it would just cause questions to sit around, creating other questions.

"Really," he said again. "It's no big thing. I guess I just sometimes let myself get to thinking too much. And in this case, there's nothing to talk about. Just something to figure out that has nothing to do with anything that's going on from day to day. As soon as I figure it out, I'll let you know. You know how it goes. Sometimes you need to figure things out on your own, from soup to nuts."

"Yeah," Scott said. That, in fact, was a true thing. "I know what you mean. Sometimes we don't even have the words to describe what we're thinking."

Jack nodded.

"That's right. And that's exactly it. And as soon as I do, like I said, I'll tell you."

Jack turned back to his lunch, seeing out of the corner of his eye Scott nodding as well.

Which was fine. For now.

If he had been alone, he would have sighed. But he didn't and just turned his attention to his own sandwich.

And to wondering what the hell he could come up with, what the hell he could ever say. That wouldn't seem contrived.

When, suddenly, his whole world seemed contrived.

## Chapter 48

THEY SET up a large old boiler by the forge and by doing some plumbing made it possible to maintain its water level by way of the house water supply. From the boiler ran another pipe, large and insulated, to carry steam to the four steam boxes. They made the steam boxes about twenty feet long and a little more than two feet square, piled up and forming what looked on the end like four pigeonholes, with doors. At intervals along the sides holes were bored for iron rods which would support and keep apart the ribs to be steamed. Each box could steam sixteen ribs.

It took five hours to steam the four and a half inch timbers of white oak. It was beautiful wood, perfectly straight-grained. The lumber supplier back east was experienced with boat lumber—at the specification for rib material, instead of just cutting up logs to the correct shape, had split the logs first to get a flat, straight-grained edge to cut from.

By necessity, it was fast work. Even if a rib had been in the steam box for hours it cooled quickly and returned to its original, formidable strength, impossible to bend.

With all speed and wearing heavy gloves Scott would pull a hot rib from the steam box and carry it to where Jack was waiting inside the ribbanded hull mold. Jack would pull it inside, score a line using a pre-set adjustable square, cut the end to the angle it would mate to the keel, and then jam the rib's end down into the place made for it. While he was doing so, Scott would clamber up and over to join him inside and they would pull back on the rib like springing a big, steaming-hot bow and push it over against the ribbands, forcing it against the curve. Scott would loosely clamp the rib in place while Jack climbed up with a heavy wooden mallet to give the top end of the rib a solid whack, forcing it to lay tight against the ribbands all the way down to the keel and forever wedding it to its destined bend as an upcurving boat rib.

Setting ribs was both hectic and slow work, with their frantic exertions forcing them to pause between each emplacement. But there was never any real resting. They were constantly checking earlier ribs. When cooled, the ribs were temporarily screwed to the ribbands and their clamps removed. As slowly as the work went, gradually the spaces between the big molds were filled up by the true ribs and suddenly, at last, the real boat's hull was now being built. Up to that point Scott had not been able to share much of Deborah's insistence that they were creating a work of art. But there daily, as more of the ribs went in, steam hanging heavy and warm around them in the cool December air, he began to appreciate her point of view. After a while, even Jack had to agree there was something to it.

Of course, they hadn't been immune to the beauty of boats. To work on boats is to love them in some way. It had always been the working of the wood, though, and the care and fitting of the different pieces which had been the main appeal. Suddenly though, simply from Deborah's persistent presence in the shop, a presence itself a tribute to unearthly beauty more than to her continual aesthetic insistence, they began to feel they were making something that was much more than what had been originally conceived.

Deborah would sit by one wall in an old armchair they had brought in for her and she would read, or write in a little notebook, but mostly she would watch the progress, entranced, as though watching a performance in a theater. Jack had felt amazed, when not irritated, at how anyone could sit and watch someone else working without getting bored. For himself, that sort of passivity would have made him feel nervous.

She was something like a cheerleader now, as well. Delighted each time Jack or Scott calculated and notched the bottom of the rib to set itself so cleanly down upon the corner of the keel when the bending was completed. She even clapped as they strained to bend the thick oak ribs and then wallop them into place. It got to be a ritual, each rib set was like yards gained on a football field. Jack and Scott, even in the midst of the hot, furious activity found themselves grinning every time they set a new one in place.

"This is the way to work," Scott said. "Every working man would love to have all this appreciation."

Jack nodded. "If he could stand it."

"I suppose it depends on who's doing the appreciation."

They both looked over at Deborah and without realizing the other was doing it, winked at her.

In spite of all the years of avoiding innuendo, or even the most light-hearted allusions to sex, Deborah found herself smiling back.

269

What was more, she found she enjoyed it, because they liked her. Suddenly it didn't bother her at all that they might imply they liked her even better because she was a woman.

"I can't see either of you being self-conscious about your work," she returned brightly, liking them back and wanting to flatter them as well.

Jack, although he wouldn't have admitted it even to himself, was indeed flattered. He took on an impassive air.

"Truth is, I typically prefer to work alone. Especially on things that aren't routine. Trial and error is boring to watch. Or maybe even embarrassing."

He smiled at her suddenly, and genuinely. He liked the feeling of explaining something about his work that was normally so intrinsic and arcane it wasn't seen. It was flattering, even. And seeing she looked truly interested, he continued, although now with a different inspiration. He realized he wanted to actually impress her.

With something.

"The trouble with working alone is nobody ever sees the trouble you take and how it takes a lot of ingenuity. That's the best part of work, and what makes it fun. All anyone sees is what is finished and maybe they like it if it's well done. But not in the same way as the person who built it. In the way that each piece of it represents a little victory."

As he was speaking, he felt how Scott was looking at him. Jack knew he was out-and-out copying the way Scott talked about things. But he didn't care. Why shouldn't he be able to have the same feelings? Even if he didn't usually bother with it? Scott didn't have a monopoly on philosophic depth around there.

Of course, Deborah didn't know much about that. She had never really been around Scott enough to know what he was capable of saying at times. So, and even though he knew he was stealing Scott's lines and making no friend in doing so, he knew he would also get away with it. Wicked, true. But for some reason it made him feel good.

"That's wonderful!" Deborah said, her eyes glistening.

None of what was transpiring was lost on Scott, but he knew there was nothing to be done about it. Despite that, he couldn't help taking a shot at Jack.

"Yeah," Scott said, looking carefully away from Jack to Deborah. "It's great to be recognized for being a genius. Even if you aren't."

Deborah felt irritated by Scott's attempt to make light of Jack's statement. Even though, she supposed, it was the normal reaction people have in the face of sincerity. Scott, of course, would always have the normal reaction well at hand. But this wasn't the normal situation. Nobody else was watching or judging. She felt his efforts to pull away from Jack's deep feelings distasteful.

"You feel that way?" Deborah said to Jack, ignoring Scott as politely as she could.

She had never expected either of them to have much of a developed idea of the psychology of work, and she now waited for a response with a tranquil look on her face. She knew she had to have inspired some of this. It was possibly a direct result of her being there.

A gratifying thought.

Here was Jack, for the first time, expressing these feelings. Perhaps even feeling them for the first time, as thoughts. She felt oddly pleased with the idea, and slightly amused.

It must be the feeling, she told herself with a little smile, that a mother hen must have. She raised her eyebrows in expectation.

"Of course," Jack said. "So, you see now, why it is so nice to have you here. It's nice to show off to beautiful ladies."

Deborah's heart sank. It couldn't have been a more disappointing thing for Jack to say. She might have expected such a thing from Scott, the tradesman. From Jack though, it seemed awful.

Then she let it pass. Because she could understand.

Deep down, she felt there were qualities hidden within Jack that they both shared. She was convinced that artists of any sort, because they were people with more highly developed sensitivities, were bound to be a little shy. She would never have mentioned that to Jack, of course. She was much too intelligent and sensitive, herself, to point out something painful in another. She knew all about her own painful shyness and how it often brought her to the brink of saying embarrassing things if only to try to make contact with other people. So she could forgive Jack's blunderbuss of a remark. Obviously, he had gone back into concealment.

As for the other ....

Scott was laughing, or at least his face was. Which didn't surprise her. He, of course, would be insensitive to Jack's feelings.

But worse, he obviously wanted to rub salt in his employer's wounds. She felt herself sigh inwardly in frustration. What he said didn't surprise her, either ... the coward: making fun of fine

271

natures.

"We all just love to be appreciated," he said. She saw his face go serious. "I was just about convinced for a few seconds that imitation, indeed, was the sincerest form of flattery. But now I'm thinking that nothing beats pure flattery."

He seemed to be fumbling for a second, frowning as he thought about something. Obviously, Deborah thought, he was realizing what an ass he was being. His next words, though, proved even that wrong.

"But in any case," he went on, "it doesn't matter. I guess any form of appreciation is better than none at all, sometimes. And we take what we can get, whether we deserve it or not."

"We deserve it," Jack said bluntly.

Scott gave him an open, cheerful look. "I can't argue with that."

She remarked how there seemed the hint of a knowing leer in his eyes. It was a shame that such a craftsman could be so repugnant sometimes. She smiled back at him as well. There were larger things to consider, and she wouldn't let them be spoiled or derailed by sarcasm.

"I'm sure you wouldn't," she said.

Jack gave her a broad grin. Scott though, suddenly turned and gave her a look she had never seen before. Calm, but at the same time with a deep intensity, his eyes half lowered as though he was thinking of something in looking at her, brooding.

It was probably one of the most handsome looks she'd ever seen on a man and for a moment she could barely look away. Then she did, managing to shift her gaze to the forge.

She was determined not to think about it, either that look, or what it might mean. In fact, that wasn't what was suddenly bothering her.

Somewhere, a chord had been struck. Not even a chord, but a faint and uneasy note, a shadowy suspicion of something not rung true. She didn't know where, or when, or by whom ….

Except that it had happened.

For the rest of that afternoon, she was less demonstrative as the work progressed. Occasionally, Scott or Jack would glance over in her direction and see her watching them intensely, as if trying to look right through them. It seemed she'd gone back to the way she'd been in the early days. The glaze in the eyes had gone dreamy, as she was again deeply sunk into her transcendental thoughts.

In truth though, she was neither looking at them, nor were her thoughts somewhere else, but rather her mind had emptied itself amid the warmth of that corner of the shop. The pounding and buzzing sounds of the workplace, the roaring fire in the forge and the scalding steam rising thickly through the hazy shop lighting, blurring or obscuring the air above her, leant an unreal quality to the scene. She had become malleable to that unreality. As always, a scene of unreality could take hold of her more forcibly than any instance of blinding clarity.

She was dimly aware of some strange process taking place in her. As though a new world had reached slowly into her chest and was lifting her as though by the handle of her heart alone. But this new world she was so intimate with as to be held by that vulnerable organ, an intimacy so much deeper than any physical sacrifice, she couldn't understand.

What she did know as she sat there with her heart beating heavily, was that it was something she was going to recognize for the first time. As though she was new born. Alive, and not just an idea of being alive. It made all her earlier beliefs pale in comparison.

The boatbuilders worked, glistening naked backs begrimed with sweat and sawdust inside the gleaming golden webs of flowing wood. Darker shades of brown and black beyond the reach of the illumination made them distinct even in the steam.

Something very old, a paradise lost, or misplaced, she couldn't tell. There, in that hazy, primordial atmosphere was growing the boat, each steaming timber an accretion of life. A shadowy Flying Dutchman, bigger and more awful in its power than any of them had imagined.

Somehow, because they had talked about it—Jack awkwardly, Scott with his enigmatic cynicism—they had lost themselves to it.

Slaves to it.

She couldn't say what had bothered her. Some word, somewhere. She could almost feel frightened, or at least nervous. Maybe. But somehow, by talking about it, it was like watching, now publicly, something very private.

She couldn't put her finger on why that should bother her. She felt it, though, and was sure they felt it as well. This tension, sharp and twisting, and clear.

Somehow too clear.

She wondered what it was.

# Chapter 49

"I SWEAR," Scott went on. "Ninety percent of the time she's just staring at our butts."

"I thought you said she was a perfectionist."

Scott gave her an appreciate look, thinking once again how lucky he was. "More like a misdirected idealist."

She gave him back a sly look. "The divine mystery?"

"Ah …," he said, even more appreciatively. "Nice combo. You remembered."

"You think I don't pay attention?"

The divine mystery allusion was indeed a good one.

He'd told her how, when he'd been a boy growing up in Port Orchard and then Seattle as his father went around looking for carpentry work in those boom days long before anyone could have believed that a crash at Boeing's could wipe out the region—he and his sister had been dragged through every denomination of protestant church it was possible to find. A result of his old man's personal quest to find something that rang of the truth. His father had been big on divine mysteries and in those days the church seemed to be where it was expected to be found. Regular people just assumed that, in those days. It went with everything else regular people assumed in a Norman Rockwell, Saturday Evening Post sort of way.

"But there's a difference," he said. "Dealing with my old man's form of it was a hell of a different matter than Deborah Sumners' way."

"You sure? I'm not. Not the way you told it."

Scott had learned that when Sydney was serious, she was serious all the way. And when she showed serious interest, he now had confidence that she really wanted to know. She was never politely bored. So he thought for a moment, trying to put in words what he generally didn't think much about anymore.

"In some ways it's the same I suppose. For my dad, life was a deep mystery that he covered over with black and white rules. Everything he looked at, whether it was his work, or art, which he loved to death, or even his family, was incomprehensible to him. Like the way he never figured art out."

"Was it really that obvious?" Sydney couldn't imagine. Her own parents had never seemed to her anything other than what they were. But on the other hand, she knew Scott's childhood had been different.

He had told her about the lectures, the ramblings—getting hauled off by the shoulder to some museum where the great stuff hung on the walls, to be instilled with yet another diatribe on how to be a great art appreciator. They either learned that, the family was told, or they would grow up like a bunch of animals. It was the difference between men and the animals. Sydney's dad had never, once, talked like that.

"Pretty obvious," Scott said. "And in some ways I guess Deborah does remind me of him. My old man was big on believing that standing before a painting in a museum ... that the more he stood there, the greater the experience was, until at last the thing got so big it caused a spiritual change."

"Well, it can do that," Sydney said. "Art can do that. You become mesmerized and engaged with ...," she thought of her art appreciation class, a required class for freshmen, "... the movement of the structure, the balance, colors, theme, technique and conception. And pretty soon, you're beyond it. I've had it happen. That doesn't mean you're off into the divine mystery."

How to explain? What had ground on Scott was how his father had lifted any attempt at art out of the possible into some other place. Instead of seeing a painting as an effort by some poor slob somewhere who had a paintbrush in his hand, some guy who maybe had a headache, a sore back, a hangover, bad teeth, who fought with his wife, who was maybe a real bastard, but who could simply paint like an angel—instead of all that, his old man saw the painting as a symbol of man's potential. Abilities and hopes. A metaphor of the God within man, if not God himself.

He remembered how his father would get, nearly breathless and all but inarticulate. Art that was Great Art, he believed in the depths of his soul, could not be produced by mere man. Only, perhaps, a sort of superman. A genius. And that was the difference.

"No, but there's an irony in my dad's form of it. Art being on that pedestal, he shied away from knowing much about artists. He'd go on and on in awe about buildings of inspiration, the great cathedrals especially, but never came anywhere near thinking about how those heaps of stones had been built by regular folk, stonemasons and glasswork artisans, and over centuries. He just took it all in as a whole and pulled it down to his level. He just ...."

Scott suddenly laughed.

Sydney watched him for a moment, and then said, "what?"

"I'd just forgotten how frustrated I'd get in those days. Eventually, I didn't mind the paintings and museums. I'd love to see a cathedral someday. But there's no way I'd put myself up in comparison." Scott laughed again. "You would have had to have been there. I mean, he simply preferred to get carried away with the spiritual impossibility that he, himself, ever could have been capable of doing something like that."

Sydney thought about it, and then looked up at him.

"That's sad."

"It's not the worst of it. Like Jack's been liking to say lately, what goes around, comes around. My old man never saw the men behind the work, and he never found his God either. All those years. All those churches. He could never figure out why his idea of God never seemed to be where people congregated."

"You don't believe in God?"

"Believe in something that explains things just because we think we can't explain them for ourselves?"

"People do, you know."

"I know, and that's all right. It's just that part of the package doesn't work anymore."

"So there's part of the package you do believe."

"I got way too much of Him, and Art, to care ... or to know."

"So what *do* you know?"

"That man probably has something to do with it."

"But you say Deborah Sumners has it differently from your father."

Scott thought about it, and shook his head. "I was wrong."

Scott felt an old irritation with his father wander in. Too bad the old guy wasn't still alive, he thought. He and Deborah Sumners could have sat down next to the boat and just sailed away with it.

Sydney examining him for a long moment, and then something in her face changed.

"I like the way you said that."

## Chapter 50

To HAVE a mistress was like watching porn films or taking strong drugs, Jack was thinking. The first few times there's just the craving for the drug of excitement, the drug of turned on hormones. Later on though it's no longer a high, but an addiction. In this case, the addiction was to a new way of having sex. Nobody exploded in artificial ecstasy, but nobody could walk away from it either.

Jack's fears about Ellen and Catherine calmed over the next two weeks. The initial excitements of his new relationship with Catherine quickly wore off and he began to see how unspectacular a thing it could be. His blood pressure now never rose when he was in the same room with both of them.

Anymore, he thought, he felt more and more natural carrying on conversations with the two together. Without worrying about tripping up. Things slipped back to being flat again and it seemed funny how life's anticipations of wonderful or awful events was often followed by nothing at all.

Maybe it was television or the movies which had gotten people used to big action scenes. But it was never so. Life was a snowfall, not the avalanche people expected. The earthshaking revelation, of either good or evil, never came.

As well it shouldn't, he thought. Anyway, avalanches couldn't mean much to anyone, except that you could get a hint that you were going to die someday, if not right then. As a lesson, knowing you were going to die someday was no revelation at all. Anyway, there seemed no avalanche hiding, one way or the other, where Ellen was concerned. If a revelation came, it would drift down easily. Of that, he felt sure; and it was comforting to feel that way, he decided.

Nothing to worry about.

If a gentle snow of reasoning seemed to be falling in Jack's life, a gentle snow also fell upon Bellingham a week before Christmas. Unusual for that time of year. Snow normally waited until sometime in January and then only for a few days or, at best, a week. That year the snow came ever so lightly, but steadily, and continued day after day until the city was muffled quiet except for the occasional clanging of snow chains or the growling of heavy truck motors as the traffic made its way around the blanketed streets.

Plodding through the snow back from Micky's one night, Jack and Ellen were arm in arm, steadying each other against stumbling, heading for home. They were silent, not thinking of much as they went along, but they were basking beneath their heavy coats in the warmth of a long, quiet conversation they'd had back at the tavern. About a lot of things. The boat. The business. The Sumners and themselves. Nothing really deep but very much on things touching their day-to-day lives. Finding mutual agreements and a general sensation of seeing things as a couple. Rarely did they have long, drawn out conversations about anything anymore, and it had been pleasurable.

As they went along a thought began to grow suddenly in Jack. But it wasn't until they passed the Moore's, that unhappy, childless couple, that the associations there made the idea flash into being, complete.

Well, sure, he wasn't going to use the Moores as the jumping off point for bringing the subject up. But he could feel, finally, it was the time.

It would take care of so many things so neatly, he thought. Ellen would be occupied, and happy. Completely distracted. Why not admit the idea of making his wife pregnant at the same time as having a mistress gave him a thrill? Why pretend otherwise?

Of course, you should never admit such a thing publicly. But there was no good reason not to be truthful with yourself, he thought. Perhaps it was even unhealthy not to do so. Think it, at least, but don't say it.

He waited to say what he had on mind while they ate a late dinner. He waited as they sat in the living room, in the dark, looking out the window at the snow—illuminated by the guard light high on the boatshed—falling silently in the night. He waited even more in bed until Ellen finally came out of the bathroom and joined him there. She too, though for simpler reasons, was also ready for him.

"Honey?" he said as he turned to her expectant arms.

Ellen took a breath and brought her mind back out of the depths of the preludes of sex. "Hmmm?"

"I've been thinking about something a lot lately."

Ellen heard the serious note in his voice and a strange sensation came over her. As though she knew what he was about to say.

"Yes?"

"Why don't we start the family?"

There was a long moment of silence, and then Ellen shrieked, throwing her arms around him in a way that nearly crushed him.

"Yes!"

It became frantic with them kicking the sheets and blankets down. Ellen, though, stopped for a moment and held them still.

"I love you," she said.

Somewhat of a rarity anymore, Jack had to respond. He didn't feel he had to force himself, though, as he had on occasion. He could feel a true love for her right then.

"Me, too."

But where he thought that would be all, she still held him and asked him to do something a bit different and unknown for them. She even had a name for it, calling it a Love Knot. And it was different, although for him no longer entirely unknown.

It took a while for Jack to recapture his concentration.

# Chapter 51

Eʀɪᴄ sᴀᴡ the opportunity and moved on it. The Hartman deal was going to work one way or the other and it was getting closer with each passing hour. But if he was excited, Eric also found himself in that strange contradiction of before-the-fact dissatisfaction. As if he had already taken possession of a new toy, played with it to the exclusion of everything else, and now had tired of it.

The irony of hope's largest ambitions is that the successful attaining of a midpoint goal gives only a few moments of satisfaction. The Hartman deal, big as it was, was only part of the package. Difficult as it would be in itself—and exhilarating in how he was an integral part of it, having won out over any other possible rival to be in that position—it was just the start of something else.

Simply, he knew he was coming into possession of keys which would finally lead to the real thing. His lifelong dream. He almost felt nervous, so true it seemed.

He couldn't tamper down that muted, tingling excitement.

No matter what his business did, how large the projects got, how much more wealthy he became, it all paled in comparison with his dream of politics.

It was like a blood poison.

He wanted to get into that world, and it was with a desire almost more powerful than that of sex.

No, he thought, it was a more powerful attraction than sex, period. Because sex only repeated itself in a mindless merry-go-round of desire and satiation, where the allures of power kept growing the more you reached for it, the more you attained it, and the more you used it.

Eric felt it very near, and he could tremble. He smiled at himself, recognizing the wild feeling. It was unmistakably like that of a boy's upon making a date and knowing absolutely he would be having sex, if not for the first time, at least for the first time with one of the girls he had dreamed about or had really wanted.

Eric pursed his lips. Perhaps, he thought, the drive towards success and ambition wasn't that far removed from sex after all. It was just age and experience which made the difference. In the early years, you desire something only because you want it, later, you desire something more profoundly if it is something, whether it be sexual or social, that is also useful to you somehow.

Eric leaned back in his chair and laughed. He had exactly that feeling. It was as strong, as powerful, as invincible a feeling as he had ever felt.

His political career was in sight. It was all suddenly here.

His, very nearly, for the taking.

Where before he felt there was nothing he could do, he now had options. And it was time to get at them.

He stopped grinning, bent forward towards his desk, and begin to think with every ounce of that intense and terrible concentration and speed of calculation that he possessed, on schemes, counter-schemes, risks, possibilities, connections, finances and manpower.

Anyone seeing him at that moment—that still figure in suit and tie leaning immobile onto the writing pad of his desk—would have thought they were looking at a statue of a man dozing at his desk.

Unaware of the churning magma chamber within.

## Chapter 52

ERIC WAS the sort of man who can concentrate for long periods on a specific thing. Meticulously, and with a gift for forgetting nothing, not even the smallest detail, he could plan out an action. He could even juggle various scenarios, comparing and analyzing one against the others. But as well, he was fast at doing so, his concentration permitting him to come to decisions in a half an hour which another man would have needed hours or even days to achieve—with much use and contemplation of notes and charts to boot.

The only thing, in this case, that Eric needed to contemplate was his desk calendar. Looking at the progression of days, with the progression of events he was building in his mind.

The idea was just possible, and again it was a matter of timing. The Hartman deal—itself very time restricted—was ushering Eric into a development situation that placed him in a very advantageous light with the local political power-brokers.

Never before had that happened.

A great deal of what people call reality is in fact based on appearances. He knew that. He also knew that no matter how much money he donated to local charity, how much time he apportioned to beneficial work, the local conventional wisdom among the political people had him pegged as a hardnosed businessman whose fundamental concerns lay in commercial development.

Ridiculous as it seemed, he thought, and as unnecessary as it truly was, if you wanted to pass muster with those people, they had to have the impression that deep within your makeup there was a conviction of faith, an ideology of some sort.

Nobody, of course, expected you to be a crusader. The Crusades were finished. And they certainly didn't need saviors either. Saviors had a tendency to get crucified and political party officials didn't find that an interesting sort of political career to promote.

But, cynical as it was, the crusading, save-the-world element gave off the odor of political correctness, the necessary spice to the stew. What they wanted to find was someone who knew what was what in the world, and could take it all on without withering—whether it be public opinion, public debate, the press, or the opposition. But who also, ironically enough, gave the impression that deep, deep down there was a naïve boy who just wanted to do good for everyone.

That was the miracle politician. The guy who could grow up to be everybody's faithful brother, uncle, father, or grandfather.

Your good ol' dad or uncle, so the thinking went, could be an ornery son-of-a-bitch, but you knew he always kept your best interests at heart.

The Fairhaven Project had that aura of political correctness, those elements of vast aspiration and ideal which a man could promote in a way beneficial to his appearance. No longer would Eric have to take a diffident stance with the local party officials. He could simply wander up to them and say Hey Bill, or Charley, or Mac, you need to get off your fat ass and get behind this thing ... it's good for the city, the county, for the whole goddamn region.

Eric could see himself talking to them in that vein, take them by the throats with it.

It was a neat bundle, all right, and they would not be able to avoid seeing that of all the people they had promoted for the previous fifteen years, not one had been able to bring so many real benefits into the area.

Then, through a simple sleight of hand, Eric could tip their attention towards the fact he had a vision of other things that could happen.

He could talk intelligently and knowingly then of the need to balance jobs and the environment, bring in money for education, promote trade, and provide better police protection. Just like that, he would have the upper hand on them because he had been able to make something happen. And it wouldn't take a genius, let alone any of them, to see they had found an interesting new, local element that could get things done on a grand scale. Maybe more than just local. Maybe even on a statewide or national scale.

Eric saw it all as clearly as if it had begun. Which pleased him, because his long experience with new projects had taught him that the ones that were the most sure, were the ones which had seemed finished before they had even started. The ones where you saw the beginning, the middle and the end in one smooth, sequential dream.

The only problem, as far as Eric could see, was to decide the timing of when to set things in motion. Where and when to make the announcements of intention.

He couldn't say anything, of course, until the Hartman project was sewn up. But he saw he could start laying in some groundwork.

Where to begin, though? He looked again at his calendar.

His appointment schedule—if he wanted things to start off with a casual-looking inception to it—wasn't too promising for that particular week. Although there was a meeting with the Port Commissioner the next day concerning the possible leasing of dock space. He thought about it. Without the Hartman deal fully inked, it was a dangerous, delicate undertaking to start even the smallest idea, launch the smallest insinuation, let alone float any but the most subtle appearances. And certainly not with the Commissioner.

Carl Ivarsson was an old, salt-of-the-earth sort. A former teamsters leader who had managed to get himself promoted off the shop floor back in the days when Big Dave Beck's inheritors were still running not only the shop but the management upstairs.

Carl ran the port like it was some sort of neighborhood hardware store. Knew all the local administrators in a way that meant he never had to argue with anyone, anywhere. And he was not really an elected official—nobody ever ran against him—so nobody ever had to test the depths of his pockets or those of his backers.

He was respected. Like any former labor organizer, he was a tough negotiator for the benefit of management. Ideologically, Eric knew that Carl looked upon all shoreline property in Bellingham Bay as though subject to some sort of Manifest Destiny. Carl was descended from the same bunch of Swedes who'd come out there in the 1880s to cut down the giant Douglas fir and hemlock of the high Cascades. Men who knew all about what was required, using their double-bitted axes and two-hand saws, to slash and hew out a life for themselves in that new world—a world that didn't have time for the environment. Which was perhaps the key to understanding or dealing with Carl.

If you want beautiful, Carl would say, go to a park, sit under a tree and eat nuts with the squirrels. If you want a house, food and clothes for the kids and retirement pay, you just let the people running the town get on with running the town.

And let spotted owls emigrate to Canada.

But the best thing about Carl was how he was in big with the local political parties. Both sides. He was a trusted outsider whose advice everyone knew had no personal side to it. Eric knew that to have Carl on your side went a long way around there.

Eric sat there for a few more minutes, considering hows and wheres. Then he reached over and pushed down the intercom button. It would take more than a meeting. More even than a lunch. It had been quite a while since Carl had been out to the house. One thing about Carl, he never turned down the offer of a home cooked meal.

His secretary said she would arrange things with Carl's secretary.

That finished, Eric could only sit in his chair for a few more minutes, and then got up and put on his coat. He couldn't sit around in that office one second longer.

He was going to do it, goddamn it. Finally going to do it.

He nodded at his secretary, as he passed her. Holding his breath.

He had to get out, or else explode.

Go somewhere.

Anywhere.

Just go the hell for a drive.

Because he was finally going to do it.

## Chapter 53

Q<small>UITTING FOR</small> lunch, Jack and Scott stepped out of the shop onto the hard packed snow in the parking lot and found Eric on the porch, holding the door ajar, talking into the house.

"Good day." Jack called to him. "Come down to see the frames being set?"

Eric turned, nodded at Scott and looked back at Jack.

"Yes."

"Have a cup of coffee?" Jack offered.

"In a minute. Why don't you show me what's been happening, first."

Jack looked beyond Eric into the kitchen. Everyone was there—Ellen, Catherine and the apprentices. And none of them seemed to show the slightest interest in their conversation, which Jack knew was just appearances. He looked back at Scott, who made a minute shake of his head. Jack almost smiled. Scott went into the kitchen, and Jack took Eric back out to the boathouse to explain the apparatus for steaming and the work done so far.

Out there, Eric seemed genuinely interested.

"I can now see why Deborah speaks so much about this," he said. "And if you'll have me for lunch, I wouldn't mind staying to watch a little this afternoon."

Jack nodded, figuring that might happen, and went on to explain the work they would continue that afternoon. He was getting used to giving guided tours.

As Jack spoke, Eric leaned back against the ribbands of the boat, his arms crossed as though hugging himself, staring around himself with a blank expression. But if he seemed to be looking at the work, his mind was working in other directions.

All this activity, he was thinking, this entire world down here, was up for grabs.

That news would certainly be a shock for these people when it saw the light of day, but he had little or nothing to say about it. Whatever relationship he or his wife had with these people would have to be dropped. There was a future much larger than all of this, larger than himself even. What Eric needed to calculate now was the time frame.

Depending on the politics of going easy, with no big counter-interests suddenly muscling in on the Fairhaven waterfront project, Colby could have half a year to relocate. If it didn't go easy, he might be reading it over his morning coffee as the bulldozers arrived at his door. Eric's guess was that Colby, if he got lucky, still had a year. That was a relief. Things would have been complicated enough, without getting stuck abandoning the boat project.

Timing. Always timing.

Hartman could get all the leases secured, the proposal made. And even with the rest of the properties being reconditioned they could leave Colby's standing long enough to finish. But if politics forced them to clean this property off fast, to avoid the slightest possibility of a re-sell or re-lease to Jack or someone else, Eric could see no way to move this work. Not from what he was seeing right there.

For the moment, from what Jack was telling him, there was structurally no boat to be moved. The main structure, which almost looked like a boat, were just molds and frames with their ribbands tied into the building for stability. The boat itself was just the keel and several dozen ribs clamped up against the forming ribbands. Take the forms away, they'd just sag and fall to the floor. Nothing that could be moved in one piece, neither barged nor trucked away.

Eric eyed the work with cold objectivity. If things stopped within the next month or so, it would mean irretrievably disassembling all the work done so far. At that point, only an idiot would consider it anything other than a tax write-off.

His eyes narrowed. The real problem, of course, would be Deborah. In light of new developments, he couldn't help but admit that the project no longer seemed the inspiration it had been before. And perhaps even a great, looming mistake. A complication, if not an outright obstacle.

As always, Eric had been thorough. He now knew a great deal about Colby Boatbuilding going well beyond its boatbuilding capacities.

Except for the tools and the furniture, it was true that Jack Colby didn't own a square inch of the place. But that wasn't really an asset. According to Eric's sources, Colby had been more than once in a position to buy the place. Setting aside how that affected him, that fact alone didn't raise Jack much in Eric's esteem. Jack, evidently had never realized what a mistake he was making turning down what were, basically, no-risk offers. No way to lose. Property down there, whether by the slow rebuilding of the historic district, or by a mega-project like Hartman's, could only go up. No matter what you were doing with it.

And without looking at the land, strictly looking at the business, that was also a major mistake not to cover. To Eric, it just made no sense. This was the last boatbuilding facility in the area and if Colby wanted to start up again he would have to build one himself. Banks will finance existing property, and are easily persuaded to support the move of their clients. But they often balk at helping construct new low-yield businesses. And a boatyard couldn't be considered high-yield, present company included.

For Eric it seemed clear enough, and he was beginning to see Colby in a different light. A man who does not secure himself is not a man you can trust with much. He's a man who thinks the future will never be anything but what he looks at when he gets up in the morning.

Following Jack, who was pointing out some damn thing about the ribs, Eric's face suddenly went hard. He could actually feel angry with people who allowed themselves to be chaff in the wind, who didn't realize it wasn't enough to just find a place ... that they had to secure what they had gained. He stared at Jack for a moment, half wanting to spin him around and wake him up to the facts of life. His life.

But then he sighed to himself.

Why the hell was he getting so upset about it? Because he'd let himself get to know these people? Got involved in this boatbuilding project?

Did he want to provide himself a salve for a guilty conscience?

Fact was, he told himself with a sobering honesty he knew was right, people got uprooted all the time. And sometimes at the worst of times.

Progress worked like that. And progress meant a lot of things. For Eric, for starters, it often meant having to lay out all sorts of money, go into full-sized partnerships with banks, putting oneself on the line unavoidably. Uprooting him from whatever business model comfort zone he'd been inhabiting.

All that was synonymous with business.

Eric would get uprooted and have to chip in quite a few dozens of millions. Just like that. Geronimo. And wouldn't think twice when the time came and everything was thought out. Because in the end he would get those back and much more.

If Jack had shown some common sense he would have been in an incredibly strong and—for him--unbelievably profitable position. But he wasn't, and no matter what happened, short term or long, when he realized what was happening to him ….

God, Eric thought, Jack was going to hate his guts. As though he cared. But it did mean saying farewell to all that effort at friendliness, interest, and shared goals … and so on.

Well, hell … this was what came from wanting to chum around on the shop floor. Messy personal relations.

Deborah, somehow, had to be warned off this as well, considering how she was doing it way more than he had done.

Time to pull back the traces. Slowly but surely. But not to be so abrupt ….

… As to be noticed.

For a moment, a small regret, of the having one's cake and eating it variety. It was true … Eric was in a position where he could help these people immensely. Put them in the way of one hell of a lot of money, if he wanted to make a little side deal that Hartman wouldn't know about and would have to buy out at a much steeper price.

But that was just not the way things worked. You don't go around making people wealthy just because of some guilt over getting wealthier because of them. Just because you had gotten friendly with them. That didn't make them friends. And certainly not family.

There was no helping it. The personal side was to be a disaster.

Eric turned his attentions back to Jack, as he continued his explanations, but in his heart was the now solid conviction there was more separating them than just money.

That they truly stood on different ground.

Always had and always would.

That some men were born to be lords and others peasantry was a historical fact that hadn't changed from the very beginning of time.

That small whim he'd had of personal contact with these people, a whim he had allowed himself to get carried away with because of his wife, was now easily seen as utter nonsense. Eric had the power to move freely, to buy in or out. These people never would. That was the difference.

Jack was droning to a finish. "It's going to be the most magnificent wooden yacht built out here in the last four decades!"

Eric almost waved his hands in frustration.

Never again, he promised himself, would he get involved down here in the basement of these projects.

He gave Jack a smile.

"Perfect," he said. It was the word he always used when he had absolutely nothing to say.

They went back into the house for lunch.

In the kitchen, Eric took off his suit jacket, undid the buttons on his vest and sat down to hot ham sandwiches and a bowl of thick clam soup. A good meal, and he enjoyed it.

After all, he thought, it could work out—maybe—for them. They could get out of it no worse off than they'd been at first. And if they got really lucky, there was still a chance things could be finished in time. They could cash out.

Even if he would not have bet a cent on it.

He looked up from his soup, and looked at the people around the table. At the very least, he thought, they were having a good time.

Having some fun.

You don't get that all the time, he thought. And sometimes, he thought, maybe for some people the best thing they could do was learn that there were worse things in life.

As he looked across the table, he saw Catherine glance at him. And he smiled at her.

Feeling guilty about having done something wrong, that was one thing, he said to himself. But to feel guilty about something that was right and natural, was false guilt. Blaming oneself for things one has no control over. Or being afraid of what other people might think. A form of conceit and pre-occupation. Smug, hair-shirt flagellation.

No sir, he wasn't going to be having any of that.

He was no longer feeling angry, and in fact felt almost merry. And he noticed how Catherine had obviously noticed his good mood, and was smiling back at him. He gave her a wink, picking up his sandwich and taking a satisfying bite out of it.

# Chapter 54

SHE DIDN'T know exactly what it was, but the way he had excused himself she knew it was not just words.

Maybe it was the way he looked at her. Or maybe in the way he carried himself, or the way his hands moved. Wherever it had been, she could feel it and how it affected her.

Eric, she was sure now, was a very good man who, in some secret way, was trying to be very good to her.

After his surprise visit and sharing of lunch Eric had stuck around afterwards, in fact for quite a while afterwards. Evidently in a happy, floating sort of mood.

He idled over a cup of coffee with Ellen and Catherine, planning to go watch the rib steaming spectacle. Deborah had called and said she'd be coming down in a hour or so.

"She keeps at it, doesn't she?" Eric said to Ellen. "You should have either started charging her spectator fees or put her to work, long ago."

"No need," Ellen said. "With her being around you'll get the boat three months ahead of schedule."

Naturally, he had no idea she was implying anything. Other than that as the family's main representative down there, she spurred things along. For him, it was a compliment for his wife, and Eric smiled.

"How about you?" Catherine said. "Have you been picking up the buzz the way she has?"

"The buzz?"

"The excitement of it. Now that the ribs are going in you can really feel it."

He smiled at her, and for a brief second—very brief—let his mind whip around an appraisal of her presence. He was admittedly and immensely attracted to her, even though now, in his mind, she was a member of the losing side.

"I honestly think I get more out of it than her," he said, feeling that earlier thrill of mutual attraction as he spoke.

"In what way?" she smiled back.

Eric returned her a steady gaze. No guilt.

"Well, for her ...," he said easily, "she's all wrapped up in the aesthetics of it, you know. It's all symbolic and she thinks this is like the search for some ideal. A platonic lion hunt."

"And you? What? A non-platonic hunt?"

It had popped out of her without thinking and she could barely believe she'd said it. But she managed not to make any sign of her embarrassment.

Eric, was indeed surprised. But didn't care. In the mood he was in, nothing, anywhere, was wrong. And a little flirting was the cherry on the cake.

"It does have its own advantages, I suppose."

What he thought he was meaning to say, was that he could enjoy the pretense of flirting. But then he suddenly saw in Catherine's eyes the something else that told him: it wasn't just pretense, and they both knew it. He felt something come up in himself. A small grain of excitement. And without willing it, his eyes gleamed.

And Catherine, who was also noticing everything—and whose own eyes were now stinging a bit and causing her to blink rapidly-- couldn't resist glancing over at Ellen, who was rinsing dishes at the sink. Ellen didn't seem to be noticing the conversation. And, especially, she wasn't noticing the exchange of looks which was utterly changing its meaning.

Catherine looked back at Eric. The signs of emotion in his eyes making her suddenly feel bold. Much bolder than she would have ever expected to be around him.

"And its dangers, as well," she said.

Eric actually had to swallow. But then did it quite easily: glancing suddenly over at Ellen in just the way Catherine had, and then back. They now were openly sharing how what they were saying had a clear, double meaning. But only for them. Not to be shared by Ellen. And just like that, they had entered the world of secrets.

"Just have to keep the boat balanced, as it were."

Ellen turned to them at that point.

"Keep what boat balanced?"

Catherine smiled at her. "I suppose he means the marriage boat." She turned back to Eric. "Isn't that right?"

He looked at her calmly. "That's one way to look at it."

"What's another?" Ellen said.

It was obvious to both Eric and Catherine that Ellen had just dropped into the conversation out of nowhere, and had no idea of what was going on. In a sense, it made whatever they were saying absurd, but at the same time gave it an intoxicating quality. Pure play, with more than just a grain of excitingly candid lust being all but openly confessed to.

Catherine told herself that, of course, that was all they were doing. Playing. And so had no problem continuing to play with it as a cat toys a mouse. And not even a mouse. A dust ball.

"I'll explain it to you sometime."

"I'd love to hear it," Eric said.

Playful, maybe. But that was a step too far for Catherine. Even if Ellen had not been there, Catherine wouldn't have dared venture any suggestion towards fulfilling that request.

"You can imagine already, I think."

Eric, having now shed his embarrassment at finding himself in a serious flirt with Catherine, was now having fun in precisely the way he had been looking for. All the tension about the Fairhaven project and the complications with the boat was gone.

Innocuous verbal parries and thrusts with Catherine, was exactly the thing he needed. He looked at her there, laughing and joking with him from the other side of the table, her pretty, intelligent eyes amused and searching at the same time, and he suddenly realized she had not only momentarily relieved his worries, but that he'd been seeking out her company on purpose over the past few minutes.

That he felt more attracted to her than he had realized. Which, still, was all right, he decided.

"Imagine?" he said. "Yes, I guess I could at that."

He gave her a long look which, if not as natural as the one before, at least fit in with the mood. She gave him back an expression of innocence which was meant to be interpreted as anything but innocent.

"Want more coffee?" Ellen said.

He sighed, looking suddenly at his watch. Fun as things were, he realized he had no time left. In any case, the conversation, let alone the tone of it, could not continue indefinitely ... going, ineluctably from fun to awkward. Best to quit while they were both ahead.

"Nope, thanks," he said, but he couldn't help one last jab at Catherine. He took a quick swig of his coffee and winked at her. "There's a time for everything."

At that he excused himself, grabbed his jacket, and headed out the door.

It was a good exit, he thought, and he enjoyed how the atmosphere of the kitchen remained floating around him in a lingering memory. He told himself there weren't that many good, really simple things in life that were traded in pure pleasure between people. Between men and women.

Some of them, sometimes, could oddly enough seem like complications if looked at in a bad light.

But they weren't really all that complicated or entangling —or to put it in a more honest way, didn't need to be.

There needed to be no entanglement just because a man and a woman felt attracted to each other. No reason not to enjoy attraction for what it was.

So there was also no reason to be constantly crushing small human connections for the sake of worrying about whether they might create obstacles on the road ahead.

There were no roadblocks ahead, now, as far as he was concerned.

Just some very straightforward things to do, and say.

Everywhere.

\*

Catherine, for different reasons, felt exactly the same way, and hours later discovered she felt happy and calm. She was looking out her windows into the dark winter night lying upon Bellingham, distant lights twinkling hard and bright in the clear air.

Then a thought stopped her reverie. What, she thought grimly, had she meant by thinking of Eric as a very good man?

In truth, she reasoned, there were a lot of things about him that weren't all that interesting to her. His money and social position, being so impossibly out of her sense of things, seemed actually boring. He wasn't boring at all, though. How could a man be so concentrated upon one thing, be so drawn to one occupation as to be fused with it in body and soul, and still be interesting?

All that, though, was peripheral to the main point. Eric Sumners was very simply a wonderful guy.

She could think of particular qualities. His attractiveness, physically and intellectually. There was also his personality. His way of being very sure of himself, of who he was, which was not at all egotistical.

That was a big thing.

Because having a strong sense of self, but not being lost in it, meant he could understand the selves of others. In a man, that meant being able to enjoy others. If the other was a woman, it was quite a flattering prospect.

Simply, he found her attractive. And was a generous man, a real man, not afraid to show her he felt that. He gave to a woman.

Of course, all that didn't make her forget Jack.

Jack.

Yes ... Jack ... well, yes, he was wonderful in his own way. She would always be grateful for his kindness. But Eric seemed more aware of the tidal surge of passions, where Jack managed to make passion seem like something you were duty bound to.

For her, Eric seemed to make passion like it was part of the air, something you could breathe.

Which led Catherine to think of the one thing she couldn't understand about him. She could like his wife all right. Sometimes Deborah nearly rose to the level of a humanness among them all, let her hair down and joined in. But for the most part she was just that unworldly, otherworldly, lost girl.

As Eric's wife, she was inexplicable.

She was rigidly ethereal. If that wasn't a contradiction in terms.

Where Eric so obviously loved life. The real life. The deep rich life, the earth, the ground, the substance, gritty and sticky, crumbly and warm and real and full of immediacy. He loved the experience of knowing people directly, and deeply. So, take that and put Deborah up against it. The question had to be asked: what the hell was happening in his own home?

Catherine stopped herself. She wasn't being fair to him, she supposed. She couldn't say she knew Deborah on any private level well enough to be able to speculate about her.

It was possible, considering that marble exterior, there was an inner personality she kept strictly invisible from the public eye.

She stared for a moment out the window at the black night. White streetlights and the dim yellow and blue lights in windows of houses, spread away down the hill and across the snowy town. The houses and homes—of families, fathers and mothers and their children, couples, and lovers—of lives being lived out in that multitude of hearth-warmed lights, some dim, some bright, but each an instance of that vital gift so many took for granted.

She thought of another house, an impressive one, and how two people were there, and how they were being there together. Sharing their hearth. A quiet conversation. A gesture, a smile. How, even early, they may feel tired with having stayed so long watching the boat. Feeling their bodies calling them to rest, to bed. How they were perhaps climbing steps, undressing, brushing teeth. Or, even now, sliding into sheets, feeling the warmth there spreading, or seeking each other for warmth. Or then, in that warmth of comfort, letting their bodies came together ....

A sudden horror came over her at what she was doing ... but against her will she let the vision continue a bit longer.

Finally though, with a violent shake of her head, she stopped it.

Stopped it all. And realized with not a little dismay that among the other things she felt about Deborah, she was now able to add jealousy to the list. And worse, it was a jealousy of superiority.

Because the girl, who barely knew what life was, wasn't right for much of anything except a nuthouse. She certainly wasn't right for her husband. Who did know about life.

Yet here I am, she thought. As always. Alive but alone, waiting for life to begin.

She sighed out loud to the loneliness lurking in the corners of the empty room. Wishing, simply and honestly with every cell of her aching body, that Jack could have been there.

# Chapter 55

Eric and Deborah were entwined, but not nakedly as Catherine was imagining. They sat together on the soft leather couch in their living room watching in silence the crackling fire in their hearth, the low light from the flames leaping and dancing into the darkness of the room.

Deborah stared intently at the hissing fire, listening to the occasional soft pop of resin bursting and watching sparks fly up the draft of the chimney going out into the cold winter air. Alive, animal and vital, she was pensive with new thoughts on the verge of being heard by the inner ear. It was a feeling so different and unexpected as to be almost ... frightening.

It had all come to her while she had sat by the other fire down at the boathouse where Tom or Will would throw split, green logs of alder into the wildly exploding flames beneath the steam boiler. Inside, the coals were creaking, and the mournful low groans from the boiler sent steam up in humid, sweaty clouds holding the heat of the fire. The black rafters high above beaded and dripped down upon them as though a rain shower in a steamy equatorial jungle, the drips spattering quietly into the sawdust on the floor.

She had sat next to the steam box watching the long, wet ribs being drawn out fast, another cloud rising, the trap snapping shut to cut off the thick, white exhalation. The steamy rib then taken down inside the boat mold, worked quickly, and then with a violent confidence like the killing of an animal, bent and pounded into place. The rib was clamped and finished off with Jack's mallet and Scott's screws. She had understood the way they worked. Uncompromising to the ultimate destiny, but somehow with sympathy. Tenderly. They ... what could it be ...?

They handled the wood as if it were alive and struggling to be free, but at the same time becoming pliantly acquiescent with their coaxing. As though there was not only a muse within their work, but an animal mistress to care for. A violent physical love the work at first resisted, and then succumbed to.

This permissiveness excited her, the warm rush of thoughts and how they gave substance to what before had only been a beautiful light. Only the light had been beautiful, before. Now even the dark, even the blackest nothingness of this violent mistress muse had a beauty and music of its own.

Such smells and sensations within the dense, hot grip of the atmosphere at the boathouse that day! Enveloped and worked upon like a limber, steamed rib, the dark senses within her had simply yielded of their own accord.

Deborah was taking shallow breaths now, trying to back away from this new sensation a bit. She looked at Eric who was also staring into the ballet of flames in the fireplace. His gaze, transfixed, seemed deep in thought.

She wondered if all this was something he had always known, and had always been unable to explain to her. Unable to penetrate through the hard shell of her understanding of the world.

Now she knew.

It was not an act of violence to bend and to set in place, but an act of a larger design. There was something deep and knowing in his eyes as he looked at the fire, something she did not fully understand but now fully trusted. She would wait for him then, she thought suddenly, she would try to understand what he was always trying to tell her. Trying to bend her to …

Funny how, she thought, this was bringing them so much closer together. Even then, she felt she was so much nearer to him. Almost as though she could practically read his mind.

That close.

She reached out then and touched his hand, and he stirred and looked at her, patting her hand in return. And then he looked back at the fire.

Eric would have preferred to be alone with his thoughts about her. An intimate thought sometimes needs privacy to be fully enjoyed. But one of the realities of marriage was that thoughts had to be entertained at any moment, and not when it was convenient. So he made do.

It had been such a small thing. First, during lunch as he had been watching her eat. How ridiculous a thing, but it was true.

She had a lovely and natural way of eating. Eric had almost smiled with a sudden impression she was politely devouring her lunch like a healthy carnivore. An intellectual carnivore at that. A little later, when she had joined into the conversation, he had observed how she livened things with what she said, not mirrored them, or worse, just provided punctuation. It was a sign of a mind which created and devoured ideas. Which formed a life of its own, rather than contenting itself to be a leaf in the breeze of other's lives.

Life was for the taking then, the devouring. It was a pleasure to be taken and devoured as well.

That one spark of conversation just before he left. Was it only a spark? No ... he knew. Something had momentarily leapt up between them. Something living and happy and eager. There in the kitchen at Colby's.

She had a sensuality exactly as he imagined he liked it. Earthy but tempered by the knowledge of itself. A dignity which knew how time and place can increase an attraction. She commanded her attractiveness.

There it was. The reverse of just ... being it.

In that taut, thrusting body of hers, so different from the filled out, floating cloud of Deborah, was the intense language of sex speaking directly to him. Not in a secret, shamed whisper, but a joyful noise. Where the language and music of Deborah's body was a muffled, unaccountably garbled message, Catherine's was a full chorus of delight. Laughs and shrieks of delight.

Such a brief message, but Eric felt it go through him, lingering and adding to what he already had. It was a rare thing, he reflected, to have one small experience give such a turn of improvement. Like owning a wonderful wine cellar, and knowing a great deal about those wines there hidden from the eyes of the world, and then suddenly learning something which made the entire cellar expand again in value.

So it was with Catherine. So it was now with Eric's life. Or else, very simply, his cellar of love as well.

In an absentminded way he reached over and stroked Deborah's hair. Then he looked at her and at how the fire set its glow there upon her hair in a soft halo, a golden luminescence in the blackened oranges and dusky reds of the living room. Deborah, he realized, had been looking at him in a quiet gaze. At his look she turned back to a peaceful contemplation of the fire. He watched her tranquil face, but he was suddenly saddened.

He could see she knew he was looking at her, yet was undisturbed by it, could not feel him as though he was devouring her. She could think things, but couldn't feel them.

He could have wished she could have tried to understand these

299

things, understand him and the realities of his world and the world in general.

Instead of only accepting their existence.

And shaming him for his insistence that she should someday … *know*.

How much better, he thought, those people who already did, and dealt with the heartaches and joys on the level of what truly existed.

## Chapter 56

LIGHT RAINS had transformed the miracle of the snowfall into dreary mush. Winds blew around the buildings of an emptied downtown, blowing up the numbing cold off the slush runneled on the streets and the standing puddles of half frozen water. Barely discernible from the streets beneath the filthy snow and ice, the slick sidewalks were treacherous where the gusts, sweeping down upon pedestrians, hurled the cold into red-pinched wet faces with runny noses and thickened lips. A jaw-paining cold. Bellingham was wet and dead with only an occasional car in search of something forgotten, spraying slush down the street. Otherwise, just another Christmas Day.

Scott was out walking because it didn't make any difference to stay home. Except that Christmas made it more difficult to be indifferent about staying home. To be indifferent meant there was a choice.

But there was no place to go. Still no place to go. Even after all those years.

Jack and Ellen had gone to be with her folks that year. They alternated on the years they didn't spend Christmas alone. Sydney was with her family for winter break. She would stay there the entire three weeks although she had offered to make other plans.

And as for anyone else ... there was nobody else.

Scott had told Sydney she might as well take the entire time with her family because her vacation didn't have anything in common with the pattern of his own life. They wouldn't have had any more time together than before.

But the fact was, Scott would have disliked an inactive Sydney hanging around waiting for him to get off work. Expecting him to make up for a day of little done.

Not that Sydney was easily bored. She was creative enough about what she did with herself. It was mainly that Scott didn't feel like being the focus point, for the moment, for anyone's decisions about whether to stay or go somewhere else.

Surely it couldn't be easy for her to be involved with such an unsupportive person, he thought ruefully.

Perhaps he was ruining her by destroying her ability to have certain creature comforts. Standards of expectation.

Which he ignored, sometimes consciously, and most probably as well sometimes unconsciously. Perhaps what Sydney actually needed were exactly those things—and a style of life rather more enthusiastic—which she was losing to his selfishness.

Sydney. She would sit on the other side of the breakfast table, that huge mass of curly brown hair tumbling around down the young face and shoulders. Her eyes, when he could see them, were honest, mischievous, laughing, or hurt, shy and uncertain; and she would roll, or crinkle them, or make them go sly as she smiled with beautiful, straight small teeth, her mouth wide and full lipped with an alluring and unconscious hint of cynical abandon and desire at the corners.

Her mouth gave it all away, he thought. Or at least to him it did. It was innocent at the center, but the extreme ends tipped up with anything but. Raw sexuality and mocking lust. Or, if not going there … simply intelligence.

He really did like her.

An absolute, watching creature. An almost-woman, but also a girl of the tentative hand upon the arm. Always trying to make contact. On a couch … always exactly there beside him, leaning against him. Standing still … always up against. Only at night, with sleep at last, might she forget. Even then not often and he would awake to find an arm or leg thrown across him.

Sydney, whose concerns had seemed to have run not much deeper than how to best breathe the daily air, who still had little more to say for herself now than she had at the start, very possibly still had no clear image of what he was. And yet, she was becoming an attachment of such an extent for him, that even when he didn't want her around he wanted her around. As though a part of her, slowly extending from her in a budlike manner, had slipped now, in a way at the same time both tenderly loving and frankly obscene, in through his side and was making root there.

He knew it. He knew she could end up his wife. Where before, such a thought with some other woman always had a questioning feeling about it. Here … no. He couldn't explain it, except that here … no.

Scott stepped along, chilled, wheezing in the cold, the freezing wind whipping him until even his mind became numb. He needed heat.

The Horseshoe Cafe was open, thank Christ.

He went inside and found the bar was open as well. Even better.

He took a seat at the bar, letting the cold fall off himself onto the floor like a shower of icicles. Letting the heat in. And there was a lot of it. It felt like it was about ninety degrees in there.

Somebody had taped a football game. Evidently, conversation or watching Bing's White Christmas wasn't the atmosphere of choice.

So it was Christmas day and it was third down and fucking eight to go, and fat alcoholic bellies propped themselves up against the bar. Watching and making angry comments, but mostly just sitting there. Like flies on something dead.

Something dead all right, Scott thought. With nail holes.

"What'll you have?"

A Rusty Nail, Scott thought, then: "Rye."

It came, and there he was. There he certainly was.

Happy Christmas, fellas.

Bunch of dead goons with blotchy faces and varicose noses.

Scott had a pickled egg. Sydney would be having ham. The Pryce family always had a cured ham brought up every year by Uncle Willard, who was very funny and smart, and only four years older than her, and worked as a pharmacist in Winston-Salem and lived next to a golf course. He wasn't married, but he was funny, and also cute, and he and Sydney were best friends and would go for drives. He always had a nice car. BMWs or Audis or something.

At her family's Christmas get-together there would be seventy or eighty people, and every year someone had a new baby to show off, and there was her great-grandmother, who was ninety-seven and could still walk and could hear but had stopped talking a few years back. Sydney hadn't been able to tell how many great-grandchildren there were, like her, but there were over thirty grandchildren.

That was something, he'd said.

When they were all together, she said, everyone talked at once. Scott wouldn't believe it.

He could. No wonder the old lady had stopped talking. The way old people are ignored, it's bad enough to have no one listening when the family is small, but to be ignored by a crowd must be a royal pain in the ass.

As for himself, he hadn't come from a big family. And after his art-struck father died, taking his massive presence with him, what little was left around his mother seemed even smaller. And then she died.

Anymore, they rarely thought of one another at all. Only at Christmastime did anyone get guilty about it and send a card. Self-consciously.

Scott didn't mind that. He himself sent Harry & David's California fruit and nuts. At least it gave people something to munch on. Saying they loved each other wasn't exactly a habit amongst them. Honesty also played a part in that. Honest, quiet, private, his people were also very stingy and selfish. Not too surprising, then, to notice that in himself.

Christmas with some remnant of his family, therefore, was nothing he might have wished on. He knew he wasn't being very normal in that sense. These days, he thought, the normal thing was to hang on to your illusions all your life. It was considered the positive, pro-active approach.

Don't worry. It was only the rest of the world going to hell.

Cheer up.

He didn't know if he loved Sydney.

He didn't have much training for knowing. He thought about her when she wasn't there, and he thought about her when she was there. He avoided thinking of things when she wasn't there, and he avoided thinking of them when she was. He didn't know if that was love … if what they had was love … or if she loved him, or had the same worries about it that he had. He didn't know shit. Although he supposed he did know one thing.

He authentically and unequivocally knew how he would have loved to have picked up funny and cute Uncle Willard's ham, Willard of the long car rides telling his niece all sorts of funny things … picked up that ham by the shinbone, and pasted funny Uncle Willard a goddamned *good one*—he'd picked up that phrase from her—across the head with it.

That, he knew he would have loved. With an absolute and trusting heart.

Scott picked up his glass as if to make a toast. But then, realizing he was alone in his action, changed the motion in mid-air to that of just taking another drink.

Christ, he thought as he set the glass down, you couldn't ask for a more classic, alcoholic's shtick than that. Toasting drunken nothings all by yourself.

Scott glanced sideways at the others. Christmas zombies. Nobody seemed to be paying any mind to him. Or each other.

Insensibility. Another drunk's shtick.

Which seemed to be the general situation, he thought.

He nodded at that thought, and no longer gave a damn and that time lifted his glass in a toast to the bar mirror. Toasting nothing, and everything. Sydney, Jack and Ellen, the Sumners, and the boat. Especially the boat. The real boat, the imaginary boat, the whatever boat, the ideal ... or even the biblical, if anyone wanted to bother.

That last thought struck him. It was suitable enough. Forty days and forty nights at full flood and up they go, two by two ...

"We should have built it out of Dogwood," he said aloud, and drained his glass.

Scrooge couldn't have done it any better.

# Chapter 57

Down at the boathouse, in the silence, all was a grey, filtered darkness.

The forge and steaming box were cold, with whatever leftover moisture frozen into frost patterns or drips into small icicles. The boat elements were glistened with frost as well, the ribs frozen and stiff. The ribs, themselves, were almost all in place now with only a few open gaps left to be filled—some at the rearmost, places along the horn timber where the hull of the boat would come out of the water, and some at the bow, which had to be set at angles forward to catch the tapering run of the hull.

The rest were finished, describing now perfectly the shape of the boat with actual members. The line of the hull swept upward from the keel, bellied big and curved back with a slight tumble-home to where the rail would sit upon the sheer line at the deck.

Yet still fragile—ribs only clamped against the horizontal ribband moldings defining her shape. Only when the beam shelves were in place, running the entire length of the hull near the top of the ribs and holding them in position with the sheer clamp on the outside, and with the transversal beams then half-notched and bolted in place on the beam shelves, locking the two halves of the rib structures in position, would the hull begin to develop any strength to stand alone.

But that in itself meant a line had been crossed.

Before, all the work had gone into creating the forms of the hull, its complex curves both fore and aft and vertical; those curves which would determine her seaworthiness and maneuverability and also, incidentally, her beauty. Now, though, while the necessity to carefully measure, cut and form the pieces of wood to follow would be much the same, that wood's contribution would be of the more plebian variety, creating her inner solidity through her crossbeams and hanging and lodging knees, and her overall stiffening and ability to float by way of her planking.

One hundred and thirty-five feet of her sat there on massive keel blocks with myriad molding braces crossing up into the rafters of the shed to lock the frames in place, keeping her still, like a giant animal caught in a huge spider's web. Or Gulliver on the beach. Somehow helpless and innocent. And somehow not at all. Depending on who was looking at it, and why.

Scott stood there in the doorway, holding the door half open, just checking before heading home. His Christmas party down at the Horseshoe hadn't lasted too long, and he'd finally decided the best present he could give himself was a good night's sleep.

In the gloom, but with enough light filtering in from outside to give it a strange near-twilight or early morning gloaming, he could make out the thin frost shining from wood surfaces. The wood would be dead cold, near frozen, and hard and catchy to drill in or cut.

He thought for a moment, looking over at one of the space heaters. He could light the thing up and bring temperatures in the shed to above freezing. Keep the place at a workable degree. But he decided against it. He didn't trust those heaters enough to leave them running alone, and there was no way he was going to stay down their watching them.

Or ...?

For a moment, he looked over at Deborah's overstuffed chair, itself probably cold as an iceberg—or as cold as her, he thought—but it would pick up body heat eventually, and he could find a sleeping bag and it wouldn't be too uncomfortable ....

Then ... no. No way.

Even though keeping the work warm down there was something he would prefer, himself, he suddenly, simply wasn't going to do it.

His mind flirted with a few wisecracks, things about how there had been enough sacrificial crucifixions going on, and not only on that day. But he dropped them. He didn't feel that dour. In fact, if anything, he was surprisingly feeling a way he had once been quite naturally: generally optimistic and cheerful, looking for the good in the bad—rather than how he had been feeling about things for quite too long a while.

And he knew why.

He stepped back, pulling the door closed, and went to his car, which was idling away, warm inside, a thin film of steam rising off the hood and from the exhaust. Almost as though it was stamping its hooves to get back to where the hearth is.

# Chapter 58

A FEW days after Christmas, Eric was driving back towards town from a day spent out on the Nooksack River. From the sort of day he almost never had anymore.

Out there.

Alone.

Trying to catch a steelhead or something.

Pretty much the last of the holidays for him, the idea hadn't been anything thought out. He'd just woken early and decided to go.

No guide.

No boat.

Deborah had wanted to get up and make him breakfast, but he insisted that she didn't. For some reason he preferred to just take a thermos of coffee and some glazed cinnamon rolls. He'd gone to his study for his steelhead gear, then gone out to the garage and started up his compact pickup truck.

The early morning had promised a quietly melancholy day as he drove out along the north shore of Lake Whatcom. A feathery mist draped down through the dark firs like Spanish moss, but underneath clear, and out over the dark green water he could see on the mirror-still calm the occasional expanding vee in the water of a swimming duck.

Even in winter, with all the underbrush and hardwood stands stripped bare, the Northwest forest was breathtaking in its dusky wintergreen shroud of hemlocks, firs and cedars, almost black beneath the drizzling rain and chill winds blowing down from the north. A stark beauty reined where dormant timber towered over the exposed, giant rocks at its feet, the summer's rushing, hillside cascades reduced to dark, trickling rivulets beneath the bright tan fronds of dead ferns.

The road he followed worked its way along the plunging hillsides above the lake until he finally reached the farther end where lone cabins, or old family homes, a bar and a small general store, sat amongst the trees. At Agate Bay he turned onto a road running north, and drove up a long, narrow valley of what had been old stump farms and dairies. At last, sweeping up and over a low hill, he came to an intersection with Mt. Baker Highway. The highway was fifty miles of two-lane road running east from Bellingham, stretching out and up into the Cascades, curving up into the foothills and then the forests, first dense hemlock and fir, and then alpine, twisting and tailing upon itself until finally ending, at treeline, as a parking lot at the Mt. Baker ski area.

Where Eric was, six miles east from Bellingham, the highway was running along the foothill spur creating the southern side of the bowled up American-Canadian flatland which the Nooksack River and her bigger sister to the north, the Fraser, flowed across.

At that intersection with the highway Eric could see beneath the rising cloud cover, through air clear as glass, all the way up to the border and beyond to where he could see the dark forest of the northern, boundary foothills.

In the flatland, in the towns, Lynden, Everson and Sumas, twenty miles away, he could see smoke rising from early morning wood stoves and fireplaces. Thin, straight lines going up through the cold air into the white mist above, looking then like white threads dangling down. The countryside of farms and meadows was brown, interspersed here and there with fuzzy, purpling patches of bare woods or dark clutches of evergreens. Eric turned the car to the right onto the highway. He headed east in the direction of Mt. Baker, but only drove another five miles to where the Nooksack River, rushing out of the mountains onto the valley floor, met the highway bridge. The place was called Nugent's Corner, an emplacement for a supermarket—"Where Friends Meet Friends"— a gas pump, a biker tavern, a bakery and a real estate office.

Eric had decided not to try driving up into the foothills and then looking around for a spot to clamber over to the river, but to try right there at the highway bridge. He drove down under the highway approach and then out onto the wide, gravely floodway alongside the river. He followed the scours between clumps of willow and river alder until he could make his way out between two small patches of trees onto a pebbly expanse right at the edge of the riverbank.

He stopped his motor on the wide, gravel bank, his front tires twenty feet from where the river ran smoothly past, settled into its deep, winter channel. With no overhanging brush the spot was very open and cold and Eric wondered how many years it had been since anyone had been able to pull anything out of that stretch of river.

It didn't matter, he thought. Sometimes, putting a hook in the water was all that counted. Besides, there was always the idea that he might by accident catch something by a method no one had done before.

Fat chance of that, though, he thought equably. If he did, one thing was for certain: his method would guarantee he would always have this way of fishing for himself.

He let himself have a clubhouse grin.

No one else would be dumb enough to want to copy it.

So, in an amiable mood, knowing he was basically doing nothing, he went through the motions of fishing. He got his gear out and set the long pole up and then put on a bright, fluorescent-red steelhead lure, complete with all its tassels and party-favors.

Except for purists, like fly fishermen, who went after steelhead with big wet flies, everyone used these incredibly gaudy lures. The gaudier, the more childish looking, the better.

Steelhead, although difficult to catch, were also basically the bimbos of the fish world when it came to their sense of what looked good to eat. Eric's lure that morning, flaming red and whorehouse pink, was supposed to resemble a clump of fresh salmon eggs broken free and drifting downriver, attended by various other miscellaneous ejectae falling out of the salmon doe as she let loose upstream.

But Eric didn't plan to be so active as to simulate drifting in order to catch roving steelhead eyes. About ten feet up from the semi-floating lure he hooked on a swiveled piece of surgical tubing and then worked into the tubing a thin, five-inch stick of lead, giving the lead a few gentle bends and crooks so that it would be less likely to catch between big river rocks out mid-channel. He then walked over to the edge of the river, twisted the pole back, flipped open the bail of the spinning reel, and jacked the lead weight and lure out as far as he could upstream.

The lead and lure went in with a satisfying smash mid-channel, dropping quickly, and he let the line drift and drop until he figured the lead was down and holding and he reeled in the slack line that had been making a big arc downstream. He cleared a few of the rocks at his feet, exposing deeper, rocky sand, and jammed and worked the long wooden handle of his rod down into it. He put some larger rocks in front and back of it, and then propped an even larger rock up against it, holding it firmly at a high angle away from the line going out. He then took from his pocket a small brass bell and clamped it onto the shank of the rod, positioning it so that the little clapper hung free. Then he went back to his pickup and climbed inside. There, he dozed, drank coffee, and gobbled down cinnamon rolls.

At first he had left the motor off so he could hear the bell, but after a while figured he could watch to see if the pole jerked, and kept the motor running. It was cold as hell.

His mind wandering, occasionally he would start, jerk upright, and check to see if a fish had come and was taking his line off the reel, which had its drag set fairly heavy but not locked. But he never saw anything like that. It was always the same with the same angle of the line swung out into the flow, and murky green glacier water there tugging gently, upwelling and playing in silent, sliding whirlpools around the line.

Sometimes mewling seagulls, either alone or in pairs, would come wheeling up the river. Or an occasional bald eagle flapped down to sit in a tree for a while. From time to time came the deep braying motors of the logging trucks as they rushed in a symphony of groans, crashes and jingles across the new highway bridge, which had replaced the old, iron highway bridge which the state had needed thirty years, from its first promise, to replace. But mostly it was dead quiet except for the rushing river.

As quiet as it was, though, Eric sat in his pickup with a deep sense of foreboding. Because he wasn't out there for no reason at all.

He had taken himself out into the solitude of that morning. All he had wanted was to move through that countryside, or to sit in it and let it take him out of himself, take him away from whatever it was he felt was about to happen to him.

He knew he was no longer content with his life.

His life: Eric shook his head, thinking, and what *is* life?

This, of course, wasn't about his business dealings, or his political ambitions. But his *life* life. The thing he had less control over. The part of life that determined who he really was as a man.

It was getting to the point where he wasn't sure anymore whether he wasn't drifting towards a pattern that had more of lifestyle than of life to it.

Lifestyle was easy. An affordable reward.

You want a vacation, he thought, you fly to Europe, dive into restaurants, take excursions. Gastronomy and shopping in Paris. Theater in London. Strolling in the Highlands or the hills around

Seville or in Tuscany. And come back with a few cases of Chateau Saint Yquen, or Haut-Brion, or Romanée Comte. Luxury based on knowing something. Or else take a flyboat up for a week's fishing in Canada, or jet down to Mexico for a doze in the sun. Or Singapore. Or Tokyo. Or even stupid luxury based on what glitters rather than knowledge: a champagne class super-jumbo to Dubai for the ultimate in fake luxury. Maybe even mix business with pleasure, dragging along some clients to play golf and boozy poker with, when everything else got boring.

Lifestyle embossed on a credit card.

But bad as that was, there was something that made it worse: to be doing whatever it was you were doing, even if just making and spending money, if no one knew what you were doing or why you were doing it. No one to appreciate it.

No one was paying attention to the pattern of your life, watching you evolve, watching you work it to your advantage, struggle, make deals, find the strategies to succeed, and fully understand and cheer your victories. Then, when you took time off, spent some of the profit margin on a semi-precious lifestyle, the purchase was understood for what it was. Rather than being despised as just an ostentatious expenditure of disposable wealth.

Eric shifted his weight and gazed sullenly out at the swift-flowing water, feeling irritated. For two conflicting reasons.

The first was that no matter how much money he spent, no matter how obvious it was that he was attaining high ambition … what he lacked—to be honest—was a little goddamn applause.

But what galled him just as much, was that he should be stooping to be irritated by such things, in the first place.

# Chapter 59

ERIC STARED at the river, deliberating letting his irritation float away with the rushing current. Letting his thoughts return to things that didn't gall him.

His meeting with the port commissioner, Carl Ivarsson, had been everything he had been hoping for and more. Long-time acquaintances, they were on a first name basis and many things that ordinarily might have had to have been said—possibly ruinous, overt things—could be set aside. After a lunch of a succulent, Dungeness crab-stuffed lingcod with wild rice, and an excellent, dry and crisp Muscadet, and after Deborah had excused herself to do some errands in town, they'd gone into the den to speak—Carl turning down the Havana but happily accepting the Armagnac. There, Eric only had to say a very, very few words and Carl caught on quickly to the situation without Eric having had to come right out and say it. It had to be Carl opening the door. It was the way it had to work. Anything else would be deniably ignored.

Eric had simply shifted the conversation around, based on mutual but unspoken knowledge of the Fairhaven Project, to a soothsaying series of predictions, economic and demographic, for the area. Carl had done the rest.

He had given Eric a good, hard stare, straight in the eye, with his age-blunted Swedish features. The heavy chin was still solid at nearly seventy years of age, bracing a full set of ivory white teeth set firmly with over fifty years' experience in dealing with men as determined and ambitious as himself. But Eric knew the stare meant nothing. It was just Carl's habitual way of taking on information. Of course, Carl wasn't going to let on what he was thinking, either.

But as Eric spoke, he began to see the hard look around Carl's eyes softening to that of shaded humor. When Eric finished, Carl put up a big, rough hand and pushed it back over the thick white hair he kept cut short like a brush over his high forehead, and then nodded.

"You know, Eric," he said, the deep, old, never lost accent still bottoming along just beneath his words, "I'm surprised you haven't yet stepped into politics around here."

It was strictly rhetorical, as Eric's answer had to be.

"It's crossed my mind," he said. "But I've never taken much of a swing at more than speculation. It seems a bit of a closed house, anyway."

Ivarsson nodded exactly in the grave, thoughtful way he was supposed to.

"Well, yes. I suppose it can seem that way to anyone, at first. But once you get inside, you'd see it isn't as closed up as all that."

Eric nodded back. He could see Carl not only understood, but agreed with the idea. The time for rhetoric was finished.

Eric raised his eyebrows in an open, frank expression of admission. Time to just get it out.

"I wouldn't mind talking to a few of those people, sometime. If ever you thought I might have a chance."

Carl shrugged, and accepted fully how they were talking openly about it. Never in his life had he been either coy or evasive, playing a role when serious issues were at hand. Which they were here.

"You have a chance. That's not the problem." Carl said flatly, and began waving his hand back and forth over the table as though a boat being washed back and forth on the waves as he went on.

"It's all a question of temperament and so forth. It's a rough game. As rough as you're bound to find. But the worst thing about it is, no matter how rough it gets, you aren't permitted to let the roughness show. Ever. Not around here, anyhow. We like to consider ourselves civilized."

Carl smiled at Eric. "But I'm sure you can handle that. I know you're solid. You know what the priorities are. Beyond that, it's just a matter of avoiding lulling yourself into ever feeling you're safe. By the way, you and Deborah don't have any kids, do you? I guess that shows you how long it's been since I've been up here at your house, much to my embarrassment and regret."

Eric gazed, a bit startled, at the Port Commissioner.

Carl nodded at him.

"Never mind, "he said. "An Old Boy's question, I suppose." He looked down at his hands for a moment, as if in thought.

Eric waited for as long as he could, then interrupted whatever Carl was thinking.

"So you really feel I have a chance at this?"

He couldn't help asking again. It had simply sounded so

wonderful the first time that he wanted to bask in the confirmation once again.

Carl Ivarsson was a very old hand at these sorts of things. Somewhat in the same way as Eric had—but for a much longer time—he too had become unimpressed by those things he knew he could do, and was only really interested by the challenge of making something he had always wanted to happen, happen.

He gave Eric a look, and then nodded. There was plenty of time to think about the uses of someone like Eric Sumners. For the moment, there were concrete things which had to be done. If they were to do it. New projects opened up new opportunities. And you never knew where things could go until you'd examined them carefully. Carl had too much experience to just let him dive into things. Too often, golden opportunities and projects had turned sour, just because of being too rash. Especially projects involving a lot of people, and all the disparate interests those people implied.

People, when given opportunities, he thought with a congenial, cynical humor, could screw up a great new idea almost faster than you could have thought it up in the first place.

"Maybe so, Eric," he said. "I've always felt you had a lot of good qualities to offer this community."

He smiled warmly, but then, with a well-practiced air of vagueness, pulled a small pair of half-moon reading glasses out of his shirt pocket and pulled a small black book out from his jacket pocket. Taking a good sip of the Armagnac and smacking his lips appreciatively, he thumbed the book open and looked down the list of names.

"Now," he said, "I just have to see who's in town."

Eric knew, then and there, he was in.

*

He shifted himself around a bit in the cab of the pickup, suddenly uncomfortable in the cramped space. That was pretty much a summation of the whole picture, he thought, and a summation of the reasons for his irritation.

No, of course he wasn't squirming with a sort of claustrophobic unease at what he was piling on himself. Always wanting something else. Like the old saying, that the answer to what you give to a man who has everything is always more. It wasn't an unease with gluttony.

It was, maybe, with how easy it came to him?

No. That wasn't what he meant. It wasn't that they just came to him. He made them happen. It was how easily he made things happen, based on his abilities and instincts. That was the thing.

Sure he wanted it all, and then he wanted more than that. Because he could.

But not only did he want those things, and knew he could get them, but he wanted to be seen, and appreciated for his success and his achievements.

That was it.

A great void suddenly opened up as he realized that, no matter how much of his dream was about to be coming into fulfillment, the backdrop of his life against which to set it in perspective was sadly inappropriate. As things stood, only his mind, with its sense of the realities and ways of the world, could properly appreciate what he was accomplishing.

It took a moment or two, but then—just as he had known—the magic worked and he began tingling with both excitement and irritation, letting his inner gyroscope set him upon whatever equilibrium it felt necessary.

One occasion led to another. But it was a question of being open to them, and reactive.

There were occasions, he told himself, when a man should let his instincts have their way.

Eric squinted across the cold water at the far bank, letting time drift, nodding his head in silent agreement to thoughts he had suppressed, and others he had not yet allowed himself to think openly about, even to himself.

At noon, the sky went dark and flurries of a strengthening wind blew an increasing number of dead leaves along the bank and into the clumps of bare trees. The first drops of rain on the windshield beaded slowly and ran down, and then beaded up again. Then the sky went darker with heavy clouds scudding in from the Pacific, and the rain increased in strength. In no time, it finally just came drumming down, shimmering out across the river, a fine spray dancing up.

For a while Eric just watched. But then, realizing it wasn't going to let up, he elbowed the cab's door open and scrambled out over to the river's edge and yanked the rod up out of the rocks, plucked the bell off, and reeled in the pornographic lure he'd had out bobbling around three feet off the river bottom all morning.

It came in and out of the frigid water in much the same state, he figured, as his thoughts had been all morning, looking like a worthless, messy floozy with a hangover.

He wasn't immune to the simile.

Personal ambition aside, he knew what that morning, and what those unacknowledged thoughts, had all been about.

The rain, heavy and cold, bounced high and white on the highway as Eric drove back to Bellingham.

When he'd left the river, he'd turned on his headlights. It was the only way to be seen. For that reason, he didn't notice the unlighted pickup that followed him at a distance, following him all the way up from the gravel riverbank onto the highway. Following him all the way into town.

There was something about the trip back that, upon reaching town, prevented Eric from driving immediately home. There was something like fate in the air. A luring, red and pink fate twisting slowly in the murkiness of his mind.

Instead of turning off James Street onto Alabama and then shooting straight out and up the hill to Lake Whatcom, he continued on down into town along State Street and then onto Jackson, as though heading for Fairhaven. Still aimless.

Then less so.

He went up into the neighborhoods laid out on the hillsides beneath where the college sat like a fortress.

He drove casually, as though a tourist, looking at old Victorian homes and turn of the century mansions mixed in with the big family houses of the 'tens and early 'twenties. Then he drove down into Fairhaven, quickly, and drove past Colby's.

He saw the light on in the kitchen and smoke coming out of the chimney. But he didn't stop.

He turned back up towards Bellingham, taking Jackson as if to skirt Sehome Hill to the downtown, and get back to Alabama. But at the last minute again, he turned off and went up into those homes again.

He was just driving around. Take this turn. That turn. Go up this street. That street. Higher and higher on the hill until he was suddenly on it.

The street.

He almost turned off, but kept on, driving right at it.

Which one was it? He grinned in derision at how his heart was beating heavily. There was next to no risk, but that also meant that there was a slight chance of risk. What if she did show up? Coming home. Or going out. Or looking out.

He realized he didn't know whether she even had windows facing the street.

On the other hand, why should she recognize him? She didn't know his pickup. Nobody did. Or, at least, he hadn't driven it for months and she wouldn't recognize him in unfamiliar circumstances. And he was bundled up as well.

It was ridiculous.

Then he saw the house. Curiosity overtook him. A large, modest house. Nothing special about it. Nicely trimmed lawn. A few old trees along the sides and down in back. Big windows on the second floor, curtained but showing lights, looking right out onto the street.

He kept on.

Six blocks later, because of how far he'd gone, and how long it had taken him to finally do it, he turned around and drove back again. Looking and not looking at the same time.

He was so involved with taking one last look that he never noticed a car passing him the other way, or how it was Jack who was driving it.

If he had made another turn he might have seen Jack parking around on a side street and hurrying back through the rain to her place. But he did not turn, just continuing on homewards, splashing back along rainy streets.

Jack hadn't noticed Eric, either. Nor did Catherine, whose windows on that side were now kept more or less permanently curtained shut.

But that didn't mean nobody had noticed nobody.

# Chapter 60

IT WAS just an idea, as usual.

Scott wondered then why he didn't just drive home as though he hadn't seen anything. Which he probably hadn't seen, anyway. Or, that was to say, hadn't really seen in any particular way worth seeing.

But he didn't, and he drove down to the boatshed and into the parking lot.

Except for Jack's pickup by the office the lot was empty. Scott drove over by the boatshed and parked. He could have parked by the house, and considering the downpour should have. But for some reason he preferred to park as far from Jack's truck as possible. As though, somehow, it made his own presence there as disconnected as possible from the place.

Or whatever, he thought.

Ellen was in the kitchen and waved him in as he stepped up onto the porch.

"What are you doing out on a day like today," she said as he came in.

The sky outside was so dark, and the rain was coming down so relentlessly it was indeed a little hard to imagine there was any good reason for anyone to be outside. And just when he got inside, it suddenly came down even heavier, a deafening roar overwhelmed the house and the rain took on the look of a waterfall, the parking lot, and everything else disappearing in a blur of water. They looked out the window for a moment, and then they both had to laugh at how ridiculous the weather was.

"It's the end of the world," Scott said.

"God, you'd think so."

"You got any coffee?"

"A little bit is left."

Scott got a cup off the dish rack and Ellen brought the percolator over from the stove and filled it for him.

"So, what are you doing?"

Scott gave a vague look, hoping it didn't look too vague.

"A few errands."

Ellen looked at him for a moment. It was true that Scott had, as she put it, cleaned up his act lately. For whatever reason. Either because of the work, which she knew he felt partly responsible for, and which she also knew he had to love, or because of Sydney, although one didn't get the impression Sydney was the sort of girl it was necessary for anyone to clean up their act for.

But the results were there, for whatever reason, and it was no longer the case that you could see on a daily basis the results of Scott's drinking. Of course, she knew he had to have been drinking.

Not that it was obvious. He wasn't drunk and didn't smell of drink. Nonetheless she knew. No way was Scott out wandering around in the rain just doing errands. Sure as day followed night he would have stopped in somewhere and had a few. It was what he did when he wasn't doing anything else.

In the end, though, it didn't matter. As long as he continued to keep it under control, it had finally become just his own business.

Even so, Ellen felt herself get irritated. History after all, was history and Scott's history was well stocked with bottles. So even if it was only a little episode now and then, it all added to the backlog.

What were you going to do, she thought? You couldn't go backwards. You can't undo the past and just walk away from it.

The fact was that, unless Scott decided one day to stop, every time he had even a single drink he would remind her, and everyone, of all the rest. It was either irritating, for those times she didn't like him, or disappointing for those times she did.

She almost sighed.

Right then she felt she liked Scott. She just wished, in light of what seemed like a forthright, intelligent man, she didn't always have to end up feeling like he was such a sham. That under all that workman's sturdiness was this weak creature who couldn't resist the temptation to blot himself out in some bar.

There was nothing she could do, though. Even though Scott had been more open to trying to do new things, to adjust to new opportunities, he just never would be as reliable as Jack.

And that was the crux of the matter, she realized. Because what woman wouldn't prefer reliability and consistency to anything else?

She took the coffee pot back to the stove.

Scott, a bit thoughtfully, had been glancing at her, and saw she was in a quiet mood. He couldn't help it: the thought swarmed up like it always did.

It was simply incomprehensible, he said to himself for the millionth time, how this handsome woman, this person who had so much clear-sightedness, who was so straightforward and generous ... had ended up with a guy like Jack.

And for the millionth time, found himself feeling a well-worn resentment. But he set it aside, knowing it was pointless, and in a sense irrelevant. It was now just a thing to wonder at, rather than feel.

Because, otherwise, things were going fairly well, those days. The work had its own rhythm, progress was daily, and there was no doubt now in anyone's mind that the boat could be built. Even Jack had grown to accept it as a fact and no longer pulled any long faces when either he or Ellen talked about the project. In fact, Jack had soaked up the whole thing to the point he seemed to have forgotten his earlier resistance.

Now, and sometimes unbelievably, he even started snapping at anyone making negative remarks about some aspect of the work.

Mr. Positive.

It made Scott smile. A few times he had even laughed, which got a dirty look in return. But outside of his usual frustrations Scott hadn't really minded all that.

Now, though, things had changed. Everything. Like a bomb going off. Things had now so radically changed, and in ways he had never suspected. Almost impossibly changed, and he was struggling.

"So ...,"Scott said, going over and taking a seat at the table, "the holidays were all right for you two?" It pleased him that his voice was calm and stable.

Ellen smiled and waved the air with her hand.

"Oh, yeah. I don't know. Christmas and all that. Anymore, it's funny, but I look forward to it and don't look forward to it at all. When it's over, I feel happy about it, and sad, at the same time."

"Sounds normal to me."

Scott gave her a clear smile and Ellen had to admit she liked the way he didn't try to explain, in any manner, the sort of Christmas she knew he'd spent. That was one difference between Scott and her husband. If Jack had passed even one day, let alone an entire holiday, like that, everyone would have had to listen to the moaning.

It made her suddenly want to help Scott a little. After all, in a way he had become like family—albeit the black sheep—and there was no reason not to show him once in a while that people could care about him.

"And you," she said, "have a good Christmas?"

She gave him a very frank, but sympathetic look and he saw what she meant. That she wanted to truly like him and not, for once, be critical. To the depths of his soul he could have wished it was something he could always get from her, but he didn't dwell on it. And it was no longer a question of appreciation, or some stupid notion like that. More, frankly, getting credit where it was due was quite enough.

"It was all right," he said, and then added without thinking. "And Sydney will be back in another week."

Ellen nodded but said nothing. She wasn't about to sit around discussing his private life—she'd learned her lesson!—or especially not that college girl. Not that she didn't like Sydney. It was simply, for her, like imagining discussing cardboard.

Of course, for Scott, it might be a different matter. God knew what he and she were like together in private. In public though, there was nothing and Ellen preferred it that way.

Although—and this she had to suddenly admit to herself—she had indeed lately been wondering what Scott was like in private.

And why not?

Just curiosity, lit by his suddenly seeming to have a private life, at last. Funny thing, and of course it was just an inkling and it made her smile to think of it, but she wouldn't have doubted one second to have learned he was a real pussycat.

"Well ...," she said, "I guess we'll get back into things the day after tomorrow."

"Fine with me."

"As it is, we have to make some pretty big decisions about the planking delivery schedules. Catherine has them set out, but Jack has to make the final decision. We'll be doing that when he gets back tonight."

Something, Ellen couldn't tell, suddenly changed in the kitchen's atmosphere. Like a switch being thrown. Scott was sitting at the table, his face seeming relaxed, but she saw how stiff his body had become. At something she'd said. She felt herself get angry.

Always that, she thought. She was well aware of Scott's jealousy about Jack's abilities and, perhaps even, of her and Jack as a couple, nearly a family, and the business they ran. Evidently, she thought, some things never changed. Whether drunk, or sober.

Right then and there, she was finished with the conversation. She had been having a relatively happy day, despite the awful weather outside. She could see Scott getting suddenly worked up about something, and she didn't want it.

More than once she had gotten involved in major conversations with him about things he considered serious. But today wasn't the day for it.

Some free time had shown up, just like that, where she would have a full day to herself, and she feared its being frittered away. She had been right in the middle of a major housecleaning effort when Scott had shown up, and although she hadn't resented his appearance, or his having a cup of coffee, she had other things to do.

She moved over to the counter where she had been putting up new shelf paper, and went back to work. No reason not to show him she was busy.

"So, I'll tell Jack you stopped by. Do you want him to call you, or anything?"

Ellen didn't look at Scott, but it was obvious now she was all business again. It was a good thing she didn't look at him, or she would have seen a full confirmation of what she'd been thinking: a frowning proof of anger at the mention of her husband's name.

"Maybe so," Scott said, taking care to keep his voice level. He was, of course, far from being anything like jealous about Jack, or Ellen and Jack, or anything else. Frankly, he didn't give a shit.

He couldn't ask straight out where Jack was. That wouldn't sound like any of his business. Nor, for the same reason, although it might seem more that way to Scott than it might to Ellen, could he ask what time Jack would get back.

Those were two questions Scott had to avoid making for the exact reason he didn't want Jack to hear they had been asked.

"I'm going home for a while, but I may be out later, in case Jack needs to call."

It worked exactly as he'd hoped, and Ellen provided all the details herself. "He won't be back until tonight. He said he probably only had to go down to Mount Vernon. If he doesn't find what he needs there, he might have to go all the way to Everett."

Scott nodded, as though uninterested in wherever Jack might be.

"All right," he said. "No big thing, anyway."

Ellen kept on with her work, and from there until Scott finished his coffee, they talked about the weather, and about the boat, and how it was a good thing the timing on the boat was such that all the wood bending was being done during the Northwest's monsoon season, rather than varnishing or painting, which needed warmer, drier weather.

All the time they talked, Scott watched Ellen, but not in the way he had always watched her before. Now, it was in a way that made him not want to stay much longer, himself. As soon as he could, he thanked her for the coffee and went back out to his pickup.

Unbelievably, it was raining even harder, and the clouds were even darker.

It is indeed the end of the world he thought as he ran across the lot to his pickup and jumped in.

Driving away up the road towards Fairhaven he almost turned off the side street towards his house, as he had been almost turning to go there all day long, but hadn't.

Once again he kept right on.

Just to be sure about what he didn't want to be sure about.

# Chapter 61

IT HAD started innocently enough, as things generally do. Which made Scott later contemplate on the reliability of innocence … when it seems that, all too often, all hell breaks loose in connection with it.

He'd been down at Nugent's Corner, out by the Nooksack River, having a bite to eat and a drink at the tavern there—just as Ellen expected. But he'd had just one beer … one … and had gone in there only because he was hungry and sincerely thirsty, having spent most of the early part of the day out in the county, in an overwarm car, trying to locate a pottery store Sydney had told him about. A place that she really *really* liked. Which, of course, was a hint about what she'd like as a present. If he actually got her something. Not that she expected it. She never said such a thing directly and so didn't mean him to do any such thing. Which meant he went looking for that store like he was looking for the Holy Grail.

And he found it and then went and got some lunch, feeling maybe not like Arthur, or even some sort of knight, but at the very least a bit relieved considering how vague her recollection of where that store had been located.

At first though, before driving into the bar's parking lot, he'd taken the road back from the highway bridge down to check out the river. He did that once in a while, especially in the winter when the water was riding high, and he'd drive down along the floodway and out onto the gravel. Sometimes he would even take a few beers down there and talk to the fishermen, who are generally amenable people and especially when someone shows up with a few beers.

And driving down there that morning, and bit surprised at first only because it's always a surprise to run into people outside of the circumstances you know them—but then not really giving it a thought afterwards—he had seen that yellow rig of Sumners.

He remembered it, even though he hadn't seen Sumners drive it since that first day he'd shown up at the boathouse. He also remembered how he hadn't liked the look of Sumners then, nor his little pickup.

Going past, Scott saw how Sumners had a bell pole rigged up on the gravel bank, and how Sumners was hunched down in the cab as though he was asleep.

Although he supposed it would have been a regular, sociable thing to do, Scott didn't feel at all like going over and talking to the guy. He had no particular revulsion at running into Sumners way out there. But, frankly, seeing him and his wife constantly around the boathouse was enough.

Those two, Scott thought, could go slumming all they wanted—for the sake of being sociable, or however they saw it. But it didn't feel right, somehow, to go the other way. To go sociable with either of them at the drop of a hat, or whenever they crossed paths.

Or maybe it was more than that, he thought. Shadows of despicable pride?

Or, he smiled to himself, just common sense. You never knew what might come out of an impromptu conversation with Sumners, who might feel that from his position of moral, or at least social, superiority, he had to say some damn thing ....

Who knew? And ... Scott thought with a grin ... who cared?

He drove back out and up to the bar, had the beer with one of their fat, juicy and hot Reuben sandwiches, and then left.

As he pulled onto the highway, he saw Sumners' pickup come up from below the bridge and turned onto the highway a hundred yards ahead of Scott. The rain was pouring down and Sumners turned on his lights, and Scott found himself following Sumners back to town. Probably, Scott was thinking, if they both pulled up to a light or something, he'd end up giving the guy a wave.

They both passed into town through the lights without having to stop.

At first, Scott figured Sumners would turn off at Alabama and head out to Lake Whatcom. But then Sumners kept on past downtown Bellingham and started on Jackson down around the bay towards Fairhaven. Scott thought he was heading for the boatyard. When the pickup turned off Jackson towards Sehome Hill, Scott had kept on straight, heading home. He stopped in Fairhaven to buy some spaghetti sauce and beer, and when he got back to his car and was almost out on the street again, Sumners pickup went by and, once again, Scott found himself following it.

Scott had laughed. Cosmic, he thought. Sydney would have come up with all sorts of explanations about paths crossing—a rare juxtaposition of fate, and so on. She liked to do that even though, he had discovered, she didn't believe in things like that any more than he did.

Sumners beat him out of the red light at the Fairhaven intersection, turning down the road towards the boathouse. Scott figured he was going down to talk to Jack and Ellen.

Scott figured he, himself, was going home.

When the light changed and he turned down the road, he could see, even in the pouring rain, the bright yellow pickup all the way down by the waterside and how it went past the Colby's without stopping. Scott kept on going down the hill, his house being closer to the waterfront than to the Fairhaven business district. It was by that fact, as he descended, that he could see both Jack's pickup and Ellen's car in the lot. And what Sumners was doing.

Sumners had obviously seen them as well, but had not stopped.

Suddenly Scott found himself curious about Sumners. It was obvious he was checking up on the Colbys. Which, in itself, was something Scott didn't like.

Even so he had been determined to just go home. Sumners pickup came up the road and went by him in the driving rain with no sign of recognition as they passed. Scott kept on and turned down his street, feeling—for the he-didn't-know-how-many-eth time—pissed off with their client.

He had turned his pickup around at the far end of the street where it dead-ended and had gotten back to his house when he saw, down at the intersection, Ellen's car go up the hill towards Fairhaven.

It was just the mixture of circumstances. A built up backlog of previous reflections about Ellen ... and Scott put the car into gear and went back out to the road.

Scott wasn't yet thinking any particular thing.

Just impressions:

Sumners driving past the boathouse with a very visible pickup.

A pickup that, Scott knew, Jack had probably never seen.

Then, five minutes later, Ellen goes up the hill.

Right after it.

And that was all.

Just this thing and that.

But Scott, suddenly, had to know.

No, of course it was all a garbled and in many ways now an ancient mess, his original jealous feelings of attraction for Ellen. Of course, there was nothing there. There had never been anything there. Except whatever he had been harboring there on his side of the fence. But that didn't change some deeper things he'd always acknowledged. His attraction, as a man, and sometimes a very lonely man, and his feelings about Jack, the jealousy, sexual and otherwise. Which he'd come to grip with.

But none of that mattered. This was something else.

He had to know. Even if it no longer had anything personal left within it. So he followed her, and in doing so he smiled suddenly at the appearance of a richly embarrassing little memory. The sort that always makes a guy shudder. The sort one could wish one could forget forever. And whenever it comes back, it's always with that sweet cruelty ... that stabbing reminder, as painful as it is ridiculous, of having done such a damn fool thing.

No, it wasn't the same thing here and now, but there were elements in it that triggered the memory.

He'd been twenty one. And he'd fallen in love with an older woman who had managed to humiliate him in public. That was to say, she and he knew of his humiliation, if no one else did. The fact was, he had been way too young for her, and certainly not ready to accept the instantaneous family that would have come with a divorcee and two children. And she had been pragmatic about it, and even nice. But then, she'd also been fairly hard about it, making him have to accept, in a friendly sort of way, the fact she was seeing other men. After she'd come to her pragmatic decision, that was.

But she wasn't all that pragmatic, either, and had a few twists of her own to deal with. And she'd sometimes call him, wondering why he hadn't been around.

It had been his first experience, his first schooling, in the flows and eddies of where loneliness and love—or lovesickness and self-deception to be more precise—could lead people.

One night, after way too many drinks, he'd ended up creeping along the neighbor's moonlit fence. And there he'd been caught. A drunken idiot. But not by her and her one-night boyfriend. The neighbor had thought he was stealing something.

There, out on the street, he'd tried to move away, saying he was doing nothing, not stealing anything. The neighbor followed, challenging, holding a crowbar and not in the mood for anything that didn't sound like the absolute truth.

Scott, drunk as he was—although sobering quickly—had realized that only an honest confession of the most abject sort would be believed. So he gave it. The shameful, horrifyingly pathetic, naked truth—reducing himself in his own eyes, let alone to a perfect stranger ... crowbar notwithstanding.

The stranger, though, had understood, evidently knowing a thing or two about the woman who lived next door. Or just knowing a thing or two, period.

He'd hefted the crowbar in his hand, patting it in the other, but not in a menacing way. A thoughtful way. As though saying, yes, he remembered a time he would have liked to have known, himself.

Supposedly, Scott suddenly thought as he followed Ellen, times had changed. But, no. Maybe not. He could see now it was still there—things like that—the jealousy of the unknown. And it would probably always be there. Well, maybe not jealousy this time. Nor humiliation, of course. There wasn't anything in the world, anymore, that could get him to creep along a fence. But surely just to know something for what it was, he guessed.

So he followed. And this time it was all deliberate.

He didn't know where the yellow pickup was but he could see Ellen's car. He followed it at a careful distance as it went through Fairhaven and then down along Jackson towards Bellingham.

Scott had begun to figure he was making a mistake, that Ellen was heading into town and it was all nothing, when she suddenly turned and headed up Sehome Hill.

Well of course, he thought, Catherine lived up there on "B" Street, and that was that. He began to be ashamed of himself, despising this reappearance of ... whatever it was.

But then he saw the yellow pickup again.

None of it made sense.

Zero.

Scott frowned.

There they all were, driving around in circles up on Sehome Hill and for no reason he could understand.

Ellen, perhaps, was understandable.

Ellen and Sumners though, there was no way Scott could figure that one out. Catherine was part of the operations and needed to be consulted on things, of course. But, surely the telephone or email was easier? So, in terms of business, it made no sense; and in social terms, even less. Catherine hadn't shown any particular relationship which might include Ellen and Sumners. Scott ended by parking down the street from Catherine's. Amazingly enough, he had somehow got in front of Sumners' pickup, which appeared again a few blocks behind him. Stranger and stranger. With a sinking, somewhat tired feeling, her turned off his engine and crouched down low as the pickup went past. When he sat up he saw how the pickup slowed as it approached Catherine's house.

No doubt about it. Sumners had checked out not only the Colby's, but then Catherine's place.

He didn't check out my place, Scott thought morosely.

His attention completely focused on Sumners' interest in Catherine's house, he had forgotten completely about Ellen. Then Ellen's car came down the street and passed right by the pickup going the other way.

Not even the slightest sign of recognition.

It was obvious that Ellen didn't know Sumners' pickup, and Scott could see how Sumners' attention was on the house. There seemed no linkup at all. And, finally, the yellow pickup drove off down the street.

Ellen, though, didn't stop at Catherine's house either, turning off on a side street.

Scott sat there for a moment, wondering if that was it, and wondering what the hell it was all about. And it was there ... when he'd decided he'd had enough and was about to start his motor again to go find out where she'd gone ... that he saw Jack go running around the corner from where Ellen's car had turned, and go up to Catherine's house, knock, and be let in.

Scott sat in his pickup for a while, staring ahead blankly while his windows fogged up, and then did start his engine.

He drove up the street, turned a corner and found where Ellen's car had been parked in a rather well hid spot, behind a bush a little ways up a side-alley. No one else inside.

There was plenty of parking on the street in front of Catherine's house. It was raining like hell. Like the end of the world. It was a lot shorter distance to get to her front porch from the curb in front, if you didn't care about anyone seeing your car.

He knew exactly what he was looking at. Scott had some experience with discrete car-parking as well.

That was when Scott had driven down to the Colby's, had a cup of coffee with Ellen, and then had left again.

Going home. Then ... once again ... not.

One last look.

But he promised himself he wasn't about to sit around like a private detective. Although, interestingly enough, he could see how ridiculously easy it was to do the largest part of that profession: people who didn't think they were being followed but took precautions anyway, practically handed out maps.

Up to Fairhaven. Through the light again. Up the hill now, taking a side street and not directly on "B" Street. Then all the way up to "A" Street looking down where he could see, from a crossing street, no one out on the sidewalk in the rain, nor were the curtains open. Then down across "B" street and, yes, there was Ellen's car still there stuck up the alleyway.

Nowhere near Mount Vernon. Let alone all the way to Everett.

But even farther away than that.

Scott stared for a moment, then finally drove home, very much in the mood—now—for a good, stiff drink.

# Chapter 62

DEBORAH WAS sitting in her comfortable armchair, which the men carefully cleaned of sawdust and brushed down each morning in case she needed it, watching Jack slowly cutting out the curving edge of a midships floor on the band saw. She watched his round-sloping shoulders hunching in concentration, and his heavy muscled sides and back twisting, and then, the tight, slowly shifting movements of his buttocks. There her eyes remained.

Scott hadn't just been telling stories to Sydney.

At another time, she would have only permitted herself a surreptitious glance which nobody—of course—would have noticed. But now she lingered as a sculptress must do. A necessary shedding of modesty in order to understand.

She concentrated on how he moved his pelvis, the slow turning and pushing, as if urging the wood through the singing blade by the sheer force of his loins. She was drawn into the movement and a dark concentration gathered deep within her as she too became a party to the thrust of his body, his hips, as he slowly twisted the heavy oak upon the saw table.

Her fingers suddenly fluttered at her sides, her heart beat rapidly and her stomach tightened. She broke from her trance momentarily startled, almost crying out in fear. But also with a joy of having discovered the animal force and nature in the work, the absolute sexuality, which was as much a part of the work as the concepts of making form align with the original idea.

At another time, she might have considered such a thing disfiguring. Now, though, it lent a terrible, tragic beauty to the work. She recognized now the great, tender and tearing pathos within the act, and within these men. And it made her feel tenderness for them.

She could pity them for what they were and what they would never be. Jack and Scott were not animals, but now she clearly understood how they were laden with the tragedy of all animals. Good men, and pure, but so full of the sensual music of their work, they were doomed never to be better than their work.

There was a suspended feeling in the air for Deborah. A twitching in her soul, making it a strange agony to watch them work, watch how they were blind to their own fate.

Everything in the days to come held this agony of comprehension and clarity. She felt a cloying freedom in her new powers of understanding, but she didn't mind at all. How could she! She couldn't change where she had been and what she had learned.

It had all been so difficult for her once, all those years hoping to find that one idea which would save her from the beastliness she saw in life. Art, of course, had saved her from that beast. Yet strangely enough, now there was another beast, so tangible as almost to be seen, sitting on its heavy haunches watching her, as she watched back. Its yellow eyes gleamed at her with lust, and yet at the same time an awful compassion which seemed to know her better than she knew herself. She knew it was a battle of wills—a renewed and more terrible battle—which she must not lose.

As she sat there in her chair, she held herself even more primly. For now, quite often, as she watched the two men wrestling their material, piece by piece, down into the boat, she felt quite conspicuous. As if her thoughts could be read. As if she was forcibly naked there in the world for anyone to see if they were looking.

As it was looking.

If only people knew how hard it all really was for her. If only they could see, and applaud, how she dealt with all of this. If only they, Eric, could understand.

But, of course, how could he? It was her combat, as it would always be for any sensitive person, to go alone into that combat for knowledge and understanding.

Others, then, could only profit from the spoils brought back from that battle. Eric could only profit, in that manner.

So, in a way, this was her duty ... for if there was a way for him to profit from her efforts to understand, she must not fail.

She would not fail, she told herself, looking sternly at the physiques of Jack and Scott—their loins and sinews—knowing now fully and clearly that those, too, were part of that duty.

Even if, she had to admit, the lust of the beast did indeed arouse her.

## Chapter 63

MID-AFTERNOON, quiet as a Thursday could be with nothing pressing, Eric told his secretary to hold all calls. He couldn't concentrate anymore.

He slumped in his chair and looked out over rain-soaked Bellingham, over the flat, asphalted roofs studded with hot air vents and chimneys.

Below on the streets traffic lights directed the few cars around the downtown where no one was out walking in that miserable weather. In all honesty, he thought, it was an ugly little town from above, in the winter.

He sighed and got up to stretch and walked across his office to the windows looking south over the downtown. He stared out across it to the bay with the college hill rising steeply to one side. He stared at that for a moment, looking at the brown haze of leafless trees following the old streets and houses below the school and then his eyes followed the shore farther on down to old Fairhaven.

Blank for a moment. Then the thought came to him, sharply focused and direct. A yearning to see if it was there at all. He turned abruptly away with a look of distaste crossing his face.

Good God, he thought, going over and flopping back onto his office couch. This was all he needed. As if things didn't get complicated enough on their own. He had a million things to contemplate. Politics. Hartman. Especially Hartman. The developer was preparing to pounce, but Eric had discovered another possibility to the Fairhaven project. A possibility which wouldn't please Hartman. At all. But one thing at a time.

It was complicated and risky, as all such ideas had always been. But he could handle it. He could seemingly handle anything when it came to business. His life in that arena was always in a cool, controlled order. As he had thought everything else was.

Except it wasn't. The everything else, that was.

Suddenly, all that seemed out of control.

There was no doubt now. He was aching for another woman.

He stared at the ceiling, slowly clenching and unclenching his fists. She had something he desired. To be brutally honest, coldly honest, that thing he desired was exactly what was lacking in Deborah.

He had never permitted himself that thought before. At least, not in so many words, thought out with precision, one brutally following the other. Something lacking. Especially lately.

When he thought of himself, there in his world of business, and especially there now when things were going to get very hard-boiled in the next few months, what he needed was a way he could share his trust with someone. The pressure lately had been tremendous.

Worse than that was Deborah's ever more entangled adoration of those wood workers. On and on she would go about how deep they were, how intricate their relationship was with what they were doing down there. Yet little did she, or they, realize, how little they knew about what was going on around them. Blind. They were blind puppets dancing beneath a sword of Damocles.

He hadn't told her yet about the Fairhaven project. But that was nothing new. He had long before learned that she was more or less indifferent to his business and so he didn't bother discussing it. Lives were overturned, mountains of money and influence came into play, and she would just nod and return to her private dreams.

The thought had come to him slowly … crept up on him nearly unawares over the past couple of months. But it was now there, and present: there were times now he regretted having married her. Almost as much as he regretted this boat thing.

Just an idle thought … but there was always divorce. The thought had wafted through, never really given much attention, but in the past few days he'd given it more than just a few idle moments of his time.

Not a simple matter. Rich men never have simple divorces. It would be a messy business, and her parents would make sure it got even messier.

Yet, on the other hand, there were no children and it was obvious his success had been established long before he had met her. Still, probably a few million to settle. He hadn't believed in pre-nuptial agreements. But now he felt it was too bad there wasn't a built-in set of agreements which everyone, without having to make a big deal out of it, would have to abide by. A black and white set of legal expectations in marriage which were outside the grasp of legal interpretation. That was to say, lawyers, and in her case—meaning her family's—practically every goddamn lawyer in Salt Lake City.

Well, he thought, you get in the end what you deserve. In the business world, he had always understood that fact very lucidly and never allowed himself to deviate from his purposes. He either got what he wanted, or let things drop. Discipline, and a willingness to sacrifice desires and self-interest when things didn't work—to walk away from obsessive attempts to cling—was the key to success. And maybe even happiness.

Where Deborah had been concerned, though, he had let all that slide. He hadn't been able to resist the creature comforts of her stunning presence, ignoring his own knowledge that what was not complete, could never be so.

So, in effect, what had he to lose? Now, evidently, he could no longer have it all as far as his private life was concerned. That was to say, complete happiness.

Divorce? Maybe not. It was so final and of an unknown quality. But, and here he was thinking something he'd never considered before, why not see if it was possible to have bits and pieces of happiness?

Already, there was some of that.

He dreamed about Catherine Wilkins at night as he lay there next to Deborah. Distant dreams, where he was with groups of people, or his wife, and in the distance, with other people, would be Catherine. She would always see him, but always something happened which tore them away from each other. Sometimes the dreams reenacted the scenario over and over again. But not just with her. At other times he would find himself in a sudden rush of fantasies with another woman: perhaps a woman executive he knew in Chicago, or some woman he might have noticed on the street. One of the secretaries in his own office. A movie star. Once even he found himself bizarrely blazing away with that college girlfriend of Scott McKay.

He would wake in a sweat, spent and worried. But gratefully, his wife always slept through it all.

But it was having a very serious effect, at other times.

Lately the case had been that, while he hadn't been so impotent as not to become ready, he often lost his concentration badly because of his growing disinterest. All it took was the hint of a problem and it all became just a process, his body in full response and loaded, but the trigger no longer there and no amount of concentration could find it, and effort seemed ludicrous.

Eric stood up suddenly. A violent reaction of irritation. Then, just as quickly, he sat back down again. Tiredly.

What the hell was he doing, he thought dismally? He was being torn into disarray by the whipping gusts of desire and disappointment. And at some point, it was going to spill over into too many other things.

He simply had to do something. That was eminently clear.

"But what?" he said aloud.

He sat there for another minute, knowing what he wanted to do, exactly what he needed to do, and pretending he didn't know it.

And then knowing and no longer pretending, he reached over and buzzed his secretary.

# Chapter 64

WHEN CATHERINE came back from a long lunch and a trip across town to check on an order of brass fittings, she was told to take some architect's plans over to Eric Sumners. Evidently, there were some last modifications he wanted to have made to the interior layout and would be going to Seattle to see Fletcher in the days to come. Jack, informed about the call, cautioned her in an unnecessarily long monologue about reminding Eric that the hull shape was now unchangeable with the ribs and floors in place.

Catherine had listened patiently to all that, feeling how, with Ellen there in the kitchen, Jack had needed to go on longer than usual; to seem like Mr. Pedantic with her, handing her all this boss-employee blah-blah to paper over any sign of intimacy. Even as he spoke, Catherine was thinking how, all things considered, if Jack had been a single man she would have considered they were well on their way towards something serious. Of course, he was not and therefore they were not. They were simply being adults about it, acknowledging that if they were going to share a bed with each other they might as well take it for all it was worth. No holding back.

The afterglow, though, took a little managing.

Jack finished at last and went back to the shop. Then Ellen left, and Catherine went and sat at her desk and thought about her next duty. Within minutes, she found her heart racing with an excited feeling of anticipation. She had never had a chance to meet Eric alone anywhere. Although she had often felt a mutual attraction between the two of them, it had always had to be let drift away into a dreamy speculation.

Perhaps, she thought, it was all a delusion. It was easily possible that Eric's seeming attraction was simply a manifestation of how he dealt with everyone.

Charisma. Or else, it was also possible she was misreading things because of the fact she was, those days, feeling a great deal better about herself.

There was no doubt. She felt buoyant. Sexy. Outside, it was

raining all the time but her life was full of sunshine. She had Jack coming to see her. When he was with her it was as though she had won something grand. And maybe she had. What was best of all was how she was also free. No strings, although it was obvious that Jack and she were getting deep. Deeper, he had been telling her, than he got with Ellen.

It was natural. A mistress was bound to carry a sense of a deeper complicity because of the shared secret and risks. It was therefore somewhat unfair for the mistress to take advantage of it. But on the other hand, happiness was hard enough to come by without throwing it away. If they could be happy together, that was a larger good for which sacrifices had to be made.

Things, therefore, were as good as they were going to get for the time being. She was attractive again, to herself as well as to others. If there really was something mutual there with Eric, God knew what else could fall into her life. When it rained, it poured.

Perhaps nothing was there to happen anyway. Catherine smiled.

Okay, at the moment, she felt like the Belle of the Ball—jokes aside. But Eric and Jack weren't exactly the same sort of guys at all. Where Jack followed out his instincts, and his sympathies and feelings of tenderness, to their logical conclusions, Eric was a businessman, whatever that meant as far as his innermost feelings were concerned.

An excitement possessed her, almost a feeling of that doom where emotions are spread upon a pyre of hopes and expectations and then lit with fears of rejection. A trembling desire backlit with the knowledge of impossibility.

Catherine could smile. But with that, she stood up and put on her coat and went out the door. Daydreams aside, she thought grimly, she still had a job to do.

As she passed through the shop on her way over to the loft stairs she glanced at the work. Jack and Scott were finishing putting in the floor bracings on the ribs. Meticulous work which had them crawling slowly, rib by rib, down the spine of the boat. Not very exciting to watch, and yet, there in the corner of the shop sat Deborah Sumners, drawing sketches of the work.

Catherine stood on the stairs for a moment. The skeleton of the boat glowed bright in the gray shed, sawdust and wood chips lay everywhere in a thick yellow scatter. In another golden point of light sat Deborah, her heavy red-orange hair pulled back from her face in a loose ponytail, the sunlight from a high, shop window, creating a thin halo of brilliant orange around her golden features. She wore a white sweater and she had pushed the sleeves up her arms for her sketch work, concentrating on the big artist's pad anchored against the pit of her stomach.

Jealousy? There was no doubt for Catherine that being attracted to these married men had a terrible side to it. It was also very real, though, and it was the very real things which always happened.

With a feeling of determination, she went up to get the plans.

# Chapter 65

Between the time he had called down to Colby's until the time he expected her to show up Eric fiddled with a number of budget sheets. His accountant had been at him about dead wood in the office, especially in light of new projects on the horizon. It meant letting some people go in order to make room for others. Around there, they called it restructuring. But he didn't like it.

Eric wasn't necessarily worried about the idea of firing people. Cash flow was good and that was always the best time to lay people off. And the situation was right. It wasn't as though Bellingham was a depressed economy where people couldn't find work. But the timing was wrong. Even under the best of circumstances layoffs were always news and the last thing he wanted right then was that sort of publicity.

He stared stubbornly at the papers in front of himself, but he gradually lost his concentration, and finally let it all drop with a rebellious urge of impatience, deciding he could well afford everybody for the time being and just let the others join in. Besides, all this staff shakeup business had been sprung on him as a surprise. Obvious candidates for restructuring had been pushed forward despite no obvious reasons. Very probably there was a carefully constructed bit of lower deck politics being filtered up through Newell Briggs' department. Eric smiled ruefully.

His accountant was not averse to office politics. In fact, if anything, he could often be the center of the storm.

All of that didn't bother Eric, either. His inclination was to let things take their course on the floors below. A form of natural selection it was better not to meddle in. So, for the time being, everybody lived.

He was then left with nothing to do, idly playing with his pen set right up to the moment his secretary buzzed that Catherine had arrived.

Eric's mind emptied. Carefully manufactured pretenses and motivations suddenly disappeared, giving him no defenses, no support. He had nothing to say to her at all, and his heart dropped.

Then she walked in.

She was wearing her overcoat unbuttoned and she carried the plans under her arm in their cardboard tube. Her other hand was thrust deep into a jacket pocket. There was something almost military in the way she carried herself stiffly into the center of his office.

Eric smiled anxiously. Then stood up.

"Hi," he said. "Thanks for coming." He waved vaguely at the sofas for her to sit down. "Would you like some coffee?"

"I just stopped by to drop off these plans of the boat," she said, and as she did so she realized how obvious and awkward a statement that was.

Eric, crossing to the coffee maker, didn't see her suddenly look at the carpet and make a face of consternation with herself. He was having his own problems with awkwardness.

His back to her, he played with the coffee cups and the pot. He filled one cup to the brim, suddenly his, and then filled another to only about a third of that. He couldn't remember the last time he had felt so inept.

Picking up his overflowing cup, he poured some into hers, spilling some scaldingly upon his fingers. Taking a slow breath, he dried his hand with a napkin, picked up the cups and turned and carried them over to her even as she stood there, still in her overcoat, still with the tube under her arm.

"Here you go," he said. Suddenly, he realized he hadn't heard her say if she wanted any or not.

Fumbling to get her hand out of her pocket, she took the coffee without a word and, as though catching up with her own thoughts, smiled at him. She set the cup on a low table by his sofa, and then the tube, and took her overcoat off.

"Oh, God," she heard him say softly behind her, and then with a firmer voice, "please, sit down."

At the core of human nature is an absolute nakedness which, regardless of how heavily clothed and hidden it is, is constantly seeking for a way to uncover itself despite its fears of exposure. Maybe just once in a lifetime one soul uncovers completely. For others perhaps, there are many instances of revealing ... although for the sake of sanity, those revealings are few and far between and usually politely ignored. For some, revealings never occur—out of absolute fear. As is quite normal. But Eric was not a man to fear his impulses, and especially not when he wanted something.

That is, he thought, once he'd regained his composure and a modicum of courage.

Catherine, as well, had recovered her composure, and watched him closely, waiting.

Then she saw him sigh, one last time, and give her the look she had been waiting for. And at that moment, she might have believed she had been waiting for it, for all of her life.

## Chapter 66

THE BIG, annual boat show was going on up in Vancouver. Jack
and Scott took a day off to drive up and see what was newer, bigger,
faster, and more expensive than last year. Most of the morning they
browsed inside the coliseum amidst the shining hulls and towering
rigging. They made a few contacts and left a few business cards
behind. It was later, at a lunch counter having fish and chips and
one of those Canuck microbrews, that Jack finally noticed how
Scott was in a very quiet mood.

It couldn't be the boat, Jack thought. There had been just a hint,
earlier on, that the project had disturbed Scott. Even though—and
Jack could be big enough to now admit it—that Scott had been
partly behind its inception. But where was the problem? It had
disturbed all of them. Look at himself and Ellen. It was a big shakeup, all this. Ellen was almost continually in a happy frame of mind,
and with reason. For once, they had plenty of money in the bank,
and great prospects for the future.

And more: she was maybe pregnant.

But what the hell, though, you can get used to success as much
as you can get used to failure. The problem with Scott, he just
hadn't gotten used to the success of it.

Or maybe he was jealous of it. Just couldn't handle it. You go
along one way with your friends and colleagues for a long time, and
then one day things change. Life evolves, people evolve, Jack
thought. In the long run, the best policy was to avoid getting mired
down by the past. Or the people who were mired there.

Why the hell Scott wouldn't be happy with things, wasn't
obvious. Jack had never outwardly insinuated, even if he had
occasionally considered, that he might let Scott go. Frankly, though,
Scot either had to get used to things somehow, or make other plans.
They just couldn't keep lugging Scott and his problems around with
them forever.

It was a shame, though. Scott was a skilled boatbuilder. After all,
the drinking hadn't really ever affected his work. More just an
irritation for Jack and Ellen to have had to deal with. The sloppy

looking mornings and the grumbling and all. Minor pain in the ass, to be honest about it.

But then, they had a right not to have to put up with that hangover shit either. It was unfair for Ellen to have had to put up with all that. Nobody needed someone else's problems dragged in across the rug.

If it was jealousy, then Scott could just plain fuck off.

Maybe though, Jack reflected, it wasn't that.

The other possibility for all this morose bullshit, of course, could very well be his girlfriend. More likely, in fact. A little more pathetic, but preferable to the other thing.

Okay, nobody around there was an Einstein. On the other hand, airheads were another story. If Scott wanted to shack up with these twit-twat college girls, he ought to know damn well what he was getting himself into.

Jack almost smiled.

She had a hot body, that was sure. It was easy enough to imagine how Scott had managed to get pulled in. Older guy, young babes. Down there in the bars watching all the young girls and figuring you didn't have a chance with any of them. Especially a guy like Scott who had more than your regular baggage of woman problems. Then along comes some girl like Sydney, all happy-go-lucky and not too picky, like a goddamn Gift from Above, and all the rest.

Yet, even so, there was Scott, sort of hang-dogging around once again.

Jack was about fed up with it. When he had problems, he didn't fucking shovel them all over everyone else. Maybe, he thought, what Scott needed to hear were a few hard truths.

He took a look over at Scott's closed face.

Jack sighed. "Is something bothering you?"

For Scott—indeed feeling hard about something he didn't want to either know or think about--Jack's words made him feel like he was suddenly torn up by the roots. Right out of the ground. Was something bothering him? Well, Jack, he thought, yes and no. No, in the sense that there weren't any real good reasons to be bothered about anything that was any of his business in the first place. But yes, in the sense that just the sight of Jack made him feel ill.

He had often swallowed whatever pride he had, kept his mouth shut, and kept his job. Before, to say nothing was no big loss. What people thought of him was less important than keeping his work and to produce good work, at that.

This time, there was an enormous temptation to not keeping his mouth shut.

You go along, he thought, some days good, others not so good. Some days understood, some days under a cloud of suspicion. But the important thing was to try to keep things straight in your own life. It wasn't that big a struggle. Actually it was simple. Don't get too frustrated, or too envious, and don't use other people to relieve your woes.

Times were, though, you could get tired.

Bothered? Perhaps it was paranoia, but the fact was that he felt, somehow, once this newest form of really bad shit set in, it was going to end up in some manner on his own doorstep.

Do something about it? Highly doubtful.

It was amazing how people managed to screw up, just when everything starts to go well. The problem is, it's awfully easy to be a failure. There's a perfection of simplicity to the equation of losing. To fail, all you have to do is avoid making hard decisions about obvious things.

To say all that to Jack, though, would be incomprehensible. So Scott dissimulated, and hoped for the best.

"No," he said. "Just a few things in the home life."

It was a lie, of course. Home was the only place things were going pretty well. But he was willing to pretend it was about Sydney. Discussing women was always an easy way out, since it was a subject that took up a lot of internal space anyway. It was easy to convince any man that it had, once again, become the center of things.

"You know …," he went on in a dull monotone, "just trying to go along without thinking too much about things."

"Oh, yeah," Jack said "that's just one of life's big lessons."

He turned and gave Scott a grin. "There comes a time though, with women, that you have to set the guidelines for them. They need that, you know. Otherwise, they feel they're being used."

There hadn't been much of a chance. Scott immediately felt white hot. Even if Jack hadn't said anything at all, things would have been on the razor's edge, Scott realized. And he knew he was trapped. His anger had exactly no place to put itself, and anything at all coming from Jack that had any personal ring to it, anything that wasn't strictly about work—and even then tethered firmly to the physical and mental activities involved in putting one piece of wood up against another one—just set it all off like a bomb.

It was too much and Scott couldn't help it. He had a sudden desire to bury Jack in it. And he knew of no better way right then than to pretend to be objective about things. Talking about one thing, when in fact it was about another.

"Well, I'll tell you," he said, feeling the nasty wickedness of it, but not caring. "I suppose people sometimes think I never take things as they come, for what they are. Maybe even that there's always some manipulating going on. What it comes down to is this. Everybody's got their lives. I've got mine. I don't ask much of anyone. I don't want anyone to have to trouble themselves with me and my shit. My major concern is that my shit doesn't end up someone else's problem."

It had all come out in one piece and there was more. Much more. But Scott suddenly felt tired and was willing to let it go at that. Unfortunately, Jack had no idea there were words behind the words.

"That's for sure," he said, with an air of ageless wisdom. "Burn and learn."

Scott felt it come up, hard and mean, and he knew there was no way to get around it. He just couldn't. Although he also knew he wasn't going to start a knock down drag out. Nevertheless, what came out next was nearly in a snarl.

"Yeah, right," he said. "Burn and learn. I figure that's the best we can do, eh? Me, I like more the idea of loyalty and keeping my crap to a minimum. For myself, if I can be as loyal to that idea as I can, then, as far as I'm concerned, I'm a loyal person. Loyal people don't use their friends, or lie to them."

He looked over at Jack, still talking about one thing and meaning another. But suddenly, as well, defending himself and Sydney from Jack's insinuation that he knew something about them. Or that he had the right to say anything.

"If anyone can show me how I'm using Sydney," he went on evenly, "I'll be ready to listen. I'm willing to hear anyone out. But if all anyone's got against me is only based on assumptions— assumptions people work up out of their own particular viewpoints—then I don't give a shit."

Jack was nearly staring at him. If he hadn't understood the rest, he certainly understood that, Scott thought. He nearly smiled. It wasn't often that he said more than three words to Jack about his own life, and Jack probably thought that was all he was capable of. And suddenly, even if he was going a long way from explaining things, it felt good to let Jack know someone else was able to get sensitive about things.

Scott, feeling inspired, decided to go with it. Not caring where it went anymore.

"It's hard," he said, enjoying now the ambiguity of his explanation, "not to frame in people using your own feelings and personality ... as though everything they do should be seen based on what you would have done in the same situation. But that won't wash. I fight my evil, you fight yours, and the battles take place on totally different ground. So I don't make any judgment. I'll tell you, though, sometimes it's goddamn hard. You know ... some people absolutely manage to fuck things up. And it always seems, you know, that those are exactly the same people who are ready to hand you all the advice in the world."

Jack had taken to sipping his beer and nodding through it all, unsure of where this was all coming from. But he'd been right about one thing, he thought. Scott had got himself all worked up about the whole show. Feeling sorry for himself and so on. Not that what he'd said wasn't, on the whole, fairly sensible. But it was also obvious the guy was feeling penned in by Sydney. You don't have these torrents gushing out if you're not twisted up about something. But at the same time, there was something about what Scott had said, that made him feel nervous. Jack couldn't put his finger on it, so he just tried to ignore it. All this, of course, wasn't his problem, it was Scott's. And another thing was sure: Scott just didn't know shit about women. The guy just didn't see how important it was to communicate with them. Women needed a lot of attention. Someone needed to tell him about how it was.

Evidently, Scott could barely make one girl happy. And he thought *that* was difficult? Hell, what would he have done with two?

Jack felt a moment's sympathy for Scott. He would have liked to be able to tell the guy that everything would be fine. But to be really helpful, he thought suddenly, the real and best thing a friend could do was to sometimes say things, right out. And this, he realized, was one of those times. He set his beer down and gave Scott as diplomatic a look as he could, both sympathetic and understanding.

"Listen, I just want you to think about this, okay? But just consider this: maybe you need to really think about things. About Sydney, I mean. Maybe not just about yourself so much."

Scott would have stared in disbelief except for the fact he wasn't at all surprised.

Which permitted Jack to continue, sure now that Scott was truly listening.

"Those guys up at the college ...," he said, "for example. When things are going slow, she's probably comparing you to them. I'm not saying they have much to offer in exchange ... but they are, after all, her age, studying and getting degrees. Maybe they're not what she really wants, but they probably make a lot more effort with her than you do. Probably manage to show a lot more of their feelings than you have."

Scott now felt chastened, but not for anything he was hearing, but for how ridiculous it was that he'd opened the door to all this in the first place. Despite himself, the sarcasm couldn't be held back.

"That's good. I never realized how much respect you had for how complicated and sensitive college boys are."

"Don't tell me you weren't complicated and sensitive at that age."

Scott was stuck. Obviously, what he really wanted to discuss, attack, or deal with, wasn't discussable. So there he was, talking about himself, and in the stupidest way imaginable. Under any other circumstance, he would have laughed.

"In some ways, yes," he said, deciding to pretend they were having a real conversation. Not caring anymore. "In others, not at all. I'm not going to sit here and feel sorry for, or try to compete with, these poor complicated college boys. Nothing is more tortured and complicated than some poor, lonely boy who wants and needs desperately to fuck Sydney. And to do it, might even have to pretend he likes her."

Jack was beginning to feel prickly with irritation, himself. These guys, he thought, who went on and on. Never once thinking how certain subjects could bother other people. No way, of course, could Scott know about himself and Catherine. But if he knew about it, he might understand how Jack wasn't just talking off the top of his head. How it was true that because of Catherine, Jack was even more sensitive now about Ellen's needs. He knew though, that probably no one was really capable of understanding. People expected the worst out of other people. That was the way it went.

"So ...," he now said flatly, with a tone of open disapproval and making a gesture of changing the subject, or the tone of things, with his hand, "things are just going along."

Scott was ready to change the subject. What did it matter in the end what Jack did? What was important was finishing the boat.

He nodded.

"Yeah, things are going along. But it's more than that too. She's very good for me. She's got that sincerity ... the young kind where you're still willing to act on it without thinking. She makes me feel that way, as well. I don't think she'll ever get smart the way all of us got so fucking smart. That's probably the best thing about her. It's the thing that makes her loyal. And even more so. Faithful, I guess, is the right word."

Jack liked that. It sounded like Scott had learned a few things. He liked how Scott spoke of his girlfriend, with respect. A man has to respect his woman, women, or else nothing else can come of it. He looked over at Scott and gave him a grin. In the end, he was an OK guy.

Scott looked back, saw the grin and returned it ... not out of some shared camaraderie, but in amusement and a sudden relief at realizing something. In the end, Jack was an idiot and had the ability to spread that idiocy in dangerous directions. And he could really screw you up.

If you weren't on to him.

# Chapter 67

KNOWING BAD things makes you feel normal; but balanced normality, what some might call a moderate state, is a flat and lonely place to passion-scoured eyes. Despite his until-lately willful flings at self-forgetting debauchery, if Scott considered himself a moderate man, that did not mean that he considered it a desirable state to be always pursued or nurtured. More, he felt things should be like a sort of pendulum which always fell to center, dead, until the next impetus to passion's swinging was brought about by external events.

Never internal, though, it seemed. The fact was, he realized he was a much more moderate man than he had guessed.

He was in an irritated mood, and had plenty of sources he could point to, for that irritation. In fact, just about everyone he knew excepting Sydney, was a source. And he felt worried he might even include her at some moment. It was possible, all this irritation wasn't based on actual injustice, but self-righteousness. He could admit that possibility, and was wary. But, on the other hand, his irritations sure seemed real enough. Jack. Ellen. Catherine. The Sumners, each in their own special way ....

It was hard not to believe his irritation was genuine. And, right there that morning, he could have picked any one of them to be grumbling about. And, somehow, as though sort of a toss of the die, he was grumbling to himself about Deborah. Why? Perhaps just because it was her turn ... or perhaps, in fact, because of the proximity of the boat. His irritations for the others could happen anywhere, but whenever he got around the boat Deborah's presence came to hover and poison things.

Not that he was thinking specifically of her. But in a tangential fashion, the boat-Deborah connection—because he was there beside the boat—was making him feel dissatisfied with everything, and even himself ... even making him feel dissatisfied with his seeming moderation.

He felt like a very bland man.

Compared with what everyone else was getting up to.

He could start anywhere with all this dissatisfaction, and let it run around and around in circles. And he did.

The idea that his passions were not self-induced, for example, nettled him, and he shrugged indignantly. He was sitting out in the shop, drinking coffee by the boat on a cold, late winter morning, watching over the space heaters pouring warmth into the air. Although he had been there less than a half an hour, he felt as though he was finishing a night's guard duty. Partly he was tired, just flat-out fatigue, which contributed to the better part of a stale, used-up feeling. The rest was contained in a solid discontentment with himself and life.

He felt like an empty shell, battered back and forth by the actions of others as they set themselves to swinging wildly either to misadventure or to glory—hard to separate which was which. He seemed to pale in their light. Lacking imagination or something. Originality. Willing to just slog away, move as though a marionette. Protesting, but not really. Sydney—who he liked and found deeply attractive though she could be no one's fatal dream of a woman— had been accepted by him, and him by her, in the same way you accepted the fact you needed a new pair of work boots. It seemed. Passion coming, if you could call it that, later.

Disagreeable as those thoughts were ... there was another, even more bothersome, source of frustration.

If he little felt the author of his own well-being, or simply his own ability to direct himself at anything, he felt even less his participation in the larger patterns. A question of choice.

He had felt, earlier, that this boat project had been brought into being by his efforts. First with the little rowing skiff which no one had wanted or seemed to appreciate. Then with his immediate decision to push forward with Sumners' original queries.

Where before he might have considered himself the seminal motor to all that, he was now an appendage. Strangely usurped by the others. He worked at Colby's, and the Colbys were building this great, goddamn yacht. And for all the world it had become as though it was only the latest in a steady stream of production which had been going on since Christ only knew when.

Goddamn it to hell, not even a decent pay raise in keeping with the general flow of money around there. Not a word about future security, either. On top of that came the rest of it, the implied, or direct, criticism. He drank too much, or had. He was so much flotsam, not even jetsam—something once perhaps useful. He ought to do this, he ought to do that. He ought to settle down. But Good God, why with her? And so on.

Once you got put in a category, he thought sourly, trimmed to size and boxed up, you never got out. Around there, Scott was this thing the Colbys had decided upon. Nothing he could do could change the impression they had, and it was the sort of impression which would deny him the ability to take credit for anything worthwhile. It wasn't just the Colbys. People in general were like that if they considered someone insubstantial.

Scott felt a galling irritation with himself. Possibly all this was self-pity. But probably not. Reality was: no new respect. He wasn't living around complicated people. He knew simple people, and he knew complicated people. And one of the differences was that simple people, regardless of intentions, always let you know what they thought of you.

And now, this new thing he had to carry around. It got so, some days, he could barely look at, let alone speak to, either Jack or Catherine.

Scott looked over at the boat. He had felt a number of ways about her over the ensuing months but never had he felt sick of her. He was aware that there is always a point in any project when you get disgusted with the sheer effort. The point where there is a cut off feeling, or unreality, which damns the desire to finish as much as the idea to have started in the first place. All endeavor becomes ridiculous. But however absurd the effort might be, it was a lot easier when you at least got credit for it.

Everyone was slogging away at something. God damn if it was only decent that you at least got credit for not giving in, lying down and croaking. That you at least got out of bed in the morning.

It was true, he thought: the best people could do for each other—if not actually helping—was to at least give each other credit for trying. Trying to work. Trying to be honest. Trying to be loyal. Trying to be unselfish. It was a more pragmatic and more easily executable form of the Golden Rule.

It had all started out so simple. Build a boat, and make sure it would float. Now it had to be always more, and always less, than it could have been. Bad enough on one hand that it had become such a smug object of satisfaction. What was worse was how she had become such a monstrous object of deluded fantasy.

Which brought him back to what was probably the original source for his irritation that morning.

Deborah Sumners. She made it all worse. Or Sumners himself.

That last one was too much. Give your wife a hundred and thirty-five foot dildo to play with. Then down she came with her big tits, sighing with an excited innocence which was obviously not so innocent anymore.

And lately, it had just gotten worse and worse. Deborah Sumners was in a hot groove all right. A real soul-sucker. Scott had been joking to Sydney about all that before. Somewhat joking. But it was a joke no longer.

She stared at them. Which was one thing. But now she did that, and also followed them around, telling them all about it. In a sort of strange fever.

Scott wished her husband could see what she was doing. He'd never let her come down there again.

He looked over the construction. The floors, locking the ribs from side to side down at the keel, were all in, as well as the beam shelves. And many of the main beams were in place. Very nearly, the hull was to the point of being self-supporting. That, of course, wouldn't come until the planking was nearly finished and all the beams and bulkheads were in place. A lot of work.

And he wished they could get on with it without those eyes, and that attitude, glomming all over them.

First it had been all the stellar inquiries into the meaning of life. Now it was becoming one big Live Sex Show down there. Anymore, he didn't know if he shouldn't take his pants off and start humping a sawhorse.

God knew what it all would lead to. Maybe this was what Sumners had been hoping for in the first place. But how could he have?

Maybe, at rock bottom, all this art shit was exactly what everyone said it was. Freud wasn't just a dirty old man; and Sumners knew exactly what he was doing.

Lighting up his wife.

As for feeling put upon, it was a fairly complete package. Even Sydney—and here he gave free reign to his frustrations, despite himself—to some extent, managed on bad days to make him feel like a reluctant Svengali. But, okay, that was nothing compared to what the others were putting on him .... He'd never known anything like it.

Ellen had him pegged for a derelict. Jack, for a whiner. Deborah, for a ... who knew what? Sumners, maybe for a gigolo.

But the worst was how Jack and Catherine had him feeling like Peeping Tom, hiding in the closet of a whorehouse.

It was getting to be a serious problem.

Not being able to look at Ellen anymore had gotten to be an affectation which, sooner or later, she was going to start noticing. And oddly enough, he not only didn't feel the same way about her as he had before, but he couldn't find himself feeling sorry for her, either.

She was happier than ever, it seemed. And he was glad for her, as far as that went. But it was amazing to him how the old latent lust he had always carried around for that taut dark body had vanished.

He knew why, and knew it wasn't very gentlemanly, but it was the truth. It was a cold shower to watch someone who was living so blissfully unaware of reality. She was no fool. She simply didn't know. Which, unfortunately, made her a fool.

Knowing some things made you feel normal, but they also make you wonder.

How long it had been going on, he couldn't guess. He had tried to think back about specific times he had seen them together down there before. Parties the previous Fall, or in the kitchen at lunchtime. With nothing to be aware of, he had seen nothing. Now, though, he could see straight through them.

They were careful, that was for sure. Even when Scott was preoccupied, or pretending to be, or Ellen wasn't around, Jack and Catherine didn't slip up. No signs, no looks. Once you knew, though, it was as good as seeing them naked in bed with each other.

He sighed and took a drink of his coffee. This was a very bad way to start off a day.

Worse, it was just another in a string of bad days, where his crowded thoughts and irritations swirled, seemingly endlessly. But there was one last thing to top all this off, which made it all even more worrisome.

When he had told Sydney about all this, recounting that rainy day up on Sehome Hill, she had made a lucid point. A very lucid point.

Sumners wasn't the sort of man who wandered around aimlessly. There was a reason for his lurking around Catherine's house.

Perhaps, Scott had suggested, Sumners knew about Jack up there, and was the sort of guy who, once knowing something, checked up on it.

Got things on people.

It fit very well, although having something on Jack seemed like pretty small potatoes. What would Sumners do with that knowledge? Get out of paying for the boat?

But Sydney pointed out that Scott had seen Sumners drive past the Colby's first, and it was only afterwards that Jack went to Catherine's. If Sumners had been checking on Jack and Catherine, then he went about it like a fortune teller—as though all he had to do was see both of the Colby's cars in the parking lot to know Jack, shortly afterwards, would be making a little excursion.

"When I first saw him drive down there, and then Ellen's car not long after, I thought he'd made a signal."

Sydney laughed. "And you *followed* ....," she drawled out the syllables in an exaggerated version of her southern accent, as she tended to do when she was making fun of him. "I would *never* have *guessed* you were so *interested* in the goings on around town."

Scott had a moment of embarrassment, remembering other reasons why, at the time, he'd been interested in following Ellen's car up the hill. But that was behind him now, and he could smile.

"It *could* have still been a signal."

"For Jack? Mr. Sumners is going down there to signal Jack that the coast is clear?"

"Yeah, yeah. OK."

"Well, look at it another way then. What is obvious about it? "

Scott pursed his lips.

"All I saw was Sumners driving around Catherine's. God knows why he swung down by the boatyard, but maybe it didn't matter and the main thing was happening up at Catherine's. I can't figure her out anymore. I thought I had, at one point. When she first started, it was simple to see. You know, you take a good looking woman who's alone, and it's clear she's only putting up with that state of things, but eventually expects something else to come along. I mean, she lets you know what she's feeling about things. But lately she doesn't need to do that anymore. Who knows where Sumners fits into that? Jack, I think, is the easy one. He was up there, he hid the car, and he lied to Ellen about where he was. Simple as that."

"So they're doing it together up there."

Scott laughed. That was Sydney's favorite euphemism, making it sound like an activity people took up out of lack of imagination to divert themselves. Like origami. Crossword puzzles.

"Looks that way."

"Looks that way to me, too. But just don't forget about Eric Sumners, and whatever it was that he was doing up there."

"What do you think? There's a big conspiracy going on?"

"Why not?"

Scott grinned. "Pretty original way to go about plotting a revolution, or a bank heist, or something."

She tossed her hair. "I wouldn't treat it all as a joke."

"I don't. But if there's something else going on besides peter-dunking, I doubt any more could happen to me—me personally—outside of losing a job. I mean, if they find out I know."

"That's what you think. A friend of my fathers? Was working at this place? Next thing you knew some people broke in one night, and you know what happened? Well ... I don't know how it happened, but I knew him and knew he wouldn't have done anything ... but they put him in jail. I mean, after that he couldn't get a job selling used cars."

Indeed, Scott was now reflecting later, sitting there in next to the boat, his coffee going cold, that was something else to think about.

Although he could sympathize with the distrust for the system-being a natural secessionist himself—hers wasn't merely a poignantly lower-middle-class, sentimental and southern-fried paranoia which he could easily dismiss. He was willing to admit that Sydney had a better feel for real nastiness than he did.

That was something, maybe, to really think about. And maybe the most important thing to think about. More than all the rest of his morning worries, which was just carping and grousing in comparison. Because regardless of how Jack and Catherine were troubling the waters down there, the moment you threw Sumners in, you had a shark swimming in them.

## Chapter 68

Scott suddenly laughed at himself. True enough, he'd been cranky, grumpy, angry and frustrated. And for days on end. Jealous, envious and feeling put upon and unappreciated. Wondering what horrible thing could possibly happen to him next. But as Sydney had pointed out, finally boiling over at watching him bounce off walls after work, you just couldn't keep doing that forever. Or, as Sydney flatly put it, you might as well croak. At some point, she'd reminded him, all of this *'ol stuff* would get washed away with the tide. Just one great big tidal flow taking it all out to sea.

He looked down the shop towards the water end, out past the trawler the boys had been scraping down. Bellingham Bay was flat calm gray and quiet. Even the gulls were quiet as they planed across the surface looking for the occasional herring that might have risen.

Sometimes you could feel something just by looking at it. And in this case, Scott could feel the bay.

Cold was the water, but even colder was the air, and fine, thin wisps of vapor thread in streamers out towards the black hulk of Lummi Island looming far across the mist. There was still some residual darkness out to the west, beyond the San Juans, but somewhere behind him, back over the Cascades, there had to be some clearing in the overcast because the higher trees on Lummi were showing tinges of color, heavy dark greens in the firs and hemlocks and the occasional bluish blur of a stand of spruce. And that was another thing Sydney was right about. Even on the ugliest of days, Bellingham and the bay were always a beautiful thing to look at.

The shop was getting warmer, at least at that end. Now, when he breathed out, it wasn't with a cloud of steam. He looked down at his coffee cup, thinking about going and getting more. It suddenly felt like he'd been down there for ages. He was almost at the point of stirring himself when he heard the steps coming down the length of the boatshed. Light, women's steps. Scott looked at his watch. It was still very early for anyone to be up and around, even for Ellen.

The footsteps stopped for a moment, came farther along the

other side of the boat, stopped again, and then continued the rest of the way. Annie Moore, now stepping into his sight, didn't immediately see him there on the other side. He didn't want to startle her, but the way she was looking at the boat told him it would be quite a while before she noticed him.

"Annie," he called over to her, not too loudly, although it made her jump anyway. "Sorry," he said, "I didn't mean to scare you."

Annie's eyes, at first wide with surprise, quickly turned in his direction, searching for him in the gloom on that side of the shop. Then she saw him and smiled.

"I had to get up early," she said, walking towards him, "and thought I'd sneak over here to see how you were all doing. I guess there's no such thing as sneaking around you, Scott."

Scott smiled back at her. "It's not on purpose. I've just got a habit of being in the wrong place at the same time."

"Tell me about it," she said with a laden sound to it, but she smiled as though it were a joke.

She glanced back along the way she'd come for a moment, almost as if she thought someone was following her, and then she gave a sigh, her shoulders slumping a little, and she leaned against one of the struts supporting the stern construction. Looking, and oddly so for that early in the morning, worn out already.

Scott had seen Annie Moore in plenty of lights, all the way from giddy with laughter to mad as hell. He didn't consider her a moody woman though, her state always seeming well connected with what was happening around her. When she was happy, you knew why and when she was cross, you also had a pretty damn good idea why. But of all the things he had seen, never had Annie appeared so tired in that way. Not the physical way.

Although he could feel a lot of things, Scott knew he was lucky that he had rarely felt the kind of tired Annie was feeling. But it only took once, to know how it felt, and he knew how it could suddenly overwhelm a person, or worse in how it could creep up on a person a little at a time without their knowing it. And then one day the world caved in.

Annie Moore, of course, didn't look as though she was going to collapse, either physically or mentally. Her back was straight enough. After her small, semi-confessional slump, her shoulders went back again, her head came up and she looked at him with open friendliness. But if she smiled, he couldn't help noticing the lassitude somewhere around her eyes, in the down curved set of her mouth, or in the lank way her hands moved upon her bare arms as she rubbed them against the morning air. Sharp quickness of eye and word had always been the main impression Annie left upon people. And for someone who knew her, its absence was noticeable.

Well, Scott thought, it wouldn't take a genius to figure out why Annie might be a little down. The way things were going those days, everyone was getting crushed by an economy rigged against them. Of the money, by the money, for the money. The idea of a future had been stripped from them. Even the illusion of security had crumbled.

Scott knew that while he might complain about his lack of acknowledgment down there, at the very least he had a paycheck for the time being, and no real responsibilities beyond himself. Bad as it was, it wasn't as though he had a family to feed or mortgage to cover. But there were plenty of people like that. Very few people he knew had a cent to spare. No one had a cent, period. Nothing in the bank. Nothing for anything used. Let alone new. The only thing left to pray for was good health. Only a very, very few had any leeway at all.

Which reminded him, very easily, of someone else.

"Would you like some coffee? Something warm to drink?" he offered.

"No, thanks." For a moment, he thought she was going to say something else, but then she just looked at the boat again, giving it a long, long appraisal. "Like I said, I was just going for a stroll this morning."

He suddenly felt embarrassed. Getting shoved around. That must have been how it felt. And worse, by a guy whose money made him immune to knowing what it was like to get shoved around.

It was the old, class thing, and it had been around for a long time. The problem was how, anymore, it was getting so completely out of control. It wasn't, of course, a subject he was going to launch into with Annie, right there. The one percent, and all that. Although it was something people were beginning to talk about. People ... after that long slumbering afterglow finally wore off from the hazy paradise of that time—now long ago—when a single paycheck could cover everything ... were beginning to wake up to discover how they were slowly being stripped of even that nostalgic dream.

Toys, of course, and more toys. People had more toys than ever. But for a vast lot, there was very little of the earlier dignity left. That dignity which the rich had let—for a while—the middle class, and even the poor, believe they might possess.

In the good old days—g.o.d. for short—salaried people had thought that by working hard, and chipping in, they were going to be allowed to share in it a little bit. But now the poor knew at last they were truly and forever poor because it had been discovered there were even poorer people, in other places, barely earning a living making the things the poor used to make.

Because, in the end, it wasn't important what got made, or sold, or helped people in general make a living. The only thing that mattered was the investors' profit margin. G.o.d. was dead.

Anymore, if people were going to live, it was on credit, and from the same companies that made the things people couldn't afford to buy with cash. People had learned that life, now, was defined as endless debt. You lived in debt. You died in debt. Your children would live in debt, and that was how it had all ended up.

Which meant, sure, you could buy things. Just get it for credit. A new refrigerator or dishwasher. A car. Whatever. But even by credit, there were times when you didn't buy just anything.

Like a boat. And maybe not even a used boat. And certainly not a new one off a boat lot, like Clyde and Annie's. That was for people who didn't know what counting money meant. For people for whom money just existed.

Of course, boat money had always existed around the Puget Sound. Small boat money. Big boat money. Even there in the Sound where boats were everywhere, so ubiquitous as to be nearly an invisible part of the landscape, the really big boat had always been the summit of conspicuous consumption. If you had anything at all, you crowned it with a boat. But few people were doing even that anymore except the techie millionaires down south in Seattle. And, Scott thought grimly, a notable exception up here in the north.

So he could easily figure how Clyde and Annie Moore were going through a bad spell. No matter what platitudes people might offer—things were no worse than they had been for a long time, or people get used to anything, even bankruptcy—it didn't change how it felt. She was obviously depressed, and she hadn't meant to find him there, and was making no effort to engage in any small talk. Because, simply, with that huge goddamn boat sitting there, anything other than that for a subject was just plain stupid.

Scott would have bet serious money that no one at the Colby's had ever had a word with either Clyde or Annie about the boat. But now that she was there, Scott decided he wouldn't let it slide by. He and Annie, and even he and Clyde, had always been on a friendly basis towards each other, and he didn't want that changed.

"You know," Scott said, stepping over and giving one of the ribbands a pat, "there are days I get up and come down here, and I get to feeling I'm working here on something that doesn't really exist."

Annie gave him a long look, and then glanced at the hull. "It looks pretty real to me."

Scott, for the second time that morning, was ashamed. She had seen right through that lame attempt of his to take the sting out of things by belittling in some way his own work. He could see he was just going to have to say the obvious thing, or they would be stuck forever.

"Yeah," he said. "It's real enough. And I'll bet it looks even more real enough to you, Annie. But that's only because you've still got a big fat unreality of your own sitting over there at your show dock."

For the first time that morning, Annie gave him a genuine, if bitter smile. "Thanks for reminding me."

"My apologies. I can guess how you feel."

Annie was looking at the boat again, putting her hand through the ribbands to touch one of the ribs. "Do you really?" she said in a vague way.

What Scott didn't know, was that her depression about the boat wasn't just a question of money. That, in fact, she'd been trying for months to purge herself of the ominous feeling that, somehow, she'd been at fault. That she had single-handedly ruined her and Clyde's last chance to get out from under things once and for all.

Of course, Clyde had never said that—and surely his insistence at bringing Eric Sumners over here hadn't helped—but she couldn't help it. And Clyde's continual repeating of how it wasn't her fault, over and over, sometimes left her feeling he was only trying to make her feel better, when in fact it *was* somehow her fault.

"Well, maybe not," he admitted. "But when I said this wasn't real, I meant it. You know, up until Sumners strolled in here, most of what this place consisted of was scraping a year's worth of algae off the bottoms of boats."

"Well, you aren't anymore."

"That's where you got it wrong," he said. "We're still barnacle scrapers. If you think this has really changed everything for once and for all, you come back here in six months' time and take a look again. I guarantee you won't be thinking what you're thinking now."

"And what am I thinking now?"

"That this was your big chance, and it didn't happen."

Annie didn't even look at him at that, now staring aimlessly towards the shop's ways stretching down away from them towards the bay, following how they ran down and then beneath the dark water slowly heaving there at the foot of the boathouse … the morning's high tide standing in there against the waterfront as though expectantly waiting to be put to work. Or just as ready to go away when nothing showed up. Where, before, she had felt a bit depressed, she was feeling irritated. She hadn't come over here, expecting to get into all this. She gave him a sudden, angry look.

"What's your problem?" she said. "I didn't ask you for your opinion or anything. I don't need you telling me what you think I feel. It's enough I feel what I feel without having you or anyone else tell me sympathetically all about it."

Even as it came out, Annie realized how true that was, and her sudden anger included Clyde. And as well, his now clearly seen tactic of telling her how it wasn't her fault, bringing up the whole subject again, to comfort her, any time they got to on the subject of lack of money. When it really had been his fault.

That bastard.

"OK. Fine," Scott said. "But this really is an aberration. The bad thing is that some people get to thinking something like this is the new reality."

"We could have used a bit of aberration, as you call it, over on our side. It was an opportunity to get rid of that fucking ketch."

Scott nodded. "Well, you'll probably do that at *some* point." He looked away from her and down the shed towards the water and then spoke, but quietly and not really to her. "But when this is finished, we, or I that is, goes back to being whatever."

She smiled. "You don't look like Cinderella."

"And Eric Sumners," he said back, "regardless of what the ladies might think, ain't no Prince Charming."

"What ladies do you have in mind?"

"Any of 'em."

Annie gave him a solemn look. "You don't think much of ladies."

Scott gave her a droll look. "He's a good enough looking guy, don't you think?"

For a half a second, her eyes flickered, but then she said with a casual indifference, "Sure."

Scott saw and interpreted correctly that flicker, and was too much of a gentleman to ignore it.

"Well," he said, "throw a billion bucks on top of that, and you've got Prince Charming."

Annie opened her mouth to argue, but then stopped. She, like Scott, liked to keep things nearer the truth whenever it was possible.

"OK," she said. "And why not?"

He nodded. "Indeed."

"And for the moment, he's *your* Prince. Your boat's come in."

He grimaced.

"Bad joke," she agreed.

"Nah," he said, "it's not that. It's that this isn't really like it's our boat that came in. But just the waves kicked up by someone else's boat, which came in for them."

Annie looked at him for a moment, and then she suddenly realized something. "Can I ask you a question?"

Scott nodded his head.

"Are you, like … a partner over here? I guess I never really knew what status you had when you first came."

"Do I look like a partner?"

She shrugged. "I understand you're building it just as much as Jack is. That's the talk around town, anyways."

"The talk … around town?" Scott frowned, scratching his head.

"Yeah, down at the cannery, and over in Lummi, and I even heard it at the bank."

The apprentice, Tom, Scott thought. That would account for the cannery. But he would never have guessed Tom was watching all that much, or had anything to say about it. But now he thought about it, it didn't surprise him. The apprentice knew boats, and most of what he'd learned down there at Colby's, Scott had taught him. Him and Will. Will accounted for Lummi.

Well, he thought. That was all right. At the very least, it was nice someone, somewhere, could appreciate his work.

"I'm not a partner. Just a fucking employee."

Annie had nothing to say to that, considering how flat and brutal he'd said it and obviously not at all wanting to go any farther in that direction.

She sighed. "Jeez," she said, "I'm freezing. Aren't you cold?"

"Not so much. When I first came down it was a lot colder."

"I can feel goose bumps all the way from my neck to my ankles. I don't know about you, but I'm getting the hell out of here."

But she didn't move for a second, as though she'd just thought of something. And then she saw Scott staring at her.

"Sorry," she went on. "Just thinking."

"Yeah," he said. "About getting the hell out of here …."

He was suddenly embarrassed. A dumb joke.

Really embarrassed. A really dumb joke.

But they smiled at each other and Annie disappeared, her footsteps ticking away up and then out of the shop.

Scott looked down at his cup, saw it was empty, and picked up his thermos, feeling a heavy slosh meaning there were still two or three cups inside. For some strange reason that made him feel good and he opened the top and poured himself another steaming hot cup.

He'd started the morning in a truly rotten mood, then had got better, then had got depressed, and was suddenly perilously close to going back to the rotten mood.

But he resisted, and it didn't happen. Because he thought that if he let it, it would be sort of stupid.

Bad enough to be that way by accident, but to let yourself slip into bad humor knowing you could avoid it, was just greedy. Especially when you've just been confronted by someone who's in just about as bad a mood as you are in, or were. Because it's all relative, in the end, he thought. No matter how bad a mood you're in, you can always find someone who is feeling worse. And when that happens, you've only got two choices. You can get angry with them in some competitive way, or you can feel better.

Scott took a sip of coffee, and then another. And then it started growing in him, slowly at first, and then it just burst and he found himself grinning and then laughing, full and easy.

So much his eyes watered.

Good Christ. He could see he did indeed have a problem down there at Colby's.

Evidently, he couldn't even find a way to maintain a deep sense of perpetual outrage.

That, surely, was no way to ever get to the top.

# Chapter 69

ERIC AND Catherine made their meticulously planned escape one long weekend the end of February. Taking a seaplane out of Vancouver at a little before noon on the Friday, they flew straight up north along the inland channel between the humping barrier islands and the fjorded mainland. Eric knew a lake resort, having taken businessmen there on fishing trips. He had tried to get the company to make a beeline for the lake, but the pilot deferred. Even though the DHC Beaver had the range, he didn't like flying over too much land, and especially not the rugged coastal mountain range. Admittedly, over 400 miles was a long way to go for a tryst, but the secluded resort was the first place that came to his mind. Deep in the interior of British Columbia, the lake, called Tetachuck, was well north of Bella Coola on the fringe of that part of the Chilcotin next to Entiako.

Eric had showed the place to Catherine on a map. She had never been anywhere so remote in her life. And although she was never nervous to fly, she'd never done so in a seaplane, or any plane that small for that matter, and for several minutes before and after takeoff from Vancouver Harbor, she'd never felt more scared. Three hours of flying took them far north. Looking down at the stark, glacier laden mountains and snow covered forest of the coast range, she felt as though they were heading for the North Pole.

They talked only in general ways on the way up. When she'd finally gotten used to feeling the more direct movements of a small plane, she enjoyed the feeling of being able to see so much more only several thousand instead of tens of thousands of feet in the air. No wonder people were drawn to flying small planes, she thought. You felt like you owned everything.

Around noon, the pilot finally dove the Beaver down into the dark, snow-swept mountains, and touched down on the cold waters of Lake Tetachuck—the pilot having confirmed that the lake wasn't frozen over that year—and swam the plane over to the lodge's dock and seaplane fuel depot jutting out from the heavy, spruce and sitka dominated forest. When they came up off the dock, an SUV with its engine running was waiting for them, and its driver took them along the lake road, through the trees, towards the lodge. Catherine realized there was nothing else there. No store, no restaurant, just the log house style lodge and cabins with their river rock chimneys.

"Are there any towns near here?" she asked the driver.

There was a moment of silence, and then the driver spoke with the deep, deliberate accent of First Nation people. "Vanderhoof. Ninety miles from Nechako Lodge."

"You mean Tetachuck Lodge, where we're going."

"No, Nechako, which from here is two hours up lake by boat."

Catherine digested that information for a moment, then looked at the driver, a thickset man with a long pony tail falling behind a wide brimmed, felt Stetson. "You mean, to get groceries and things, you have to go all the way there?"

"No. I live at the village."

"There's no store at the village?"

Another pause, then the driver said, "No."

"It must be hard living here all winter?"

The driver hunched his shoulders. "I don't stay here. I came down because they wanted me to open up the place for you. We don't normally get visitors this time of year."

"Ah," Catherine said. She looked over at Eric, but he was looking out at the lake, not really listening. She turned back to the driver.

"Your people are the ...?" Catherine was going to say the name of the lake or something, but suddenly felt shy. As though her ignorance was somehow her fault.

"*Dakelh*," the driver said. "Up here, we're mostly that or Wet'suwet'en. But my wife is Tsilhqot'in."

Catherine was nervous, talking just for the sake of talking. But she didn't know what else to say, after that, so she just looked out the window at the lake and the big trees going past.

Pulling into the lodge compound, they were driven straight over to their cabin. The driver got out and helped them take their suitcases and bags of groceries up the steps and onto the porch and then turned to leave. "See you Monday morning," he said. "If you need anything, my number is on the notice." Eric nodded thanks, passing the Dakelh a bill in their handshake.

Watching the SUV drive off, disappearing back into the dark trees, Catherine and Eric stood on the porch for a moment, surveying the place they had found themselves.

Before them, a small, cleared path led down through the trees and snow-buried ground to the lake. Drifts of snow lay deep in some places but wind off the lake had swept others clear and bare, and there, brown needles carpeting the path were as dry as in summer. The lake itself, big, deep and long, mirrored the high hillsides and mountains on the other side, and as they watched they suddenly heard the idling sound of the floatplane, somewhere unseen, go into a throaty growl as the pilot took off to return to Vancouver.

Already it was beginning to darken. There were no lights along the other side of the lake, nor even there along their edge. There were other cabins, tucked into the forest like theirs, here and there along the lake. But nobody was there. They were alone.

No wind stirred the trees, but it was cold, and Eric and Catherine turned and went across the cedar porch. Eric, though, had her wait outside for a moment. Unlocking the door, he went inside as Catherine waited. Not that he expected a bear or a mountain lion, or even a lynx or wolverine. But even with the mice or a raccoon he knew from previous experience it was good to go in and stomp around. After a minute, he stuck his head out the door.

"All clear," he said.

They put the groceries away in the kitchen and their bags back in the small bedroom off the main room. It wasn't until Catherine found an old aluminum coffee pot and began making some coffee on the stove that either one of them had much of a word for the other.

"How're you doing?" Eric said.

"Guess." Catherine continued to play with the stove, turning knobs until she had the gas jets turned to the right height.

He went over to the sofa. Behind the sofa were big windows looking out across the porch and down through the trees to the darkening lake. He sat down, still wearing his jacket zipped up tight, running his arm along the back of the couch and patting his hand there, absentmindedly, in a way that reminded Catherine of someone else. A sudden emptiness swirled through her.

Eric let out a breath. "We're probably the only people here since last fall. The first for the year, that is."

He gazed absently out the window, his voice hollow sounding in the cabin, his breath coming out in white plumes in the frozen air of the living room. Catherine turned back to the kitchen.

Strange, she thought, to have walked in and made themselves at home in this cabin which had sat here unused and silent among the trees for months on end. A place no one lived in, but just used. Vacationers, fishermen, and now herself and Eric.

Not a home, she thought, and almost not even a house but more like a whore, this cabin waited docilely, served its purpose, and then was left behind. How many had passed through this door as if, for a brief moment, it was their door, or cooked in the little kitchen as if it were their kitchen, or made love in the bed.

"Yes," was all she said, looking at the coffee pot and watching coffee begin to perk up into a the glass telltale.

She had been so happy with the idea, and then driving up the highway to Vancouver, and then most of the way flying. Maybe it had been all the forced non-conversation in the plane with the pilot, there just in front. But the idle fact they couldn't have said anything even if they had wanted to, weighed on her.

She couldn't help how she felt right then. Not talking about anything at all seemed to wrap up the whole situation all too neatly. A somewhat depressing idea. The moment she had realized all that, in the plane, she had begun thinking about things. Then, she really did have something she couldn't talk about ... and on, and on. It had become a vicious circle which had enforced itself and even made Eric feel its presence after a while.

Suddenly, floating in on silent, deadly wings, had come this awareness of who they were and what they were doing together.

God, it was cold, she thought, hugging herself.

Why did he just sit there and not get the fire going, she thought?

But somehow, that silence made her incapable of remonstrating and she just stood there before the stove in the kitchen until the coffee had bubbled through the glass telltale knob for a while. When it was dark enough she took the percolator off the flame and carried it with a potholder, two cups dangling from her other hand, over to him and set it all on a low table there. She poured him a cup and stood there in front of him as he continued to gaze quietly back at her. This was the man she wanted to be with more than any other man on earth. He was her will and desire and the result of dreams barely dared. A commitment to plunge beyond limiting fears; that woman's need to give, and then give way in a death defying act of faith which is what she thought her woman's courage was made of.

He continued to look at her, if not directly into her eyes. He seemed, if anything, more lost than she was. But where he seemed frozen, she felt her determination come back to her and his immobility put her in motion.

As if in a trance, slowly and vaguely but with a gathering confidence, she began removing her clothes. Her dress slipping down, and then the rest, like plucking leaves away and letting them fall, loosening fetters until she stood there in front of him, her skin barely feeling the cold air of the cabin.

He sat enthralled. She leaned over and picked up his untouched cup of coffee, returning to her stance, sipping the coffee, her legs slightly spread and straight, her shoulders back.

"Well, I made your goddamn coffee like a good little girl," she said. "So now you had better make a fire because I'm not putting anything back on."

"Oh, god. Sorry," Eric said. His heart choking him, he practically fell off the couch towards the fireplace.

Catherine stood above him as he worked, drinking her coffee and not shivering despite the glacial cold of the cabin, her cool white thighs waiting as the flames began to rise up, tenderly and shyly at first, through the kindling and logs.

After a minute or so a pitchy smell of smoke came into the cold air of the room, a crackling of growing flames. She looked at him sternly but was not angry. She was simply and intensely resolved to be there not only as his woman, but as her own woman. Not as something hidden there in the heart of the great northern forest. Alone and naked. She defied all that, and stood there, unclothed and calm. Until he let go as well.

They said nothing to each other while Eric continued throwing logs on until a true blaze roared up the wide open flu out to the frigid mountain air. Heat flared out like knives into the cold of the living room. The warmth of the cabin slowly rose until it could begin to absorb the fire's heat, enfold what it offered with a capacity for warmth of its own. As he watched the fire he now felt something break, suddenly, within himself.

Turning, he placed his hands upon Catherine's ankles, steadying his grasp upon the cold flesh. He moved his hands up behind her legs, pushing his face in against her thighs, breathing her in as the fire lashed out at him from behind.

For a while, like that, neither of them felt any discontentment anymore. Catherine, perhaps, even quite happy again. They were alone there at last, and made to themselves a very, very small world.

## Chapter 70

AFTER ALL the determined nights. After all the false starts and where there had been a growing sense of frustration it was finally just a simple thing. Looking at the calendar, Ellen noticed she wasn't feeling puffy. In fact, if she was feeling anything, it was more like throwing up. No excitement. Just nausea.

She was surprised at how something she had hoped so much for, now left her feeling empty. She wondered how Jack would react, although she had a sudden conviction he wouldn't be thrilled, either. If anything could thrill him. And especially those days when he gave off the impression that nothing satisfied him. Jack had been quiet lately. Worried about things, as usual ... but also, somehow, more than usual.

It seemed to her there was always a stone, right there at the center of his brain, which his mind had to work its way around but could never penetrate or assimilate. But the stone, lately, had become a boulder.

The poor bastard, she thought. Always that ability to worry up trouble within the silence of that rocky substrate of doubts.

Jack's problem was simply that he could never deal with abstractions. When they finally arrived, though, he was usually all right.

Her own fears, those creepy, flesh-crawling things that had been sneaking up upon her lately, she knew would also disappear. A heavily-moored realist, she distrusted implicitly all forms of either optimism or pessimism, and knew it all would pass. Because regardless of anything else, she knew what she and Jack had, both singly and together. And she knew Jack.

So first, she would tell Catherine. An ovarian celebration between women to get herself started down the proper road to contentment.

You decided to be content, she told herself with conviction, and you built upon the proper foundations.

A woman's reaction was the logical place to start. To get things moving on the right road. Regardless of how her new found friend might feel about babies, fulfillment, women's roles, men, and all the rest, there would be only one possible social response. Then Ellen would present it to Jack, moving the known into the unknown.

Jack didn't realize how wonderful she had managed to be. Always, she had looked for ways to move closer to him, rejecting any reflex on his or her own part to move away. The pity of it was how he had never had the slightest suspicion of how involved the battle had been.

Ellen, with completeness, could now see she could be not only true to Jack, but be a form of truth as well.

She must not pity the man. It had been her private struggle all those years, convincing him, convincing herself. One of them had had, by necessity, to be the stronger one, the one more resilient and able to handle the truth.

That she was stronger was a fact. And in ways Jack couldn't even have guessed. Even in terms of faithfulness.

He would have been shocked to know it, and she had always kept it as her deepest secret from him, but she had never believed in the conventions of marriage the way he did. She felt that the giving, or withholding of her body had nothing to do with convictions or vows. Her loyalty, therefore, was just a gift to him, and a pact to herself to not belittle—rather than betray, which she didn't consider to be the appropriate definition—his trust.

How little did he know that she could have easily slept with any number of men. She'd had the opportunities, had seen the signs of interest. And she could have done so without the slightest qualm. Perhaps—most shocking of all—even have born children by them. And have still remained faithful on her own terms with Jack.

She couldn't help smile at how naïve he was about her. She could have taken advantage of his own blindness, his conventional nature which was not attuned to the limitless possibilities of unconventionality. So little he knew about life! But she had made a private vow of conventionality for his sake. That vow being more important than anything they would ever say to each other.

Because, in the end, that was the part she was given to play.

She looked back in the mirror, and looked at her smile. It was a clear and honest smile, aware and appreciative of realities. Then she looked down at her abdomen, spreading her fingers across the still flat expanse there, gazing at it as though at something she'd never seen before. And she thought again of Jack, and how he would react on learning this great, new truth in their lives.

Well, it *had* been his idea, after all. At least, that was, the initiating of it.

But she knew Jack, and how just because he could think of doing something, it was a great deal different from actually doing it.

And maybe that was better for him. It made it possible for him to deal with life's hard realities.

She looked back up at the mirror, still smiling. How little one could know, she thought. Or should.

# Chapter 71

C LYDE M OORE had seen how the planking, twenty foot long lengths of mahogany in two thicknesses, thinner for the inner layer, had been delivered that morning.

Curious about the work and restless in the midst of a strange feeling he'd been having lately, he slipped across the gravel of his silent boatyard to the Colby's to watch. Although they didn't say anything to him after their initial greetings they didn't seem to mind his presence and not even when he followed them around, taking care to stay out of their way.

Clyde looked on with sincere interest as Jack and Scott, taking measurements onto a spiling board, then transferred the run for the sheer edge of the boat from that board to a length of planking. The plank was cut along with a mirror image plank for the other side. Both were then scooped slightly to fit to the curves of the ribs and clamped in place. Counterboring holes and screwing the planks down tight onto the ribs, they continued with another set of planks, and then another until they had finished the first run all along the length of the sheer where the hull and the deck joined. Clyde was impressed by how easy they made it look, although he knew it wasn't easy at all.

Looking at the hull, and seeing how much planking would have to be done, Clyde could see that a massive amount of slow-going work lay ahead of them. He had no way of knowing that it would be even more than that. Long before, it had been decided that the entire hull of the ketch would be double-planked, running a thicker layer of planks over the first set. It was a lot of work, but it would make for a sleek and very resilient hull which would need no caulking.

But for Jack and Scott, even with the massive slowness of the work ahead of them, there was a tangible impression to having entered the downhill side of it. There was a feeling of satisfaction in being able to give each successive plank a good, resounding slap, feeling there the strength of it bent to the ribs, as though that shape had always been its own, now forever wedded.

Even Clyde picked it up, watching them and—despite himself—even feeling a bit of envious admiration. A sense of seeing something strong and solid. And later that evening, sitting up at Micky's, he reflected on that sense of unhurried movement, and then on the imminent sense of stagnancy in his own life.

He was doing his best, he thought. It just didn't seem to be enough.

Try as he might, nothing got anywhere.

He put all the effort he could into that boatyard and ... little or nothing. He'd sold only four boats that year. With little mark up. And all the rest had sat out there all that time, covered with a heavy polish to protect them from the weather, and would probably be sitting there the same way next year.

Another year older. Like himself. And unsold.

He looked up at the mirror behind the bar, saw himself, and grimaced. He supposed, he thought, he could also count on, in another year, sitting there in Micky's having the same goddamn thoughts. Instead of being somewhere, lost, warm and calm ... as he dreamed every Summer of his life.

Nope. He would only be there, nursing lukewarm beer while Annie, as usual, was back home thinking her lukewarm thoughts about him.

He snorted to himself, ignoring a quizzical glance from Micky.

Lukewarm wasn't exactly the right word for it, he thought. More like the fucking frozen ice of downtown Siberia.

His depression, his eternal springtime Gift, washed through him once again. Suddenly, and not for the first time by a long shot, Clyde felt very sorry for his lot.

Honestly, he thought, what could you do? She was making it awfully difficult for him. Somewhere, they had just gotten onto the wrong track. If he tried to say anything, she threw it back at him. If he did anything, she held it against him. If he didn't say anything at all, she provided the words for him whether he had thought them or not. Damned either way. And if by some fucking miracle something actually worked? He got no thanks. The goddamn woman was diabolical.

Sure, he maybe wasn't the greatest catch she could have made. Who was ever the greatest catch for anyone? He wasn't the fucking worst, either. She had just given up noticing his efforts. How all winter they had hung in there because of his efforts alone. He had managed to sell that one thirty-foot cruiser, which hadn't been any day at the beach to offload on the guy. Endless questions. Endless worries. Another Puget Sound boating newbie.

But while Annie's chewing his ass hadn't been dragging him down, there were other things. Some damn thing. This odd thing he'd come across and which had got him thinking ....

Funny shit with the lease.

But *no*, he thought, naturally she wouldn't be noticing that either. All she wanted to do was just go down inside all that anger she had, just sit in that stinking pile of boiling shit, and feed off it. Lately, she seemed to get her only satisfaction out of that. Something, somewhere, had really ticked her off.

Well, if feeling angry was all it took to make her happy, he was going to let her have it. Anyway, what else was there to do? Fight against it? Good Christ, all he would get then was a stream of nonstop shit from morning to night.

Silence, he thought, was vastly preferable. And at that reflection, he nodded his head and made a gesture with his hand in front of him as though presenting someone with a point of irrefutable logic.

And then, without thinking, brought his fist down with a bang on the counter.

"What's the matter, Clyde?"

Micky came down the bar and gave Clyde a long, ironic and very studied grin. He had his bar side psychology turned up full.

Defuse, defuse, defuse, he was telling himself. He was in no mood to listen to litanies that day.

About pressure. Or the crap these guys dragged in.

Sometimes, all that even got to him ....

No one, Micky reflected without too much bitterness, ever took bartenders into account. Bartenders always got treated as though they were part of the bar. A congenial and indivisible part of some convenient spot to wash away the misery.

What if one day he just got up on the bar and told the whole goddamn bunch of wet-eyed assholes to get the fuck out and go straighten up their lives somewhere else? What if? That would surprise the hell out of them, for sure.

What if, one day, he started sniveling back at them, bending their ears for hours about his problems?

He could do that just as well as them.

He could tell them about how he could get ill listening to them. How the payments on the place got so far behind it became surreal, like living in the future without a net.

Or for example how, lately, there had been something funny coming up about his lease arrangement. He was especially sensitive about that. Nothing had been said outright, but when the bastards even mentioned it, even in passing, you knew you had better start paying attention.

What would the fuckers think of *that*, he wondered.

Micky looked at Clyde's hang-dog face, defying him to respond and knowing it would probably work. He knew that by asking these guys what the matter was—one of the oldest tricks in the bartender's book—you basically denied a full and proper response.

The tactic worked, corking up Clyde like a bottle of gas.

"Nothing much," he said.

Like a comic, working with a heckler, keeping the heat on until he was sure the guy would shut the fuck up permanently, Micky drove at him.

"You look like your house just burned down."

Clyde looked at Micky, and gave him an unpleasant smile.

"Nothing so nice as that."

"Just the usual shit, huh?"

The statement was explicit. If it was the usual shit, there was no reason to go into it. Bring the curtain down, boys, the show's over.

"Yeah. I guess. Although burning the house down wouldn't be such a bad idea, now that you mention it."

It wasn't quite the effect Micky had hoped for. Getting Clyde into a twisted sense of depression, though, was better than tears.

"Oh, yeah?" he said, for lack of anything else. But then, what else were you supposed to say? Maybe Clyde just needed a minute or two.

Micky sighed to himself. OK, he thought, he could have it. Clyde didn't do this very often … in fact almost never. So he'd sort of built up credit for being able to complain a bit. He watched Clyde shake his head.

"I really mean it," Clyde said. "Fucking hell. All the time, build, build, build, you know. Like you're a goddamn slave or something. You're not even supposed to think about it. And what do you get for your efforts? The bank, or creditors, or landlords, or someone, shoves it all straight up your ass. Sideways. Red-hot. I get sick of it, sometimes. There you are down there, trying to keep your own life from going down the hole, paying them their goddamn pound of flesh every month and they don't have to do a thing except collect, and do you think they give a shit? No way. I'm telling you, when you're on the bottom rung, it's not enough they want to keep you there, but they want to have the power to kick you right off down into the shit any time they want."

"That," Micky said noncommittally, "I don't know." Although, in fact, he *did* know. And, oddly, he'd been thinking the exact same things lately.

"I'm not kidding, Mick. I wish we were still back in the good old days when there were much simpler ways to take care of things. Someone fucks you over, you just go straight out and fuck *them* over. All these civil property rights, tort laws, all these courts and regulations, they're all built to take power out of the hands of the people on the bottom. Day was when a man could defend himself against assholes. You just had to go out and boot their damn balls up into their tonsils. Now, if you did that, they'd throw away the key."

"Somebody's fucking you over?"

"Oh, on top of everything else, I'm getting to feel that way. You know the feeling? Something a little off somewhere. I think the pig fuckers are trying to set me up to raise the rent on me. Buttering my ass up for the next good reaming."

"That's funny."

"It's not that goddamn funny. That's the truth."

Micky felt a small twinge of worry. For years and years, when he would get to looking around his place down there at Fairhaven, bullshitting with all the bullshitters about life, liberty, and the pursuit of politics, there had always been a fairly constant thread to the conversation. Fairhaven was this, Fairhaven was that. Property development always looming on the horizon, but nothing in particular. You got used to it. It was part of the reason Micky had held on to the place so long. Knowing that even if things took off, he'd just rise with it. He'd long had a dream. Not just a waterside bar, but one day, with the old part of town spruced up, new housing built and, God knew, a better clientele ... Micky would open up a restaurant. Nothing fancy, just good food at good prices. Nice and clean and ... well, fuck it ... elegant. With table cloths and candles. Wear a tie and supervise.

It was his most secret wish. To get out from behind the beer-soaked bar, forever quit of wiping endless glasses and noses. Get off his poor, flat feet and finally be able to go home at a reasonable hour.

You get paranoid when you have dreams.

Life can happen.

And life, when it does, takes turnings that often have nothing to do with your dreams. Sometimes those turnings are so small they seem like nothing, just a little hint here and there. But even a microscopic turning can destroy a dream ... and when it has to do with your life, the simple fact that you're attuned to a turning, no matter how small it is, makes you sit up and take notice. Like a radar on the Distant Early Warning line pinging away at you how Out There, somewhere, were uncontrollable things coming at you.

Ten years, Micky had been waiting to see the developers come in, to see them start planting houses down the hill from the brick remnants of downtown Fairhaven to the waterside, planting them like potted plants. Ten years he'd had his eyes out for surveyors, and seeing them he would sidle over and inquire. But, no, always just a sewer line, or the adjustment of a property line, but never anything substantial he could have planned for.

It could very probably be a hell of a battle for him to remain there, to keep his fortress in place while the builders moved in, ensuring he would have something to start with. But he had always been ready for that. The worst nightmare though, was to get the rug pulled out from under him. Anyone could see how it could happen. Even Clyde could see it, if it was obvious.

Should he mention it? No. No reason to worry the bastard any more than he already was. Nevertheless, suddenly, Micky was feeling as prickly as a porcupine, the spines rising on his back like a field of sharpened stakes.

"You think that's all they want?" he said guardedly.

"Who the hell knows? All I did was give them a call asking for a small postponement on the rent. We always get it in the springtime. It's normal. They know we don't have fuck-all until at least May. This time, instead of just agreeing to it like every year, I get told they didn't have the time to discuss it and would contact me a little later. The cold shoulder. What the hell is there to discuss? We've been doing it for so long it might as well be part of the contract. You tell me."

Half of Micky's mind was thinking flippantly: you bet, I could tell you all about it. But suddenly, the other half woke up and he realized Clyde was telling him something that fit right in.

Micky looked at Clyde, now carefully, and felt his Distant Early Warning go from pinging to now clanging like a fire alarm. Suddenly, it was more than paranoia. You could only have paranoia one way: your own. But when someone else had it the same exact way, it was time to look out.

Micky stood up straight behind the bar … and felt a true shiver go down his spine.

He could see Clyde wasn't yet paranoid. But Micky knew all he would have to do was mention some of the fudged-over proclamations and outright avoidances he'd been getting about his own lease, and Clyde would be tracking right down the same alley.

This was far from paranoia. Something was on. And people were fucking up by keeping things too close to their chests.

That meant it was big. Or, at least, bigger than any of them down there were. Otherwise, there would have been no hint of it. But the hint, mainly in how inflexible people were getting about waterfront leases, was coming through.

Because no one became more inflexible than when the ground began to shake.

Micky looked down the bar at the other men strung along it at intervals like unsociable birds on a wire, and suddenly wished they'd all just go the hell home.

A bar was a place you could make a hell of a good living off of other people's worries, but right then he had a few too many of his own to have time for theirs.

He looked at Clyde for a moment, and then made up his mind. He leaned over, close to Clyde's ear, and said: "So … what do you think is going on …?"

# Chapter 72

IT WAS with a heavy sense of foreboding that Jack felt how he had fallen out of love with Ellen. And heavy irony.

She was now pregnant.

An unremarkable thing after all the years of discussing it. And now that it had happened, incredibly, he felt freed from her. There was no other way to explain it. God knew, he had given the woman finally, exactly what she wanted. And in doing so, he felt no longer necessary. No longer responsible. Although, of course, he was.

But, goddamn it to hell, at the same time he wasn't.

And there was no way to figure how or why.

If it hadn't been obvious all those years how he had been lukewarm to the idea of children, it now was glaringly so. At least to him. Ellen was obviously so caught up with her pregnancy that she could notice nothing much beyond the periphery of her swelling breasts.

Jack felt alienated all right. Damn straight he did!

Of course, he was surprised how he suddenly had no feelings of sentiment for her. He hadn't expected this, although from time to time he'd felt a flatness in his marriage come and go. Taking things for granted. Which, he'd heard, was normal and which didn't last forever.

But this time ... the falling out of love was not the normal thing it had been in the past. He had found someone else to turn to, at least to paper over the flatness. Or he had thought so. He wasn't sure anymore. That also seemed to be changing on him. His desire for Catherine was now permanent. But lately though it had become immense.

Of course, part of that could have come from the risk. But now it seemed that Catherine had found the risk too much. Was pulling away from him somehow. And, he couldn't help it: it was driving him crazy.

Amazing, he thought. A woman comes crying on your doorstep for attention, and when she gets it, she starts making demands.

Before, he'd understood her when she had said it would be just for a while. But now, the tone of what she said had changed. Now she would say how she preferred fast liaisons. That she was getting fidgety. That she wasn't completely comfortable anymore.

She sure hadn't said anything in that way in the beginning and Jack wasn't buying it. There was a definite feeling of rejection in the air.

Even if, in reality, there was none. But what the hell, he thought. You felt what you felt, whether it was real or not.

Funny though, that unreal little sense of rejection, added to the risk, made his desire for her all the more poignant.

Supposedly, she was feeling better about herself. She said she was more capable of handling the loneliness those days. She admitted she now even had a few prospects. Nothing serious, or able to equal what he gave her, she had added quickly at a sharp look from him. A statement which did, indeed, sooth him a bit but nevertheless stabbed at a jealousy he hadn't ever had for her before. And in the end, that jealousy, slight as it was, only added to a desire for her which was now next to overpowering.

When things became overpowering, he thought, it meant even more care had to be taken. And having to be that careful, double, triple careful, worried him. Now, when she was down there working, he could barely look at her. Which was difficult, but helped by how the planking of the boat was such an endless, nitpicky job. And through forcing himself to concentrate entirely on making the work go well, he was able to avoid the office.

But one day in March he couldn't. They had been stopped well before lunch, waiting for another shipment of wood. He and Scott had been out in the shed, looking over their stock, when Ellen told him to come in and take a call.

Catherine was sitting at the desk in the office making inventories. She didn't look at him when he picked up the phone. He looked around for a second. Ellen was preparing lunch in the kitchen. He looked back at Catherine but she still didn't look up at him. He put the receiver to his ear and said hello and found Micky on the other end.

"Hey, Mick, What's up?"

"Right. Listen, Jack. Can you come over? I need to talk to you about something."

"You can talk to me now."

"Maybe so. Maybe not."

"What do you mean, maybe not?"

"I don't know, Jack. That's the point. I've got to go somewhere at noon. I'm going with Moore, and you should come along."

Jack frowned at the telephone.

"Why him?"

A movement in the kitchen caught his eye and he turned to see Ellen gesturing.

"Hold on a second, Micky." He turned to her, cupping his fingers around the mouthpiece. "What?"

"I've got nothing here at all for lunch. I'm going to have to make a run."

"Yeah, yeah. Okay."

"You guys will have to wait a little."

"Scott's having lunch with Sydney. It'll just be us," Jack said.

"Hmmm. We don't even have that much. But just for a couple of sandwiches, maybe."

"I don't need anything," Catherine said. "I've got my yoghurt and stuff."

"Jack?" Ellen said.

"I don't really need anything. Just a sandwich."

Ellen thought for a moment.

"If that's the case, then I won't only do a run, but I'll go down to Anacortes and pick up the sealant you ordered."

Between the layers of planking, Jack and Scott were applying a moisture seal. Nothing heavy, a breathable organic product ... something to inhibit dry rot. Ellen looked over at Catherine.

"You want to come along?"

Catherine looked up from her ledger book.

"I'd like to finish this up. Then I thought I'd run the newest figures over to Eric."

It was when she glanced over at Jack, that he suddenly had the idea.

"Sounds fine," he said to Ellen. He uncupped his fingers. "Micky? Listen, what's the problem, anyway?"

"I'm not sure, Jack. But I think it's important."

Jack shifted from one leg to another with impatience.

"Christ Almighty."

"Can you come?"

Jack looked at Ellen, who was preparing to leave.

"What time did you say?"

"Noon. Noon and a half."

"An hour?"

383

"Yeah, fine. But don't be late."

"OK. I'll be over."

Jack wasn't thinking about Micky as he turned back towards Ellen and Catherine. Scott wouldn't be back for over an hour, Ellen was heading out the door and easily wouldn't be back for three hours, and he and Catherine were alone.

There was nothing preplanned, nothing had passed through his mind until that instance, but now, looking at Catherine finishing her bookwork, a raging torrent began flowing down through him.

The next minute passed in a flash. Ellen swept quickly out the door, leaving him still standing by the desk, Catherine still looking at the ledger. She didn't look up at him, but he watched her.

She made a shuffle of papers and closed the book, and giving him a friendly little squinting nod, stood up and went to the sink to rinse out her coffee cup. He turned to watch her.

He could hear Ellen's car start up and then crunch out of the parking lot. Jack looked at how Catherine's dress fell there to the back of her knees.

Her thoughts couldn't have been farther from Jack's. She was thinking about her promise to go see Eric. She had done everything she could to make it possible to go that afternoon. They had both agreed that if she could get away, he would be waiting at his office. Of course, things were complicated enough as it was without trying anything crazy, even though Eric's office staff and his secretary had gotten used to her comings and goings. It was just to see each other.

Ever since the trip to Canada, Catherine had felt the growing weight of her relationship with Eric. Of course, now they didn't go through such elaborate schemes to be together. She didn't mind the motels scattered around the county. What counted was each other.

She knew. And she knew it was getting complicated. There was something there, but she barely dared to think about it. The old, push-pull was installing itself. Sometimes it was her backing off as he came on, sometimes the other way around. Normal. Timing was everything, and it was hard to have the same thoughts at the same time when the world outside of their relationship took no account of how they felt.

A warm glow came over her at the idea of them both feeling things about each other. She knew how she felt. She knew he was feeling something as well. Winter had passed, and now they were on the verge of Spring, and rebirth—what else could one call it—was in the air.

The excitement was the fact she could have caused him to feel those things. How she handled things from here on out would determine how those feelings either evolved, or disintegrated. That excited her as well, because for the first time she knew she was capable of dealing with things.

For a while, she hadn't been against the idea of eventual disintegration. As a side thing, like it had been with Jack. But more so with Eric because it was incredible, the numbers of complications involved.

Lately, though, she had begun thinking the unthinkable. You never, never knew. She had decided to be careful. Make no demands but to maintain things to the point that, if they were going to stick, they would start sticking. She had made the decision that it would not be of her doing if things came undone.

But it wasn't just her. She wouldn't have thought any of that at all, if Eric hadn't started hinting it. He said, of course, that he loved her. And had said that whatever happened, there would be a lot of time involved. He could do nothing about it. And he didn't want her to get hurt, or be bothered.

And she had said she wasn't bothered at all.

Catherine finished rinsing her cup. Her thoughts being all for Eric, she gasped in surprise as Jack came up behind her, taking her about the waist and pushing up against her there at the sink.

She smiled. Even giggled when she thought suddenly of how they appeared there in the kitchen. Sort of like one of those Victorian post-cards with the husband making advances towards the maid.

All they lacked, she thought, was the sub-title.

But funny as it was, it was also a stern reminder that Jack was something else she would have to deal with.

Of course, she liked Jack. She was grateful, as well. But things were changing. Even to the point that, she had to admit, having his arms suddenly around her like that in the kitchen when she had been thinking of something else, was ... well, maybe even a little irritating.

She sighed.

Jack, hearing her, began pushing himself up against her more forcefully, moving his hands down along her hips.

She tried to laugh. "*Jack*," she complained a little whiningly. She wanted to leave right then and wondered how much snuggling it would take before she could get out of there.

Snuggling was the last thing Jack had on his mind.

"Yeah?" he said, pressing her up against the sink and running his hands up to her breasts."

"Jack," she said again, losing her patience a bit. "I've got to go."

"Do you?"

There was a note of indifference in his voice. Also a self-assurance. He knew she would like it. He could feel himself becoming excited and he pushed himself against her, letting her know.

"Oh my God, Jack," she breathed out, realizing what was happening. "Not here."

Suddenly, she was no longer irritated. If anything, frightened. Where, before, she had been partly responsible, wanting him, wanting it, this was a monster that she did not want.

"Jack, no," she breathed out as the movements of his hands upon her became more insistent.

Suddenly his hand went under her skirt, pulling it up until he could slide his hand beneath her underwear. She felt trapped and didn't struggle, but it was with a feeling of revulsion that she knew there was no stopping him. She shuddered as he dragged down her underwear, destroying them in his excitement.

"Bend more," he said, her skirt now entirely up.

His voice was calm, but there was a tense abruptness in it, an ugliness she could not find any way to resist. She leaned farther over the sink, his feet pushing her feet apart, far from ready. It was painful, and from that angle he was crushing her hips against the counter. To reduce his weight upon her she tried to steady herself against the counter. But she could not maintain her hold and her hands slipped down into the bottom of the sink. It was unreal how she felt almost nothing. She could lift her head just high enough to see out the kitchen window, scanning the parking lot and the street carefully. There was no one there, but she continued watching. For as long as it took.

It seemed to take forever.

# Chapter 73

No one was home. There was a note on the table. Jack had gone off to Micky's at some point. Catherine had gone on her errands.

Ellen went back out to the car and brought in the rest of the groceries. After that, with nothing else to do, she went to the living room, flicked on some Chopin, and flopped into an armchair, enjoying the music. After a while, she picked up a book, a novel Catherine had lent her ... something about foolish, complicated, well-off people living in New York and having fancy dinners and cocktails on high terraces ... and read, enjoying the music and the book. Feeling even more relaxed, she got up and went to the kitchen to boil some water for tea. She went back to her book and now enjoyed it again, along with the music and her tea.

Several chapters later, she took the teapot back to the kitchen and took out the teabags. She leaned over to put the used bags into the garbage pail under the sink and, seeing it was full, tossed the teabags into it and pulled it out and carried it outside to the barrel.

There, she jammed the edges of the paper sack liner together so they wouldn't get stuck, and tipped the pail over into the barrel. The paper sack fell out, not sticking for once, but as it often did the bottom split open as it fell into the barrel, dispersing into the barrel its contents of smashed eggshells, orange peels, black coffee grounds, carrot and potato trimmings, brown apple cores, slimy banana skins and several wet and crumpled paper towels which came apart revealing the torn remnants of light cotton underwear the size and style of which she had never worn. The paper towels, with that familiar musky smell, had been carefully shoved to the bottom of the pail. It should have probably just been taken away. But who would have thought that the contents of a garbage pail, emptied out upside down, would have caught anyone's attention? sometimes tearing open on the bottom, sometimes opening up like a sodden flower, exposing to the light of day those things which should never be seen? Who else but someone who never really thought that far ahead, or who had any inkling how other people thought, or that they were even capable of thinking?

Ellen stood for a moment, trying to take in what she was looking at. But unable to stop looking. Then she reached down, her fingers moving tentatively and carefully. When she was sure she knew what she was looking at, if not what it represented exactly, she picked things out, put the lid back on the can, and returned to the house.

# Chapter 74

J<small>ACK, WHO</small> normally paid little attention to the cheap thrills side of sex, was intoxicated. He'd never done anything like that.

It hadn't been enough, then, just to take her like that at the kitchen sink.

She had been surprised, of course. But he could tell how she had found it exciting as well, trembling constantly beneath him and so much so that he had become excited again afterwards as he got busy with paper towels and then took her damaged underwear and shoved them down into the garbage sack while she calmed herself, smoothing her dress back down.

But actually shaking from head to toe.

He remembered every detail. There had been this strange smile on her face. She hadn't been able to look at him.

He knew she had loved it.

Which made him want her all the more.

So he had gone with it, taking her up to her place to continue.

He had never dreamed taking risks could be such a powerful drug. He believed he had never experienced anything as powerful, physically, as he had felt there at the sink.

God knew he had been needing something lately. All this baby business, and the boat work. All this pressure now that he was finally on the top, or getting there. A family man, and a successful boatbuilder. He wished he could have just cleared a bit of space around himself. Slowed things down for a moment and caught his breath. But that seemed impossible. Like going down a water slide. Just rushing downward, ever more rapidly with the stream. He needed Catherine now more than ever. She was the small clearing for him. The little sunlit glade in the heavy forest.

He lay with his arms around her in her apartment ... uncaring about how to explain this disappearance to Ellen or Scott. Just needing it, feeling her warm body, caressing her breasts or running his hand down between her legs and hold her like that as though to comfort himself with her reality. She lay unspeaking, although he could feel how her heart was beating rapidly. But docile.

He pulled her against himself, once again feeling his desire returning. Feeling her breath quicken. She let out a small sound, almost a whimper if more than a sigh.

Was it love that made him want to have her like this?

Whether it was or not, the thing absolutely sure was that she was his, now. As he was hers. Arrangements, contracts, agreements notwithstanding, they were now something else. Together.

The word came as almost an emotion. Hot and stinging. Heat again rising as his own heartbeat began to race, as he hunched his back and ground against her.

To just blank things out for a time. To push everything away and create a separate universe there with her. Get a chance to think clearly about the things that really mattered.

Jack pushed his face against Catherine's neck, pulling her around again.

She moaned.

*

Several hours later she was alone. She felt very tired. It was amazing how tired you could feel, she thought, when faced with the necessity to do a great deal of thinking.

What, she asked herself, could she have done? What, in herself, could she trust? What could she know?

He, of course, couldn't help her with this. Not that he would want to, of course.

Trapped.

Just trapped. And tired.

So, so tired.

Of the mistake. Of all the mistakes.

Of all the times she had thought she had known, and which had turned out to be just guessing, and guessing as wrong as wrong could be.

But the one thing Ellen did not have to guess about was that now she would be looking. Ellen would be looking. With her eyes wide open.

## Chapter 75

W HEN JACK didn't show up, Micky and Clyde went alone to pay a visit on a very old lady living on Sehome Hill. They didn't talk much. Mrs. Wilson was very old, and strangely very trusting of the two younger men who came to visit her so politely that afternoon. They had a pleasant chat because they were all, of course, somehow involved with each other as business and land owners in the old Fairhaven waterfront area.

They didn't stay long.

Mrs. Wilson was pretty vivacious for her age and all, they said, but they were concerned they were making her tired and so forth, anyway, with all this nonsense.

It was so nice for Mrs. Wilson to have company. Lately, always about the same thing. She had been having several visitors.

All these young men. Such a memorable March.

It was something she was also proud of, knowing that most of the women friends of her age were all such a bunch of biddies, no longer involved with the world. But she was still much a part of it. Still having people come to see her and talk business with her.

These two, though, Mr. Moore and Mr. Przworski, didn't actually talk contracts as the others did. It was just a nice, general chat. In a way, she preferred these two polite men to the young fellows who came in with their beautiful, expensive tailored suits, but who hadn't learned how to be relaxed about life.

She and Mr. Moore and Mr. Przworski all agreed that, what with things being the way they were, it would be a good thing to stay in contact with each other. A sort of merchants association, Mr. Moore had said.

Mrs. Wilson rather liked that. It had a nice ring to it and made her feel part of something. She liked the idea of being part of something. They would keep in touch.

Micky and Clyde went back down to the bar. Micky had a lot of bartending to do when they got back, which left Clyde deep in concentration.

How to put all this in its place? It was strange indeed how all this was happening, and how at the same time both he and Micky were having troubles through the bank, when the real owner, that sweet little old lady up on the hill, didn't seem to have the slightest ill will towards them. Didn't mention a thing about the leasing arrangements.

Even though she, in the end, was the owner.

Something was going on. Clyde was worried enough to wonder if it wasn't time to get himself and Annie the hell out of it for once and for all. Bad enough to be trying to keep a business from caving in, than to get it yanked right out from underneath you.

With, he thought, several fucking dozens of back inventory items sitting on blocks or floating around down at the dock.

Four beers later, Clyde was looking wistfully down at Micky, wishing he could talk with him about all this. Turn it over with him. He thought he had something figured out.

But, the truth was ... he was used to having Annie at these times. He was used to having her to bounce these ideas off of.

But even that wasn't enough this time. Although she often helped him get things clear, he needed more. He wished he could find someone who could be objective about it. Who didn't give a shit. Who wouldn't blame him. Or, who wouldn't try to screw him over. Someone who ....

He felt someone clap him on the shoulder.

Clyde looked up to see who it was, and found Scott grinning at him.

# Chapter 76

MARCH WAS dragging on at an interminable pace for Eric. So much to do, but so much depended on timing. There were days which passed where he could do nothing but wait for the next day. Waiting for everyone.

This particular day, he had been waiting for Catherine. But he was also waiting for Carl Ivarsson to give him a sign. And, as always, he was waiting for Hartman.

As far as the Hartman deal was concerned, timing was getting crucial. Now, what had been the slow process of getting Deborah out and away from the Colby's—out of the way and clearing the field—was becoming unbearable.

In many ways.

And then there was the boat. Probably the most pressing problem of all.

As far as that was concerned, he had thought he might wean Deborah of going down there. Prepare her for giving up on seeing it built. Find other activities around town for her to get involved in. There were always plenty of charitable things a rich woman could be called upon to do. But he could see now it was impossible. Deborah was determined to see the boat finished before her eyes. They were putting the planks on. The Muse was very nearly to the point of being able to be floated.

At one point, he had even considered finding out if the goddamn thing actually *could* be put in the water. He couldn't figure out how to say it, though, without getting everyone suspicious.

Hartman was becoming threatening about it. The time frame was getting tight, and if they couldn't get in and flatten everything soon, they would lose a great deal of leverage.

But Eric had discovered some new information. Fascinating information. His earlier inklings had been confirmed.

Things weren't as sewn up as Hartman had wanted him to believe.

In fact, Hartman didn't have complete control, and amazingly enough, there were a couple of property owners down there still presenting him with room to maneuver. One was an old lady, the one with the ancient land rights, and the other, was the lease holder of Jack Colby's.

Eric didn't know exactly what he was going to do with his knowledge. But he knew exactly the situation.

Hartman still had most of the cards.

Hartman still wanted Eric in on the deal.

And it was still a very attractive proposition as it stood.

Eric would be a fool, though, if he didn't examine any alternatives that presented themselves.

But he had to be extremely careful. If Hartman got the slightest hint, there would be all hell to pay. Hartman wasn't a man who gave his word lightly. To offer trust, for a man who spent most of his time dealing from a position of mistrust, was an enormous risk. So it was only with the gravest sort of decision that Eric would step outside their plans.

If only that damn boat was out of there. Gone, vanished. Then there would be clear sailing—if that phrase was appropriate.

Eric sighed. And then realizing what he looked like there, sighed again.

He was sitting at his desk, the lord of his empire, his jacket draped over the back of his chair, his suspenders drooping on his chest, fiddling with a paper knife. If they could only see him, he thought. All his employees down below pounding away at their desks, making him enough money so that he would be happy with their work, and not get upset or something and fire them. Their jobs were to make him so much money, make him ever so much richer, that he would pay them their salaries at the end of the month.

It was laughable to think of.

They were glad to be working like slaves to make him rich. Goddamn glad. Because there wasn't a goddamn thing they could do about it. So they might as well like it.

And they did.

They were even proud when they managed to go beyond themselves and make him even richer than he expected they could.

What were you going to do, Eric thought? What could you do in a world like this?

There he sat, on top of it all. Richer by the minute. Fiddling around on his desk pad, stretching his suspenders. Itching and mumbling to himself. Wondering about Hartman. Whether he could be screwed. Waiting for Catherine. And wondering—with a sudden, bleak, and vulgar inspiration of humor—where they could screw next.

If his people could only see him as he was right then. What would they think? What would they do?

There would be a fucking riot, is what there would be, he thought.

But then again, maybe not. Maybe the world was made in such a way that most people liked being treated like assholes as long as they were paid, and left alone on the weekends.

He sighed again. Going back to the first of his irritations.

Where the hell was she, anyway?

She had been steady, a rock. She had understood exactly the difficulty and confusion, and had been patient.

That trip to the backwoods of Canada had been like a fine present for her. And then all the others. And all the things they had said.

Of course, it wasn't possible to think of the future. They had both had this thing happen to them as though some mad comet had streaked in from outer space, landing on them in one giant smash which they could have no more avoided than they could have changed its course.

She was aware of that.

He loved looking into her eyes as they talked, seeing that total awareness, the tender irony. She knew the price of life, and of love, and knew that nothing at all was ever free.

This woman—and she was so much a woman, much more than any he had ever known—was so alive to realities, yet so warm and sensitive. She gave off an aura that she secretly knew the true values to things, knew what true quality was, and found him not at all wanting within her framework for judgment.

For the first time in his life, Eric was with a woman who showed she was aware of all his parts. Not just his good but his bad parts as well. And she accepted him as he was. She accepted his actions, showed she understood he was not simply instinctual about everything, but was calculating sums of right and wrong. And ... why not? ... sums of things like honor and decency.

He had a right to be honorable and decent.

If he was trying to reach for some ideal in a world which didn't allow itself to be perfect, which despite everything people might say refused to be bothered with finding a better way—like the ants working for him below—then he felt he had the right to a certain amount of respect.

To be admired. As a man.

And as a man, if he had some deep carnal urge, she went up to it unafraid and appeased it with no more shame or embarrassment, or criticism, than she held for herself. In fact, fully agreed with it.

So where was she?

Eric flipped his desk calendar up to April, running his fingers down the days.

Just a matter of planning, he thought. They couldn't rely, he could see, upon the informal anymore. They had tried, once they had got back from Canada. Heres and theres. But she now was so caught up in her duties down at Colby's. Her responsibilities to Jack Colby were snagging her up.

That's the problem with responsibilities, he thought, nodding. He understood. You gave yourself to them by decision. Made yourself available to them. From that moment forward you become a slave to them. You went where and when they demanded.

The point was, it seemed to him, that to control the situation meant making yourself a responsibility as well for others. His happiness was his employees' responsibility, and they were well paid for maintaining it. And he, here, now had a new responsibility.

So it was just a matter of organization.

He'd have to organize things.

He looked at his desk clock. It was now too late for anything. She knew how long he had been able to be free.

He could see it would be up to him to now always organize things. For her, and for himself. After all, he was thinking for the benefit of both of them. She would understand. That's what her Sex Knot was all about.

But she would have to organize herself as well. Get her priorities figured out.

# Chapter 77

IN THE still of those spring mornings, Scott would go early to the shop to cut and set plugs, that tedious chore. But he liked tedious chores. They dulled his mind to other things.

Taking scraps of mahogany to the drill press, he bore out plug after plug until the piece of scrap was little more than dozens of holes held together by something that used to be called wood. He would gather his plugs in a canvas work pouch tied around his waist and, with a small mallet and a pot of waterproof glue, start tapping the plugs into the holes over the tops of the planking screws. When he had filled the morning's holes he would go back over those of the previous day, their glue now dry, striking off the protruding ends of those plugs with a chisel and shaving them down flush to the surface of the hull planking. A dull procedure, but one which resulted as much as anything, through their regular perfection, in lending workmanship and beauty to the hull. It was one thing to stand back twenty feet and admire the grand, sweeping lines of the huge hull. It was another to come up close to the exquisite grain of the dark, red-brown mahogany. To examine the way the various lengths of wood fit together, lines and angles precisely mated, set in counterpoint with the plugs, their grain aligned with that of the planks, as though not separate pieces of wood, but only small, drawn circles.

On several of these mornings, bringing him out a cup of coffee, Catherine had stayed to watch what he was doing.

He noticed on those occasions that there was something jumpy and nervous about her. He had a pretty good idea as to why and, not too strangely, could feel a bit of sympathy for her. Because of that, as much as he disliked her, he had no particular desire to make her feel worse. And certainly not by showing or intimating he knew anything about her.

He pretended to be friendly and ignorant. That last one being the easier of the two. He'd spent quite a bit of time lately pretending to be ignorant.

"It's a shame to have to paint over this," she said after watching him for a while on one of those mornings.

"There'll be plenty of varnished wood up top," he said, unable not to agree with her feelings, "starting right at the rail. But it's the truth that the naked wood on the hull gives you the idea of what it's all about, of all the work, and is the one thing that will end up hidden. She'll be so smooth, you won't be able to tell she wasn't made of plastic."

Catherine laid her hand on the wood.

"Amazing. It's really mahogany. A boat made with mahogany. I'd gotten so used to the idea of only furniture being made out of these woods. And oak too. You usually think they're too precious, like gold or silver, to be used for anything else."

"These are good, strong woods. You know, back East and in Europe, these were always historically the woods used for serious construction. The sort that lasts for centuries."

Catherine's motives for being there in the morning were indeed along the lines of what Scott suspected. To be somewhere where things seemed neutral and normal and not fraught with undercurrents. And what had started as a sort of momentary escape had become something she enjoyed. It made it easier to go to work in the morning, starting off the day with the calming effect of those first few minutes out there in the shop with him. And in so doing, she had of late begun to truly appreciate Scott's work, and enjoyed watching him. Despite his aura of marginality, there was a sense of gentle resolution about the way he approached materials he used. He dominated the wood and the tools but at the same time took them up with a respect and tenderness that, for lack of any other word, came close to a form of love.

So she watched and watched and soon understood the way he went about his work those mornings.

He was chiseling off the protruding parts of plugs he had set, a fairly basic job, but she saw how he judged each plug individually, considering it in itself, and then cut so softly there was almost no sound on the stroke. He made a first cut, out a bit from the plank to find the true run of the plug's grain, and then went down close to cut smooth and sharp. The chisel was honed to a razor edge and cut the plugs as fine and smooth as the polished surface of a varnished table.

As he moved along she would sometimes go closer to look at the finished plugs, instinctively touching where they set in the satiny surroundings of the semi-sanded mahogany planking. But mostly, and discretely, she watched him, with his big, hard shoulders and arms, his strong back creasing and flexing beneath the light flannel shirt, the tight muscles of his forearms playing beneath the surface of his freckled, but oddly dark skin.

She'd never noticed that before. Most freckled people had skin white as ivory. His had a richer hue, as though lightly but permanently bronzed. A strange coloration, and yet it touched her in some way, as though it made him seem more ancient, of some long disappeared race. A picture of brute force, she thought, and yet ... so delicately tapping his chisel as to give the impression it, and he, had a butterfly lightness, moving from plug to plug.

She had come to like his quiet, slightly sardonic way. She had also come to realize that of all the other people, Scott was the one she felt the most relaxed to be near. More than even Eric, perhaps.

Maybe because she wasn't involved with him, because he was so smoothly quiescent about his relations with others. Even, it seemed to her, with his girlfriend. A strong, hard man physically, but the humor in his clear blue eyes gave proof, always, that never once would he force upon anyone his own desires or opinions. Of all of them, his was not a forceful presence where all the rest of them had such strong personalities.

Yet, she reflected, for all that, he seemed to get what he wanted and needed anyway. You could feel—slightly—jealous, she thought, about these people who were able to enjoy the simple things, simply, and wanted no more than that. Of course, if you had a strong sense of will, the power of personality she and Eric, or Jack and Ellen had, you were doomed to higher aspirations.

Nevertheless, Scott's easygoing happiness was of a wonder to her, and she frowned at the thought of it. She could even admit to feeling curious about him. Hard, though, to know these silent, contented types. Only the discontented let you right in to their very depths.

Those days, for her for example, were certainly not happy ones for her. She had decided that, no, it had not been rape ... not really.

There had been a ferocity in it, yes. Unbridled lack of restraint and dominance, which had her nervous. Something bordering on the feeling of being trapped. As though a deer run to ground by hounds and hunters. He had taken, absolutely, his way with her and then all the rest of it up at her place. Just taken everything.

But, no. Not rape.

She had been physically hurt by him, bruised and sharply aching when he had finally left her alone.

She had, indeed, been stunned, unable to think.

And she had missed her rendezvous with Eric. She had not been able to talk to anyone, and it had taken days for her to feel more normal down at the Colby's.

Jack had not approached her since that day. They exchanged an occasional glance though, and when they did she had seen the gleam was still there in his eyes, whatever it was.

It hadn't been rape.

She had needed room to think. To calm her nerves. You could wish the world could be turned off for a time so you could get your bearings, get yourself back on steady ground. But it kept turning, always moving one step ahead of you.

And it was part of the reason she was out there with Scott. And … why? Because, somewhere, she felt she could trust him? Or that, simply, he was neither Eric nor Jack?

She didn't know. Although, oddly enough, there was something soothing about his presence. Something safe, neutral, strong and sure.

Instinctively, she followed Scott's work, moving with him incrementally down the hull as he moved his step ladder from ribline to ribline. And as she watched him, moving as though carrying out an act a thousand years old, she felt a glow and personal warmth of her own … towards him … come up. She smiled, approaching him, and asking with a quiet, silky voice that she knew men liked, but also with real curiosity.

"Have you always worked on boats?"

# Chapter 78

Scott blinked once, slowly. Half a year gone and it was the first time she had ever asked him about himself.

All those lunches, and dinners, and little parties and odd moments where he had heard everything he felt it was possible to know about her, her ex-jobs, her ex-husbands, their wives, her ex-boyfriends, her ex-friends in Seattle and their ex-husbands, and so on—and she'd only just then become somewhat interested in him. It was odd enough to make him wonder why she should.

Perhaps, he thought, life was getting a bit too complicated for her. She was in need of human solidarity. And there he was again, the convenient man at the bottom of the barrel.

Not that it mattered. Scott's recent bitterness had washed through him as though a hard rain had cleared the air. He didn't really care about Jack and her, or more precisely, he was past caring. That was their problem. Black clouds rolled in, black clouds rolled away. In another month, God only knew how he would feel again. But for the time being, life was good.

Good enough, that was, compared to these poor saps.

Had he always worked on boats? In one sense no. In another .... His head moved vaguely.

"All my life"

Catherine was leaning back against the hull, sipping her coffee. "That's funny."

"Why's that?" He climbed down to move his ladder over and then went back up to the next set of plugs.

"I don't know. Maybe because you don't seem so absolutely a boat builder. Like Jack, I mean. He is so seriously a boat builder, you know. I guess it's sort of like, for Jack, there's nothing more important than these boats, it's his whole life."

Scott took a tentative tap at the plug he was working on. Very carefully.

"I think you said you once went to school," she kept on.

Scott set the chisel close, and then struck. Another perfect plug. Somehow.

"Everybody goes to school."

"Where?"

"Oh, lots of places."

Catherine was fascinated by the thought of Scott as a student. It wasn't at all evident.

"Really."

For a second, blankly, Scott stared at the expanse of wood in front of him. Despite how her line of questioning was annoying and how he was trying to find some diplomatic way to get somewhere else, he felt himself go into it.

He normally didn't spend much time examining his past. But she had brought his memories of those days back.

As usual, and being the main reason he and most other people set those thoughts aside, he found himself wondering about the myriad lost opportunities. Who didn't have those thoughts? But he'd found it never really helped because, no matter how you raked out your past, in the end it was awfully hard to tell.

You go one way or another and later on it all looks like there was a pattern to it. Even if there wasn't, really.

Amazing, that habit, of trying to assign meaning.

But he knew better. He'd come to a separate peace with that way of thinking, and understood that as long as he made sure he was doing what he wanted, then the pattern of his life would never be something he could regret. Or, at least, he hoped so. Some people mapped it all out, and from there on either had successes or failures. A continual cost/benefit, bean-counting analysis of everything. Some people even did that with friends. Good friends.

Of course, he'd done that enough where his current job was concerned, and with Jack, and with Ellen. But that was different. At least in terms of friendship. Because he knew only a masochist would consider what he shared with them—on anything other than a professional level—as friendship. But even there his philosophy held true, as it held true for the past. If your method was to keep things as enjoyable as possible on the day to day level, it seemed to him there was a better percentage of feeling good about both the present and what happened when it became the past. So in those terms, and applying it to his checkered school career, he didn't feel particularly bad. He really didn't. He looked at her and smiled.

"Believe it or not, I've got about twice the credits of a regular, graduating senior. I'm probably about six months away from four separate majors."

Catherine was actually shocked.

"So why not finish up? If you're so close?" She nodded her head in the direction of the college hill.

"Why?"

She looked down at her shoes, angered at the cavalier sounding answer. Why should anyone do anything, she thought? Sometimes, things were just there to be picked up so easily there was no reason not to. She herself had gone back. She found his attitude irritating. It was bothersome how he could pick something up, to later drop it as inconsequential. As though, in the end, he didn't give a damn about anything. Which, pretty obviously, was exactly the case with him.

"I don't know," she said. "It just seems like it wouldn't hurt anything."

Scott nodded, setting his chisel to another plug. Catherine saw he was dismissing the entire importance of the point.

She became suddenly infuriated.

"I guess you don't need it. I suppose you are the sort of person who only uses things that seem useful to you at the moment."

Her vehemence stunned him. And rather than considering where all that might really be coming from, all he could feel was the possibility of an insinuation about Sydney.

But a moment later, he even let that slide. He was no angel, he knew. But he most surely wasn't alone in that, and wasn't going to let some undercurrent of accusation bother him. Whatever his social shortcomings might or might not be, he honestly felt he could be worse as a human being. And was prepared to live and let live, even in the face of someone's need to imply disapproval.

He just didn't care.

As long as no one said anything right out at him, he wasn't about to waste his time getting into a fight. Although he knew that it was only when people tell you things to your face, that you knew they'd lost all respect for you. Which meant, if things were important, some sort of a defense was called upon.

This wasn't the case.

"In some ways, I suppose," he said equably, eyeing the next plug in line. "But to be honest, if I did finish, the only thing I could really do with it would be to mail the diploma to my mother. She could hang it up and look at it."

He was about to tap his chisel, but then he stopped, dropping his hands for a moment, and looked at her. Solemnly.

"I guess it does come down to using or not using things. And I've come to the point in my life that I don't just do things for the hell of it, without thinking how it affects me or ...," he knew what he was about to add was tangential to what he was talking about, but it fit in well with his feelings and carried a message he thought she should hear, "... anything or anyone else I care about."

By the way he'd looked at her, she sensed how he suspected she'd made a cut about Sydney. She hadn't meant that, though. Not really.

Nonetheless, and despite having been surprised by her anger at the thought, she was sure of her feeling that Scott came along and used things as he wanted to, whether he needed them or not, and then put them to the side. Despite anything he might say. As he so obviously would with Sydney. Which made him, unfortunately, a bit of a phony. But, in the end, what did that matter?

"So what would you have graduated as?" she asked, deciding to change the tone of the conversation.

She figured something, at best, like biology or chemistry. He probably was clever and methodical enough for those. Intelligent enough. He didn't seem the business school type, of course. That was obvious. Maybe even geology, out picking up rocks. Or some hippy social science. At worst, of course, and considering his build, some sort of physical education degree. No doubt he'd been a jock.

"Liberal Arts."

Well, she thought, of course. That made sense most of all. Dabbling at painting or—she looked at the chisel in his hands—sculpture. Utterly useless, except at how it explained the comfort he had, and his enjoyment, for working with his hands. She nodded.

"Art. Yes, I can see that."

"No, although I took a lot of art classes. Liberal Arts."

She frowned.

"You mean, oh ... you mean, sociology or the humanities. English?"

Scott laughed.

"Oh, shit no. Although that was in there. A lot. No, mostly philosophy and comparative literature. It's my father's fault, but that's a long story." He laughed again. "Anyway, so I figure I'm doing exactly what I would have been doing even with one of those degrees."

"*What?*" Catherine was stunned. Here, in front of her, was the one man in the whole place who had actually studied the books she read. Not once, in the entire time she had been down there, had she ever detected it in him.

Scott heard the touch of wonder in her voice, how she evidently found such a thing almost impossible to believe. He found that annoying, disliking the implied condescension, but then realized he was probably annoying her even worse. He smiled again.

"Why? Do I look more like MBA material? If I was, I doubt I would have ended up like this, pounding nails and sawing boards."

"It's not so bad, what you're doing." she said. Obviously, she had touched a nerve. He really had nothing to be ashamed of. Manual labor was not valueless. Of course, he might struggle with these sorts of things, this life, having been exposed to the intellectual life. But, really, she thought, he shouldn't feel bitter.

She waved her hand lightly in the air in a way she hoped would tactfully and graciously relay those feelings.

Scott stopped and looked at her.

Evidently, she thought, tactfulness wasn't going to do it.

"Okay," she said. "You didn't say it was bad. Obviously, you like it, in fact."

"You could say that."

"But," she said, now suddenly unable to resist wanting to push at him a little, like making a recalcitrant child straighten up or own up and be honest, for once, "how much do you really like it?"

Scott hated theatrical gestures, and hated finding himself suddenly motivated to making them himself. But he couldn't help it. It was all just so ... grotesque. He took his eyes off her and looked up, glancing at the windows high on the side of the building where the bright morning sunshine sent in a feathery light.

Such a lovely day out there.

He took a long breath, then looked back down and over at her, ... and let go with it.

"If you don't know that, Catherine, then you don't know fuck-all. About me. About anything. Sometimes, to be perfectly honest, that gets to be my guess."

It was totally unexpected, and for a second a wild thing came up into her throat, choking her. She swallowed, trying to say something, but Scott turned back to the boat's flank.

She stared at him. Never had she heard him say anything with that sort of cold hardness. It shocked her. She hadn't even known he was capable of doing so, so generally soft-spoken he seemed. Or of even harboring such anger.

She could say nothing, and for a moment stood motionless, both her mind and her feet petrified. Horrified, suddenly, with the unnerving feeling he knew everything about what she might say to him, even before she could think of it herself. But then the simple instinct of flight kicked in, and regardless of how it might look, she found herself first backing away, and then turning to go, somewhat shakily, back to the office.

She had never had that sort of an experience with a man at any time.

Anywhere.

She went into the office and sat down at her desk, composing herself and looked at the orders she had to deal with that morning.

Blanking her mind. Blanking. Blanking.

More white oak for reinforcing the deck beams, teak for decking and red Philippine mahogany for interior work.

Plenty to do.

She frowned for a second, being businesslike. Professional. Getting back to work. She picked up the phone. But then set it down again, her hand shaking.

\*

Out in the shed, Scott kept tapping away at the plugs.

Too damn bad, he thought. She still seemed smart as hell. Still seemed attractive. He could think about her legs, all day long, no problem at all. Pounding nails or whatever, and he could have thought about those legs.

Setting aside all her pretense at conversation and all the rest of that supercilious crap that had gone with it, he had seen that she was promoting all right. Recent events convinced him of that, and she was smart enough to try. Digging herself out. But, whatever she thought she was going for, he couldn't make out.

Jack?

That possibility flickered for a second in his mind, but he set it aside. Scott wasn't really interested in getting to the bottom of her problems.

Suddenly, he let his mind wander as he continued trimming plugs. Letting his irritation dissipate with impressionistic thoughts. One, and then another. As though letting his unconscious sort all that out. Random images. What was she after, now?

He thought about Jack again. Wondered, and set it aside again.

Jack, he thought, couldn't be it. Jack was a dead end.

Jack was all neon and brass bands, but at the bottom he couldn't tie his shoes. At least not in terms of making life-changing decisions.

So ... no way she could win, he thought, if that was it.

Especially not now.

For what it was worth, for the next year or so at least, Ellen had the high ground; love being politics carried out by other means.

Catherine, normally, was smart enough to see that.

So what the hell was going on?

Scott set his lips grimly.

"Getting pretty creepy around here," he muttered.

He reached out and patted the boat.

At least *she* was still solid, he thought, and he pulled another plug from the pouch.

# Chapter 79

JACK AND Scott were working in a fury, moving from planking the hull to setting the curved deck beams and removing, station by station, the first of the hull molds. The interior of the *Muse* opened up enough that the day finally came when men from the engine manufacturer could bring the big diesels over.

The motor blocks were built and the motors were lowered and bolted into place within the hull: gleaming, green and chrome monsters. Over the next few days the specialists then installed the shafts with their housings for the propellers, and set up the electrical systems, the conduits for water and exhaust, and the fuel tanks and lines. After the engine men had left, having made a final inspection to their satisfaction, Jack and Scott built the engine compartment, the first interior structure, making it big enough for a man to work on the engines without having to crawl.

It was when they completed that construction, and walked back along the inside of the huge hull to contemplate the space, that it suddenly struck them.

That huge space, needing to be filled with frames, cross-beams, floors, and bulkheads—not to mention all the fine cabinetry involved in the finishing work—suddenly was too much for them to accomplish. At least, not within Sumners' time frame.

Jack said only a half dozen words to Scott, with Scott nodding, and then went to make the phone call they both knew had been a long time in coming.

*

An hour and a half later, Jack and Sumners were up in the loft. For the first fifteen minutes of that meeting, Scott didn't need to be anywhere near that end of the shop to understand what they were saying, or the tone of it. Sumners voice was the first to go rising in volume into a heavy, furious bellowing, but soon enough Jack was doing the same. And for a while Scott thought it would never end and everything was just headed towards a total blowup.

Quickly, though, the voices went down. So quickly, it was almost as though nobody was up there. But Scott knew better. At a couple of points, he very nearly gave in to the temptation to find a reason to stick his head in up there. But he finally decided if Jack didn't call for him, he was not only not needed but not wanted.

In any case, Scott thought, for whatever else Jack was capable of, he at least knew exactly what was needed to finish the Muse within any reasonable time-frame. Especially the much more urgent time-frame Sumners had been pushing lately.

There was no doubt that Jack would spell it out. Time, in this case, meant money. The shorter, the more expensive.

And either Sumners would opt for the one, or the other.

It would be interesting to see which one, Scott thought. For himself, he didn't mind at all the idea of working for another year, just him and Jack, on the boat. He'd gotten comfortable with the lifestyle, and supposed Jack was as well. But there was no doubt there was a monstrous amount of work to be done. All the careful framing. All the creation of spaces. Not to mention all the endless cabinetry work, which Scott knew would fall mostly on him. And on top of that was all the fitting of sailing gear, and the rudder and steering cockpit, and all the million other minute and skilled tasks to be done.

All the things which Jack was explaining right at that moment.

All told, it took about an hour of quiet time before they came back down the stairs. They didn't say goodbye to each other, or look at each other, and Sumners didn't look over at Scott either, just going out to his car carrying a very large roll of drawings.

Jack wandered up to Scott with a dark look of fatigue.

Scott nodded. "I see he's off with my interior plans."

"He took the whole lot."

"Didn't want us to handle the arrangements?"

Jack frowned at the insinuation. But after a moment had to smile.

"Yeah. He'll feel better taking part in the solution. Give him a chance to be part of the team."

They could have left it like that, with just the insinuation covered with diplomacy, but Scott decided he preferred things openly said. "And assure himself that things are properly back under control."

Jack shrugged, and then actually laughed.

"Right. Properly back under control of the person who knows how to best keep things under control."

"Well, it's understandable."

"I suppose so," Jack sighed. "But be prepared. We're going to have a change around here, and pretty quickly."

That, as it turned out, was an understatement.

*

There were times, Scott thought, when life, teetering on expectations, just ground to a halt. That was how things felt for the next two days. Then the workers began to drift in. Within four days, twenty men were working on the hull. And life turned into a runaway train.

Where they had come from—a motley of old workers and young … balding heads, bald heads, pony tails, moustaches … beards black, red, brown or gray … blue eyes, brown, blue, green … exhibiting friendly garrulousness or concentrated silence … and evidently all experienced wooden boat builders—there was no way of telling. Another Sumners miracle of organization and efficiency. And, as well, they were evidently under Sumners' direct orders and pay because they all went at their work as though it had all the urgency of the building of the Ark. Work went into a tunnel so concentrated and so deep, that time seemed literally to have disappeared as a dimension.

Work, eat, sleep.

All told, that went on for six weeks.

*

Jack, even at the big yards back east, had never seen so much done in so little time. A person looked one day, and there was an empty hull, two days later, the inside was planked, the bilge drains set, and subflooring for the lowest decks in place. In another two days, bulkheads fore and aft were set up. Then the other decks, compartments and spaces, with all the electricals and plumbing set where it had to go. On some days, Jack and Scott actually felt they were getting in the way. Deborah, in the face of the implacable pragmatism—and frank and open stares—of her husband's mercenaries … for they were no other, regardless of their woodworking skills and qualifications … basically fled.

By the end of the third week, several big trucks showed up, and Scott and Jack, having little else to do, helped direct the unloading of heavy crates which had been flown in from overseas. Manila, Ceylon, or Singapore. Manhandled inside, the crates were unpacked, and large pieces of fine cabinetry began to be taken up and set down inside the boat. Whirl-oak panels for cabins, maple, oak and walnut for counters, doors, cabinets and shelving. Biggest of all were the bedroom and main cabinet furniture, the finely scrolled and massive bedframes for the two master suites, which were built to flow into the framing of the suite as though of a single unit. Every inch of it exactly to the specifications Scott had designed and meticulously drawn out all winter in his spare time.

Naturally, all that had to be in place before the cabin roofs were built, but once in place the final work began on the topsides, the work crew doing in a day what Scott and Jack would have taken a month to accomplish.

The deck beams were completed—heavy, gently curving arcs of white oak. Big gaps in the deck, made with half beams, allowed for the main and forward cabins as well as for the cockpit, and heavy blocks had been screwed between beams for stress points where rigging or rigging equipment would be anchored.

Two massively blocked emplacements, with corresponding timbers at the keel, were prepared for where the masts, main and mizzen, would be stepped. Each beam, each block or half beam, was different and had to be mitered and shaped, a grinding form of ship's carpentry, but at last it was finished in preparation for the exacting work of decking.

Work was moving quickly now not only because of the incessant rushing change of simultaneous tasks which were events in themselves—each a large, similar job like planking, but now reduced to but one among many—but also because of how the giant boat, except for the rawness of the appearance of the untreated wood, looked finished. There was still a great deal to do, but they were now much closer to the end point than the far distant beginning to all this, receding now at a backwards rush into history.

By the fifth week, the subdecking was in place. And, there, Jack finally joined in fully with the crew rather than finding odd jobs, beginning the process of laying the inch and a half square strips of Burma teak decking, running the long strips of teak over the heavy under-decking they'd laid across the deck beams ... then boring holes, setting screws, and seating teak bungs over the heads of the screws. While both he and Scott shared expertise in almost every area of boatbuilding, teak deckwork was Jack's particular specialty and, seeing his work, even Sumners' hired guns finally let him direct that job.

Scott, finally getting to setting up the cabinet and joinery work below, attached himself to another part of the crew doing the finishing work. Which was strange, in a sense. Because he found himself fitting and screwing into places pieces of joinery and furniture which, otherwise, he would have made with his own hands. They were, indeed, his designed work. And he had to admit they were all perfectly performed, the fitting of wood grain in panels aligned within a hair, the fluted molding flawless.

It had all, somehow, been done in shops out somewhere on the Pacific Rim. And had all, somehow, been done ... that fast.

Sumners had known where to go to get the best work done the most quickly. And while he didn't seem to have cared, he had saved money in the bargain.

But Scott finally decided it wasn't so bad. It wasn't as though the boat had been taken out of his and Jack's hands. It was still their boat. These were still his galley cabinets, his rails and closets, panels, deckfloor design, cabin door details. Regardless if they were made half a world away, and installed by a gang of skilled fortune hunters.

Up to then during that whirlwind, Jack and Scott had worked on particular projects, the rudder, or mast blocks, side by side. Mainly, almost, to stay out of the way of Sumners' men. But now they were separated and for the next week or so, rarely saw each other.

It was a little strange at first, at least for Scott, to find himself working at opposite ends of the hull from Jack. As though he was working at a different company. But for Scott, as well, he could admit that it came as a relief to not have to be around Jack all day. Those few weeks they'd been doing odd jobs alongside each other while the gang completed the boat, Jack had become more and more strange, moody even—and Scott preferred to let him stew alone.

He then, working sometimes twenty hour days alongside the others, set up the interior. Hard, highly crafted work, it was extremely tiring, but represented major progress, and he enjoyed seeing the realization of Fletcher's beautiful arrangements. Each bulkhead or doorway was placed to take best advantage of space and provide strength to the hull. There was the large working cabin, luxurious appointed, back of the mizzen mast, with the navigation station to one side, and stairs at either end, one towards the crew cabins and the engine compartment, the other towards the galley and the corridor leading forward to the main salon.

That cabin, set over guest bedrooms, showers, bathrooms, closets and hallways below decks, took up almost the entire expanse at deck level between the mizzen and mainmast. Following Fletcher's plans, the salon was supposed to be an open and spacious area, very simple, where the Sumners would be using normal furniture rather than marine-style booths and hinged tables. They had plenty of room.

For the furniture, one of the best interior decorators in New York had selected a number of well-padded sofas and chairs, delivered in protective plastic wrapping, with accompanying oak end tables and accessories. It would all end up looking like a large, comfortable living room with the exception that everything would be bolted down. Perhaps more cozy than a New York apartment overlooking Central Park, but Scott could see the inspiration. Deborah Sumners was an avid reader of The New Yorker.

By the seventh week, almost finished, there was a sort of party. Bratwurst and beer. Fun. Girlfriends.

Which, for Scott, meant Sydney had been able to join all the rest of them with no undercurrents, now, of being considered an outsider. After the two months they had just passed, they all felt a bit like outsiders. So she did. And in doing so, Scott found himself thinking she was the most natural female element there.

Where Deborah, Ellen, and Catherine represented something else.

A big group picture. Smiles of pride and happiness.

Then, in the days that followed, the Sumners' gang drifted away in the same way it had come … in twos and threes for a couple of days, and then gone all at once. Leaving Jack and Scott standing there, one morning, feeling as though a hurricane had left.

Except with one difference.

In all the time those workers had been there, Jack had made almost no effort to get to know them. Scott had seen how Jack could barely remember the names of any of them. But Scott, once the shock of all the manpower had worn off, had gradually befriended in a fashion almost all of them, learned where they came from and what they'd done before. He'd found they were almost like a sort of guild, like old-fashioned masons and journeymen carpenters, travelling from worksite to worksite. Most of them knew each other from other projects both on the east and west coasts and, he discovered, would often recommend each other for jobs. Few of them worked long anywhere—and exactly in order to avoid working in the way Scott worked year-round at the Colby's.

They were boatbuilders, one grizzled boatwright had said, not barnacle scrapers, and unless a yard had another job lined up directly behind the first one, they moved on.

A few of them ribbed Scott about how he had become a barnacle, himself, calcified over and just feeding on whatever drifted his way. He took all that lightly, but secretly felt a little jealous. They all seemed to have something figured out, and many of them had families. It wasn't as though they were tramps.

In the end, Scott just shrugged his jealousy away, not thinking about it. But he couldn't help feeling secretly proud of how they reacted to him, complementing him on his skills, and he accepted good-naturedly their business cards and invitations for him to stay in touch, in the future, if he ever wanted to join in on other jobs. It made him smile but, in fact, warmed his heart. He had forgotten how that felt, both good … and just.

*

On that first morning after Sumners' crew were all finally and truly gone, when Jack and Scott came out to the shed with no one else there, the silence seemed incredible. For the first time they were able to take stock of what had happened.

Without a word but with the same thoughts, they went up the stairs towards the loft, stopping half way and turning to look at the *Muse*. It was as though a different boat sat in the boatshed.

A person now visiting the boat could step up onto the boat's clean, black-seamed teak deck, looking through doorways at fine oak parquet floors and mahogany-paneled cabin sides, all unvarnished, and go inside and see doors and passageways, and at the galley and hatchways leading down into storage areas and the engine compartment, and at all the cabinets and storage bins, as yet doorless. But perfectly finished.

Even cabin fenestration was finished.

In the midst of the other work, two teams of glaziers had come. One set up the big, shatterproof windows that would be making the main cabins light and airy. The other, piercing the first holes in the finished hull, had cut out and set the discrete cabin windows, small and built slightly above waterline, which would provide working quarters, and even crew cabins, with light and a view.

But for the painting and varnishing, the *Muse* was finished. At least the boatshed part. Once that was done, she would be launched down the ways and taken to the pier extending from the boatworks, where a crane would step her masts, and her rigging would be set up. The only thing they really had to do now, was get the immense amount of wood dust in the place under control. So much dust, that even the slightest draft set fine clouds dancing into the air. The remains of the furies. They felt it. Both of them. They had worked as though in a dream, or a nightmare, driven by a motivation to finish which was only partly aligned with Sumners' demands, but mostly by that giant feeling of rush and effort that comes at the end of any project. A motivation of wanting it to happen, which becomes nearly a form of fear.

The fear of something happening.

A disaster.

A last minute change of heart.

Financial ruin.

Acts of God.

The self- protective urge to push things through to a finish.

And now, there she was. Her presence was nearly overwhelming in trying to take in how quickly she had taken form.

Jack shook his head, staring at the boat. "What in the world happened to us?"

Scott wiped dust from his forehead. "Money."

They stood on the stairs looking at it and feeling it a little longer. Then they went down as they'd come up, in silence and in silent agreement. In the same way, they didn't go straight to work but went back out of the shop to the house to get more coffee and to get Ellen and Catherine, who then came back out with them to also stand there with them again, looking at it and feeling it.

Getting used to how fast things could change when people who had the power to make them change, did.

Someone, of course, normally might have said something to that effect. Stating the obvious. But there are times when the obvious, especially when it highlights differences bordering on the painful and embarrassing, is better left alone.

# Chapter 80

ONE DAY near the end of the month Eric came down on a weekend with Deborah to examine the interior of the boat. It was the one thing he could feel happy about.

He had pressing worries by then. Hartman had now given him weeks, instead of months, to sign. The moment he signed, Colby, as well as all the rest of the business and land owners down there, would be history.

He had his city hall people on standby, but his hands were tied as long as the boat sat in the shed. Even though he understood it was now basically finished, he couldn't just have it yanked out of there. Not yet. The day before, he had even tried convincing Jack to paint the hull. Jack had only stared at him as though he was, once again, just an idiot tyro. It had been a mistake, and he knew it even as he was asking.

But that didn't stop him from letting a deeper sense of resentment about Jack come bubbling up. Eric now felt a profound distaste for Jack. The fact the man had no idea what was about to happen to him, didn't help. Eric knew it was unfair to judge a man that way, solely based on the fact he was ignorant of his fate. But he couldn't help it. And yet, that wasn't what made Eric pity the man. Because he also knew that Jack had had many an opportunity to consolidate his lease or even ownership of that property, and had refused over and over again. Simply going along on the assumption that all would be, forever, well.

It was a deeply mule-headed—if not stupid—way to go through life. And if there was one thing Eric couldn't abide, it was any man who generated pity. And it was hard to hide those feelings. And he knew he wasn't always successful. Luckily, though, he could see that Colby just interpreted it all as impatience.

Jack, also luckily for Eric, was not the sort of man to wonder about strange signs of nervousness and hurry, and had just patiently explained that there was still too much sawdust in the air, and that they needed a few degrees more of temperature in the morning. Especially for the clear-coating inside, but also for the hull. Just a few weeks away. No time at all. It was a hard argument to counter. In fact, impossible.

Even so, Eric had tried. Stubbornly and angrily. His and Jack's second big blow-up. But that time, Eric had backed down. Because it seemed so unreasonable. At that point, given everything else, he didn't suddenly want to seem irrational or panicked. Or give the impression that, for some reason, he seemed paranoid about the timing of things. Which, in fact, he was. Which made him feel paranoid about being paranoid.

Simply, he was afraid of spilling the beans.

Deborah had spoken to him about that. That was to say, she hadn't spoken to him about paranoia or the fear of bean spilling, since she had no idea those existed or what they were based on. But by his pushing attitude towards the boat. She didn't often do such a thing. But lately he'd been a bit too much.

As an irrational request, the paint-it-now fight had even sparked a suspicion in her. And that had caused him to back down, as well.

Suspicion, from anyone at that point, was something he couldn't risk. Luckily, no one down there knew anything. He was confident Hartman had done his work thoroughly.

He now stood there in the main cabin looking around himself at this great gift to his wife—with her off somewhere in the bowels of the monster examining some details or other.

He was pleased.

He could see it really was as close to being finished as he could wish. Painting, or no, he could get it out of there. Either launched, to float keel-less to another yard, or trucked out on a special flatbed. But where he could have contemplated all that with happy satisfaction, his thoughts were anything but where they needed to be—even with a dozen important details crowding in on him thanks to Hartman. Right there, all his foremost thoughts were about his wife. Thinking almost exclusively of her.

But in a way far from what people might have expected.

He had tried, but could not avoid the fact of it. His attachment to Catherine had become so strong lately that, not to put too fine a point on it, he had stopped thinking of himself as Deborah's husband. Or, at least, it was no longer the definition he felt.

If he was clear about that, and felt he had arrived at a logical juncture in his life for which no one was truly to blame, he couldn't, however, avoid the inevitable guilt.

He would look at Deborah, still seeing the lovely young girl he had had so many hopes and dreams for. Now, though, those hopes and dreams, rather than being just over the horizon—worthy goals to pursue for an entire lifetime—seemed more like chains and weights. A drag upon him where Catherine tracked effortlessly along beside him.

So the finishing of the *Muse*—or whatever it was it would end up being named—had taken on another urgent aspect.

He had thought long and hard about it. He had developed in his mind very specific conversations he would have with Deborah. To see how she felt. And he had come to the conclusions that, in fact, Deborah saw the boat as a very personal thing, highly unconnected to their marriage, but in an ever more bizarre fashion.

And this was what he was going to have to deal with, along with the rest of what happened. Along with what would happen with Catherine.

The way Deborah talked about it, strangely enough, now pained him.

Despite the changes in his life, he could remember the original joy he had felt at the idea of giving this thing to her. Something that had been symbolic of his love for her.

But to be honest, and it was almost humorous now to think of it, just as that love and that symbolism had withered within himself, there had never truly been any response in that quarter from her, either. At least, not in any way he had hoped for. And she had been hesitant to even talk to him about it.

Very nearly, it almost seemed more right and just that the original idea had sunk. It clarified everything.

Guilt, hell. He could also get enraged if he thought about all that. How, for her, she had never acknowledged the love that had generated it. And now it was too late—and he damn well wasn't going to belittle himself, by trying to point all that out to her. No, he just got angry, now. In a cold, clear light, he had decided it would not be a gift of love, but a gift of rupture.

Once he got the damn monster out of there, he could be quit of it all. There would be a charade, of course, to act out.

But in the end, he thought, she would get the fucking boat and, in all probability, be just as happy in the long run.

He looked around at the finishing work. Thank god, he thought, he'd finally taken things in hand and got that crew in. It showed, once again, that no matter how much trust you gave to people, there was always a time when you had to intervene.

And now it was almost done. Surreptitiously, he had even called around to find a company which would be capable of hauling that goddamn boat out of the shop.

He'd force things, if he had to. But for the moment, he knew he'd have to wait. On all scores.

So down to the sea they went. To look at the boat.

He shook himself out of his thoughts and went to look for her. When he found her, he followed her, watching her examine everything. He could see how she was so far gone into it, whatever it was to her. She was so distant, and preoccupied. Yet perfectly content.

He knew, seeing that, he was right. In time, she wouldn't even remember he existed, except for his monthly check or whatever.

He grunted to himself in astonishment at that truth. But as was his habit, once he had made his mind up or come to a conclusion about something, he would finish with it rather than continue to dwell on it. So there, wandering around those dark cabins at the lower levels, he put his thoughts aside with a sigh. And, as though on a vacation from his own thoughts, he focused his eyes and began looking at the boat he'd been sulking around in ever since they'd first come down there.

He smiled.

He might as well look at it, he thought, considering how much it was costing him. Originally a couple of million? Now, it was running towards six, reinsured, of course. Although he wondered if he could be reimbursed for the damages that would be caused by having it hauled bodily out of the shop like moving a house, or launched prematurely—without painting.

The fitting of the interior work was indisputably excellent. It was now clear who had been responsible for the perfection of the joinery work on the little rowing skiff. Scott's excellence in the designs in cabinets, rails, in the steps leading down from the deck to the main cabin and in the oak paneling, was flawlessly evident, even beneath the fine coat of sawdust that lay everywhere. Eric, as well as Deborah, continually ran his hands over everything, coating himself with a light, flourlike dusting.

Resigning himself to her inspections, he went with her up and down the passageways, looking into cabins, examining the woodwork and the sea bunks and clothes closets Scott had been installing. The details he hadn't let even the work crew touch. In each cabin Scott had left a box full of brass fittings, door knobs, coat hooks, cabinet latches, light switches and the lights themselves—pieces of brass and painted, frosted glass which Deborah had picked out of a marine decorator's catalogue.

All the while, Deborah was humming with delight.

Eric watched her, aware of how she swept from cabin to cabin with a passionate curiosity. She was changed, he thought then again as he had been thinking nearly continuously lately. That was for sure. She wasn't the same woman as the one he had married. But the woman had not moved forward in the sense of moving forward with *him*. Or towards him. She had moved, if anything, at an oblique angle to him. He didn't know how to put it. But he no longer cared to understand.

Because he now had someone who didn't have to be understood at such cost and effort.

He didn't dislike Deborah. That would have been going too far. There was no need to create a false antipathy for her, in order to appease himself somehow. He wanted her, somehow, to remain as a friend. Even though, he admitted, that his money—as he'd reflected before—would create quite a few pitfalls.

Lawyers being a breed of people who had no real conception of what the term friendship meant.

Expectations and pressures.

God, he thought, the excitement of possibilities, and the fatalism of a deeper pessimism. Those could trip a man into making mistakes.

He needed to look towards the stronger shore. With no excuses. Life was tough enough. He would make no pleas for understanding either. Excusing himself. After all, and all things considered, he could have been a worse man. Luckily for her.

He had to get clear of it. All these exhortations of a nervous conscience were the outlines for decency, but not the actual thing.

Sometimes, real decency came in simply being true to what you had to do.

There, he thought, was real ethics. Beyond the idiotic mouthings about duty and responsibility.

# Chapter 81

CATHERINE WAS sitting in her apartment, watching the evening sky and reflecting on how she had simply had the most wonderful month of her life.

Each week of April—that awful event with Scott now far in the past—she was able to go to work with a sense of security she had rarely felt before. At last, her life was singing along.

There were snags, of course. She knew, though, all that worrying about Jack had been unnecessary. All that wild grappling—she had come to see that it had been predictable. He had obviously begun picking up how she had changed. He must have seen she was no longer dependent on him and tried to impose himself back on her again. Subconsciously trying to get her back.

She could understand. But in the end there was nothing he could do, even if she brought him to an abrupt halt. She held all the cards.

That is, unless Jack was simply nuts insane and didn't mind losing his business, as well as Ellen. One word would do it.

These weren't exactly the most elevating thoughts, she realized. There were simply times in life when you had to be tough as a nut.

She smiled. As a nut. Almost a joke.

And she smiled at something else. Where before it had sometimes annoyed her, she now enjoyed how Ellen gave off the air of a woman who could not be gotten around. Catherine could appreciate that as far as Jack would be concerned.

It gave Catherine a clear field, simply by letting it be so.

Which brought her thoughts back to Eric, and his wife. If Ellen was one thing ... when it came to Deborah, it was hard to say what the situation was. Eric had yet to broach that subject directly, although it was evident that Deborah couldn't give him what he needed, and that Catherine did ... and on an average of twice a week, even during the crazy weeks they'd just been through. If anything, Eric seemed even more in need of a tranquil harbor.

Deborah, clearly, was not right for Eric. She was stunningly beautiful of course. Perfect. If ideals of perfection tended towards the overdeveloped side.

But Deborah's was also a dreamy, distant beauty. Men, it was well known, secretly like a little bit of hard, prancing reality shining out of their women's eyes. They want their women to show they like it, even if they don't say it.

She wasn't suitable for him. Eventually that truth would win out and Eric would find himself deeply unhappy.

Catherine, with the satisfaction that it was at least honest, intended to be there when it happened.

Could she make it happen? That was certainly a question. She didn't know if she could go quite that far with it. On the other hand, something had already begun anyway. With herself as catalyst. Almost in pure innocence.

Yes, innocence! Why the hell shouldn't she feel it was that? She hadn't schemed for him. It had all grown out of the natural attraction between two people who were right for each other.

But if she had not plotted anything, maybe it was time to nudge things a bit. It was fine to take things as they came if you were twenty and had your whole life ahead of you. But there came a time when you had to get on with it. You had to say that hanging out is all very well and good, but there is going to have to be an eventual point to it. Or not.

Catherine, for better or worse, in sickness or in health, had become the other woman. The famous worst situation a woman could put herself into. And she loved it.

*

The evening sky stayed with them longer now, each day that passed. That night was particularly beautiful as there were no clouds except on the horizon, out towards Vancouver Island and the Straits where bright fire reds and oranges burst past the purple hues of a far-off evening storm coming in. She looked at her watch. Eric had promised to stop by, and she got up to make some tea.

Just as the teapot began to whistle the phone rang and Eric said he couldn't come by, but set a firm date for later in the week. Tenderly and wonderfully apologetic. She didn't mind, and went to bed in peace. But even if she knew what she wanted, and could sleep easily, things were not all that much easier all the same. It was a sad time in so many ways. For that exact reason Catherine knew she must not deny herself any happiness she felt. But, as with all states of passion, she could run hot and cold.

There beneath the enveloping folds of her soft, warm quilts, Catherine fell quickly into a warm, soft dream, sailing on blue waters, the green wonder of the land was safely there if they wanted, but also very far away. And then she slept.

But even there, one small grain of sand ... she wasn't as peaceful as she thought she was.

*

The next morning, sitting alone at her kitchen table and looking at the cloud laden gray sky, she idly drummed her fingers on the edge, thinking coldly of the day ahead. Feeling a sudden panic.

Things were advancing so fast at Colby's everything else seemed to move too slow in comparison. That last month and a half had gone by in a rush of work, buried beneath the wild effort of that work crew. But now they were gone. Things were back to normal. And without warning, she felt very lonely and insecure. She wished someone could be there.

Anyone.

Eric, or Jack, or just someone who would come in and be kind and put their arms around her and tell her she was fine.

Not forever. Just until she felt better.

She felt ill. She had to bring her hand up under her breasts. But nothing helped, and agony of loneliness coursed through her like waves coming through the breakwater, her lips, closed upon themselves, trembled. She closed her eyes then and the tears of misery squeezed through and ran as though frightened down her face.

With the freedom of having no one there, she let go and burst her poor soul, crying over the pain of the million shattered pieces of it.

Eric was so good to her. He had conscientiously made a schedule they could both meet. It had been his commitment to her, and he had made sure she knew he was thinking of her.

It was just that, sometimes, real life intervened.

For the moment.

It was all just so good. All so near. And she hadn't cried like that in a long time. In anticipation of happiness.

Happiness, she could see, was just as messy as unhappiness.

# Chapter 82

ELLEN KNEW it was much more than just one of their occasional lapses into a mutually blank acceptance of one another. Watching, she could see there was something deeply sinister in the way Jack talked, or didn't talk. In the way he looked at her, or, more importantly, didn't look at her. She could feel it again: something big, moving heavily in the depths. Her old nightmare.

At first, she'd wanted to convince herself that it was just a mistake. That she had been mistaken. Totally. The last seven weeks had blown through the boatyard in such a way, nobody had time to think. Everyone was distracted. Rushed, irritated, nervous and concentrated. And where Jack wasn't always the most sensitive and aware person around, those circumstances basically turned him into a human wall. But that wasn't it.

Something was indeed there. Something that had been there during the frantic burst of work, but did not dissipate as the work went back to normal. She had noticed it, dismissed it, but seeing it was still there even now, she noticed it even more. She was sensitive to it.

She took to observing him with growing purpose. Now that she was actually looking for it, she could see it all. And she didn't need to stumble across any more garbage cans to be sure.

At first, a lot of possibilities had gone through her mind. But none of them fit. One idea was that since Jack could be subject to peevishness, it was easy enough to believe his strange, semi-concealed attempts to distance himself were connected with the pressures of work. Or else, she was willing to concede, that the shock of actually being on the road to fatherhood was a substantial one. But Ellen couldn't convince herself. It didn't work. Jack got used to things. He'd gotten over his private, sullen stubbornness about the boat. He eventually accepted realities. For anyone, it's hard to actually become what you think you want to be. But now, Jack had made that plunge. So it couldn't be the work, nor the baby.

The deep, lurking thing swam up a little higher in the darkness of her suspicions, trying to make its own darkness more readily seen.

As it slowly rose, dark and obscene, it became ever more than an inkling.

Then the day finally came, and Ellen allowed herself to think the unthinkable and that awful thing opened its sickening maw wider and wider, and her fears fell helplessly into its unfeeling belly. She felt the presence of someone there, in the absolute darkness.

She knew.

She went down into herself in those days, trying desperately to sort things out, to figure out what to do. She didn't know how she was going to manage without cracking up. Which would have been the worst thing.

The first thing she knew she had to do, was to put him right up against the wall. It was strangely shameful to have to do so, as though by bringing it all out in the open, she was dragging her own dignity through the mud.

She felt very alone. There was no way she could talk about it with anyone else, not even Catherine. It was hurtful, but she didn't want anyone's sympathy and even less their advice.

She needed to get her feet back on the ground. Then, she was determined to have it straight out with the one person concerned. Or at the very least, she thought angrily, have his goddamn balls.

In her growing anger and resentment, every time she saw him come in after work, washing his hands in the sink, whistling, sitting down at her table with his cheerful expression, she also saw the furtiveness, trying always to slide around her. But she waited, wanting to be very sure of him, and of herself.

It was amazing to be so calmly positive Jack was involved with another woman. If her anger had burned, it had become a low and steady flame. Perhaps it was exactly Jack's furtiveness which permitted her to stay cool. Jack was obviously on guard in his own stupid way. As though he knew, somehow, he could end up crushed by her. That weakness of his gave her strength.

Bad as the present situation was, what was worse was how her suspicions destroyed her faith ... to the point she could no longer trust him for any time they hadn't been together.

He'd always been so ready, she recalled, to tell her everything and anything.

Hell, she herself couldn't always remember what she'd done the day before, and there had been Jack, who occasionally didn't even know what day it was, outlining in concrete terms what he had been doing for weeks on end while he had been away.

She remembered with bitterness how he would be nonchalant, but precise. Never had to search his memory.

It was that bad.

Ellen's heart sank day by day, and there were mornings—sick as she already was—where if not for the work and keeping up appearances, she would have rather stayed in bed. To sleep away an inner misery that had little to do with the physical nausea of pregnancy.

In those days, the only way anyone could have told anything about her would have been to have caught her alone, twisting a dishrag violently, staring off into space with eyes that burned ... or staring fiercely into the unturned pages of a book, or into a cold, undrunk cup of coffee, with a grim, tight smile which would have turned any man, let alone Jack, to stone.

The rest of the time she was very much herself, neither more quiet nor more cheerful. She was just as attentive to Catherine's verbal wanderings about the nature of life and men, or to Deborah's musings about life, boats and the universe. Ellen would nod. She still had a radiant smile.

But she kept a sharp eye on Jack. Biding her time. The one thing she knew for sure, though, was that she would not let it slide. She believed in swift retribution. Payment for lying and Jack would pay for it, dearly.

She just wondered who the hell it was. But her mind just stopped there.

She had never felt so much fear in her life.

Sometimes, the thing you want to know more than anything else in the world, is the last thing you want to know. And sometimes, which is worse, you already know it but don't want at all to acknowledge it.

# Chapter 83

SITTING BY the big window, accompanied only by the tiny glow from a desk lamp far back in the darkness behind him, Eric looked down the sloping, landscaped hillside, down through the trees to the lake, studying the evening's deep blue settling over the black shoreline.

It was one of the rare times in the year when Eric was alone. Deborah was over at the university for one of those interminable Board of Trustees parties which Eric usually accompanied her to as one of the pillars of the community. He hadn't been able to bring himself to go with her. One phone call had ruined his night so badly he couldn't be sure it hadn't ruined his life.

A gloomy feeling of depression hovered over him. Even in that expansive room vaulting up to the dark rafters as though to stretch out into the largeness of the evening sky, he felt a strangling claustrophobia. The effect, he knew, of realizing he had made a serious mistake.

How could he have been so utterly stupid as to risk his entire life for a woman he barely knew?

The infamous Death Wish.

He felt a wave of revulsion at his own weakness and stupidity, and awful as it was to admit, he was now less preoccupied with how to escape the situation than with avoiding the possibility of discovery.

To what point could he say he had faith in Catherine?

Good God, after all, considering what now was at stake, he realized he didn't really know her at all.

As it stood, he might have to actually claim such a thing someday. He wished suddenly he could have really said such a thing in perfect truth. Plenty of men in the public eye had been forced to make such statements.

Those men, though, customarily had the sense to keep their affairs far back in the shadows. Maximum deniability.

If the truth got out on this one, though, there would be too many witnesses.

He tried to think his way through it all logically.

All people had motives and methods, he reflected coldly. Under certain circumstances, though, methods became unpredictable. To what extent would Catherine become unpredictable?

He knew part of the ease of the relationship had been built upon her intense loneliness. But however it was, all questions of honor or decency aside, there was no way to wipe away the previous three months. No way to even lie about it. She could get testimony to that. The requisite two witnesses, in fact. Forcing him to consider the costs of buying off one bush pilot and one lodge keeper … as well as her.

God! … and he had thought a divorce would be expensive. That, now, seemed like pocket change.

If it was one thing to buy yourself a ticket of freedom, it was another to be forced to purchase silence, to hide something away.

Eric closed his eyes, feeling his body folding in upon itself, his life collapsing around him until there was just one big constricted heartbeat at the center of a hopeless void.

That phone call.

Just as they had been readying to leave for the party the phone in his office, just off the main entryway, began to buzz. Deborah had been reaching for her coat and turned to look at Eric, rolling her eyes. He just held his hands out helplessly and went into the study and picked up the phone, saying "yes?"

"Hello, Eric. Tom Hoaglund, here."

Eric nodded, as though there couldn't have been a thing more natural than to get a call from the treasurer of the one of the state's political parties.

Of course, they knew each other. God knew, they knew each other.

How many times had Eric seen Hoaglund at some fundraiser? Had a general chat now and again? How many years had Eric tried to engage him in talk of politics only to always be reminded that the last thing one of the most powerful political handlers in the state wanted to talk about, was politics?

Sure, they knew each other, knew all about each other. How long now? Ten years? Then suddenly, out of the blue, he's called right to the house. For the first time ever.

Well, it wasn't all that much of a surprise. Eric had wondered where that conversation with Carl Ivarsson was going to resurface. But he hadn't expected so much, so soon.

Even though this was an auspicious moment, Eric knew he must be very cautious. Hoaglund, of course, would only be scouting. Eric would never have been contacted by the state party chairman, or even vice-chairman. He was just at the first level.

But nevertheless, for the first time in so many years he couldn't remember anymore, Eric found himself almost breathless in excitement.

"Tom," he said in as even a voice as he could manage, lowering himself into the chair by the desk, "you've caught me by surprise."

Hoaglund chuckled dryly on the other end.

"I suppose so. I hope I'm not calling at a bad moment."

"No, of course not. We were just getting ready to head over to the Campus."

"Oh, yeah. Luckily for me, I twisted my knee last weekend out on my boat and I can't go." Hoaglund laughed. "Not that I don't enjoy going to the Trustees' functions. Anyway, Nancy will go for me and make sure no one is talking behind my back."

Eric stared at the top of the desk for a moment, unsure what to say next. It was an extraordinary situation.

Year after year he had built up his business, brokered deals, set up partnerships, hired, fired ... and with time had become used to dealing directly with whatever it was he wanted people to do, or know.

His mind, in its most purely professional mode, could methodically run down mental outlines of ideas, ticking off in a logical manner those points he needed to make so as to, in the most efficient manner, get some aspect of a project in motion. He knew how to edit his thoughts, revealing only the information strictly necessary at any given moment ... that last not so much for secrecy—although that sometimes had something to do with things—but mostly for the case of expediency. His ability to communicate, therefore, was finely honed and polished and was easily one of the most important skills he brought to bear as he went out into the world.

Yet, suddenly, there he was hanging on the phone like a sweaty adolescent. And once again, the image of himself as a teenager asking for his first date, swarmed up into his mind. For just a second, his brain swirled, and he had to put a hand over the receiver so that he could take a deep breath without Hoaglund hearing him.

He imagined Tom Hoaglund for a second, a large, crumpled-suit sort of guy who wore a closely-trimmed beard. If there had been the slightest mischief in Hoaglund's eyes, you might have even thought he was jovial looking. But there was nothing either mischievous or jovial about Hoaglund. For proof, all you had to do was get up close enough to see the real look in his eyes, as straight and unwavering as eyes looking over a gun sight.

Eric sat there at his desk, staring off into the gloom of his unlit office. And all he could see was those eyes staring back at him.

Cold. Flat. Almost clinical, or reptilian, in their lack of expression. Examining, judging with utter objectivity:

Him.

## Chapter 84

"You still there?" Hoaglund said.

Eric nodded again, and then said, "sure, sure." He pulled himself together rapidly, and he swallowed. "Listen, Tom, we're not heading right out the door this instant, but if you need to discuss something in depth, I can call you tomorrow."

The moment he said it, Eric damned himself to the bottom of his soul. If he had wanted to find a way to shoot himself in the foot, he couldn't have found a better one. He knew, himself, how much he detested when this sort of obvious, self-esteem protecting gambit was being handed his way. He expected Hoaglund, also, would see through it, make a fast decision, and that would be the end of everything.

Hoaglund, though, wasn't through with his surprises. He laughed. Loudly and good-naturedly.

"Yeah, sure, Eric," he said. "You'll make some time for me tomorrow, huh?" He laughed again, and then his voice got serious.

"Listen. All right, so I caught you a little off base by calling you like this. You know what I want to talk about. I should have called your secretary, given you a chance to prepare. I'm sorry about that, but things are moving fast these days and I don't have time for the niceties. Down our way, we've got a little problem, and as we were talking about it the other day your name came up."

Eric knew better than to acknowledge that with anything more than a grunt.

"So," Hoaglund went on, "we have done some serious talking about this ... we have come to the conclusion that, based on our files and some fairly important recommendations we've had from not only Old Man Ivarsson but from down in Seattle, that you could be a good shot for us not just for Olympia, but for the big one nineteen months from now. We want to know what you think."

Eric, instead of resenting the way Hoaglund had slapped him back into the arena of professionalism, in fact now appreciated the reproach. His reply, therefore, was as direct as if he was now talking to a business associate of fifteen years.

"You know as well as I do what my response is, Tom," he said. "I've been thinking about this for a long time. I'm only surprised you want to go for the federal election. After all, I'm politically unknown."

Hoaglund's voice came across with no stern hint of rebuke left, now natural as he discussed what was, in fact, the very breath of life for him.

"We'll talk more about that. But I can tell you we've looked at this carefully, and at the way you've been doing business up here, and it fits together beautifully."

"A lot of people will wonder if I'm not a wolf in sheep's clothing."

"Oh, shit. Nobody draws that republican-democrat line anymore based on how much money you have or what you've done before. You worried about that? Don't be. I mean, maybe the other side has been talking to you? I don't know anything about that. But whether they have or haven't, I can tell you that we can get you in, and they can't. As a matter of fact, for the next ten years or so, around here, they're going to have a hell of a time getting anyone in. And, frankly, if you go in with them, the only thing anyone's going to see is your business first, and you afterwards."

Of course, no one from the other party had contacted Eric. But if they had, he would have taken just as seriously anything they had to say. He wasn't trying to make any deals with Hoaglund, though. It was just so much, so fast, and he could barely believe he was hearing exactly those things he had so long wished for.

"That is the main point, I suppose," Eric said. "What happens to my business?"

"Well, my boy," Hoaglund said with a tone as flat as Eric had ever heard any partner, business rival, bank officer, or stockbroker intone, "you've got just about two months to get from it whatever it is you can, and then you kiss it goodbye for the duration. Which could be forever. That is the deal. Where we want to send you, and with what your business is doing, and what you will be dealing with back there, there is no way for you to work your way around your company's interests. I think that's about as plain as day."

Eric nodded. It was, indeed, as plain as day. Two months. That would be enough. He had been working hard on the Fairhaven Project, had finally brought a few people from his staff into the scheme. And his people had made some giant inroads on Hartman's control of things.

Hartman was still pushing … still thought he had Eric and the downtown people sewn up. But Eric had the edge. He, after all, was from the area. His was no outside interest, and that fact was playing the right tune for the right people.

Two months from there, almost with certainty, he would have milked this last, biggest project of his business career for every cent he could get.

Afterwards, there would have been what?

With nowhere else to go, he would have taken his company's efforts out of state. Maybe overseas. Just the same as Hartman had. But at that point, his political aspirations would have been finished.

Too big, too spread out, too high on the Fortune 500 list, he would have been just too successful to ever make it in.

You can have a billion dollars. You can wield an incredible amount of power, have the ear of everyone right up to the president. But you'll never, ever, get in. Not unless you're willing to just about give the whole amount away. Because until the day comes when there are no more poor people, the super rich will not be able to buy enough words to hide the fact they are still rich, and intent on remaining so.

They can only wield power through buying what they can.

That, Eric thought glumly, was why democracy produced so many shams, so many half-men. But that was one of the truths. He knew his answer.

"Tom, I'd sell it all tomorrow if I had to. I have to tell you though, I've got to have a bit of time to dismantle things. Too many irons in the fire. Too many people depending on me, you know. I've got to think of my people, too."

There was now a pause at the other end, and then a jubilant sounding Hoaglund.

"That, my friend, was your first stump speech, and it was pretty good. I knew we were barking up the right tree. But," the warning sound came back into his voice, "let me tell you something, and you might as well get it straight, right from the start. You've got ideas. That's good. We've heard about them, know your positions pretty good. And we agree. And you can keep most of them as far as we're concerned. It's also pretty obvious you know how to control yourself, keep the right impression flowing. You're going to have to make that the priority from here on out. But just remember this one thing: don't ever, for one goddamn second, try to bullshit your way past us. We've got a long road ahead of us, and we have to be

433

traveling in the same direction, in the same bus as it were, at the same time. Otherwise, we're going to end up with absolutely nothing. Once we get started, things happen just too fast to have it any other way. Understand?"

"All right. You got it," Eric said. "So I might as well admit things like: I want this so bad I can taste it?"

"For example."

"What else?"

There was a fairly long pause before Hoaglund answered.

"Not much," he finally said, "except the usual formalities."

"Formalities?" Eric could not figure out what formalities could come to play. "You mean, an oath? A signature? A giant contribution? That last one wouldn't come as a surprise."

"No, no. I mean the usual formalities of living life in a glass bubble. I guess what I should have said is comportment. You might as well get pretty straight on this as well. As far as we could find out, you're a clean number. But, amazing as it might seem, we've found we actually need to remind people that if they do have anything in the closet, it had better be cleaned out for good before we get started. And I mean really clean. We've had to deal with the mess created by one of our last guys, you know, and it takes one hell of a lot of work and you don't get very far anymore with the women's lobbies, for example. You don't have anything like that to surprise us with, do you Eric?"

All the time Hoaglund had been talking, Eric had felt his heart both pounding and sinking at the same time. A knot of fear forming in his stomach. But on Hoaglund's direct question, he found that instead of trying to sidestep it, he was suddenly ready, and belligerent.

"Absolutely not," Eric said, glaring at the telephone as if defying it to answer back.

"Good to hear that."

"Are things going to have to get this personal?"

"Worse, and before the press starts asking, you're going to get it from us first. So get used to it. You'll be asked just about anything. You watch. They'll find out whether you've been circumcised or not." Hoaglund laughed. "Have you?"

"What?" Eric said, startled.

"I'm not kidding. Get used to it. Get used to anything. Even about your wife. How is your wife?"

"Fine, thanks."

"Deborah's going to help you quite a bit, we think. By the way, someone mentioned it might be a problem that you two are childless. Any reason for that?"

"For Christ's sake, Tom," Eric complained. "You don't have to use shock tactics to show me what's ahead."

There was a pause at the other end, and it was long enough to almost convince Eric that his outburst had been justified and necessary. But Hoaglund's next words showed him, once again, how easily he could be on the wrong side of all these new ideas.

"I'm not using shock tactics, Eric. I'm being dead serious about this. I'm asking things that will have as much an effect on the campaign as your ideas for the future. I want to know now, is there any particular reason, after all these years of your marriage, why you have no children? Is it a medical reason?"

Eric looked up and towards the door out to the hallway. Deborah had poked her head in a couple of times already, giving him a quizzical look and pointing at her watch. But she was not there, and he knew she was not standing out in the hallway listening, either. He could always trust her in that way.

"No," he said, "there's no medical reason."

"Have you thought about it?"

"Well, yes."

"Are you for, or against it?"

"Neither."

"And how about Deborah?"

"I guess she'd want them."

"You guess? Don't you know? So, it's you that doesn't want them, I take it. Not really a good thing, Eric. But, you don't know how she feels? Do you have a close marriage or not?"

Anyone else, Eric would have hung up.

"It's close enough, Tom. Don't worry about that. The fact is, up to now, Deborah and I have had other interests."

"All right," Hoaglund's voice now came over heavy and deep, with a sadness almost, as though speaking words he didn't enjoy, but was forced to say because of circumstances ... because of his understanding of the world and how it worked. And in a manner, with such sincerity, that it almost sounded the voice of a friend.

"Consider this: we're still more than a year and a half away, and you can tell me to go jump in the lake, but the fact is, if ever before you and Deborah had considered starting a family, you might just consider it a little more carefully, now. As a matter of fact, pregnancy, a birth, and a new family are all elements which make it all just about a shoe-in."

Eric was practically dumbfounded.

"I can't believe I'm hearing this."

"You are."

"Is this what it's really all about?"

"No, but it's a big part of how you get there."

"I never really thought about all this, Tom."

"Are you still interested?"

Deborah chose that moment to stick her head in the door again and Eric looked up at her. She had the same look on her face as before, but that time, instead of just making a point and leaving, she now stayed. Something in the way Eric was looking at her—looking at his wife—made her feel as though he wanted her to be part of whatever it was he was talking about on the phone.

Eric stared at her for a moment longer, and then said, "Yes, Tom, I am."

"Good. So when do we see each other? Tomorrow?"

"Just give me a call in the morning."

"I'll do that."

Hoaglund didn't even say goodbye. Evidently, when the conversation was finished, he hung up in the same way he walked away from people at parties. Conversation over, he turned a shoulder and left.

Eric hung up the phone and nodded. Momentarily, he forgot Deborah was even in the room.

So here, he thought, was where it all began.

He looked up then to find Deborah still standing by the desk. She asked him if something was the matter, and he told her. And then told her he had to think. No way could he hobnob with the Trustees. She agreed. She could see he'd be socially useless. And she went alone. He told her to be on the lookout for Nancy Hoaglund. She'd probably appreciate sharing the woe of being spouseless for the evening.

Later, after she had left and as he sat alone in the house and had already thought about all the obvious things, he began thinking that he probably should have gone to the party with Deborah. Tom's wife would report back that Eric hadn't made it.

Pretty obvious.

But what the hell? He wasn't into the campaign yet. He didn't have to force himself out into the public yet. He didn't have to prove himself to anyone yet. And that was good, because for the moment he could certainly say he wasn't ready.

There was an awful lot he had to get settled before he could say he was ready. Holy Mother of Christ, if that wasn't true.

He looked down at his hands, twisted together there in his lap. He had always admired his own hands. Now there they were, wringing themselves in desperation like the anxious hands of a child. Making themselves into a knot.

Sex knot indeed.

Peeved, suddenly, he spread them smooth upon his legs, forcing them flat against the muscles of his thighs.

You had fucking better get yourself together, he thought, remembering Tom's admonishments.

The party wouldn't expect anything less of him.

# Chapter 85

LATER, AND later, and later, he was still sitting there when he saw the lights finally appear at the gate down below in the trees.

The car made its way up the hill and then across in front of the house over to the garage, the headlights sweeping white across the lawns and bushes and over the crushed gravel of the drive.

Eric closed his eyes for a moment, trying to blank his mind.

He knew that to avoid thinking was the worst type of procrastination. But there was nothing to be done.

Deborah came lightly into that night filled room, the delicate smell of her perfume reinvigorating the scent of stale flowers in the air. Her hair fell across him as she kissed him.

He reached out to her and pulled her down upon himself, pulling her close and warm, to breathe her warmth. To force himself to remember what he must never forget again.

Deborah must always be his wife.

The fact was that, no matter how other-worldly she might be, she was ultimately much more suited to being the wife of a United States Senator than Catherine could ever be.

He nodded his head ruefully. Angrily. Emphatically. Looking off across the room while her own head lay on his shoulder. Unknowing.

True love, for God's sake! How had he never considered that one day, especially not long after having talked to Carl, the party's committee would approach him?

But it had, and for the first time in his life, he knew he was finally setting off after what he had always been meant for. There were so many things he could do; and now there were so many other things he had to do first.

But at the top of the immediate list was Catherine, and his choices were limited to two. Tell her what was happening and work things out over time. Or cut things off clean.

Neither was an attractive idea, but taking things slow was, naturally, the most attractive course. To work things out, in some ways, could be easier at first. Or seemed easier.

He had never made any overt commitments to her and for a while, at least, things wouldn't have to change all that much. They could even continue to see each other for a while.

But down the line ....

Eric knew all about taking the easy way. And he knew how often it was the wrong way. Letting things slide didn't fix anything and very often just made things worse. Made them more complicated and even more difficult to take care of later.

Eric saw there were too many variables. Too many temptations. Regardless of who they were now, eventually their relationship would change with him gaining stature.

One misstep and Catherine would have something on him that could be used for tremendous, one-time, profit. Or hellish damage. Everybody had seen that happen. Although, admittedly, Catherine seemed more intelligent than most of the women who made up the public parade of vengeful mistresses.

But who the hell knew? Who could bet on human nature?

Eric never had. He had never put any of his people in the way of temptation, never permitted anyone getting anything but the most temporary sorts of advantages upon him. Never any long term advantages, those sorts you could seal away as though in a bank vault. A redeemable certificate which would be as good in ten years as it was today. And who could say where Catherine would be in ten years.

One thing for certain, Washington D.C. would be the most unlikely place to find her. But that was also the last place he would want to run across her.

They could string things along for a while, it was true, but eventually it would have to be over. That was all there was to it.

Of course, everyone knew that plenty of congressmen and senators had long-standing affairs. But, as with any new enterprise, Eric didn't want to be going into an unknown arena with anything which might help an opponent.

God knew what things would be like once inside, but that was something else. He didn't want to suddenly see her popping up out of nowhere, looking for a way to cash in. Or, worse, to get even.

Everyone had seen that, as well.

Maybe he *could* work something out, he wavered. Maybe Catherine and he could go on like this forever. No one needed to know, no harm would come of it. He knew, though, that was impossible. Certain limits had been passed. They had become too intimate, shared too many needs and described too many disappointments, building up too many ways of supporting each other.

At the time it had seemed like a Godsend. Now it was all a giant, ticking bomb.

Catherine would eventually see herself as the one true partner for him, and him for her, or else have them both damned.

In all honesty, he couldn't blame her, and in fact could find it admirable that she would probably ruin him for the sake of scorned love rather than money. But ruination is an absolute thing, no matter by what path you arrive at it. And there would be no consolation to know he'd been dragged down because of some higher motive.

So, there was to be no lingering, slow tapering off. He had to cut things cleanly. But, how? That was to say, how, without it being too much of a shock and creating a rebound.

Very probably there would be hell to pay of some sort. Big hell. But in the long term, things would be finished for good.

What could she do? Right there and then, of course, she could make him very uncomfortable. She could confront Deborah, or, considering the abruptness, she could topple over into simple hatred and demand money.

He'd have to take that chance.

He ran his hand over Deborah's back, feeling her laying quietly against him, letting him think. She knew he was thinking, and knew she was somehow helping.

Catherine, he thought. How to go about it?

It was a real problem, he realized, because the problem wasn't the end result. The problem was the peripheral consequences. That made it way more complicated. He contemplated the worst aspects:

First, even as awful as it was to think of it—he knew that Deborah would forgive him. In the exact same way he had earlier realized she would have accepted divorce.

She would be hurt and disappointed, terribly so, but Deborah was simply not like anyone else he knew. She had an entirely different frame of reference to life. Whatever happened, she would accept it. So that end result wasn't the problem. Which, in itself was a bit depressing. Eric had now just realized something he had perhaps spent most of his marriage avoiding the thought of:

The bottom line was that Eric could make Deborah accept just about anything.

Unlike most people who, when pushed too far, eventually will draw a line in the dirt and say, this is as far as they will go, Deborah had no lines to draw. Everything being possible, everything a part of the explanation, everything was therefore, if not permitted, at least forgivable.

He would be forgiven and, strangely enough, eventually as loved by Deborah as he had ever been. She loved him in her own, serene, disconnected way.

There was no choice to Eric's choice. The idyll was over, and it was time to get back to business.

And business consisted of the other worst aspects ... the peripheral consequences which could linger.

Because he only had two months to do it.

The question was how, if not to eliminate them, at least mute and diffuse them.

The words tumbled in his mind: Mute. Diffuse.

Eliminate.

He stared off into the darkness of his office, the weight of Deborah upon him as though anchoring him in place, feeling a great, rushing wave, a tsunami of disaster, gathering out there somewhere. Just out of sight.

## Chapter 86

IN HIS wanderings, Scott had noticed the For Sale sign stuck out on the road and he had driven down a lane through the trees to look at the property.

He wasn't there ten minutes before he felt terrible.

Useful buildings already stood on the property. Big, well-built storage sheds and a good-sized office up near the road. Long and sloping, the five acre site went right down to the shore. Deep water, he knew, lay no more than twenty feet or so from water's edge, the shallows shelving steeply out to the drop-off. Perfect for launching or hauling boats, even the biggest.

God knew what the asking price was. Out there, half way around the north shore of Bellingham Bay towards the reservation there was little or no development taking place. A forgotten quarter. Eventually it would be one long strip of either homes or industry, depending on which got a toehold first. Not right then, though, and it was possible the land was still reasonable. Scott felt a sense of urgency come over him.

The day would come when there would be no such thing as a reasonable land price. That would be the true finish to the last frontier. Scott knew that people would someday hang on to property forever. Because one day, even the scraps would be worth fighting over.

Scott's eyes took in the property with an assessor's acuity, but his mind spun around in a dizzying dream. He knew exactly what he could try to do. Go straight to Eric. Before the boat was delivered, of course. While they were all still one big happy family and before the Sumners moved on.

The money from the *Muse* could cover any down payment. There would even be money left over. Enough to secure a loan to cover the materials for the building of a sister yacht free and clear of any owner.

He would advertise it all over the world. Already, they had been the subject of a few local articles, and someone from Seattle had come up as well. The national magazines were yet to be cracked.

That was once again Jack's fault. Scott had told him he ought to put a glossy ad in a few magazines and create a little excitement. Jack had done nothing. Scott had even tried his old tactic of edging Ellen around. But these days she no longer had much ambition either, it seemed. Strangely vacant. She had let the idea just float off in the air, Scott standing there in front of her. As if she was thinking of other things.

He had just gone back to the shop to brood. He hated when ideas were so good he could not resist trying to get someone to listen. Ellen was indeed being vague, those days. So publicity ideas had fallen down flat.

Scott, though, couldn't stop the visions. They already had the lines lofted, the Alexandrite plans rolled and stored in the driest building by the boathouse, a steel hut on the other side of the house. And they had all the molds built, and those and all the ribbands were stacked along the far fence, numbered and sorted, and protected by heavy canvas tarpaulins. They could be building the second boat's keel from day one.

He could see it. He would cart all the molds and ribbands over to the new place as soon as the contract was signed. He would have even thought about looking for a new place to live out there on the north shore. For a few minutes even more plans came popping into his head. But then he laughed.

Dreaming was always exciting. In comparison to the normal world. But eventually the normal world reclaimed its rights.

Scott stood near water's edge looking south over Bellingham Bay. His thoughts becoming reasonable again.

But he refused to let them make him feel sour. It was such a pretty spot as well, he conceded without rancor, looking across the water over at big Lummi Island to the east. To the west, Bellingham was a mottled smear along the edge of the bay, Sehome Hill piling up behind. A clear day, Mt. Baker rose gleaming in the bright sunlight. A beautiful spot to build a home.

For someone, Scott thought dryly.

Certainly not him.

Because, in truth, he had no say in anything except his paycheck. Jack, as was his right, would pocket the lion's share of the profit. And Jack would decide what to do after that.

Even if Scott persuaded Jack and Ellen to come out here and look at this place, he could already feel the bitterness of giving away, once again, another thing of his own to that couple.

The problem was, Jack hated new ideas, and worse, hated listening to them. Trying to drag Jack around to another point of view was a waste of time. He hadn't wanted to build the *Muse*. Had barely listened. To this, he wouldn't even listen.

Scott went back to his car, wishing he'd never seen the property. He always hated it when his imagination ran amok, and ran counter to the satisfactions he'd been able to find in life. Through his compromises, which made things livable.

But something about this particular dream had, evidently, taken a much deeper hold than he'd thought it had. And he was about halfway back to Bellingham when the idea hit him.

It came fully formed, and it was not a nice idea.

In fact, it was just plain dirty.

But Scott, suddenly—and in light of the bitterness he felt about people who could not recognize opportunity lapping at their feet, washing over them like the biggest tidal wave in the world—was not in an edifyingly upstanding mood.

It was time to put up a fight. And perhaps right down in the dirt.

It was so clear.

Ever since they had started building the boat, it had become easy to see how things might be different. All it would take was incentive, and the funds to get started.

Neither the money nor the incentive had been there before. But money now made both possible.

All that lacked, now, was setting that incentive to motion. Somehow.

It seemed such a waste to let everything slide away because of lack of incentive. Jack, Scott knew, wouldn't do anything. Once again, if anyone was going to show any incentive, it was Scott.

Unfortunately, incentive in this case meant, in some very real ways, screwing Jack over. Really screwing him, rather than just going behind his back as he'd done with the *Muse*.

It meant not only cutting him out of an opportunity, but using what normally belonged only to him to build that opportunity, even though—in all truth—Scott had been the one to provide all that in the first place.

What was hard, what was making all this difficult, was that he knew some scruple was bound to get squashed. Or more than one.

Scott didn't like the feeling. That, he told himself, was exactly his problem. What he needed was a little moral support. Someone to tell him it was all right to be a real asshole.

Sydney for example.

If anyone saw the world free of ethical considerations—or at least the sort which could get so tangled up you weren't sure the end result was all that ethical—it was her. For his girlfriend, if the thing was immediately right or wrong seeming, it managed miraculously to stay that way. Right on down the road.

If she told him it was the wrong thing to do, he'd drop it. Flat.

But if she told him to see what he could do …?

He just might do it.

The thing is, there were so many other details.

Other things happening.

Another conversation he'd had with Clyde the other night at Micky's.

Things he knew and had seen.

It was a question of fitting it all together.

And then fitting this into it.

He'd have to see what she thought.

# Chapter 87

CATHERINE DIDN'T know how she could feel so confused and guilty and sure and righteous at the same time.

She and Eric must find a way to be with each other. The consequences, though perhaps momentarily horrible, must be viewed as being the best for everyone in the long run.

Eric couldn't be happy with Deborah and that would eventually come to the surface. Deborah would therefore suffer, any way it came.

You can't fight fate, she told herself. Life had its pain as a matter of course. Catherine knew that it was best then, in the end, to face it courageously, to make the hard choices.

As she had done.

So, despite the difficulties ahead, she was resolved.

There were so many things to do. One of which was Jack.

She hadn't called him over for quite a while. There was now a cloying atmosphere between them, how he thought he could grab her anytime he wanted her. She had to put a stop to it.

She called him, asking him to come up to her place.

With all good intentions she meant to be direct with him, but when she saw his smiling, browned face at her door she felt herself falter.

It was the history of their meetings which suddenly took over and held them both in its grip. Intimate relationships were the purchased property of the human heart. And it is a hard won property that the heart finds difficult to give up, as one is always owned by one's own property.

She could do nothing else but put herself into his arms, feeling a spasm of rebellion. It could also seem unfair to have to give him up as well. So soon.

She could need Jack.

But where he was ready to provide her with everything she had originally asked for, tenderness and a feeling of companionship and understanding, she now wanted more. If only she could tell him everything. To enlist his aid for the dangerous days ahead.

She could admit that, to be honest about the whole thing, it was a shame to end it.

She felt no guilt as far as Ellen was concerned. Her relationship with Jack—thank God for that at least—was a straightforward understanding.

Jack was not and could never be her man. So she had not been stealing his soul from Ellen's possession, but merely borrowing some of his time.

Which she now could stop.

Of course, she couldn't repay it. Not directly. Except that it was possible she had done Ellen a favor as well, by being straightforward with Jack. She had made it possible for him to come to grips with his own states of emotion.

"It's so good to see you again," he said to her.

Catherine leaned back in his arms, looking up into his eyes. "I'm glad you could come."

"Never worry about that."

She felt a pang of pity for him, and loosened herself from him.

"Would you like something to drink? I've got some scotch."

Eric drank scotch, and that was all she kept in stock.

"Sure," he said.

While she went to pour the drinks he sat down on the couch, watching her from there. As usual, just looking at her, he felt the desires begin to surge.

Ever since that wild possession of her he had become infused with the power which it had unleashed. It was exactly that absolute moment of possession which had crystallized his feelings for her. Perhaps it was just the situation, with them meeting surreptitiously all those months, but all he knew was that he now wanted her, and could have sworn he needed her.

Catherine brought the drinks over and sat down next to him. For a few minutes they said little to each other, there being so much emotion in the air. There was nothing to be done about it.

Catherine felt her own desires, as an oblique reference to the intensity of her thoughts about Eric and the future, become excited. Feeling the need to let pressure off.

It was incredible, she thought, how she had never before wanted Jack in her bed so badly.

As Jack's own desire increased, so rose a new form of guilt. There was no longer any question in his mind that he loved Catherine. Or that he would have to explain all this to her.

Even as his eyes traveled freely over Catherine's body, his mind was partially captured by the need to tell her, propelling his need to possess her again.

Love, sex, love, sex. Like a wheel of fortune spinning so fast that the prizes were blurred together.

He looked at her breasts filling out within her blouse, letting his eyes travel down farther to her waist and then to her legs.

He loved her.

Catherine, enjoying Jack's gaze, flushing with a heat of her own desire, at the same time felt a tremendous dread. At one time she had been able to convince herself that she hadn't wanted any more of Jack than this. But she would always be able to want more of him.

It was natural, the desire to follow things to their logical end when you, alone, possess something. Privacy and secrecy, with their enormous proprietorial demands, seemed to have the power to destroy ethical resolve more thoroughly than mere lack of moral willpower could ever manage.

What a contradiction! She had had no time to resolve why she could contemplate so coldly the taking away of Deborah's husband … and so forlornly, Ellen's.

Because, in the end, she knew that either would have been equally correct, if the circumstances warranted it.

When juxtaposed, though, the two directions became a thing at the same time beautiful and hideous. A strange, perfect and perfectly ugly equation.

She needed to make it all fit now, she suddenly thought coldly.

The fact was, she needed what she needed.

Ellen, as her friend, had these same needs for Jack that she did, and soon, she could have them fully back. Catherine would then, elsewhere, have something to possess of her own as concrete and solid as what Ellen had been unknowingly sharing.

Her life would then be fulfilled, making what transpired between herself and Jack just the physical motion it was.

She suddenly realized Jack was looking at her with animal heat, a slim smile on his face. And she realized how she had been unconsciously translating her reflections into a slow twisting of her hips as Jack's eyes lay upon them.

She smiled, herself.

Look at yourself, she thought! Grinding your hips like a whore, your legs shivering in anticipation of the poor guy!

She almost laughed.

To continue much longer with Jack would be the worst form of selfishness. But for the moment ... for the moment it was all right.

In the cold reality of the aftermath, she would make herself do what was called for.

Ironically, it would be the decent thing.

But honestly, who could think of that now? Who could think of anything when sex, both desired and available, was so near?

Catherine, at that second, couldn't even bring herself to think Eric's name. She moved towards Jack.

Time disappeared, but somewhere she knew an entirely different future was opening ... and that what was about to happen was a culmination with a past.

Jack put his glass down and, unbuttoning her blouse from the neck to her beltline, began to stroke his fingers across the exposed hollow in her throat and down between her breasts.

Catherine pulled her blouse farther apart and unhooked her bra in front. As he bent towards her she felt a last shudder, as though descending with him was a dark curtain falling over her heart. Resolution to be destroyed one last time, set to rout by the pleasure of witnessing once again a man enthralled by the sight of her naked flesh.

In the end, it would make things a little more difficult to explain to Jack, mingled, as they were, with feelings of tender pity and also worry that he would become distraught.

But handle them she would, and even as she lifted her hips to receive him, she felt as though she was soaring towards true freedom for the first time in her life.

She would tell him afterwards, she thought as the first waves of pleasure began to flow over her.

It would be a disaster of sorts.

A disaster.

A fucking .... She gasped.

Disaster ....

But survivable .... As they all were.

But first there was this.

For ... herself.

# Chapter 88

LATER, SHE found the note mixed in among some bills and some junk mail in her mailbox. The envelope had no stamp, no return address, no nothing.

She knew it was from Eric, an elegantly masculine scrawl where Jack's was a rough, semi-printed sort of handwriting. Her first love letter.

As she went to open the letter she suddenly felt anguish, reminded of how complicated it all was. What would this letter bring? What worse forms of complications were to be found in the future, both immediate and far?

In spite of the twinge of insecurity with all that, there was at least small, comforting warmth in the knowledge that he was out there somewhere, and he was thinking of her.

She thought of how he had snuck the note into her mailbox and that now she was alone with it. Of how their thoughts were together even now. That image swept away any last trace of ache and worry from her heart, and she sat down and opened the envelope.

Dearest no name and unsigned with forever love and remembrance.

Very short and careful. As though copied out.

Short as it was it seemed an eternity for Catherine to read to the end of it. As though there were a million nuances to be read between the lines.

# Chapter 89

THE ENTIRE world was with someone.

Scott was off with Sydney, doing their usual bar crawling stint. No doubt.

Jack—having been told what was what—was back down with Ellen, licking his wounds but now cut off from Catherine forever.

And Eric ... was with his eternal bride.

Catherine needed desperately to reread the letter but on trying could only stare down into the center of it. The words said exactly nothing, but that all was absolutely and by necessity finished. No appeal was possible. She finally set the letter to one side and looked out her windows to the bay, letting her body relax back into the sofa. A sudden, short laugh flew up out of her. She smiled then, and then out came another little laugh.

She reached for the letter, her eyes beginning to stream, and then laughed again.

Forever love.

If she felt anything at all, it was an inner revulsion at herself.

Anything that might have had healing powers, whether narcissism, bitterness, cynicism, or even something she might have read in one of her hundreds of well-thumbed books, were wrenched brutally away.

She was defenseless, even against her own feelings.

She looked at herself with a cynical mirth and despised herself with a triumphant magnanimity and tolerance towards how pathetically small a creature she was, there crumpled on her couch.

Tolerant hatred.

The apartment was absolutely empty of sound except for the ticking of the clock on the mantelpiece. Empty of life except for her breathing, a rhythm in and out, in and out, right out to the end of her life.

She was far beyond crying, although her face was doing so. But much farther than anywhere tears can go.

Far now beyond even dreams.

# Chapter 90

It is always a bit of a shock, Jack was thinking as he looked out the living room window, to find it raining so hard so early in the morning. It was really coming down and nearly loud as it pounded on the house and swooshed into the gravel of the parking lot..

Except for the rain pissing down though, it was very quiet in all other ways. Quiet being the deepest level of hell. As bad as it looked outside, he would have given practically anything to have had an excuse to be out there. He didn't have one.

Scott and the apprentices wouldn't show up until afternoon. It was cold for that time of year. They were, those days, down inside the boat varnishing. The work was extremely slow, coatings taking forever to dry. They had even rigged a canvas tent around the entire boat.

It looked like Ringling Brothers inside the shed. The idea was to close off the boat from cold waterside drafts, and then direct into the tent the two ancient kerosene space heaters—those long, rocket-like air throwers used normally around the shop in wintertime.

Making a few ventilation ports, they got the air warming under the canvas until temperatures were in the normal working range of the coatings and varnish. It took time, usually all morning, to get all that air shifting around inside the boat warmed.

Over Fairhaven, the cloud-smothered sky was dark, moving shaggily in from the sea. The rain fell continually. Although streetlights hadn't come back on, lights of cars swept through the downpour. Gutters overflowed and intersections became big ponds, splashing up with passing tires. Nobody went outside unless they absolutely had to.

A bad day all around, Jack thought.

He and Ellen were sitting in their living room with the fireplace roaring to keep the damp out, drinking coffee and occasionally glancing out at the rain. Mostly they just sat there avoiding each other's eyes. Feeling the hell in the air.

First to have come was the news that morning that Clyde's wife,

Annie, had left him. Or something. It wasn't clear if it was permanent or not. It wasn't said explicitly what was happening, leaving things to the usual conjectures people made about other couple's problems. The problems, generally, can be easily seen, but they don't always explain the fallout.

There had been plenty of signs that things had not been going well. But neither Jack nor Ellen could recall any direct sign she was going to get up and go. That was to say, neither Jack, in his own mind, nor Ellen in hers, since between the two of them weren't discussing much those days. There was nothing related, of course.

Clyde and Annie's problems neither influenced nor were connected in any way with the undercurrents next door. But it was true, the known problems in one couple often tend to remind other couples of their own.

Jack could feel the undercurrents shifting around his ankles like the sinister, serpent-like swirlings of a rip tide.

Clyde had told them that morning, coming over early. It was a complete surprise, both the news and his presence. He hadn't come over to tell them out of some neighborly, let alone friendly, relation he had with them. Or to vent his grief and pain, or to find consolation at the first place at hand. But just to find out if they had seen her. He simply had no idea where she had gone.

He was undoubtedly a mess, with whatever he was feeling. He told them he was all right, but there was an indefinite quality in the way he would look at them. Movements and gestures. Odds and ends of physical habit. Perhaps, even if he wasn't looking for sympathy, he certainly seemed in need of being absolved. He wasn't asking questions or offering explanations. The unsaid conjectures stood on their own plain enough for anyone to see.

But for Jack, Clyde's visit wasn't what made the morning seem like Black Death. There had been something foreboding in the air long before Clyde had come over. Clyde's presence just put all that in a glaring spotlight.

Something.

Something had been stirring these last few days and, casting back, perhaps even a few weeks.

Something, in the way Ellen had been barely speaking to him. Something that, even when she did, made her face tighten into an inscrutable mask.

He had seen that mask before, of course. And he conceded he had probably made it a few times himself—that mask of stifling reactions and thoughts which bordered on the dangerous, the irreparable, and irreversible. Although much less than her, he felt, suddenly bitter at thinking of the times she had been unfair to him. The other times she had been ... well, why not just say it? A pure bitch.

He had seen it. Or, rather, he had seen versions of it. He had never seen it, though, so set and absolute.

At other times, the way it worked, she would eventually be able to relax it a bit, especially when asked a direct question. Or she would force herself to maintain a calm composure as the details of the daily routine asserted themselves ... only reverting to the mask when the essential question came up again.

This time, the mask was of hard steel.

Because of that, he had been making coffee and pretending to be busy in the kitchen, practically hiding from her as she took her shower and dressed, when Clyde knocked.

When Clyde came up on the porch, Jack had almost sighed with relief ... expecting, at the very least, it would provide some sort of diversion for Ellen's mood. With a bit of the outside world visiting, she would be forced to soften a bit. And, hopefully, that softening could be, if not nurtured, kept alive enough to carry forward to another softening. Take the strain off things.

But the moment Jack saw Clyde's face, he knew things across the way had gone from bad to worse, and would not lend towards anything distracting, whether professional or otherwise.

"Jack," Clyde said tonelessly, then nodding at Ellen as she came to the kitchen entry. "Ellen."

For a long moment, his face preventing either of them from saying anything, he stared at a space somewhere halfway between the two of them as though a third person were standing there.

They might have thought he was searching for words except that the look on his face showed he knew what he wanted to say, he was just trying to believe they were true. His eyes continued to stare while he spoke.

"Annie left. She's gone. Last night. She was ...."

Clyde, never at a loss for words, suddenly didn't have a thing. His mouth worked a bit, as though words were trying to form. But then he just ran his tongue between his lips and looked up at them.

"Has she ...?"

They all just stood there. The kitchen seemed like a dead thing. Then Ellen spoke, moving towards the table and pulling out a chair.

"Sit down, Clyde."

"No, thanks. So she didn't …?"

Ellen shook her head.

He looked at Jack, and got the same response. "OK," Clyde said. "Uh … thanks. I have to go. I've got to …." He stopped again, his eyes squinting with thoughts, or with the effort of forming them.

"You sure you're all right?" Ellen said.

Clyde stared around slowly, but it was obvious that, that time, he really hadn't heard her.

"S'okay. You know," he looked at his shoes, seeming to be thinking of something, "but if you do hear from her …."

"Clyde …," Ellen began, but stopped. "Of course."

He looked at her, vaguely for a moment, and then it all broke loose.

"I saw it coming. But just couldn't hold it all back. She said a million times that she felt like she was drowning. That she couldn't find a way to feel good. She gets, got, depressed all the time. Well, so do I. So does everybody. The only difference I saw was that lately, instead of giving me Holy Hell like normal, she just let it go."

Clyde's eyes began to water, looking back and forth between Jack and Ellen.

How in the world could he explain it? To these people, he thought, surely not. And to himself, barely. Because the simple fact was, whatever his neighbors thought the problems might have been—and they were partially right: problems about money and self-esteem, and the esteem and confidence a couple had for each other—it was way more complicated.

Clyde wasn't just shocked, but flabbergasted. Because it wasn't what people, and even Annie, might assume. In a way, Annie had left for all the right reasons in the world, and none of them really fit the realities of the situation.

She just hadn't known.

And the worst thing was that he hadn't told her, or been able to tell her. Because this time, he hadn't wanted her to get too far ahead of things. He'd, therefore, for the first time in his life, been trying to be careful. This was what was wracking him, tearing him between feelings of guilt and feelings of frustration.

Things were more complicated than Annie had known. Maybe worse. But—and this was what made it all so terrible—maybe much, much better.

He had learned, or thought he'd learned, not to get her hopes up too high. He knew the consequences of that. Thought it better to wait until he knew, himself. Really and truly.

And it had blown up in his face.

He'd been hiding it. If only because he hadn't yet been able to put all the pieces together.

Signs.

The problem of the lease was the main one. And under normal circumstances it would have been a serious worry. But there seemed nothing normal about it, no normal explanation. He had gone directly to confront the people at the bank for an explanation, and had found them avoiding any admission they had ever shown him any seasonal leniencies.

In so many words, they had tried to get him to agree to let his lease go. It had made zero sense.

Well, he'd taken care of that, going straight around to his lawyer, who had then written the owners about a long-term clause that had always existed in the lease contract but had never been invoked. Clyde had always managed to avoid that clause, year after year. But now he had no choice. He'd called them on it. So, now, instead of being stuck with trying desperately each year to make the lease payments, he was committed to three years of struggling, with no guarantee he would make good. But there had been no other solution and his lawyer had agreed: regardless of what happened, sink or swim, with the three year lease enacted the bank would be forced to lighten up. That had been a relief, but as was seeming to be the case more and more those days, there was yet another strange element to the deal.

His lawyer, unable to put his finger on it, had made some enquiries and said he'd discovered that the resistance had come not so much from the bank but from the owners. Although he couldn't be sure, it had almost seemed as though the owners might have not only tried to buy Clyde's lease up, but his business as well. Incredible. Who would do something like that? And why?

At the time, Clyde had been so happy at the thought of having saved his business, having out-foxed the bank, that it hadn't immediately occurred to him that he might have come close to getting right out from under it. Gotten rid of everything, the whole inventory, including the Nickerson Ketch. Only later had he begun to realize what might be happening. And then he'd talked to a few other people up the hill, including Micky.

But like a fool, he hadn't told Annie any of that.

It had been years, in fact, since Clyde would have felt comfortable telling her about a serious mistake. Or for that matter, anything complicated.

The three year lease, and how he had seemed to have blocked his bank from pulling the lease, seemed a victory of sorts. But because there seemed something else happening, he hadn't wanted to worry Annie—that telling her that there seemed something mysterious going on, wouldn't have helped in any way.

He would, now, if she came back. But he didn't even know where she'd gone.

He looked at Jack and Ellen, and suddenly felt sour, with some of the old self-pity returning.

The happy couple, he thought. There looking at him with compassion from within their safe little bubble of contentment.

Someday, Clyde thought, someone would figure out what the hell life was really all about. But he wasn't the one. He was just one poor guy trying to make a living selling sailboats and boat cushions. All he knew was that the next breath, the next word, the next step always did seem worth making, and it was better not to ask why if you didn't want to drive yourself nuts.

He looked at Jack and Ellen, feeling he needed them to know something other than what they thought they knew. In case they did know where she was.

"Annie's mistaken." He gave them a sharp look. "She needs to know things aren't what she thought ...." He hesitated, again. Should he tell them? Only a week or so before, he'd found himself looking at a whole new plan. A way to get out from under the lease and everything else. And had even discovered someone who'd be willing to run his business for a while for nothing, on speculation. Someone who was connected to someone who might surprise the hell out of Jack and Ellen.

Really surprise them.

At that thought, he looked at Ellen and Jack again, and decided against it. If there was one thing Clyde knew about business, it was never to not only not count your chickens before they hatched, but to even discuss the possibility of having them.

And the more people knew, the more the possibility of it all going to hell and gone.

He nodded at them. "I'll be getting back," he said, and just turned and left.

They watched him make his way back across the parking lot and over to his office, the rain driving down upon his shoulders.

"Well," Jack said finally, "That was one hell of a visit."

Ellen didn't say anything, didn't look at him, and just went back into the living room, leaving Jack feeling a sudden, enormous emptiness. And wondering suddenly what it was, whatever sort of life they had for themselves, that seemed to be going so fast sideways.

So much for a softening.

Clyde's visit, instead of offering a pause, seemed to just underline whatever was happening. For what seemed forever, Jack stood there in the kitchen, unable to move. His whole body wanted to go out the door into the boatyard, but his connection was too deep, his need to know too intense, his fear too great, to step in any direction except towards her.

There was no getting around it. She knew something.

He walked into the living room, feeling the time had come to find out what it was.

Not having the slightest clue that it was going to be much worse than anything he could have imagined.

Jack having always carried that one last assurance: that as bad as things could get, the worst things could never happen to himself.

## Chapter 91

For Ellen, it had been an excruciating visit. If the heaviness of the disaster next door was bad, it seemed only another drop of woe in the ocean of sorrows surrounding her.

Normally, the problems of someone you knew could make the world seem fragile and desperately unfair, ripping any sense of security away with an almost callous disregard. But when the world already seemed like hell itself, bad news got soaked up by the much larger, all-encompassing sponge of smashed up expectations. Annie's leaving seemed like a confirmation of something.

Jack came in and stood in the middle of the living room, staring out the window at Moore's boatyard. An office light there glowed yellow across the gray of the gravel lot and the dull whites of the dripping boats scattered around with gaily colored little flags hanging like wet handkerchiefs from their rigging.

There had to be a limit to how far down things could go, he thought.

He sighed. God knew how they could get bad enough as it was.

"Pretty awful," Jack remarked.

With that, suddenly, the terrible gloom hanging over their heads became visible, and they looked at each other and saw it in each other's eyes.

It had arrived, and their marriage now stood physically in the room like an uncomfortable guest, crowding out all intimacy or sense of ease.

Even the simple act of breathing seemed oppressed, each action staged and presented. As they looked at each other, they both felt a deep sickness of confusion and pain, the need to inflict pain, the need to be utterly forgiven, and of knowing that there was no way to make a full length leap to the other side of the horror laying between them.

Ellen could see most of it without asking any questions. She little needed to talk to him, or even respond to him. However, she was a creature of habit.

"What is, Jack?"

It was no question at all. Just the wooden announcement of the next act in the ongoing *danse macabre* they were destined to live out.

Jack's eyebrows came together. Those were her first words to him that morning, and they came as a shock. As though he'd been gaffed by the chin.

He nearly damned himself by sinking back into pitiful, self-pitying darkness.

He wanted to cry out. Ask why. Ask for forgiveness for … whatever it was. Plead innocence or, at the very least, ignorance. But he couldn't, feeling no matter what he said would light off the powder keg.

He couldn't bring himself to tempt it, to do anything. He was suddenly that much afraid.

Ellen watched him, watching the shadows cross his face, and saw the confirmation of everything there.

She didn't have any details. Her lack of that knowledge mattered little, though, now that the beast was loosed.

She suddenly knew that, if only just for her sanity, she was going to let it fly. Let it tear up all that lay around them.

Jack, glancing at her, saw it in her. Saw he didn't have the choice to light it off, or not, himself. That she was going to do it anyway.

It was coming. At any second. He was about to know. It was coming and bringing the worst dread Jack had ever experienced. He had never felt so much his connection with life, and what that life consisted of. Never had he seen how delicate the balance could be. Now tipped by a wild, cancerous offshoot of an earlier sense of security and satisfaction. He struggled with it, and fidgeted. Speech seemed blasted from his brain.

"Ellen … I." He stopped. Hopeful. But no.

He saw she was going to wait for him. Forever and mercilessly.

He slumped and looked back out the window. It was morning, incredibly, and it was raining like hell itself, and they had the whole day of it ahead of them. He plunged.

"You should never have had to hear such a thing from me. I wish to God, now, it had never been."

He paused, she still waited. But as he was working on his next words, whatever they might be, her eyes lost their focus upon him, widening suddenly and shining, as she now dealt with taking on confirmation.

It would first be this. And then of … who.

Ellen's mind raced back over the months. Now letting it all

develop, overwhelming her. The incredible, blind naïveté ....

She suddenly knew.

And was just as suddenly furious for how she'd blinded herself!

She couldn't believe how much she'd willed herself to go other directions. Any other direction.

Her hand came up to her mouth, feeling nauseated with anger and hatred, thinking of the contents of that garbage pail. Why else would it be in *their* pail, in *their* kitchen, in *their* house?

"Ellen ...." Jack was terrified by the look on her face.

"Don't." She calmed herself, and then finally said, "I knew something was wrong around here lately."

Jack nodded. But, stupidly, as though there was any shred of hope left it might be something else, thinking maybe he could push it somewhere else, he said, "yes, well, with everything going on, I suppose I've been ...."

That was as far as he got. Ellen didn't move a muscle in her face, but said with flat devastation.

"If you think you're going to lie your way around the reasons you've been fucking Catherine, you're a fucking idiot."

Jack's guts dissolved beneath the sheer, flat horror of the statement. And in the absolute silence which followed, every heartbeat pounded deeper and deeper the confirmation of it.

His only hope would have been to jump, to shout, to scream his innocence ... maybe.

But he was unable to respond, every second drifting ever farther from the safety of the shoreline, drowning within sight of land. Within sight of Ellen.

Worse, his only life-ring, his heretofore hard won sense of rightness about what he'd been doing with Catherine, had been stripped from him, become in itself an obscenity.

Where, before, scenes of Catherine and himself making love seemed erotic or romantic, if not practically admirable for their generosity and humanity, now, with Ellen's eyes upon it, there in their own living room as though in the cheapest, most obscene film of flat-faced whores and squinting brutes, was the picture of Jack and Catherine together, naked. Their writhing efforts as though pigs copulating.

Jack saw himself no longer as a man in some sort of hopelessly romantic moral balancing act, but as a ludicrous, rutting dog. Running around with a mindless grin and a big, red, boner.

An electric charge went through Ellen's body as she watched

how her words had entered Jack as though the ice-cold thrust of a spear. Deflating him like some cheap balloon toy punched by its own play stick.

She didn't need any details now. Confirmation was enough. She didn't need to know how long they had been doing it. Or how often. Or where, or how they did it. Or if hers was sweeter, or tighter, or if she liked it, as well, it up her goddamn ....

She could suddenly remember a time, in fact not long after Catherine had come to work, when Jack had begun to show a surprising new adeptness and imagination in bed. Or for that matter, herself. Innocent conversation among friends ....

Sex Knots ....

She suddenly found herself staring at him.

"I never planned anything," Jack's lips said.

Still staring, she nevertheless managed: "Do you ever?"

It had come out easily. Too easily. And she now wished it hadn't sounded so bitterly complacent. She would have preferred something truly glacial, or at least frightfully detached.

All that time, she thought, the beast had been right there alongside her, chewing at her ear.

She would never feel the same about him. Never.

Unquestioned trust had been stripped away, her body exposed and no longer innocent. Never again could Jack be considered a good man for all his faults. Now he was Fault itself, and every day would be a test, for the rest of his life.

The question was, could she live with that? All things considered, for the moment she didn't have the slightest idea what she could or could not live with.

Jack was still suffering the humiliating vision of himself and Catherine.

"So ...," he said, his tongue wallowing in the muddy sensation of his mouth, "well ...."

Ellen studied him. Evidently, Catherine had taken him a long way down the path. Christ only knew, she thought, how much that cunt had taken.

For what it was worth, though, all of that had taken place in the shadows, in the dark. Which weakened Catherine's grasp, no matter what she might have thought. Because things that live in the dark always wither in the open light.

Ellen's rage burned.

The bitch probably even believed she had an advantage of some sort.

Suddenly, Ellen's mind cleared, and logical once again, she was in control of herself.

"I don't know what is going on in your head, but if you're planning to go with her, you can be sure there's no way she's going to get you on a silver platter. If you both think I will give anything else up, then both of you are going to get a surprise. I promise you, you think things are bad now, just wait and see."

With a coldness she would have never thought capable of, she looked at her husband. He had nothing to say, so she went on:

"Think about it, Jack. Think about that, and yourself, and that goddamned treacherous cunt, and then think of this house, that boat out there, your business, and the baby you're going to be paying for, for the rest of your life ... if you can see what I mean. Or maybe you can't. That certainly wouldn't surprise me. Not anymore. Anyway, think of all that," she finished, "just for starters."

She squinted at him with contempt.

"As for the rest," she continued, "you can think of all your bigger things later. You know what I mean ... all those bigger issues of ethics, truth, duty, or whatever else you're always spouting on about in order to make sure that no one ever thinks they can fuck you over or take the moral high ground from you."

She had got that out. Neat and precise. She examined him, and found she couldn't stand the sight of him.

With Jack's face hung open like a moron's, she lifted quickly out of her chair and went out to the kitchen to get more coffee, and to contemplate her revenge; and to keep herself from screaming with disgust at the mere sight of him.

In the kitchen she came to a dead stop, staring at the floor, feeling all the pure, wrenching hatred the world had to offer.

She knew Jack was just standing back there, staring at the rain. Staring at goddamn whatever. The bastard idiot of all time.

Putting her coffee cup down she reached out to steady herself on the dishrack full of plates and cups and silverware.

And threw it onto the floor.

## Chapter 92

Eric could do nothing. Deborah was down there again and he was irritated and felt put upon, as though waiting at a station for a train he didn't want to be on.

It might not be done straight out.

Or it might be done straight out with a terrible, shrieking scene with everything out on the ground, bleeding, where everyone could see it.

Everything about Eric. His stupidity. His weakness.

Especially that.

The most dangerous and idiotic weakness he had ever fallen prey to.

Bad as that could be, if not bringing on a crisis in his marriage, worse was how he could become so vulnerable.

In the pack, if the lead dog falls, the tendency is to tear it to shreds. With people, overjoyed to find an idiot to tear apart, the first reaction would be a gratefully, and a gleefully, righteous indignation. Nobody could stand much scrutiny, therefore it was a great relief to let fly in savage abandon at someone else, unscathed and safe from repercussions.

Nothing of course absolutely said that anyone needed to find out. Everyone did, indeed, have their price. But he could do nothing with that knowledge, as though at battle with a storm at sea he'd been given a handful of water as a weapon.

He couldn't have kept Deborah from going down there. He had no explicable means at his disposal, no control over her daily movements. He had never realized how much of his life was determined by hers. But that wasn't what was galling him.

The damning truth was: he had never realized how much better off she was than him.

All those years of their marriage where she had been left to go where she wanted, she had always found ways to center herself upon him. Without faltering she found something constant and committed herself to it.

That, he thought, was the secret to her serenity.

The ultimate attraction of her soul.

She wasn't in search of everything at once. She only seemed that. She did search, did find one small thing after another, and enlarged upon her discoveries. Enthralled herself with her explorations. But her freedom wasn't there.

Her freedom came from being faultless. Irreproachable.

He sat back in his chair, staring blindly at the wall. Finally, he dropped his hands onto his desk.

"Shit," he said. "Shit. Fuck and shit."

Why, oh why, had he fucking *written* it?

He looked at the clock on the mantle, that goddamned clock they'd picked up in Naples from that thief of an antiques dealer. She had been gone three hours. She said she might be there for lunch, but if she wasn't there by noon she was lunching with her friends.

Her friends, those days, consisted of Ellen and Catherine.

Good God.

Why hadn't he gone to see Catherine and talked it all out? Never before in his life had he shirked from even the most disagreeable task.

For those reasons alone, he probably deserved all the disaster the situation could muster. Tempting fate and taking risks was one thing and you could be destroyed or victorious. But to do nothing except cross your fingers invited ignominious annihilation, and you deserved it.

He should have gone to see her. Probably, it would have cost him plenty. Emotionally. In terms of pain and even self-respect. In time. In pointless, endless discussion. A horrible scene, no doubt.

But bad as that would have been, it would have been nothing compared to what it was probably going to cost him now.

He'd treated her miserably, and without any sense of honor or consideration. He'd fled, with his tail between his legs, like a guilty, thoughtless schoolboy. And where, before, there would have certainly been hurt and anger, there was now bound to be immeasurable fury.

The tally sheet was drawn, and he could see it was all written in his own red blood.

And worse, it really and truly was ... written.

## Chapter 93

THE NIGHTS were the worst and she tried not to think about them during the day.

But on getting home, all around her in her living room became something frightening.

A modern setting for Macbeth, her life in tattered grays and browns and dried-blood reds and black.

She couldn't tell if the god-awful mess of her life meant some sort of terrible reproach, a demonstration of reality, or if it was perhaps something worse.

Perhaps it was a mistake ... so big as to not even seem real ... and it wasn't even her life she had been dropped into.

Just an enourmous, evil pit.

A joke played on her by some ultimate malignancy somewhere. Laughing at her while, mistakenly thinking things were going a different way, she had slowly and carefully murdered every real possibility of happiness that came within her reach.

It was an old nightmare, a childhood thing: that the body and circumstances she had been dumped into—in the same way her mother had poured melted wax into candle molds at Christmastime—were only of an accidental nature. How very easily her existence, mind and consciousness might have been dumped, alternatively, into the body of her best friend up the street. Which frankly, she had often thought even as a child, would not have been so bad. Everyone else always seemed happier. What if, by some sort of mistake of routing, through cosmic bad luck or divine fumble fingers, she hadn't been meant to be herself at all?

A big, floating feeling would come into her at those times. A sad and lonely emptiness ... a crying little girl thinking about her parents and how far away and foreign they were. How strange it was they were really hers. That she couldn't feel any responsibility for them, being the accident she was.

Catherine, even in the grown up world, could feel that distant emptiness from long in the past. That teasing unkindness which, in its evil, only wanted to see her break down and cry.

466

She had been down before. But never this low.

She could almost see herself as happier dead, comforting herself with a swift, determined razor and then a gentle slipping into a warm emptiness in a bathtub. Or punishing herself and everyone else, strangling in horror at the end of a rope, her chest wracking her in terrible, fatal heaves.

She could almost search to satisfy the burning pain in self-annihilation. The screaming pain of suicide a form of conciliation with the unfairness of life. A final, and justified, complaint.

She could almost die. Plaintively. Except she didn't even deserve that, she was so worthless. Had acted so worthlessly, with no mind to any real sense of self-esteem. Because, evidently, she had none. And no one had any for her.

Total, bottomless depression.

It would have been better to stay home. To just find an excuse to quit, and do it.

She knew it was bound to show. Everywhere.

Even Ellen had been avoiding talking much to her.

There seemed almost a reproach there, as though by merely being depressed, Catherine was betraying their friendship.

Not even the slightest sign of sympathy. Which, in a way was surprising.

Despite her unhappiness, she could feel annoyed.

Couldn't Ellen tell there was a serious case of depression in front of her eyes?

Couldn't she find empathy for how despondent distress was something you didn't just "take care of."

It was disappointing to have discovered that pitiless element of human selfishness which always expected friends to be happy, or—if it had absolutely to be that way—only moderately unhappy. And that they dealt with it on their own.

And elsewhere.

God knew, Catherine had with indulgence put up with Ellen's funks.

She sighed, letting her anger pass. It didn't matter. There were certain unsavory truths to human nature which were infallible, she thought, and one was that nobody likes to be around sad people, no matter what. She now was sad people.

A week had passed. Then two. Another message never came. The phone never rang. Time crept constantly slower and hope, parched and forgotten, wilted and then withered to nearly nothing.

In earlier years, hope would have held its ground a little longer than only two weeks. But hope, like time itself, is a possession and currency of reckless youth, spent with ignorant frivolity and fleeting regret.

The first week, she had been a young girl inside hope.

But by the second week she was once again thirty-five. And rejected and doubly divorced. And less thin than she'd once been. And not really well-off with no clear future, and not doing anything truly exciting, living nothing exotic or fascinating. And for that matter neither as good-looking, athletic, witty, clever, extroverted, admired, entreated, large-breasted nor—obviously—intelligent, as she might have wished to have been. She was even too old to feel really angry.

Not too old, though—never too old and in fact gaining an ever deeper ability—to feel ever more exquisitely the depths of melancholia.

What a lovely gift for age and wisdom to bestow.

Catherine heaved a sigh, and decided to just go to bed.

But as she got up from the sofa she suddenly remembered that, bad as things were, she still had one consolation.

Maybe it wasn't the best, she thought.

But, in a way, it was remarkable she even had that.

# Chapter 94

A THURSDAY evening, she was finally able to catch Jack alone, out back of the boat. He was filling up a can with red lead paint dumped from a number of almost empty cans.

She sidled into the canvas awning hanging over the boat, checking to see no one else was around, and then went to him.

As she approached he turned his head. He did not look happy at seeing her.

She almost smiled. She could see that her depression had been affecting everyone. But she knew, no matter what, she could rely on Jack, even with all that had passed. She felt an inner calm descend over her which she had not felt for weeks.

She had let him know it was supposed to be over between them. He was probably still stinging from her rejection.

But what was absolutely essential, now, was that his pride was soothed. Quickly.

She looked around again. She didn't know why, but lately she had been feeling paranoid whenever Ellen was around. Something about Ellen those days ... so stern. Catherine had secretly smiled about that. Ellen seemed to have become something out of a novel by Nathanial Hawthorne. Prim and proper. Nearly Puritan. She would have looked perfect in a stiff-collared dress with her hair pulled back into a severe bun. But it wasn't really funny and was, in fact, uncomfortable. For Catherine to simply talk to her husband in her presence, in the normal course of the day, had become strained. Jack, himself, becoming uncomfortable.

Too bad, she thought. And maybe it was cold, but the fact was that there were winners and losers. And those that could handle stress, and those who couldn't. Ellen, who Catherine now saw as the as-yet unknowing loser, was also someone who knuckled under when life really, truly, happened. It was evidently that: some women handled their pregnancies well. Some turned into flaming bitches. You never knew. And understanding all that, although with a bit of pity, Catherine had dismissed it and just made herself even more careful than usual about finding somewhere to talk to Jack.

She looked back over her shoulder a last time. They were deep inside the tent, far down along the boat. No one else was there. Even if Ellen came out, and came inside the tent to find Jack, Catherine could slip around the stern end and up the other side without being seen. She knew she was utterly safe with Jack.

She looked at him.

"Can you come over this weekend?"

She moved closer to him. She had always admired his build and his strong way of carrying himself and moving. Once again, she could feel the heat of physical passion building within. She desired him, and—as she hadn't for a while—now actually needed him.

Jack finished pouring out another can of thick, dark red paint. It really looked for a moment like he was pouring blood and Catherine's stomach gave a lurch. He threw the empty can away and reached for another.

"You must be joking," he said. "I thought it was all over." He stared at her for a moment, but then realized he didn't even care to argue a very obvious point. "In any case," he went on flatly, "I can't."

They had always had a casual arrangement. So casual acceptances and refusals were supposed to be part of the deal. She was supposed to say, at that point, that it was all right.

But this was not the regular circumstances. In fact, it seemed a matter of life and death. She had to make him understand that. In spite of his pride.

"I wish you would try," she made her voice as serious as possible. She wanted no mistaken meaning. "I'm sorry about what I said. It was an over-reaction that day. I've been having a bad time lately. Badly sad," she tried to smile, "and all that."

Jack nodded. Sympathy, though, was far from his mind right then. He could tell her all about bad times.

"I can't, and I can't tell you why." He looked up at her. "All right?"

He didn't want a scene. It had taken all his effort to ensure that Ellen didn't say anything until the boat was out of his shop. Out and paid off.

So, until the *Muse* was finally gone, he would not feel at ease. The presence would be there like a great, evil cloud, or a great evil wave far off on the horizon.

It was like a house of cards, and the removal of even the slightest element put at risk the entire structure.

For the first time in his life, by God, he was going to make a success of things. Climb out of this hole, get rid of this poisonous inertia he'd let himself be seduced by.

He wasn't sure how he would do it, but he was going to try any way he could.

For the moment, though, there wasn't much to be done. Until they got that boat out of the shop, got the keel onto her, and got her out onto the water and out of their lives, they just had to hold on. And for him, therefore, he just had to stay cool and calm. Not make waves of his own. Just get this all over with.

He was convinced: Ellen was not going to leave him. She and the baby would stay. She hadn't said as much. In fact, given her cold and bitter silence, it certainly wasn't obvious she would. But he felt an odd confidence. They would get through this, and come out the other side with something renewed and refreshed. A new basis.

At the very least, a new financial basis. Which wouldn't hurt. This boat was going to guarantee they were a success, rather than him ending up like a Clyde Moore, washed up on the beach and picked apart by every passing gull or crab.

For that, he wasn't about to encourage Catherine in the slightest way. Even cooling to a strictly professional level their exchanges.

Avoiding any form of contact beyond the strict minimum.

One slip otherwise—if Ellen saw him sharing even the slightest form of friendly banter with Catherine—he knew he could predict utter disaster.

At that instant, there next to the boat, all he wanted was for her to go away. For her to accept, blithely, his refusal. He could and would deal with the permanent solution to her later. They had another three weeks to go with the boat, and then it would all be over.

Catherine, he reflected, would not have believed what all had transpired around her. It had been so hard to convince Ellen.

It had taken four hours.

He'd never talked non-stop to Ellen like that in their entire marriage.

In the end, angry as she was, she had agreed to say nothing. She had only made one demand: that it was to be her right to tell Catherine to get out. He had agreed.

It made Jack shudder to think of what that was going to be like.

A husband might be forgiven. Well, maybe forgiven was not the accurate word. There didn't seem a word to describe what a wife does when she decides to let the past bury itself. He was certainly not condoned. He would never be pardoned. It was as though Ellen had decided to remarry him, but the remarriage was not with the original man she had married. He was not pardoned, but converted, and then accepted back on those grounds.

What sort of husband?

Evidently, a lesser sort. He had never said, outside of his monotone wedding vow, that he would be faithful. Yet, by never having said anything at all, the assumption she could make was not a mistaken one. So he had failed her.

Well ... he had never been an angel and she had never expected it of him. But he was fallen, all the same.

It was tough, Jack thought, but he had to maintain control. After all, he was the boss. If they were going to continue, he would have to regain that position. No big scenes. No public admissions. No way could Scott ever know. Fucking Scott, and his ordered little life.

God, he thought, it was like surviving an accident. How had he ever been able to contemplate leaving Ellen for Catherine? He continued to pour the thick red paint; and he began to feel pity for Catherine.

A husband might be forgiven. His mistress, never.

"Not even a couple of hours?"

Catherine was feeling a sudden desperation as she looked at his calm, unknowing shoulders. Only by great self-effort did she keep a rising note out of her voice.

Jack looked thoughtful, twisting his head to one side as though to cock it stubbornly for the no she saw was obviously there. At that sight her desperation got too large for her to hold onto.

"Jack," she breathed out hard. "Oh, God, please. You don't understand."

She couldn't stop herself, falling upon him and wrapping her arms around him even as he was pouring the lead paint.

Sobbing.

"Jack, please say you'll come over. It's never been so bad. I can't take it. Maybe because it is all coming to an end."

Her tears ran down her face and her voice cracked and splintered as she used any excuse, any argument.

"You've said nothing. You haven't come around, haven't called. I can't help but feel afraid. All I ask is a little time."

She felt hurt and betrayed just talking about it. Even if it hadn't been that way. But now it became that way. He had left her alone. If that was the lone criteria, he had betrayed her. He owed it to her, and she was suddenly furious. There was no doubt now; he had to come see her. She would not allow him to shirk his responsibilities.

Or, she suddenly thought, he would pay. They would all pay. She could feel Jack's heart racing beneath her chest. He remained silent. She could feel how he was trying to find a way to refuse her again. A white hot rage flew up within her.

"After all, Jack," she said, her voice suddenly low and steady, "things have been going pretty good for you. It's only fair. I only want my share. I don't want to have to force you."

The threat was implicit. From that moment forward, as far as Jack was concerned, nothing else she said mattered.

Of course what she didn't know, he thought, was that blackmail no longer held the slightest threat. The world she threatened to explode, had long since been detonated.

He suddenly felt no pity. Just anger. At himself, but mostly for her.

Always feeling sorry for herself, he thought. Always grabbing for everyone else's plate.

He stood slowly, loosening her hold on him.

"How could you possibly force such a thing?" he said.

He knew perfectly well how she thought she could do it and wondered at how, by doing so, she would still enjoy his forced companionship. But he couldn't help asking all the same. It was so unbelievable.

She saw his face was hard, and she lost whatever control she had left.

"Do I really have to spell it out?" she said. "Well, as you wish. This would be no time for Ellen to find out. I think you should come over this weekend."

True, now it was all or nothing. But having nothing, she felt she had nothing to lose. She had got it straight out, and actually felt an odd sense of relief in saying it. Almost triumphantly. It felt good, for once, to not be on the absolute bottom rung.

Jack, though, wasn't impressed at all, and in fact went as brutal as a mind could get.

Look at this fucking crack, he thought, staring at me with her absolute slut's confidence I'll come running up there with a hard-on in hand to keep her mouth shut.

If she had been a man, he would have flattened her on the spot. As it was, he only had words. Chivalry be damned.

"I can't. I told you. Just shut the fuck up and let it be."

Catherine suddenly thought of Ellen, and hated her. Before, there had been a sort of honor in not taking Jack away from his wife. But Catherine no longer cared. In fact, now she thought she might just do it. Why the fuck not, she thought? What, after all, did she really have left but him?

Perhaps she momentarily hated him—hated him as much as she hated Ellen, or Eric, or everyone else—but she would also have him for herself ... all to herself, for however long it lasted. And he'd, of course, change his tune once they got into bed.

"What's the matter?" she said. "Won't Mommy let you come out and play?"

Jack looked at Catherine. At first he saw her glaring back in pure sarcasm and hatred. But, finally, the hardness in her face softened, as though her own words began to dawn on her.

Unfortunately, it was obvious she couldn't bring herself to actually believing her words, and Jack knew he would have to drive the nail all the way home, himself.

He managed a steady gaze.

"That," he said, "is exactly the state of things around here."

# Chapter 95

SOMETHING HAD been happening, but Scott hadn't paid much a mind to it at first.

Perhaps it was because the boat was almost finished that he had been feeling jumpy. But then Micky had gotten to talking one night, again, and out had come this wild stream of what seemed at first paranoia about land, an L.A. developer, lease problems, you name it. Scott was trying to put it all together. Clyde's strange offer, and now this.

Somehow, everyone down there was involved. It looked like some guy was trying to buy up the whole area.

Scott hated Californian money. The money used and then threw what was left away. If he were truthful, he knew he shouldn't be so hard on Californian money. There was plenty of asshole money in Washington State. One look at the sprawling free-for-all up and down the Puget Sound showed you that. But while Washington money was just as bad you felt that, eventually, you might control it.

Sydney thought he should go talk to Eric Sumners about it, that there might be something in it for Scott. He, of course, had had that idea. But he couldn't put the pieces together. Couldn't figure out how to not only make it all work, but work it.

And he certainly had no plan for how Sumner might be used, although it was obvious that the billionaire was the only hope.

He thought about it a lot, and then one day found himself standing in Sumners' outer office. Unprepared. But unable to resist wanting to see if there was anything there.

He hadn't made an appointment but said he hadn't needed much time. Just needed to drop something off.

The plan was to get in and get out. But also, somehow, get his foot in the door.

Standing there in the outer office, he suddenly felt the real power of the businessman. Scott could remember how, at one time, Sumners had seemed in awe of Scott. Now with the boat almost finished, it was all changed.

This guy had it, Scott thought. This was where money lived and worked and he could see it was no longer asshole money or any other sort of money. It was simply money, and it had its own rules. Not inherently evil or good. Like the old theoretical problem about God, Money fell right in.

Money was all powerful, Money was all good. But bad things happened. Somehow or other, it wasn't Money's fault and never would be.

The paneling in the outer office, Scott noted, was pecan, and the secretary's desk was fine, French oak. A very nice piece that desk, he thought, and old. Perhaps even an original.

He stood with his hands dangling at his sides, glad his boots, planted in the thick beige carpet, were clean. He gazed for a moment at Sumners' secretary. A rich man's girl Friday. Actually, she was quite attractive if you liked the smooth, look-but-don't-touch sort that wore high heels to give their legs the sexy curves, and then conscientiously kept their knees clamped vise-like together. Squashing all hope.

She ignored him with an ease he considered prodigious. However, he had been resigned to that from when he had first walked in and gotten the once over. He had seen she considered him out of place. If not something from the Black Lagoon.

From then on, he was merely the next item on the agenda.

The intercom on the secretary's desk buzzed, and she looked up at Scott, picking up a receiver. She nodded, replacing the phone.

"He can see you now. His next appointment isn't for a few *minutes*." She smiled grimly upon that last word, stood, and went over to open Sumners' door.

Scott could only admire how succinctly she had put him in his place. And there was nothing, short of making a total ass out of himself, he could do to respond. "That's fine. I just need a few minutes."

A professional smile back from the secretary and he was in.

Eric Sumners came crisply around his desk with a big smile. Evidently, this was his way in his own office. No handshake, though.

"How are you, Scott? Everything all right? I hope this isn't a bad news visit." Eric looked at Scott for a moment. It wasn't obvious that it was business, nor was it purely social. He could offer Scott a drink and they could sit on the couches. Not a hard drink, of course. Jack had warned him, off-handedly of course, about that. "Cup of coffee?"

"No, thanks," Scott said, walking over and looking out the window towards Fairhaven.

"Nice view you have from here. I've always wondered what it was like."

"It's a beautiful town."

Scott felt some humor return. Bellingham was a lot of things but beautiful wasn't one of them. Especially from above.

"Looks like the command post. You get up this high, you feel like you own it." He looked over at Eric. "Is that the way you feel?"

Eric smiled. "That old argument again?"

Scott smiled back.

"No. To be perfectly honest, I can say I can admire you for all this. Don't ask me how. Us liberals, especially the poor and jealous variety, don't like to say things like that, let alone figure out why."

"I didn't know you were jealous."

"I'm not. I thought you might be flattered if I said so." Scott looked back out over Bellingham.

Eric smiled. "So, what was it you wanted?"

Scott had got so far as to know what he was going to say, but now had to develop the words. He looked at Eric, and then began walking slowly around the office.

"It's only a hunch," he began. "Maybe you even know about it already. Word has it something big is being stewed up for Fairhaven."

Eric held his face smooth.

Scott continued. "I've got no reason, of course, to be telling you this, or even to be discussing this with you, except that there's the possibility—even if you do know what is going on—that you might not know everything about it."

As far as Eric was concerned, there was not all that much to hide. It came as no surprise there would be leaks and rumors eventually starting up. The question was, what sorts of rumors were going around? "What information do you have?"

Scott looked at Sumners. The man was smart, indeed, he thought. He knew anything else would have seemed like a lie. Suddenly, Scott needed a second to think.

"I think I'll take you up on that coffee, if you don't mind."

Eric smiled again.

"Sure ... just a second." He turned to go to his coffee machine. Scott went to look out the window.

Again.

It had been strictly a guess on Scott's part. But seeing how little Sumners responded had confirmed that the businessman knew something about it. The question now was, to what point was he inevitably involved, and how deeply?

And, as for himself, was he making a mistake?

He didn't think so. He wasn't big enough, in any sense, to create a problem for Sumners.

But if there was anything for Scott to get out of it, he couldn't see yet how it might be done. He was just playing things by ear, hoping he could gather clues from Eric's reactions as he talked. As he just had. Scott wondered how the game should be played. How much to bluff? How much to lie? Or maybe just straight-shooting.

Personally, Scott was attracted to the idea that these guys, at this level of money, didn't bluff much. They didn't have to.

Or else it was all a bluff. If that was so, then he had a chance. He decided to go that way.

Scott pursed his lips and looked at Eric. Strange, he thought, how so much had changed about the guy since the first time he had seen him. Environment seemed to be everything. You took this guy, in whatever clothes he chose, a three piece suit or a jogging outfit, and walked him around down at the waterfront, and he would always look ridiculous.

Amongst people who made their living straining their backs out of shape, someone like Sumners was an unneeded interruption. He got in the way, and his opinions didn't change the fundamental truths to manual labor. The only thing a guy like that could do was pay you better, or worse, or fire you straight away. The work, and what your body could physically accomplish in an hour, a day, a week, or a lifetime, never changed.

Up here in his tower though, firmly planted on his fine carpeting and framed in by a generous view of his town, he was resplendent. Even the walls of his office told you that. The outer office had been paneled in pecan. Sumners' was point blank oak. And not just oak veneered paneling, but real, plank cut timber.

If pecan could make you feel stupid, oak just blew you away.

# Chapter 96

HE SLID his gaze off the panelling.

Well, he thought, if he was there, he might as well see what happened. He glanced back as Sumners came over with a mug.

"Not much," Scott said. "It's just that some people working for a guy named Hartman have been all over the place down in Fairhaven since last fall, tying up property. Or trying to. You probably have heard of Hartman, considering you are both in the same business."

The fact that a few people had gotten wind of Hartman's maneuvers didn't bother Eric. That sort of thing happened all the time, and normally by the time word began to get out, things were all sewn up anyway. Which was precisely why Eric could sound casual.

"You say he's trying to get property."

"Yeah. He's been pushing a few people hard, but he hasn't got much yet. As for the main waterfront, the asking price could be tripled and he would probably go for it."

Eric gazed at Scott calmly. This was the confirmation, he thought. Hartman had indeed been lying. The meeting between them had been a stalling action, hoping to keep Eric quietly to the side. Eric's getting asked to run for office might also be a red herring, however sincere the Party's offer had been. Probably, it had been Hartman himself who had first whispered in Carl Ivarsson's crumpled old ear.

He had to admit, though, if it had been that, the desired effect was achieved. Lately, his mind had been entirely occupied with politics. Which gave Hartman more time and room to maneuver. Down the line, Eric might have gotten blackmailed between getting the public office and being involved in the project.

Conflict of interest.

It all had a nice symmetry to it, and Eric had to admire the simplicity and beauty of the leverage. Too bad they had screwed up. What's more, they obviously knew it.

Eric would have liked to have known at what point they had

realized it. The summer before, Hartman had gotten a lot of things arranged. But he'd got the cart before the horse. He had gotten all the politics sorted out, but hadn't got the property.

Asking Eric about the local political scene was all a smoke screen. Hartman already knew the answers and wanted Eric to think that was to be his turf. All the rest was just going through the motions. Pretending to get the largest local developer to buy in, and keeping him unaware of how to get at the main action.

It had practically worked, except that Hartman—as was obvious from what Scott was saying—hadn't managed to get his hands on that waterfront strip.

Maybe hadn't bowled the old lady over with enough money. Or hadn't sweet-talked her enough. An old lady would like company. A simple enough thing to arrange.

Friendship could be arranged.

Then you had to nurse it along. Something Hartman wasn't in the position, or evidently the disposition, to do. The other giant mistake was in not getting the owners of Clyde Moore's place lined up.

That, though, was now fully taken care of, or would be when Newell Briggs finished working out how to leverage a man like Moore out of his lease, lock, stock and barrel.

Eric had been amused to discover that at some point he could end up not only the owner of the *Muse*, but the Nickerson Ketch as well.

As though a weight had been lifted from him, Eric turned back to Scott.

"So, what is it you want?" He smiled. "Precisely."

Scott realized he didn't know that much about whatever it was he was supposed to know. A little knowledge more than merely dangerous.

He felt there had to be something, though, somewhere in this for him.

Eric, Jack, both these guys profited from Scott's pains. All Scott received was a pay check when what he wanted was freedom to control his own life.

The dream.

But it certainly wasn't easy to get something with nothing.

"Look," he began, "let me put it this way. Whatever is going on in Fairhaven, I don't worry too much about, because I know what could be gotten away with wouldn't be much. I'm no back-tonaturist, either, but country is country, town is town. Better something happens down there than somewhere else."

Scott paused for effect. There was none. And, in fact, he could see Eric was impatient with the little speech, and hurried on:

"Hartman doesn't have all the property. The fact is that a few other guys have gotten friendly with the owner of the key property, and I think I can help you out."

Scott stopped again, waiting for some sort of response. But once again there was nothing. He continued.

"Clyde Moore's wife left him. Clyde doesn't have the heart for much of anything, right now. What it comes down to is this: the last thing he did before she took off was to get his lawyer to force a three-year, unbreakable lease. She didn't know he'd done that. Anyway, he did that because the property owners had been getting coy."

Scott hesitated. It was always easier to talk about what other people wanted, than what you wanted for yourself. But he knew the one truth about these things: you never got anything if you didn't ask for it. Well, he thought, here goes. It's all or nothing.

"I don't talk about it much, but you should know I've always wanted a place of my own. Between you, me and the wall, Jack hasn't always been so inclined towards new business ventures. You might not know it, but I'm telling you now … if it hadn't been for me, the *Muse* would never have been taken on." Scott took a breath. "Clyde asked me if I didn't want to run his boatyard for him."

Up to hearing of what Clyde had done, Eric hadn't batted an eye. But from there on, Scott could see he was surprised. He suddenly felt a first exciting flush of confidence come into himself.

"As a matter of fact," he said. "I'm going to agree to it as soon as the boat is finished. I'll run the business, and Clyde can get away from the place for a while. But there's another thing. Clyde said that, if I wanted, if I came up with the money, he'd sign the lease over to me." Scott gave Eric a long, searching look. "The upshot is, I wouldn't have a problem breaking the lease. What I would like is to get a bank to help me start my own boatworks. I know a place out west towards the reservation that's for sale. To be honest, as it stands right now, they wouldn't give me enough to make a down payment on a bus ticket out of town."

He stopped there. It was plain enough. If Sumners wanted Clyde Moore's waterfront property, Scott could be a great help.

Where, before, there had been small signs of irritation in the businessman, Scott could now see a sort of interest. Something he had said had touched something somewhere. He had no idea of where. But suddenly Scott had another idea and went with it.

"Actually, the way things are going down at Colby's, I might be able to get Jack's lease as well."

For the past minute, Eric's mind had been calculating, but this last information sent it spinning. He'd been unprepared for that.

While Scott was just talking about things that were details on the periphery of larger things, things that could possibly be interesting ... just possibly ... Sumners hadn't been overly concerned other than to begin thinking of new possibilities. The sorts of tactical and strategic things his business mind was used to sorting out. But to hear there were things wrong at Colby's brought another worry to mind.

And there, he frowned. "There are problems?"

That frown didn't escape Scott.

There was something there.

"Not giant problems. Let's say Jack doesn't always think in terms of his own best interest. Follows his instincts a little too much. Know what I mean?"

Eric's eyes narrowed. A shadow. Scott, seeing that, knew he was onto something.

"Back against the wall, Jack could be pressured into signing over his own lease." He gave Eric a long look. "There're things, lately."

Scott hated what he was doing. Not only for the doing of it, but for how it made him feel like some sort of class traitor. But betrayal had had a logic of its own, which didn't make it always wrong.

Jack had never offered much to Scott. So Scott didn't see where his guilt might lie. He felt an old, smoldering anger. The unsaid prejudice of Jack, and even sometimes of Ellen. And Scott could feel it was time to fight back a little.

No longer comfortable, Eric had to move to his desk and sit down. He was now deeply worried about what was taking place there in his office. Scott, he thought suddenly, might actually be much more clever than any of them had given him credit for.

Was he hinting? Talking tangentially, but with each word coming closer and closer to ... the thing? Did he know? How could he? And if he did, how could he possibly profit without getting himself into some seriously dangerous waters? Didn't he know how dangerous this could be?

Eric felt that worry grow deeper.

"You know, this sounds a lot like blackmail."

"Does, doesn't it ...."

"It doesn't bother you to insinuate you have something on Jack?" Or, he thought, someone else?

Eric eyed Scott as perhaps, by necessity, becoming a potential element in his plans—depending on what he really knew—or as a potential threat. Scott, evidently, had until then unknown talents, but it was also evident from Scott's tone of voice that he wasn't used to doing these things and didn't necessarily like it.

That's what differentiated Scott from people in the business world, Eric thought, where scruples were something no one could afford. In a sense, Eric had to admire—and could even regret to a certain extent not being in the position to possess, himself—Scott's ethics. But it wasn't clear those ethics would hold Scott back, either.

Scott was now, clearly, an unknown element.

What, exactly, did he know?

Scott might, if need be, be duped out of all this by pretending it was too seedy to be contemplated. However, the implied ability to use some sort of blackmail, and a lease leverage through Moore and the old woman, had some value. Because, shadows of a ruse or not, Eric knew he now had full commitment from Tom Hoaglund which meant that any new leverage on the Fairhaven Project, anything which could be used to speed things up, must be seriously considered. No matter who it came from.

As for the other possibility, only the next minute or so would tell him how dangerous Scott really was. Eric waited.

The implications hanging in the air.

## Chapter 97

SCOTT COULD feel both the worry, and—strangely enough—a tinge of fear, in Eric. That was normal. The man was beginning to think about exactly what Scott had alluded to, without having really alluded to it. But Scott didn't want it to go any further than that for the moment. The last thing he wanted out in the open right there and then was the sordid, lopsided love triangle in Fairhaven. Something only Catherine and Scott were fully aware of, with the difference that Catherine wasn't aware of Scott's knowing.

He took a quick survey of his motives.

No, he wasn't looking to blackmail anyone. Or at least, it didn't seem necessary yet. But he was hoping he now had Eric's full attention. He didn't like, of course, the implied criticism, but he could live with the implied understanding it stood upon.

"Well," Scott answered him at last, "the way I look at it, you save someone's ass, at the very least you don't expect them to give you a boot in yours. It's enough to make you a drinking man."

It was no answer to the question, but Eric suddenly felt, by the way all his anger seemed to be directed towards the Colbys, that there was a good possibility that Scott knew nothing about himself and Catherine. He decided he could still afford to be offensive.

"From what I gather, that may be one of the problems."

Scott nodded. So, it had in fact been discussed. Probably Jack.

"As far as I'm concerned," he said flatly, "that's always been a handy excuse for a lot of things. Maybe they don't like the way I looked in the morning. Maybe you don't. But what it comes down to is this: my work is excellent, and that is all that counts. I'm not going to stand here defending who or what I am to people who don't know one goddamn thing about me. Including you."

Eric said nothing, still wondering how much Scott really knew, but also approving of the direct accounting. Despite himself, he had always felt there was something admirable about Scott, the way he talked, the way he held himself, and his approach to life.

He could remember that lunch with all the workers down at Fairhaven, and how it had been Scott, not Jack, who had provided the most interesting directions in the conversation. A man who, one might think, could even be useful in some way.

But, he thought, for the moment, evidently a man with a grudge.

Eric didn't like grudges. They made for emotions; and emotions could get very messy indeed when business became involved.

"So," he said, "you've got something on Jack, from what you said."

"That's a cheesy way to put it."

Eric brushed it off. "I suppose you have proof."

Scott paused for a second. Being the sole witness, it was his word against Jack's. Then a thought occurred to him. Eric evidently didn't have the slightest idea. And maybe giving him the information wouldn't be a good move. But on the other hand, Scott couldn't imagine a better way to destabilize Sumners than to puncture his flattered sense of self-worth. He also noticed how Sumners was fishing to see if Scott's blackmail-tinged knowledge was limited to Jack. Scott felt he should skirt that a bit. It was too precise, and would create something that could be acted on. Scott didn't want Eric acting on anything, for the moment.

"Given the circumstances, if you'd been me, you'd have seen it for yourself. A question of perspective."

Eric at first had felt a faint stirring of confusion, a prickling sensation as though a storm was threatening, unseen, over the horizon. Then with a brilliant flash of realization, he knew.

There was no other possibility. There had been no reaction following his note. No telephone call, no letter. She was still out there, though, and he began to wonder what the final bill was to be.

He had harbored the hope it would be relatively light.

But no more. He knew that now.

It was all too deliberate. Where before it had seemed only an unfortunate and maladroit series of events, his affair with Catherine and then the offer of Party support, she had obviously been playing a double game.

But how deeply? Who was she in with? Besides Scott, that was.

Partly, he could be fascinated by the possibilities of what he might be confronted with. What was her plan? To get something on both Eric and Jack? For how much? For how long? Was she working alone, or did she have help? If she'd been working Eric, she'd no doubt been working Jack.

It was suddenly very interesting how she had shown up on the jobsite after the building had begun, after the Fairhaven Project had

485

been originally proposed, and plenty of time in advance of the Party's proposal.

He was stunned by the brilliance of it. An incredible scenario, perhaps, except that Eric had actually seen such things, been aware of such women, who hired themselves out for these sorts of circumstances.

Normally, though, the women were irresistibly beautiful. Their careers were established upon that condition.

Catherine, as attractive as she was, did not entirely fit the expectations one might have for one of those women. But who knew? She was intelligent, knew what money was worth, and had a hard-nosed business sense. Attributes that Hartman would recognize. It was all just possible then, depending on who she really was, and what she really wanted out of life. He was horrified by her possible motivations.

Love, he saw, was now dead and buried. Catherine, if that was her name, was a whole new proposition.

If she had only gone after one of them, the love game might have been just that. The first time you go hunting for love, you use a rifle. Love's idealism reduces not only the number of targets, but the manner of picking them off. Where there was more than one lover, though, there was only one possibility. After a while, after a lot of misses, you turn to a shotgun. Shoot any goddamn thing that moves. Idealism falls apart that way.

But where money is concerned, no one, ever, uses anything but a shotgun. Money works that way. You go for the widest spread and you don't care how messy it is. And there was no doubt: she was someone's ringer. Hartman's?

She'd be coming around.

"Okay," he said to Scott. "You have been more or less frank with me, and in return I can say I've found some of what you said very interesting. That's all I can say, for a variety of reasons, but none of which have much to do with you, personally."

"That's not saying a hell of a lot."

"What do you expect me to say?"

Scott looked down at his boots, thinking for half a second about what he'd just done. The limits he'd just crossed.

He'd shattered his own credibility for living and letting live. He'd shown himself as capable of dirty ambition as the next guy, if not more. Now he was in the position of having nothing, except a bad reputation if Sumners didn't want, or couldn't use, any of this.

"You understand where I might be in this?"

There was the slightest pause in Eric's mind where he could have very easily said, there was nothing farther to discuss. But with all that was swirling around in his thoughts, he couldn't do it. Scott was evidently of much more value. Just the way he was handling himself, showed that. Eric prided himself on his ability to find the very best people. His greatest talent. He needed to know more.

It felt almost like a formal moment of agreement, reminding him of the ceremonial feeling he had had with Colby the day he had given him that first check on account. So he stood up from his desk and looked at how Scott was eyeing him warily.

"Let's say, yes," he said. "Is that enough for you today?"

Strangely enough, Scott felt as though he had just been hired.

Or something.

Hired wasn't the word. It wasn't an employer-employee feeling. Something really else. He almost shuddered, it was such a strange situation.

It wasn't often, Scott reflected, that you could have the serious feeling you were making a mistake at the very moment you were doing it.

In a few weeks, the adventure would be over. Maybe it was best to leave it that way. But he couldn't help trying to hang on. All that money, all that power. And all Eric had to do was lift his little finger.

Or, in Scott's case, have it pried up.

And if it all worked out, Scott told himself, the only thing he'd have to do, was learn to live with himself.

He gave Sumners another long look. But instead of feeling the inner cringing he'd felt before, he only wondered at whether he'd have to apply more pressure.

And when.

He might have shuddered. But he didn't. Although that happened just a bit later, after their meeting came to a close. As he was going back out through the reception area, he saw Sumners' secretary, giving him a frosty goodbye, pick up the phone. And he heard her say:

"Yes, Mr. Hartman, he's just finished. I ring you through."

# Chapter 98

CATHERINE SPENT a few of the darkest hours she had ever known in her life in the silence of her apartment, then gave it up as a loss.

That things were a bad mess, there was no doubt. Ellen had been playing with her, knowing full well what had been going on.

It was an excruciating memory to recall a few of Ellen's remarks. And her own blithe ignorance which permitted several, now mortifying, comments.

That woman must have a heart of ice, she thought. How the hell could she have continued smiling and chatting with her at the office?

It was frightening. The sign of a truly vengeful nature.

God knew what Ellen might do, or be planning to do. Open confrontation would be bad enough. Catherine would be disgraced publicly, and fired. Beyond that, there didn't seem much more that Ellen could extract. Obviously she had regained her hold on Jack. One time it wouldn't have seemed like such a loss.

The time when Catherine had had Eric.

But that, now, was long gone as well.

Blindingly, it came to her. She knew what the initial revenge had consisted of. How could she have been so asinine?

Of course.

Ellen had somehow come to know about her and Eric. It could only be that. The timing fit perfectly. She'd simply ruined everything by letting him know Catherine was going to be shucked for having come anywhere near Jack.

No wonder Eric had been so swift, and the stony silence had fallen upon her like the utter midnight of a tomb.

No word, no call, beyond that stupid note.

She could imagine Eric's thoughts about her. And she couldn't help feeling embarrassed how the table had turned.

Where before, she had thought he was being a bastard, taking from her and then throwing her away. Or else a coward, frightened by how far things were going. Now, she imagined his chagrin at the thought of sharing her with Jack.

But she had cut things off with Jack!

That's what he couldn't know. Especially if the knowledge came from Ellen.

As she thought about it, the more she knew what she was going to have to do. She knew Eric loved her, and she loved Eric.

They were being forced apart by circumstances.

She knew they could see it through.

But she had to explain it all to him.

She couldn't go out to the house. She wouldn't even get in that gate. She couldn't talk to him in front of Deborah anyway.

Later, they would tell Deborah together, but at first it had to be just Eric and herself.

She got up from the couch, poured herself another scotch, and went to the kitchen bar and sat on a stool. It had been, what, five weeks? Amazing how fast time goes by when life is one frantic despondency. A swirl of desperation and pain which makes every second seem like eternity. But when you look back over it, the period seems as though it was only a day.

When time has been truly lost that way, she thought, and you suddenly realize what is happening, each moment you continue becomes a moment of pain.

She made up her mind, staring at the phone on the bar for a long moment, then took a long breath and dialed. It rang three times, and Deborah answered.

"Catherine? How are you?"

"I hope I'm not calling too late?"

"Is something the matter?"

It was definitely irregular for her to be calling that late, if ever, and she had to cover whatever surprise Deborah might have. She was sure Deborah didn't have suspicions. Naïve she came, naïve she would go, right until the day she got hit between the eyes with it.

"Nothing's the matter, I just needed to check one last thing with Eric for Monday. I would have let it go, but I'm thinking of going to Seattle tomorrow, so I won't be around until late and I thought I'd ask now."

She was sure that would get Eric to the phone, even if he didn't want to. He wouldn't be able to avoid it.

Deborah proved infuriating, though. "What is it?"

It was obvious she expected to relay the question to him. Catherine had to be very controlled. She couldn't say it was highly technical. Deborah knew enough now about boats.

Catherine's voice went soft. "Well, I guess someone had to spill the beans. I don't know any way around it. You would have found out anyway, there's no way to hide these things."

Deborah made an interested little sound.

"The fact is, the launching is very close now, you know?" Catherine let that hang in the air. Then let it hang in the air even longer.

Whatever it might imply, Deborah suddenly seemed to know.

"Oh!" There was a small laugh. "And this has something to do with me."

"You might say so."

A giggle and then a rapid sigh.

"Don't worry. You haven't spoiled anything."

"You said it, I didn't."

Another laugh.

"All right. I won't let on. I'll go get him." There was a merry sound in Deborah's voice now. "It's so rare that I can get a jump on him, that I think I'll do something to surprise him in the middle of his surprise for me. What do you think of that?"

"I think he'll love it."

"Yes. Anyway, as a matter of fact, I do have an enormous surprise for everyone. Oh, thank you Catherine for spilling the beans. Even if you haven't, not legally. Do you want me to go get him, I mean, are you in a rush?"

Evidently, with the flush of happiness, Deborah was in the mood for a chat, but Catherine almost panicked at the thought of another minute of her, not bothering to think for a second what Deborah's big surprise was, nor caring.

"Actually, I'm bushed. Yeah, go get him, please."

There was quite a long silence on the other end of the phone, enough so that Catherine knew Eric was having to be convinced. She knew the effect her call would have on him. She could be glad of the fact that when he did pick up the phone, Deborah would be nowhere near to listen. Of course, she would be careful to listen for any extension being picked up. But that wasn't much like Deborah's style.

# Chapter 99

"TWENTY YEARS ago," Eric's voice said directly in her ear, "I might have expected something like this. I thought we were adults."

She was startled by the hardness of his words, but she felt suddenly safe again, just hearing his voice.

"So did I, Eric. So did I."

There was a pause, and then a sigh.

"Okay. I guess I should have expected an explanation would be in order. It was just wishful thinking on my part to think that things like Fate or Destiny could be obvious to anyone."

"Fate?"

"It just caught up with us."

Catherine's feeling of security vanished at how firmly Eric's mind seemed to have been made up. That, and the fact he had done so without consulting her in the slightest, created a new wealth of bitterness for her.

"It did?"

"Yes."

As though that was that, she thought. Fate had caught up with them, and everything was settled. For the first time, ever, she was infuriated with him. "Which fate, Eric? Yours, mine or ours?"

The taunt was plain, and Eric didn't have to answer. He was also being careful, not knowing exactly who or what he was dealing with. But he knew the best thing, for the moment, was to treat things as if their banal, sordid reality was all there was to it. So, if that was the case, of course it was his fate involved. But that had always been a reasonably foreseeable outcome. She shouldn't have been surprised by it.

"I thought it was better this way. I was sure you would see that if something like this happened there was nothing either one of us could do about it." He was being very, very careful.

Catherine felt the bitterness creeping in.

"So, everything has to be considered a waste of time."

"No, I'll never consider it that. Nothing we do, if we do it with our full hearts, should be considered a waste of time. If circumstances had been different, who knows? But they didn't, and I'm stuck with it, and so are you."

It was obvious that Catherine, genuine or otherwise, would ask him to explain what had happened. That presented Eric with the pure dilemma of truth.

What, in fact, did the truth represent in this case, and what would be the outcome of revealing it? If she already knew everything, he would have to pretend he hadn't caught on to her, somehow convince her that he was as naïve and simple about the situation as he had thought she was. But if she was for real, that was another thing.

If he lied and said that he had simply refallen in love with his wife, Catherine's belief would be stretched to an extreme. Only the week before his note, his professions of love for Catherine had seemed unchanging. If he persisted, though, she would have to accept it. If she was real.

Nevertheless, her bitterness would be unbounded.

She would hate him for the very inconstancy that had brought him to her door, and would search for revenge in one way or another. Sure as night follows day.

If he openly acknowledged the truth, what could happen? If she was real she, for one, might understand the situation and would see how impossible it was to continue with her without her putting his entry in politics in total jeopardy. She might understand that, and see herself as a victim of a Fate larger than both of them. At that point, being angry, hurt and disappointed, two things could happen. She might cling, or might disappear.

To just walk away, though, would take an emotional stamina of superhuman strength. So the clinging was a more likely possibility, although to what level it was also hard to predict. She might try to make an arrangement. It seemed she was quite good at making arrangements. But ... if she was playing a double game?

How much time she would demand, though, he could no longer judge. He had considered her a strong, intelligent woman of character. But he had been wrong. Regardless of what she was, she was mostly just intelligent. That was, of course, if he was dealing with a genuine woman and not a ringer.

But regardless of who she was, he had to play out the only scenario he had for the moment. And within that, there was suddenly a third possibility, and that was for him to go on the offensive.

He could use a combination of lie and truth. Into it he could mix the catalyst of guilt.

The moment the thought occurred to him, he knew he had to do it, even if it was the dirtiest of dirty pool and, surprisingly, the next thing she said fell right into it.

"I would have thought," she said, "you would have told me if things had changed."

Eric nodded to himself. Anything she said, at this point, was an opening for him. To drop a hint that he maybe knew something ... even if he didn't know anything. Scott had been maddeningly vague.

"We might say that was a mutual feeling."

"When did I ever not discuss things with you?"

"Indeed, that seems to be the question."

"I've never lied to you, Eric."

This was his only chance, even though he knew he was only fishing at this point. "Strictly speaking, no."

"What do you mean?"

It was only a glimmer. That Jack was part of Scott's insinuations. But Scott had never said anything directly, had never confirmed it. But assumptions are sometimes as easily believed as convictions. And in this case, it didn't matter. He played the card, without knowing—only hoping, deeply and suddenly desperately—it was true. Everything, suddenly, hinged on that one fact.

"Meaning, unless I had directly asked you about yourself and Jack, you never had need to lie."

There it was, and as the statement exploded in Catherine's brain, Eric prepared to follow it up.

But ready as he was for a hurried denial, or counterattack—anything of a strong nature from her—he was flustered to realize that the whispered sounds coming over the telephone were of her crying softly.

Total, absolute, victory. He could have shouted with joy.

And she had surrendered that without a fight. Relieved beyond measure, Eric softened the tone of his voice, now calculating with a rapidity and clarity which was exceptional, even for him.

"But, listen," he said, "that is just part of the situation."

Catherine brought her crying to a stop with a sob, and then she took a breath. Evidently, it had only been recently that he had found out. Jack, probably, had been careless. The way he had been behaving must have caught Ellen's eye. What was bothersome was to think that Ellen might have told Eric directly.

But ... why?

For a second, confusion. But that was suddenly a minor point.

She did some quick calculations of her own. Her affair with Jack was obviously known. Her relations with Eric, she had believed were camouflaged. There was no good reason for anyone to think it necessary, or worthwhile, to mention anything to Eric about it. Her thoughts led her along those paths for a moment, unsure where she was going, and then suddenly a thought appeared that chilled her heart.

Unless it was Deborah.

Desperately, Catherine cast her mind back over the past few weeks. Not once had she noticed anything changed in Deborah Sumners' demeanor. But how well did she know Deborah? Always, there had been that angelic, slightly faraway quality about her. A Venusian surface of clouds hiding the true contours below them. It was the quiet ones who could pull the rug out from under you.

The girl seemed suddenly monstrous to Catherine.

Eric knew, and to deny it was impossible. Eric was not the sort of man whose world was influenced by rumors. If he had said as much, he then was absolutely sure. That led her, though, to ask the one thing she felt she could ask, and still maintain some sort of dignity.

"What did you do, put a private eye on me?"

Because the thought had never occurred to him, he didn't think over his response.

"No," he said, "of course not."

The moment the words left his mouth, he regretted them. It would have sewed things up neatly, if a little sordidly. Now, he had a prickly situation, uncontrollable, with other personalities brought into play.

She had intended to stop there, but her curiosity was too much in need. And dignity be damned.

"I know it's childish," she said. "But how did you find out."

"I said, it's not important anyway."

There was a desperate quality in his voice, and Catherine could only reach the conclusion that it was torturing him to even discuss it. Then she knew why that could be.

"So you saw it yourself?"

Eric didn't hesitate. "It was a pure accident."

Catherine, her wits having fled, would later realize she had missed one chance to claim innocence. After all, even the rape had been so calculated there had been no chance of them being caught. Eric would never have seen a kiss. But Catherine was too upset and just fed him what he needed instead. The fatal mistake which is always made, when there's no time to think.

"Eric, please, you have to believe me. Although I have seen Jack off and on, it is over. Jack was only because I needed someone. It was a long time before you came along. But what Jack did for me was just a thing at that time. Don't you see? I'm being completely honest with you. It didn't mean anything. I never considered it wrong, just as I never considered one single thing we ever did as wrong. That was the just problem though. When we first started seeing each other, although it was wonderful, I never really expected it to go anywhere and I guess I held on to what I had with Jack as well."

She knew she was rambling. But she couldn't stop herself:

"But, really, when we became more serious, I then made every effort to break things off with Jack. The problem was just that Jack got more attached than I thought he would. You can't help these things, Eric. But now, definitely, it is over. It's totally over. There has been nothing between me and him. Only you and me. There was never anything there. I suppose, though, with Jack being so insistent, you were bound to see him one day if you passed by the house."

And there, a great weight lifted from Eric's shoulders.

He knew.

He was free of it.

If it had come at him in any other way than this outpouring of guilt, he would have known he was trapped.

The slightest hint of blackmail, of threat, he would have been utterly ruined.

But here, only tears. It was like opening a new chapter, fresh, and very nearly absolved.

It took all of several seconds to finally dawn on him how fully he had escaped disaster.

## Chapter 100

THERE WAS no deeper plan, no conspiracy, no entangled mesh. Eric could have laughed.

Maybe, far down in the future when he had real power in his hands, such things could happen. But he'd only been dreaming the paranoid dreams of a neophyte politician.

Putting the cart before the horse.

Except for an assuaged masculine pride, Eric had been listening with an increasing sense of disinterest. None of it mattered. The argument, since it could change nothing, was rendered moot and reduced to being just the sordid pleadings of a woman trying to explain away a very banal situation.

Her last statement, though, was useful. It let him off the hook, and it quieted his fears that Hartman had somehow been involved. In fact, he felt suddenly free, light and unhampered by the possibility of some sort of plot growing up around him.

For all he knew and cared, she and Jack had been going at it in the woods. Now, at least, he could claim that he had seen them in a proven location.

"Yes," he lied without the slightest feeling of guilt. "As a matter of fact, the most shocking thing about it was that if I had come by five minutes later, I would have been ringing your doorbell. I know we had made a pact not to see each other without warning, but that particular day I had just forgotten everything."

Catherine, her mind caught on the image of Jack in her bed with Eric at the door, lost any further questions.

"It was over at that point, Eric. It was absolutely over. I didn't feel anything for him anymore. I never, did. You have to believe it." Her lie was guiltless as well, with the difference being that, at that moment, she was willing to believe it was true.

Eric looked at his watch. Even with serious business partners his calls rarely lasted very long. For him to go on talking very much longer with her, would appear strange to his wife.

Deborah, he realized, knew nothing. But if there was one thing Eric had learned it was that the most dangerous moment for truth to get out, was exactly at the time when everything appeared safe again. There was a flux in events where you felt relieved, and the mind, relaxing from tensions submitted to, became less keen. A little slip now and God knew what might happen.

"I told you, it doesn't matter. The fact is, Catherine, other things have been happening and you might as well know there is nothing now I can do about it." He made his voice firm. "Absolutely nothing."

Catherine was openly crying again. "What?" was all she could say.

"I can't go into it. We've been talking too long as it is."

Eric no longer cared. The thing he had been listening for from the beginning, blackmail, had not appeared, and he knew that her double-dealing had been on a pathetic, personal level. She had not even had the sense to use what she had against him. He felt no fear now. Only aversion.

"When can you talk to me then?"

Eric almost sighed with impatience. So in the end it was to be the clinging. Not only was he going to have to dislike her for the trickery, which he had avoided becoming ensnared in, but now for her lack of control. He saw, though, that he now could forget about the problem for the time being. A permanent fix to the question could be dealt with at a later time.

And then a thought.

Maybe he should indeed maintain contact. He just couldn't quit thinking about that stupid, stupid letter. If he could only get it back somehow. His mind gave a lurch. He might even have to ….

"I'll give you a call later," he said. "When I can talk. All right?"

Catherine, although deeply upset, was also too experienced to take that sort of statement without a binding promise attached.

"When?"

"Next week."

"That is way too far away."

"Ok. I can't talk to you this weekend. So I'll call Monday. Now really, Catherine, I simply have to go."

The phone clicked in her ear, and Catherine was left alone.

That it was all over, finished and over for her and Eric, was clear. There had been no response to her explanations about Jack. What was also very clear was that something else was involved. Catherine felt she had a right to understand. And she would. She was determined she would.

It seemed possible Deborah still had something to do with it. Deborah, the little princess, whose boat launching, joyful and merry as it would be, was now a week or so away, incredible as it seemed. Once that happened, once that *Muse* was in the water, Deborah could just sail away with Eric forever. Sail right out of all their lives as if they had never come.

That fucking boat, Catherine thought. If there was a God in Heaven, that wooden whore of luxury, of pleasure and pride, of Deborah's goddamn transcendental beauty and art, would sink straight to the bottom of Bellingham Bay the moment it dropped off the ends of the skids.

That, indeed, would be something of universal relevance for mankind.

*

He'd grown used to discussing things with her, or at least he felt he was—and wasn't just using her as a wall for bouncing off thoughts and opinions. Naturally, he knew more about the ins and outs of things like boatbuilding, employers, clients, and contracts, than she did. Which naturally led to the feeling that all that extended somehow to knowing more about life, as well. Sydney had been patient with all that, and then decided it was time to not be.

He'd been going on about it, as usual, relativizing and balancing, analyzing and commenting, sitting there on the sofa with her sitting there listening to him from the armchair. The late afternoon sun was streaming in through the front windows from out over the bay, and her hair was all lit up and golden and even as he talked he was thinking somewhere else how beautiful she was.

Somehow, he'd gotten onto Jack Colby again. The usual stuff. But this time, when he paused, he didn't get from her the noncommittal shrug which showed that while she didn't really care, she did understand. This time, she actually sort of lifted her hand, and then out it came. Sydney never minced words.

"You know," she said. "Sometimes you should listen to yourself because most of the time … well, OK … but sometimes it's just, hey, you know? Petty?"

No word with her southern accent could have sounded worse.

He looked at her, and she looked back, and she kept looking at him looking at her for a long time until she saw he wasn't looking at her anymore and she got up to make some tea.

## Chapter 101

Relief wasn't the word for it. Not that Eric would have hesitated for a moment carrying out the risky and expensive solution he'd considered, if needed. But, letter aside, with Catherine's call he now knew the way was clear for him on all accounts. Or … almost. He'd have to get a full statement from Scott about whatever it was he knew. But that was a minor thing, he was sure.

He had Hartman caught up in his own time-table snare. Before, there had been an obvious snare, almost entrapment, caused by his wife's involvement with the boat, and the Colbys; something he was now sure Hartman had not only known about but had been gambling on. But Eric was now free of it. He could let things take their natural course.

It had been awfully close. He had come near to making a decision which would have been as large a crisis for his marriage as he could have managed to provoke. And not the one Catherine had almost been a part of, but one where he would have had to abandon the boat to the fates. He had almost sent in a crane and bulldozer to drag the *Muse* out of the shed. Close as she was to completion, he knew the moving would have tied his hands too much. Six million dollars' worth of boat anchoring him down just at the moment he needed pure freedom.

Business freedom.

And it would, indeed, have been strictly a business decision then. Six million, of course, was nothing to sneeze at, but in comparison with the sheer profit on the Fairhaven Project, he would not even have blinked at the idea of possibly wrecking her. It.

Within his grasp was the single, largest project of his career. A project which was about to make him one of the richest men, cash liquid, in the State of Washington, and a Senator to boot.

Deborah notwithstanding, there was no choice involved. Perhaps they would have figured something else out. Perhaps there would have been a way to save the boat. But that couldn't enter into the considerations.

But now, all those worries were moot. He had all the leases, or knew how to get them. Clyde Moore and Scott aside. Mrs. Wilson, it turned out, was capable of falling in love even with Newell Briggs. Eric had to smile at that, picturing Briggs having to sweet-talk the old lady. But then, Briggs was as good as they came. It probably hadn't taken much effort.

In any case, Eric now not only had all the cards but owned the casino as well. Time, that most dreaded of all his opponents, no longer mattered. He'd screwed not only everybody, literally and figuratively—he could allow himself that vulgar joke—but Time as well.

Eric allowed himself a big grin. A celebratory one. There would be more than just a wooden boat to launch in the days to come.

An image appeared of himself and Deborah sailing photogenically around out in the waters of his home state. An attractive picture ... sort of Kennedy-esque. Hoaglund said the public loved that sort of thing.

Youth, wealth, beauty, power, happiness.

Nothing was wrong with the picture.

He smiled. He could see he would have to learn to be able to steer that goddamn boat himself. Wouldn't do to have his own craft helmed by a crewman.

He had even thought up a better name for her. The *Swift Knot*.

Deborah, he knew, wouldn't mind that last little detail at all.

It was the thought that counts.

# Chapter 102

To have fallen flat on her face was one thing, but to have it generalized knowledge was another. Some people can manage to avoid feeling ashamed when they are alone. But with an audience, pride can find no shelter.

She called Jack the next morning.

Purposeful as she had felt while dialing his number, her mind went blank when he picked up the receiver.

Too many things to say. The silence over the wire was motionless, devoid of contact. Then Jack's voice came out to her.

"What do you want this time?"

"Okay," she said, as though continuing a conversation that had been unrolling for the last hour. "Look, the way things are, just don't tell Ellen that I know she knows."

Jack was barely awake with his first cup of coffee. He shot a glance towards the living room but Ellen was still back in the bedroom with the door shut.

"We don't say a word about it anymore," he said. "We didn't really say much in the first place and that got said pretty fast. Unless something really big comes up, we'll probably never talk about it again."

Catherine nodded to herself. Of course, given everything, it was a ridiculous point to cling to. Somehow, though, she could put up with the sham of pretending she was unaware of Ellen's knowledge. Having had a secret knowledge over Ellen for so long had made it intolerable now to be so naked. Wrapping herself in layers of awareness helped her feel clothed once more.

Better than having to deal with open understanding, in this case. Because there was nothing at all to win back, least of all her pride.

It was a small thing, but her defenses weren't that good, and whatever crumbling efforts she had at her disposal to maintain any sort of dignity at all, she had to take.

Otherwise ....

Well, she couldn't think about the otherwise.

"I'll be leaving very soon."

For some reason, it was important to hear his response to that statement. It mattered little what the response was. But, being that it was her life, she needed a feeling her existence was still something people reacted to.

Otherwise …

Otherwise, she was as good as cast loose and floating away from the world, so much undesired material heaved overboard to lighten everybody's load.

"If you stay to the end, we can still use your help, of course. But that won't be very long now. Just to finalize the orders for the masts and sails and navigational equipment. After that, it's Sumners' baby."

Jack would have infinitely preferred her to go, never to be seen again. He knew he should simply tell her the truth of what he thought was best, that she should not come down anymore. In fact, it would be a real kindness, instead of the soft-toned treatment he was handing her, given what Ellen had in store for her after the launching.

But complications being what they were and always carrying complications of their own, it was somehow better she still came down. For one thing it hid from Ellen's wrath, in so doing, that there were further conversations and understandings going on. And for another, it just felt easier to continue with patterns already set.

Just barely, he had an inkling how this last was his fatal weakness. That he could not cut himself away from the mistakes of his past. That he had a deep inability to take responsibility for them and continued to return to older grounds and patterns in hopes of annulling, somehow, whatever he had done.

Catherine, at his words, waved her hand in a vague motion there in her apartment, as though Jack were there to see it. But whether the movement signified resignation or despair, she was unconscious of it. She said she would see on Monday and hung up.

But if it was an unpleasant prospect, fraught with anxiety and dread, her mind was made up. She would handle it.

She could imagine it already: showing up early for work, as usual, setting down at her now well-loved desk, her post of action, and having to pick her way consciously around the minefields in Ellen's eyes.

She imagined trying to talk, occasionally looking into those eyes and having them look back.

She could handle it, and would. Because she had to.

Not for any other reason would she go down there.

Simply enough, getting through one more week down there, forcing herself to get through it, was practically synonymous with getting through the rest of her life.

# Chapter 103

APPLYING THE finish to the wood inside the boat was a long process and Scott felt as though he was being slowly poisoned. He wanted to have as many as seven very thin applications of clearcoating, hand rubbed in between, on all the inside wood.

Even with fans moving warm air around, the varnish fumes became unbearable down inside the cabins. Every hour or so he would have to get out to the parking lot and gulp down some fresh air, drizzle or downpour notwithstanding.

While Scott was alternatively turning blue or getting rained upon, Jack and the apprentices were painting the huge hull. After having sanded smooth the hull planking and painted below waterline with a blood-red anti-corrosion product, they'd applied to the upper planks a couple of thin undercoats, letting a dark gray sink deeply into the wood. Then they'd started in, spraying over all that the marine paint.

The boat would be a glossy black with a white line at the waterline to separate from the brick red bottom. The coats went on even and thin and within days the hull took on a mirror-like surface like polished, unbanded onyx. Even below waterline it shined with the slippery anti-fouling paint.

As that process neared completion, one of the apprentices began applying clearcoating to the cabin sides and hatches and the wood trim running around the deck.

The *Muse* was almost finished. The masts and sails, built by another company under William Fletcher's supervision, were to be delivered after the launch. As far as things looked, she would be lifted, have her keel fixed on and her rudder hung, and be in the water within ten days, ready for having her engines tested.

Nobody was rushing and when Jack and the apprentices were working with care on her final topcoating, Scott was carefully going over last details. He installed brass doorknobs and coathooks, and Deborah's cherished lighting fixtures, he set up the plumbing in the galley and in the heads, he prepared the navigation station for the expensive equipment to be fit in after the launch, he got the cabin furniture and the custom-made mattresses for the bunks put in, and even hung Deborah's carefully selected curtains on brass rods around cabin ports and windows, those curtains matching the cloth of sofas and chairs already bolted down in place.

There suddenly seemed a lot to do and all during that time, because she had absolutely nothing to do herself, Catherine had taken to climbing inside the boat to watch Scott puttering around.

She sat on one of the cabin sofas. They would talk if he was doing work nearby, but mostly she was alone in there. Nobody would come around. Deborah was rarely there, even though each final detail was a result of months of carefully developed work … the final sheen on perfection. Or, as Scott said, the final sheen of perspiration.

Eric never came down anymore. But everyone knew the Sumners had spent a night or two inside the boat after Scott had got the master bedroom set up. Evidently that was one of Deborah's ideas. Something about living within the final developments of perfection.

Not surprisingly, at least to Scott, neither Jack nor Ellen would come in with Catherine in there. Both, for their own reasons, were secretly astounded to see her show up at all. The fact that she spent almost none of her time at her desk brought no remarks from anyone. Nobody cared. So she would sit in the cabin, safe from all company, all remarks and looks, compiling a big, loose-leaf binder of the record of material ordered. A diary of what was to be ordered at any stage of the building and of where things were to be found at the best prices and quality. It was the last thing she could do. The Colby's were planning to build another big ketch, and with the diary Ellen could easily handle all the office work.

Catherine wasn't as depressed to be down there as she had imagined, but there was no doubt she was in the deepest pit of whatever her life had in store for her. When she wasn't at work, she slept. An embracement of a small sort of death, and within that, a deathly dignity.

It was amazing, in a sense, how you could survive anything by sleeping.

During the day, diminished in her own eyes as she was, she was too small to even contemplate suicide. No one, she was now sure, would think the better of her. No one would be likely to feel any return of respect for her, or even pity her for that matter. She would simply disappear.

She sat numbly in that shining, beautiful boat which was so near its launching, so near to being sailed, like her dreams, away forever. She saw how everyone else was scurrying to the final moment of completion. As if the tide was coming in and they could not wait a minute too long.

To get done.

To get on now to other things. Other boats, or lives.

Of course it was natural for all of them to feel that way, to be looking forward to their futures. For herself, painful as it was, she could have wished to slow things, if not bring them to a stop. Just one last time returning to those glorious earlier days when the beginning had drifted away into forgetfulness and there was no end in sight. Just day after wonderful day of creation and hope, happily blind to the rest of the world.

She had been so contented.

Now she could barely remember her place in the building of that boat, to see her contribution to any of it. That, perhaps, was the most horrible thing at all.

She sat in there with Scott, the neutrality of Scott moving slowly across the empty landscape of her stricken existence. And she found she needed that presence.

He wasn't involved. He had nothing to do with any of it, and especially not her. Where she was concerned, Scott neither hated nor loved her. To him, she was just what she had been before. Unchanged and unsullied by anything else. Very nearly, she almost needed that. One person who felt nothing at all about her beyond what she had contributed.

That was all. She needed his presence. His soul was not part of the landscape. Only his shadow mattered, an unknowing, unseeing shadow. He knew nothing, had never known anything. She had never realized she could feel so attracted to the quiet boatbuilder, watching him and almost yearning, in a way, for the peaceful ignorance he represented.

## Chapter 104

PEOPLE WERE bouncing off each other as though they'd suddenly become hard rubber balls. Scott could tell that if people's lives hadn't necessarily caught up with them, the truth—or certain parts of it—was out, somewhere. He had seen it, and knew.

Scott couldn't spare many sorrows for them if only because his own life seemed to be coming together. Suddenly, he was doing something he'd never done before: planning a future.

It was a question of the elements.

He knew he didn't have enough of them lined up to be fully ready to strike out on his own yet. He still needed Colby Boatworks all the more right then. To see him through.

Just a little more time, he thought, and a little patience, and he could finally make it work for himself. He was sure of it. Confident and sure. But where he now was confident, conscious and aware, he was also on his guard. Things were just too strained, and strange.

An earlier version of Scott might have felt amused by that, or even flirted with a smug contentment. But no more. Somehow, the proximity of human disaster and emotional suffering removed any temptation towards jealousy, even if he had little empathy to share.

Formerly, he would have loved to have done so, dipping into bottomless wells of rancid bitterness. But he couldn't anymore.

His visit to Sumners' office had cured him of the illusion he was above temptation. He could also see in a clear eye that not even Jack was completely at fault. At least, not in some huge, and hugely evil way. All the small steps leading up to big disasters could be explained, if not excused. Rarely was there ever one monstrous mistake, one absolutely malignant failure to distinguish between right and wrong. If that was so, very little would go wrong except in the hands of truly wicked people. It was more a matter of momentum, the inability to recognize all the possibilities, good or bad. Of where things could lead. And in this case, the question of where the sentiments could lead. Scott had got past his anger at how Jack had jeopardized so many things, and got past something much less worthy: that lurking desire and attraction he'd felt for

Ellen and that nasty form of jealousy he'd felt to think Jack not only had her, but a mistress as well. Scott couldn't claim any higher ground for himself anymore. But at the same time he knew that Jack and Catherine could and should have recognized the momentum of the mistake they were making, and of the inevitability of disaster. But they hadn't. From whatever Scott could make of it, they had tried to believe they could make a decision and then expect that ensuing events would never evolve beyond their original, pure vision.

A pure vision … of what they could get away with.

Pure visions based on lies and deception, though, either had to remain beyond anyone's grasp, or they had to have a very short life span. It was a hell of a nasty truth, and just the thought of it—mingled with the scheming he himself had been considering lately—stopped Scott cold. He stood up and nearly shuddered, and was suddenly glad for how he was working in the engine compartment, putting in light fixtures, out of sight of Catherine up in the main cabin with her loose-leaf notebook.

People fooled themselves so easily, he thought. It was always so easy and pleasant to think how so much could be spared by simply not acting on impulses. But living is done day-to-day. And hasty, unthinking and reckless hope—sadly enough the greatest enemy of common sense—arises as surely as the sun.

He didn't know how far things went. But it wasn't just Jack and Catherine who were so obviously ignoring each other. He could see something in Ellen as well, and how she and Catherine, formerly so friendly, didn't make much of anything for company anymore.

A pretty bad, pretty original situation, made even more so by how Jack wasn't stalking around in resentment for the way things had gone. Meaning that, this time, things were so truly bad that Jack had no one to point a finger at. That seemed clear enough. What Scott couldn't figure out, though, if everything was out in the open, was why and how Catherine was still around.

Of all the badly concealed pain floating around down there, Catherine's was obviously the most vulnerable and least treatable one, and for a simple reason. Regardless of anything else, any other consideration, she was the only one who had no choices left.

But worse, she hadn't realized it. Until finally and completely, every hope she might look for or cling to, had gotten smashed.

# Chapter 105

IT HAD been the day before. Scott had been working in the main cabin installing curtains and small reading lights. Catherine had helped him a bit. She had been wearing a soft, light wool skirt with a matching vest over a rather frilly blouse. And Scott, despite the discomfort of having her forcibly cheerful desperation following him around, had been admiring her figure beneath the clinging fabrics. It was more a fall or winter thing to wear, but with the weather being cool it had seemed practical enough.

They had been talking about nothing in particular—just the things they had always found mutually interesting enough to be at ease with—when Scott had seen a small, mortified glimmer peeking up shyly from deep within Catherine's heart.

Her daily share of hope, to be fondled or battered.

Under normal circumstances, he would have ignored it. But it was the externalization of a kind of hope that he could no longer deal with, knowing what he knew and understanding the state she was in. To be in the raw presence of her pain and hope, and her complete ignorance of his knowledge, was as though watching someone blind and deaf undress. Even she could see he was affected, although she couldn't know why. And it was enough to make her bolder than she felt.

"So," she had said, the subject making her voice quiver. "How are things with Sydney?"

Scott held up the brass mount for the curtain rod and made a couple of marks with a nail.

He couldn't help smile, feeling something of déjà vu in the question, and circumstances, which wasn't unlike another time earlier in the spring when she'd done this. Except for, this time, there was something somewhat different in the atmosphere. Something clanging at a much deeper level.

"Oh, you know. Sydney's Sydney, and I'm me."

Catherine laughed, a little loudly. "You really like her, huh?"

"Sure."

She flipped the curtain on another window, casually, as though to see the effect. She peered closely at the pattern on the cloth.

"Do you love her?"

Scott lined up his hand drill. He began turning the wheel. At first, he took in a long, slow breath and very nearly said what most people would have said to such a question, but then just let it out in a silent sigh.

"I don't know what to call it. But I suppose, eventually, that's what it will look like."

"But not now?"

"I don't know. Do I have to know, now?"

She laughed in a small way. "That's strange, don't you think?"

"Think so?"

"Sort of. It doesn't sound awfully clear."

"It isn't. You think it should always be clear?"

Catherine slid her hand slowly along a brass curtain rod, her fingers gently pushing the brass curtain rings along it. She tilted her head to one side.

"Well, I think people can feel things about others, and it's usually right from the start. I mean," she gave the curtain another little swish, "from the time they really start thinking about each other. Being aware of each other. Then, from that moment, they both know there's something there that doesn't exist in their feelings about anyone else."

She gave him a sharp glance, but he said nothing. Watching him seeming to be trying to be all manly and stoic about feelings and whatnot, she gave out that musical laugh of hers which went down into a wonderful deep throatiness, and then went on:

"It's funny, you know, because sometimes they didn't even know they really felt that way before. I know people who worked with each other for years, and then one day they just all of a sudden realize ...," she broke off.

Scott was staring at the holes he'd bored in a way that told her he knew, completely, what she was alluding to as if she'd thought quite a bit about it. To be honest, she hadn't really been thinking about such a thing, herself, until she'd begun speaking. But now ....

An incredible idea. But just possible.

For a moment Catherine was afraid he was going to say something. She wasn't ready for that yet. In truth, the idea had caught her by surprise, as well. And if she was going to go with the idea—and she wasn't against the idea, suddenly—she nevertheless knew she had to continue to prepare the terrain.

She needed time. Time!

If only time could stand still. Locking them there, unmoving, letting one moment slide into another as the logic and sense of the universe filled in the pieces.

But then Scott, who had indeed seemed momentarily frozen in place, moved, putting the mount up to the holes and fingering the screws into place, bringing up his screwdriver to turn them in. Each action effacing the one before and layering over, successively, that previous moment in time, so fraught with sudden awareness and import.

But hope for Catherine, had now returned in full bloom, and was not to be denied.

She sighed, now completely conscious of what she was thinking, and doing. It was an almost perfect fix. And she could, in a flash, imagine all of it, from beginning to end. She could see each and every one of its ramifications, and the incredible intricacy and elegance of it, as a solution. And ... she could imagine the shock of it. The sublime, delicious and superbly satisfying shock of it.

Besides, she thought suddenly, putting into outright words what had previously been unthinkable, he really was an attractive man.

She took a breath, and let her voice have its most vibrant quality.

"That's the way I think it can be, don't you?"

Scott turned his head to look at her. Regardless of how he knew where all of this was coming from, he deeply resented how it made him feel like bargain basement goods. But at the same time he found himself thinking, coldly, something along the lines of how on a day to day level, life's infinite possibilities are often carefully, or unconsciously, ignored. And how, in general, most people take as great comfort that the wild relativity of the universe stays firmly shoved into the shadows. Until they're desperate, and desperate hope lunges out at how opportunity—and people's lives—could be altered forever in a fleeting second. With no more than a simple nod of the head, their whole world could be spun around.

It was an interesting idea, and it was somewhat comforting to know such things could happen. But only that. Because no amount of time, whether fleeting or long, would have changed how, as far as she was concerned, he was not only determinedly, but categorically and positively, uninterested. And for just about any or every reason he could be uninterested not only in a particular woman, but in a person. He could put up with her in the regular social way, and even feel sorry for her, but beyond that was utter antipathy. He just disliked her as deeply as he had disliked anyone.

And, in the blink of an eye, that passed to Catherine.

The cordially neutral, but brutally honest look on his face was worse than passions consuming themselves to ashes. His obvious, total disdain like an immense black void more terrible than loneliness or death could ever be, echoing dully: no, and no, and no again. Which, in that instant of time it took to fully form in her consciousness, rose finally to a resounding shriek.

No. No!

Stunned, she could barely handle how, in a second, it was as if they had lived their lives out together, had passed a thousand years in each other's presence.

And it was no more. Finished.

Like everything else.

Her senses returned to her and she turned and walked away. As she'd walked away the other time. But this time, with a sense of finality which was becoming all too familiar to her these days.

Scott watched her go, knew she knew he was watching her go, and he could feel how there was no doubt that there had been yet another failure of some sort down there at the Colby's. Whether it was tragic or comic was only a question of point of view.

But tragedy or comedy, depending on the season, at least for this last one, left him unmoved. One wave, one tide too many of too many waves and too many tides, had finally left him washed up on this particular beach where he was determined to remain. His ability to be worried by or about the fate of those who were not worried by or about him, was something he could now find the ability to abandon.

All he wanted to make now—outside of his little personal project which involved some knowledge he shared with Micky and Clyde and sweet little old Mrs. Wilson—was boats, a little music, something with Sydney, and a daily effort to find ways to like himself.

That last had always been a challenge, and even more so lately, considering that crassly ignoble conversation with Sumners. But he had to try. It was the best that anyone could do for themselves, and for everyone else. And it was interesting, he thought as he watched Catherine finally slip out of sight, that sometimes some of the best things we learn about life come from people who haven't the slightest clue.

# Chapter 106

FEW THINGS end the way they begin. That is to say, few things end the way they were expected to end at the beginning of everything. Down at the boatyard, people were actually getting celebratory with the work all but finished, and were surprisingly beginning to slack off a bit from the previous, unbearable tensions. The end of everything, had that effect; it wasn't a question of forgetting about everything, but just having done with it.

Catherine found herself alone at the office well past quitting time. Jack and Ellen had gone up to visit some friends in Vancouver. Scott was off at a bar somewhere getting set up to play with a local band.

She straightened the desk, perhaps for the last time, and looked around. Things were over. The orders diary was finished and she put it in the filing cabinet. She was feeling tired, and it was late. She got her coat and went out, locking up the office, and starting towards her car. But suddenly she couldn't leave.

Her hesitation fluttered. It was just a Friday night, foggy and wet outside. But she was alone, and that made the difference. Very possibly it was going to be the last time she was alone down there like that. Her feelings resolved themselves, and she went over to the shop and let herself in.

It couldn't have been darker inside. No streetlights, no houselights or glow of the town could make its way in there through the deep fog moving in from the sea. Almost freezing. A little sea weather slipping down from the Bay of Alaska. Even in summer, you had to expect that occasionally. But, God, was it cold.

Catherine went over and turned on one of the rocket heaters. It clicked to life with a loud, whooshing sound, and began blowing, cannon-like, a column of air in through a gap in the canvas tent over the boat. She stood by it until she could feel the steady blast begin to slowly warm. Soon, whatever it was inside the propulsion unit that heated the air would be red hot and the air inside the big canvas awnings strung along and up over the huge hull would begin to circulate in boilings and turbulences and little whirlpools, a tidal race of currents ever warming from the steady blast.

Catherine could already feel how much warmer it was right there at that end of the covering and she went inside the canvas, losing now any glint of light and everything now was black blindness.

With one hand against the boat's side and one hand out to block in front of her, she made her way past the shoring timbers down to the ladder propped alongside.

She climbed up in the dark, visualizing what was there beneath her hands and feet. She made it over the top of the ladder then and stood on the deck.

The *Muse* was so big and strong, so solid feeling there beneath Catherine. She stooped over for a moment to run her hand over the strips of teak decking invisible in the dark. The teak was smooth and clean, but somehow gritty feeling, and she could smell its fresh, untreated scent even over the various smells of curing paints and varnishes.

A small, rolling wave of heated air came down the deck and Catherine went warm and cold with it as it passed.

She waited. Then another came. Soon, the air in between the waves was warmer too, and as it became comfortable she slipped over to the main cabin door and stepped down the stairs inside.

It was a little warmer inside, the working temperature not yet dispersed from the well-insulated hull.

Scott had installed some of the batteries and the ship-to-shore electrical connections. A big power cable up forward hooked up the boat to the shop's system. She stepped over to where a small light was attached to a bulkhead and turned its adjustable knob.

She kept the light dim. Just enough to see the space. Near the lamp, in the dusky yellow and orange of the low-level light, the satiny deep reds and browns of the mahogany and oak joinery work shined in a heavy, rich-grained way. Farther away from the light those woods went darker, becoming black corners of invisibility and pockets of dense shadows, denser than the shadows of sunlight could ever hope to be.

The cabin was finished. It was no longer a space, but a home. The curtains hung neatly at the brass lined windows and portholes. Deck beams above stood out dark and gleaming from the cream-enameled ceiling planking. The floor of laid oak had a large Persian rug of burgundy and blue fixed in place. Spread around the rug were the soft sofas and chairs, and there were end tables and a large coffee table with raised edges. Bookshelves and settees ran along the sides of the cabin and at one end there was a bar with all its bottles and glassware. Only small details were missing.

The bookshelves were still empty. Spaces for paintings and prints hadn't been filled. Deborah's precious art had not been installed yet to compete with the boatbuilders' art. But for the most part the yacht was already as much like a home as could be expected.

Catherine looked behind the bar. She opened a small fridge and got out an ice cube tray, dropping a few into a wide, cut crystal glass, and poured herself a generous portion of very old scotch.

That the bar was stocked was no surprise. They had all taken to toasting each night, a minor celebration of each final day. Even herself. Even with Ellen, who seemed the most celebratory about how everything was soon to be over.

Catherine didn't dwell on the reasons for that. The same way she tried not to dwell on too many other things.

She took her glass and went to the stairs going down to the sleeping compartments and there wandered along the corridor. She went into the galley. The oven and stove weren't in yet, but the big enameled sink was installed, and the counters were tiled up with dark blue ceramics of fading and deepening colors, the dark shifting depths of the sea.

It was a big workplace and there would be, she'd been told, a microwave and a grill there as well. All the modern conveniences. She opened a few cupboards, the solid oak doors resisting slightly with their self-closing mechanisms. She looked in drawers and other compartments, all with their own self-locking tricks. But everything was empty, if clean and dust free. Like a brand-new house.

The navigation station down the corridor was the most unfinished place in the boat. The desk was there, and the swiveling captain's chair. But the big square slots for the navigation equipment gaped empty. All of that had yet to be set up by the electronics company, and all of that would wait until after the launching when the masts would be stepped and could carry the radars and radio aerials.

Catherine went on deeper into the boat, switching on lights in cabins or along the corridor as she passed along. The cabins were ready. The bunks had their mattresses. There were now even the sheets and blankets and pillows upon them like a small hotel.

Deborah had been doing that. In the toilets—you couldn't call them heads so little they resembled that marine function—creamy soap sat on soap trays and thick bath towels hung from rings next to the mirrors. In the forward, main shower, there were frosted shower doors, the high quality plexiglass whorled and flowered in an etched design of a seascape.

Catherine went all the way forward to the big cabin up in the bow and she went around the double bed to the very end and unlatched the door there, looking into the sail locker with its access hatch and ladder from up above.

In the center of the locker stood a deep, heavily timbered well where the anchor chain would settle itself. She went in, walking around the chain well, up past where the sails would be bundled, all the way up to the bow where she put her hand out and felt the big stem timber curving out in the darkness away from her.

It was varnished and felt glassy and she rested there, feeling how immense and strong that piece of oak was. If a piece of wood could be lucky, she thought, it was certainly this one. But then she took her hand away, somewhat frightened by a sadness just lurking over the horizon of her thoughts.

A momentary, constricting panic.

No, no, she thought. Don't.

As though running away, she quickly turned and went out and back down the corridor to the main cabin to fix herself another drink, calming herself. Then she went across the cabin and went down another set of stairs to the back passageway.

She had made up her mind. This was going to be the last time she would look at the boat. Not wait a week for the launching. She would tell them Monday. That would be no problem. She knew nobody would mind.

She wasn't sure about Bellingham anymore, but that was a question for another day. She needed to quit the boatyard first and then go from there.

It was too bad. Too, too bad. It had been so beautiful. And this, this was beautiful. She passed her hand over the gorgeously rich paneling of the corridor. She certainly had loved being around the building of this boat. Loved that it could exist. It was a shame to leave when you could love something so simply.

A sudden wave of nausea passed through her. It was a shame to love something that you also hated.

Hated to death.

She paused there in the passageway, leaning against the paneling. Stopped by a horrifying thought.

# Chapter 107

Bᴜᴛ, ɴᴏ, she thought.

Not that.

She mustn't ever think such things. The *Muse* had nothing to do with it.

She went on into the main sleeping cabin and flicked on the light. There wasn't much to see there. It was large and it was for the Sumners. It would be a comfortable bedroom even in a house.

The centerpiece was their custom-made bed complete with box spring and mattress. A couple of overstuffed chairs and a rug completed the furniture. There were no personal details yet on the bulkheads or shelves. But when she opened a closet, she suffered a small shock at finding herself confronted by suits and dresses. It was then that she realized that Scott had long finished working on that space and it was now, slowly, being built up by Eric and Deborah as a home, as a private place. And it was suddenly a very real place to Catherine. She had never been to their house. But now she was in their bedroom.

Although her flesh crept at the idea of being there, curiosity overcame her and she rummaged, at first casually and then more deliberately, through things. In drawers were other clothes and she found herself examining Deborah's underwear. It was, of course, expensive and beautiful. Another closet was full of dresses, another held jeans and sweaters. Masculine and feminine clothes were neatly separated, but sorted by use and placed in relation to each other.

She went over and sat on the bed, sitting on the heavy, antique quilt there, and looked slowly around the cabin. Next to the bed was a little drawer, the most private drawer in any house, and she reached over at last, as though idly, but also as though vindictively exerting her rights, and pulled it out.

A packet of tissues. A bottle of aspirin. Hemorrhoid ointment. Throat lozenges. A bottle of fingernail polish. Nose drops. A box of tampons. Condoms. A sheet of birth control pills and a tube of lubricant.

For a few moments, Catherine's mind once again became lucid, her bank secretary's instincts calculating rapidly.

The pills had a starting date of the beginning of May, and were barely used. So Deborah had stopped taking them more than six weeks back. In the packet of condoms, a box of thirty-six, three were left. Catherine did some rough arithmetic, gauging back to when Eric would need to start using rubbers in replacement of the pills.

Thirty-three rubbers, forty-two days. She gave a toss of her head. Pretty arduous application of effort, she thought, for a guy just trying to convincingly pretend to his wife he's in love with her.

If that simple explanation had been all there was to it.

And it certainly wasn't, she thought bitterly … the way she had gotten to know the guy.

Catherine looked at the condoms and could allow herself to wonder whether the box had been brought down with only three left, or if the missing ones had been used there, as it seemed they must. Rubbers were not things you stocked in somewhere and left, the way you left a few emergency cans of pork and beans in your kitchen.

The tube of lubricant was interesting in its own way. She had figured Deborah for being a little blocked in spite of the overly developed body, and it was somehow a small pleasure to think Eric's wife responded so little that Eric was forced to resort to industrial help. She even smiled.

Catherine wondered which of them suffered from the other problem—perhaps both.

Although she was indifferent now, tired and a little drunk, she also wondered why they had switched to using condoms.

She was obviously off the pill. Which made for one conclusion, yet didn't explain why they had taken to using the other method, either, unless they were doing some rhythm thing.

She remembered how Deborah had been glowing lately. Was that it? If so, why hadn't Eric just said so? Told Catherine his wife was pregnant? And why would it have made a difference anyway?

Of course, that was now a true secret. A small detail in someone else's life. But it was something she could never know until a public announcement was made.

Where once she had known so many things, was part of Eric's private life, she was now just another member of his public. Regardless of the illogic, she felt so terribly outside of everything, outside from a life where there were little, private details such as a nearly empty box of condoms.

Outside of little secrets.

It was there that she discovered how you could be jealous of secrets.

She felt so tired. She held the box of condoms in her hand, and then on an impulse, pulled one of the little packets out of the box. She looked at it for a moment, and then set her glass down on the table and grasped the packet and tore it open, drawing out the condom.

There was something so intimate in the object. The ring a dark red around the translucent pink skin membrane, the little bubble reservoir tucked into the ring, ready to swing out as Eric slipped the condom on. Or as Deborah pushed it on for him.

Catherine lay back onto the bad, now placing the condom over the tips of two fingers and rolling it slowly down, pulling it down, too large and formless, but extending it until it was completely undone. It didn't seem much of a thing, but merely to know that what she had over her fingers would have been in contact with Eric, was enough to give it a power of its own.

But there was also the knowledge it would have been used with Deborah, giving her the pleasure now denied Catherine. And, eventually, Eric's seed would have filled that reservoir, drawn from him by his pleasure for Deborah. Pleasure that in another life had been meant for Catherine.

She lay there for a moment but did not cry, holding the condom between her fingers. Feeling the lubricated surface which was evidently not enough. A dry hole, indeed.

Catherine's fingers slowly began tying the condom into knots, one after another, until at last it was nothing but one big knot.

Unable to stand being there any longer, Catherine replaced everything in the drawer and, putting the knotted condom in a skirt pocket, went out and back to the main cabin.

She had been tempted to leave the drawer open and the ruined condom in plain sight on top of the bed. A small and complicating revenge. But she managed not to.

Something telling her not to burn her bridges yet.

# Chapter 108

THE AIR was warm and comfortable by then. She went over to the bar and fixed herself another drink. Her fourth? Fifth? She made it big like the others before. A little later, she would make another. And then another. And why the hell not? They could blame the empty bottle on Scott.

She sat for a very long time in the cabin, on Deborah's sofa, and felt, for a lack of any other way to describe it to herself, as though her life was flowing out of her body and floating away. Sliding away into the night. In a few months she would have been there a year. Another year of her life. Gone. She had been thirty-five. Now she was thirty-six. Look what this year had been like.

Just look at it.

With these people who a year ago hadn't existed, then had become an entire world for her, and now were to disappear entirely. With what they had brought. Look at what they had brought. A little, then a lot, and in the end ... nothing at all. A year gone.

What about the next one?

Catherine sat there for a long time thinking about the next one, and then finally shook her head.

"Good God."

She went and got the Scotch bottle, bringing it back and settling down again on the sofa. It was so warm in there, she thought. You could take all your clothes off and still be comfortable.

She laughed, her beautiful voice ringing into the silence; and time passed slowly onward there in the dim light.

Later, it was impossible to tell how long she had been there. It seemed as though it had been all her life. She let her eyes sweep around the cabin.

Well, she thought, this thing here had gotten built. This thing that had been reality, an ideal, then form with the molds, but not reality, then reality again, and on and on and blah-blah-blah.

All that shit, all year. Deborah making it a metaphor for God only knew what.

Catherine held her hand to her face.

And Jack. Now Mr. Family-man Boatbuilder.

MFB.

Mother Fucking Bastard.

And Scott.

She couldn't think up a name for him. Scott being the simple worker, crucified for the sins of simplicity. A lie, she now knew bitterly, but she preferred the lie as being easier to use.

And Eric. All that time, Eric getting the thrill of a lifetime playing footsies with the philosophy of the working class—and basically just trying to get his end in. Then successfully doing so ... with her.

With Catherine, that working class slut who had no possibility of, or right to protect herself from, her Master.

She certainly had no way to get even with him, to fuck him over as badly as he'd done her.

Amazing what they can do, she thought. They come down and diddle everyone in sight, play around as much as they want, and—in fact—the great goddamn thing actually did get built and they would now take it away and forget about the place as though it had never existed.

They had got it built and would get away with it ... exactly the thing, and this thing, that they had wanted.

This thing, whatever the fuck it was.

"And what does that mean to me?" she said out loud.

The silence in the cabin suppressed her own response for a moment, intimidating her. Suddenly she felt like hell. Total hell.

"You're fucking drunk," she said with a small voice, as if testing the brooding silence of the deserted yacht. Then, the next thing came, and she set her glass down on an end table and put both of her hands to her face and wept.

"You might as well be fucking dead."

She grabbed her purse, and pulled from it Eric's letter. Why she'd kept the goddamn thing, she didn't know. But somehow just having it, had made her feel better.

She read it again. And then: an idea.

She got out a pen, and turning it over, began to write on the back.

*Dear Eric, (you see, I too can be a hypocrite.) While ending things, as you say, is something you have no control over, remember how things started. You were the one who asked me to come to your office. You were the one who started our lovely love affair. You certainly seemed to be in control in time. But now you've lost control. So be it. You evidently don't think much of me, but I'll prove you wrong in this. I won't ruin your life. I won't tell Deborah. I won't tell Jack Colby, although I'd love him and Ellen to know who and what you are, the same as I do. Someone else might want revenge. But I won't seek it. I just want you to know these two things. Fuck you forever. And no matter how rich you are, you are no better than anyone else. Forever remembering, Catherine*

It was a sloppy mess. She looked at it again, tears welling up.

She poured herself another drink, drank it off like a longshoreman, and started crying even harder.

After a while, when her paroxysm was reduced to a last few, racking sobs, she tried to calm herself. But anything she tried made everything seem worse by steady increments. By then, even those thoughts of death didn't bother her, for misery creates a feeling of immortality within which nothing else exists, not even the final extinction.

There was no one there to make the pain go away, or simply to be conscious of it. No one to share anything at all with, or just put out a hand to her.

Her body screamed to be held, to be comforted.

She had no control. It just screamed and screamed, and as it did so the room went dark.

And she found herself screaming in terror.

She stopped, trembling with fright.

Never in her life had she lost mastery of herself like that. She had lost touch with everything. She didn't even know how long that had lasted. That was the most horrifying feeling of all. Like she'd gone completely insane.

She looked down at herself, trying to pull herself together.

Then she felt dizzy and thought she was going to get sick. Suddenly, the scotch felt sour inside her, her head thick and fuzzy, and she realized she'd passed out for a moment and that was all.

What followed would only be remembered as a dream, where some things were clear and others indistinct.

She couldn't remember much. In fact, she couldn't remember anything.

Clutching that awful letter. And her purse.

Left nothing behind.

She made sure of that.

The rest … she couldn't remember.

Getting out, somehow, of the cabin. Going up into that hot blackness. Getting out into the cold, the wet, wispy, foggy night air, even colder in hot tears.

Feeling so much like utter hell, sharp stabbing terror, somewhere a hatred, elsewhere a fear, but mostly feeling weak and ill as she made her way out to the door and into the alien world of the parking lot.

She had drank so much it scared her. Maybe a whole bottle. She should have passed out for good. It scared her that it was still inside her. It could kill her, or cause her to kill herself somehow.

She got to her car and there, fell down, fainting nearly into unconsciousness.

Nearly.

Just a momentary black-out. It seemed.

Dizzy, head swimming, hard to see there in the dark of the parking lot, the gravel feeling wet and dank on her hands.

Using her car to brace herself, she found her purse and got up and managed to get the door open and get inside. She felt better there, but barely, and she ran her window down. She needed all the air she could get.

She got the car started and drove away, slowly, half-terrified. She didn't have to go far but she took a side-street, skirting behind the Old Fairhaven, to avoid the light.

Along the way she cried, once, very hard and had to pull over. She felt so sick and insane with the scotch that she was afraid she would pass out again.

The tears finally stopped though, and the alcohol roaming around in her system took at last its final hold, and she no longer cared.

Around Fairhaven, up the parkway, onto the streets going up Sehome hill.

She got home. Left the car. Got in the door. Exhausted.

Dizzy drunk.

Of all the things in the world she wanted, it was healthy, quiet sleep. What she got was a poisoned, swimming miasma of sickness.

She went into the bathroom and got down on her knees by her toilet, and very luckily for her, got sick.

And that was where she would wake up the next day. Very, very late in the next day when she would find herself being woken up by Sydney.

But for that time it would all vanish from her tortured mind, and she would be alone at last.

Innocent again and unconscious of the hurtful world outside.

## Chapter 109

A CLEAR, cool morning, but warm there on the terrace next to the pool, Eric and Deborah were quietly sharing breakfast as each, separately, prepared for their day. Eric was going over a sheaf of notes prepared by Newell Briggs concerning Fairhaven land titles.

There was no doubt now that Eric's team had nearly sewn it all up. He was the virtual owner of a continual strip of shoreline beginning at the far south end of Bellingham Bay and working its way around to the foot of Sehome Hill at Jackson Street.

Literally, he owned Fairhaven because except for the burgeoning historic district, he also had title to most of the unused half mile or so of land stretching up to those old buildings from the shore.

Of course, there were some leases still outstanding, but the truth was, he now had the titles and he could put the project in motion, give Briggs power of attorney, and regardless of whether the project came to fruition in six months, or six years, Eric could turn his back on it as though it no longer concerned him.

Very simply, between then and six years, perhaps nearing the end of his first term as senator, his wealth would be multiplied by nearly ten and he would suffer no political consequences.

Eric reached out for his coffee and took a sip, looking out across the pool towards where the neatly mowed lawn began dipping down over the hillside towards Lake Whatcom, there a line of trees making a brilliant show beneath the morning's sun.

The lake was calm, but already Eric could catch the occasional flash of movement on the lake as boaters got early out on the water for what was promising to be a glorious day. Simply beautiful, he thought, then turning to look at Deborah and, having done so, had to suppress a laugh.

She was sitting upright at the wrought-iron breakfast table scribbling intensely in her day book. He knew she was making plans for the launching of the Swift Knot, and it was amusing how seriously she was taking all the fun intended to go with it.

Strange, he thought, how that boat had disappeared from his interests. Of course, it would be nice to have around. He had decided that it would, indeed, be a positive part of his public persona.

Hoaglund had told him that the public, rather than what one might think, did not resent a display of wealth. In that area especially, nothing seemed more down-home and regular as having a boat, regardless of what a monster it would be. Hoaglund even had ideas on special cruises that could be made which would attract the right sort of publicity.

A bit of a laugh, all that. Especially when Eric remembered back to the heady days when he had first commissioned the boat, and what the boat had meant to him then.

Amazing, how things changed. Way back last fall, he could have bought that other boat from Clyde Moore and been done with it. Deborah would have invested it with whatever she would have come up with, he would have saved a few million dollars, and would have had quit of Fairhaven and all who lived there a long time ago.

Eric set his cup back on the edge of the table and looked down at his notes again, feeling somewhat grumpy.

If he had bought that boat, he could have spared himself a few other things as well. Worries, especially. But also—he could see it now—the long-term headache of owning a wooden boat, modern as she might be. All the upkeep, the incredibly expensive upkeep. Whereas with the Nickerson Ketch, it would have just been there, more or less ready for them when they had the time for jaunts.

For half a second he let himself consider boats. They were highly photogenic, it was true. It would be good to have one, especially coming from that part of the country. Almost expected. But, maybe, the big wooden ketch was too ostentatious. Just too damn over the top and something constituents would have a hard time with, despite what Hoaglund said.

Maybe better, once it was in the water, to quietly sell it off and buy the other one. That way everyone would be happy.

Eric nodded. It was nice, he thought with a shrug, to make everyone happy once in a while. He'd go talk to Clyde Moore again.

He realized that he'd just made a decision about what had been a bit of a logjammed situation. Which was helpful, considering the other, more dangerous, logjams surrounding his private life.

Hoaglund and Party would give him pure hell if Catherine Wilkins ever sprang back into his way, but of course, Eric had not been able to tell them about it. The nomination meant too much, way too much, for such a thing to hold him back. He was just going to have to take his chances with her.

It was the awful truth: she had something she could hold over him. It's always that way with people who have less than you or nothing. They are the ones who can hold something over you, spoil your hopes and ambitions, where you can almost never have anything to hold over them.

It was a fact. What the hell could he ever hold over that woman to shut her up? Answer? Nothing. Nada. At least for right then.

But, of course, the worst thing was that she had that letter. Although, as far as he could remember, he hadn't signed it.

But it was, in fact, his handwriting.

He sighed.

No, that was just paranoia talking. He had enough experience to know that things would be taken care of, when they appeared.

Time would tell, therefore. Most regular people eventually did something, somewhere, that you could hold on them. It was a truth he had learned to put his trust in. And that Wilkins woman was a very regular sort of person.

Eric nodded to himself, and then reached out and patted Deborah's hand. She looked up at him for a moment, looking at him through the blaze of details she had been putting together concerning the social occasion of the boat.

There was so much to do, she thought with a bit of frustration. Although it was a pleasant frustration.

So many people to invite.

Especially now when Eric's career was to be reborn.

She was still excited about the boat, of course. So wonderful the time they had passed watching it being built, so interesting to have been so intimately involved with the process, but his political career was now something beginning to form itself in her mind into another great project.

Deborah could barely stifle her excitement at the life they were setting themselves out to create.

She smiled at him, and picked up his hand and brushed her lips across the backs of his fingers.

Truly, she thought, if there was inspiration in life, it was in having a challenge in the future.

She thought of all her dear friends there in Bellingham, prominent people at the university, and their wives, whom she had been so involved with over the years in trying to do something for the community. And she thought of how she would miss them when they moved to Washington D.C. It was for them that this launching would have a special significance.

That and her pregnancy.

It was all practically too exciting for words, she thought, then releasing Eric's hand and returning to her guest list.

# Chapter 110

MORNING ON the bay had come with grey filtered light, but clear and drying and, best of all, a clear blue opening out to the west.

Scott got up with the dawn. Even with only a few hours' sleep he felt like a million. He took his coffee with him in his car as he drove down to the waterfront.

His first thought, down at the boatyard, was how in the world he'd slept through this. There must have been sirens all over the place, and the smell of smoke would have been everywhere. The second was how it was a shame they hadn't let it smolder down to ashes until there was nothing left at all.

They hadn't, though.

They had wanted to try to see why it had happened and had stopped it while things were still recognizable.

The pumper trucks were long gone but the investigators, a small crew of firemen, and several police were still picking around and looking things over in the light of the creeping dawn. The investigators stood over by the police cars in the lot. Scott went over and identified himself.

He could barely bring himself to ask the first question, sounding stupid to himself.

One of the investigators, a thickset middle-aged man in a windbreaker and a Mariners hat, told him the boat had gone up first, and then the shop.

The house had been saved with part of the shop wall. But the rest had fallen, black and broken, in one long scene of devastation all the way down to the water's edge.

Luckily no workboats had been in. Or anything tied up at the dock. The building had collapsed in that direction.

From a certain distance it looked, all and all, everything and anything, like an unending heap of blackened timbers, the wood charred and cracked into knobs and fissures. Closer, the black mess took on the appearance of the giant sticks of a child's game.

Or what was left of the game, he thought, when the child had gotten tired of it and had kicked it to shit.

Laid over and around what was left of the boat were the remains of the building's roof beams and the beams and flooring of the old loft. An intermingled disaster.

Colby's Boatbuilding and the *Muse*, the Swift Knot, or whatever the hell it was, were now, truly, one.

# Chapter 111

HE STARED at it, letting it all sink in.

The air smelled acrid—sticky and poisonous. All around in the parking lot and on into what was left of the boatshed water puddled and pooled with oily rainbow sheens, small tendrils of smoke or steam curling up as though from a newly formed lava flow.

The firemen told Scott the building was totally engulfed when they got down there. For a while all they could do was manage to save the house. They had also been forced to save Moore's closer boats, dragging them over to the other side of his lot by the dock and the Nickerson Ketch where, helter-skelter, they now huddled like frightened sheep.

Scott saw that the only things of Clyde that had suffered were his once jaunty strings of plastic flags nearest to the Colby yard. Along their wires, blobs and drips, cooled and hard now, hung or sat like deformed sparrows. All the rest of his stock, the Sharktails, daysailers and the big Nickerson Ketch at the dock, looked untouched other than their being covered with the thin, streaky skuds and film of gray ash. On the Colby side, amazingly, the boat molds and braces and the keel and rudder, set against the fence, hadn't been damaged, although the canvas covering them was so badly singed it was obvious it had been a near thing they hadn't burst into combustion..

Standing next to where the shop wall had been, Scott looked at the boat's remains.

She'd fairly well consumed herself. Enough so that when the shop had collapsed, her weakened structure had been crushed outwards on all sides, shattering down her ribs and planking in strangely concentric circles like stepping on a clam shell. She was almost entirely gone. But not enough for Scott.

It was possible for him to recognize objects—now reduced to grotesque caricatures of what they had been or else blasted into fantastic shapes—he had formed with his two hands. The keel, still fairly intact, resembled the stripped and burnt spine of a fish, the black remains of the floors set grimly like vertebrae along its length with, in between, piles of ashes of what had once been inner bulkheads and joinery.

Likely enough, the interior had been an inferno for a time, gutting the boat long before escaping through the collapsing deck and cabin beams to involve the shop.

The only real remains of the boat were occasional long strips of double planking, still screwed together here or there where the center wood hadn't charred through ... still maintaining their graceful curves and attesting to the inherent strength of the steam fitted mahogany. But black and lifeless.

Scott got permission, in the form of shrugs, and stepped across into the dripping wreckage of the shop, some places sending up wreaths and clouds of steam. Everything at closer inspection was a primordial black ooze where things perhaps once well-known were now barely distinguishable. Especially, he noticed the tools. A hammer head. A warped saw blade, perhaps once his own but now utterly foreign to him. Sick looking strands of wire with globs of blackened plastic running along their lengths. A smashed space heater looking like a used tube of toothpaste. Charred canvas, now ash-fragile like embossed paper, so thin, and dissolving underfoot. Nails laying loose or protruding in bent angles from timber burnt away from them, shrinking from them like wounded flesh. A table spoon, oddly clean. Pitch-black cans of paint and varnish. Brushes burnt to metal bands, handles of charcoal. Screws and nails lying in sooty, scattered heaps once in boxes and bags. The sole of a boot curled like a despairing, thirst-stricken black tongue. Screwdrivers with melted plastic handles. The iron boat rails twisted and humped. A shattered porcelain cup. The big bandsaw bent over with its weight like a dying dinosaur. Drill bits warped and useless. An electric handsaw split like a cracked walnut, it's insides cooked into a black knob. Oddly: a wooden sawhorse, consumed to black ash but still standing in one corner. A ghost to something.

Towards the bows and amidships the boat had left a few metal fittings scattered along on both sides of the keel, a coathook here, a curtain rod or doorknob there.

At the far end the motors lay upside down in a heap of cindered timbers against the keel and deadwood, and along the keel were the springs and metal frameworks of mattresses, one lying across the starboard motor.

Scott walked along and gazed quietly, stopping to toe something now and then. A twisted porthole. The blasted refrigerator. A shattered toilet. Not one single painted or varnished surface was left untouched. Not even a blistered surface. Every single piece of wood in the boat had been burned, if not to the core.

He finally walked out of it, the sky above and behind him going bluer and brighter and the day warming with every minute.

It was funny, he was thinking, how so many of the worst things that had ever happened to him in his life, had happened while he wasn't there. He walked up to the investigator who was still jotting things down onto his aluminum clipboard.

"Arson?"

"Don't know yet," the man said. He had a long, horsey face but his eyes were just squints. Right then, Scott might have thought they were squinting suspiciously at him.

"It was going so good, it's hard to tell exactly where it might have started. Inside the boat makes arson less likely if you wanted to be sure the company burned down. But on the other hand, if that's what you wanted to burn, then that's what you would start with. Depends. A case like this has got an awful lot of possible motives, don't you think?"

"I don't know what to think."

"You the owner?"

"Nope."

"Nope for the boat, or nope for the business?"

"Nope, nope."

The investigator pulled a crumpled pack of cigarettes out of his pocket and fingered a squashed cigarette into his lips.

"Got a match?"

Scott gave him a look.

The investigator shrugged and brought out a cheap lighter.

Scott surveyed what was left of his workplace once again.

"So tell me," the investigator went on, the cigarette now dangling from the corner of his mouth, "that boat in there, you got an idea what the value of it was?"

It was a great question, Scott thought. He looked at the investigator for a moment and then shook his head.

"A lot, huh?"

"It was worth a lot of money. The insurance will cover its building costs."

"You were involved in building it, eh? I suppose, naturally, it was finished."

"There'll be photos to prove it."

"It's not me that'll want the proof."

"They'll get their proof."

"So much the better for you. So how about the business? What was it worth?"

Scott shook his head again.

"You don't know?"

"Same thing. Depends who you're talking to."

"I'm talking to you."

"You shouldn't be."

The investigator took a long pull on his cigarette and looked over at the scene of disaster for a moment. Thirty years in the business, he had seen this sort of thing time and time again. A big fire that left practically nothing standing. Desolation so complete, and so out of ordinary compared with day to day life, that it seemed to call upon him, or someone—anyone—to say something about it. But in thirty years, he had never found whatever it was you might say.

"Where are the owners?"

"Celebrating the impending launching."

The investigator tightened his lips on his cigarette, taking a long pull, and scratched his neck. But that was all.

After that, other people talked to Scott and he answered a few more questions along those lines. All with the general purpose of digging around in the personalities of Jack and Ellen Colby, and of Scott, and what their individual relationships were with each other and the business.

If a blunt question was asked, Scott answered bluntly. Otherwise, when he finally got away, the police knew very little more than he knew himself. Although not at what he could guess.

He couldn't get over how all this had happened while he and Sydney had been uptown having such a good time. Then he and Sydney whooping on home. Lately he and Sydney had whooped around everywhere, oblivious to everything.

Evidently.

It must have been in the wee hours. And it had to have been someone. The wiring in that building had been upgraded to code, as well as the wiring of the boat itself.

Someone.

The Sumners?

He had seen the signs that they'd had a few overnighters. But why, then, would they have left?

Didn't make sense.

He walked back across the soggy parking lot in the bright sun, the air still stinking and the wet gravel sloshing beneath his boots. He began to get in his car, when he noticed something trampled down into the gravel, almost covered up.

He didn't know why he felt he had to do it, but he glanced over his shoulder. No one was looking in his direction. He reached down, pulled it out and shook off the gravel. A crumpled sheet of paper. He almost opened it up but then an odd feeling come over him and, giving a look around again, shoved it in his pocket and got in his car.

He left the scene of the fire, and the police to the care and feeding of the suspicions their temperaments took to naturally, and drove up the street towards Fairhaven. Up there in the historic district people were already out taking advantage of the warmth of what seemed the beginning of summer.

He pulled his car over to the sidewalk, pulled out the piece of paper and flattened it out. Having been by some miracle far enough away from the fire and the fire trucks, it was neither singed nor too damp and the writing was intact. He read both sides, then folded it up carefully and put it in his shirt pocket. The other miracle was that nobody had noticed it. He started his car again and drove off.

He drove home and talked to Sydney, then went back out to his car.

At first he thought he might stop in and have a beer somewhere and think things through. There was no rush to go out there. But as he drove, he remembered the last thing Sydney said to him as he stepped off the porch.

"There are times it's best to believe the worst."

He'd stopped, and turned to look at her.

"What?" he'd said. "You think she's dead, or something?"

"No," she'd said. "Not that way bad. But, what with all the other things you were telling me, I *do* believe you'd better think the worst of all of them. You remember? The friend of my father?"

So he thought of the worst, and could see that there were much more important things to do than having a few beers.

# Chapter 112

Twenty minutes later, he pulled out of the parking lot beside the printer's office with the photocopies he'd made. All the while he'd been doing that, everything became clearer and clearer. He drove home, gave the original to Sydney and told her to put it away somewhere. They talked for only a few minutes and she was in complete agreement about everything. In fact, she was the one who mostly outlined how it would work. He then went out and got back in his car.

He'd go out there. He was going to go out there. But he knew he had a bit of time. They weren't expected to come down there, and Jack and Ellen wouldn't be back until much later and nobody was making an effort to find or contact them.

So he had time for a drive. Just to make sure.

Even Sydney, who had urged him to not waste any time, agreed he should go. It would resolve him, as she put it.

He drove around the bay, out along the north shore again, out to that land and buildings he'd seen before. He got there and drove down the road and parked, looking at the big sheds and the slope of the land down to the water, where the tide was in and made it obvious it could easily take a slip which could bring boats close in.

It was so perfect, it was heart-breaking. Scott figured the whole thing could be had, in the condition it was in, for under a hundred thousand. Simply because it was so isolated. For the moment. And for another fifty grand, an operation could be up and running.

It truly was nearly heart-breaking. A fateful decision. Something he hadn't done very often, and even then—not including the one he'd made with Sydney—never so seriously. It wasn't lost on him how that one, and this one, was connected. He continued to stare at the property for a few more minutes, and then felt it come over him, and he smiled the way people smile when fate happens.

He was done.

He started his car and drove back to the main road, and then the car took him back into Bellingham, pulling him quietly and steadily towards it all. There was only one place to go now. Oddly enough, it almost felt as though a boat *was* being launched. The thing sliding easily, on greased rails, down to the waiting waters of the high tide. He knew exactly what he was going to say to Eric Sumners. And he knew Sumners would take it as it had to be taken. Once, of course, he got over the initial shock.

Scott sighed, looking out over Bellingham Bay as he made his way around it, glancing down towards Fairhaven along the southern shore. It would be a fine day, by the looks of it, he thought.

He got through the downtown, and headed towards Lake Whatcom. All the while he was thinking of how Sydney had put it about how things could go. Or, that was, how they could go if he just left them to themselves and took advantage of it. Doing as anyone else, understandably, might have done. Wrapping themselves in the safety of doing what most people might do, or thought was the correct thing to do.

Sydney was right. She was right, and she was smart. Maybe smarter than all of them. Bad enough to do nothing even when there was little you could do. But there was nothing worse, she said, than doing nothing when you could do something.

In this case, though, there was no choice of could, or should. He simply had to do what he was going to do. It wasn't a simple case of opportunity; it was a case of self-preservation.

But not in terms of cashing in.

It was in terms of preserving what he now felt about himself. He'd saved those business cards and knew he could be as honest and scrupulous as anyone could be … when facing one of the most unscrupulous men he had ever met. Who deserved nothing better than the worst form of blackmail.

It didn't matter, though.

He was going to take his time this time. Where it would all go next, he had no idea, but wherever it was, was better than here.

And he was going to be careful about it, which was the other thing Sydney had urged him to understand. Even though it seemed hard not to believe that the worst thing that could happen, would be the last thing that could ever happen.

Because if there'd been one thing proved lately, it was you never, ever, knew what directions people would go, when given half a chance.

## ABOUT THE AUTHOR

Marc Lloyd Heberden was born on 20 March 1956 in Spokane, Washington. His early years were spent in Pullman and later Tacoma. After his studies at Western Washington University in Bellingham and the University of Washington in Seattle, where he earned a degree in journalism, he worked as a newspaper editor and award-winning journalist. Moving to Europe in the early 1980s he wrote for newspapers and magazines and began writing short stories, novels and screenplays. Since 1999 he has lived with his wife Christine in a small town southwest of Paris where they raised their three children, Maurine, Joyce and Cliff. His novels include Outside Man, The Big Tide, Feeney's Part, The Norman, and Feeney's Last.